Praise for Cathy Cash Spellman's
Bestselling Books

Bless the Child
"Spine-tingling. The suspense, which rivals the best of Stephen King, builds until... the final, chilling conclusion."
- *West Coast Review of Books*

"Seductive ... spellbinding ... an unrelenting sense of foreboding drives the narrative forward with power and speed." – *Publishers Weekly*

Paint The Wind
"Paint the Wind is the Gone with the Wind of the West."
- *Gerald A. Browne, author of 11 Harrowhouse.*

So Many Partings
"Almost impossible to put down. Cathy Cash Spellman has the ability to produce one powerful scene after another, and the strong plotting draws you helplessly on."
- *Publishers Weekly*

"A cross between The Thorn Birds and Ragtime!" – *New York Daily News*

An Excess of Love
"Riveting" – *Daily News (New York)*

"A lushly written saga of love and rebellion and Civil War" – *Washington Post*

Other books by Cathy Cash Spellman

FICTION

So Many Partings
An Excess of Love
Paint the Wind
Bless the Child
The Playground of the Gods

NON-FICTION

Notes to My Daughters

PROSE, PRAYER AND POETRY

Snowflake from the Hand of God

LARK'S LABYRINTH

by
Cathy Cash Spellman

This is a work of fiction. A number of actual historical people appear in these pages and others are discussed along with my fictional characters, but all the actions and dialogue attributed to my players live only in my imagination.

LARK'S LABYRINTH

by
Cathy Cash Spellman

For information:

The Wild Harp & Company, Inc.
6 Turkey Hill Road South
Westport, CT 06880

www.CathyCashSpellman.com

ISBN: 978-1461177364

Dedication

This book is for my sister Conny, who, for 15 years and against monumental odds, never once gave up on this story, and never stopped encouraging me to believe it would one day be real. For this, and for all the trust and love and laughter through the years, there aren't words adequate to express my love and gratitude to the very best sister in the world.

"But one of the soldiers with a Spear pierced his side, and forthwith came there out blood and water."

John 19, 34-37
The New Testament

❧ ❧

Adolf Hitler, in <u>Mein Kampf</u>,
describing his first encounter
with the Spear of Longinus:

"These foreigners stopped almost immediately in front of where I was standing, while their guide pointed to an ancient Spearhead. And then I heard the words which were to change my whole life:

'There is a legend associated with this Spear that whoever claims it, and solves its secrets, holds the destiny of the world in his hands for good or evil'."

Prologue

Palestine 33 A.D.

It was the Friday before the Spring Equinox. The relentless sun of Palestine beat down on the hapless bodies hanging from three wooden crosses on Golgotha, the Hill of Skulls.

Most of the crowd that had followed them from the courtroom along what the rabble called The Trail of Tears, had already dispersed. Any fun to be had was over now, and all that was left was the ignominious dying. No one had come to mourn the thieves, but the broken body on the middle cross was that of the one the Jews had called Moshioch, the Messiah.

Two women, one of whom was most likely his mother by the ravaged look of her, stood at the foot of the cross, their bodies paralyzed by anguish, backs held straight as blades in their determination to endure the unendurable. A younger man, who must have been a relative, stood with them, his face was haggard, worn thin with grief; he gripped the hand of the older woman in his own. Their eyes were on the dying face of the man who had been called King of the Jews. He had murmured something a moment ago, and they had stepped closer to hear.

Gaius Cassius Longinus was an officer of the Third Legion, serving in Syria. It was not his usual duty to oversee crucifixions, but Pilate had feared an uprising of the Nazarene's followers, so he had dispatched a Centurion and his men to keep the peace. Longinus sat immobile on his horse and tried to think what he could do to end the suffering of this decent man, who had dared to defy an empire and failed. Longinus had long been intrigued by this fisherman from Nazareth, who had caused such a rift among the

Jews. Half a dozen times he'd contrived to hear him speak of a better world than the one that Longinus served and knew so well. A world where war was not the only option.

Longinus was sick to death of war. Sick, too, of the excesses of Rome and the maniacs who sat on her throne. But there was no way out for him, he knew, until his time was up or some brave deed allowed him the chance to leave with glory and become the farmer he was born to be.

The murmuring of his troop behind him told Longinus it was time to hasten the deaths of the crucified ones, so his men could get on with more important matters. Their method of dispatching criminals was as cruel as the crucifixion itself, he thought with distaste. In another moment, a soldier would come forward with a heavy wooden mallet to break the men's legs. The weight of their own bodies would see to it that their lungs collapsed and suffocated them, poor bastards. He'd seen it done often enough to know how the victims would strangle out their last breaths in pitiful gasps of agony.

Longinus stared at the two stalwart women and the young man with the prematurely aged face, who hadn't moved from the foot of the cross. Surely, they would carry those last gasps in their nightmares forever.

On impulse, Longinus pulled the spear from his saddle mount, and urged his horse forward toward the one they called Master. He stared for a moment at the once ruggedly handsome face, now grotesque with blood and gore from the needle-sharp crown of thorns the cruel onlookers had forced onto his head at the trial.

"Forgive me, Rabbi," he murmured as he thrust the spear upward into the man's laboring heart with all his strength and skill. "There is nothing more in my power to do for you but this."

Blood and water gushed from the wound, splattering Longinus' hand as well as the spear that held it. He'd never felt anything like the shattering energy that coursed up his arm and then dispersed as quickly as if lightning had singed him.

Disoriented, Longinus returned the spear to its saddle mount, and hastily shouted orders to his men, to cover his own confusion.

"The imposter is dead! Cut him down!" he ordered. Was it his imagination that the sky had darkened, at precisely the moment his spear had pierced the man's flesh?

He turned his horse and saw that a distinguished looking older man had joined the sparse assemblage. He was fashionably dressed and his demeanor was that of one used to command.

"His body, Centurion," the man called out to him, in a deep, strong voice, that belied his years. "I've come for the body of Jeshua Ben Joseph."

The man pulled a paper from beneath his cloak with an air of authority, and handed it up to Longinus. It appeared that Joseph of Arimethea was his name. The order had been signed by Herod Agrippa himself. How curious. The old man must be influential indeed.

So it wasn't just the poor and desperate who followed the Nazarene fisherman, he thought, making mental note of the man's name, and address. He wasn't sure why. "You may take him, after my men strip the body."

"Ah, yes," said the old man. "I have heard the soldiers cast lots for the clothes of the dead. Do as you must... it is his body alone that concerns me."

Longinus watched the man hasten to the three who'd kept the vigil, enfolding them all in an emotional embrace. Longinus flexed his right hand, puzzling over the strange sensation he felt there. He looked upward at the sky, now nearly black as night, as silent lightning flashed across the barren hillside

Longinus shouted an order to his men. The cross was lowered and the women rushed forward to embrace the dead man, who had sought to make a better world and perished for his audacity.

How despicably easy it is to kill the gentle ones, he thought angrily, as he turned his horse's head back toward his men. Now, all the implausible words of peace and kindness that had sounded so possible when the Nazarene had spoken them would be forgotten, and nothing at all would be changed by the death of this man who had thought he could change the world.

Death of a Caretaker
Part I

"In the end, God will win."

Archibald MacLiesh

Greenwich, Connecticut
November 20 Late Afternoon

———————————————— **1** ————————————————

Greenwich / November

37 Year old, Dr. Cait Monahan, felt her daughter's forehead, the age-old gesture of worried mothers, and frowned. Feverish. Very feverish.

"Throat again, sweetheart?" she asked, knowing the answer. Nine year-old Lark nodded unhappily. "I feel sick, Mommy," she said in a raspier than usual voice.

"Better let me take a look," Cait answered, reaching automatically for her medical bag. These recurrent ear/throat infections were getting worrisome. It irked her that neither she, an internist, nor Lark's pediatrician, had been able to get to the source of the problem and solve it.

Obediently, the freckle-faced little redhead opened wide and stuck out her tongue. Lark's cheeks were too red and her eyes had allergic shiners under them.

Cait brushed her own auburn hair back behind her ears in a practiced gesture and took a tongue depressor from its compartment to give her daughter's throat an expert look. Then she reached back into the leather bag for her otoscope and peered into Lark's ears, quite certain now of what she'd find. She sat back with a sigh and touched the child's cheek lovingly.

"Well, my sweet, I'm afraid that old ear and throat thing is doing it again. I'll do a swab to be certain what we're dealing with here, but I'd put my money on strep and a sinus infection." It bugged Cait that she hadn't been able to keep Lark healthy since they'd moved into this old house that on all other counts was absolutely perfect for them. So many old houses had mold or fungus in the heating system that caused allergies. If, as she suspected, that turned out to be the cause of these recurrent infections, it would be hard to combat.

"I'm afraid you'll be out of commission for a day or two, love, and your sleepover will have to be postponed. Better call Bitsy with the bad news."

"But Mom, this is your anniversary, remember?" Lark pleaded. "You and Dad are going out to that fancy restaurant to get all lovey dovey and romantic, so I've got to stay at Bitsy's."

Cait popped a thermometer into her daughter's mouth before answering. She smiled a little, knowing Lark was still of an age to believe in fairytales and happily ever afters.

"Tell you what, my love," Cait answered, finally. "How about if Daddy and I have our romantic dinner at home tonight instead of going out? You tell Bitsy you'd like a raincheck on the sleepover and I'll cook up some of my special pasta that made your father fall in love with me in the first place. Okay?"

Cait took the thermometer out from under her daughter's tongue and clucked her own. 103, and still only afternoon. Not good. Temperatures tended to go up toward nightfall. She put away the thermometer on auto-pilot, planning what to do next. Call Lark's pediatrician about phoning in a scrip for an antibiotic to the drugstore, ask Mrs. Hannigan to pick up a few things from the market before leaving for her night-off, call Bitsy's mom and regroup the sleepover. Phone Jack and tell him they should probably go to Plan B for their 10th anniversary celebration. He would understand...

                    *   *   *

Cait stood back from the rosewood dining room table and did a mental inventory. Everything looked so sweetly full of memories. The linens they'd bought in Dublin on their honeymoon, the crystal that had been a gift from Jack's parents on their sixth anniversary. The James Robinson silver that was a legacy from her own parents, now long gone. She ran her fingers over the delicately entwined initials engraved on the handle of an old teaspoon, as if that somehow brought her mother and father close again. She'd been Lark's age when her mother died. Sometimes it seemed lifetimes ago; sometimes, like now, it felt like yesterday. Her father had passed on four years ago and the ache of that loss was still quick to kindle. *I love you guys*, she murmured to them both, suddenly teary at the sweet memories. *But I need to be happy tonight, so I can't think any sad thoughts. Okay?*

Satisfied that everything looked as it should, Cait took off her apron and glanced at the clock on the sideboard. Jack would be home by 6:30 and she wanted everything to be sweet and easy by then. It was a shame to cancel dinner at The Homestead Inn, but home would be fine, too. She looked around the elegant old dining room to make sure she hadn't forgotten anything, then headed for the bedroom to change her clothes. They'd searched such a long time to find their dream house, close enough to the City so Jack could get to Columbia, where he taught his rarefied mathematical magic to grad students with the brains for MIT but the geographic need to be in Manhattan. Large enough to house an office for her medical practice, near good schools for Lark, who'd inherited her father's gift for theoretical numbers. They'd settled on Greenwich because of a fluke that had made this wonderful old house affordable in an otherwise astronomical neighborhood. That, plus the bulk of their savings and some help from their parents, had made it a reach, but possible. Less than half a mile from Jack's Mom and Dad's home, it had been in the estate of old friends of the elder Monahans, and, as it hadn't been redecorated since 1926, the house had sold, far below value in a slow market.

Cait had been instantly enchanted by the elaborate Victorian wainscoting and Adamesque cherubs on the ornate ceilings. She wouldn't have said this to her so-serious medical colleagues at Greenwich Hospital, but her favorite magazine was Victoria, with all its delicate frou-frou throwbacks to a prettier, more romantic age.

The house was alive with eccentricities – a cockeyed floor plan with bedrooms and cubbies that followed a circuitous design no architect could have conceived; bedrooms added willy-nilly by each new generation. There was even a Widow's Walk atop the master bedroom, whose only access was a hidden, pull-down ladder in the closet that led first to the "luggage room" a Victorian euphemism for "attic," and then to the glassed-in cupola that provided a view of backcountry Greenwich.

She and Jack had fallen in love with the place at first sight, easily able to see beyond the dismal, outdated decorating and the dusty velvet drapes that kept out all but the most determined sunbeams. They'd walked from room to room, more excited at each new eccentricity.

As she crossed the floor of her bedroom, Cait thought of the attic stair and paused as an idea surfaced. Lark's old baby monitor was up there someplace – if she could find it, that would provide a perfect way to be able to keep an ear on Lark tonight, without having to run to the den a dozen times during dinner.

Cait climbed to the attic and felt the unheated air hit her with an icy wallop. Even the second door at the stair top couldn't quell the cold; she opened it, rubbed her arms for warmth and looked around for the box of old electronic gadgets. Silently, she blessed Jack's orderly nature that tended to keep attic, basement and garage, if not exactly pristine, at least eminently find-worthy. She untangled the speaker and monitor from the box and headed back down to take a shower. She'd intended to take a quick run before dinner, but with Mrs. Hannigan out shopping and Lark sick in bed, that wouldn't happen. Tomorrow morning would be soon enough to keep her aerobic rate in training for the marathon next spring. She hated regular exercise but loved to run, and that, plus some weight training had been enough to keep her 37 year-old body strong and trim enough, so far. She'd never make the cover of *Vogue,* she thought with a rueful smile, but nobody'd called her chubby lately, either.

2

Jack Monahan walked through the door to the den where Cait had made a temporary bed for Lark. His lanky body filled the doorframe and his daughter's face lit up at the sight of him. Tall, thin and a little gangly, with brown hair liberally laced with gray, he looked professorial in chinos and tweed jacket. Lark thought he was the handsomest man in the world, despite the irregular features of his face and the wire-rimmed glasses parked on his nose; in fact, she thought him pretty much perfect in every way.

"How's my cupcake?" Jack asked with concern in his deep, pleasant voice. "Mom tells me you've got that pesky bug again." He sat on the edge of the sofa and gathered his little girl into the safety of his arms. Her hugs always filled him with a sense of the miraculous, that something so good could have happened to his life. It had been that way for him since he'd helped Lamaze her into the world.

"I love you, Daddy," Lark murmured into his chest, burrowing into the comfort of his unquestioned love. "But I feel yucky."

He squeezed her extra hard in sympathetic response. "So Mom said, kiddo. I guess it's a good thing we decided to eat in tonight, huh?" His eyes smiled at her, crinkling up just enough at the corners to betray his 42 years.

"I didn't mean to spoil your anniversary, Daddy," she said flopping back onto the pillows. "I told Mom I could stay with Mrs. Hannigan, but you know Mom."

Jack nodded. "Your Mom's too good a doctor to run out on her favorite patient. Besides, we wouldn't have any fun if we had to worry about you all night. And you didn't spoil anything. Where is your Mom, anyway?"

"Upstairs getting all gorgeous."

Jack smiled indulgently at this precocious, shy, freckle-faced child who was so much like him. He reached over to brush a damp strand of red hair back from her flushed face. "Your mom doesn't have far to go to accomplish that feat," he said gallantly. "She takes after her daughter in gorgeosity."

Lark giggled back appreciatively at the compliment, but the giggle ended in a cough and he could see she was down for the count.

"Too tired for a quick run through the Labyrinth before supper?" he asked, just because he asked it every night.

Lark's eyes brightened for a moment; she loved Lark's Labyrinth, the computer game he'd invented for her, better than anything, and was getting really good at it despite its escalating complexities, but she just didn't feel well enough to play, so she shook her head.

"I'm really sleepy, Daddy. And it hurts to talk. I think I'll just take a nap, okay?" She snuggled down into her pillow, eyes already half closed.

"Sounds like a wise decision," he said tucking the coverlet in around her. "Want me to take you upstairs to bed?"

Lark shook her head.

"Mom said I could stay down here, Daddy. She scrounged up my old baby monitor so you guys can hear me from the dining room." She pointed to the small white transmitter on the desk.

Jack leaned over and kissed her on the cheek. "Your mom thinks of everything, kiddo. It was a lucky day we picked her out, you and me." It was an old joke between them that they'd both picked out Cait. There were so many private understandings between father and daughter that Cait sometimes felt a tiny twinge of jealousy. It wasn't just their connectedness that made her feel an outsider, but the quirky mathematical gifts they shared that made it hard not to envy the connection between them.

"You snooze now," he said softly as he stood up to go. "I'll carry you upstairs after dinner." Lark blew him a kiss and Jack made an elaborate mime of catching it, then left to find his wife.

3

Jack watched Cait's familiar movements across the dinner table, and smiled to himself. He felt content tonight – just plain content. Ten years married and still in love... that in itself was a pretty spectacular achievement considering the dismal track record of most of the couples they knew.

Cait looked happy, too, he thought watching her fuss over the pasta. It occurred to him that his wife's face, only a little changed from a decade ago, had always seemed to him just the right face, from the moment he'd seen her hurrying across the quad, her long auburn hair bouncing in the afternoon sunlight. She'd walked as if she meant it, as if she were consciously striding into the future. He remembered how he'd watched her hurry to class, trying to get up the courage to say hello, until Fate had taken matters out of his hands and mutual friends had introduced them a day later. He watched her now, as she ate her salad, ten years older, ten years more entwined with his world, and felt pretty good about life.

"I was just thinking," he mused, raising his glass toward her own, "This occasion demands a toast, so, here goes." He cleared his throat portentously, "To my wife Cait... ten years ago I only knew how lucky I was to have snagged you. Now I know how much I really love you."

The unexpected emotion she heard in his voice touched Cait to the heart. She looked intently at the husband she loved so very much, saw the spare New England frame and the earnest, weathered face, and felt the familiar thrill of knowing they belonged to each other. 'Laid Back Jack,' his students called him because of his quiet, even disposition and the fact that he always lay back and observed all details before drawing conclusions. There was nothing precipitous in Jack's nature, and the steel-trap mind that ran his internal computer was never rashly sprung. He observed, he assessed, he decided, he acted. Always in that order. Which was probably what made him so brilliant at his mathematical specialty of ciphers and encryption, a talent he'd inherited from his father. Jack had the patience to observe and assess, no matter what the obstacle. But that wasn't what she loved about him, she thought with sudden clarity. It was his unshakably kind heart and his integrity that made her feel safe and loved. Their life wasn't perfect... they had ups and downs like everybody else, but it was pretty damned good.

"Remember when we were poor overworked grad students," she asked, suddenly feeling playful, "and I used to cook this dinner for us, but we could never get all the way through it without making love?"

Jack grinned. "I always thought you put an aphrodisiac in the sauce," he said, leaning back from the table.

She laughed as she answered him, the million-dollar smile he loved lighting up her face. "And all these years I thought you just didn't like my spaghetti..."

Jack cocked his head to the side and smiled, "You know," he said, "the same phenomenon might just be kicking in right this minute..." He stood up, and tugged her out of her chair, with uncharacteristic spontaneity. Surprised, Cait laughed as she turned her mouth up to his, feeling his arms encircle her, each curve of their bodies fitting as they always had.

"This is more fun than eating spaghetti..." she murmured and Jack reached for the hand that caressed his neck and brought it to his lips, kissing her fingers softly. He was a good-natured lover – unhurried and intuitive in his lovemaking as in all other areas of life. Cait felt an urgency run through her body like liquid electricity.

"Do you think Lark's asleep?" Jack whispered into her hair. "I'd like to make love to you right here... we haven't really christened all the corners of this house yet..."

Cait laughed. "You're so right. I think we missed the kitchen sink, the hutch in the hall and maybe the clothes dryer in the basement."

She glanced at the baby monitor through which only a soft, even breathing emanated. "I haven't heard a peep from the den for quite a while, but it's probably a little risky, love. I'd hate to have her walk in on us."

"Upstairs, it is then," Jack countered, looking at the table full of dishes, "or, are we supposed to clean up our act before we celebrate?"

Cait looked at the half-eaten meal. "Dishes be damned," she said emphatically, "I'll just carry Lark upstairs to bed, while you let the cat in and lock up. The rest of the night is just for messing around."

"Let me carry her up, Cait. She's getting pretty big."

"I'm strong like bull," Cait said in a mock Russian accent. "Can't waste all those hours I spend pumping iron. Besides, I need to make sure her temperature's headed in the right direction – then I can concentrate on lust."

Jack smiled his reply. "Don't forget this thing," he said, slipping the receiver for the baby monitor into her pocket. "I'll make sure we're locked up tight. I don't want anything to interfere with the next eight hours."

Cait had reason later to remember his words.

*   *   *

Cait picked up her sleeping daughter, and pressed her damp, feverish body close. Jack was right, Lark was getting too big to be carried, but because she'd inherited his long lean frame, she was leggy as a colt, and there wasn't much meat on her bones. Lark, mostly asleep, wrapped her slender arms around her mother's neck and nestled her head onto her shoulder as Cait headed upstairs.

Mrs. Hannigan had turned down the bed and left the little stargazer night light on, so a pattern of solar lights danced across the walls and ceiling as Cait lay Lark on the cool pink sheets and covered her with a quilt. She put a knowing hand on her daughter's forehead, then satisfied that the fever wasn't any higher, she kissed her cheek and turned toward her own room. She felt giddy and sensual from the wine and anticipation.

4

Jack moved from lamp to wall switch shutting down the first floor lights, heading for the kitchen on his usual bedtime door check. He really liked the old house, but it had more doors than a Coney Island Funhouse.

Two heavily armed, dark-skinned men stood in his kitchen. The shock of seeing them there was so visceral, that for a moment Jack couldn't breathe. Adrenaline shot through his system, slamming his heart into his throat, as he struggled to control his voice.

"What do you want?" he asked, knowing exactly what they wanted, just as he'd always known they would come. *When you least expect it, son,* his father had warned him. *Never let down your guard for an instant.* But that had been long ago, and the years had unfolded without incident, so after a while it had become easy to believe that the theft would never be discovered.

Jack's mind was in instant overdrive. How many times had he played this scene over in his mind, in the years since his father had told him. He had to warn Cait – why the hell had he never found the right time to tell her what he knew? The burden had always seemed too much. The baby monitor was still in the den... she had the receiver in her pocket – *please, God don't let her have turned it off.* If he could only find a way to get these men into the den so the transmitter would pick up their voices.

The wiry, dark leader snarled a reply. "We want the Spear, Professor Monahan. We intend to take it back where it belongs." He was pointing a 9 millimeter Beretta at Jack's chest, but that wasn't the only weapon aimed at him. His companion standing behind to his left carried an uzi-like weapon Jack couldn't identify. The quick interchange in some guttural language – German, Arabic, he wasn't sure which – between the intruders was impatient.

"I haven't got any Spear," Jack said clearly, trying to think of the best way to warn Cait. *Observe. Assess. Decide...* The litany by which he'd lived his life repeated itself in his head; he used it now to force back the fear. There could be no mistakes made here, or his family would die. "I want you and your guns out of my house!" he shouted angrily, hoping his wife would hear and run.

"Don't be absurd, Professor, we are not leaving until you give us the Spear. We know your father stole the Spear of Longinus, and we know he entrusted you with its care. It will not be in your best interest to be coy with me." The second man spat out a sentence in what sounded like staccato Arabic, but the leader silenced him with a gesture.

"The Spear of Longinus is in the Hofburg," Jack snapped back, hostility seeming to raise his voice a notch. "I've seen it myself. Now get your guns out of my house before I call the police!" He had to give Cait whatever clues he could... had to buy time for her to get Lark to safety before he took his chance to act. There would be only one.

*   *   *

The baby monitor in her pocket exploded into sudden sound, catching Cait totally off guard – she'd nearly reached the door to the hall. She strained to hear what the voices were saying, but they were too far from the transmitter for clarity. Words static'd in and out maddeningly. Guns? The Spear of *who*? Some foreign words? Her heart was pounding so hard she could barely breathe, never mind hear. She thought she heard Jack say he wanted the guns out of their house. She definitely heard him threaten to call the police. A burglar must have caught him as he was locking up. She picked up the phone with trembling hands to dial 911, but there was no dialtone. Ice water shot through her and she grabbed Lark up from the bed, moving swiftly through the connecting door to the master bedroom. She slid the lock into place, a terrible pang reminding her that Jack was now on the other side of that lock.

For an instant she leaned her head against the door to clear it. *Have to get control!* she admonished herself. *Have to figure out what to do!* She forced her breathing to steady, willed her heart to stop pounding in her ears. Cait set Lark down on the bed and shook her awake. Where the hell was her cell phone? Oh, *shit!* It was in the car where she'd left it when she went to the drugstore.

"Lark!" she whispered urgently, shaking the child gently awake. "Baby, you've got to pay attention to everything I say, now. We may be in big danger and I really need your help."

Lark struggled to wake up; something in her mother's urgent voice reached through the sleep haze and medication. As she sat up and tried to understand she watched her mom slide a painted Welsh dresser against the bedroom door.

"Mommy?" she whispered, scared by what she was seeing. "What's the matter? Where's Daddy?"

Cait looked right, left, *everywhere*, assessing the possibilities, fear lapping at her like a predator. Her pistol was in the gun safe in her bedroom closet, but the key was on the keyring in her purse, left on the sideboard at the bottom of the stairs. Because Lark was growing up she had become ultra-careful about guns lately. Why the hell had she not hidden a second key in the bedroom?

"There are burglers in the house, baby," Cait said as steadily as she could. "I'm trying to figure out how to get us out of here and you've got to stay awake for me!"

*   *   *

"You know perfectly well the Spear in the Hofburg is the forgery, Professor," the leader spat the words at Jack. "Your father was equally uncooperative and now he is dead for all his stubbornness. Along with his wife. He suffered a heart attack, I believe, when my associate cut your mother's throat."

Jack launched himself backwards into the den, taking a small corner table with him noisily to the floor as he went down. He needed them to think he'd panicked... needed Cait to hear the crash. He was already a dead man. They would torture him for the information, as they had his parents, then kill him, his only hope to die quickly. But Cait and Lark must be saved. He'd played variations of this scene a thousand times in his head since he'd committed himself to the Spear. He knew exactly what he had to do next. Seeing the baby monitor's transmitter still on the desk near the couch, he raised his voice, praying to God Cait would hear him. *Why the hell had he never told her the story?* The rules said he had to pass the responsibility on before he died.

"My wife knows nothing about the Spear of Longinus!" he shouted in desperation. "Run Cait! They're after the Spear! It's yours now!" he blurted loud as he could, as he hurled his 6-foot 3-inch body directly at the man with the gun, hoping for the gift of a swift death.

5

The unmistakable crack of a gunshot smashed through the monitor as Cait jerked open the closet door and yanked down the cord that lowered the attic ladder. "Up the ladder, Lark. *Now!*" Cait grabbed her daughter's hand and pushing her toward the hatch.

"You may have killed him, you fool!" a male voice shouted furiously through the monitor. Their voices were clearer now. "We need him alive! I'll keep him breathing... you find the woman and the child. *Go!*"

The thought of Jack and the gunshot ripped at her, but Cait pushed down the horror, so she could keep moving. She knew exactly what guns could do to a body, she was not only a doctor, but she'd hunted with her father and sister since childhood. She and Lark had to get out of the house to get help for Jack. She could hear a man on the stairs – heavy feet on her grandmother's hall runner. He was confused by the arrangement of the rooms on the second floor; she heard him shout to someone else, as he slammed doors. She forced back her terror so she could function.

"Where's Daddy?" Lark rasped from the ladder top. Cait, behind her, felt the answer catch in her throat. "I think he's been shot, sweetheart" she said, wondering if that was the right thing to say, needing her to understand the urgency. She wrestled the ladder hatch up behind them. "He shouted for us to run, Lark. We've got to get help for Daddy!" The panic-stricken look in Lark's eyes matched her own.

"Are they going to shoot us, too, Mommy?" Lark whispered, tears blurring the words.

"Not if I can help it, baby. But we've got to get out of the house, *now*."

Lark nodded. "Maybe we could use the fire ladder."

Cait's head shot up. Of course! The rope ladder Jack had insisted they put up here 'just in case' was in a basket near the hatch. She heard the man moving below, smashing at the locked bedroom door.

She grabbed two sets of sneakers and two sweatshirts from the out-of-season storage rack. "Help me drag something heavy over this hatch to buy us some time, baby." She was already tugging a huge trunk over the opening. Lark ran to help her mother, and Cait dropped the handle of the trunk, and pulled the sweatshirt over her daughter's head, then pulled on her own. The two yanked on their running shoes, and scrambled up the ladder to the Widow's Walk, dragging the fire ladder behind them.

Once inside the cupola, they bolted the hatch, breathing hard. The ladder had a horseshoe shaped pair of metal clamps meant to hold it to a windowsill, Cait saw as she unfurled it. *God bless you, Jack!* she breathed, clamping it in place and throwing the rungs over the cupola's window ledge. They'd be short of the ground but maybe it wouldn't be too far to jump, because of the porch roof. She hugged Lark hard for luck, then lifted her out onto the rope ladder, praying it would hold their combined weight.

They hit the roof over the sun porch and scrambled down the trellis that held Morning Glories in the spring. Cait grabbed her daughter's hand and sprinted for the frozen trees that ringed the property. She could hear voices shouting behind them inside the house, but she didn't stop till they'd reached the heavy fringe of trees that bordered their land. There were no near neighbors in backcountry Greenwich. Her in-laws were their safest haven.

"I know a short-cut to Gram's house," Lark breathed as she saw her mother hesitate, deciding which way to run. "Daddy and I always go that way."

"Show me, Sweetheart. Daddy's still in our house. We've got to get help faster than we've ever done anything in our lives."

"These sneaks are from last summer, Mom, they're too small for me," Lark whispered with a strangled sob.

Cait hugged her tight, barely able to speak over the lump in her throat. "Just do the best you can, baby," she managed to say. "You can't run barefoot, and we've got to go." The child nodded, biting her lower lip.

"We're running for Daddy, baby," Cait whispered into her daughter's hair before letting her go. "It's not over till we give up, okay?"

"Okay." The child's voice was resolute, but there was terror in the tiny word.

"Now get us to Gram's."

There was a path underfoot, not clear, but enough to follow if you knew the woods. Backcountry Greenwich was black as pitch once you left North Street's occasional street lights behind. Cait watched her daughter edging ahead of her in the dark woods, lit only by a weakly waning moon. Thank God they ran together twice a week, not long distances, but enough to keep the child's aerobic capacity up. If Lark weren't sick she could do this half mile run with ease. But she was sick, and scared; Cait could hear her breath coming hard.

A quarter mile further on, the child tripped, sprawling flat on the cold leaves with a sharp cry and a strangled cough. She scrambled up, trying to breathe, bending over at the waist as Cait had taught her to increase lung capacity. "I gotta stop, Mommy," she gasped, coughing. "I can't breathe."

Cait crouched down beside her daughter, hearing the sounds of pursuers in the undergrowth somewhere behind them. "We've got to keep moving, baby," she whispered urgently. "Get on my back. I think I can still carry you that way." Lark grabbed hold of her mother's neck and wrapped her long legs around her waist. "I'm so sorry, Mommy," she sobbed into Cait's hair as her mother swung into motion.

"You did great, baby," Cait gasped, the extra weight dragging at her. "You're the one who showed us the shortcut, right? And we're almost to Gram's house."

"What's that light, Mommy?" Lark blurted, pointing right, "over by Gram's." A red glow hovered over the thinning trees.

Cait stared at the blazing sky as a new fear flooded her – the ominous glow was coming from the direction of her in-laws' home and she could smell smoke that wasn't from chimneys. They hit the street beyond the wood, and a clamor of voices and people shouting assaulted them. Fire engines ringed the block. People in nightclothes and overcoats stood in groups, some with tears running down their cheeks.

6

Numb with horror, Cait let Lark slide off her back and pushed forward, wordlessly gripping her daughter's hand. Flames were shooting out of windows and doors; smoke was billowing from the inferno that had been her in-laws' beautiful old Georgian home.

Cait started running again, Lark's hand still clutched in her own. She grabbed frantically at the sleeve of a huge fireman in a soot-filthy coat and boots.

"The Monahans!" she shouted above the roar of flame and rushing water. "Where are my in-laws?"

The man shook his head, his sad eyes eloquent as he pointed toward a red car that said 'Fire Chief.' "Talk to the Chief, ma'am," he said, his deep voice hoarse from smoke. "He'll help you out."

Cait glanced back toward the woods, but saw no sign of pursuers. She threaded her way fast through the crowd to the car where a large barrel-chested Irishman around sixty was spitting orders into a two way radio.

"I'm Dr. Caitlin Monahan," she shouted, struggling to make herself heard over the roar of the fire and hoses. "My husband's parents own this house. Are they safe?"

The man stepped out of the car and offered her his hand. "I'm so sorry to have to tell you this, Doctor, but no one made it out of that house. An electrical fire in an old house like this – it races through the walls and then bursts out all over the place at once. They were in their beds on the second floor. The Monahans, the maid, even the dogs..."

Cait fought hard to quell the vertigo. John and Mary, dead? Maybe Jack, too. Maybe, somebody wanted them all dead. That had to be what was happening. But why? She glanced around the sea of faces, fighting for control of head and heart. She felt the Fire Chief's eyes scrutinizing her reaction, waiting for some response.

"I need a phone," she breathed the words, nearly strangled by fear. "And I need the police. Something terrible is happening at my house on Dingletown. We came here to get help..." she lapsed in mid-sentence, it was all too horrible to take in. She looked up into compassionate eyes that understood suffering.

A staticy voice erupted on the car phone and the Chief's attention shifted instantly.

"Get this lady a phone and anything else she needs," he barked to a young aide hovering nearby. "She says she needs the police." The man snapped to, and pulled a cell from his pocket.

"A black and white just pulled up, doctor," the young fireman said, gesturing toward a police car at the edge of the crowd of fire and emergency trucks. "Take my cell phone for your call, ma'am, and I'll tell the cops you need to speak to them." He handed her his cell and took off at a lope. Lark was sobbing quietly at her side. Cait pulled her daughter close to comfort her, before turning her attention to her call.

Gripping the phone in trembling fingers, her breath coming out in little frost clouds, Cait dialed her sister's number in Manhattan, praying Meg would be there, but the answering machine picked up instead. "Meg, it's me," she said urgently. "Something terrible is happening, here. I think Jack's been shot. My in-laws are dead. Please come as fast as you can." She pushed 'End' just as the police car pulled up.

"We've got to get back to my house, fast, officer," she blurted to the cop in the driver's seat. "Men broke into our house. I think they shot my husband. I heard them struggling, shouting, then gunshots. Something about a spear they wanted, I didn't really understand. Please hurry."

The two young cops looked at each other, before one spoke. "You need to calm down, now, ma'am. Let's just take it a little easy here. Where exactly is this house you want to go to?"

"137 Dingletown Lane," she snapped, control at the breaking point. "It isn't far but you've got to get there fast. Please! Backtrack up North..."

"I know how to get to Dingletown, ma'am, but you need to take it easy so we can find out what this is all about."

"My name is Doctor Caitlin Monahan," she said, carefully trying to control her redheaded Irish temper and keep her fear from undoing her. "I need you to get me to my house right now, so I can find out what happened to my husband! He needs our help!"

"And what do you think might have happened to your husband?" the darker haired young policeman asked as if speaking to a slow child.

"I think he was shot. I heard the damned shots!" She heard the edge of hysteria in her own voice.

"And you know what gunfire sounds like from the TV?"

"I know what gunshots sound like," she blurted, frustration raising her voice even higher than terror. "I hunt... I own guns."

The two policemen exchanged glances, then the driver picked up the radio and called in to base. Static and an operator's voice kicked in.

"This is car 12 en route to 137 Dingletown with a woman who says she heard gunshots there. I'm gonna need backup. Over."

Dingletown was dark, the houses trim and elegant behind large walls or massive hedges. Nothing stirred on the foliage-rich street. Cait saw that all the lights were on in her house, although she knew Jack had been turning them off.

"You say there were armed men in your house? How many did you see?"

"I didn't *see* any of them. I heard them – over the baby monitor. First in the den with my husband, then in the halls slamming doors trying to find us. We climbed out through the Widow's Walk." She was halfway out the car door, when the policeman blocked her way.

"You and the little girl will have to stay here, ma'am. We'll go check on your husband."

"I'm a doctor, I'm going in with you. You don't understand... my husband needs me..."

"Sorry, ma'am. I can't let you go in with us. You stay right here with your little girl."

Lark grabbed Cait's hand, as if to say please don't leave me, mommy, tears were running down her cheeks. "They'll help Daddy, won't they Mommy?"

Cait wrapped her arms around Lark's shivering body, "They'll find him, Sweetheart. We just have to be brave now." Cait patted the frightened child, cradling her, trying to keep her own fear banked enough so she could think straight.

Her family was on somebody's hit list and Meg hadn't answered her phone. Maybe her sister, too, was a victim of whatever it was that was after them.

7

The second police car pulled slowly into Cait's driveway as the first cop motioned from the doorway, calling her into the house. "I think you'd better take a look here, Doctor. There's nobody here, but the place is a wreck."

"Where's my husband?" she called out as she lifted Lark into her arms and ran toward the door.

"Maybe you can tell us," he answered.

Cait's heart lurched. Jack could still be alive. Somewhere. Alive and terribly hurt.

The scene inside the door stopped her in her tracks. The house was trashed, furniture overturned, books pulled from shelves, lamps askew. A dark red stain puddled on the Heriz carpet they'd bought in Egypt when Lark was two. Cait, reluctantly let Lark slide to the floor, but held her hand tightly as she walked unsteadily forward. She then knelt to touch the sticky substance, as if touching it brought her closer to Jack. The quantity of puddled blood made her heart physically hurt and she fought the pounding of blood in her ears that could mean she was about to pass out. She battled back the bile in her throat and stood up.

"Better not touch anything, doctor. This could be a crime scene."

"*Could be* a crime scene?" she blurted in consternation. "That's blood on my rug, officer. My husband's blood! Where is he? He could still be in the house or on the grounds... Why aren't you looking for him?" she heard the rising desperation in her own voice and stopped.

"Where do *you* think he is, Doctor?" one of the policemen said quietly and something in the question made Cait look up sharply, seeing the suspicion in his eyes.

"Dear God..." she breathed in utter disbelief. "You can't be suggesting I had something to do with all this?" She gestured to the disastrous mess in the room. "Are you out of your mind? I loved my husband more than life! Why aren't you looking for Jack?"

"At the moment we have no way of knowing what happened here, Doctor, and we have only your word for the fact that your husband was even in the house tonight."

"My Daddy was so here!" Lark shouted, clinging to her mother's sleeve. "If my Mommy says somebody hurt him then you better go find him!"

Meg Fitzgibbons, tall and athletic in a dark blue suit and white starched shirt, somewhat wrinkled from a day in court followed by a cocktail party, took in the scene from the doorway, despite the best efforts of the cop who was trying to block her path. She had a good-looking make-up free face, the kind that suggested a straightforward, bring-it-on approach to the world. Her long blunt-cut brown hair and make-up free skin added to the serious persona, as did the I don't suffer fools gladly look on her face.

"What exactly is going on here?" she demanded, in her best courtroom intimidation voice. "This is my sister's home and I need to check on her safety and that of my niece. Are you alright, Cait? Lark?" she called over the man's intervening shoulders.

"Thank God you're here!" Cait started toward the door, relief at the sight of her sister flooding her. "I was afraid they'd gotten you, too."

"Excuse me, ma'am," said the more pugnacious of the two officers still body-blocking Meg's path. "I'm afraid you can't come in here right now. This is a crime scene under investigation."

Meg gave the man her most withering stare. "My name is Megan Fitzgibbons. I'm Doctor Monahan's sister, and her attorney. I need to speak with my client, immediately and in private." She pulled a card from her pocket and handed it to him in an official gesture that suggested she was ready to wage war. The cop looked to his partner for guidance. The second man shrugged and Meg walked toward her sister without waiting further permission. Two more cop cars had just pulled up to the front of the house.

"Cait, why don't you and I go into the kitchen," Meg said steadily, "and leave these officers to do their work. Lark, baby, why don't you come give your old auntie a hug – it looks to me as if it's been a rough night and we could all use a cup of that tea your mom tells me you've learned how to make really well."

"How on earth did you get here so fast?" Cait asked. "It's only twenty minutes since I called you?"

"I was on my way back to the city from New Canaan – a party at my boss's house, when I checked for messages. You sounded desperate, so I burned rubber on 95."

The three reached the kitchen and threw their arms around each other, the minute the door shut behind them.

"So, what the hell happened here?" Meg demanded. "Did you say Jack was shot? And who trashed your house?"

Cait blurted the story from the beginning, stopping only when her emotions got the better of her, and to answer Meg's pointed questions. Lark listened wide-eyed to the recital, analytical brain in high gear. Lark paid attention, too, to her aunt's succinct assessment and advice.

"Look, Cait," Meg was saying, "nobody's more of a persistent idealist than I am – but I also know how screwed up our legal system can be and how bamboozled local law enforcement can get in any case that's not simple." She paused to make sure Cait was tracking after all she'd been through. Her sister looked pretty ragged.

"Take a look at what we've got here that's weird. There's no body, but plenty of blood stains that'll turn out to be Jack's. So as of now your husband's a missing person in their book, and a possible victim of foul play. That makes you the prime suspect, spouses always are. You're going to have to get wary of everybody, very fast. That trusting nature of yours can only get you into hot water for now. Trust no one as Muldur would say, until we get a handle on what the hell's going on here. It sounds to me way beyond the Greenwich Police Department. Remember, with Jack's security clearance, this may have something to do with his work. Do you have any idea if he was into anything dangerous?"

Cait shook her head and yanked another Kleenex from the box on the counter. She blew her nose, wiped her eyes and said, "No. He never would have told me about anything classified."

Meg nodded, thinking. "OK," she said, "but that doesn't mean he wasn't doing something classified that could have triggered what's happened here. I'm going to try to get the boys in blue out of here as fast as possible by promising you'll make a full statement first thing in the morning. Even at that, it'll take time for them to comb this place for signs of Jack. The minute they're gone, you and I and that smart little cookie over there are going to sift through this house with a fine tooth comb to see what we can find out. Sound right to you, so far?"

Cait nodded, the full impact of all that had happened beginning to seep in like ice water through a crack in the wall. She was trying to keep it together for Lark's sake, but her world had just nova'd in front of her and she felt as if she were bleeding from wounds so deep they had to be mortal. Jack, *Jack. Where are you?* kept shrieking in her mind. She wanted to scream out for him... wanted to weep for all that had been lost in a heartbeat... all that would never be. She wanted to beat her breast and shout to God, "How could you do this to us?" and beg and plead for mercy for Jack, all at the same time.

She felt suddenly drained of all energy, and she couldn't get the sound of Jack's stricken voice out of her head. Or the sound of the gunshot.

"But where's Jack, Meg?" she pleaded instead of answering Meg's question. "He's lost so much blood..." her voice faltered on the words. "I've got to find him..."

Meg bit her lip, a habit from childhood she employed when trying to keep from speaking what was on her mind.

"It'll be okay, Mommy," Lark interjected, sensing her mother's despair. "We'll find Daddy, and it'll all be okay." She put her arms around her mother to comfort her. Cait and Meg's eyes met above the child's head, Meg's full of troubled question marks, Cait's full of anguish.

Meg sighed, took a deep breath and headed for the living room to try to sweet-talk the cops out of the house, that up until a few hours ago, had been the most improbably happy one she'd ever known.

—————————————————— **8** ——————————————————

The police search of the house and grounds finally came to an end, having turned up little useful evidence beyond inconclusive footprints.

Cait sat in Jack's big leather arm chair, her legs drawn up into an almost fetal position as she tried to force her brain to focus on anything that could be a clue. Her eye makeup had been cried off, and her face was drawn and colorless. Lark had finally drifted off to sleep on the living room sofa, but she tossed fitfully and a fever-flush tinged her cheeks. Cait had checked her forehead a dozen times already and as she rose to do so again, she felt her sister's eyes on her, and looked over at Meg.

"We'd better start searching while we're still on our feet," she said resolutely. "There's got to be something in this house to explain all this, Meg." The adrenaline had ebbed, and she was bone weary but knew there wouldn't be any rest tonight for either one of them.

Cait straightened up, shocked at how unsteady she felt on her feet. There was an aura of unreality about the last few hours, as if she were wrapped in cotton wool. She'd treated Post Traumatic Stress Syndrome often enough to know she wasn't operating on all cylinders, but the sense that she was trapped in an amorphous nightmare from which she would soon awaken seemed to be holding her in a state of suspended animation, somewhere just outside the reach of reality. She knew it was the body/mind's way of holding unbearable pain at bay, but if ever she'd needed all brain cells working, it was now.

"You try Jack's desk," she said to Meg, surprised her voice still worked when nothing else seemed to. "I'll head upstairs. There's a key on the ring in my purse. Just do me a favor and don't leave Lark alone even for a second, okay?"

Her sister nodded, hearing the maternal fear, so near the surface.

"Who needs a key, the drawers are all smashed open."

Cait nodded and headed for the staircase. She was pretty sure she knew every item in their bedroom, but the attic might offer possibilities. And it was a big house, with a million cubbyholes. She sighed inwardly at the thought of the dozens of boxes and crates that filled the spaces under the eaves, any one of which could hold the needle in the haystack, but doing something, anything, was better than sitting still.

The ringing doorbell startled both women. Their eyes met briefly, and Cait changed direction halfway up the stairs, heading toward the door. Four dark-suited men, tall and clone-like in the similarity of their builds, bearing and wardrobes, filled the porch beyond the front hall. The man closest to the door seemed in charge; he held up an official looking badge for a fleeting moment, then put it back in his pocket.

"I'm Special Agent Royce," he said, in a voice out of central casting for government agent. "May we come in?"

Cait felt Meg move past her and reach out her hand toward the man.

"May I see that ID, please?" she asked, and the man reluctantly pulled the leather case from his pocket again and handed it to her.

"NSA?" Meg said wonderingly. "What's NSA doing here? And how did you get the news so soon?"

"I'd prefer to tell you inside," the man said steadily.

"And I'd prefer you answer the question here, or you're not going inside," Meg replied in precisely the same tone.

"We have questions for Dr. Monahan about the whereabouts of her husband."

"I'm Dr. Monahan," Cait said, stepping forward. "Are you here to help us find my husband?"

"We should discuss that inside," the man persisted.

"I'm Dr. Monahan's counsel," Meg interjected. "She's been through a great deal tonight and this really isn't a good time…"

"No, Meg," Cait interrupted. "Maybe they can help us."

Meg took a deep breath, held it, then moved aside grudgingly. Cait tended to trust people too quickly; she herself trusted no one, and the priority was searching the house for clues to what was happening. As the men filed past, she pulled her sister aside. "For God's sake, be careful," she whispered. "We don't know why they're here. Don't assume they're on our side!"

Cait nodded and started walking towards the den, as two of the men peeled off and headed for the stairs.

"Just a minute," Cait called after them. "Where are you going?"

"To search the premises for evidence, Dr. Monahan," Agent Royce answered.

"Not without telling me why you're here, you're not!" Cait said emphatically. Suddenly, she realized she'd had enough violation for one night, and Meg's instincts right now were more reliable than her own.

"We don't need your permission, doctor," Royce answered.

"But without it, you do need a search warrant," Meg put in, as much starch in her voice as there'd been in his.

"You're going to have to tell us what you know whether you want to or not, Dr. Monahan," he countered.

"What the hell is the matter with you people?" Cait exploded. "I've already told the police everything I know and that surly attitude of yours is not going to elicit anything at all from me, unless you explain exactly who you are, what your interest is in my husband, and why you're here. If you've come to help me find Jack, I'll be happy to cooperate, otherwise you can consider this conversation at an end."

"Your husband has top level security clearance, Dr. Monahan. He works on highly sensitive government matters. Now he's missing and we intend to know why."

"Was Jack working on some project involving terrorists?" Cait asked, involuntarily glancing into the next room to where Lark was sleeping.

"We're not at liberty to tell you that," Royce replied.

"I have a child who may be at risk here, Special Agent Royce. I need to know exactly what I'm up against. Do you know who did this to my husband?"

"That information is classified, I'm afraid, Doctor. But if you'll let us take a look around, maybe we'll find something useful."

"Which you also won't tell me about?" she retaliated, anger rising again. She had a long fuse, but a redhead's temper. "I don't think so. I'd like you and your men to leave now – it's been a long, ugly night and I have a sick child."

The expression on his face said he'd dealt with difficult women before. "We'll be back, Doctor. With or without a warrant, we can search, but tomorrow morning can work, too."

Cait held the door open wordlessly as they filed through. When they'd gone she turned to Meg.

"If there's anything in this house we need to find, we've got to find it now," she said. "I didn't like the look of that crowd – all ice water in the arteries. I wish the police hadn't taken my guns," she added as an afterthought, as she locked the door emphatically behind the retreating men.

"They'll check your weapons against any evidence they've found, then return them as long as you're not charged with a felony."

"Could that really happen?"

"Highly unlikely, but if they want to squeeze you.... Let's not worry till we have to, okay? We've got enough on our plates without that possibility."

Both women were excellent shots, the result of their father's tutelage and a summer house in the mountains of western North Carolina, where they'd hunted with him and his best friend Jake Many Feathers, from the local Indian res, during every school holiday for nearly 20 years.

Meg started back toward the den. If anything that would help them find Jack was in the house, they'd only have a few hours to find it. "Do you know Jack's computer password?"

Cait stopped. "Lark can get in. They work on his computer all the time. But if there's anything sensitive there, it'll be encrypted."

"Still... let's copy everything on the hard drive in case they confiscate the computer in the morning. I hate to wake up the Baby Bird, but I think we may have to. They'll be back with a warrant as soon as they can roust a judge out of bed."

Cait nodded. "There are thumb drives on my desk. Maybe Lark can just tell us the password so we can upload the files while we search. But let's let her sleep a little longer before we do that. When she wakes up she'll have to face what's happened..." Cait let the thought trail off.

Methodically, the two women scoured the large house until exhaustion finally forced them to stop. After waking Lark for the password and downloading everything she could, Meg slipped the thumb drives into her handbag and she and Cait loaded a box of files and discs from Jack's desk, and another from the attic, into her car before calling it quits. The night was icy clear and full of stars; their breath made frost clouds as they moved back toward the house.

Cait peeled off her coat and furry earmuffs, then collapsed heavily onto one of the sofas that flanked the living room fireplace – the small pile of objects she'd collected in her search sat on the table in front of her. None looked promising for leads, but some were just too personal to leave behind for the prying eyes she knew would be there in the morning. She tried not to look at Jack's photo out of self-preservation, but it drew her gaze magnetically, so she slipped it into her pocket.

Meg carried in two cups of tea from the kitchen on a small wooden tray. "The Irish panacea," Cait said ruefully. "A cup of tea for whatever ails you, from heartache to nuclear war…"

Meg sat down on the opposite couch.

"Can you sleep if you go to bed?" she asked with concern.

Cait shook her head. "There are two blankets in the armoire with the TV. I'll get pillows and we can camp out here on the couches for what's left of the night. I can't go back to our bedroom…" her voice wavered on the last few words. "I don't think we should separate, do you?"

"No way. I've got a .380 in my handbag. It's not much of a canon, but I don't want to risk any more visitors tonight without some sort of protection."

The women drank the steaming tea without speaking, and settled in on their makeshift beds, the kitchen light left on for comfort, Lark sprawled out on the armchair and ottoman in the corner. Neither fell asleep.

"I was thinking about Papa," Cait said finally into the semi-darkness. "About how he must have felt when Mamma died. How there was always that secret sorrow in him after that, that nothing could reach, not even us. He must have missed her so damned much."

Meg bit her lip before she spoke.

"We don't know Jack's dead, Cait. Not yet."

For a long moment Cait didn't reply.

"I don't know how I know this, Meg – but I know he's not coming back. Just like I knew about Mamma. Something's gone that was there… like a note I've always heard with my heart and now it's silent. Jack's not coming home."

Meg forced back the platitudes of reassurance she might have used to comfort someone else. Cait had always been fey, a quality understood in Irish families. Born with a caul, she'd always had some kind of sixth sense, especially about death. They'd been eight and nine when their mother went to the hospital to deliver a baby brother and Meg had found her sister sitting on the sunporch, knees drawn up, arms around them, staring into space, tears running down her face.

"What's wrong with you," she'd asked, annoyed that Cait was down on such a happy day. "Daddy said we can go see them this afternoon at the hospital."

But Cait had turned a stricken face toward her and whispered, "Something terrible's happening, Meggy. Something terrible's happening to both of them."

No words of comfort had worked then either. And who could have known that a hidden aneurysm would burst during labor and in the time it took to figure out what was killing the mother, the baby boy she carried would choke on his own umbilical cord. Who but Cait?

"I love you, Caitlin," Meg whispered now into the darkness, defeated by the memory. "Somehow, it'll be alright." Their father's words of comfort in the worst of times, echoing in her head. *This too shall pass.*

Both women lay staring into the silent darkness for a long, long while before they fell into troubled slumber.

9

The sharp rap on the front door broke through the sleep haze. Cait sat up, disoriented and saw Meg do the same on the other sofa.

The rap, sharper this time, was accompanied by a voice calling Cait's name.

"You in there, Dr. Monahan?" a deep male voice was shouting. "I'm Detective Aurelio from the Greenwich Police."

Cait opened the door and knew by the Detective's face that the news was grim. She motioned him into the house, steeling herself for his message.

Lark, too, had wakened at the sound. She stood like a bedraggled puppy next to Meg, her aunt's arm around her small shoulders.

Cait took a deep breath, held it a moment, then followed the man to the living room and sat down next to her sister and child.

"You've found my husband, haven't you?" she asked, reaching instinctively for her daughter.

The man nodded, reluctant to put words to it.

"I'm afraid the news isn't good, Doctor," he said, clearing his throat. "The Westport Police found your husband's body just off Exit 18. He'd been dead several hours before we found him."

"The gunshot wound?" she asked, hoping he'd died quickly, the only possible comfort.

Detective Aurelio cleared his throat again. This was the toughest part of his job, breaking the news. "It appears he was tortured some, Doctor. His fingers were broken... there were burn marks... other wounds." He glanced at the child. "He died from blood loss, we think. Of course, we'll know more after the autopsy." He watched carefully to see how much she could take -- the woman was a doctor, but they were talking about her husband.

Cait put up her hand involuntarily as if it could ward off the news. "No more..." she managed to say. "Not yet..." She dug her nails into her palm. Jack's gone. *Jack's gone.* The words were a litany of confirmation of the worst fear she'd ever had. Jack's gone and I'm still here... how can that be?

Detective Aurelio was talking, saying things she couldn't really connect with except on the most perfunctory level. She heard her own voice replying, just as if the world hadn't come to an end. Meg was saying something to the man, showing him out the door.

Cait sat very still, waiting for her heart to stop hammering in her ears, waiting to be able to focus on something just beyond her grasp. She couldn't let herself think of Jack tortured. She'd volunteered for three summers at Amnesty International, years before... had read the files, had talked to survivors of torture. She felt her sister's arms go around her shoulders... felt Lark's sobbing body curl in next to hers on the sofa and tried to come back for their sake, but some instinct begged her to stay in limbo just a little longer before the full impact of the pain would come crashing down. She put her arms around both of them and clung there silently until she began to cry, softly at first, then great wracking sobs that shook all three as they clung together.

I will miss you forever, she said the words silently to her husband, wherever he was. *I love you all there is and I will miss you forever.*

10

The triple funeral for Jack and his parents was a horror mitigated only by exhaustion. Cait was numb with grief, Meg was knee-walking from overseeing all the funeral details and trying to keep Cait going. There were few relatives to worry about, although dozens of friends, neighbors and students had called or appeared to pay their last respects.

The religious service at the gravesite ended and the well-wishers dispersed, but Cait remained steadfast beside her husband's coffin, desperate to touch him one more time, wondering how she could endure a lifetime of imagining him trapped inside this ugly casket, buried forever in the cold, uncaring earth. *I am not resigned to the hiding away of loving hearts in the cold ground*, Millay had said, with good reason.

Lark and Meg stood hand in hand just behind her. Cait could feel Lark's quiet sobbing, as the child came forward and wrapped her arms around her mother's body. The antibiotics had her respiratory infection on the run but the horror of the past few days meant she was feeling far from well. Cait bent down to hold her daughter until the sobbing stilled a little. The limo that was to drive them home stood patiently at the bottom of the hill, but she couldn't bear the thought of leaving Jack alone in so sorrowful a place, so she stood again, frozen as the Victorian angel statuary that surrounded her in the cemetery.

The man who approached them was tall, elegant and elderly. He walked with the determined step of a much younger man and stopped just short of the casket, making the sign of the cross reverently as he waited to be acknowledged.

Cait looked up into his face, wondering why anyone would choose such a terrible moment to intrude. But she was struck by the compassionate expression she saw on a face that must once have been very handsome.

"Do I know you?" she asked. "I saw you earlier at St. Mary's."

"Permit me to introduce myself, Dr. Monahan, and to offer my sincerest condolences for your inconceivable loss. My name is Anthony Delafield, Earl of Urnbridge. I was a close friend of your late father-in-law. I would never presume to intrude at such a moment except for the extreme urgency of my mission. May I speak with you privately?"

Blade-straight at 6'4", with snowy hair, and a courtly manner, Anthony Delafield exuded the patrician air of British privilege. He seemed determined to engage their attention.

Cait and Meg exchanged looks and Cait instinctively reached for Lark and pressed her close to her side.

"I have no secrets from my sister," she said, "but I think my daughter has had too much to cope with already."

"Might she wait in your car for a few moments, then, Dr. Monahan? We could speak in mine," he motioned toward a Rolls Silver Cloud parked on the circular road beside the hill. All cars but theirs and his had departed. "I don't mean to sound melodramatic, doctor, but I can't stress strongly enough that this is a matter of life and death."

Cait placed Lark in the care of the limo driver and the two women followed the Earl to his automobile.

"Your father-in-law, John, was both a scholar and an idealist, Dr. Monahan," he began. "I admired him greatly. I first knew him when we both served in Allied Intelligence during World War II. He was employed as a cypher expert, but as you perhaps know, his great predilection was for history – it was his delight and his passion. One which we shared."

"Yes, I know about his erudition, Mr. Delafield," Cait replied, a tired edge to her voice. "I'm afraid I don't see the relevance..."

"But did you also know, my dear," Delafield interjected, "that in April, 1945, John Monahan was with General George Patton when he liberated a certain bunker under St. Katherine's Church in Berlin?"

Cait and Meg exchanged puzzled glances.

"And that he and three other young soldiers were made party to a conspiracy there -- one which has the most profound significance for humankind?"

Cait sat up straighter, wondering if the old man might be unhinged.

"I have no idea what you're talking about," she replied carefully.

"What they found, my dear Caitlin – may I call you by your given name?" He hesitated and she nodded affirmatively. "... was the Spear of Longinus. The legendary weapon that pierced Christ's side on the Cross."

"I've never heard of that legend," Meg interjected.

But Cait recognized the name she hadn't been able to remember... the unfamiliar words Jack had shouted on the night he died.

"I assure you, it is more than legend, Ms. Fitzgibbons. It is a fact. You see, the Spear of Longinus has been venerated for two thousand years as an object of rare occult power. Many of history's most famous men believed that by possessing it, one inherited the ability to rule the world."

"Who were these men and why would they believe such a fairytale?" Cait asked, trying to digest his extraordinary statement.

"My dear, I realize in your current grief, this all sounds a bit mad and certainly irrelevant. But I give you my word that everything I tell you is true and of great consequence to you and to your daughter. Please, hear me out, before you judge.

"According to legend," he continued, now with both women's complete attention, "Gaius Cassius Longinus, the Roman Centurion who thrust his Spear into Christ's side on that terrible day on Cavalry, set a strange destiny in motion, which, over the centuries, has played a hidden but dominant role in world history. Longinus was, we believe, a secret convert to Christianity – some have posited that he may have pierced Christ's side as an act of mercy, not malice, and to assure fulfillment of an Old Testament prophecy. Whatever his religious convictions, after the Crucifixion, Longinus the Centurion, managed to deliver the Spear, which was covered in Christ's blood, to Joseph of Arimathea. He may also have helped the man spirit it out of Palestine.

"Over the centuries, the Spear of Longinus has been owned by a succession of extraordinarily powerful men – Charlemagne, Constantine, Otto the Barbarian, Tamarlane, the Knights Templar, to name but a few of them – and, finally, by Adolf Hitler – all of whom fervently believed that it gave them the power to rule the world."

"How do you know all this and what has any of it to do with my sister and my niece?" Meg interrupted, skepticism obvious in her tone.

Delafield smiled. "You are just as I'd imagined you, Ms. Fitzgibbons – direct and ready to do battle, if need be. I admire both characteristics.

"You see, John Monahan, I, and two other young Americans, were the first to enter that bunker, along with General Patton. We discovered the Spear and the counterfeit Hitler had made to protect the real Spear from theft. I knew of its occult significance and when I apprised the General of the Spear's history and its occult powers, he – being both an amateur historian and no stranger to the unseen universe – was disturbed by the implications of the find. I'm afraid that acting on impulse – or perhaps inspired by those who guide humanity's destiny – the General made a rash decision. One which I believe has now, my dear Caitlin, ended my friend John's life prematurely, as well as that of his son, your husband."

Delafield seemed to drift backwards in time for a heartbeat. Then he said steadily, "I'm afraid that, with the General's blessing, we four young men stole the Spear of Longinus."

Cait's eyes widened in disbelief.

"Are you telling us that General George Patton, the most famous general of the Second World War, was complicit in the theft of an historic relic?" she asked incredulously. "That seems inconceivable to me."

"Perhaps it would be more accurate to say he allowed the theft to transpire, for humanitarian reasons. Please let me attempt to explain what I believe his motives were, Caitlin, before you decide. The General was a most remarkable man. I knew him fairly well, you see, as he was a good friend of my father's.

"George Patton, was a man marked by history, his own and the world's. He'd come from a long line of soldiers – fathers, uncles, grandfather, all military men. All proud of it. So young George had always expected he would grow up to be a soldier, and he'd prepared himself, body, mind and spirit for that role.

"But it wasn't merely the events of this lifetime that called him to battle, you see. Ever since boyhood he'd experienced vivid memories of previous lifetimes. Countless wars, endless battlefields, all lived within him, he said. And in great detail. He knew, for example, that he'd led the brave but doomed Spartan forces – the fabled 300 – at Thermopylae. He knew how it felt to lead men into the euphoria of victory or the misery of defeat. He was a warrior. Always had been. And he reveled in that knowledge.

"After we'd made the discovery in St. Katherine's, the General took me aside for a private conversation. He knew of my family's, shall we say, unusual spiritual inclinations. He asked me all I knew of the Spear's occult history, and seemed quite moved by the story. And quite troubled, I might add.

"He said when he'd held the two Spears – the real and the counterfeit – in his hands in that bunker, he had known in an instant which Spear was the One. He'd felt the unmistakable power course through him, he said, and, like Frodo with the One Ring, he'd also sensed its danger. 'Power of this magnitude has the ability to corrupt,' he told me emphatically. Power's a damned slippery slope and politics is a damned dirty business,' he said, and it was obvious he was deeply troubled by the moral responsibility of determining what to do with our find. He asked me to search my own conscience for answers, and said he'd do the same.

"That night, perhaps with the guidance of Divine Providence, a plan formed in my mind quite clearly. I felt it might provide the answer – for the General, for myself, and for humanity, so I presented it to Patton the next morning and as luck would have it, he agreed. He would return the counterfeit to the Hapsburg family – they had owned the Spear before Hitler stole it – and we four men who had been with him for the discovery, would spirit away the real one, to be placed somewhere safe and secret, until such time as mankind seemed ready for its responsibilities.

"The General told me he had no qualms at all about three of us co-conspirators. He was a good judge of men, he said, and three of us seemed well chosen by a higher power for this task. But the fourth soldier – a chap named Ruddy Dandridge – troubled him. He was a bit of a spoiled brat, I believe you Yanks would say. Over-privileged, under-disciplined and rather full of his own importance. Patton asked me if I thought that Ruddy Dandridge had been chosen to be there in that bunker with us for God's own purpose? You see, neither of us believed any of us had been there by accident.

"The General then pulled out an old journal of his, and handed it to me, open to a particular page. He showed me a poem about his own soul's past, that he'd written years before. It was called *Through a Glass, Darkly*. He said it now seemed prophetic, and he thought, perhaps, once I'd read the poem, I'd understand why this matter was so important to him." And he was quite right. In the poem he spoke of his many remembered lives as a soldier, and even posed the question of whether he could have been the one who stabbed Jesus in the side, while the Savior was on the Cross."

Delafield reached into his breast pocket and pulled out a piece of paper, handing it to Cait and Meg, so they, too, could read the poem.

"You see, my dear young ladies," Delafield said as Cait and Meg exchanged glances after having read the moving poem, "the General was an extraordinary man, and I believe he was chosen by Fate to determine the next stop for the Spear of Longinus on its circuitous journey through the corridors of power."

"And you want us to believe that you, yourself, were there for this discovery," Meg pressed, trying to get the story straight. "You must have been a very young man, Lord Delafield, to have been on the general's staff in 1945..." she began.

He smiled ruefully at the question, "Yes, you are quite right about that – it seems to me several lifetimes ago, now looking back. I was 24 years old, an officer in British Intelligence and I'd been seconded to the General when his Third Army was on its way to Berlin. My father, who knew and admired George Patton... as a general and as an honorable man, had pulled a few strings to make this happen, you may be sure.

Delafield glanced at the expression on the women's faces.

"I can see how troubled you both are by what I'm telling you, and the timing of our conversation is so unfortunate... but if you'll indulge me for a moment more, I believe it would help you to know something about the four of us who became the Caretakers. You see, having convinced the General to allow this theft to transpire, I next had to convince my would-be accomplices to cooperate... let me tell you how I remember that conversation, as it speaks to the characters of all involved...

The Conspirator's Tale
Berlin 1945 April

Anthony Delafield looked again at the three troubled faces of the young men seated around the table in the Officers' quarters. Lincoln Tremaine, one of the Negroes Patton had made a point of admitting to his command, sat quietly at one end. Large and broad-shouldered, the man looked like a rugby lock-forward, but his immense musculature was most likely the result of hard work, not hard play. From what Delafield knew of the bloke, he was poor as a church-mouse, but brilliant enough to have begun a college education before enlisting, no mean feat for a poor colored boy from rural Alabama.

Rutherford Dandridge, called Ruddy because of his initials and a somewhat florid complexion, sat on his left. He was cut from far different cloth. Blond, blue-eyed, the picture of New England WASP breeding, he had grown perfectly into the patrician expectations of a prominent New Hampshire family. Seated next to him was John Monahan, a mathematical genius with a gift for ciphers and a quirky sense of humor. Something of a prodigy, he'd been teaching at Harvard since he was 19 years of age. Brains were the common link at this table. That, and the bizarre mission Fate seemed to have bestowed on the four of them yesterday. Delafield, because of his family's occult knowledge, at least had an inkling of what this conspiracy would require, the rest needed to be told before they took on such grave responsibility.

"We must assume, gentlemen," Delafield began, "that we have not been chosen for this mission by chance."

"Why must we assume that?" asked Ruddy, with a wry laugh. "Perhaps we were simply in the wrong place at the wrong time."

He was smart, but a trifle too over-privileged to accept anything at face value, thought Delafield. He'd be the hardest of the bunch to trust.

"You and John are intelligence experts," he continued unfazed. "Lincoln is the most resourceful brain in the unit, I bring certain unusual credentials to the party that are of an occult nature, which is what led me to conclude that our merry band is not an accident. You see, gentlemen, whether you believe me or not, the relic we've just uncovered in St. Katharine's has supernatural powers that can be extremely dangerous in the wrong hands." He held up a hand to stay the explosion of disbelief and derision, around the table. "I do not believe for a moment that the Universe would permit this sacred object to fall into the hands of just any ragtag and random group of men. I believe we've been chosen."

"Very dramatic and compelling, Delafield," said Ruddy, "and we all know your grandfather dabbled in all sorts of occult nonsense and wrote books on the subject, but let me submit that the Universe seems to have permitted this very Spear to fall into the hands of an utter madman in the person of Herr Hitler."

"Let's hear him out, Ruddy," Lincoln interrupted thoughtfully. He sounded not argumentative, but rather as if he were carefully considering the whole situation.

Monahan cleared his throat and came to Linc's defense. "The General doesn't do things rashly," he offered. "If he's decided to protect this Spear by extraordinary means, who are we to say no? He told me just this morning that the battle between good and evil depended on men's choices... Remember what he said to us? That he was choosing us for our integrity, just as the Universe had chosen him..." he let the thought trail off.

"That's all very noble and high-minded, John," Ruddy interjected, "but you're asking us to be involved in a conspiracy that could be construed as treason. I, for one, want no part of it."

Lincoln moved his chair back a little, as if he were having a hard time containing his huge frame in so small a space. "But you are involved now, Ruddy, aren't you?" he said. "We all are. Take a rational look at your choices here. Would you sell out the old man and turn him in for theft? He seemed utterly sincere in his concerns about this Spear... Tony here told me some things about its history. For centuries powerful men have believed this Spear had some kind of magical power. Did you know Attila the Hun captured it, and actually gave it away because he said he could feel the power it possessed, but didn't serve the God it belonged to?"

"Legends," scoffed Ruddy. "Nothing more than overblown legends."

"Then what's the harm?" Linc shot back, and Delafield smiled. He'd noticed few men ever won a verbal battle with Lincoln Tremaine. The big man's quiet logic tended always to provide the last word in any confrontation.

"Look," John Monahan placated. "I don't believe in magic, but I believe in the General. He's an irascible son of a bitch, but honorable to the bone. If he's willing to take this chance – after all, it'd be his hide they'd go after if anybody finds out – we're just following orders."

"Like all those good Germans?" Ruddy asked contemptuously.

"I'm in," John countered, not bothering to argue. He'd always found Ruddy to be a consummate pain in the ass. "Who else is?"

Tremaine and Delafield nodded affirmatively.

"Ok. Ok." Ruddy said. "I won't rat on you or the General. You have my word on it as a gentleman. But I also don't want to know where the spear gets hidden. If things ever get dicey, or Herr Schickelgruber comes to collect it, I want no part of the damned thing."

The other three men considered this for a moment, then nodded their agreement. Linc spoke again. "Ruddy may have a point. Maybe not everyone involved should know exactly where the Spear is kept. If only one of us knows, there's less chance of the secret getting out if we're ever interrogated."

"Good point," Delafield agreed. "Perhaps the fairest way to decide who hides it is if we all draw lots.. One man knows... the rest of us support him if he ever needs us."

Monahan and Tremaine nodded assent. Dandridge held up a hand. "No lot for me," he said. "I'll keep the secret, but that's as far as I'm willing to go with this hare-brained scheme."

"What happens when we die?" Linc asked quietly. "Does the Spear just disappear forever?"

"Isn't that the whole bloody purpose of this exercise?" Ruddy said with a short laugh.

Delafield put the crumpled pieces of paper he'd been fiddling with into his hat and held it out to the others.

"We'll draw lots," he said. "Whoever picks the paper with the X on it, hides the Spear. Before he dies, he arranges for someone he trusts to take on the responsibility for the next generation. Agreed?"

They all nodded, then three of them pulled a paper from the hat.

"Oh shit!" John Monahan said fervently, as he stared at the paper he'd drawn. "How the hell will I ever get this thing out of Germany without getting caught?"

"I can arrange that," Delafield answered, obviously having thought it through. "I have diplomatic immunity and access to the diplomatic pouch. When the war ends, I'll see that the Spear is returned to you."

John, obviously concerned, finally nodded his consent. The full impact of the responsibility he'd taken on, had just hit home.

Delafield finished his story and returned to the here and now... he had told the tale so compellingly, both women felt they'd seen it all unfold.

"I realize this is a complex story, my dears," Lord Delafield continued with concern, seeing the consternation on both women's faces. "But on my honor as a gentleman, every word of it is true."

Cait and Meg exchanged troubled glances.

"I've got to get back to my home, Lord Delafield," Cait said, to avoid commenting on what they'd just heard, and because her heart and brain were already on circuitry overload. "People will be gathering there after the funeral, and I'm pretty much holding on to my emotions by a thread right now. I barely know what to say to you... except this: In order to believe what you've told me, I'll need to know a great deal more... I just can't cope with any of it today."

Meg interjected, "Could we three meet tomorrow, Lord Delafield? That would give my sister and me a chance to digest what you've said."

The old man nodded. "I understand completely. But please know we can wait no longer than that. You are all in extreme danger and my ability to protect you in this country is limited. Tomorrow, I will tell you what I propose."

He offered his hand to both women, squeezing their fingers in an oddly protective way, then helped them from the car.

"Until then," he said handing Cait an engraved card with a Park Avenue address. "Come at 6 tomorrow and all will be explained."

"Until then," Cait replied, doubting seriously that one meeting could make sense of all that had happened to her well-ordered life.

The Masters of the Hunt
Part II

"Tactics is knowing what to do
when there is something to do.
Strategy is knowing what to do
when there is nothing to do."

Chessmaster
Savielly Grigorievitch
Tartakower

11

The Delafield address on Park Avenue turned out not to be a coop building, but an old townhouse, more like an Embassy than a private residence.

A uniformed butler received the women and led them to a two story library, where a fire crackled in a massive hearth. Lord Delafield rose when the sisters entered, as did two other men, one Delafield's age, one closer to 40.

"Permit me to introduce you to Prince Siegfried von Hochburg, and to my son Hugh," Delafield said as the two men walked toward the newcomers, and the old Prince greeted Cait and Meg with the courtliness of a bygone age. He was tall and slender, with a fencer's grace, and an angular, aristocratic face softened by a warm smile and the bluest eyes Cait had ever seen.

"My cousin Siegfried," Delafield explained, "knows a great deal about your current problems, my dears. He was one of those who sought to assassinate Hitler and he knew the Führer well. Both he and Hugh wish to help us – I think you'll find each brings a different kind of expertise to that effort."

Hugh Delafield took Cait's hand with the same courtly grace as his father and uncle. He had an athlete's build, broader and more muscular than the older men, and a remarkable face, too craggy to be called handsome, too compelling to be called anything else. There was an intensity about the man that went beyond good looks – the word gravitas popped into her mind. Odd for a man in his 40's.

"Prince Siegfried worked unrelentingly during the war on humanitarian efforts to feed and protect the needy, at great risk to himself and his family," Delafield was saying, and Cait pulled her gaze away from Hugh's to study the older man's face. She thought she saw both courage and compassion there.

"You are a bona fide *Prince*?" Meg asked. "Forgive me, but I didn't think there were any of those left in Germany."

"I am, Ms. Fitzgibbons," von Hochburg answered with an amused smile, obviously not offended by the question, "although that anachronism holds little sway in these times, of course. I'm afraid our Principality no longer officially exists. But my castle is one of the few in Germany kept substantially intact from the 13th Century. It was badly damaged during the war, but was restored after, and remains the von Hochburg family seat, although there are few of us left in the family now."

"I trust you won't be put off by our unexpected presence," he added gently, "but you see, there is so much for you both to know, and so little time... Tony – Lord Delafield – and I believed it would be easiest if we all were to sit together to tell the story as we know it." His German accent was faint and highly educated, but there was an elegant old world cadence that Cait found charming.

"And you came all the way from Germany to do this?" Meg pursued.

"I did," von Hochburg answered, "and Hugh from England. You see, we felt it was imperative. So you could understand the urgency."

Cait glanced at Hugh, who was now standing next to the fire; his body language carried all the easy grace of generations of privilege. He turned his eyes to hers, and said with studied directness, "Perhaps, we should begin as close to the beginning as we can for you, Doctor. My uncle is the true expert here, so perhaps he should start by telling you of the uncanny fascination Hitler had for the Spear of Longinus, and how passionately it had captured his imagination. He called it The Heilege Lanze, by the way... The Holy Lance."

Prince Siegfried nodded at his nephew. "This tale was told to me by Walter Stein himself," he began, "who was a close friend of Adolf's in his youth, and told me of being taken by Hitler one day, to visit the Spear at the Hofburg..." The old man cleared his throat and began to recount what he had been told:

Vienna 1912

The aggressively scruffy-looking young art student sped his friend up the staircase that led into the depths of the Hofburg Treasure House. Young Adolf's face was flushed with excitement and anticipation. He strode down the gangway toward his destination, a wolf on the hunt – the place where the Heilege Lanze rested on its faded velvet cushion was just ahead.

*"It has **powers**, Walter," he breathed excitedly, as he barreled toward the case where the prize lay. "You'll see!"*

Walter Stein hurried behind Adolf, wondering what wild passion possessed his friend today. Not that it was ever easy to fathom the endless mood swings, the strange leaps from near lethargy to wildly strident diatribes on politics, or whatever else happened to set the boy off on a given day, but something had whipped Adolf into a near frenzy of excitement this morning.

Hitler drew to a halt before the case and dropped his voice to a reverent whisper. "Whoever carries this Spear and solves its secrets, holds the destiny of the world in his hands for good or evil, Walter," he breathed. "Can you conceive of such power?"

Walter Johanness Stein looked at his friend more closely, to see if he were serious or jesting. Adolf had a weird sense of humor, so it was never easy to know for certain. He saw the boy's near black eyes were blazing with that strange glaze that sometimes suffused them. He looked almost drugged and there was a thin film of sweat on his pallid brow.

"It's just a legend, Adolf," Stein whispered, fearing that the young man was about to make a fool of himself by fainting as he

had done once before when in this frenzied state. "It's just like those other old relics the Church claims can cure your gout or take away your sins. Just an old farce."

Hitler snapped his head around and fastened his dark gaze on his companion, reproachfully.

"It speaks to me, Walter," he breathed, eyes shining with that strange incandescence. "It has been mine in other times. It will be mine again."

---------------------------------- **12** ----------------------------------

The butler appeared silently in the doorway, as von Hochburg's account ended. He announced that dinner was served, and ushered them into a dining room, resplendent with the opulent grace of an old world, now gone. A roaring fire blazed in a hearth large enough to roast an ox, and the baronial table, glittering with silver and crystal, was lit by candelabra worth a king's ransom in another age. Mesmerized, Cait and Meg seated themselves at the table, both feeling they'd fallen down the rabbit hole.

Delafield was the first to speak. "What we've told you thus far, my dears, is just the tip of the iceberg, as you Yanks would say. And much of what you'll learn this evening will strain credulity. But without the knowledge we hope to impart, we fear you cannot defend yourselves – which is why my cousin and son have come all this way to lend their voices and knowledge to this discussion. So I beg you to hear us out with an open mind. I give you my word we'll answer every question as best we can."

"I understand why *you* are involved in this, Lord Delafield," Cait said, "But, I'm still confused by how Prince Siegfried is involved."

A look passed among the men, and the old prince answered for himself.

"My cousin Tony was a member of the original Conspirators, as you already know," he explained, in his elegant old world diction. "It was he who chose to involve me – and a number of others, whom you may one day meet – in a pact to protect the Spear, and in that way, to protect the world. You see..." he spoke carefully, as if considering where to start a long and complex story, "there are many secrets of great importance to humanity that the world knows little of. We three, who are offering our services to you both tonight, are members of a most discreet and private society – one that has existed in one form or another for centuries – let us call it for the moment, the Hunting Lodge. Our members act as a sort of bulwark for humanity in the battle between Good and Evil. We are watchdogs, if you will, and, when called upon to be, soldiers. Our resources, which are considerable and worldwide, are called into play in many instances and arenas, but especially in those which involve occult power. We are, you see, practitioners of certain esoteric arts that have been long forgotten by most of humanity."

"So, basically, you're telling us you're Dumbledore?" Meg said, both amused and incredulous.

Delafield and von Hochburg exchanged glances, but there was a twinkle in their old eyes as Delafield answered, "Yes my dear, something rather like that, I suppose."

"It's important you understand," Hugh interjected, "that whether you believe in Magic or not, the Spear of Longinus carries immense power, as well as the charisma of legend. During the Reich, Hitler actually convinced all his high ranking officers that the Spear was his god-given key to world domination. He created a Nazi Occult Bureau, called *Ahnenerbe,* and gave it the job of protecting the Spear and other mystical artifacts – by both mundane and arcane means. The powerful occult inner circle of Ahnenerbe was named The Thule Society – it exists to this day."

Seeing how skeptical Cait looked, von Hochburg added gravely, "Adolf Hitler was a practitioner of Black Magic, my dear Caitlin, make no mistake about it. Hard as this may be for you to accept, I have personal knowledge of the fact that he was initiated into the ranks of the Dark Force by a Black Magician of High Degree whom I knew well – a dreadful man named Dietrich Eckart, who was one of the seven founders of the Nazi Party. Eisenhower and Roosevelt knew this, too, of course – Churchill as well – but the Allies went to great lengths to keep the implications of this dark knowledge from the public, as they believed it would cause terror and panic of unprecedented proportions, if Hitler's black magic predilections were known.

"The simple truth is that Hitler, who was at the time of their meeting merely an arrogant and belligerent young malcontent – met Dietrich Eckart, who was already a power-broker extraordinaire – and was instantly seduced by Eckart's stories of the secret dark powers he could learn to command. He was also fascinated by Eckart's conviction that an Aryan race of genetically superior Supermen existed in the "true German" – the blond haired, blue eyed specimen that later became the goal of the Nazi breeding program. Eckart was a master story-teller, and his tales played perfectly into Hitler's Messianic fantasies. Adolf had already fallen in love with the Spear, but it was Eckart who convinced him that his destiny as world ruler was assured by his possessing this relic."

Delafield, drew two books from beneath his chair. "I'm sure you know of *Mein Kampf*, the book that turned a ne'r do well like Hitler into the most infamous tyrant of our century," he said, handing Hitler's famous manifesto to her. "I believe it would help your understanding if you were to read what Hitler himself said of the Spear in his autobiography. If you wouldn't mind reading it aloud, so your sister can hear as well...?"

Cait opened the book to a marked page and began read:

"These foreigners stopped almost immediately in front of where I was standing, while their guide pointed to an ancient Spearhead. At first I didn't even bother to listen to what this expert had to say about it, merely regarding the presence of the party as an intrusion into the privacy of my own despairing thoughts. And then I heard the words which were to change my whole life:

'There is a legend associated with this Spear that whoever claims it, and solves its secrets, holds the destiny of the world in his hands for good or evil'.

"The Spear appeared to be some sort of magical medium of revelation for it brought the world of ideas into such close and living perspective that human imagination became more real than the world of sense.

"I felt as though I myself had held it in my hands before in some earlier century of history – that I myself had once claimed it as my talisman of power and held the destiny of the world in my hands. Yet how could this be possible? What sort of madness was this that was invading my mind and creating such turmoil in my breast?"

When she'd finished reading, Delafield handed a second book to Meg. "This is the memoir of Herr Eckart, written shortly before his death. If you wouldn't mind reading aloud for your sister, the passage I've marked, I believe you will both find it most illuminating and corroborative of all we've been telling you."

Meg opened the bookmarked page and read the marked passage as Cait had done with the other book:

"Follow Hitler! He will dance, but it is I who have called the tune! I have initiated him into the 'Secret Doctrine,' opened his centers in visions and given him the means to communicate with the Powers. Do not mourn for me: I shall have influenced history more than any other German."

Meg laid the book down, a thoughtful expression on her face.

"Der Führer," Delafield said quietly, using the title with obvious contempt, "not only practiced Black Magic, but he forced his highest ranking Generals to take initiation into his infamous Black Magic confraternity. It was dedicated to Evil and world domination *then,* and I assure you it's no less dedicated, *now,* although it's gone underground and few know of its existence. They have metamorphosed into something called simply The Order of the 13, a secret cabal comprised of members of 13 of the most powerful families and institutions on earth."

"The 13," Cait repeated, "that hardly sounds like a lucky number."

"Precisely my dear. You see The 13 aspire to bring about an Armageddon of sorts."

"What does 'of sorts' mean?" Meg interrupted.

"It means they intend to destroy the current order just as Hitler did, and bring about a New World Order under their control."

"From the ashes of World War III, they will take not only monster fortunes, just as they did after World War II, but they will have built the New World Order they so ardently desire. Germany surrendered after the war, you see, but the Nazis never did."

Seeing he had their full attention Delafield continued, "The 13 has its own agenda that has evolved just as the world has. They've infiltrated every fascist country, particularly those in the Middle East, and they have riches and power you can't imagine at their disposal. Between the spoils taken out of Germany by high ranking Nazis at the war's end, the current Arab oil fortunes they tap into, the untold millions in family-controlled banks, and the tendrils they have interwoven into the most lucrative illegal enterprises on earth, their resources are virtually limitless."

13

Cait was still trying to absorb this extraordinary story, when Hugh added with deep concern, "There's one further complication in this very dangerous game that you must be made aware of, Cait. I'm afraid your CIA is a player here." Seeing her disbelief, he went on rapidly. "They're protecting a very old, very ugly secret of their own. Have you heard of Gustav Gruner?"

"Surely, everyone knows of Gruner," she replied impatiently. "Ambassador-at-large... confidant of kings and presidents... *eminence grise* at political and social functions..."

Hugh nodded, his face serious. "Gruner was once famous for something else entirely, I'm afraid. In the Reich, he was Dr. Helmut Guttman, the brilliant and ruthless young medical prodigy who was both a member of Hitler's secret occult bureau and a favorite protégé of Heinrich Himmler, head of the SS. He was personally responsible for helping Himmler devise some of the most brutal concentration camp medical experiments, to fit his occult agenda.

"You see, it wasn't simply that torturing helpless victims provided him sexual gratification – which it did and still does – but he had devised ways of using both their anguish and the energy of their dying in occult rituals, in much the same way a sacrifice's energy is used in the Black Mass."

Cait, listened in increasingly disturbed silence. Her eyes met her sister's, but Meg seemed equally at a loss for words.

"As the war neared an end," Prince Siegfried interjected gravely "Guttman – who was always a brilliant political strategist and opportunist – armed himself with certain secret scientific and medical documents desired by the Allies. These had to do with both the genetics and mind control experiments the Nazis had been conducting with great success since the early '30s. He used them as a bargaining chip with your Central Intelligence Division to save himself from the Nuremburg War Crimes Trials. Because of his cleverness, this butcher was given safe passage by the OSS – the pre-cursor of your CIA – and has prospered in America ever since. Guttman/Gruner doesn't just *believe* himself to be above the law – he *knows* he is."

Siegfried looked both pained and angry at the injustice he was chronicling, but he continued the story:

"Guttman was given his new identity as Gustav Gruner in 1945 by Odessa, the underground railroad of Nazi Sympathizers whose job it was to hide important Nazis from the Allied War Crimes Tribunal at Nuremberg. The OSS then spirited him out of Germany via the Odessa Rat Line and a Vatican passport, just as they did Adolf Eichman. Thus, a new man was "born" who went on to a stellar career in international politics. His face was altered by Odessa surgeons in Paraguay, but he is *the one,* Cait. He is Guttman.

"Now the CIA will do *anything* to keep secret the fact that it brought war criminals of such stature into the U.S. and covered their tracks. The clandestine operation was called Project Paperclip, and although its existence has now been well documented by historians, its deceptions are still quite hidden from the American public at large. The fact that one such as Guttman has access to your President and the highest levels of national security, is something you may be certain the CIA will attempt to cover up at any cost.

"Despite his high profile as benevolent diplomat-at-large," Hugh interrupted, "it is Guttman in his new Gruner identity, who now secretly heads The 13."

"But isn't he about 150 years old, by now?" Meg asked wryly.

"He's quite old, of course," von Hochburg replied with a small chuckle, "but then so am I and so is Delafield, yet I assure you my dear, we are still capable of wielding quite a lot of power, and in Gruner's case, he has a vast network of young fanatics whose strings can be pulled by him and his cohort. And he has a son, Fritz, quite as evil as he, although with perhaps, slightly different motives from his father's. We think the younger man's motivation is primarily greed and a hunger to outdo his father."

"The 13 is all about power and money, Cait," Hugh added. "There's a vast amount of both to be had as a result of any war, if you hold the right purse strings and can manipulate at a high enough level. We need you to believe what we're telling you because your life and Lark's most certainly depend on it."

"Why, exactly, is that?" Cait pressed, her sense of foreboding rising with each new revelation.

"The simple truth is this," the old Prince answered soberly. "Gruner wants the Spear and thinks you have it. We must find the Spear before Gruner does, before they capture you, and torture you or Lark to get the information they *think* you possess."

"Not only do I *not* know where the Spear is," Cait replied hotly, "but I don't understand why this is all happening now, when the Spear has been hidden for 60 years. Why *now*?"

Father and son look at each other as if deciding how much to say, then Delafield continued.

"Have either of you ever heard of Neuschwabenland?"

"Neuschwabenland?" Cait repeated, as Meg said, "No, I don't think so."

"Toward the last days of the war, Hitler sent an expedition under the command of a man named Hartmann – a trusted U Boat Captain – to a place called Neuschwabenland – it was a secret air and naval base located in Antarctica. Hartmann told certain of his men that the expedition was to take the Holy Spear to a secret place for safekeeping, and it has been documented that in 1945, he made this trip.

"At the turn of the current Millennium, Gruner called for its retrieval. We do *not* know why, and can only speculate on the escalating urgency of his desire to obtain it. The Middle East was a tinder box... perhaps a war was being contemplated by those in power. China, India, North Korea and Pakistan all had the bomb, so opportunities for mayhem abounded. We think he may have decided a symbol was needed, and the Spear carried both symbolic and genuine power. *Whatever* the reason, Gruner sent a retrieval team. The box was brought back, but when Gruner had it opened, he found not the Spear, but documents stating that the original and the forgery had been stashed in the St. Katherine's bunker. That's when he dispatched a team to track the original. They appear to have found your family."

Cait sat up straighter in her chair as the full magnitude of the danger to herself and her loved ones settled into her bones. She realized she no longer thought these people at the dinner table were crackpots.

"Your father-in-law, John Monahan, Sr.," Delafield continued, "was the only one of our original four Caretakers who actually *knew* the whereabouts of the Spear, since we Conspirators had drawn lots to determine who would know where it would be kept. We have, however, stayed in contact every few years, since the war, you see. A few issues emerged over the decades and we kept our word by helping John deal with them – all of us but Ruddy, of course. On his 60th birthday, John sent word to me and to Lincoln that because of ailing health, he'd passed the knowledge of the Spear's whereabouts, and the responsibility, on to his son – your husband, Jack."

14

"Even if I accept all of this as gospel," Cait said, tension tautening her voice, "and God help me, I'm beginning to think I might... the Nazi regime seems ancient history now. I can't imagine why this 13 group would need the Spear *now* as its rallying point. Half the world barely remembers the Third Reich."

Hugh leaned forward. "But everyone understands the terror coming out of the Middle East, don't they, Cait? The 13 is knee deep in that debacle. Do *you* know the connection between the

Nazis and the current Middle Eastern tinderbox? Do you understand how deeply the roots of Al Qaeda are entwined with Nazism?"

Cait's large eyes widened at that thought – she looked to her sister to see if Meg knew more than she, but Meg shook her head.

"The terrorist agendas of men like Saddam Hussein, Yasir Arafat, Osama bin Laden, plus organizations like Al Qaeda and Hamas," Hugh said gravely, "can all be traced back to World War II. There were two key figures in the beginning, Adolf Hitler and Amin al-Husseini, the Grand Mufti of Jerusalem.

"Adolf Eichmann, the Nazi butcher who eluded capture for so long, was sent to meet with the British-appointed Mufti in Palestine in 1937, specifically to make him an agent of Nazi Germany. The Mufti was given the job by Hitler of arranging funding and organizing of pro-Nazi organizations in Egypt, Syria, Palestine and Iraq. All this came out at Adolph Eichmann's war crimes trial.

"In '41, Hitler even sent the Mufti to Nazi-occupied Bosnia, where he was given the title 'Protector of Islam.' And when in 1943, Hitler ordered the creation of the Nazi SS Division there, nearly 100,000 Bosnian Muslims volunteered. In many ways, all these pro-Nazi activities set the stage for today's Islamic terrorism."

"But why?" Cait asked, genuinely puzzled. "What do the Nazis and the Radical Islamic Extremists have in common?"

"I'll bet I can answer that one," Meg interjected. "They have a common goal and common enemies, haven't they? Hatred of Judaism, hatred of democracy and the United States. Wars have been fought for far less."

Hugh smiled approvingly. "Precisely." he answered her. "There's been close cooperation between Muslim extremists and Fascists ever since the founding of the Nazi movement in the 1920's. The National Socialism of Hitler had a profound impact on the political philosophies of many radical Islamic political organizations – the Muslim Brotherhood, Nasser's Young Egypt movement, the Social Nationalist Party of Syria and the Ba'ath Party of Iraq. Saddam Hussein's uncle and guardian, Khairallah

Tulfah, was one of the main leaders of the 1941 pro-Nazi coup in Iraq.

"The rise of Al Qaeda and the explosion of neo-Nazi activity in Germany and elsewhere coincided with the breakup of the USSR in the early 1990's. Neo-Nazis in both Europe and the United States began making overtures to Islamic terrorists. The resulting mixture of Nazi and Islamic ideologies is very real and it's very dangerous. The Order of the 13 is stirring this stew of power, money, bigotry and fundamentalist hatred to further its own agenda."

"If all this is true," Cait responds, "why don't we in the U.S. know *any* of this?"

"For the most part, my dear Cait," Prince Siegfried replied, "Nazism is considered old news in your country – and even in mine, I'm afraid, where so many have reason to wish it forgotten. The Holocaust survivors are dying off and the world too easily forgets history and other people's suffering. You might be interested to know however, that much of the coordination of worldwide neo-Nazi/Muslim terrorist activities is still done in the United States. Since overt Nazi activity is outlawed in Germany and many other European countries, neo-Nazis and Islamic extremists have taken advantage of America's First Amendment protections. In fact, the headquarters today of the *Nationalsozialistische Deutsche Arbeiterrpartei* is in Nebraska. The Internet and electronic banking makes communication and the transfer of funds instantaneous, and American rights to privacy afford excellent cover and protection.

"Do you recall how recently President Mahmoud Ahmadinejad of Iran has been making headlines with his Holocaust-denial speeches? He's trying to rewrite history, because he knows so well that Iran welcomed Nazi Gestapo agents and other operatives to Tehran during the prewar and war years, and allowed them to use the city as a base for Middle East agitation against the British and the region's Jews."

"Do either of you know the meaning of the word Iran?" Hugh asked suddenly. Both women shook their heads *no*.

"The Shah of Iran so identified with the Third Reich, that in 1935 he changed his country's ancient name from Persia to Iran, because in Farsi, Iran means Aryan. Both Nazi racial theorists and Persian ethnologists believed they share a common lineage that makes them the Master Race.

"We don't know for certain *why* the Order of the 13 wants the Spear so badly now. Maybe it's a rallying point for reassembling the old myths of a God-given mandate to rule the world. Maybe there's another agenda entirely. Maybe once they've got the Spear, some dictator of their choosing will be made to look like an anointed leader. There are plenty of candidates in the Middle East to choose from."

"So what do you believe is their *real* agenda?" Meg asked.

"We live in explosive political times, Meg," Hugh answered her. "We know with absolute certainty, The 13 plans world-wide anarchy, subversion of individual currencies, and the seizure of overt power, far beyond the shadow power they already possess. They have nearly unlimited money, and tendrils into the Military/Industrial complex, politics, governments, aerospace, drugs legal and illegal, banking, crime – in short, every powerbase on the planet. The 13 wants the Spear, and believe me, no matter how far-fetched the idea of Magic may seem to you, these men know how to work with its occult power. And even if you don't believe in magical powers, you mustn't underestimate the power of mass hysteria, and the value of symbols in manipulating mass consciousness. Fundamentalist religious sects, whether they're Evangelicals or Wahabi Muslims, are easy to manipulate for political purpose. And the fundamentalists of a great many countries hate the United States and would love to destroy her hold on geo-political power.

"The 13 know that the Spear in the Hofburg is the forgery, not the original," von Hochburg continued, "but it has taken them 'til now to track the *real* Spear's whereabouts. For whatever

nefarious reason they want it, they intend to get it back. We believe
Jack and his father and mother were the first casualties in their new
war. We must believe that you and Lark are slated to be next, Cait
– and perhaps, Meg, too. With Jack and his father gone, these
ruthless men have every reason to believe one of you has been
chosen as the new Caretaker for the Spear."

"I'll bet Jack could untangle these threads, if he were here,"
Cait said ruefully, thinking out loud, "he was a genius at solving
puzzles." As she heard herself say the words, the thought triggered
an epiphany.

"Oh my God!" she blurted. "Could it be *that's* what *Lark's
Labyrinth* is all about? If my husband knew he'd someday have to
pass the Spear's whereabouts on to *someone* trustworthy, and he
didn't choose me, could he have chosen Lark, because she's
inherited the family gift for ciphers? What if the secret's hidden in
Lark's Labyrinth?"

"What is *Lark's Labyrinth?*" a chorus of voices asked around
the table.

"A complex computer game," she answered hurriedly. "A
sort of *Dungeons and Dragons* Jack designed for Lark when she
was very little... right around the time he realized she had the same
intellectual gifts he and his father did. Lark could solve the most
complex riddles even as a toddler – her IQ is off the charts, but it
seems to manifest primarily in this weird rarefied gift for numbers
and for solving ciphers. I always figured he was just expanding on
her obvious strengths, by making so much of the game.

"Jack and his father were forever testing her skill with the
Labyrinth, because they always said she'd need it for life. I *thought*
they meant that the intricacies of the game would prepare her for
life's complexities – but what if the game is really the key to the
Spear's whereabouts?"

The four agreed the idea was plausible, but none was adept
enough with computers to offer to be the experts.

"I have a friend in the Foreign Office," Hugh said, eagerly.
"His specialty is ciphers..."

"Let's keep this in the family for now," Meg cut in. "My partner used to be with the FBI Intelligence Division and now has her own Cyber Security business. Let's start with Carter. The game leads too directly back to Lark for us to let anybody else in on this possibility yet."

Cait nodded vigorously. "I couldn't agree more. I could be wrong about this game connection, and I don't want to make my daughter even more of a target..."

"Good call," Hugh said quietly. "The game could play some part in this, although from what I've learned of your husband's extraordinary mind, my instinct tells me a computer game would be too obvious a basket for him to have put all his eggs in. But until we know for certain, I agree you must play it very close to the vest for safety."

Dinner ended before ten and the sisters headed back to Meg's apartment where Lark and Cait intended to stay the night.

*   *   *

After the women left, the three men sat together to discuss the events of the evening.

"You saw in her what I had seen, my boy?" Delafield asked his son.

Hugh, pensive and troubled, raised his eyes to his father's. "I did, Father," he answered quietly, as if measuring his words carefully. "And much more, I'm afraid."

Delafield and von Hochburg exchanged glances, but something in Hugh's voice kept them from pressing him further about what he'd meant by that cryptic remark.

15

Meg slipped the key in the lock of the apartment she shared with Carter, and then held it wide to let Cait walk in ahead of her. Lark ran forward to wrap her mother and aunt in a bear hug.

"Where's Carter, Sweetie?" Meg asked, but it was Matt McCormack who answered as he rose from the sofa and stretched his lanky frame. He was wearing jeans and an old khaki sweater with sleeves pushed up, revealing the muscular arms and Army Rangers tattoo that were so much part of his cop persona.

"Carter's in the shower," he said easily. "She had a rough day and only got here fifteen minutes ago. I've been the chief babysitter, which worked out just fine because the kid, here," he smiled as he flicked his head in Lark's direction, "plays a mean game of gin. We were just about to move on to poker."

Lark giggled as he knew she would. He thought she had a crush on him, which made babysitting easier.

Meg shook off her coat, grabbed Cait's, too, and headed for the hall closet. "Let me see if I can nudge Carter out of the shower – she tends to go into some kind of water-induced trance in there. We all need to talk."

Cait looked up at Matt and smiled indulgently. From a family of cops in the Bronx, he had the kind of manly, lived-in Irish face and husky 6' 2" body that drove women crazy.

Cait had always liked the man, ever since Meg and Carter had met him – a cop, getting a law degree nights at Fordham – and they'd all clicked, somehow. Over the years since, Meg and Carter had practically adopted Matt as part of the family, so Jack and Cait had done the same. Of the ten Christmases she and Jack had shared as a family, Matt had probably been there for five of them.

"Thanks for the babysitting, Matt," she said easily, as she reached up to kiss his cheek. "And for wanting to help us figure out what the hell is going on."

"Full service friendship," he responded with a wry smile, as he held her at arm's length so he could look her over judiciously.

"You're not looking so good, kid," he said, seeing the obvious marks of strain. "No surprise there, of course, considering..."

Cait nodded agreement, registering the genuine concern in his voice. For the first time she noticed that new lines had formed at the corners of his eyes. Matt had great eyes, grey with flecks of gold that gave him a vaguely animal look that was oddly compelling – as was the fact that he genuinely liked women, although he was as baffled by them as all men are. Cait knew Matt's wife had left him sometime in the late 90's, because she'd hated his job, and despite having a rep for being able to attract any girl he wanted, Matt hadn't yet found anyone to replace her. Sometimes Cait wondered if he ever would, as there was still a closed-down place in him that was clearly visible whenever Deirdre's name was mentioned, and being a cop didn't seem to bode well for marriages. Maybe, if he ever decided to practice law, instead of police work, it would be a different story.

Jack and Cait had spent enough late nights conversing around the fire with him, Meg and Carter, to know what a complex combination of idealist and realist the man was. Which was probably why he liked being a cop so much, she thought, although he was over-educated for the job. She knew he was a closet writer, too, and wondered if maybe he stayed on the job to collect stories he'd someday write about. If so, they had a humdinger for him tonight.

Cynthia Carter – called Carter since captaining the high school swim team – joined the group in sweats, the towel she'd been drying her carrot colored hair with, draped prize-fighter-style around her strong, swimmer's shoulders. Slender and agile, she moved with the easy assurance of a natural athlete.

"Well, it's good to see the merry band assembled again," she said as she plopped down unceremoniously next to Matt. "Meg's making coffee – she said to go ahead without her – she'll only be a minute."

"Just enough time to take this little cupcake to bed," Cait announced, tugging Lark out of her seat, against protest. But seeing her mother meant business, Lark finally kissed everybody and trudged off grudgingly toward the guestroom.

Five minutes later, Cait closed the bedroom door softly behind her, and stood for a few moments at the place where the hall met the arch to the living room, surveying the easy camaraderie of the friends gathered there. She felt deeply touched by their willingness to help with this strange, dangerous riddle.

She watched Meg come in with a tray of coffee and cups – Carter getting up to help, ditching the damp towel and shaking her strawberry curls like a small dog coming in from the rain. She smiled at the loosed halo of red gold now thoroughly unfurled, that made Carter look so much like a super-annuated Orphan Annie. She knew the girl kept her hair slicked into a tight bun during the day at work, in an effort to squelch just that imagery.

Her computer geekiness had helped Carter breeze through schools her family could never have afforded and most people never applied to. Savvy and street-smart, she'd been recruited straight out of law school by the FBI because it had appealed to her idealism. Saving the world had seemed eminently doable at 23.

She'd stuck it out for four and a half years, learning the ins and outs of law enforcement, politics, and the big business of government. She'd even loved her job for a while – loved the edgy, state-of-the-art equipment, the sense of being in the loop with people who, like her, intended to protect the world in a rarefied way. She'd thrived on the intellectual challenge, the brilliant colleagues, the high sense of purpose, until she realized that her conscience and sense of justice didn't mesh with the secrecy, the lies and obfuscations the work entailed. *Who's watching the watchers?* she'd asked Meg, with more and more frequency. How can we really trust these covert policemen whose job it is to cover the tracks of governments, to spin what the public is permitted to know, to make choices no man or group of men is really wise enough to make, and to cover their tracks when the outcome is other than what had been planned?

Carter didn't consider herself wise enough to know if the decisions being made by these men were right or wrong in the long run. Perhaps most decisions were actually motivated by insider knowledge far above her paygrade. But in the absence of such wisdom, she didn't want to be part of it anymore. She didn't regret any of it – was grateful, in fact, for all she'd learned and all the smart, good friends and important acquaintances the job had provided – but there was too much covert about the Bureau for her very overt nature.

And, then the serendipity of her software invention had provided freedom. She was financially independent by the age of 28 and a half, so nobody really questioned it when she resigned from the Bureau, and assured her bosses that any secrets of national security she'd been privy to would go with her to her grave. All the dire threats and admonitions they responded with, were *not* the reason Carter would keep silent. She would do so because she loved her country, and because she didn't think she knew enough to sort through the terrible choices other people in such government agencies had to make. She just hoped some among the choice-makers were men and women of wisdom and rectitude will far beyond the ordinary.

So, she'd taken the money from her software windfall, and started her own cyber security business, offering combined IT and law enforcement skills to those businesses that needed both. Clients found her – a trickle at first, then a torrent. She turned away more business than she took on. Money in the bank allowed a spirit of independence that made choices possible. The clients ranged from a chic Private Detective Agency run by an elegant Irishman she adored, to corporate giants, to freelancing for the kind of government agencies she'd just left.

She and Meg had been friends, then lovers during most of it. They were open about their commitment to each other and had as good a partnership as Cait had ever witnessed. Standing in the doorway, looking at them on the sofa next to Matt, it eased Cait's heart to see the obvious love and camaraderie they shared, and the easy friendship they'd found with Matt years ago, that had only grown with time.

Meg saw her sister standing in the doorway and signaled with her expression that she could carry the ball for a while, then she started to fill in Carter and Matt on the night's history lesson. Cait was grateful to be able to listen, not talk. She felt drained by everything that had happened, and she needed to think about all she'd heard tonight. Listening to Meg tell the story was helpful. Meg had that laser-brained ability common among litigators, to be able to tell a story succinctly, with meticulous detail, and without digression. It was a kind of mind-radar that Cait had always admired in her sister. She smiled now, as she watched and listened from the doorway, transported back to when she was a kid, not all that much older than Lark...

Cedar Mountain
North Carolina 1983

The snow lay heavily on the hills and had collected in the stillness of the valleys, in great powdery drifts. They'd tracked the buck through thick North Carolina woodland, Cait secretly hoping the great deer would outwit them, knowing that was unlikely. She saw her father nod to Meg. The younger girl shouldered her bow and took aim with the utter concentration that always marked her in the woods. Cait knew her sister was gifted with some kind of inner guidance system when it came to hunting Cait didn't possess even though she was the older. Meg could always find her way, could always bring down a clean kill so the animal didn't suffer. It wasn't that she didn't care about the deer, rather that she understood some other balance in nature that made the use of her skills acceptable, even laudable.

"There isn't enough food in the forest for all the deer, once winter comes, girls," their father had explained more than once.

"If the herd isn't thinned in late fall, they will starve during the snowy months. That isn't a good death for such noble animals."

Her father had learned to hunt and track like an Indian because his best boyhood friend, Jake Many Feathers, who had taught him wood lore, was a full blood Cherokee who'd been raised in these mountains, where her father's family had maintained the log house by the lake, nearly back to the time of the war between the states.

Meg's arrow arc'd through the air with its usual accuracy and the large deer buckled and fell to its knees, then to earth. Cait watched half awestruck by her sister's skill, half horrified by the blood on the magnificent animal's chest where the arrow had come to rest. Her own instinct would have been to heal him, although she knew that was foolishness. Maybe it was because she'd always known she was supposed to be a doctor, that she had such a hard time accepting the reality of death. Or maybe it was just that her mother's death had taken so much from all of them...

The thoughts of life and death jolted Cait abruptly back to the present. "I am *losing* it!" she chided herself, trying to get a grip, despite her fatigue.

"I've been thinking as you were telling the story, Meg," she said, rejoining the small assemblage. "I'm not sure we have a choice but to take these people up on their offer to help us. They know more about what's going on than we do – which isn't saying much, God knows – but they seem to have some kind of network – this Hunting Lodge of theirs – that's got influence. Lark and I can't go home right now, and we can't camp with you forever. If we split up, maybe I can use Delafield's help to find things out in Europe, while you guys ferret out all the information you can here. I can get Mrs. Hannigan to keep an eye on the house and the cat while we're gone for a few weeks, and I'll get somebody to cover my practice..."

"What about Lark and school?" Matt cut in.

"She's smart," Cait answered. "She'll catch up, or I'll get her a tutor for the summer. Right now, safety trumps schoolwork. I don't know if this is the right thing to do or not, but it seems like there's a chance it could give me a starting point." She looked so troubled and forlorn, Matt decided not to argue. Hell, maybe it was a good idea to get out of Dodge right now.

"I'll check out the Brit and the Kraut in the morning," he said irreverently, "At least we should make sure they're not ax murderers. This Hunting Lodge occulty crap, is pretty weird, but far be it from me to nay-say the unseen Universe and its little quirks."

Everyone in the room knew Matt's Aunt Nell was a genuinely gifted trance medium, who'd earned her living as a storefront reader of cards and tea leaves after her husband died, until she wrote a book about it and became Oprah's guest du jour. Being Irish, Matt knew there was more to life than meets the eye, so he never dismissed the mystical out of hand – but he also didn't take any wooden nickels. Cait smiled a little at the man's funny contradictions.

"Ok," she said, "so I won't book flights until the old boys pass the ax murderer test, but I'm leaning toward getting out of here as soon as possible. I just can't go back to our house right now."

No one asked why. Before they'd dispersed at 1:40 a.m., the group had a tentative plan of action.

16

Lark lay in her bed staring at the darkened ceiling. She'd let her mother think she was asleep because she knew the grownups wanted to talk, but she wasn't tired. She was just so sad. Everything that had happened to them kept buzzing around and around in her head, like when you forget to close the screen door in the summer, and then something big and buzzy keeps you up all night zooming in endless noisy circles around your room.

She missed her daddy with all her heart. Matt was great, and everybody was being so nice to her because they wanted to cheer her up, but she didn't want to be cheered up. She just wanted to cry and cry. And she was mad at God, too. How could God let somebody hurt her daddy and take him away from her like this? She loved her mother but she thought maybe she couldn't tell her how she felt about God, and about daddy, and about everything. Her mother was trying to act okay but she *wasn't* okay. She was sad and lonely and afraid, and pretending everything was going to be alright, but Lark wasn't so sure about that, and even though her mommy was trying to be brave just like she was trying to be, *nothing* would ever be the same...

The child pulled the covers back from the laptop that lay beside her in the bed. Playing *Labyrinth* made her feel a little better... or not exactly better... it was more like she just escaped out of the real world where things were so sad and wrong and popped up in a different world where her daddy still held her hand and talked to her in his own voice, and that made things feel better for a little while.

The screen began to glow and the great stone entrance to the Labyrinth morphed into form. Lark typed in her password and her father's smiling face appeared on the screen. "Hi Cupcake," he said in the voice she loved so much. Then the screen dissolved into a world of wonders, as he handed her the reins to her coal black horse and buckled on his sword. "Ready for an adventure, My Lady?" the voice asked, as her father's avatar on the screen bowed toward her in salute.

Lark's fingers reached out and touched the screen, which was really not a good thing to do, but she didn't care tonight.

"I love you daddy," she whispered, tears making her voice sound strangled. "I miss you all the time."

17

Matt was really worried about them. His cop-radar said this trouble wasn't just going away easily. He'd puzzled all night after their meeting, trying to figure out where to start digging. A sixty year old cold case would be no easy matter to unravel, even if he'd had jurisdiction, which he didn't.

His early morning identity-search on the two elderly European men had turned up nothing suspicious. As far as he could see, the two old guys were pretty much what they said they were – aging aristocrats with impeccable reputations. Of course, their kind of money and social position could whitewash a lot of unsavory history, but his gut wasn't telling him either man was dangerous. He could understand Cait's wanting to get out of town for a while, he just didn't like having her and Lark so far out of his sight while they were in danger.

He'd decided to get the ball rolling by calling Chris Richardson, an old army buddy, who was now with the Judge Advocate General's office, to see if he could mine the CIA connection to Gruner's past. If the old guy's story was right about Gruner's original identity and his lifetime ties to the Company, that might be a place to start. This Order of the 13 stuff sounded like something out of a Conspiracy Theorists wet dream, but hey, you never could tell what was under the rock 'til you turned it over. Chris had said he'd meet him for a burger at 12:30, so Matt glanced at his watch and headed out of the precinct house.

Richardson was already seated at a table in the corner of the dingy-chic little tavern near the South Street Seaport. Matt sat down, ordered a beer and gave Richardson the bare bones of what he was looking for. They'd done a few favors for each other over the years since the Gulf. The rule of thumb was 'don't tell me too much about what you're asking for, and don't ask for anything that will send up red flags.'

"What do you know about the Company?" Matt asked after taking a swallow of his beer.

"Enough to stay as far away from those guys as possible," Richardson answered. "Why?"

"I'm following up on a lead that goes way back to the beginning – you know, right after World War II. I'm not sure what I'm after, other than that it has to do with some old Nazi scientists they got new identities for, back in the day."

Richardson relaxed a little. What Matt was asking about sounded old enough not to be dangerous. "Anything that old is probably easier found on the internet than through the Company, don't you think, pal?"

Matt shook his head. "I need to dig a little deeper than that, Chris – kind of get a feel for the climate back then, you know? So I can figure out how much of what you find on the internet might actually be true. I need to know who was pulling the strings after the war, how much power did they have to keep their dirty laundry under wraps, and how high up the food chain did it go. Stuff like that."

Richardson thought a minute, obviously not wanting to know too much about why Matt was asking. "And this affects a current case...?" he let the question trail off.

"Maybe. There's three homicides that might have some weird old connections. I need to get close to some source who can point me in the right direction, so I don't just spin my wheels. But it's a hell of a long time ago, so most people in the know back then are probably dead by now."

Richardson played with his glass a minute before answering. "Maybe not," he said thoughtfully. "There's this smart old lady. I've had a couple of dealings with her over the years. She's a real piece of work, but she was right in the thick of things in the early days of the Company because she was some kind of archivist at the CIA's pet law firm. She wasn't a player, but she knew pretty much all that was going on. She's cagey, but she's not a lawyer, so she might speak to you, and if anybody could point you to where you need to poke around, she's the girl. I'll see if I can get her to talk to you if you want."

Matt thanked him and the rest of the lunch was spent talking about guys they both knew and where they were now. Talking about the old lady made Matt think about his Aunt Nell and the fact that he owed her a visit. He decided he'd stop by on his way home from work and talk to her about this whole weird business.

18

"Matthew Christopher McCormack!" Aunt Nell called out, stretching her arms up to reach his face for a kiss. As he was a foot and a half taller than his diminutive aunt, this wasn't easy. "You are a sight for sore eyes, my *darling* boy!" she said, an exuberant grin animating her late middle-aged face.

Matt simply picked the small woman up in a bear hug, and swung her around several times, provoking whoops of laughter, and making the glasses she perpetually wore on top of her head, fling themselves across the large circular entrance foyer of her Apthorp apartment.

Matt remembered the lean days, after Aunt Nell's much-loved husband had been killed in the line of duty, and his police pension hadn't provided any luxuries whatsoever for Nell and her five young children, all under the age of eight. Her digs in those days had been a small apartment in Queens – a far cry from the opulence she lived in now. A four bedroom coop in the Apthorp, one of New York's grandest pre-war buildings. This was all part of what she called the Pot of Gold for her Golden Years, Matt thought with a smile, as he put her down on the circular black and white marble foyer floor. And all because of her psychic gifts, plus the three bestselling books and the TV show they'd spawned about a psychic, who was a cross between Aunt Nell and Auntie Mame.

Matt retrieved her glasses in gentlemanly fashion, and propped them back onto the cotton candy white halo of hair. Nell, a lifelong redhead, had fought the white hair as long as possible, but finally acquiesced, not because of surrendering to old age, but because the fluffy white halo made her look like a pre-Raphaelite angel, on TV.

Nell beamed at her adored nephew. Of all her sisters' children, he'd always been her favorite, she thought, looking him up and down with a practiced eye. "And to what do I owe the pleasure of such a mostly-unannounced visit, might I ask?" The questions in her bright blue eyes were as apparent as the twinkle of delight at seeing him. "I know I'm a psychic and supposed to know *all*, but I confess your motivations more than most, are hidden behind an *impenetrable veil*." She emphasized the last words, making them sound spooky, mysterious and playful, all at the same time.

Matt laughed with her. Nell had always had the gift of laughter as much as insight, he knew. In his darkest days, both in boyhood and manhood, Nell had been the one able to cut through the brooding melancholia he so easily fell into, and make him roar.

Without asking if he wanted it, Nell poured three fingers of John Jameson into a handsome cut crystal glass, plopped in three ice cubes and handed it to him, then made another for herself. She had, he knew from long experience, the McCormack family hollow-leg – a capacity to drink any man under the table, without ever showing a hint of inebriation. She called it, "My Other Gift" and dismissed it as one of God's special commitments to the Irish, and a skill she'd always found most useful in negotiating new contracts.

"Out with it, boyo," she said now, motioning him to his favorite chair in the huge living room. "What's up?"

He smiled. "I've got a friend..."

"A woman-friend, I hope to God," she interjected. "It's way past time for a fabulous woman in your life."

"There's a woman involved," he answered, ignoring the jibe, "but not in that way. Well, not exactly, anyway."

Nell cocked an eyebrow questioningly.

"Truth is, I've always been attracted to her, and if you tell anybody that, I'll be forced to kill you, which would be a very great loss to me and the television public." She laughed as he knew she would.

"Does she know about this 'always attracted to her' thing?" she probed, and he shook his head, no.

"Up to a week or two ago she was happily married to a very nice guy..." he said. "Her husband was recently killed, and his death has opened up a weird can of worms..." he let the words trail off.

"My, *my*, Matthew dear," she said, "this tale becomes more and more interesting by the minute. Is there something in all this that has to do with me? I mean, besides the fact that I'd love to see you married and happy and surrounded by little Matthews of your own making? How can I help?"

Matt stood up, took off his jacket, loosened his tie, then, on second thought, pulled it off completely, unbuttoned the top button of his shirt, rolled up his sleeves, and sat back down, his long arms stretched across the back of the white sofa that faced the one she occupied.

His aunt looked amused. He was a gorgeous male specimen with a heart the size of Montana – a pushover for anyone in trouble, especially women and children. His body language tonight told her he had a lot to unburden himself of.

"If you've got an hour, I want to tell you about it," he said earnestly. "And then I'd really like to hear what you think."

"For you, dear boy," she said, meaning every word, "I have all the time in this world, or the next."

Two hours, and a very satisfying dinner later, Matt had unburdened himself of the whole story, and Nell, touched and more than a little concerned, had said she'd see what she could find out that might help him. Images had begun to seep into her vision-field as he'd laid out the problem, but there were too many, and too confusing to deal with until she was alone. There appeared to be multiple layers, multiple agendas in play – even multiple time-frames to make it more confusing. After she kissed him good-bye and shut the door behind him, she walked down the hall to the place where answers usually could be found.

Nell opened the door to what she referred to as God's Bedroom. The apartment's second biggest bedroom in a bygone day, now candles burned there and an altar dominated the center of the chapel-like space. The walls and shelves were filled with sacred images: one wall praised the Feminine Principle, Sypi Gualmo, Quan Yin, Isis, Gaia – she called them the Mothers, who brought the energies of love and compassion to humanity, but could also fight evil with all the power and rage of a mother protecting her young. Jesus, Buddha, Krishna and Lord Mahavir occupied another wall – the male principle that drove power, reason, sexuality. Immense wall murals of Michael, Gabriel, Raphael, Uriel – the four Archangels who guarded the four directions – stood like winged sentinels, at the South, West, East, North compass points.

Nell slipped off the satin slippers she'd been wearing and left them at the door. She breathed a reverent prayer, asking both protection and permission to petition for answers. Then she lit the five white candles, strategically positioned for this purpose, entered the circle of light, and left the mundane world behind as a rush of images washed through her and she braced herself for the onslaught.

The Quest

Part III

"Unless he is already doomed, fortune is apt to favor the man who keeps his nerve."

Beowolf

19

England

Cait sat back in the well-cushioned seat of the old Bentley and watched the English countryside sail by, trying not to cry, not to fold in front of Lark, not to think of Jack and her own loneliness, not to fall apart with fear and misgivings about this trip. Cait had been concerned about letting Lark fly so soon after being ill, so they'd waited one extra day for her to recuperate, and then taken the redeye out of JFK to Heathrow, and she'd slept on the plane. She stared out the window now, into the slate colored sky, remembering, *remembering…*

Lark, beside her, was staring out the window, too, mesmerized by all she was seeing. They'd left the city's grit and bustle behind, and the suburban crowding of row houses had thinned to reveal elegant countryside.

"It looks just like in my King Arthur books, Mom," Lark said, as she watched the landscape change to hills and fields.

Cait was hoping the diversion of being in a new place and the delight of an unexpected school holiday would help a little with her daughter's grief, so deep and so like her own. She worried that Lark was holding much too much of it inside, not sharing the worst of her loss, but she understood only too well how impossible it was for a child to put into words the unutterable anguish of losing a beloved parent. The memory of her own loss of her mother was still an unhealable knife wound in her heart after nearly three decades.

"We'll be entering the grounds in a moment, Doctor," the driver said in a broad Scottish burr. "The heath is luvely even in winter. I think the wee bairn might want to keep her eye out for deer and peacocks. Visitors seem to fancy them."

"They have peacocks?" Lark piped up. She sat up closer to the window, on full alert now.

A moment later they passed through massive stone gates and entered what could easily have been fairyland. Ancient trees overhung the road, and sprawling hills rolled off in every direction. The land was dotted by ponds, pathways and gardens, exquisitely trimmed and cared for. Stately old-growth trees and endless lawn finally gave way to a view of the house, if house were an adequate word for it. An immense stone edifice rose ahead of them, its crenellated battlements belying the gracious placidity of so bucolic a setting. It seemed more castle than manor house, a fact that wasn't lost on awestruck Lark.

The driver brought the car to a halt at the imposing front entrance, as massive doors were opened on cue, and two servants emerged to greet them and to negotiate with the driver about luggage.

Nearly as startled as her daughter by the exquisite, last century grandeur of the place, Cait exited the car after Lark, who had already scampered out in the direction of two massive wolfhounds that had emerged behind the servants.

"Wait, Sweetheart!" she called quickly. "We don't know how the dogs feel about visitors."

"Bran! Scanlan!" A deep male voice called from the doorway. "Say a nice hello to our guests." Anthony Lord Delafield moved toward them with a smile of welcome. "The hounds are superb judges of character, Cait. They're as delighted to see you both as I am."

The genuine warmth in the old man's eyes was unmistakable. Cait took his proffered hand and found she was comforted by his touch.

"I imagine you'd like to rest a bit after your long trip from the Colonies," he said with good-humor in his voice, as he led her into the vast entry hall. "But I know you're also most anxious to begin your plans, so let's get you settled in and after that a cup of tea would probably be in order."

"Then," he said putting her hand on his arm, "perhaps a tour of the old place so Lark can begin to feel at home here. There are dozens of rooms and corridors, and it can all be a bit daunting to visitors at first, but once you get the hang of it, as you Yanks say, it's fairly easy to navigate."

"That would be perfect," Cait replied with a grateful smile. What a sweet courtly old man he is, she thought as he continued talking. It was easy to see he was trying to put her at ease.

"I had thought of tucking Lark into the nursery suite," Delafield continued in his amiable tone, "it's quite charming and colorful, full of generations of toys and books, you know – but it's rather far from the grown ups and I thought under the circumstances, she might feel safer next to your rooms."

Cait smiled again. "You're being very kind to us," she responded, wanting to say more, but not sure what.

"I assure you, my dear," he answered her with a reassuring pat of her hand, "it is my great pleasure to welcome you both to my home, I've asked Mrs. Dunleavey to show you to your rooms," he added, nodding toward a small, smiling, round-faced woman who was waiting patiently at the foot of the great staircase.

Lark reached for Cait's hand as they headed for the stair. It was hard not to feel dwarfed by the scale of this old house, she thought as they climbed, and by the eerie sense that they were taking the first step on a journey into the unknown.

20

A half hour later, Cait left Lark in the care of the cheery little housekeeper, who'd promised the child a full tour, including the kitchen where she said cocoa awaited them. She found Lord Delafield in the drawing room.

"How are you feeling my dear," he asked, greeting her warmly.

"Most grateful for all your kindness Lord Delafield, but I have to confess this is all so... bewildering for me. I feel as if I've fallen down the rabbit hole and I can't seem to regain enough equilibrium to climb back out."

Delafield smiled gently as he leaned toward her. He was seated in a wing chair beside a fire that crackled and popped vigorously. "My dear, how could it be otherwise? You've been through a terrible tragedy and loss... you've realized the extent of the danger you're in, but you aren't certain how to protect yourself or Lark. It would be most odd if you were not thrown off balance by all that's happened to you."

"I don't even know where to start,' she said honestly, as she sat down in the chair he'd motioned her toward. "My whole life has been so goal directed... up to now, even if I didn't know *how* to do whatever needed doing, I at least knew how to get started. Now... in this..." she just put up her hands in a gesture of futility. "I wish so desperately that Jack had trusted me more..." Her voice carried a note of heartsickness that touched the old man.

"I believe it wasn't a matter of lack of trust, my dear," he said gently, "but rather of protectiveness. No man who loved you would have wished to share such a burden with you. And from all I know of your marriage, your husband loved you very much, indeed. And of course, you were both still so young. Your Jack would have believed he had all the time in the world ahead of him in which to prepare you..." he left the thought unfinished.

Cait nodded, grateful for the compassionate kindness behind the speech. She sighed, took a breath and looked at him very directly.

"I'm so hoping you can help me know how to begin," she said, hating the plaintive note in her own voice. "I feel so lost without my husband…"

"Indeed I can help you, my dear. But it will be Hugh who will be your guide and champion through this labyrinth, Cait. I will help you both, with every means at my disposal, as will my cousin Siegfried, of course. But this sacred quest of yours needs youth, strength and courage.... Yours and Hugh's."

"Sacred quest?" her forehead wrinkled a little at the odd choice of words.

"Oh yes, indeed, it is that... and more. You've been chosen to retrieve the Spear of Longinus. That is the sacred task of the Caretaker – I'm afraid that when your husband shouted those last words to you, he passed the mantle of responsibility. We may never know if it had previously been his intention to pass the Caretakership to Lark at some point in the future, perhaps through her game. But at the moment of truth, it was you, Caitlin, to whom he passed the torch."

"But Lord Delafield," she said, weighing the possibility, "I know nothing of what I need to know to do the job."

Delafield sat back in his great armchair for a moment, thinking about how to respond to what lay beneath the words. He focused his kind gaze directly on her when he spoke.

"But that isn't true, my dear," he said quietly. "Perhaps you are not consciously aware of your capabilities... perhaps not even from this lifetime. But you would not have been chosen if you couldn't fulfill the mission. The Caretaker is chosen by the Universe for this task."

So Hitler was chosen for this job, too? she almost blurted, but caught herself before speaking the words. She couldn't repay kindness with rudeness, and besides, she had no one else to turn to.

Seeing her hesitancy, Delafield went on.

"Hugh is formulating a plan – there are others involved – this quest will require a fair amount of coordination, if we are to keep you and Lark safe. I assume your sister has allies in New York who will perform the same function for her?"

Cait nodded.

"Then I will leave it to Hugh to apprise you of the arrangements he's making. Do you and your daughter ride, by any chance, Cait?"

The abrupt change of topic took her by surprise. "We do," she said. "We both love horses."

"Then may I suggest you go to the stables when you are ready, and Arthur, my stable manager will help you select appropriate mounts. I'll have cook prepare a picnic lunch..."

"Isn't it a bit chilly for a picnic?" Cait asked.

"Indeed it would be, if there were no shelter on the heath, but there is a lovely old cottage and gazebo with a fine view of the sea – it's one of Hugh's favorite riding destinations. It would make a perfect stopping place for lunch. I believe you three need to get to know one another."

He saw Cait's uncertainty.

"The Universe never leaves the Caretaker without appropriate allies, Cait. You will learn a great deal about this in the days to come, I suspect. It doesn't mean you can't fail in your task – you may even be called on to give your life for it, as your Jack has, but it means you'll be given a fighting chance to succeed."

Then, the old man rose and walking toward her chair, placed an elegant, long-fingered hand on her shoulder reassuringly.

"Have faith, my dear," he said gently. "There are larger forces at play here than you yet know."

21

"You have a gift for horses it seems," Hugh told Lark with a knowing smile, as he watched her slide easily down from her saddle.

She grinned back at him, full of shy nine-year-old pride and the excitement of the ride.

"He has a comfy back," she said, patting the horse's flank, "especially when he canters."

"Arthur is very good at selecting the proper mount for each guest," Hugh replied with a smile.

Lark giggled as the horse nuzzled her hand, searching for a treat.

"If you'd like, and your mother gives permission, of course, you may consider him yours alone, whenever you come to visit. Arthur will be delighted to have such an excellent rider to help him exercise Excalibur."

"Why did you name him after King Arthur's sword?" she asked.

"Truth be known, I really wanted to name him after King Arthur's horse, you see, but nobody seems to know what his name was. So I simply chose the next best thing."

"You could have named him Merlin," Lark said thoughtfully.

"Indeed, that would have been an excellent name for such a magical creature. Why don't we tell Arthur that the next foal to need naming will be called Merlin? Would you like that?"

Lark's eyes lit up. "Only if it's a magical looking foal though, right?" she said.

"Oh, quite so," Hugh replied. "We mustn't forget to tell him that. Names are very significant, don't you think?"

Lark nodded vigorously. "Oh yes. My grandpa had a best friend who's an Indian, and he said your name helps make you who you are. He says names carry special energies, like sound waves, you know," she looked at him to make sure he was following, "and that makes lots of sense because everything is really math and electromagnetic fields, so you have to try to get the names right."

Hugh nodded sagely. "Did your father tell you that – about the math, I mean? I understand he was a gifted mathematician."

The child's face clouded for a moment then cleared. "He was a genius," she said proudly. "Everybody said so. He taught me all kinds of cool stuff about numbers."

"I'm certain he did," Hugh said, the expression on his face very gentle. Cait could see he was going out of his way to win the child's trust. But she thought there was something more in his face. Something sad.

"Are you any good at math?" Lark asked suddenly brightening.

Hugh smiled at the precocious child. "Excellent question," he said taking the query seriously. "I'd have to say I'm good with some numbers, I suppose, he said judiciously. "Three and six are my favorites."

Lark giggled. "I like nine best," she said, playing along. "Nine is a magic number because no matter what other number you multiply it by, when you add up the digits, it always equals nine again."

Hugh looked suitably impressed by this information. "You mean like 9 x 3 is 27, and then 2 plus 7 equals nine?"

"Yup!" she said, "and 9 x 2368 is 21,312!"

"Oh, dear, now you've left me in the dust, haven't you?"

Lark grinned. "Don't worry. I could teach you how to multiply really fast in your head. I know a trick that makes it easy even with really *big* numbers!"

"That would be marvelous!" Hugh answered with obvious enthusiasm. "I've always wanted to know such mysterious things."

Cait smiled to herself, thinking it was always easy to spot a man who genuinely liked children. They never spoke down to them.

They tethered the horses to the iron posts outside the cottage and Hugh opened the creaky door.

"Oh!" both Cait and Lark gasped in unison, and then laughed together. Hugh thought it a lovely sound.

"It's like a people-sized dollhouse!" Lark exclaimed walking ahead of the grownups and looking all around.

"She's right, Hugh," Cait agreed. "This is an enchanted dollhouse made big enough to walk around in."

He helped her out of her jacket and tossed it on a rack in the entry hall. "It is, indeed, called The Dollhouse, and may very well be enchanted," he said with a light laugh. "It was built by a romantic and whimsical ancestor of mine as a love nest. It is a place constructed entirely for pleasure – no one but he and his lady love were ever permitted inside."

Cait laughed, nodding toward the fire that blazed in the hearth. "It appears someone else was allowed in today, however," she said, "someone kind enough to start a fire and set the table for us."

"Quite," he answered. "I'm a bit more practical than my great-grandfather – I love the cottage, but I'm not averse to having help with its maintenance."

They ate lunch, the conversation mainly monopolized by Lark asking questions about the estate. Her analytical turn of mind was apparent in her unexpected queries and insights. It was obvious she saw things differently from most children, but Hugh could see she was also just a little girl, fragile, shy, and sweet-natured, who was carrying a huge burden of sadness in as stoic a way as she could manage.

The sun had warmed the land a little, by the time lunch was done.

As they rode into the stable yard, Hugh pulled his horse up beside Cait's.

"We have a good deal to talk about," he said, "much of it best spoken of without small ears listening. There are so many things I feel I must tell you before we leave here, Cait."

"Before we leave here..." Cait repeated as if trying to digest that. "Where exactly will we be going and when?"

Hugh hesitated, glancing at Lark. "To find the Spear, Cait – and we should leave as quickly as possible. That's why we need to talk..."

She nodded, dreading the conversation, yet anxious for it. Dismounting, she handed the reins to a waiting groom, then turned to face Hugh.

"Thank you for being so good to Lark," she said quietly, "she seems to have taken to you."

"And I to her," he said. He seemed about to say more, but changed his mind.

"Cait, why not let Lark spend some time with Arthur and the horses, so we can talk right now. Will you walk with me?"

She nodded agreement and five minutes later they were following a path that wound its way in intricate geometric patterns, past well-marked specimen plants, a Shakespeare garden and a medieval herb garden, on its way toward the high hedges of a maze.

"We've mobilized the Friends of the Hunt," Hugh began. "It's important that you know you are not alone in this quest of yours, Cait. You might think of them as our standing army... people of like mind and heart who are willing to do their part to help hold evil at bay in the world."

"Are all these people you speak of involved in the Occult?" she asked not certain what that would really mean if the answer were yes.

"For the most part. At varying levels, of course, depending on their circumstances and degree of training. There are circles within the great circle if you will... one must pass certain initiatory steps to climb from level to level. Not everyone is willing – nor able – to make such a commitment. Some are content to act as helpers in whatever way they can best serve. Intelligence gathering, running interference, supplying necessary equipment or transport, providing safe houses – that sort of thing. You would be astounded by how many ways there are for one to serve, if one is determined to do so. It's a bit like what the Resistance did in the Great War. One and all, they are believers in our cause."

"And that is...?"

"The unwavering belief that a constant war is waged between the forces of Good and the forces of Evil. That those who fight the good fight, battle for the evolution of humanity itself."

"And you believe you can win this battle?"

"We believe that we *must* win, Cait. Everything we cherish hangs in the balance. Evil doesn't build civilizations... it tears them down, so that all the hard won accumulation of humanity's efforts to evolve toward enlightenment is turned to ashes."

She thought he wished to say more, but changed his mind, and they walked on a while in silence.

"Do you believe in reincarnation, Cait?" he asked her suddenly.

"I don't really know," she answered, carefully. "I was raised a Catholic and so I suppose I'm steeped in the idea of heaven and hell everlasting, foolish as that sounds when you say it out loud. I haven't given it much thought except to hope with all my heart that I get to see again the people I've loved, who've died.

"My Mother, my Father..." she hesitated. "Now Jack. It's unbearable for me to think I've lost them forever."

He heard the catch in her voice and nodded. "It is my belief – and that of our fellowship," he said quietly, "that the soul continues in consciousness beyond the gates of death. We believe our souls are on a journey back to God... a journey that takes us, in many incarnations, down many roads and many off ramps, if you will. Each lifetime adds to our accumulated experience and wisdom. The closest we come to believing in heaven, is the idea that between lifetimes, our souls reside somewhere beyond the veil – we simply call it the Other Side. When enough enlightenment about our human condition has been accumulated, our souls, with all their myriad memories, will be absorbed back into the perfection of the God-consciousness. In the meantime, while we wander, striving to live and to learn, God experiences humanity, through our efforts. Along the way, we accumulate friends, enemies... karmic connections."

"And what exactly is Karma?" she asked.

"Exactly? I don't know, really. There are many theories. The Jain Monks for example, say it's a substance that collects like dust motes adhering to our souls, based on our everyday actions and decisions. I think of it simply as a long continuum of experience in which we accumulate friends, enemies, debts, obligations and gifts – all of which may have a bearing on the events of our current lifetime."

"Why are you telling me all this?" She asked the question, and stopped, sitting down on a small stone bench in the rose garden.

"Because I believe you and I are connected by old ties, Cait. I believe we've worked together in past lives, for the purpose of protecting the Spear of Longinus and keeping it out of the hands of evil men."

Cait started to protest, but he cut her off, "My father and uncle and I belong to a fraternity that can help you protect the Spear, Cait, but I believe you are the one who has the responsibility for retrieving it."

"Why in the world would *that* be?" she asked, miffed and unsettled by the turn the conversation was taking. "The Spear was Jack's secret, not mine."

"But what if that isn't so?" Hugh replied earnestly. "What if your karma and that of the Spear are inextricably intertwined, and have been so since Calvary. What if this *isn't* the first time you've been the Spear's Caretaker?"

"What on earth are you talking about, Hugh?" Cait blurted with exasperation. "Forgive me for being rude, but I think that's just ridiculous speculation! And come to think of it, maybe this whole medieval fantasy of stately homes and secret societies and henchmen of dark forces, is just as crackpot." Cait's frustration was bubbling over. "I'm trying not to deny *any* possibility, no matter how improbable, that can help me and Lark and Meg stay alive, but I'm also trying to stay rational here, Hugh. My family's safety depends on my keeping a clear head and figuring out a whole host of imponderables I've barely scratched the surface of.

"All I want to do, is to keep us safe. I think it's terribly unfair of you to suggest I'm supposed to save some old relic *and* the world, while I'm at it – especially considering that I only learned the damned thing existed less than a week ago!"

She stood up and Hugh followed.

"You *can* trust us, Cait," he said, urgently. "I understand your distress – this is a damned unsettling business – but don't you see, we of the Lodge have been sent to you, to help you find your way."

"I don't know *what* I see anymore," she blurted. "Maybe it's the fact that I haven't slept since Jack died, that's unhinging me. I've got to get a grip on myself and I've got to find that damned Spear, if that's what it takes to get us out of this mess. But that's about all I can handle right now. I do think you're trying to help me, Hugh... I just don't know what's real and what's not anymore."

Impulsively, he reached out and touched her hand with his own. "Don't you remember me, Cait?" he asked, as if her answer were very important to him. "I remember *you*." He said it so gravely she felt her gut tighten.

"Don't you see, I think we have a job to do together," he added, hurriedly, to stop her protest... "we just don't have all the pieces of this puzzle yet, but I mean to help you do whatever you must."

Cait stared at the man, half believing in his sincerity, half wondering if this could be some bizarre pick-up line. She turned, intending to head back toward the house, but Hugh grabbed her arm. He wanted to comfort her, but more than that, he wanted to convince her of the truth. Disconcerting flashes of the past and present zinged through Cait at his touch, as if Hugh's powerful energy field had triggered something in her she didn't understand at all. She caught her breath, and pulled her arm away with more force than necessary.

"Please don't touch me, Hugh," she blurted, struggling to keep her voice steady. "I know you're trying to help me... but everyone I hold dear is at stake here. I need to be clear-headed enough to figure all this out and I can't afford to be more unnerved than I already am!" She shook her head in consternation at her own ridiculously inadequate explanation.   Feeling foolish and vulnerable, she managed to stammer, "I'm so sorry, Hugh... please... just don't touch me again."

Shocked by her own outburst, she hurried off, feeling anything but clear-headed. Hugh stood looking bewildered, and staring after her.

22

Cait looked at the clock and sighed – maybe she could take half an hour to compose herself before having to face reality, dinner, and seeing Hugh again. She was embarrassed by how badly she'd handled their earlier conversation. She knew she'd been rude and needlessly abrupt, but the truth was she felt unsettled by the idea of traveling alone with him. Of course, she felt unsettled by just about *everything* that was happening to her now. No matter how hard she tried, she couldn't seem to regain her equilibrium. The awful, disconnected-from-reality feeling that had plagued her since Jack's death – the feeling of being fogbound or wrapped in cottonwool -- had been followed by a visceral pain that seemed to grip her heart now in an unrelenting vice. The ache of loss was so deep it seemed capable of blotting out life itself. She felt she had to remind herself to breathe.

Cait lay back, and willed the water in the huge antique claw foot tub to spread warmth into her icy bones; she wanted to lie there forever, adrift with nothing expected of her that she didn't know how to accomplish. She felt as if all the warmth in the world had been extinguished with Jack's death.

Jack was *dead*. The hideous cruelty of the word reverberated somewhere within her, just out of reach. It was so alien, so unreal a concept, she couldn't let it in, and all the ghastly euphemisms people substituted for the word seemed disrespectful, insipid, too pallid for so horrific a truth. Passed away... gone... passed on... as if he'd been a train that missed the station. But *dead* was unrelenting, final. Unbearable.

Cait glanced at the clock on the marble dressing table and realized the time for maudlin self-indulgence was over. And besides, inertia was a mind killer – she needed to get out of these seductive bubbles and back into the game. She owed it to Hugh to hear what she had to say. She wasn't sure what to make of the man who made her so uneasy, yet seemed only to be trying to help.

Cait rose from the tub, looked around for a towel, and caught an unexpected glimpse of herself in the huge gilt-framed mirror that covered one wall of the bathroom. The enormous antique mirror gave her a startling perspective on herself. Naked, she looked as vulnerable as she felt, and that wouldn't do at all. She took a deep breath and spoke to her own confronting alter-ego in the mirror.

"I know you're scared and exhausted," she said aloud to her mirror-twin, as if saying the words could force clarity to surface. "You know nothing about detective work, or international intrigue, or any of the secrets in Jack's past. You're in this fairytale castle, with people from a time warp, who say they're going to help, but, it's really just you and me who have to figure this out and keep us all safe. Right?"

She stared at herself, for a few seconds more, daunted by the enormity of it all, then stood up straighter, squared her shoulders, and said very deliberately, "But, we're not going down without one hell of a fight, are we Caitlin?" The sound of her own voice reverberating in the huge marble bathroom made her laugh out loud.

Feeling both ridiculous and heartened by her pep talk to herself, Cait stepped onto the cold marble floor, wrapped a warmed fluffy towel the size of a beach blanket around her, and walked with equal parts trepidation and determination into whatever would come next.

*   *   *

In the next room, Lark stood staring out the window at the gathering dusk. The scene outside was like something out of a book about olden times when there were knights and ladies and kings and queens. It would be interesting to look in all the rooms and to check out all the suits of armor in the hallways. Maybe Hugh would let her do that. He seemed to like kids and he was pretty easy to talk to.

The child sighed. She heard her mother, in the adjoining bathroom. Her mom always took to the bubble bath when she was sad or upset. Kind of like what spending time in the Labyrinth did for her own mood.

Lark walked to the bed where the laptop lay, opened it, booted it up and hit the desktop icon for the Labyrinth. When she was in the Labyrinth, her daddy was alive again and he was her champion and defender. Together they slew wizards, visited Fairy queens, flew on the backs of dragons, and conquered evil. She knew almost every centimeter of the Labyrinth, even the hard parts.

That was the trouble.

Where could anything be hidden in this so-familiar game? Could it be that Daddy hadn't put the real clues in yet? He'd added layers of complex algorithms every year, but what if the really important stuff just wasn't there yet? Or what if it was, but without her Daddy's help, she could never find it? She sensed how important it was to her Mom to find out where Daddy and Grandpa had hidden the Spear. When her mommy first told her the answer could be in the game, she was positive she could find it... now she wasn't sure at all.

She was very worried about her mom. Never, ever had she seen her so sad. Mom was a doctor, she knew stuff other people's moms didn't know. She always knew what to say and what to do and how to make things turn out OK. But now everything was different...

Lark turned her attention to the screen, and felt the familiar change sweep through her, opening her senses to an altered reality, expanding her consciousness to an almost supernatural awareness. She'd never known what to call it, always known it was there, this strange ability that set her apart. The gift of another self inside her that was called forth by the game, the computer, the numbers, the Daddy Things.

She knew the Gift made her special... everybody said so, even her teachers at school. Not that she ever *felt* special, except when she could use the "gift" to do things other kids couldn't do and that wasn't so great anyway, because it just set her apart from the others and made her feel lonely. Daddy had explained it to her once... how the Gift let her think in numbers, like other kids thought in words. It wasn't that she didn't *like* words – she loved books and stories, especially fantasies. It was that she had this other thing that happened to her – where ideas came to her in numbers and number sequences... where shapes became geometry and things that baffled grown-ups looked like algorithms to her. And then there was the weird connection she felt with computers – she didn't think of them as machines like Mommy did. They were more like other intelligences that just didn't come in people-bodies. But they were definitely intelligences to play with, not hard to understand, just different – more like her own intelligence and Daddy's.

Even Grandpa had the gift, she knew, which is what had made him famous in the big war, and that was part of why Daddy had been so proud of *his* Daddy. But Grandpa had lived in the olden days, when there were no computers and you had to use all kinds of other cool stuff to dis-encrypt messages and play the games. He had shown some of them to her, and explained how King Solomon and Alexander the Great, and Queen Elizabeth I had sent their secret messages, and how philosophers and mathematicians had created all these cool Ciphers, like the Magic Squares of Solomon and Alberti's Disc, or the Atbash Cipher, the Templar Knights used when they traveled. Grandpa and Daddy had taught her about lots of tricks people had used in the olden days before computers, when they wanted to keep secrets.

She thought of the *other* Lark – the one who popped out when the gift was in use – as her Secret Self. It was her Secret Self who would have to figure this out, she thought with consternation, letting her consciousness morph into the one on the screen. Daddy and Grandpa were gone and Mommy was afraid and wouldn't have known how to help anyway.

Lark took a deep breath and entered the game.

"Where did you hide it, Daddy?" she breathed the words out softly to the computer screen image. A large tear welled up and then spilled down her cheek, but she just blinked hard and ignored the interruption.

23

Lark stood on tiptoe trying to see inside the immense suit of armor that stood, like a sentinel, at the far end of the dark corridor that ran outside their bedrooms, as her mother dressed for dinner. She was not quite tall-enough to peek inside, and that frustrated her. Now, that she'd seen all these suits of armor up close, all she thought she knew about knights in shining armor seemed wrong. The suits that lined the hallway looked more like crosses between an automobile and a giant can of tuna.

"Would you like me to lift you up so you could peek inside?" a pleasant male voice behind her asked, and Lark jumped back, startled that she'd been discovered, not sure if what she'd wanted to do was even allowed. Hugh had been on his way to dinner, when he'd spotted Lark in the corridor of the bedroom wing.

"I'm sorry," she stammered to Hugh, who was smiling down at her. "I just wanted to see how it works. I mean, it doesn't look like anybody could move fast enough to fight in these suits, and it would be pretty hard to see out, wouldn't it?"

Hugh grinned at the child's accurate appraisal. "You're quite right of course," he said, "this type of full body armor was really only useful if you were mounted on horseback for a joust or a cavalry attack. And even then, it had a good many drawbacks."

"Poor horse!" she blurted, and they both laughed.

"Yes, quite right, I'm afraid the horses must have suffered gravely, and I'd wager they did a good deal more plodding than galloping. But you see, in olden times it was prestigious to own a horse. It meant you had wealth and stature in the community. And it meant you could offer your services as a liege man to your local Lordship or to the King." He saw she wanted to know more.

On sudden impulse, he bowed to her.

"Milady," he said in a courtly manner. "If you'd care to come with me, I'll show you what the Templar Knights wore in battle. Their garb was quite dashing and far more practical for fighting."

She looked up at him and he saw that although she meant to smile, there were sudden tears in her eyes. "My daddy always called me that," she explained, when she saw his troubled look, "in the game, I mean. He was my knight, so he called me Milady."

Hugh coughed to give himself a moment to figure out how to cover this blunder, without further distressing the child. "But of course he would, wouldn't he?" he said finally. "He was your most chivalrous protector and your champion. Is that right?"

Lark nodded gravely.

"And did he also have leave to wear your colors?" he asked. Lark's eyes widened, and she nodded her head, yes.

"Well there you are," Hugh said with cheery conviction. "Then you probably know what chivalry is, Lark, don't you?" he asked it and simultaneously offered her his arm, as if she were a grown up. She hesitated, then put her hand on his arm, as she had seen people do in books.

"It was the Code of the Knights," she recited, speaking words obviously learned by rote. "'Protect the weak, defenseless, and helpless, and fight for your King and Sovereign and the general welfare of all.'" She thought a moment, then added, "And they were very nice to ladies and they could slay dragons!"

"Excellent!" he applauded as they turned a corner, and entered another long corridor. "Becoming a knight was a very great honor, so I believe your daddy was the perfect choice, judging by everything I've heard of him." He paused a moment, then said, "And did you know that when a lady's Champion had the misfortune to be slain in battle, it was the privilege and duty of another knight to offer her his protection?"

Lark shook her head no. "I didn't know that," she said uncertainly.

They had reached a figure dressed in full Templar regalia, that stood near the head of the staircase. Hugh stopped in front of it, and made a sweeping gesture, "And here we have..." he began but Lark cut in, eager to show off her knowledge.

"He's a Knight of the Temple, I can tell by the big red cross on his chest. They had the nicest outfits."

Hugh managed not to laugh, but his eyes were merry. "Indeed," he said, "their garb was also the most practical gear for fighting. You see they were a Holy Order, not just a military one. The Templars, most of whom were from noble families, gave up their fortunes to join the Order. They vowed poverty, chastity, obedience, and holiness. So their garments were part military and part priestly. They didn't wear armor, only long chain mail under their tabards – that's the proper name for that tunic with the red cross emblazoned on it.

"Their mail was fashioned much like the cassocks of priestly orders, except that it was open from waist to hem, so they could easily sit a horse, joust, dual in the field – that sort of knightly enterprise. And of course, the great rosy cross marked them as Knights Templar, which was somewhat like being a Marine or a Navy Seal, I imagine, in your country, or a Paratrooper in mine. It meant everyone knew you followed a strict code of honor, and would fight to the death for a just cause..."

"Or a damsel in distress!" she added triumphantly, and he smiled.

"That was one of their first priorities," he agreed.

"And they had these great cloaks!" she added, warming to the discussion.

"Ah, yes," he replied as if she'd made an astute discovery. "These cloaks were a hot fashion item in the 12th century, as I recall."

Lark giggled her appreciation.

"I must say, you are quite well schooled in matters of knighthood," Hugh complimented, genuine warmth in his voice. "Especially for an American young lady. I had no idea you were taught so well in your schools about such things as chivalry."

"Not school," she corrected, with an emphatic headshake. "The game my Daddy made for me, the one we played a lot..." she faltered a moment, deciding what to say, then went on. "It was all about a magical kingdom with portals for time travel and inter-dimensional shifts and wormholes and other cool stuff, but my daddy's avatar was a Knight and mine was a Princess, and my daddy was my protector so I could learn everything I needed to know to pass through all the portals, and win the prize and save the world..." It had all come out in one big breath, the words propelled by happy memory, but then, as suddenly as the joy had appeared, it evaporated.

Hugh nodded his understanding, and sighed. "That's a very big task for a young princess, isn't it, Lark?" he said gently.

"My daddy said I could do it!" she flung back instantly.

"Oh, I have no doubt of it," he agreed. "Your daddy was an extraordinary man, and he knew better than anyone what remarkable things you are capable of. I was simply thinking that you shouldn't have to do all that alone..." He stopped and she looked up at his face, because of a note she'd heard in his voice that was both emotional and determined, as if he'd just made an important decision. To her surprise he suddenly reached out, and pulled the sword from the Templar's scabbard, then dropped to one knee in front of her. With great dignity and the appearance of long-practice, he laid the large sword across his bent knee.

"Milady," he said with great seriousness, "Inasmuch as your brave champion and knight has fallen in battle, I have come to offer you my services, my allegiance and my sacred honor – not to take his place, as that can never be – but to pledge myself your liegeman, your protector, and your most humble servant. Will you accept me into your service?"

Lark looked momentarily dumbstruck, by the words and the vision of the kneeling man before her. Hugh saw her eyes take in absolutely every detail, watched her assess his sincerity, saw her decide – all in the space of a few heartbeats.

Then her fiery head came up, her back straightened perceptibly, and her eyes met his.

"I accept your pledge, Sir Knight," she said, as gravely as he. "And I give you leave to wear my colors." She thought for a moment, then yanked the bright blue hair ribbon from one of her pigtails and handed it to him.

"My token, Sir Knight," she said.

Hugh accepted the ribbon reverently and tucked it into his pocket. Then he took the great sword from his knee, and holding it upright before him with both hands, he touched it to his lips and his heart, then stood up effortlessly, and with full ceremonial gravity, returned it to its engraved scabbard.

"So, then..." he said, to lighten the moment, and get control of his own emotions that had been so touched by the child's sweet gesture, "would you like to try on the cloak?"

Lark giggled. This was a very interesting man. 'Yes, please. And I'd like you to tell me more about Knights and Ladies."

Hugh smiled at her. "My knowledge and my sword are entirely at your service, Milady" he said. "And may I ask a favor in return?"

She looked at him quizzically.

"Will you teach me your game?"

Lark cocked her head to the side, examining him with a critical eye. Finally, she said, "I'll try, but it's pretty hard..."

"Lovely," he answered her, sealing the pact. "Now, why don't you ask your mother if you may join me in the library for tea. You see, I have some books with wonderful old engravings from medieval times. I think you might very much enjoy seeing them."

"Ok." Lark said. "I'll go find Mom and ask her."

Hugh watched her scamper back up the hall until she turned the corner and was out of sight. She was a little girl with a very large burden. He wondered what he could do to help her carry it.

24

Lord Delafield found Cait in the library before breakfast the next morning, half dozing in a chair, near an embering fire, surrounded by stacks of books. He perused a few of the titles and chuckled good naturedly. She'd clearly spent much of the night there poring through books on the occult, reincarnation, the Crucifixion, and Nazism.

"I see from the books you've chosen, and the dark circles under your eyes, that you've taken up the quest," Delafield said approvingly and she gave him a weary smile, stretching herself into wakefulness.

"Not much choice that I can see," she answered, yawning. "But your amazing library has helped me learn a great deal since last evening. I couldn't sleep – I feel such urgency to get going..."

"Have you found your way to your starting point, then, my dear?"

"Germany. The trail has to start there. Hugh and I talked about it last night. He said your cousin Siegfried will open doors for me..."

He nodded agreement. "He will do so gladly. You and Hugh should leave as soon as you feel up to it. Siegfried is connected to the Hapsburgs through his mother's line, and his home is not far from Wewelsburg – you should see what remains of that nefarious Nazi fortress."

"I'd like to see the counterfeit Spear in the Hofburg, too," she added. "I need to get a feel for what I'm seeking, so Germany and Austria make sense as a starting point."

"Your enemies will, of course, make the same assumption," he said thoughtfully.

"We talked about that, too, Lord Delafield. Which is why I think that much as I hate the idea, I can't take Lark with me. Is it possible she could stay with you until we return? I need to be certain she's safe."

The old man could see how hard a struggle it was for her to make the choice between keeping her daughter close under her wing or leaving her with strangers, who might keep her safer.

"My dear Caitlin," he said, laying a kindly hand on her arm. "I know how difficult this is for you. During the war, when the blitz was at its worst, thousands of mothers in London were faced with the same terrible choice – to keep their children close and risk the bombs, or to send them away to be cared for by strangers in the country. My wife and I took in a great many children here at the Manor until the worst of it was over. I can tell you with great honesty that it was a wise plan – so many were saved, you see – and it gave the mothers the freedom to go about their work with the knowledge they'd made the right and loving choice. Lark will be well cared for in your absence, you may count on it. And she will be safe, I'll see to it."

"I believe you," she said, grateful for his kindness, "and I just don't see any other way, but I think it will be very hard for her to understand. She's just lost her father and now I need to leave her to find this damned Spear..." she looked at him, her eyes filling with tears against her will.

He patted her hand, "You go and find your Spear, Cait. That's what will keep you and Lark safest. Hugh will make travel arrangements for you both – you should go quickly – a day or two at most. I'll telephone Siegfried to tell him you will shortly be on the way to him. But first, there is a group of friends you must meet. It took a bit of doing to gather them on such short notice, but they'll be here. I think the ballroom would be best – at 10 this evening. There will be many who will want to wish you well on your journey."

"I'll look forward to it," Cait said, curious about what the gathering would hold.

25

Hugh found Cait after breakfast and told her Lark had agreed to initiate him into the game. "Do you play it with her?" he asked.

She smiled. "Not very well, I'm afraid. That was Jack's territory. You see, the game is simple in concept, but it quickly becomes incredibly hard to play. Lark's Labyrinth is a magical puzzle-realm. It's basic storyline seems to involve a particularly brave and trustworthy knight – that's Jack's character or avatar in game-speak – who has been sent to be the guardian and protector of a beautiful young princess – that's Lark's avatar, of course – who thinks she's just an ordinary Princess, but in truth she, in some mysterious way that even she doesn't fully understand, holds the fate of the Galaxy in her hands."

Hugh smiled indulgently at her, charmed by her earnest expression and the obvious love she bore her talented husband and daughter.

"Sounds like a game I'll enjoy playing," he said and she went on.

"Neither the Knight nor the Princess knows what will be asked of them at the Final Beckoning, as it's portentously called. But the knight knows he's been given the task by the PTB – they're the Powers That Be, you see – Gods, Goddesses, Divine Beings of all sorts, and they pop in and out of the game as they please, being divine – but it seems they've given this knight the task of being the Princess's protector. They've also given him special powers that allow him to travel inter-dimensionally, to journey into other realities of hyperspace, to time jump, teleport, call on other Galactic Species for help, *whatever,* depending on just what kind of trouble the Dreadlords – they're the bad guys – have thrown into her Princessly path." Cait stopped for breath and to acknowledge her own lack of comprehension. "That's about as far as I understand it," she said with a self-deprecating shrug. But seeing he was eager to learn more, she continued.

"Now, obviously I knew nothing about the Spear, until that awful night... so I believed what Jack told me about the game... that he and his father conceived of it as a sort of one-stop-shopping experience of education – to help Lark develop her gifts, and become a well-rounded, educated person. They said young geniuses are too often cubbyholed into only their own prodigious skill-set, so they're never truly educated. They wanted to expose Lark to math, physics, history, science, maybe even metaphysics and spirituality – remember the knightly honor code was pretty strict and comprehensive. The game was to lure her into learnings beyond her own area of giftedness."

Cait looked into Hugh's eyes to see if he understood.

"Of course I didn't have a clue then, that the game was more than he said it was..." Cait's voice trailed off, lost in thought and sudden sadness.

"And perhaps it isn't," Hugh answered, watching her troubled expression. "Perhaps the game is unfinished, or merely a Red Herring of some kind..."

She looked startled. "Meant to throw us off the track?"

"Meant to throw *everyone* off the track." He said the words as if he'd given this a great deal of thought, then added, "I'm off to my first lesson in Lark's Labyrinth right after breakfast."

Cait smiled. "You're in for a fun ride, my friend. The early levels are a marvel of fantasy and creativity. Harry Potter, King Arthur, Star Wars and the Ring Trilogy all rolled into one. The path gets noticeably steeper around Level Three, and by Level Four, only math geniuses need apply, I'm afraid."

Hugh stood up and stretched his large frame, then swatted at the air vigorously, as if preparing for a cricket match. "Not a moment to lose then, before I get into training. One should never say 'no' to a once in a lifetime challenge."

Cait smiled to herself as she watched the man exit the room. He was throwing air punches at an imaginary opponent, and humming softly. What an intriguing enigma he is, she thought, watching him. A quirky, wry humor overlaying intense gravitas. She wondered what had made him who he was. Wondered, too, if she were insane to be going off with a stranger and leaving her daughter in the care of another one. But just how many choices did she really have?

26

Inside the Labyrinth

Hugh stared in wonder at the astonishing world that had just materialized before him on the computer screen. They'd entered the Labyrinth through the Great Gate of the Good, and as they did so, they'd been greeted by the White Knight, the avatar that had been Jack's, and the beautiful young princess, who was Milady Lark. She'd introduced him to the Knight Errant avatar which was to be his own persona in the game. He hadn't known what to expect, but the exquisite beauty of the world around them and the detail that made it seem both real and surreal at the same time, took him by surprise.

"There are all kinds of things you'll need to know about how to stay safe here in the Labyrinth," Lark warned him, "because nothing is exactly what it seems like." Then the Milady figure on the screen reached up toward a brilliantly plumed bird, flying in lazy circles above them, and at the gesture, the bird swooped to her upstretched hand and trilled a soft series of repeating notes.

"She flies for the Harper," Lark said matter of factly. "She's a sort of "familiar" – you know, like witches used to have? – Malfazador, the wicked Dreadlord sorcerer cast a spell on her, so for half of everyday, she looks like a bird and not a girl. But that's okay because when she's a bird she can help the Harper, by traveling all over the realms to find things out for the Knight and me, and she flies to get me when there's important news from the Nexus."

"And who is the Harper and what is the Nexus?" Hugh asked, not knowing for certain if he were talking to the child at the computer, or her alter-ego on the screen.

"You'll meet the Harper in a minute," Lark answered emphatically, "and Nexus is the Last Stronghold, there's a staircase to the Akashic Record there, so we can teleport to wherever we need to go to win." She looked up at him quizzically to see if he were following, and seeing the rapt expression on his face as he stared at the screen, she knew he was hooked.

"Quite so," he said. "Carry on, then. What did the bird have to say?"

Lark giggled. "She just wanted to know if we'd been summoned or were here for our own pleasure. That's because you can just invite somebody in to play the game with you if you want to, or you can go on the big Quest."

"And you told her *what* exactly?" he asked with a grin.

Lark moved her mouse expertly and the Lark figure on the screen raised its hand so the little bird was close to her lips, as if delivering a message or a kiss. Hugh realized how easily one could be mesmerized by this game into believing it's action to be real, and better understood why Lark was so enchanted by it.

"I told her to take us to the Harper," she said judiciously. "That's where new players usually start, because he's programmed to explain things and he has an enchanted harp that gives really cool clues." She thought for a moment, then added, "and he may send you to visit the Gatekeeper."

"Oh dear," Hugh said, with a smile behind his eyes. "And who exactly is this Gatekeeper?"

"Every portal has a Gatekeeper," Lark said as if it were a well-known fact he'd somehow overlooked. "He's the one who knows *all* the secrets. Even more than the Minstrel, I think."

Hugh nodded sagely. "So I shall have to pass muster with him, too, I suppose?"

"Don't worry," Lark assured him. "I'll help you."

Jack had been not merely a genius, Hugh realized with rueful admiration – he was also a romantic with a noble heart. These were even bigger shoes to fill than he had imagined.

*   *   *

The immense ornate gate creaked open to reveal the interior of the Labyrinth in all its surreal beauty. Hugh's knight followed Milady, leading his horse by its halter. The exquisite silver gelding suddenly reared and whinnied, as an apparition shimmered into view before them on the path.

The huge dark presence before them had the fierce yet oddly benevolent face of a gigantic Foo Dog, but its body was unmistakably that of a dragon. Its long, thick reptilian tale swished dramatically, knocking over a few trees, as its form fully materialized.

"Have you brought chocolate?" it asked in a stentorian voice that seemed to emanate from the depths of its enormous body, and Hugh was so startled by the unexpected question he laughed aloud.

Milady Lark bowed low before the creature and pulled what appeared to be a Hershey Bar from the folds of her gown.

"Gatekeeper, dear," the figure on the screen said sweetly, "I've brought a new player to meet you. And, of course, an offering of chocolate for the introduction."

Hugh couldn't help but chuckle, as the great beast accepted the chocolate bar with immense dignity, then consumed it with a happy smacking of his lips before acknowledging the presence of a new player. This was amazingly sophisticated software, he realized, as he settled in to enjoy the experience.

"And who might you be, Knight Errant?" the Gatekeeper asked, settling back on his vast haunches and seeming to regard the new arrival.

"Go ahead," the real Lark prompted Hugh in a whisper, "You can talk to him. He has lots of fun responses programmed in. Or you can type in your answer, if you want to."

Wonderingly, Hugh spoke, "I'm Hugh, Earl of Delafield, new champion to Milady Lark," he said feeling only slightly foolish. "And may I ask who *you* are?"

"I am the Gatekeeper of this Labyrinth," the creature answered, "bound to this place eons ago, by an accident of Fate and a profound act of ritual magic. Please be advised this is a Sacred Portal, and must be approached with respect." The Gatekeeper's voice seemed to emanate from a subterranean cavern.

"I didn't know the Labyrinth was a *Portal?*" Hugh said.

"A Portal is a doorway between dimensions," the Gatekeeper replied. "And now I suppose you'll want to know what *dimensions* are!"

Hugh laughed again. "Thank you, but no – I believe I do know that. But I'd like to know more about what you do here. What is your task, Gatekeeper?"

"Excellent question," replied the Gatekeeper approvingly. "I keep the riffraff out."

"What kind of riffraff?"

"Oh, all sorts. A Portal of this magnitude attracts entities from practically everywhere. Other planets, other levels of consciousness, other time slots..."

"Then you're a Time Portal, too?" Hugh asked.

"Indeed I am," the Gatekeeper replied generously. "I have very few limitations."

"He knows *all* the secrets of the Labyrinth," Lark prompted. "He knows math and magic and the way the universe *really* works... that's why the game gets so complicated."

"Mine is a lonely job," the creature intoned with a sigh, "so I'm happy when Milady visits me." Hugh was once again awed by the complexity of what Jack and his father had created. He wondered if any of his grad students had been involved in the project.

"Gatekeeper's my friend," Lark told Hugh conspiratorially, "but he's not supposed to tell me the answers. I have to do that for myself."

"I know many things," the Gatekeeper interjected. "I was once worshipped as a deity on your planet, in fact." He sighed audibly. "But that was long ago in Persia, and hardly worth mentioning, I suppose."

Lark typed something in and the Gatekeeper asked, "Where do you wish to go today, Milady?"

"I'm taking Knight Errant to Minstrel, so he can learn to play the game, Gatekeeper. May we pass?"

"You may," said the Gatekeeper. "I wish you fair journey and bid you watch for troll treachery – they have been unusually cranky of late." The large beast then moved aside and began to shimmer out of view. Just as he was almost gone entirely, his voice once again emanated from the dancing, sparkling molecules that marked the spot where he'd been a moment before.

"Snickers!" the voice cried out, the words wavering in the air, as if coming from afar. "Next time, bring Snickers."

Hugh was almost too dumbstruck by all this to remember to follow after Milady down the path. Then he remembered that Lewis Carroll, a Professor of Mathematics, had created Alice in Wonderland to teach math concepts to a child he was tutoring.

Ahead of them he saw a charming thatch-roofed cottage emerge, surrounded by fanciful statuary, flora and twittering strange creatures.

A minstrel sat cross-legged on a giant toadstool, in front of the cottage. He was playing a lute. The brilliantly plumed bird they'd seen earlier, sat on his shoulder, her iridescent feathers gleaming in the light of the sun that shone above them. She appeared to be accompanying him in song.

"Hail, Minstrel," Milady called out as they approached, and her fingers flew over the keyboard. "I bring a new player to our game."

The Minstrel looked up from his instrument, his eyes were a brilliant aqua that matched the feathers of the bird.

"A new player, eh?" he said gliding forward. "If Milady vouches for you and the Gatekeeper let you pass, then let us begin. Would you like to know some trifling facts about our game?"

"I would, indeed," Hugh agreed eagerly.

"Good. I shall compose an epic poem for you," the Minstrel said magnanimously. "Come back in a fortnight."

"Oh, no, Minstrel!" Lark corrected, and typed a command. "We have a mission, and no time for poems. Just this once could you tell him the rules without rhyming?"

The Minstrel cocked his head as if he'd been challenged. "But you know the rules, Milady. If I do that, then the puzzles must be all the more arduous on the path!"

"That's OK. I'll have to help him, anyway, because he doesn't know how to play at all, Minstrel."

The Minstrel's brows came together in a frown. "No verses, then, Milady. Let us begin..."

Hugh saw that two new toadstools had sprouted beside the first, and when Milady climbed up to sit on one, he moved his mouse so his knight perched on the other.

"The game is very simple, and nearly impossible, for it is a mirror of life," the Minstrel began matter-of-factly, strumming the lute to accompany his words, which, while they were not in verse or song, sounded mellifluous.

"The Labyrinth is a multi-dimensional Omniverse – a place where an infinite number of worlds intersect. Like the Universe you inhabit, there is the seen and the unseen and the perfectly implausible. After all, we must consider the Microverse and the Macroverse as well as any other Verses the Maestro chooses to sing into the program." He strummed a few bars, then repeated his last sentence, but with musical accompaniment.

"Tell him about Port!" Milady urged. "She's an awesome portal!"

The Minstrel, strummed again, and sang his answer.

Port, Port
She's just your sort.
She cries and she laughs
And she seldom makes gaffs
She'll take you to meet
The outrageous elite
She'll find you a saint
Or find you a sinner
The whole galaxy's yours
And you'll be home by dinner!"

He finished the song with a flourish, then said quite seriously, "Port is a superconducting super-computer, who was endowed by her creator with the personality of his beloved wife – she has the heart and soul of a human, but the powers of a super-computer. She likes to provoke dialogues with the great thinkers of other ages, and she's always happy to entertain visitors. If she likes you, she'll help you with your quest. But she's quirky, mind you. Always full of surprises, our Port is."

Hugh shook his head in amazement. "I'm astounded by all this, Lark," he said meaning it. "Utterly gobsmacked. How is all this possible?"

Lark grinned. "My daddy could do anything. He was really smart."

"I should say he was!" Hugh agreed, then turning back to the screen, he asked, "Are there more characters for me to know about?"

"Lots... but some are *really* important." She typed in a command then said, "You have to tell him about the Ferryman, Minstrel."

"Ah yes, the Ferryman," the screen character responded. "Tricky bugger, he is. The Ferryman is a mysterious figure – rather dark, if I may say so. He pilots a subterranean boat that can take you to other dimensions of time/space, or let you travel inter-galactically, if you wish. But you must possess the Sigil that will allow you to return home, otherwise you'd be stranded in the Elsewhere forever, wouldn't you? To acquire the sigil you must pass the Ferryman's tests. And I feel I must warn you, they are never easy."

"I'll remember that," Hugh said, "Is there anything else I should fear?"

"Goblins and Dragonspawn and Toadwallopers and Mumpits, of course," sang the Minstrel. "Outliers, Ogres, Metamorphs, Wildings and Werebunnies, too. Mindmelders, Soulbenders, Timetakers, I suppose. Of course, the Dreadosphere and the Dreadlords, Malthazaar and Malfazadore – that sort of thing. But you'll be fine if you stick to the path, listen to Milady and answer the riddles."

Lark turned to Hugh and asked, "Did you ever play Chutes and Ladders when you were little?"

Hugh shook his head no.

"Well, it's a little like that game... sometimes you could be going along just fine on the path and then all of a sudden you fall into another realm quite by accident! Or you might answer a question right and get beamed up to another dimension. If that happens, you have to go in a whole new direction. My daddy said sometimes that happens to you in life, too. And then you're in a whole new game." She stopped short and Hugh realized she'd made the connection to the fact that her description perfectly fitted what had happened to her own real life.

"Type in the words Nine Gates, now," Lark said abruptly.

He did and the Minstrel spoke again.

"Nine Gates must be passed in order to complete the game. Each gate is a level guarded by The Gatekeeper. If you answer the gate's math question right, you get to collect a word clue for the Final Beckoning." At each gate you'll meet a Philosopher or a Physilosopher, who plays chess with The Gatekeeper to keep him entertained."

"What is a physilosopher, please?" Hugh whispered to Lark.

"He's a philosopher of physics," Lark answered. "My Daddy said when you get beyond quantum physics you have to take everything on faith, so he invented Physilosophers."

Hugh shook his head in wonder and then the Minstrel spoke again.

"At the end of the Game, when the Final Beckoning takes place, you will be rewarded with a prize that is of great consequence to the world's well-being – but until the prize is won, it's never identified. And I feel conscience-bound to tell you, Knight Errant – thus far, no one has ever reached the prize."

Lark touched Hugh's hand with her own.

"See, I told you it was a little hard, but don't worry – I'll help you, Ok?"

Hugh nodded grateful assent. "And here I thought all I'd have to do as your Champion was to slay a few dark knights and dragons – perhaps apprehend an occasional flying monkey or two..."

Lark giggled and returned her attention to the screen.

27

After lunch, Cait braced herself, said a prayer for courage, then told Lark of her plans to leave her in England while she tried to find the Spear. The revelation was just as devastating for both of them as she'd feared it would be. She tried not to let their shared misery derail her resolve for what she had to do. Tried, too, to help her beloved, and oh-so-wounded child, understand she had no choice but to go, but how could a nine year old understand such a thing, when she herself could barely cope? Finally, more out of fatigue than understanding, Lark had said she'd try to be brave while her mother was away, and she'd made Cait promise to be gone no more than a week. Cait had acquiesced in a desperate effort to calm Lark's fears, but now, several hours after their gut-wrenching conversation, as she sat beside her daughter on the big bed in her room, she knew the odds were wildly against her being able to keep her promise.

A book Lark had found in the old nursery was in Cait's hand. She'd always loved reading bedtime stories to Lark – she and Jack had alternated reading nights, so the child had always kept two separate piles of books next to her bed, insisting some books were for "Mommy reading" and some for "Daddy reading." Just the thought made Cait's eyes well up, as so very many trigger-points did now, the sorrow within her like a bottomless well that could be tapped by the barest thought of Jack.

She knew most all of the "Daddy reading" books were connected to math, or puzzles or numbers, the common thread for her husband and child. Some were tales of knights and dragons, leftovers from Jack's own childhood – tales of honor and courage and adventure he wanted Lark to share. She wondered who could ever fill that need now for Lark – not just the need for a loving father, but for one with such special gifts that matched her own, and such special love that had wrapped them both in such certainty of safety.

Lark settled back against the big bolster.

"Mommy," she said softly, after a while, "do you think Daddy's in heaven?"

Cait's voice caught as she tried to answer. "He deserves to be, love, that's for sure. Your daddy was a very good man, Lark – a wonderful husband and the best daddy ever. So, I guess, if there is a heaven, that's where he is now, keeping an eye on us."

Lark nodded. "But do you think there really *is* a heaven, Mommy?" Cait could imagine how important the answer to this question would be for the grieving child, but she tried never to lie to Lark, so she chose her words carefully.

"I believe we'll be with him again someday, *somewhere*, love," she said, meaning it. "I believe he's always with us in some way we don't understand, even now. But there's no way I know of to prove if heaven really exists or what it's like, sweetheart, so I think we just get to decide what we *want* to believe, Lark... and I've decided to believe there's a place where we'll be with him again, one day. I think maybe you have to decide what *you* want to believe... I think maybe this is one of those times when nobody else can tell you what to believe. It just has to feel right to your heart."

Lark nodded. "I asked Hugh about it," she said matter of factly.

That startled Cait. "You did? When did you do that?"

"He's really nice, Mommy," Lark answered in non-sequiter. "When he was showing me his books about knights and all, he told me lots of things about what it was like to be a Knight in shining armor. But I know a lot already, because of Daddy's Avatar and all, so I had stuff to tell him, too. Hugh was really interested in all the things Daddy taught me, especially the cipher stuff." It was the longest sentence Cait had heard Lark utter since Jack died.

"Wow!" she responded. "That's *great* that you two had a lot to talk about. But why did you ask him about heaven, sweetheart?"

Lark looked up into Cait's face, meeting her eyes almost shyly. "Because..." she began, faltering just a little before she went on, "...because knights used to die a lot in battle, so I thought he might know. I think he's some kind of knight, Mommy, but he keeps it a secret."

The poignant longing in her child's voice made tears rise again in Cait's eyes. "And did he know – about heaven, I mean?" she managed to ask, over the lump in her throat.

Lark nodded vigorously. "He didn't have any doubts at all, Mommy. He said he doesn't call it heaven, though. He calls it the Other Side, and he said he knows lots of people who know for sure that Daddy's okay now and that he's watching over us all the time, so we'll be safe." She saw the hesitancy in her mother's face and wanted to reassure her. "Hugh's really smart, Mom," she said. "Not smart like Daddy... not like a genius or anything, but he's smart about a lot of other things, and he seemed pretty sure about this."

Cait took a deep breath. "I'm so glad to hear that, love. It makes you feel better doesn't it?"

Lark smiled and nodded affirmatively again. "I still miss Daddy, though," she added plaintively. "I miss him all the time."

Cait wrapped her daughter in her arms once again. "Me, too, baby. Me, too."

28

Lark and Hugh had been sitting at the laptop for two hours. Seeing Lark's bereft expression and knowing Cait had told her about their trip, Hugh had decided to play the game with the child a while longer, to take her mind off his and Cait's imminent departure.

The battle he'd just fought at the Forgetful Forge had gone quite well, he thought. He'd had to fight because he'd missed yet another answer to a math problem. But he was getting good at the swordplay his avatar was capable of, and the gymnastic skills that let him leapfrog an opponent from a standing start, or scale a wall in a heartbeat, or do battle on the tops of trees –was all such a delightful improvement on the real-world battlefields he'd experienced.

Suddenly, a golden *something* rose from behind a gate on the Labyrinth's path and hovered overhead. It appeared to be the mathematical sign for Pi, gleaming and plump and somehow playful.

"What's *that* doing up there," Hugh asked, amused.

"That's Pi in the Sky," Lark answered, matter of factly. "That means Pythagoras or Euclid must be here with the Gatekeeper. They're really cool! Wait 'til you see..."

The Gate swung open and seated behind it were the Gatekeeper and Pythagoras, who was dwarfed by the Dragon's great bulk. Both were concentrating on a game of three-dimensional chess, the triple layered board hovering in the air between them, held up by butterflies, hummingbirds and a battalion of Ladybugs.

The Princess curtsied gracefully and Pythagoras rose to greet the visitors.

"Do you wish to consider a problem of geometry today, Milady?" he asked in a kindly voice. Instantly, a circle and a trapezoid materialized in front of them. One read *Oh yes please!* the other read *No way!* Lark had Milady touch the circle of *yes,* and the problem blinked into view in front of them.

"What concerns does my Theorem have with the area of squares?" Pythagoras asked on the screen.

Lark thought a moment, doodled something on her pad, then answered enthusiastically. "A square placed on the hypotenuse of a right triangle, whose side length is the length of the hypotenuse, has an area equal to the sum of the areas of two other squares. One has the side length of one of the legs of the triangle, and the other has the side length of the other leg.

Pythagoras smiled, and made a sweeping gesture toward the path ahead.

"You may continue on your way young mathematician," he said, as they sped on past the gate. "I *love* geometry!" Lark told Hugh with a grin.

"I believe I liked it, too," Hugh answered, "although my geometry career was brief and rather a long time ago. But, I think I recall there's something about geometry that appealed to my sense of order. And geometric shapes are like building blocks in time/space, aren't they?"

As he said it, Lark giggled, a lilting sound, and Milady bent to open a small door in a tree, out of which tumbled a riot of geometric shapes, circles, squares, triangles, rhomboids, tetrahedrons, all colors and sizes, cavorting and tumbling all over themselves and each other, forming the shapes of buildings and bridges and walls and towers, just as if a child were building structures with colored blocks.

"You can build something if you'd like," Lark told him, whipping her mouse about and causing the blocks to assemble and disassemble themselves, making shapes and then other shapes. "I used to do this a lot when I was little and my Daddy was teaching me geometry."

"My word, Milady," Hugh said, impressed, "what a lovely way to learn."

She nodded vigorously. "There's a Tesseract Tree, too," she said enthusiastically. "It's even cooler. Want to see?"

Hugh laughed, "I'm sure I would, if I remembered precisely what a Tesseract might be," he said, "but perhaps we could save that for another day?" He smiled warmly at Lark. "I'm afraid I'm rather anxious to see what lies further on the path and I have a good deal to do to prepare for our travels tomorrow." He was beginning to get the hang of the game, so he directed his avatar down the path ahead of the Princess, just as Lark shouted a warning.

"Trolls!" she cried out. "Watch where you step!" but the warning came too late and Hugh saw his avatar suddenly sucked out of sight, tumbling, horse and all down a long dark tunnel and landing with a thump, in a mist-enshrouded place where shadows lurked everywhere, just out of reach.

Milady stood for a moment, peering over the edge of the giant hole that had swallowed Knight Errant. Lark typed, *Oh dear!* into her game, and Milady spoke the words, then leaped headfirst into the hole, and followed the knight down to the Dreadosphere where the Ferryman awaited.

There was a compassionate expression on Lark's face, as she looked up from the screen at the consternation on Hugh's face. On the screen, Milady and Knight Errant had both landed hard at the Ferryman's feet. Hugh saw that instead of her usual speed and determination to show him the game, she was simply sitting motionless, staring at the screen.

"Are you alright, Lark?" he asked.

She didn't look at him. "I don't want you and Mommy to go." She said the words in a small voice, with tears beneath.

"We are going to find the Spear in order to keep you safe, Lark. Nothing less than your safety would cause your mother to leave you, even for a little while. I give you my word that I will be her liegeman, too, and protect her every step of the way. Do you understand this?"

After a long moment, Lark nodded, and then she turned to look at him, her large eyes brimming with tears. "Sometimes knights die," she said, her voice almost inaudible. "My Daddy died."

Hugh felt the moisture flood his own eyes. "My dear, sweet child," he said, wishing he knew how to comfort her. "I will not let her come to harm," he said reaching out to fold her into his arms as he saw her dissolve into helpless tears. "I give you my solemn promise, Lark. On my honor, I will bring her back to you."

29

It was just after 10 that night when Anthony Delafield looked around the gathering. He'd called this emergency meeting to introduce Cait to the assemblage.

For the most part they were old, these men and women of his beloved Hunting Lodge, he thought as he scanned the familiar faces. He was heartened, however, to see how many were accompanied by younger family members like Hugh, or trusted initiates being trained by them, but the faces he knew best were growing old. He silently thanked Providence there were now so many new young members worldwide, capable of taking up the torch. It was a small miracle so many in this new generation were willing to devote themselves so selflessly to the common good, and to the rigors of a classical occult initiation process. But then, perhaps miracles were what the Lodge had always been about.

"Ladies and gentlemen," he began, "the game is afoot again. It appears we have a great deal of work to do."

He turned to Cait, who was seated on his right between himself and Hugh. "We have the rare privilege today of welcoming to our Lodge the newest Caretaker." All eyes turned toward Cait, assessingly. "Her name is Dr. Caitlin Monahan, and the task of Caretaker was passed to her from her husband Jack, who received it from his father, John.

"As Fate would have it, because of the unexpected nature of Jack's demise, he had no time to explain to Caitlin the full history of the Spear, nor the obligations of The Caretaker. Thus it has fallen to us of the Lodge to give her the information she will need in order to begin her sacred Quest.

"My son Hugh has offered to be her champion on this mission, and he felt it best that before they both leave England, we assemble the Friends of the Hunt, so that Dr. Monahan can learn of us, and we of her. And so that the story of the Spear can be told in detail once more – for some gathered here, it will be a well-known tale, for others, perhaps a new one."

He looked around the sea of assembled faces and smiled. "Knights, Ladies, and trusted friends of the Hunting Lodge of the Ancient Order of the Poor Knights of the Temple of Solomon, it is my great honor to commend to your eternal care and unquestioning loyalty, Doctor Caitlin Monahan, The Caretaker."

A chorus of welcome rose from the curious assemblage that contained both the obvious gentry and many who appeared to be of the working classes, and Cait, already stunned by the use of the terms Knights and Ladies, and by the realization that their Order was in some incomprehensible manner that of the Knights Templar itself, alive and well in England in the year 2010, acknowledged the gracious introduction with a nervous smile, a bow and a murmured thank you. Lord Delafield beamed his approval then spoke again to the group.

"Are there any here too young to know the full history of our Order with the Spear?"

A number of hands rose in the room, including Cait's.

"Well, then," he said, clearing his throat portentously, "let us begin at the beginning..."

Palestine A.D. 33

Longinus, The Centurion, looked furtively in all directions before knocking at the ornate door. He could hear the soft patter of water falling into a fountain somewhere within. He had taken great pains to insure that he hadn't been followed. If he were to be found consorting with the friends of the crucified Rabbi, who was now whispered to have risen from the dead, he could be accused of treason and find himself the next victim on Golgotha. Longinus had enemies enough within the Legion to be sure he would not go unhumiliated or unpunished. His early ascension to the coveted rank of centurion had made the older legionnaires envious.

The woman who answered the knock was young and diffident in her greeting. Large, Semitic eyes assessed him, then turned demurely downward. "My father is in the garden," she said softly, "I will take you to him."

Joseph of Arimethea, Longinus had learned, was both a wealthy merchant and an influential member of the Sanhedrin, the governing body within the Jewish sector. The older man rose to greet the newcomer, the three young children with whom he had been playing, scattered amidst suppressed giggles, except for one boy, about 7 years of age, who stood his ground.

"Is he a soldier, Grandfather?" the boy asked with seriousness. "He walks like a soldier."

"He is, Jacob," said the imposing man, who now stood in front of Longinus. "You are most observant, but I'm afraid it is time for you to run along to your tutor. I have business with this man."

The boy hesitated another moment, staring pointedly at the sword that hung like an extra appendage at Longinus' belt. Then, reluctantly, he moved toward the door, turned abruptly then blurted:

"What is in that big parcel, sir?"

Longinus smiled. He had a son this age at home and understood the insatiable curiosity of boys.

"A gift for your grandfather, Jacob," he replied solemnly. "But it is for his eyes only, I'm afraid."

The boy's own eyes widened. A secret was even better than a gift. At a gesture from Joseph, he reluctantly left the room.

"I have been expecting you," Joseph said without preamble.

"Have you?" Longinus replied, not trying to conceal the heavy skepticism in his voice. "I myself didn't know I was coming here until an hour ago."

"My Master knows what we do not," Joseph replied simply, gesturing to a cushioned seat beside a small gurgling fountain. "I was told you would be coming."

Longinus looked carefully at the older man, as if trying to be certain he was not being made a fool.

"I've been told to give you my spear," he said, finally, thrusting the long parcel at the man. "I've had three dreams in a row, each one stranger than the last. They are undream-like. Urgent. Demanding. I want it gone." He averted his eyes as if embarrassed, then said in a softer voice, "Last night, an angel told me to return it to you." The Centurian shook his head and sighed audibly, as if to say he understood the absurdity of what he'd just said.

"Tell me the words," Joseph replied gravely.

Longinus looked into the man's eyes again, before trusting himself to speak. "'You are the first Caretaker,' is what he told me. 'There will be others. It is a sacred duty. You may be called upon to give your life to protect what has been entrusted to you. You carry mankind's destiny in your saddle mount.'"

Joseph nodded, satisfied by the revelation, not surprised. "And what did this angel look like?"

"He looked like a great warrior. He was heavily armed, fierce and imposing. He was made of light, and great wings of light emanated from his shoulders. He was..." the man hesitated, groping for a word... "he was quite terrifying."

"Indeed, he is a most formidable warrior, our Michael," said Joseph with a small hint of a smile. 'Archangel of Fire, Regent of the South, Captain of the Angelic Army. He sits at the right hand of God."

*Longinus looked relieved that he was being taken seriously. He nodded, trying to understand. "The Rabbi we crucified... he was... the **one** you've been waiting for, then? Your Messiah?"*

"He was the One," Joseph said simply.

Longinus nodded again, as if to say this news was not unexpected. "This Spear," he said, "it has power." It wasn't a question.

Joseph inclined his head. "His blood has baptized it. Are you aware of the prophecy that you fulfilled with this instrument?"

Longinus, puzzled, shook his head.

"'A bone of him shall not be broken,' it says in scripture... you saved him from the breaking of the legs that is the norm for criminals on the cross..."

"I sought a more merciful death for him than for the others. He seemed so gentle..."

Joseph nodded. "You, too, were baptized by his blood. Did you not feel the power when it touched you?"

"I felt... as if I'd been struck by lightning. As if..." he hesitated. "As if I'd been touched by God himself." Joseph could hear in the man's hushed voice that he was struggling to control his emotions.

"You may go in peace, Longinus," Joseph said, gently. "The Master has blessed you for your good intent. You have now passed the Spear to the next Caretaker, for I am he."

Longinus nodded and not knowing what to say turned for the door. Then hesitated.

"The Caretaker," he said. "What is expected of this Caretaker?"

Joseph smiled sadly. "Whatever God chooses to demand of him."

Longinus nodded, accepting the responsibility that had been laid upon each of them.

"Forever?" Longinus asked.

"Forever," was the solemn reply.

The story of the Spear's astounding journey through the centuries continued far into the night. Cait sat, mesmerized by the sound of Lord Delafield's voice, and by the marvelous, magical tales he told as he carried his audience along with him through nearly two thousand years of history, peopled by kings and emperors, commoners and Caretakers. Visions and voices rose within her as the tales unfolded, and she realized, somewhere in the night, that she could no longer be certain where Delafield's stories ended and her own began, because they weren't stories anymore. They were lives she'd led and places she'd lived and deaths she'd died, knowledge that could not be denied or forgotten.

But none of that meant she had a clue what to do about any of it.

*   *   *

Hugh, watching her closely as the night wore on toward morning, knew that it had all begun in earnest for Cait, now. After tonight, nothing would ever be the same for her. The knowledge made him happy and sad in equal measure.

Curiouser & Curiouser

Part IV

*"Religion hinges upon faith,
politics hinges upon who can tell
the most convincing lies…"*
                              Ian Stewart

30

Rome. The Vatican.

Opus Dei was not the only covert power within the Vatican, it was simply the secret society the whole world knew about, which allowed the others to flourish unnoticed.

Giacomo Cardinal Andretti, head of the far more covert cabal, *Deus Vult,* moved his large girth back from the outsized desk in his exquisitely paneled office in the Vatican Secretariat to allow himself some breathing room. His chubby fingers clutched the message he'd been reading for a long moment, as he glanced absently out the window into the Court of St. Damascus below.

So Gustav Gruner had actually sent a hit team to America to secure the Spear of Longinus – *tagliatevi dai piedi!* – how *absurd.* Worse yet, they had failed, and murders had taken place that could stir up old secrets and shine a light into places better left in shadow. Gruner's monumental ego had obviously slipped its bonds. The man was too used to having all wishes fulfilled. But of course this particular wish was ludicrous. What could be motivating the head of the most powerful secret society on earth to send thugs on such a quest after half a century? It wasn't like Gruner to be rash. Cunning and evil were adjectives that fit him more aptly.

The Cardinal reached for his phone. He had no intention of letting this stupid Spear catastrophe interfere with his well-ordered plans. Bringing the world's attention to the Spear and Hitler and a time best forgotten, could only interfere with his own Papal agenda. He intended to see to it that Pius XII was canonized before the end of this decade, and by doing so, he would enhance his own chance for the Papacy a thousand fold. He would not let something as inconsequential as the Spear of Longinus subvert this goal.

The Cardinal drummed his fingers on the desk, thinking a moment longer before picking up the receiver. Whatever measures must be taken to keep the old Nazi nonsense from surfacing would be taken. It was a pity there was a child involved with this business in the States, but nits make lice, as Cromwell had said, and who knew what the distraught mother might have said to so precocious a girl. It would certainly be in his best interests to find out. Why that damned old relic wouldn't stay buried was beyond him. Two thousand years of popping up at odd moments in odd hands... one could almost believe the tales of its supernatural powers.

It was unfortunate Gruner's blunder was making serious damage-control measures necessary now, but it was all for the greater honor and glory of God, after all. The words of another religious pragmatist were suddenly in his head... the Apostolic Delegate who slew the Cathari heretics, man, woman and child. "Kill them all," he'd said when his orders to do so had been questioned by reluctant soldiers. "Let God sort out his own." He, too, might have to leave the sorting to God, if this stupid business could not quickly and quietly be contained.

Andretti made up his mind and jiggled the line for an operator. Where had his exasperating secretary disappeared to *now*? No matter.

"I need a secure line," he told the voice on the line, then dialed the number that would bring this Spear nonsense to a hasty and satisfactory conclusion. The 13 wasn't the only covert organization with a stake in this ridiculous business in America. *Deus Vult* – his own secret group within the Vatican – had just as much to lose if the Spear's secrets came to light – perhaps more. To have Deus Vult's leader on the Papal Throne would mean the agenda they had worked so hard for could finally be achieved, and the insanity of Pope John XXIII and his so-called liberal reforms would be repealed. True Catholicism would be restored, and the liberal lunacy of the past five decades would be erased forever. Whatever it took to achieve that end was surely in God's best interest. *Deus vult.* God wills it.

Gruner's 13 might be a secret society of the world's most powerful families and corporations, playing brilliantly at the game of greed and power, but the Roman Catholic Church had seen such power as theirs come and go through two millennia, and always, always, the Church had remained intact. It was the one power base that would never be toppled because it was protected by God Almighty Himself, and Deus Vult were His ground troops.

Pius XII was about to become a Saint. The Beatification process was well on its way to completion, after that, Canonization was an easy leap. The one further miracle needed wouldn't be hard to find, as long as there were over-pious nuns and laity all too willing to believe. This was certainly not the time for ugly stories from the past to surface.

The Jews had already tried to stop Pius XII's canonization, but fortunately he'd been able to make their attempt seem like petty sour grapes. However, if the story of the Spear and, God forbid, the Church's involvement with the likes of Gruner and the American CIA, became common knowledge, it would almost certainly get people focusing on facts in Pius XII's life that were in sympathy with Hitler. Before becoming Pope, he'd spent all those years as Papal Nuncio in Berlin, and Hitler had shown such kindness to the Church, the survival of which was after all, of far more importance to the world's well-being than the endless whinings of Jewry.

The Holocaust was unfortunate, of course, but those people were always winging about mistreatment of one kind or another, so it wasn't all that hard to deflect criticism. Andretti sighed. Of course, that was before the infernal internet – Satan's own invention. Now any busybody could investigate things best kept buried, and secrets were popping up like toadstools on a damp day. Thank God for the ease with which true believers could be manipulated. Thank God for the foresight of whoever had been smart enough to invent the concept of blind Faith.

Inwardly, Andretti congratulated himself on having had the good sense to stay involved with Gruner for so many decades. His own participation in the affairs of The 13 had yielded a number of lucrative deals for the Church over the years, and it had earned him a place at The 13's table. His not inconsiderable negotiating skills had been useful to the group more than once, and the Vatican's worldwide power base was unparallelled. In return, priceless information had made its way to him for more than a quarter century.

Nonetheless, Gruner had been a servant of Satan when he was Guttman in the Reich – and he certainly hadn't changed his allegiance when he'd changed his name and his face. Even if the Americans had been fooled, Andretti had not. But the virtue of keeping your friends close and your enemies closer, was, after all, a most Italian concept.

The Cardinal silently blessed his own perspicacity in having realized so early on that while the Germans had surrendered at the end of the war, the Nazi agenda would continue under a new banner forwarded by Gruner and others like him. Those high ranking survivors had escaped the consequences of their crimes by being smart, rich and ruthless. And they knew secrets others would kill for. The Vatican had never taken the danger posed by such men lightly. And neither had Giacomo Cardinal Andretti, their point man in such matters of statecraft.

He waited impatiently for the phone to be answered – the voice at the other end of the line would be just the one he'd need to help sort this out discreetly.

*   *   *

The pious Sicilian named Vincenzo, bowed his head at the alter rail and wondered why God had chosen this difficult path for him. He frequently pondered this, when he knew that a call from his patron, the Cardinal, was imminent.

The small country church he prayed in now, was so like the one of his childhood memories. It made him think of his mother and the others like her, who attended early mass each day, dressed in black shroud-like garments from another age. What would she think of the rocky road the Saviour had placed him on? What would she think of the things he had been called on to do over the years, or the deeds he had perpetrated, to fulfill his obligations to God.

He had never meant to be an assassin, despite the reputation his homeland had for vendetta. But he had been given this special gift by God Himself: this almost supernatural ability to kill at great distances with his rifle, and the courage to kill at close range, even staring an opponent in the face, as he did so. Two unique gifts, that were given to few men. If the Almighty had not wanted him to become an instrument of destruction, why would He have given him these gifts?

God's will. His mother had spoken of it often. When his father had been killed in the war... when he himself had volunteered for war zones that enhanced his killing skills... when his brother had become a priest... when his sister had died in childbirth. When he had been recruited by the Cardinal to be the instrument of justice. All these events were God's will. *Deus Vult.*

The special cell phone he had been given by the Cardinal began to vibrate. Vincenzo blessed himself piously, then hurried to the back of the tiny roadside church. It would be sacrilege to speak of bloody deeds near the Blessed Sacrament – even if it was a Cardinal who demanded them.

"I have an important mission for you, my son," Cardinal Andretti began, in his most unctuous tone, once reserved only for the pulpit and large donors. "It is most delicate, and of the utmost importance to our Cause."

"I understand, Eminence," the man said dutifully. "Someone is to be eliminated?"

"Perhaps that will be the final need, Vincenzo," the Cardinal replied judiciously, "but first we must get certain information from a woman."

"A woman, Excellency?" the man responded, genuinely aghast. "Never have you sent me to harm a woman!"

"So true, my son," Andretti replied with equanimity, "but the ways of the Lord are sometimes mysterious, are they not? And her gender is precisely why I am counseling that we proceed with utmost caution – she may not need to be harmed. In fact, she may need to be protected. It is a complex issue. This woman holds the key to a sacred mystery, Vincenzo – one she has no business possessing. The Lord never intended that women be trusted with sacred knowledge. Do you recall this teaching from your catechism?" The Cardinal's tone held just the right hint of reproach to motivate the Sicilian and his simple faith.

Vincenzo had always wondered about this Church teaching regarding women. From what he had observed in life, women were the stronger ones. Not physically of course, but in other ways, in endurance and piety, compassion and love. He supposed the Cardinal and the Lord had their reasons for not trusting women, but he, himself, would not have had such reservations.

"You know best, Eminence," he said finally, believing that was so. "How can I serve you in this matter?"

"A packet of information will come to you by the usual means, my son. It will contain photographs of two women and a child," Vincenzo's heart sank.

"*Maria Santissima!* You wish me to harm a child?" Vincenzo whispered, in horrified disbelief. What could God be thinking to demand such a thing of him?

"Not necessarily, my son," the Cardinal amended hastily, hearing the revulsion in the man's voice.

"We believe it is the redheaded woman who holds the information we desire, but her child could also be used as a pawn of the devil. The sister, the dark haired woman, is the least likely to know the secret we seek, but because she is an attorney, there is always the possibility that something may have been placed in her care for safe-keeping – something that would enlighten us."

"And what will be expected of me, pertaining to these three, Eminence?" Without thinking, Vincenzo walked back into the empty church and again knelt, leaning hard against the altar rail.

"For now, Vincenzo," said the Cardinal, "you will follow the red haired one. If you must choose only one of the three to pursue, follow her. Allow no one to kidnap her or harm her in any way, as others may be seeking this knowledge she possesses, and they cannot be allowed to achieve their ends. Our hope is that she will simply lead us to a certain treasure which belongs to the Church, but is now hidden... in which case, you will take it from her and bring it here to me. If that does not transpire quickly, it may be necessary for you to capture and interrogate her or the child, or the sister. You will receive further instructions, if that is the case. For now, simply do as the packet tells you. And *only* what it tells you. Is this understood?"

"I understand, Eminence. I am relieved this is all you wish of me, for the moment. *Madre Mia*, it would be hard for me to harm a woman or a child."

The Cardinal frowned. "But you *will* follow orders, Vincenzo, no matter what they may be? Am I correct in this assumption, my son?"

The large shaggy-haired man hesitated, hating himself for the spiritual weakness this indecision showed. He was a soldier of *Deus Vult*. A soldier in the army of Christ. There was no excuse for this hesitancy on his part, if duty called.

"I will do as you bid me, Eminence," he said in a hoarse voice. "I am a simple man and there is much I do not understand. But I always do as I am instructed by you, Eminence. As I have done in all the years you have permitted me the honor of serving you."

Andretti, relieved, let out the breath he'd been holding. "We knew you could be counted on, Vincenzo," he said with great solemnity and the royal plural. "You have never failed us, my son."

The connection was broken abruptly after that, and the big, simple man, who had been called on by Fate to do many things he did not understand, lowered his head to his arms, now folded on the altar rail, and wept.

*   *   *

Andretti, satisfied that the women would now be kept under his scrutiny, laid down the receiver, then picked it up again.

"A secure line to America, Peter," he said to his secretary, who had reappeared. "I wish to speak with Director Farnsworth?"

"Of the CIA, Eminence?" his secretary responded, then regretted the words, even as they left his lips.

"You know of another director by that name, then?" Andretti rebuked, in a weary, but not unkind voice.

"No, Eminence," Peter stammered. "I'll put the call through for you immediately."

Andretti sighed. Peter was a good boy, for an American, but he did not understand the Italian subtleties, and he often spoke without thinking. He must break him of this foolishness or replace him, which would be a shame, as his billionaire parents in Chicago were contributors of great merit.

31

New York

Matt sat at his desk at the Precinct House and drummed his pencil on the wood, raising a few annoyed eyebrows in the small sea of desks outside his cramped, institutionally dingy and paper-strewn office. He picked up the folder he'd just thrown down, and reread the contents, frowning.

A familiar stocky form appeared in the doorway. Matt motioned him in with a head gesture.

Croce moved his weight-lifter heft to the steel chair that faced the desk. He was as rectangular as a refrigerator. "What's up?" he asked, nodding toward the pencil in Matt's hand. "The drum beat called to me." Croce was Matt's closest buddy on the force and the nearest thing he had to a best friend.

"You want I should close the door?" Croce asked and then did so without waiting for a reply.

"You remember my friend Meg, right?"

Croce nodded. "Sure. She's the great looking Lesbo from Kramer Crowley – sheesh, what a waste. The one with the nice family you like so much – you introduced me a while back. I saw the story in the paper about the murders in Greenwich, and figured you'd tell me what's going on when you were in the mood."

"If I knew what was going on, I'd do just that. This one's got a few weirder than usual twists and since we've got no jurisdiction I've got to nose around carefully..."

"And you'd like me to help with the snoopage?" Croce finished for him. "You know me – I live to serve."

Matt smirked. "Thanks, Croce, I could really use your eyes and ears on this one – what I know so far is pretty strange. I've been digging discretely for a couple of days..."

"So we grab a beer after work and you tell me what you know or don't know, and we'll see where that takes us, yeah?"

Matt handed him the file he'd been putting together. "Don't leave this lying around – it's pretty ugly stuff and I got most of it under the table."

Croce's eyebrows rose. "But, of course," he said in his best Inspector Clouseau French accent. "Zat is why zey gave us ze Gold Shields – zo we could *detect,*" he emphasized the last word.

Croce let himself out and took the folder to his desk. Twenty minutes later, he slid it back under Matt's phone.

"One beer ain't gonna be enough," he said, and walked out the door.

32

Washington, D.C.

"What a consummate pain in the arse!" CIA Director, H. Burton Farnsworth growled, slapping the file onto his enormous and uncluttered desk for emphasis. "After all this time, not only have these fools dredged up the deadly dead, but they've hooked us into a scandal of fucking epic proportion for no earthly reason. That Nazi son of a bitch should have died years ago, but probably not even Satan can stand Gruner's stench."

"It's not too late to arrange his untimely demise," said Winfield Livingston III, sitting unperturbed on the other side of the desk. He was known for his sangfroid. It would be easy enough to give the job to Blackwater or Greystone or whatever it was those ubiquitous and ever-useful mercenaries were calling themselves this week.

"Don't tempt me," his boss snapped back, in his characteristic guttural growl. Gruner had been a thorn in his side for decades. Once the arrogant old Nazi was dead, if that felicitous day ever arrived, the whole file on Project Paperclip and all its disturbing sub-projects, could be blessedly put to rest. It wasn't that there weren't other old Nazis happily ensconced in lucrative new lives all over the globe, especially in South America, but none was as visible, and therefore potentially dangerous to the CIA's ancient dirty secrets, as Gruner. And the filthy son of a bitch seemed to have found the goddamned Fountain of Youth.

"Maybe that sociopath son of his will get tired of waiting for his inheritance," Farnsworth said finally, brightening at the thought of patricide.

Livingston chuckled without mirth, "And quite an inheritance it will be," he said with the equanimity that was his hallmark as well as a legacy of his Wasp heritage. "It would take 10 lifetimes to deplete what Gruner stashed in Swiss accounts before his inglorious departure from the Fatherland."

"Why do you think Gruner's muddying the water with this ridiculous Spear of Longinus business now, after all this time?" Farnsworth asked abruptly. "It couldn't be of less consequence on the world scene."

"Are we so certain he's the one responsible for those murders in Greenwich, then?" Livingston countered, both to let his boss know he was on top of that, and because it was an interesting possibility. "Isn't it possible some of those young jihadists or skinhead fanatics they breed like homunculi under bell jars, were just out for a good time or to make their bones?"

Farnsworth shook his head. "My sources believe the murders tie into the fact that Gruner's after the Spear. God alone knows why." He didn't add he'd been keeping Gruner on his special watchlist for decades. That wasn't Livingston's business yet.

"Speaking of God, have you asked our friend at the Vatican for an explanation?"

"Actually," Farnsworth replied with a small laugh, "His Eminence called me. I wish to God our intelligence network functioned as efficiently as the Vatican's."

"Ah, but they have a direct line to the Almighty," his second-in-command suggested with an amused twitch of his lip.

Farnsworth snorted derisively, "What makes you think the Almighty is the one at the other end of that line?"

Livingston smiled again, this time genuinely amused. "What did your friend the Cardinal have to say?"

"It was a courtesy call, according to His Eminence. Just a heads up that the game had begun. He's sicced his Deus Vult team onto it... said he'll keep us in the loop."

Livingston's left eyebrow rose a little. "And what will we be doing in the meantime?"

"I'd just as soon take the Spear out of play altogether. These religious icons are a tricky business. Like those Virgin sightings on a pizza crust – the sheeple line up for the wolves to feast on them."

He liked the idea of people and sheep combined – it covered so much ground.

"Find the woman... Dr. Caitlin Monahan is her name, as I'm sure you know by now. She and her prodigy daughter, plus a lawyer sister, constitute the whole family according to the dossier I've had drawn up for you. One of them knows where the Spear is. Find them, get them to relinquish it 'for the sake of National Security' or some such. Frighten them with whatever terrorist twaddle you can cook up, and go collect the damned thing as quickly as possible. We can bury it in the Smithsonian basement or use it as a bargaining chip with Gruner's cronies. Whatever. Just get the damned thing out of circulation."

Livingston rose, his 6'3" frame just the faintest bit stooped from years of willingly taking orders. "Shouldn't be hard to do, sir," he said.

"You think not?" snorted Farnsworth, derisively. "We'll see. Better check to see if the Jebbies are after it, too."

Livingston looked up, surprised. "The Jesuits, too?" he asked. "Why on earth would *they* want it?"

"The man who's the Postulator for Pius XII's Beatification process is a Jesuit," he answered, "Although there appears to be some kind of bad blood between him and Andretti."

"This gets more and more Byzantine," Livingston said thoughtfully. "Most likely the good Cardinal who's so intent on getting Hitler's Pope canonized, simply doesn't want the dirty laundry from the war hanging in St. Peter's Square."

"Indeed. That's certainly what's at the bottom of his interest in all this."

"Ah, those sheeple," Livingston said with a world-weary sigh. "Imagine believing a Pope who didn't have the balls to denounce Hitler's atrocities, being considered a source of miracles. That's a miracle in itself, I suppose."

Farnsworth watched the man leave. Livingston was a superb lieutenant. Proper credentials, perfect demeanor, utterly without conscience, and with a wicked dry humor that could be most entertaining. But he was being a bit shortsighted about this Spear thing, perhaps. Of course Farnsworth had history with Gruner and knew it was never good to underestimate an old nemesis. The queer little prickle of intuition at the back of his neck that always alerted him to potential hazards, had been prickling ever since he'd heard the Spear was in play again. He hadn't gotten to be Director by ignoring signs and portents. This Spear business was going to need damage control. He just wasn't yet certain what damage they'd be controlling.

33

Winfield Livingston pondered all that Farnsworth had said, as he prepared to set up surveillance. The old man was canny and seldom wrong about this sort of thing – practically had second sight when it came to skullduggery.

He rather liked the old boy, if the truth be told. Farnsworth had come up the hard way. On sheer talent, not family wealth and political connections. *That* and the fact that no one knew more dark secrets about nearly everyone of political consequence, than Farnsworth. Maybe Wild Bill Donovan in his time, or the Dulles brothers had known as much, but no one now alive knew what Farnsworth knew. Livingston hadn't gotten this far in the Company without being smart enough to know when the chief was light years ahead of him. He'd have to catch up fast...

But *why the Spear, and why now? The Papacy?* Gruner wouldn't give a rat's testicle about that. *Magical powers?* The church would dismiss that poppycock in a heartbeat. Some other faction that could use Project Paperclip against the CIA? *That* could be a reason... but who, and how? And why *now?*

He'd need to choose precisely the right people to strongarm the two women into revealing whatever it was they knew. One in

New York... one in England. The international aspect shouldn't be a problem. The company had reciprocal privileges with MI5 and MI6. As long as they weren't planning to kill anyone just yet, it shouldn't even raise an eyebrow. A few judiciously chosen threats should do the trick and he'd be able to see that the Spear was back in Farnsworth's hands, most expeditiously. On the assumption that was really all the Old Boy wanted here. The Director was a notoriously Byzantine thinker, and there were so many old secrets...

He had asked for the file folder on the newly deceased Professor Jack Monahan and had read it through with considerable interest. It contained the specifics of every project the Professor had ever worked on for NSA. Monahan had possessed an unusual clearance level for a college professor, and he'd been called on in half a dozen sensitive cases, any of which could be useful as a manipulative tool for dealing with his widow. But it was obvious to Livingston, the man's work for the government had had nothing to do with his untimely death.

The Director was right, as usual. Everything about the man's murder led back to the ridiculous Spear and Gruner's obsession with it. And clearly the Director knew a great deal more about Gruner and the Spear than he was letting on. So be it. The good news was that Professor Monahan's occasional employment by government agencies would provide the perfect cover for what Winfield intended to set in motion. The man's high level clearance, and the phrase "in the interest of National Security," would be enough to allow the Company considerable latitude in pressuring the two women who might have knowledge of the Spear's whereabouts. Armed with both, he could harass these women into submission pretty much any way he pleased.

Any threat to National Security allowed him to invoke the Patriot Act, which in turn enabled him to avoid the Justice System altogether. He could threaten them with so much trouble they'd have to accede. Most of all, he could get back the Spear Farnsworth seemed to want so badly *and* impose a gag order so no one could find out how he'd gone about it. *Delightful.*

Win Livingston drummed his fingers on the file folder and considered his options. Better test their resolve with pressure first. If that didn't do the trick, there'd be time for sterner measures, later.

The first thing to do was the wiretapping, so much easier these days than it had been before Bush, Cheney and Rumsfeld had gotten the red tape out of the way. Harold Thornby over at Homeland might be useful, too, if only to up the pressure in the pot.

While he was at it, he'd better make sure he was notified about any new interest in Paperclip or Gruner that cropped up anywhere. It was unlikely the woman had friends with access to anything classified, but you just never knew. Intelligent amateurs could surprise you.

Livingston drummed his fingers on the Monahan file. *Why the Spear? Why now?* The Middle East and the Af-Pak alliance were tinderboxes, and a Christian relic could have no meaning he could see, in that arena. Something else was in play here. But what the hell was it?

Minding Rats at a Crossroad

Part V

"Better to reign in Hell than serve in Heaven."

John Milton
Paradise Lost

34

Germany

Dr. Gustav Gruner, born Helmut Guttman, retained the ramrod posture of his youthful SS training, as he stood at the head of the immense conference table, around which sat some of the most powerful men and women on earth. Gruner's emotionless blue eyes were ice floes in a face that betrayed no hint of either humanity or compassion. He thought of himself as a shape-shifter with the chameleon-like ability to act any role with such perfect attention to detail that every impersonation became a second skin.

This face was not the one he had worn in the Reich. *That* face had been left behind in Costa Rica decades before, and the current one had been nipped and tucked as needed over his ninety years, so that, tall and slender as he was, he could easily have passed for closer to seventy. The biogenetically engineered enhancements he received monthly at the private clinic he funded, didn't hurt either. The placental and umbilical stem cell injections were painful, but worth it. The medical experiments at Auschwitz and Buchenwald had yielded extraordinary information about the human endocrine system and had gotten the Nazi genetic engineering program off to a brilliant start. Playing by nobody's outdated rules of medical ethics had made possible scientific leaps it had taken the rest of the world decades to catch up with – some still had not been made public. The V-2 rocket scientists weren't the only Aryans who had gone light-years beyond their inferior rivals.

The Order of the 13, assembled now before him, was a formidable group of the richest families and the most influential corporations and enterprises on earth. There was little of consequence that happened on the world stage that didn't have their fingerprints on it, but they were proving to be shortsighted when it came to the importance of the Spear. They considered it his personal obsession and were willing to indulge him up to a point, as long as his success with all other Order business continued to provide both money and political power for their enterprises. And he had never disappointed them. The mind control research alone, that he'd begun in the Reich and his son Fritz had continued to supply to the highest military bidders, had increased their fortunes exponentially. As had his manipulation of certain markets that had served their collective purpose for half a century.

But then, of course, The Order didn't know that the Spear's mystical properties were only half the story. The true Spear of Longinus held the only key to one of history's greatest unsolved mysteries, and Gruner was the last man left alive who knew the truth.

*   *   *

From his place near the foot of the vast conference table, Fritz Gruner, wiry, intelligent and filled with carefully banked rage, watched his father with the same shark-like intensity his father bestowed on the assembling power-brokers. Fritz made a point of being respectful toward the old man, as impeccable in this as in all other areas of life that were observable. Places into which his father didn't delve, allowed Fritz ample opportunity for his own set of perversions.

About the old man's character he had no illusions. Gustav Gruner was motivated by self-interest, his greed for power so monumental, it bordered on the obsessional. But that was nothing his psychologist son needed to be concerned about. Despite the old man's will, he simply couldn't live forever. It was essential to Fritz's plan that he force himself to exercise a patience that didn't come to him naturally. He had no illusions about what his father would do to him if he suspected disloyalty of any kind. So he had to bide his time – but only for a little longer. If he played his cards right, this Spear stupidity would be his father's undoing. Fritz smiled a little to himself... his father wasn't after all, the only superb card player in the family.

The sharp rap of the gavel called the assemblage to order and Fritz turned his full concentration back to the task at hand. He had been given a place at the table because of his father's position at its head, but respect from those who sat here was something he'd always known he'd have to earn for himself.

35

The thirteen men and women seated at the table represented raw power, cloaked by the silken trappings of privilege and wealth that, for the most part, placed them far beyond the rules that governed ordinary people. Many were recognizable from the media, some would never allow their faces to be seen, or if seen, they took pains to appear something entirely other than what they were.

Much of the money and power represented here was inherited. It wasn't easy to learn the proper exercise of such sovereignty in a single lifetime, and being born to it, and trained from infancy to rulership, was a distinct advantage. Others had won their places at the table by their own utterly ruthless acquisition of wealth and influence, climbing over bodies, corporations or countries to do so. One was there because of the inestimable wealth and influence of his religion. Some were products of the breeding program so assiduously practiced in the latter days of the Reich, others were obviously the product of Fate's own breeding program, the Darwinian attrition that assured survival of the fittest. Some had come to the table through humankind's frailties and addictions. Two decades ago, the lords of the drug cartels had been crude and thug-like, now, like the Mafia before them, they'd sent their sons and daughters to the best schools, so they no longer were an embarrassment in civilized company.

"I have a number of matters to bring before you today," Gruner began, looking around the table, knowing everyone there to the marrow. Ten men and two women stared back implacably. They would expect an accounting from him of what he'd accomplished in the twelve months since they'd last assembled, as well as his plan for the year to come. The larger agenda had been set and agreed upon long ago, but had to be constantly adjusted to accommodate current needs. Pulling the strings of governments and the banking establishment behind the scenes had grown somewhat more complex in this age of electronic media and the proliferating numbers of governments. Of course, governments could be manipulated both from within and without.

Gruner had won the respect of the assemblage over the years, with his pragmatic intellect, his ruthlessness, and his ability to remain in both the spotlight and shadows with equal skill. But he could never be thought secure in his tenure as Chairman of The Order of The 13. Every man and woman at this table was adept at the game of dominance, and his incomprehensible quest for a religious artifact had made several of them wonder if it betrayed a weakness on Gruner's part that could be exploited in some way for their own benefit. He'd have to deal with that today.

"As you are all aware," Gruner said, his voice strong and confident, "our strategy for narrowing the number of banks to a more handle-able number worldwide, has succeeded even better than we'd anticipated. Public debt is at an all-time high, fear and unrest are mounting and the shift we have engineered, via the housing and derivatives debacles, and the devaluation of currencies worldwide will eventually permit our complete covert control of the monetary system. Much of our economic agenda is well under way."

"How do you propose to handle the public outcry as the financial stranglehold becomes more pronounced, and the hoped-for recovery remains elusive?" a sharp Asian female voice interrupted from the right side of the table. All eyes turned toward the formidable matriarch whose concerns were never to be ignored or taken lightly.

"My dear Madame Eight," Gruner responded smoothly, although he never enjoyed being interrupted, "your query is as always, a useful one." She nodded just enough to show that his compliments were of no consequence to her whatsoever.

"We will deal with it using the usual disinformation," he answered, "and by feeding to the media only what we wish them to disseminate to the masses. Seventy percent of the world's media is now in the hands of eight corporations into which we have placed strategic partners and unwitting dupes. Control of dissemination of dis-information is one of our strengths, as you well know. The few dissenters can usually be bribed or threatened sufficiently so that I anticipate no trouble from that sector in the coming year.

"When dissatisfaction and financial distress reach the right crescendo, we will take the usual measures to distract the people with a war. As you know, the masses are easily enough manipulated when we label all dissenters and critics as traitors, and assure the rest that their sacrifices are saving the world for democracy. A simple system, but it has never failed us in the past. If we keep them busy enough with the current recession and inflation struggling to put food on their tables and roofs over their heads, and then offer them the jobs and prosperity that inevitably come with a major war, they'll do our bidding as they always have."

"It has worked well enough in the past," a heavily accented Russian voice barked from the far side of the table, "And now we have several on-going conflicts that can be escalated at a moment's notice, if need arises. Afghanistan is a bottomless pit for armies... ours, yours, anyone who has ever attempted to conquer it. Af-Pak makes Vietnam look like child's play. And let us not forget the blessings of Terrorism. We accomplished a good deal with the demolition of the Towers." He emphasized the word to underline its sinister usefulness. "Another 9/11 and they'll welcome Martial

Law. Two more such events on American soil and they'll let us Microchip them for safety. An easy progression, and a lucrative one, I might add."

Heads nodded all around, then returned to the business of the day. There was a great deal to accomplish before they took leave of one another for another year. The price of gold and diamonds had to be set, a rogue African dictatorship had to be dealt with, and, there was the question of how best to deal with the expected revision of oil prices because the American President was promoting wind power. Off-shore drilling needed to be protected despite the BP disaster in the Gulf of Mexico. How they could exploit the spill and direct attention away from those responsible, required going over the original sabotage plan and its aftermath. Questions had to be answered regarding the stock-dumps by major players that had preceded the spill, and a host of other serious business issues were on the docket for discussion.

Colonization plans for both Moon and Mars would have to be handled, as would covert control of the major Communication Satellite companies. The Haarp Project in Alaska had yielded some interesting mass mind and weather control possibilities with valuable military potential. Gruner was eyeing his agenda, deciding which item to tackle first. The group seemed feistier than usual today, although assessing relative viciousness among piranhas was silly.

"Has this Spear you have been seeking, been found yet, Number One?" a voice with a distinctly British accent broke into his thoughts. Although the man who had spoken wore Arab garb, all present knew the Sheik had been educated in London. "Perhaps you would be good enough to remind us why we are seeking it?"

Gruner's eyebrows came together in a frown. The Sheik's immeasurable wealth and influence, coupled with his complete lack of conscience, allowed him certain latitudes, but Gruner found his amused and supercilious tone irritating. Nonetheless, he too, smiled.

"I would have thought anything reputed to have power to rule the world would be most appealing to you, Number Three," he answered with precisely the same degree of lightly veiled contempt, in his voice he'd heard in the Sheik's. "By all accounts, you have similar ambitions?"

The Sheik smiled again, and Fritz, watching, was reminded of the upturned mouth of the boa constrictor he had kept as a pet when he was a child.

"Should I decide to fulfill such ambitions," the Sheik replied with frosty equanimity, "you may rest assured it will be accomplished with resources far more appropriate than an ancient relic with supposed magical powers that only a fool would believe in."

"Would the Holy Stone at Mecca fall into that same category, Number Three?" Gruner countered ingenuously. "I was under the impression that you often make mention of that *ancient relic* with supposed *magical powers* when you rouse your clerics and their faithful followers to jihad. But perhaps, I'm mistaken about this?"

It was the Sheik's turn to frown. "The Hajar-ul-Aswad is a true sacred object!" he replied coldly. "It was given to Abraham by the Archangel Gabriel himself, and is the cornerstone of the Ka'aba, at the heart of Islam, itself."

Gruner's smile was generous. "As the Spear is a sacred relic of Christianity, my dear Number Three. Made sacred by Jesus Christ himself. And if the truth be told, even if *neither* of these objects has any true magical power whatsoever, perhaps you would not disagree with me that they hold the power of *imagination* for the masses, eh?" He didn't wait for an answer.

The Sheik, assessing the effect Gruner's words and demeanor were having on the others at the table, chose a strategic retreat. He would deal with this arrogant infidel another day.

"You have a point, my dear doctor," he allowed, smoothly. "I asked to be reminded of your reasoning and you have presented a plausible case. Perhaps, we should move on to more pressing business, eh?"

Gruner nodded, a pleasantly mild expression overtaking his features.

"As you wish, Number Three," he replied, amiably. "But before we do so let me inform you of a mission with reference to this Spear, that I recently dispatched to the United States. While the agents chosen for the task were unable to take possession of the Spear because it has been passed on from one Caretaker to another, they were able to gain a considerable amount of valuable intelligence for their troubles." He looked pointedly at the Sheik, "I believe they were two of your countrymen, who'd been volunteered for this task by your chief of operations?" He let the thought settle in a moment then continued. "While, as you quite rightly have reminded us, the Spears retrieval is hardly on a par with the other topics on our agenda today, I feel duty bound to keep all members current about our retrieval efforts."

A tiny, gnome-like woman wearing more diamonds than usual, cleared her throat, and leaned toward the table. Gruner took the cue and focused on her unusual face, one well known to the media. She had a sharp brain and an equally sharp tongue, if provoked.

"I tire of this foolish distraction," she said peremptorily. "The issue of the American presidency is of paramount importance to us all." Her voice was surprisingly deep and cultured. "Surely that must be the next order of business for us, not these matters of absurd religious speculation!"

Gruner nodded acquiescence. "As always, Number Four, a superb suggestion.

"Let us then, move to more pressing matters, as Number Four suggests. Number Seven has amassed a considerable amount of critical information that will be useful in our decision as to which candidate in the next American election will best serve our needs. His cabinet position provides us access to the West Wing at a level we haven't occupied before. I believe you will find his talk most enlightening.

"And bear in mind, now that blacks and women have joined the political field so prominently in America, there are new vulnerabilities in each party that offer superb emotional side issues for us to exploit. I've asked my son Fritz to work with Number Seven on assessing the psychological implications of these developments. They have explored possibilities with the best brains in the field and Fritz will add his findings to Seven's overview. His mind control work has also yielded certain breakthroughs I expect you'll find interesting. Working with the concept of Rendition of prisoners, and using several black facilities as his experimental laboratories, he has some very interesting findings to share with you regarding psychopharmaceutical interrogation techniques when used in concert with physical duress. Now that even the U.S. is sanctioning the use of torture as long as others do it for them, breakthroughs have been made." He paused to make certain they'd followed. "We'll hear from both shortly."

"As Aerospace, Pharmaceuticals, Banking, Insurance and, of course, the Military, all have important representation at this table, Number Five has prepared a comprehensive overview of how these industries best fit into our agenda. He's drawn up a strategic plan for us to consider and improve upon, if need be. As usual, there are weighty matters to finalize, so we'll divide ourselves into smaller discussion groups after lunch, to consider options and plausible scenarios with everyone's input and needs taken into account. Then, hopefully, at tomorrow's assembly, we can finalize the year's work, and decide just what measures we shall adopt. As always, both our plans and our strategies for achieving them must be agreed upon by all members. I look forward to stimulating debate."

Gruner waved his hand gracefully toward a large, easily recognizable figure in uniform on his far left. "General," he said amiably, "the floor is now yours..."

36

Germany

The three day meeting of The 13 had tired him more than usual, Gruner admitted begrudgingly. It hadn't been an easy three days, and the mission in Greenwich having failed so miserably, had started the weekend off on the wrong foot – not for the assemblage, but for himself. He had minimized the failed attempt, but it galled him not to have been able to report a successful run at the target.

The two scowling Arabs stood before him now at mute attention, as so many other soldiers had stood over the decades, awaiting word of their punishment. The house was finally cleared of all visiting Order Members so he could deal with this matter privately.

"You are incompetent imbeciles," he said in a deadly cold and contemptuous monotone, "You killed the two men we *know* had the knowledge we seek, and then let escape the two other people most likely to have the knowledge itself, or the means of finding it."

One of the men found the courage to respond. Who was this infidel, after all, to speak to a servant of Allah in such a way? "The man was stronger than he looked," he growled belligerently. "He withstood pain far better than such a man should have done. And he had lost so much blood, we did not have long enough to interrogate him properly."

Gruner's eyes narrowed. These two had been offered to him by his Middle Eastern Section Head specifically for the task of prying the Spear's whereabouts from the Caretaker – surely not difficult now that the Caretaker had been identified as a mere college professor. *Specialists* they had been called. In the Reich these two idiots would have been considered unfit to clean horse manure off officers' boots.

Gruner's voice was low and precise when he spoke again.

He said with quiet menace, "Let us now take inventory. In a single night you managed to kill two Caretakers, burn down the house that might have held evidence, and allowed yourselves to be outwitted by an unarmed woman and a child. Am I correct?"

The chin of the Arab who had spoken came up pugnaciously. "You misled us," he said boldly, although his voice was thick with fear. "You told us the old man would be no problem, a helpless invalid. And you made no mention of the old woman. She was a hellcat, protecting her husband with a pistol she produced from Allah knows where, and screaming words no woman should ever know. It was a pleasure to cut her throat. How was I to know the man would have a heart attack and die when I did this? As to the fire, there was no time for anything else to cover what had been done. We made it look like an electrical fire, so the authorities would be delayed in their investigation and then we went immediately to the home of the man's son, which was not even part of our original mission, but which we undertook on our own initiative."

Gruner's left eyebrow raised a bit.

"And do you know what we in the Reich do with a soldier who acts on his own initiative, when he has already been given specific orders?" he asked.

The sullen man shook his head.

"This is what we do," Gruner replied, picking up the pistol he had been fondling in his lap under the desk, and firing it quite casually.

The second man stared in disbelief at the hole that had appeared between his partner's eyes. Gruner had not even seemed to aim. The man began to babble prayers in Arabic, and Gruner fingered the gun, lips pursed as if in indecision. Finally, he placed the Lugar back on his desk and spoke.

"Clean up this mess, and report to your superiors how merciful I have been toward you." Then he returned to the papers on his desk, never looking up until he was again, the only one left in the room.

*   *   *

Fritz had watched the interchange from behind a slightly ajar door between his office and his father's. Gruner knew he was there, but saw no reason to acknowledge his presence, any more than Fritz felt the need to engage his father's attention.

You have to hand it to the old man, he thought admiringly. He knows discipline. It comes to him as naturally as breathing. Fritz preferred to rule those around him by cunning and deception and thought his father's methods needlessly messy. Effective, of course, but old fashioned.

He'd wondered before the meeting how his father would handle giving the news of this bungled kidnapping attempt to the 13, thinking *that* would be worth the price of admission. But as usual his father had deftly turned the story to his own advantage. His father was a master of politics and statecraft and he had made it seem as if the blunder had furthered the hunt. *And* he'd used the men's nationality to insult the quarrelsome Sheik. Of course it was apparent to Fritz that the members of The 13 couldn't care less about the Spear – in fact, he was certain they all considered the Spear to be his father's private folly, an old man's obsession. It was the man's golden rolodex that kept them in line – the one with the private numbers of presidents, potentates and popes, any of whom, he could get on the line with a single phone call. That, and his ruthlessness. Even those with all the money and power in the world knew better than to make an enemy of his father.

Fritz watched for a minute or two, the frenetic, trembling efforts of the now marked man, to deal with the heavy body of his partner, and with cleaning the blood puddle from the priceless Persian carpet on which he'd fallen. Then tiring of the entertainment, Fritz, like his father, went about his work.

He realized as he walked out of his office and into the hallway beyond, that he felt a rising warmth in his loins, an excitement no doubt engendered by the violence and fear he'd just witnessed. Both emotions always had that effect on him. Perhaps that maid he'd had his eye on for a while would bring relief. Martha,

Margaret, she was called by one of those M names. He made a mental note to ask about her, and hummed softly at the pleasant thought of bedding her. He wondered idly if she liked pain. Not that it mattered much what she liked.

37

Marta Rosen eyed her own perfect breasts in the mirror, assessing her next move. She'd always considered them her secret weapons, a genetic gift from her *Bubbe*, who'd had the same superb proportions and presumably, had had precisely the same effect on men as Marta. Flawless breasts, tiny waist, amply seductive hips and perfectly proportioned ass. She had fine legs, too, but she'd never known a single man to care, once he'd seen her breasts. She'd kept all her assets judiciously under wraps during the time she'd been employed in Herr Gruner's house of horrors, but it might be time to let Fritz have a glimpse.

Marta had used her body when necessary in the service of her government, although she generally preferred to use her brain. But she was getting a bit impatient, and so, it seemed, were her handlers.

Today was her first day off in two weeks. No one would think it odd for her to go into town for some recreation. Marta hummed a little as she dressed in street clothes, instead the stupidly anachronistic maid's uniform she wore for her job. She buttoned her breasts into submission beneath the prim shirt, chosen for its dowdy propriety, pulled on the dreary, ill-fitting coat expected of her station in life, and left her room. She gritted her teeth, put a demure expression on her face and headed for the door.

*   *   *

The place her handler had indicated she was to receive her intel today, was above the little bookseller's shop near the center of town. How the powers at Mossad's Intelligence center in Tel Aviv chose and organized such meetings was not her problem. All she had to do was go where she was told and report what she knew. They, and a loose-knit coalition of dedicated Nazi Hunting factions, had been after Gruner for decades, and had planted her in his household in hopes that she could finally find evidence substantive enough to take him into custody.

Marta dawdled outside the shop's grimy window, as if deciding whether or not to enter, then walked through the glass door with the tinkly bell attached, and entered the dim interior, making it clear she was there to browse. She smiled at the proprietor and wandered between the stacks, patiently marking time until she could make her way unobtrusively to a door marked Private.

Satisfied that no customer was near enough to see her next moves, she slipped into the tiny room. Once inside, she took a key from her pocket, opened and entered what appeared to be a janitorial closet, locking the door behind her. She hurried up the hidden stairs to where her handler awaited her report. She'd been following this Nazi bastard for over a year, hoping to find absolutely irrefutable proof of his former identity, and some weakness by which he could finally be brought down.

The key to catching this one lay with his son. She was sure of it now. But the younger man was as dangerous as his father and she wasn't about to take him on without the sanction of her superiors and without both back up and an exit strategy.

Scientitia est Potentia
Knowledge is Power
Part VI

*"Victory goes to the player who
makes the next-to-last mistake."*

Chessmaster
Savielly Grigorievitch
Tartakower

38

New York

Meg spotted Sally Kittridge on the bench they'd chosen as a meeting place, far from prying ears and eyes. Sally was a rangy brunette with piercing dark eyes and short, spiky brown hair currently whipping around the red fur earmuffs she always wore in winter to the accompaniment of endless ribbing. The collar of her dark navy coat was pulled up and she looked both cold and agitated. She was a rising star at the Department of Justice and had been a close friend of Meg's and Carter's since Meg was at the DOJ.

"Let's walk," Sally said without the usual cheery preamble. She looked worried.

"You think you were followed?" Meg asked, falling into step with Sally's long strides.

"Not me. You're the one on somebody's goddamned radar."

"OK," Meg answered, digesting that news. "Do you know whose and why?"

"Only that your name is flagged... your sister's, too. Something about a murder that could be linked to National Security. It's a *Watch and Report Activity* flag."

Meg took a deep breath. "Were you able to get the info I asked for?"

Sally looked at her with an unreadable expression. "Only for you," she said, "and only this once, understand? I'm in deep shit if *anybody* finds out what I've done. There's something funky about these files, Meg. I'm pretty sure they're booby-trapped. There are weird references I'm trying to follow up on... crazy stuff about Nuremberg, and mind-control experiments and about how maybe the Germans really had a Uranium bomb before we got the Plutonium one? And cover-ups up the wazoo. I think this is really dangerous to dig into and I'm afraid there could be tripwires. I didn't realize how toxic this would be or how high up this all goes..."

Meg bit her lip, feeling guilty for having asked so big a favor.

"I'm *so* sorry, Sally," she said, meaning it. "I wouldn't have asked at all, except its about Cait and Lark, and I'm scared to death for their safety."

"I know," Sally snapped. "That's why I did it." She walked another minute, getting herself under control.

"Just listen, OK? I got plenty, and I think I know where to get more. Even though a lot of it is redacted in the files, there's still a lot there and all of it's ugly and unsavory. I have an envelope with notes I made for you – threads to follow – you know? But we need a more secluded spot for that, so let's keep walking 'til we find some cover. I'll put down my bag – the envelope's right on top – you'll reach in and get it out, surreptitiously, please. Meg, I think your sister has tripped over some things that are really, really dangerous! I'm not being melodramatic..." She drew in a deep breath then continued.

"Let me give you the big picture, but it's just the tip of the iceberg. It starts with something called Project Paperclip, that was authorized in 1945 by Truman, for the Joint Intelligence Objectives Agency of the OSS. Their mission was to recruit smart Germans with either crucial medical, genetic or rocketry expertise, bleach their real records, give them new identities and/or faces and names where needed, then shepherd them into the U.S. military, business and medical establishments."

"Charming," Meg said with maximum contempt.

"First they had to identify the ones they wanted – some of the rats, of course, came scampering in on their own. At that point it was called Operation Overcast, but soon got dubbed Paperclip, because they would paperclip the old identities to the new dossiers."

They'd reached a secluded spot, and Sally stopped at a wooden bench, and lay her tote bag down, half hidden on the ground between them. Then, as she leaned down ostensibly to remove a pebble from her shoe, so that her coat draped over the bag, Meg snaked her hand into the tote, grabbed the envelope and slipped it under her own coat.

"Aerodynamics, guidance systems, and rocket fuel experts were hot tickets," Sally continued as they started walking again. "Everybody knows we snagged Werner Von Braun, not everybody knows how many other Nazis populated NASA. It looks like the Army Signal Corps grabbed 24 of them, 86 aeronautical engineers landed at Wright Field, which was then dubbed Operation Lusty, for Luftwaffe Secret Technology. There were a pile of other acronyms, Applepie, Dustbin, Eclipse, Safehaven, Project 63 – the notorious M K Ultra Mind Control Project – all part and parcel of the same black op. All dirty little secrets and every one with a specific purpose: Project 63 got jobs for Nazis at big corporations and defense contractors. Physicists were seeded into all kinds of top secret government and military projects by several other projects."

"No wonder Eisenhower warned against trusting the military industrial complex in his farewell address," Meg said with distaste. "But, what about medicine? The guy I'm after was a doctor."

"Only if you use the term *very* loosely," Sally responded, her eyes darting right and left nervously, as she spoke. "Radiation, genetics and mind control were Guttman's – or should we say Gruner's – specialties. Your guy was a bloody butcher. A soulless, conscienceless, merciless, bottomless pit of evil."

Meg looked up quickly at Sally's face. This kind of emotional invective was very unlike her. "Whoa, Nellie!" she said trying to lighten the moment. "Tell me what you *really* think!"

"Read the notes in the envelope," her friend snapped. "And whatever the hell you do with what's there, don't let it lead back to me. Maybe Carter and her crew can dig further – she told me she's got two new kid geniuses she can tap. And for the love of God, Meg, watch your ass. The cover-up on all this goes very high up. Maybe all the way to the top.

"I'll be in touch if any of the leads I set in motion pays off. OK? Is there any safe place to send you stuff if any more comes through?" Sally asked obviously getting ready to leave. "I don't think we should meet again."

"Carter's office maybe?" Meg offered tentatively. "Or the two geeks you mentioned?" Sally was really spooked. The young woman nodded assent, then without another word, she turned and hurried away, leaving Meg standing, wondering and alone in the freezing wind – the envelope now clasped firmly under her arm inside the coat, seemed to have taken on a life of its own.

39

Carter finished sweeping the apartment for surveillance devices, then nodded the OK to talk... the group hunkered around the triangular Nogucci cocktail table that sat between the twin sofas, looked up. "Can't be too careful when it comes to bugs in New York City," Carter said brightly, to no one in particular. "Damned little critters can be anywhere."

Matt, Croce and Meg absently nodded agreement.

"I'm the low man on the totem poll here, guys," Croce piped up, "but I got a real methodical mind... so start talking and I'll catch up with you."

"'His strength is as the strength of ten,'" Matt quipped with a good-natured smirk, "'because his heart is pure.'"

Croce replied with a smirk of his own. "So what do we know so far about Herr Guttman/Gruner?"

"I think we have to start with Project Paperclip," Meg began. "The intel I got from my informant and Carter got from some old pals at the FBI and Cyber-Space is on the table – you should all read it for details – but the gist is this:

"After WWII ended in 1945 – and maybe even before – Russian and American intelligence teams began a treasure hunt throughout occupied Germany for military and scientific secrets. They were looking for rocket and aircraft designs, anti-gravity research, medicines, biological warfare specimens, you name it.

And, of course, the most precious "spoils" of all: the scientists whose brains had nearly won the war for Germany.

"Originally, it was made to look like the U.S. Military intended to identify those Nazi scientists and bring them to America, just to debrief them, then send them back to face their crimes at Nuremburg. But, that was mostly a lie. Once they'd seen how far ahead of us the Germans were with the flying discs they called Foo Fighters, particle/laser beam weaponry, anti-gravity devices like something called the Bell, genetic engineering, and maybe even the technology for the Bomb, the War Department decided that NASA and the CIA needed to control this technology, and they'd better control the brains of the Nazis who'd created it all, too.

"But that, of course, was illegal. U.S. law explicitly prohibited Nazis from immigrating to America. So Harry Truman authorized "Project Paperclip," a covert program designed to get select German scientists to work on America's behalf. Now in fairness to old Give'em-Hell-Harry, Truman expressly excluded anyone found 'to have been a member of the Nazi party and more than a nominal participant in its activities, or an active supporter of Nazism or militarism.' So when the War Department's Joint Intelligence Objectives Agency (JIOA) conducted background investigations on these scientists and learned they were mostly *all* Nazi bastards, they had to find a political way around Truman's order.

"Enter stage left, Nazi Intelligence Specialist Reinhard Gehler, a master spy for Germany, who badly wanted asylum in the west, and who had a lot of secrets to trade to save his own ass. Gehler and the CIA's Allen Dulles hit it off bigtime, and Dulles saw Gehler as the place to get all the covert intel he needed about Nazis. So he simply annexed Gehler's whole spy network into the CIA, and called it the Nazi Intelligence Unit."

"Well, I'll be damned," Matt said, looking disgusted as he felt.

Meg continued, "MK Ultra – the scary-as-hell mind control op – Operation Artichoke, Operation Midnight and other notorious Black Ops that Conspiracy Theorists are always trying to find out about, were initiated there, and all the participating scientists' dossiers were whitewashed by the CIA, taking out any mention of their incriminating Nazi pasts.

"At any rate, in September 1946, Project Paperclip was approved, with a mission to bring no fewer than 1,000 Nazi scientists into the United States. Among them were many of the vilest criminals of the war. There were doctors from Dachau concentration camp who had killed prisoners by putting them through excruciating high altitude tests, or frozen their victims, or drowned them in ice water. There were doctors who had tested Sarin nerve gas on prisoners at Auschwitz, and ones who had simulated battlefield traumas by taking women prisoners at Ravensbruck, wounding them grievously, then filling their wounds with gangrene cultures, sawdust, mustard gas, and glass, and sewing them up and treating some with doses of sulfa drugs, while timing others to see how long it took for them to develop lethal cases of gangrene and die excruciating deaths."

She took a breath to calm herself.

"Which brings us to our boy Guttman/Gruner."

"Why don't you get yourself a drink, Meg," Carter interjected, looking at her partner with concern. "I can do the next lap – this stuff is too lethal to talk about in large doses without throwing up."

Meg nodded and headed off toward the kitchen, glad to be able to hide the tears of anger that had welled behind her eyes.

Carter moved her own notes to the center of the table, like a school teacher about to begin a lesson, and took up the tale.

"Gustav Gruner, current upper-crust advisor to Presidents and kings, Ambassador at large, dinner speaker extraordinaire – was born Helmut Guttman, brilliant child prodigy son of Helga and Gunther Guttman of Stuttgart. Recognized early for his prodigious brain and phenomenal eidetic memory, he was propelled through schools, skipping four grades in all. He entered Medical School on full scholarship, aced that, too, graduated the University of Heidelburg with M.D. and Ph.D. degrees by age 19. His brilliance had only one flaw that was ever noted in his records. It seems he was completely without feelings or compassion, which you might think would be a big problem for a medical doctor, but the professor who made notation of this in Guttman/Gruner's record suggested being a sociopath might actually be useful for one devoted to pure scientific research.

"Guttman brought himself to the attention of SS Chief Heinrich Himmler – architect of the Final Solution to the Jewish problem – by designing a study suggesting they use concentration camp captives in a series of medical experiments that would provide research about battlefield trauma, torture, and mind control. He argued that allowing testing on human subjects without pesky medical ethics getting in the way, would be very efficient, and Himmler loved efficiency. Just to be clear about Herr Doctor Guttman, his research subjects always died in torment. He burned them, forced salt water down their throats or into their veins, put them into pressure chambers until their heads exploded, conducted autopsies on living subjects..."

"No wonder they pay him the big bucks to speak at fancy political dinners," Croce quipped, his face a thundercloud.

"And don't forget he had a few specialties," Matt broke in. "According to my buddy from the Gulf, Gruner in his Guttman days, had a thing for torturing mothers and children in front of each other. He also liked to bury the kids alive, then send the mothers to find them, while he, in turn, would hunt the mothers. Remember that short story, 'The Dangerous Game,' where the guy invites people to dinner, then tells them they can only leave alive if they can outwit him as he hunts them down? It seems Gruner used to boast to friends that the idea for the story came from him."

"Maybe this is something we'd better let Cait know about," Carter said, sounding very concerned.

"I really hate to do it – it'll freak her out – but I think you're right," Meg said.

All eyes around the table were grim.

"And that's *all* you got for me so far?" Croce asked dryly.

"Not quite," Matt said, clearing his throat. "Although I don't know what you'll make of this little piece of intel that comes from my Aunt Nell."

That got everyone's attention.

"Have you all heard about Wewelsburg Castle?"

Negative nods around the table.

Well," he drew out the word as if what he was about to say might be considered ridiculous. "According to Aunt Nell, who's clued into the mystic hotline, and knows stuff most of the world doesn't, Hitler and Himmler were 100% into the occult. Black Magicians, occult sacrifices, blood rituals for the elite SS troops, fearsome blood oaths, weird séances in the crypt, all taken very seriously and a lot of it happening at Wewelsburg Castle, which Himmler believed to be built on a convergence of mystical power lines – she calls them leylines – Aunt Nell says this location made it some kind of portal to other dimensions."

"Sounds plausible to me," Croce said with a short laugh.

"Now, hang on everybody," Matt said seriously, "This could be important, considering that this Spear we're after is an occult relic. You know, if you'd hang out around Aunt Nell for a while you wouldn't be so quick to judge what's possible. I've seen a few pretty hinky things..."

He cleared his throat, looking slightly embarrassed, then continued.

Carter broke in. "My research told me pretty much the same thing, guys, so whether we believe in magic or not, we'd better take this seriously because Guttman/Gruner, Hitler and Himmler did."

Matt nodded and went on.

"Anyway, it seems our Guttman/Gruner guy was really big into this black magic stuff, or maybe he just had Himmler's number, but it appears he came to Himmler early in the concentration camp days and told him that just like in the Black Mass, the suffering and death throes of the inmates could be used to raise some kind of intense mystical power. And if Himmler would give him carte blanche to invent particularly heinous kinds of tortures and deaths, and you multiplied that by the thousands of inmates, well..." he hesitated, looking for the right words.

"You could raise a lot of hell," Meg supplied.

"She also said there are several agendas going on here at the same time, so we have to be really careful about sorting out who's doing what to who."

Carter reorganized her papers to make sure she hadn't forgotten anything. "Oh! Wait a minute," she said flipping through her notes. "We also have indications that there may be ties to Al Qaeda and some other terrorist groups in the Middle East, but we're not sure exactly how that works yet, so we've put out feelers wherever possible to see what we can dig up on that."

Croce looked at the horrified faces around the table, and decided he needed to ease the tension. "OK, then," he said, judiciously. "This is good. We know a lot more about the opposition than we did before. So now all we have to do is make a plan to get this sick son of a bitch... without pissing off the CIA, NASA, the whole U.S. government, the Neo Nazis and Al Qaeda."

"Damned straight!" Carter responded with wry cheer. "Good thing there's four of us, then."

After they'd finished laughing, they started to make lists of what each of them needed to do next.

40

New York. Murray Street.

Carter thought long and hard about what she could do to pull her weight in the current crisis. She loved Meg. Anything that disturbed her partner's life was important, and this particular disturbance was epic. She knew exactly how worried Meg was about her sister and her niece, and after four years in law enforcement, she knew the dangers worrying Meg were the real thing. There were very bad people out there, and sometimes they weren't street thugs. They were men of power and influence, men who were protected by cadres of lawyers and spin doctors and flunkies whose job it was to obfuscate truths, to muddy waters and to protect old secrets at any cost. She also knew how many briefcases filled with money changed hands in DC every week, in order to protect such agendas. And this case was further complicated, not only by Gruner's high profile in government, but by his diplomatic immunity.

She put down the 9mm semi-automatic she'd been firing and pushed the button that would activate the pulley and bring her target in closer to her station at the gun range. She often went to the range to think hard issues through. People who feared guns thought they were about violence, but that had never been the case for Carter. They were precision instruments that allowed her to pit herself against herself – her eye-hand coordination, her ability to steady nerves and breathing at will, her capacity for speed, accuracy and precision, against whatever Fate threw into her path. And all in perfect solitude, the sound of gunfire, the only distraction, and *that* muffled by the requisite ear protection that banished sound into the realm of white noise, unimportant and barely acknowledged except as a means of counting her spent rounds – a need drilled into her early on by her first pistol instructor. *If you don't count your rounds, you don't know how many shots you have left. If you don't*

know that, you can be dead before you get the spare magazine out
of your pocket.

The pulley came to a halt. A large figure of a man was hanging from one metal clip, a small bullseye from the other. Carter smiled at the tight grouping in the center of the figure's head, another at its heart. These days, you never knew who wore body armor, so she tended to concentrate her practice on headshots. If she ever needed to bring down a bad guy who was gripping a struggling hostage, there'd be no margin for misstep. Not that it seemed likely she'd ever have to do that again – not in her new position as business owner and Cyber Security Specialist.

The small target had a gaping hole in its center where the bullseye had been, Carter noted with satisfaction. She'd emptied her whole magazine rapid-fire into its center, and shredded the target into orderly nothingness.

Carter pulled two more targets from the floor behind her and set them up, pushing the lever to send the targets to the far end of the range. She missed the combat range at Quantico, but this would do for the moment. Her work might keep her at a computer screen or in meetings all day and a lot of nights, but her private time was active. She liked the balance – play hard, work hard, think hard. Who said geeks were one dimensional? The digerati she knew had more dimensions than a Polyoctahedron Hypercube.

By the time she left the range, she'd decided what it was she'd do next.

41

Carter waited outside the old factory building loft in Dumbo, while the five locks on the industrial strength door were opened from within by Damon. She'd started calling the boys Damon and Pythias when she'd first realized how brilliant they were, and how much they needed a mentor who could help them stay firmly tethered to the real world while they did their thing.

They were both named Henry, which was ridiculously confusing, so she'd proffered the nicknames, and been tickled that they both seemed so inordinately delighted about being renamed for the most faithful friends in history. Of course it helped that the original Damon and Pythias had been disciples of Pythagoras, so that was part of it, but she couldn't help but wonder if, in their cerebral past, no one had ever called either of them by an affectionate pet name.

Carter wasn't sure anymore which of them had found her, because they seemed always joined at the hip, or maybe the circuit board. They'd been looking for an internship, and she'd been looking for off-the-wall talent for the new enterprise she was starting after leaving the Bureau. The fit had been terrific, if sporadic, as they had no intention of ever seeking long term employment – so they came and went as they pleased, which suited Carter perfectly.

Damon's specialty was cryptoanalysis and applied math, Pythias was into Mathematical Physics and some things so arcane even Carter wasn't certain what they were. Both oddball geniuses had minimal social skills and maximal social paranoia, based as far as she could learn, on all the Conspiracy Theory-web surfing they'd done since they'd been able to access the Internet via a computer keyboard. Probably, she judged now, after knowing them for nearly three years, that had been when they were around age 2½. "Trust No One," their hero Agent Fox Mulder had said, and they concurred. Except that they trusted Carter, who was both amused by their whacked out dual-personality, and awestruck by their gifts. Truth was, she liked them very much.

She hadn't exactly hired them, she thought now, as she entered their stainless steel and grunge sanctuary. They worked only on what they wished to, and only on a freelance basis, and only on their own weird timetable. They were paid in cash and gave her a friends-and-family discount that was staggering, despite the fact that her business was now quite comfortably lucrative.

Damon led her into their electronic sanctuary, and Pythias stared up at her from his multi-screened computer nest. He was wearing a tee shirt showing a molecular structure she knew was the chemical formula for caffeine. He looked like a baby owl disturbed by the arrival of the dawn. The loft reminded her of the deck of Battlestar Galactica, crossed with a frat house. Empty Red Bull cans littered the counter tops and discarded, somewhat malodorous clothes, lay in heaps. She knew they often went days without sleep if they were following some thread of information into the ozone.

She also knew they ate next to nothing that ordinary humans ate, as they distrusted the genetically engineered Frankenfoods they felt had destroyed the world's food supply. They did drink copious amounts of some weird smelling green drinks that came out of a restaurant-sized juicer that stood blessedly far away from where she stood now, in the loft's kitchen. The smell when you neared it was that of a green compost heap. How they squared their self-imposed dietary restrictions with the Red Bull that kept them awake, she had no clue.

But the computer nest where the boys spent most waking hours, was pristine and way beyond state-of-the-art. She walked toward it now, smiling at them both with genuine affection.

Damon's eyes were enlarged by glasses. Pythias wore no such visual aids, but his eyes were larger than ordinary, and had a tendency to look perpetually startled, like Nancy Pelosi.

"I need to ask you guys to do something big for me," she said as she pulled up a chair without waiting to be asked. "Something really important that's maybe a matter of life and death for people I care a lot about."

She saw the immediate excitement and willingness in both sets of eyes.

"But, just to be clear and up front, this is definitely top secret and probably dangerous."

"Illegal, too?" Damon asked hopefully, but Pythias, the more laid back of the two, just smiled his lazy smile and looked pleased at the prospect of good things to come.

"Without a doubt," Carter answered, trying not to smile at their eagerness.

She opened her briefcase and began to lay out the notes she'd made. She needed to start them on the scent by downloading everything she knew or intuited, then set them free to see what they could ferret out. Carter had seen often enough how they'd follow threads of information until the threads began to weave themselves into discernible patterns, that then would morph into new threads and more complex patterns. Once she'd set them in motion the best thing she could do was step back until the data started pouring in.

It occurred to her that she should probably also tell them about the Labyrinth, too, but not get them into the game. They'd have enough to do without that distraction.

42

Forest Hills Gardens, New York

The elegant old woman to whom Chris Richardson had wangled him an introduction, had to be 90, Matt thought. Yet, as she entered the room and extended a well-manicured hand, he could see in the way she carried herself, and the confidence she exuded, that she must have been quite a beauty when she worked at the CIA's pet law firm after WWII. She was tall, slender, and conservatively, but stylishly dressed, the soft, mellifluous accent betraying Southern roots. The house, too, displayed a certain Southern charm to his cop's eye. The woman appeared to be not wealthy, but comfortable, everything in the small house carefully chosen.

Matt wondered if she had a pension of some kind from her 30 year stint at the law firm, or if, perhaps, her deceased husband had left her an income sufficient for a comfortable lifestyle in Forest Hills Gardens. Maybe both. He made a mental note to ask Croce to check on her financial situation when he got back to the precinct, and to ask Chris more about her. He was intrigued by the absence of any of the little old lady frailty, he had expected when he'd calculated her age.

"Thank you for seeing me, Mrs. Sinclair," he began, but she genteelly cut him off.

"I'm not at all certain I can be of any help to you, Detective McCormack," she interjected smoothly. "Our mutual acquaintance tells me you'd like to discuss certain issues relating to a time just after World War II, is that right? But you see, nearly all of what I dealt with then at the Firm, would be covered by attorney/client privilege, and, of course it was all a very, very long time ago." She smiled benignly. She'd said *The Firm* as if speaking of some hallowed institution.

Matt's cop-intuition told him there was probably not one syllable of what this woman had archived at *The Firm*, that she didn't remember verbatim. He smiled his best you-can-trust-me-with-all-your-secrets-smile, and she smiled back, her best all-the-charm-in-the-world-won't-cajole-a-word-out-of-me-that-I-don't-want-to-let-slip smile. Mexican standoff. *OK.*

"May I offer you some tea?" Mrs. Sinclair asked, reaching for the tea-cozy covered pot in the silver service on the table that stood between them. "I do hope this visit won't be just a waste of your time."

"Yes, thank you, ma'am," he said, feeling once again like a seven year old, invited into the nun's parlour. "But you weren't an attorney were you?" he prompted, as if he didn't already know the answer. Her eyes came up to meet his. "I mean, attorney/client privilege wouldn't have extended to you, would it?"

She poured the tea, handed over the cup and fussed a bit with milk and sugar lumps, before answering.

"We were not *just* an ordinary law firm, Detective McCormack," she said, choosing her words carefully. "You already know *that*, or you wouldn't be here asking questions."

"Yes, ma'am," he admitted. "I know of your law firm's close ties to the CIA."

"Well then, you also know we were keepers of many of our country's most potent secrets – secrets that impacted national security and national policy. Because of that, every employee in the Firm was vetted in extraordinary depth. And, after that vetting, we all took oaths of non-disclosure that were binding in perpetuity. Even now, more than 50 years later, I'm afraid I am still bound – both by these oaths and by my own conscience." She sipped her tea with equanimity.

Matt considered how to proceed, knowing all inquiries would probably be dead-ended, but worth a try, nonetheless.

"Mrs. Sinclair," he began, putting down his cup and leaning forward with his elbows on his knees and his hands folded between them, his best Catholic schoolboy earnestness clearly written on his face. "I'm not asking you to violate any oaths here," he said, "but I'll be forthright with you, if that's alright with you – no beating around the bush, ok? There are a couple of lives at stake here... maybe more than just a couple. I'm trying to put together some very old puzzle pieces that might shed light on why these lives are currently in jeopardy. The only way I can get at the truth here, is by talking to people who lived through the war and its aftermath. I'm not asking you to share any classified information, Mrs. Sinclair, only whatever personal remembrances you may have that could help me unravel this mystery."

She, too, put down her cup.

"And what remembrances might they be, Detective?" she asked sweetly.

"Operation Paperclip," he replied and saw her eyes narrow just enough to let him know she knew everything he needed.

"I suggest you go to the internet about that, Detective. Its hardly a secret that many high-ranking Germans were needed by our government after the war. Their scientists were miles ahead of ours in certain respects... anti-gravity, V-2 rocket engineering, genetic engineering... a few other specialties. Our government found the scientists we needed and rehabilitated them, you might say. Their politics were unimportant, their brain-power was very important. I and my colleagues, if any are still alive, would surely make no apologies for this. Wars make strange bedfellows. But that was all long ago and I can conceive of no relevance it would have today, even if I could speak of it, which I can't." She smiled sweetly again and – *oh my God – did this 90 year old woman just bat her eyelashes at me?* Matt thought. She must have been some piece of work in her hey-day.

"Do you personally know of any men or women still alive, who are currently in positions of power in this country who were brought here by Project Paperclip?" he urged, suppressing a smile.

"If I did, I could not and *would not* tell you who they are," she said with sweet finality.

Matt sighed audibly and rose to go.

"Thank you for seeing me, Mrs. Sinclair," he said. "I hope I haven't brought up any unpleasant memories for you."

She smiled, and he could see clearly the beauty she must have been a half century ago. "Quite the contrary, Detective," she answered him. "They were the best and most exciting years of my life. It isn't often one has the opportunity to contribute to the cause of freedom, when one's country is in need. That was my privilege, you see."

"I can let myself out," he said. "No need to trouble yourself."

"No indeed, you may *not*, my dear boy," she said in the same steel magnolia voice. "I shall lock the door behind you."

Matt smiled at Mrs. Sinclair approvingly. "You're very wise to be so careful," he said, "especially when you're alone in the house."

"What makes you think I'm alone, Detective?" she answered enigmatically, as she let him out the door and closed it firmly behind him.

Well, she certainly swallowed the kool-aid, he thought as he bounded down her front steps. *Waterboarding wouldn't get anything out of that old bat.* Whatever Mrs. Sinclair knew about Project Paperclip would go to the grave with her.

Harriet Sinclair watched him hurry down her steps and hail a cab. Then she turned her gaze to the man who had quietly come up behind her.

"Was that satisfactory for your purposes, Agent Dexter?" she asked sweetly, pleased with being back in the game that had given purpose to her life.

"Perfectly, Mrs. Sinclair," the tall dark haired man answered. "I'll tell the Director you have once again rendered a great service to your country. You did the right thing by calling us."

"Thank you, dear boy," she said magnanimously. "I assure you I have never forgotten for a moment how important it is to our dear country to keep old secrets, shall we say... secret."

43

New York.

The noise in Rosie O'Grady's Pub was a deafening blend of laughter, singing, shouting and general Irish mayhem.

Meg, Carter, Croce and Matt occupied a booth close to the front door of the place, hoping to avoid the worst of the happy cacophony, while they waited for the take-out they'd ordered. The pub didn't do take-out for just anybody, but cops were special. Matt had just finished telling them about his Sinclair visit. A pint of beer stood in front of each of them, except for Matt, who'd ordered a Guinness.

Croce was eyeing the molasses colored stout in his friend's glass with an expression of distaste.

"You know that stuff tastes like raw sewage, right?" he asked, not having been asked for an opinion.

"Only because you're not Irish," Matt countered, good naturedly. "If you were raised on it, you know it's the Nectar of the Gods."

"Yeah, well, any God who couldn't order up anything better than that swill, needs to go back to God school," Croce answered, with his characteristic smirk.

Meg leaned over the table, so as not to have to shout, "Would you two Bickersons remind me why we're here?"

"We're here because the odds on everyplace else we could go to being bugged, are around 110%," Matt answered. "And I'm hungry."

"I concur," said Carter brightly. "Just because you're not paranoid doesn't mean they're not out to get you. And I'm hungry, too."

"I had a crazy idea about that, actually, that I wanted to run by you guys," Meg said. "I was thinking about who we could get to help us, who won't get fired or pressured not to, or worse... and I suddenly thought about Jake."

"Your dad's old Indian buddy?" Croce asked with interest. "Matt told me about him."

"I thought Jake was dead," Carter interrupted.

"He is," Meg answered, "but his son, Johnny Many Feathers is still around, and *his* two sons. Anyway it occurred to me that an Indian Res is a sovereign nation... not subject to our laws and law enforcement, etc., etc. Soooo," she drew out the single syllable, "maybe it'd be a safe haven for us, should we need one. And maybe it's also an unlikely place to get wire-tapped."

Matt, Carter and Croce all looked impressed as they considered it. "Except for the fact that it's in North Carolina," Matt said finally, "it sounds like the perfect place for us."

Meg swatted his shoulder and made a wry face at him. "Nobody likes a smartass, McCormack. And North Carolina hasn't the only Indian Reservation on the planet. There are several within spitting distance of Manhattan, as a matter of fact. I thought I'd snail-mail Johnny Eagle Tree and see if there's some kind of reciprocal 'professional courtesy' thing going on between tribes that would give us an *in* on some Res in the Tri-State."

"Snail mail because..." Croce pressed.

"If they're surveilling our phones, they may be capturing stuff from our computers, too," Carter pronounced.

"If our Resident Geek says they can do that," Matt said, "I believe... but considering the IT ineptitude of the NYPD it sounds pretty far fetched to me."

Carter reached for a pretzel. "Not far fetched for the Feds, though," she said. "They've got an army of geeks on the payroll. And they've got Echelon and Autonomy – mega-computer networks that can be programmed to capture any keywords they want, from any electronic device, anywhere on the planet. Autonomy scans phone, fax, email, video, you name it in 116 languages, so I am not saying avoidance is easy, even for geeks like me."

"There are no geeks like you, Sweetie Pie," Meg smiled. "You are simply one of a kind." Carter responded by kissing her partner lightly on the cheek.

"So what are we saying here, everybody?" Croce asked sensibly, "That we need to banish ourselves to an Indian Reservation or an Irish Bedlam in order to get privacy?"

Carter shook her head. "Damned inconvenient to do *that* when you've got me to hold the snoops at bay, don't you think? Maybe we can save the trek to the Res for when we all have to take it on the lam, *after* this is over."

"What are you, like those Lone Gunman geeks from the X-Files?" Croce asked with a short laugh. "I knew from Matt you used to be with the Bureau, but I didn't know the Lone Gunman part."

"Nah... I'm better looking than Lone Gunman," she bantered, "I'm pretty sure *I'm* on somebody's radar because of my relationship with Meg, but I have this pair of geeky-kid-protégés who make Lone Gunman look like Luddites. They could hack the Pentagon if properly motivated by the whiff of a good conspiracy theory."

"And you think they're not on law enforcement's radar already with creds like that?" Matt asked.

Carter grinned, "I think we have a small window of opportunity before they do something to set either the Feds or the banking establishment on their trail."

"Can we afford them?" Matt asked, "they sound like they should be working for Bill Gates."

"Should be, but wouldn't think of it," Carter laughed. "Too pure for crass-commercialization at the moment, even though they could make a killing in commerce. They'll do it for me, if I ask them to. I've already put them on the case – worked up a list for them to get started on."

All heads around the table nodded approval, but Matt registered Meg's worried expression. "No word yet from across the pond?"

She shook her head. "A couple of short, nervous and cryptic messages from Cait in shorthand/code/doublespeak and a bunch of tweets. Very unsatisfying. I talk to Lark a lot via email but that doesn't get us any news. Carter's working on a way to get us secure phones of some kind."

Croce looked unconvinced. "You really think there *is* such an animal these days? Since 9/11 we're all surveilled at every street corner, never mind on every airwave."

"I'm working on it, but you're right, of course," Carter answered. "Sat phones are the worst and everything else is vulnerable, but maybe we can make it harder for them."

A many-voiced, mega-decibel drunken chorus of *The Minstrel Boy* suddenly assaulted their ears.

"Ok," Matt said, with a grin. "That's it. I vote for the Indians next time."

"Me, too," Croce added. "Let's get the kind with a Casino"

They picked up the burgers they'd ordered when they came in, paid the tab and left the Pub to go back to Meg and Carter's place. Matt fell into step beside Meg. "We'll figure out a way to help them, Meg," he said, "and to keep all of you safe. I give you my word on it."

44

New York.

Meg sat in her small, genteelly-paneled office at Kramer Crowley Crookfield and stared at the closed folder on her desk. She knew every word in it now, a nearly eidetic memory was one of the gifts that had put her on the Harvard Law Review, provided a clerkship with Justice Lincoln Tremaine, and secured her a place on the partner fast track of a fine old white shoe law firm in Manhattan. Not that she was sure Kramer Crowley Crookfield was where she'd like to spend the rest of her career, among over-privileged white bread clients with sanctimonious lawyers to match. She missed the DOJ and wondered if she'd made the right choice in chucking it for this New York opportunity. But Manhattan was where Carter hung her hat, so Manhattan it was for now.

Meg stared at the phone, willing it to ring. She was really worried about Cait and Lark's safety, to say nothing of her own. Was it just her imagination that the van that had side-swiped her car yesterday on the Merritt Parkway, had done so intentionally? Or was it paranoia? Cait was an ocean away and that made her anxiety about her sister's safety worse. Several years ago, Meg had started carrying a gun in her purse at all times, when a felon had threatened her life after losing at trial. It gave her a certain sense of confidence about being able to protect herself. But Cait had no such weapon in England, and she was in the company of strangers.

Meg sat for a moment staring into space, deciding what to do next. She was always better off *doing*, rather than sitting around feeling bogged in cement. She reached for the telephone, and dialed the number for the Supreme Court office of Justice Lincoln Tremaine. She had no idea if the old man could or would help them in this, but it was important that he be made aware of what was happening. Was it just the weirdest coincidence on earth that he had been one of the original Spear discoverers, or was it remotely possible that there was something bigger going on here, that she just couldn't fathom yet?

Meg asked the secretary who answered the line, if she could book an appointment with Justice Tremaine on a most urgent and personal matter that concerned his time with General Patton. She was gratified to learn, when the voice returned, that the Justice remembered her well and would be happy to see her the following morning if she could get to D.C. that quickly.

Meg pulled the shuttle schedule up on her computer screen. She spent a good deal of time in Washington in the course of her job. No one would think it odd if she made an unscheduled trip to D.C. for half a day, but she'd make the arrangements herself, not through her secretary, Emily. From this point on, the fewer people who knew where she was going or why, the safer she would feel.

On second thought, she'd better tell Cait. Carter had warned her to beware of phone taps, to keep messages brief and vague, and she'd tried to do that, but most every crisis of Cait's and her own life had been shared and their custom was to speak to each other by phone each day. Tweeting really didn't cut it.

Meg picked up the phone again and placed the transatlantic call to her sister.

*   *   *

"Oh, God, I'm so glad to hear your voice, Meg!" Cait said when she realized who the call was from. "I feel like I've landed on the moon and I'd give anything to be in the same room with you."

Meg nodded agreement, as if her sister were there with her. "You do feel pretty far away, Cait, and I hate that. How are you holding up?"

"I don't honestly know how I am, Meggie," Cait answered honestly, and her sister heard the tears behind the words. "I feel inadequate about absolutely everything. I don't know how to help Lark and I'm pretty sure she's holding much too much inside, but you know she has more layers than an onion and I think she's just shut herself in to try to cope..."

"It's a lot to cope with, Cait," Meg interrupted, wanting to comfort her. "Jack, the new surroundings, being so far from home...I think she's a pretty amazing kid to be coping at all."

"You're right, Meggie," Cait responded. "The problem is I'm not sure if I'm doing the right thing by being here, and contemplating leaving her behind while I try to find out how to solve this riddle is pretty overwhelming. They couldn't be nicer to us, but it's all so old-world weird, and I still don't know for sure who or *what* they are, and I can't bear the idea of leaving her to go off on some quest I'm ill-equipped for... I just don't know what else to do." She paused then added "And mostly I'm just scared to death."

Meg winced. "I know, Cait...me, too. But for what it's worth, I think you're doing the right thing. My gut says they're decent men and they've got resources we haven't. *And* I really don't think you should be in the States now."

Cait let out a relieved breath. "I'm glad you think so, Meg, because to tell you the truth, I'm not a bit sure I'm thinking straight. I'm just so heartsick over Jack, and so frightened about the idea we're on somebody's hit list, while I don't have a fucking clue how to defend us, that it's probably clouding my judgment. But Delafield called this amazing meeting of his allies so I could meet them, and they do seem to know things and they definitely want to help us...so I've decided to go. But the whole gathering was like something out of Camelot and   I'm dying to tell you all about it before we go to Germany..."

Meg broke in hurriedly, "No specifics, OK, sweetie? I can't stand not hearing every detail but I think it's not safe... Carter says we have to be *very* careful until she gets a handle on who's listening."

"You're right," Cait agreed with a short rueful laugh. "Not that I *know* anything concrete yet to tell anybody... how about you?"

"Matt and Carter are pulling out all the stops, and I have an appointment with Justice Tremaine tomorrow in DC."

"That's gutsy," Cait said. "Probably a really brilliant idea, too. At least he can verify what's true and what's not. Hugh and I have a plan for us here, too. As soon as I'm clearer on details I'll call or send snail mail, if you think that's safer. But to tell you the truth, I just don't know what other options I have but to try to find the damned Spear. We really need some kind of bargaining chip if push comes to shove."

"Easier said than done," Meg answered.

"Meggie," Cait said, trying hard to control her voice, "Please be careful... I *hate* being so far away from you..."

"Don't worry about me. I've got backup. It's you I'm worried about. You're all alone over there..."

"Not entirely. I *think* Hugh is a good guy... I'm just not trusting my own judgment much these days."

"Yeah, yeah, I'm sure he's a nice guy, but I think you need a hulk with an uzi to watch your back, not some candy ass English Lord."

Cait laughed, as Meg had hoped she would. "Call me after your Tremaine reunion, will you? I know you think the world of him."

Meg sighed. "Let's just hope he thinks the world of what I have to tell him."

They each hung up, buoyed by having heard the other's voice, but feeling the full weight of an ocean's separation and all the unanswered questions. Meg put down the phone, her heart aching for the pain and uncertainty she'd heard in every word her sister had said.

45

Washington, D.C.
Offices of the Supreme Court

Abraham Lincoln Tremaine, called Linc by the lucky few who were truly his friends, was years over 80 and well over 6' 5". His imposing stature had altered a bit with the years... the belly no longer flat as a linebacker's, but his height was curiously untouched by time, perhaps because standing up to whatever the Fates had in store was what Linc did best.

He rose from behind his desk to greet Meg, and a lot of the same awestruck wonder she'd felt all those years ago flooded in as she walked across the carpet toward the man she admired more than any Supreme Court Justice of the last hundred years. Could it really be nearly fifteen years since she'd first stood in this office, trembling and tongue-tied by the honor and responsibility of being his clerk, and he'd put her at ease with the kindly, courtly manner that was his way.

"I'm grateful you were willing to see me on such short notice, sir," she said now, holding out her hand toward his outstretched one.

His all-enveloping smile was just as she remembered it. "And I'm touched that you've reached out to me in what appears from what you said on the phone to be a most urgent personal matter." There it was again. That ineffable generosity of spirit. It heartened her.

He beckoned her toward the two small facing sofas in the corner of his office, and they sat down.

"Now, then," he prompted in the soft Alabama drawl that had mesmerized juries for fifty years, "What brings you here?"

It took twenty minutes for Meg to lay out her story, in her succinct rapid-fire, linear way. Tremaine smiled with remembrance of the girl at 22, nervous, smart and nearly as capable of this kind of razor-sharp clarity then, as now. He interrupted only three times with questions and when she was done he leaned forward toward her.

He looked her in the eye and said, "First, every word of what Delafield told you both about how the Spear came into our possession is true. Second, it has power. I've held it in my own two hands and I know that for a certainty. Third, Delafield's a fine, fine man, Megan. I've known him since I was very young and I give you my word, your sister is in good hands. He has resources and integrity she can count on." He paused a moment to think. "As to this Gruner connection – *that* disturbs me. I've met the man on many occasions and I can't say I find what you're telling me farfetched. Something about those ice cold eyes of his always gave me the willies. But, that said, he's a mighty important fella around D.C., so my instinct tells me you'd best tread real lightly until we have our facts straight. I'll speak with Delafield and I'll pull a few strings to see what I can find out about him, beyond what the media tells us. How's that for starters?"

"I'm not asking for anything specific at the moment, sir," she replied, "mostly because I don't yet know what to ask for. I thought you'd want to know the Spear is in play again, and there may be sources of information you can access that I can't. I hope I've done the right thing in coming here... I hope I haven't presumed..."

"You did exactly right, child," he said quite gently. "But, now *I* need to do some thinking about all this, and maybe a bit of soul search, as well. I confess that after 60 years, I'm a little out of practice worrying about that old Spear. But rest assured, if I can learn more, I shall do so."

They talked for a few more minutes before he was reminded by his secretary that their time was up. Meg left feeling marginally relieved, although nothing had really changed, it was just good to feel they had so special an ally.

*   *   *

Lincoln Tremaine sat in his office for a few minutes after Meg Fitzgibbons had departed. She'd grown up to be a fine young woman. Smart, strong, honorable. Just as he'd expected she would. What was *unexpected* was the turn of events she'd related. My, *my*, but that story of hers had provoked a flood of memories. Of the war. Of the General. Of the bizarre mix of idealism, patriotism, segregation, anger... all the powerful emotions a black man couldn't help but feel in a time of inequality, danger, and the heady chance for heroism. Delafield had already told him of John Monahan's death and he'd said he would pass the word to Ruddy, although he'd dragged his feet more than a week about doing that.

If the truth be told, he'd been giving thought to the Spear ever since Delafield's call. He wondered why Tony had not gone into further detail; perhaps, he'd been worried about eavesdropping. But ever since the call, he'd been praying for guidance. Back in '45, he'd been the most genuinely religious of the four of them. Ruddy was too arrogant to think God of much consequence. John was a good man, led best by reason not religion, if he had to guess. Delafield... now *he* was of a different stripe. Certainly of a mystic bent... he knew things, secret things. The kind of old knowledge that ran in aristocratic British families whose secrets went back centuries. Lincoln smiled to realize his own assessment of the men whom Fate had chosen as his fellow Caretakers hadn't changed one whit with the years. It had never occurred to him that their being in that bunker was an accident. God didn't permit accidents and it had never occurred to him that the hand of God hadn't been in play where the Spear was concerned.

That old Spear had power alright – Linc had held it in his own hands and felt some kind of healing energy surge through him. And there was something else, too – another kind of power not easy to describe. It felt as if that old Spear awakened some power in his own soul he hadn't known was there before. Maybe Ruddy'd felt something personal, too, when he'd touched it. Maybe that's what had scared him so badly. Of course, anything that wasn't self-serving scared Ruddy, so maybe he was just letting his old imagination ascribe too much to the man's motivations. The thought made Lincoln chuckle.

He rested his large frame against the high-backed leather chair he always sat in, and shook his old grey head in wonder at the ways of the Lord. Just when he'd begun to think that God had no more use for his services in this world, this old mystery was surfacing, and in such an interesting way. A line from Dr. King came to him from somewhere, "In the end, we will remember not the words of our enemies," he had said, "but the silence of our friends."

He just wasn't sure yet what he'd be called upon to say in this matter.

But of one thing he was absolutely certain. He'd be called to say something.

46

The two Federal Officers caught up with Meg as she left the Supreme Court Building after her meeting with Tremaine. She had her cell phone in her hand, poised for dialing. They were unmistakable, even before they whipped out their badges.

"Ms. Fitzgibbons?" the older one said in a sonorous baritone, "I'm Special Agent Lennon and this is Special Agent Cuccio. We need you to come with us. We have some questions for you."

Meg, startled by the intrusion and the peremptory tone, to buy time asked to examine their badges which had disappeared as quickly as they'd been flashed. "Questions about what exactly,

Agent... Lennon, is it?" she asked, making a mental note of his name and the CIA logo on the badges.

"We're not at liberty to say, Ma'am," Cuccio answered, getting a stern look from Lennon for his troubles. "If you'll just come with us..."

"If you're not at liberty to say what we're going to talk about, how exactly do you expect to ask me any questions?" she asked dryly, but she had no illusions about having to go with them. She pulled up her cell phone and pressed her secretary's speed dial number. "I'll just let my secretary know where I'll be..." she began, but Lennon reached out for her phone and pressed the end-call button, then pocketed it.

"We'd like you to step into this car quietly, Ms. Fitzgibbons," Lennon said, taking a firm grip on her arm and steering her toward the curb and a waiting black sedan with government plates and darkened windows. Obviously, this little scene was all about intimidation, something the CIA with their spooky dark glasses and robotic behaviors, excelled at.

"You're sure you wouldn't rather just question me in a coffee shop," she said to lighten the tone of the ridiculous situation. "There's a Starbucks on the next block. They have great doughnuts." She realized how terrifying their tactics would seem to the average citizen and every lawyerly cell in her body bristled. God bless the ACLU, flashed into her mind. She was an attorney who knew her rights and was part of a big law firm. She lived with a former FBI Agent, and she had committed no crime, and she still felt the sense of helpless victim-hood these guys provoked. Her heart was pounding in her chest but she told herself to stay cool and learn all she could from whatever questions they threw at her.

The building they took her to was not CIA Headquarters at Langley, as she'd expected, but rather, a large nondescript warehouse somewhere on the outskirts of D.C.. OK. This was getting a little scary.

"Are you at liberty to tell me where the hell we are, Agent Lennon?" she asked as they led her from the car toward the building.

"Where we are doesn't really matter, Ma'am," he answered.

Not to you, maybe, she thought as she followed.

At least the building wasn't deserted, she noted as they walked briskly through the lobby, cleared a metal detector and arrived at what she took to be an interrogation room, with institutional grey walls and a two-way mirror. They told her to be seated, and that someone would be in soon to interrogate her. It was the first time in her life she'd ever found the word *interrogate* disturbing.

Suddenly the words of a wry Irish street ballad from Belfast that Tommy Makem used to sing, came into her head and she started to sing it, hoping somebody on the other side of the mirror could hear.

> *"Whatever you say, say nothing*
> *when you talk about you know what,*
> *for if you know who should hear you,*
> *you know what you'll get... "*

Megan smiled to herself at the absurdity of finding herself in a situation in which these paranoid lyrics made all the sense in the world.

One hour and thirty-seven minutes after she'd arrived, a tall, slender middle-aged man in wire-rimmed glasses and tweedy jacket arrived and seated himself on the opposite side of the table. Lennon was with him, Cuccio wasn't.

"You are probably wondering why we've brought you here," he began in the toney nasal diction of the New England Prep School-educated.

"I am," she replied, determined to hold her temper. "And *you* are?"

"Harold Thornby," he replied amiably enough. "You've bounced off our radar, Ms. Fitzgibbons, in a number of ways in the past week. We have a few questions we'd like answered."

"And they couldn't have been answered in my office, without the cloak and dagger routine?"

"What do you know of the Spear of Longinus?" he asked, ignoring her question.

"Only what I've been able to learn on the Internet." she replied, "and that someone seems to think my sister's husband knew something about it."

"And did he?"

"I have no idea. He certainly never spoke of it to me."

"And did he speak of it to your sister or her daughter?"

"My sister has told me she never heard of the Spear of Longinus until the night her husband was murdered, and my niece is nine years old. It's hard to believe anyone thinks she knows more than the grown ups do."

"I see," he said, in a tone meant to say he didn't. "And are you aware that your sister's husband is suspected of espionage."

Meg nearly burst out laughing. "*That* is utterly preposterous!" she said, meaning it. "Jack was as loyal to this country as anyone I've ever known."

"You are aware he did classified work for the government?"

"He never mentioned to me that he was doing anything classified," she said quietly, "but I heard of that possibility when two Federal Agents appeared at my sister's house the night Jack died. It doesn't surprise me however, as he was one of the country's leading encryption experts. I can imagine he might have been called on to deal with classified projects."

Thornsby was watching her responses carefully.

"Are you aware that your sister has fled the country?" he said suddenly.

Meg frowned at the terminology. "I'm aware that my sister has *left* the country temporarily, but the only thing she has *fled* is the memory of a terrible tragedy."

"Your sister is a suspect in her husband's murder and as such should not have left Connecticut."

Meg's eyes met his. "That is patently ridiculous and you know it," she said. "Cait is *not* a suspect, has not been charged with anything, was not admonished to remain in the jurisdiction, and is the last person on this planet who would have wished her husband harm. She adored him. He adored her. They both adored their daughter. And by the way, let me go on record to say, this whole nonsensical charade today is an absurd abuse of power. You know it, as well as I do. So why don't we just cut to the chase, and you tell me why the hell you've brought me here, wherever *here* is, and I'll tell you if I can help you with whatever it is you want to know."

Thornby was quiet a moment, then pushed his glasses back up the bridge of his long, thin nose.

"Your sister," he said finally, "her husband, his parents, and perhaps you yourself, are suspected of an unsavory involvement in a matter of National Security. You are up to date enough on the Patriot Act, I imagine, Ms. Fitzgibbons, so you understand that the laws that apply in ordinary judicial proceedings do not apply in matters of Homeland Security." He stared at her with cold eyes. "Do not be so foolish as to think that we would hesitate to remove your entire family from the playing field, if we felt it was in the best interest of the security of the United States to do so."

Meg stared at him, half in disbelief and half in the horrified knowledge that such powers now existed in the United States of America and resided in the hands of men like Thornby.

"What were you meeting with Justice Tremaine about this morning," he asked in a non-sequitur that took her by surprise.

"I clerked for him several years ago," she answered. "I asked his advice about a legal matter in a case I'm preparing." How the hell had they known she was seeing Tremaine? The phone call to Cait! That had to be it. Carter was right. They had her phones bugged.

Thornby's thin lips moved in what might have been a challenging smile. "You see, Ms. Fitzgibbons, that is precisely the kind of lie that could cause me to distrust the rest of what you have to say."

"What in God's name is it you think we know?" she asked quietly.

He tapped his pen against the side of his nose thoughtfully, then put it into his breast pocket with finality.

"That will be all for today, Ms. Fitzgibbons," he said without answering. "For your sake and your sister's, I hope we need not meet again. Next time, our interchange will not be so cordial."

Thornby rose and left the room. Lennon rose next, cleared his throat and said, "I'll have someone return you to the Courthouse." Then he, too, was gone and Meg was left alone with the realization that life as they'd known it before Jack's death, was over.

47

"Harold?" Winfield Livingston said into the receiver. "I'm very much looking forward to hearing your opinion of the Fitzgibbons woman." Harold Thornby had been his opening gambit against the two sisters, and he was anxious to move on to the next steps.

Harold Thornby had been with Winfield at both Choate and Harvard. His current position with Homeland Security had proven invaluable to Livingston since he'd been given the post. Thornby was the kind of well-credentialed bureaucrat with an above average I.Q. and a below average conscience who did very well in Washington, and knew who his friends were.

Win waited. He knew it was Thornby's style to take his time.

"She is rather feisty," Thornby said finally, in the nasal drawl he and Winfield shared, "as one would expect from an attorney. I think she does *not* have the information you seek, but that her sister might know how to get it."

Win's eyebrows came together in a furrow. He knew he'd chosen the right man for his initial pass at the women.

"Does that mean you feel that pressure should be brought to bear only on the sister, then?"

"Oh, no indeed," Thornby replied heartily. "I'd keep up the pressure on both, if I were you. This one is very protective of her sister and niece. She wouldn't want to see them harassed. That vulnerability can be a useful tool, I should think. Perhaps, a bit of physical coercion would have merit as well? Let them know you mean business, eh? I'd do it sooner than later, while the nerves are still raw."

"Hmmm." Winfield answered noncommittally. "I'll give it a think, Harold. Perhaps throwing a scare into one would up the ante on the other's cooperation... you could be quite right about that."

"Or perhaps scare them both?" Thornby suggested. "Just a thought to consider, of course, Win. Not a recommendation."

Win smiled. Nothing would ever come home to roost in that well-feathered nest.

"Yes," he answered. "I'll take what you've said under consideration."

Time to change the subject. "Will you and Lily be at the wedding on Saturday?" Livingston asked knowing that Thornby and his wife were sure to be guests at an A-list wedding like that of the Senator who was planning to tie the knot on Saturday. "I hear they've commandeered the entire Corcoran for the festivities. Emma is looking forward to the trip."

"I'll tell Lily you'll be there," Thornby responded, not having to ask which wedding. "In the meantime, would you like me to put a few men on this business of yours, Win? Not a problem for me to apply a bit of pressure for you."

"Not yet, Harold," Winfield replied, "But I do appreciate the offer. I believe I'll put a few ducks in line first, see what I can scare out of the woodwork first, if you'll forgive a bit of a mixed metaphor. I'll be in touch if I need further assistance. Kind of you to offer."

"See you Saturday, then," Thornby said as he hung up the phone. *I wonder what old Win has up his sleeve*? he mused with a small smile. Sounds to me as if he sees this as an opportunity. Perhaps it wouldn't hurt to have my boys keep an eye on those two women, as well – with or without Win's sanction.

48

Lark stared at the problem on the Labyrinth's path for a long minute before picking up her pencil. It was just simple algebra she thought happily – practically a freebie. Even Hugh could do this one... well, maybe anyway. Every problem in the Labyrinth didn't earn you a clue. Some were just for fun or math practice.

The question on the path in front of her read:

> The zookeeper has lost his ability to distinguish between Wildings and Werebunnies. However, he is able to count eyes and feet. He counts fifty-eight eyes and eighty-four feet. *How many Wildings and how many Werebunnies* are there?

Both Wildings and Werebunnies only had two eyes each, so that made it easy. Wildings had two legs and Werebunnies had four, so Lark talked herself through the problem a step at a time, like Daddy said you should always do, even with the easy stuff, so you don't make some silly mistake.

Fifty-eight eyes means that there are twenty-nine animals in total.   Let X equal the number of Werebunnies and 29 – x the number of animals minus the number of Werebunnies equals the number of Wildings... she mumbled the calculations under her breath, scribbled some numbers on her note pad and nibbled the end of her pencil, as she stared at her equation a moment, then smiled.

"There are thirteen Werebunnies and sixteen Wildings!" she said out loud to the empty room. Then she typed it into her laptop.

"Excellent!" said a familiar voice from the screen. "You've earned another clue, haven't you?"

This clue was in a cipher. *Cool!* It read:

> *Srh tivzevh ziv Tlow*
> *Srh svzig rh Uriv*
> *Srh Kldvi slowsh*
> *Vgvimzo riv.*

Lark stared at the screen a moment, puzzling out how to proceed, then spotted a Templar Cross lying in the grass just off the path. "It's gotta be Atbash!" she thought, excitedly. Her Grandpa had taught her how to do Atbash when she was little. It was a really easy substitution code, where the first letter of the alphabet was exchanged with the last letter and so on.

She didn't need crib notes anymore – all she had to do was close her eyes and she could visualize the substitution graph.

A	B	C	D	E	F	G	H	I	J	K	L	M	N	O	P	Q	R	S	T	U	V	W	X	Y	Z
Z	Y	X	W	V	U	T	S	R	Q	P	O	N	M	L	K	J	I	H	G	F	E	D	C	B	A

She began to translate
His greaves are gold
His heart is fire
His Power holds
Eternal ire.

As soon as she found out what greaves and ire meant, it would probably make a lot of sense. Lark wrote the clue into her diary, then looked up the words on her laptop.

Greaves pl n. (used with singular or plural verb) grēvz
    Ornate metal armor worn on the shins of warriors in ancient Greece. The soldiers of Thrace, Sparta and other ancient city-states could be identified by the insignia on their greaves.

Ire n. (īr) Middle English from Old French, from Latin
    Anger, rage, wrath, often righteous and justified, as in anger shown against an evil enemy.

Lark's eyebrows wrinkled into a frown. The math was easy, but the clue wasn't. Although, maybe it made sense because she was looking for a Spear like soldiers carried. But she couldn't imagine what somebody angry, wearing old fashioned leg armor, had to do with her puzzle.

Into the Labyrinth

Part VII

"To Believe in a Supernatural source of evil is not necessary; men alone are capable of every wickedness."

Joseph Conrad

49

Germany

Gruner seldom brooded. It wasn't his nature. He did, however, strategize. It was important to leave nothing to chance. Which was why his lifetime of journals – his and der Führer's – were concealed in his secret chamber. Even though the precious Book of Secrets would have confounded anyone not extraordinarily well versed in ritual magic, it was still essential that no one know of its existence.

Gruner's safe chamber held most of the materials on which he'd built his empire. Particularly those from the war years that chronicled the truth of his experiments at Auschwitz, Buchenwald, Sobibor and other camps. He hadn't shared all he knew with those who'd gotten him his freedom. Not by a long-shot. The American fools had settled for a small fraction of the secret experimental data he'd worked on himself, or stolen from others. Of course, the U.S. hadn't been the only bidders he'd done business with, just the most useful and gullible.

He didn't spend enough time here in Germany now, Gruner thought looking around appreciatively at his home. He felt at peace here. The secret cache of treasures so easily stored in the vaults... the elegance of the surroundings, the sense of continuity... and, of course, it served as a grand arena in which to entertain The 13. Lavish enough to impress even those rich as Croesus, well-appointed enough to establish his rarefied tastes. Private enough for his special needs. Neither the house in Georgetown, nor the estate in Bedford, provided for his pleasures quite so well, although the seclusion of the woods surrounding the Bedford house made it an excellent hunting preserve, and more than a hundred acres were enough to keep prying eyes away.

The electronic mechanism Gruner activated next, made a barely discernible hum, somewhat like a hive of well-behaved bumble bees, he thought with a smile. The device was his own design – it caused the large stone fireplace to swallow whole the burning logs that had blazed there just a moment before, as a new slate floor slithered into place above the spot where the burning logs had been. A panel opened within the hearth and a staircase revealed itself. Gruner entered the hidden stairwell, and, triggering the closing mechanism from within, followed the well-known route to the secret chamber.

Once there, he did not stop to admire the staggering display of old masters and French Impressionists that adorned the walls, or stood stacked for his personal perusal. All had been stolen from Jews and from museums in the final days of the war. He went straight to the safe, removed Hitler's most prized possession – The Spear's Book of Secrets, and his own translation of it, from among der Führer's diaries, and sat down to read one more time what had been written there. It had taken him years to unravel all the secrets of this occult masterpiece as he trusted no one enough to ask for help with the encryption. What was contained here was the key to the last and greatest treasure on earth.

*   *   *

His own dis-encryption, which had been worked out over five decades began the day when Himmler had shown him the Spear and told him it was the key to the greater treasure, he had known it would help him achieve everything he dreamed.

Whether or not Himmler had realized the true enormity of what he held in his vault at Wewelsburg Castle Gruner didn't know. Himmler had been so proud that der Führer had trusted him to keep his sacred artifact, and the encoded book that held its occult secrets. The code was a difficult one, he'd boasted, and Hitler had trusted him alone of all men to break it.

Himmler, a mathematician by genetic gift and an accountant by training, had spent his life solving riddles of one sort or another. Which was how he had been able to plan the solution to the Jewish problem so efficiently. It was really only a matter of applying mathematics to the problem and then eliminating wrong answers one by one as they came up. Simple subtraction, really: Europe minus six to ten million.

The first time Gruner, then Guttman, had heard anything about the immortality issue, had been on the eve of the great turning point of his own career. He had gone to a dinner party to which only the most elite officers of the SS had been invited to share a meal with their Führer. The youngest man there by several years, Gruner had been told the invitation was a reward for how well his use of prisoners in medical experiments, had succeeded. This success had marked him as a prodigy of sorts, whose ruthless brilliance would prove invaluable both to the Reich and to Himmler's and Hitler's personal agendas.

After dinner, the conversation had drifted to various occult matters, and finally the issue of immortality had been raised. Der Führer himself had asked the question as if the matter under discussion were an ordinary one. "And so, my dear young doctor, where do you stand on the question of immortality?"

Startled, Guttman had answered with his usual political sagacity. "If there were something that would keep those in this room alive forever, for the good of the Reich, I would willingly spend my whole life in the pursuit of such knowledge, no matter the cost to me, mein Führer."

"You are aware, perhaps," Hitler persisted, "that the Holy Grail, to which our Teutonic Order is dedicated, possesses the power to make men immortal?"

Guttman had considered his response to this startling question carefully, as there could be no missteps in the presence of the Führer. "I have heard the inspiring stories, mein Führer," he'd said, "and had hoped that they were not merely legends."

"And what would you say, Herr Doktor," Hitler had asked him in a most serious voice, "if I were to tell you that I intend to possess this Grail, and with it, to become immortal?"

Gruner remembered still, the ferocious hammering he had felt in his chest at this statement, that somehow coming as it did from der Führer, was no longer preposterous.

He remembered, too, that he had stammered his reply in a nearly inaudible whisper.

"The Grail quest has been my own personal dream since boyhood, mein Führer," he had managed to say, and Hitler had raised a dark brow thoughtfully, and studied him for several long seconds before replying.

"Has it, indeed?" he had said, finally, then he'd turned his attention abruptly away, as if the conversation had never taken place. He had begun a conversation on a completely different subject with his personal mystic advisor Haushoffer, and ignored Guttman for the remainder of the evening, but the Book and Spear had been mentioned.

Guttman had fretted about the exchange later that night, worrying that he had blundered, but it became apparent soon enough that he had passed the test. From that night on more and more power and access had been granted him. From that point, too, he'd enjoyed Himmler's occasional confidences and absolute carte blanche to do as he wished with the prisoners.

The Book of Secrets, the Spear, the Grail. He had discovered their connection later, but Hitler's obsession with immortality had been made clear to him that night. For half a century now, these had been Gruner's obsession, too.

It had taken him decades to break the code. He had used the work done by Himmler as a starting point, and little by little had learned what had inspired Hitler to believe that immortality was nearly within his grasp. He alone of all men knew not only the *location* of the Grail, but that the true Spear was the one key that could unlock its hiding place. Once he had the Spear, he would collect the Grail, and he alone would possess the greatest prize of all – immortality. Not even der Führer, with all his powers and pretensions, had achieved that.

Gruner finished reading the particular passage he'd sought, replaced the precious document into its airtight container and retraced his steps. The Spear was the key to everything and it must elude him no longer. Perhaps it was time to enlist Fritz's talents more fully. Both his brain and single-mindedness might be useful in bringing this business to a satisfactory conclusion. There was no need for his son to know the true nature of his need for the Spear, of course – it was enough that he, like the others of the Order assumed it was an old man's obsession. He'd seen the evidence of the change in Fritz's approval rating by The 13, in the covert glances signaling admiration during his son's monetary fund presentation.

Fritz was a sterling example of the Aryan breeding program at its best, as well as the strict discipline that had been employed in raising him. The business ventures Gruner had entrusted to his son had been handled with ruthless efficiency, and many of his son's ideas for innovation had proved even more lucrative than Gruner had thought possible. Fritz's own predilection for psychology had made him invaluable in the implementation of the mind control programs Gruner had begun in the Reich. And the approbation for Fritz's presentation about the manipulation of the masses using media coverage as a catalyst for controlled chaos, had been most gratifying.

Fritz mustn't know of the Grail connection, of course. He was smart enough to put 2 and 2 together, and no son wanted his father to be immortal. But he could help with the issue of retrieval. Gruner could see no downside to that.

50

Fritz Gruner knew the answers he sought lay in his father's secret chamber. He'd found the hidden entrance years ago, but hadn't yet managed sufficient access to inventory its contents. And there was the safe to contend with. He would have to wait until he was ready to make his final move against his father to breach the safe. Once he showed his hand, one of them would die, and he had no intention of being the one.

He'd been just a boy when he'd heard his father speak of the chamber with the one lackey the old man had ever trusted with his darkest secrets. Hans Ruder had worked for his father in the camps and was loyal in the way of a well-fed dog whose master is to be saved and protected at all costs, a ferocious Rottweiler of disciplined, conscienceless obedience.

Fritz had spent a lifetime trying to discover the secret of what lay hidden in the chamber but had never succeeded. Frau Ruder. Hans' wife and their longtime cook, had told him pieces of the story over time, but during one such conversation, Hans had come into the kitchen at precisely the wrong moment, and the terrified look in Frau Ruder's eyes had told Fritz all he needed to know of the importance of this particular secret. She was the only person on earth he had ever loved, or felt loved by, and she'd doted on the brilliant, lonely and, in her view, abused, boy, baking special treats for him and letting him linger in her warm kitchen, rather than sending him back to his solitary cell of a room, to prepare the endless lessons his father demanded he excel at. When she occasionally would hug him to her capacious bosom, he had felt the only semblance of mothering he would ever know. Perhaps, he'd often thought, that was why he was so inordinately drawn to women's breasts.

Frau Ruder had been sent away after that, or perhaps killed. He never saw her again and was forbidden to inquire about her or even speak her name. But with wheedling, she had let slip a number of pieces of the Gruner past, and even as a boy, he had been good at puzzles. Perhaps he would one day make his father pay for the loss of Frau Ruder, given the approval he'd seen in the eyes of The 13 at this year's Summit, perhaps that day was no longer far off.

Fritz saw his father emerge from the study. The old man looked conspicuously content. Something new was afoot, something important, Fritz felt with certainty, and the Spear was part of it. He'd hoped, as his father grew old, that the man would mellow and let some truths begin to emerge, but quite the opposite seemed true, so now Fritz watched and waited, every sense alert to every nuance.

He would have to make his move soon – perhaps as soon as his father left for his next visit to America – but not before he discovered the true secret of the chamber. His father had a subtle intellect, for all his heavy-handed cruelties, and there might be treasures yet unimagined that could be accessed, if all the secrets of his private sanctuary were plumbed.

Marta watched Fritz watch his father. She smiled provocatively as he passed her by, and, making a mental note to find out more about the girl, Fritz smiled back. But right now, not even sex mattered more than the game of cat and mouse he was playing with the old man.

Marta watched Fritz disappear around a corner. Gathering intel on this family of elegant psychotics was harder than any undercover op she'd ever worked. Her baby-faced beauty and perfect German, to say nothing of the fact her family had been a sleeper-cell in Berlin for decades, had gotten her this assignment nearly a year before, but so far she had bubkis to show for all her dusting and snooping. Marta hummed a nursery ditty from her German-Jewish childhood, turned and left the hall. She was about to fix all that.

51

Being a housemaid had suited Marta's purposes before – such maids were nearly invisible to most of the truly rich – functional as clocks, expected to perform and go utterly unnoticed. In earlier times, special hallways were built for servants, parallel to the corridors used by those who employed them, lest the servants be seen by family or guests as they scurried about their endless chores.

But invisibility was no longer helping her cause. Inasmuch as her handlers had agreed to her plan, Marta wanted, *needed* to be noticed by Fritz. She'd decided to ask Inga the cook for advice. Maybe ask if she could help Marta be elevated to wait-staff. If she could pull *that* off, she could contrive to flash her assets at Fritz in ways he couldn't help but notice. Marta had absolute confidence in the power of her assets. There had never been a man who'd been able to resist her, if she chose to seduce him.

Once she'd gotten Fritz into her bed, there would be a window of opportunity – not for intimacy beyond the obvious sexual kind – but for pillow talk, which had never before failed to provide her with information she sought. Sooner or later, of course, he would tire of her and the window would close – men like Fritz generally had massive sexual appetites which they satisfied with a constant stream of new talent in their beds. Timing was always the tricky part – figuring out how to keep the interest-window open long enough that she could establish sufficient comfort to accumulate valuable data.

It was always a subtle game, and all the more so with a man as cold blooded as Fritz appeared to be. But Marta had watched him intently for nearly a year now, and had listened to the below-stairs gossip about his habits. And she'd made a special study of his eyes – dead cold eyes that nonetheless flashed malevolence in his father's presence. Servants saw people's weaknesses better than their surface strengths. Marta had catalogued a number of genuine emotions in Fritz. Hurt. Sorrow. Rage. Frigid calculation, too, of course, but underneath all that, there was some kind of desperate, terrible loneliness. A bottomless well of it. *That* was the weak link she sought – the vulnerability that could be exploited.

Marta adjusted her demeanor for the necessary conversation with Inga – cooks tended to be the most emotionally accessible among the help in any household – and headed for the kitchen.

52

It hadn't been as difficult as Marta feared to have her duties elevated. In exchange for her grandmother's strudel recipe, the promise of helping out when needed in the kitchen without extra pay, and some salacious gossip about one of the other housemaids, she'd gotten Inga to agree.

Now, Marta bent to retrieve the napkin she'd so artfully contrived to drop next to Fritz's chair, as he sat alone in his study. She'd set down the drink he'd requested on the table beside his armchair, and then managed to fumble just enough to be sure the napkin landed where she wanted it to be.

Appearing chagrined by her mistake, she looked up innocently into the man's frowning face, and gently replaced the napkin on his lap, as she mumbled a contrite and breathy apology. Then, she watched his eyes as they strayed to the deliberately opened buttons of her uniform blouse, and noted the change of his expression, as he took in the sight of her breasts, now straining against the fabric of her shirt, as she attempted to rise from the floor where she'd knelt beside him to retrieve the napkin. She felt Fritz's hand move from the napkin she'd just replaced on his lap, to the collar of her uniform, and paused in her rise, looking up at him questioningly.

"Your name is...?" he asked letting his fingers toy with the fabric of her collar.

"Marta, sir," she answered deferentially, but the flirtatious look in her eyes belied her deference. "I'm terribly sorry to have disturbed you..."

"Perhaps, I rather like being disturbed," he answered, as his fingers moved from the shirt collar to brush the throat beneath.

Marta arched her neck a little to allow him better access, without seeming too bold. She'd save the boldness for later.

"I've been noticing you lately, Marta," Fritz said, with a smile in his voice. "You seem to have taken on several new duties of late. Is that true?"

She relaxed a little, letting her buttocks rest back on her heels, no longer attempting to rise. "Oh, yes, sir," she breathed, arching her neck like a cat stretching languidly beneath its master's touch. She felt his fingers drift lower on her throat. She'd purposely left the top buttons of her uniform undone, and worn her most enticing French-lace half bra beneath. It never hurt to showcase your assets. "I like my new duties very much, sir. It's been a great pleasure to serve..."

Fritz smiled again as his fingers grazed the top of one breast, and he felt himself begin to strain pleasantly against the fabric of his trousers.

"And is it possible there are other... shall we say... more *personal* services your duties might allow?" His hand was now well within the lacy confines of her bra, grazing an ill-concealed nipple with his thumb.

"Oh yes, sir," she whispered breathlessly, moving a little with the rhythm of his fingers, as if he were driving her wild with his touch. "I think there are many services I could perform that might please you..." she left the thought unfinished.

Fritz let his hand cup her full breast beneath its lacy covering, and gave it a proprietary and somewhat playful squeeze.

"Then, perhaps, we might explore a few of those services this very evening, Marta," he said. "Why don't you lock the door and the let us see what we shall see."

Marta smiled guilelessly, rose and glided in a most provocative way toward the door to lock it. She unfastened her uniform as she walked. Then, turning toward him again, she shrugged out of the boring cotton servant-schmatta and let it slip to the floor. Seeing that she had his full attention now, she reached behind her back to unfasten her bra, letting it too fall before she began a slow and tantalizing walk back toward where he sat, quite mesmerized by the brazen display. She could see in his hooded eyes, and in his earnest fumbling with his belt buckle, that she'd succeeded.

Gotcha! she thought as she arrived back in front of his chair and he reached for her greedily with both hands.

Gotcha! You smarmy son of a bitch.

Trip to Castle Perilous

Part VIII

*"History is an account, mostly false
of events, mostly unimportant
Brought about by rulers, mostly knaves
and soldiers, mostly fools."*

Ambrose Bierce

53

Germany

Hugh took the wheel of the Mercedes and sped out of the airport parking lot as if jet propelled.

"Where did you learn to drive," Cait blurted as her body lurched against the seat belt, "the Indy 500?"

Hugh laughed, "I did drive race cars for a bit, a long time ago, but in response to your question, I take it you've never been to Germany? Everyone here drives this way. In fact, it's worth your life to drive under 80 on the Autobahn."

"Well, at least it makes the danger from the Spear chasers seem pale by comparison," she replied dryly. "I noticed all those photos of you, your father has in his study – big game hunting, fencing, boxing, skydiving – cars aren't your only dangerous sport, are they? And yet you don't strike me as the frivolous playboy type who just dabbles at everything. Are you an adrenaline junkie, by any chance?"

She thought the question would amuse him, but instead she saw Hugh's mouth go into a grim hard line, and realized she'd hit a nerve.

"They are skills I find useful in my work," he said enigmatically.

She cocked her head to get a better look at his face, the tense expression giving her pause. "What exactly does one, who lives in a place like Heredon, work at?" she asked, genuinely intrigued.

"Handle family investments? Run the estate? Your world is so different from mine, Hugh, I can't help but wonder."

"I do all of that to help my father, of course," he answered, "and whatever I can for the Hunting Lodge. I expect you'll understand better soon."

"Can you tell me more about the Lodge? I was pretty stunned by the gathering your father arranged, but I'm still not absolutely clear on how it all works."

"Why don't we wait until you've met a few more of our members in the next few days? I think it will all become clearer for you then. I'm not being evasive, Cait... its just not an easy question to answer. And I believe Uncle Siegfried has a good deal he'd like to tell you about what's in play here, so perhaps we should table the question until we reach him."

Cait frowned at the enigmatic response and rode in silence for a while before attempting further conversation.

"Do we have far to go?" she asked. "I've been wondering if the von Hochburg castle would turn out to be as beautiful as Heredon. My experience of castles is pretty slim."

"The von Hochburg castle predates us by four or five centuries – and makes Heredon look like a poor relation, I'm afraid," he said with a chuckle. "As to beauty... I'm a bit prejudiced towards my own home, but the von Hochburg fortress is spectacularly stalwart and mighty. Any edifice that has stood for eight hundred years is an impressive monument to man's desire for immortality at the very least. It has its own kind of austere beauty. We'll be there in an hour... you can decide for yourself."

Cait was about to answer, when she felt herself thrown violently sideways by a sudden impact. Her neck snapped left, then right so abruptly, she saw stars.

The black paneled van that had rammed them had materialized out of nowhere.

"Hang on!" Hugh shouted, "the road narrows up ahead and there's a sheer drop. That's where he'll try to push us over."

The Mercedes leaped forward with the ease of expensive engineering that expected to be pushed to its limits and beyond. Cait hoped fleetingly the van wasn't also a Mercedes, but she was still focused on the words *push us over.*

Hugh clutched the wheel in a death grip as he attempted to swerve out of range of the marauding vehicle that had now accelerated to stratospheric speed. There were no visible cutoffs on the road ahead, but a wall of rock suddenly loomed to their right, and the view to the left dropped away precipitously, as if cut by a giant scythe. The van smashed into their rear bumper with bone-rattling force, making them veer sharply to the left, but Hugh managed to control the spin, and, as the van once again accelerated, trying to wedge its way between them and the wall of rock, she saw it was angling for a way to send them careening over the precipice, with the next massive thrust.

Heart racing, Cait gripped the door and dashboard in a last ditch attempt to protect herself from the inevitable plunge down the side of the cliff. Time seemed to be condensing into slow motion, as she caught sight of a dilapidated yellow truck, clearing the bend in the cliff face ahead. It was coming straight at them in the opposite lane. She sucked in her breath involuntarily and prepared to die. What happened next came so fast, so improbably, her brain barely took it in, but somehow, impossibly, they were past the truck in a squeal of rubber, and a cascade of rock and rubble like a cosmic hailstorm. Looking back, she saw the van was trying to clear the narrow space they'd just squeaked through, but the truck was now blocking its way. The van's driver was out of the car and running toward the truck, waving his hands and screaming at the truck driver who had climbed from his cab, too, and now stood implacably beside his vehicle, with what appeared to be a weapon of some kind in his hand.

Their own car was traveling so fast there was no plausible way for it to take the hairpin curves they still had to navigate, but then just as suddenly as the imprisoning rock wall had appeared, it fell away and they were careening down the other side of the mountain, free and clear. Hugh was speaking urgently into his mobile in German, and the only word she could understand was "danke" which he said more than once. She didn't even attempt to speak over the pounding of her heart.

The car slowed to a more autobahn-like speed and Hugh reached a hand toward Cait, then, as if suddenly remembering her admonition not to touch, he pulled it back quickly.

"Are you alright?" he asked urgently. "I thought there might be trouble but couldn't be sure. Perhaps I should have warned you?"

"You mean you *knew* that would happen and *didn't* warn me?" she barked, turning toward him.

Trying to defuse the tension he said, "At least I know two admirable new things about you, now, Cait. You don't panic easily and you don't scream."

"And now you're going to learn a third thing about me, you arrogant bastard!" she shot back. "I also have a temper that could topple buildings if you set it off. Don't you *dare* hold out on me again, do you understand? If I find out you know something I need to know and you keep it from me, I swear I will leave you where you stand, and find that fucking relic by myself!"

The road had widened, with farm and woodlands to their right. Hugh said nothing, but pulled the car toward what appeared to be a service road of some kind, only partially paved, and veered onto it. He stopped, but left the motor running in neutral as he turned to face her.

"I understand," he said, not contritely, but gravely. "It won't happen again. I had no way of knowing for certain that they'd try to intercept us... but I guessed that if they somehow *did* know where we were headed, or if they had us under surveillance, there was only one logical place for them to try a takedown. So I alerted the Friends of the Hunt to be prepared. They sent the truck – although I wasn't at all sure of *who* was in it, when it first came 'round that curve. It could have been a pincer move by the opposition to catch us between the two vehicles. There was no time after that to explain, just to react."

Cait felt some of her anger drain, realizing the enormity of the split second decision he'd had to make, and the skill it had taken to keep them on the road and alive.

She managed a wan smile. "At the rate we're going, Hugh, by the time the opposition gets around to torturing me, it'll seem like child's play." She took a breath, let it out and said evenly, "I should tell you that I'm slow to anger, but once I'm mad, the first three rows damned well better step back."

He laughed aloud, obviously relieved. "Fair warning then. I should have known better than to take on a redhead of Irish extraction. I believe a good many of us Brits have learned the futility of that, over the years."

He threw the car into gear and the rest of the trip to the Von Hochburg castle was silent and without incident.

54

The Rhine River rises in Switzerland, before making its turbulent way through Austria, Lichtenstein, France, Germany and the Netherlands, to the frigid North Sea. But before leaving Switzerland's glacial majesty behind, it wends its way through a picturesque gorge between the Vosges Mountains and the Black Forest. On this fabled stretch of nature's best handiwork, only 35 miles in length, are more castles than in any other river valley on earth.

Hugh pointed to a magnificent fortress at the top of the jagged mountain looming above them. It was surmounted by a buttressed tower that soared fifty feet above the crenellated battlements, a proud stone sentinel.

"The view from those windows," she gasped, "must be breathtaking!"

"There are magnificent terraces outside the family's apartments," Hugh agreed, "Outside the ballroom, there's a fountained terrace where knights and their ladies danced under starlight on inlaid marble floors, in an age that could support such grandeur."

"What a pity I forgot to pack my ball gown," she said and they both laughed easily, the earlier problem miles behind them.

*   *   *

Inside the 800 year old castle, Prince Siegfried von Hochburg put the phone down thoughtfully and reached for the key he wore on the same chain that held his watch fob and the exquisite rose gold Girard-Perregaux pocket watch that had been made for his great grandfather. The remarkable Complications of the watch – the perpetual calendar, tourbillion and moon-phase minder, split-second chronograph functions, and all the other brilliant examples of the chronographer's art, meant little to him beyond their practical use, but the memory of his grandfather and father each explaining these features to him in his boyhood meant a great deal.

The small key opened a hidden spring-locked drawer in his desk and a leather bound book with a few words inscribed on the cover in gold leaf, became visible. Nowadays he knew, the ways to contact people through mobile numbers, faxes, e-mail addresses, and all the other electronic magic of this new age, had grown exponentially, so all the numbers he needed could more efficiently be kept in an electronic gadget of some sort. But this list must never fall into the hands of the enemy – and besides, the ancient set of books just like this one, dating back centuries, were in his vault, and it wouldn't do to change the format now. At least not for his lifetime. He sighed at the sudden thought of his own advancing age. He seldom actually *felt* old, but reality demanded that he occasionally acknowledge that he *was*. He shook off a momentary chill and squared his shoulders. There was work to do.

Von Hochburg thumbed through the pages, jotting down numbers as he found them, then smiled at the compilation that included one who, in other times, would have been an Emperor, another, a Prime Minister, as well as a plumber, a policeman, a Mother Superior and an ex-resistance fighter, now over 90. The unifying allegiance of this egalitarian band was written in Latin on the hand-tooled leather cover. *Amici Venatio*, it said. Friends of the Hunt. As Master of the Hunt, it was his privilege and responsibility to alert those whose skills would soon be needed, to their tasks.

Prince Siegfried von Hochburg slipped the list into his pocket and closed the book, satisfied. He would greet his esteemed guests and then make the rest of his calls.

55

The old Prince clasped Cait's hand in both his aged ones, and led her, with a broad smile of welcome, into the Great Hall of his castle.

"I've been awaiting your arrival, my dear," he said, as warmly as if she were his long lost child. "And Hugh's arrival is *always* a most welcome treat. I understand you've just had a sample of my godson's daredevil driving skills. It delights me to see you've survived."

He bestowed a smile of great pride and benevolence on Hugh, clapping him affectionately on the shoulder.

"Up 'til this ride I thought finding the Spear was my biggest problem," Cait answered with a smile of her own, "now I know better."

"I knew you were a brave girl the moment we met." Siegfried replied, with an approving chuckle. "I've ordered tea to be served in the conservatory – I thought after your harrowing welcome to

Germany, you'd probably need a warm drink, or perhaps you'd prefer something a bit stronger."

He saw Cait gazing upward with wonder, at the vaulted ceiling that soared 50 feet above their heads. "I'd be delighted to tell you about my home as we walk, my dear, if you'd care to hear. Nearly a millennium of Europe's history has been enshrined in this citadel."

"I'd be honored if you'd give me a tour," she responded, meaning it.

Siegfried nodded approval, offered her his arm, and they started off.

"The first stones were laid in 1209, according to our most trusted ancestral source. The castle has been sacked, burned, overrun, and, of course, occupied by the Allies during the war, but somehow by the grace of God or some architecturally inclined angel, enough has always survived so it could be rebuilt. The Byzantine Hall we're passing through was inspired by the Hagia Sophia in Constantinople, and dates from the time of the Crusades, when returning knights brought Middle Eastern artwork, and Muslim craftsmen, home with them, to recreate in Europe, what had so impressed them in the palaces of the Caliphs and Sultans."

Cait didn't know where to gaze first. Her eyes traveled upward along the mosaic tiled arches that stood in turquoise and gilded tiers, one gallery atop the next, to 40 or 50 feet above where they stood. Each one of the dozen arches on ground level appeared to house artwork from a variety of centuries. The mosaic'd floor was a vast zodiac of astrological symbols and magical sigils.

Cait breathed, "Even kings would be cowed by such grandeur."

The old man chuckled. "That, my dear, was precisely what the builders hoped for. How clever of you to have discerned it. Each ruler needed to assert his power and sovereignty by every means possible, and remember, these walls have entertained emperors and popes. It wouldn't have done at all to show weakness or vulnerability to any such predators, so artful splendour was, in its own way, a protective device as much as a show of vanity and pride."

He patted her hand, as if commending a clever child.

"Let me show you my most beloved spot, my dear. It is not as full of wonder as it was in my boyhood, alas, but it is still my sanctuary."

The old Prince led them out of the vast entry hall and into a small corridor beyond. He opened one of a great pair of arched oak doors, and Cait gasped involuntarily at the scene before her. The chapel was small and human-scale, compared to the rest of what she'd just seen, and its richly carved walls and ceiling were covered by an intricate masterwork of scenes from the life of Christ. But Cait barely registered the art and carvings because her gaze was riveted by the soaring windows in the adjacent tower. They vaulted skyward, graceful, elegant and seemingly suspended by some magical means between heaven and earth. The light from them spilled in richly colored puddles onto the white marble floor beneath her feet, and she stood transfixed by the sheer beauty that bathed her.

Seeing her rapt expression, Siegfried smiled with utter satisfaction. "Do you know the story of the *Spiritus Mundi*, Cait? The Breath of the World?"

She shook her head no, too dazzled to break the spell of the moment with inadequate words.

"When the Templar Knights were sent to Jerusalem to Solomon's temple, they were not, as history has suggested, a group of nine noble policemen sent to protect the pilgrims on the road to the Holy Land. Far from it. They were men of noble lineage, great education, impeccable moral fiber, and vast wealth, dispatched by St. Bernard of Clairvaux, and entrusted with a singular mission: they were to find the Treasure of King Solomon beneath the ruins of his Temple.

"The knights occupied Solomon's Temple for 200 years, during which time they excavated the intricate network of stables and catacombs in which the fabled Emperor had stored his most prized possessions. But they accomplished a great deal more than that – much of which is relevant to your current quest, my dear:

"The knights, over time, were befriended by the Sufis, the great and learned sages of the desert world, and many secrets passed between those two groups of learned and pious men. The science of what later came to be known as Gothic architecture, which is based upon the secret of the flying buttress, was one such treasure. Did you know that the Guild of Masons who created the great Cathedrals of Europe learned their Sacred Geometry at Cistercian monasteries, which had been founded by the same Bernard of Clairvaux, who dispatched the Knights Templar to Jerusalem? The Cistercian monasteries formed a network of repositories and libraries, filled with mystic knowledge brought back from those exotic lands by the Templars. The alchemy of *Spiritus Mundi* was another of their gifts to us."

"And what exactly is this Breath of the World?" Cait asked, entranced.

"Exactly? I cannot say, *exactly,* dear child, as the secret has been lost for 600 years. What I can tell you, is that it produced a kind of stained glass that has never been equaled. Glass that captures the light itself, and holds it, even once the sun had set."

Cait's forehead wrinkled. "How can that be?"

"Sadly my dear, no one knows. And the two great examples of this alchemical magic – my chapel, and the Rose Window at Chartres, were both shattered in the war. Only remnants remain." His regret at the loss was palpable.

"Look to your left my dear, Caitlin... do you see how the vision of Christ in Gethsemani glows with an unearthly splendor, despite the lateness of the hour, the dreariness of the day, and the fact that this particular window is now in late-day shadow?"

Cait looked sharply left to the praying Christ figure, head bowed and hands clasped on the great rock he knelt before, and realized this was the source of the extraordinary puddle of light at her feet. Without thinking, she leaned down, as if to dip her fingers into the ruby and cobalt pool in which she stood. Her eyes were filled with tears when she turned them back toward the old prince.

"I'd like to say a prayer for my husband's soul in this beautiful place," she whispered. "May I light a candle on your altar?"

"You may consider my chapel to be *your* chapel while you are here, Caitlin, dear. It will be open to you night and day. I have mourned many whom I have loved, within these walls. I believe you will find it to be a place of peace and comfort."

She nodded, unable to speak, and walked to the beautifully carved altar rail behind which a row of lit candles stood flickering, a row of unlit candles standing in a rack beneath them. She placed a fresh candle into a votive holder, and lit it with a taper. Folding her hands, and resting her elbows on the altar rail, she lowered her head to her hands and prayed.

When she was done, Cait rose and turned toward the prince, who took her arm to lead her toward the door. She saw that Hugh, too, had quietly taken a candle from the box. He placed it close to hers, lighted it and then lowered his head in prayer.

"Hugh, too, has much to mourn," Prince Siegfried said gently, then without further explanation, he led her out into the hall, where they waited for the younger man to join them.

56

"I understand from Hugh that you wish to visit Wewelsburg and see the counterfeit Spear," Siegfried said over his teacup. "Is this true?"

Cait nodded and swallowed a mouthful of scone before answering. "I know there must be answers in Germany and Austria. I'd like to see the fake Spear in hopes it's physical size and shape might give me some clue as to where Jack might have hidden the real thing. As to Wewelsburg, I know from Lord Delafield's books there's not much left to see, so it will probably be a waste of time, but I thought I might get some kind of psychic hit from the place. You know, an inspiration of some kind."

"Indeed I do know and I think it's a valid possibility. You are Irish after all... the Celts are a highly psychic genetic strain, you know. And redheads in particular."

"You're joking," she said, smiling.

"Not in the least. There's quite a bit of evidence in mystical circles that connects the redheaded Celts to the Faery bloodlines, and they are surely the most psychic race to ever have inhabited our planet."

"Faery bloodlines?" she repeated, startled, "Are you saying there really are faeries? I remember a story in the New York Times a few years ago about the Irish re-routing a super highway, because it would have disturbed a faery hill. I thought at the time it was pretty enlightened of them – I can't imagine the state of New York or Connecticut doing such a thing."

"The faeries are – or were – quite real, Cait," he said. "They were once known as the Race of the Wise, a noble caste. They were called The Sidhe by the Celts and were probably of Scythian stock, perhaps out of Atlantis before the great flood and inundation. The faeries could see and interact with the subtle dimensions more easily than we can, and were tuned to a higher frequency than humans. But they intermarried with humans nonetheless, and the Celts were born as a hybrid race – the redheaded ones carried more of the DNA of faery psychism than the others, hence in the older cultures, they were regarded either as royalty, or as witches."

Cait cocked her head, listening with great fascination. It actually sounded plausible when said with such conviction.

"How did I live this long on this planet without any hint of all I've learned in these last few days?" she mused, almost to herself.

"You've known much of the psychic realm, I'd wager, Cait," Siegfried said, "you just call it by a different name, perhaps. Haven't you always known things other people didn't? Perhaps you call it intuition or a hunch. Haven't you sometimes sensed the coming of events before they happen?"

She took a deep breath and exhaled it before answering. "Yes, to both questions... but I've never really been able to trust what I know, because its so random. I can't rely on it. Why didn't I know something terrible would happen to Jack that awful night? I was just happy and excited about our anniversary – not terrified by some vision of disaster. If my psychism is real, why didn't I have a vision that could have stopped the chain of events?" She sounded both resentful and sad.

"But you *do* have visions?" Siegfried pressed.

"Yes. All my life. But unfortunately not when I need them, it seems."

"May I ask what form these visions take?" Hugh interjected.

"Usually, they start in a dream," Cait answered slowly, "then I wake up and see the rest of the vision unfold, as if I were watching it on a large movie screen." She saw Hugh and Siegfried exchange knowing glances.

"And sometimes, I just *know* things that are happening somewhere else. Like when my mother and baby brother died. I felt their dying, deep inside me. And with Jack... I knew he was gone forever, long before the police told me they'd found him."

"Such gifts are rare, Cait, and they are almost always random. You can be taught to become better able to control your gifts – but there will always be areas across which a veil is drawn. Some things we are simply not permitted to know, or not permitted to interfere with."

She saw Hugh turn his face away, but before he did so, she saw an expression of raw pain and anger there that startled her.

"I see," she said, somewhat bitterly, "So, nothing is fair. Is God Himself just? Or are we simply random pawns in some strange game He plays with us mortals?"

"I understand your frustration and even anger, Cait. You've suffered a great loss, and are now trapped in a demanding game, not of your own choosing. And there is so much more for you to know." He shook his head, as if having made a decision.

"Tomorrow you must journey to the home of my cousin, Maria. She is a Hapsburg by birth, and possessed of both knowledge and wisdom. She can introduce you to the counterfeit Spear, and she can, if she chooses, open certain pathways to you. She is a long-time Friend of the Hunt, but she is didactic and capricious. One never quite knows what Maria will do in fulfilling her obligations to the Hunters.

"But tonight, I think you must simply rest – there is a long journey ahead of you."

"How far from here does she live?" she asked.

"That is not the journey of which I speak, Cait. Maria's home is only a few hours drive. But I believe you will find that it is just an on-ramp to the far longer road you must now travel."

Siegfried von Hochburg pulled himself from the wing chair teetering a little, and waved away the footman who rushed to his side to help him.

"I am *fine*, Friedrich," he said emphatically. "I am merely feeling the weight of my years tonight." He turned to Cait and Hugh.

"Would you think me an inadequate host if I were to suggest a small nap before dinner?"

"As a doctor," Cait replied with a smile, "that's precisely what I'd prescribe – for all of us."

"Then we should reconvene at 9:00 if that suits you both?" He was already moving toward the door, as they murmured their assent.

57

Germany

A small dining table had been set up before the hearth in the Prince's study. The room was a satinwood haven, warmed by rare books in exquisite bindings and paintings that appeared to span centuries, as well as many schools of mastery.

"I trust you don't mind dining casually," the Prince began as they seated themselves at a round table set for three, before the crackling fire. "The formal dining room is vast, as you've seen, and so in the winter, I've taken a fancy to dining here instead, by the fire. For whatever reason, one feels lonelier in winter, don't you agree? And sitting by one's self at a huge table calls to mind other times, other faces..." he paused for a moment almost reverently, then continued "...those who are no longer with us. In winter there is a sadness, a *tiefe Traurigkeit* that pervades my dining room through no fault of its own." He laughed a little at his own foolishness.

"Great books, a soothing fire and fine company," Cait responded. "What more could one ask?"

The old Prince smiled benevolently at his guest, then glanced at Hugh, who seemed quite taken with the young doctor, too. "I confess to having another reason for suggesting the intimacy of this room," he went on. "You see, we have much to speak about that requires the utmost secrecy, and this room is not only my safe haven, but it is protected from outside interference on this material plane, and on others, as well. It has been well warded against unwanted intrusion."

Cait's eyebrows rose and Hugh hurried to explain. "Warding involves an intentionally imposed shifting of energies to surround a space with a wall of protection."

"Sounds sensible," Cait responded, managing to keep the smile she felt out of her voice.

"How much do you know of our Sacred Order, Caitlin?" the old man asked as the first course was served by an obviously trusted elderly servant.

"Hugh and Lord Delafield introduced me to a gathering of your..." she sought the right word, "allies, I expect you would call them?" She looked to Hugh for help.

"Actually, we call them the Friends of Hunt, for the most part... or the Amici of the Hunting Lodge. We have been known by many names in many countries because of the need for secrecy about the work we do."

"And that work is what precisely?" she asked, with studied directness. "I'm trying to wrap my mind around all this but you must know it's a lot to take in."

"We are Knights of an ancient Order, Cait," Siegfried answered with great gravity. "As you learned at Heredon, we have pledged our sacred honor to do battle for humanity against the forces of darkness. Our Order preserves the old ways, the old teachings and initiations, so that we are equipped to meet whatever challenges are sent by the Universe."

"So, you're mystics of some sort?"

"Mystics, psychics, clairvoyants, psychometrists, mages... again, *many* names have been used to describe a large range of disciplines we practice that are beyond the ordinary. Our special perceptive abilities and our cognizance of the Inner Planes – those parts of the universe which are not visible to ordinary sight – give us the ability to protect humanity against those who have similar access to occult power, but use it for selfish or unscrupulous ends."

Hugh leaned toward her, anxious for her to understand. "There is a balance in the Universe, Cait. Life is a school-room, and we are given the chance through all we learn here, to strive either toward enlightenment, or toward temporal and temporary power and self-gratification. But, there is a Higher Law to be served – a code of spiritual conduct that reflects the Divine Will which created it. When these Higher Laws are breached by those who use their unique powers to undermine balance and enlightenment, those who possess similar abilities, are called upon to restore order. Our Amici are trained to use their gifts to deal with offenders and to protect those of good heart and intent."

"And all of this must be kept secret, of course," she said trying to understand, "because in the ordinary everyday world, you'd all be thought quite mad. Am I right?"

Hugh nodded.

"But, Hugh, if all this is true, why can't you simply use this magic of yours to get back the Spear and save my family? Why all this questing, picking up breadcrumbs of knowledge, as we stumble along not knowing where to go next..."

The old prince reached across the table for her hand and patted it gently. "Remember the schoolroom analogy, Caitlin. We are here so that our souls can make choices, and learn the consequences of those choices. *Nothing* is made easy for us – in fact, the higher we climb, the more obstacles we encounter.

"But we are never alone in our battles. We have our code of honor and our God-given skills, we have help on the Inner Planes from the great Beings – perhaps you know them as Angels and Archangels, those who guide humanity's destiny. And we have each other – we have our Amici... our standing army of those who will not let Evil win without fighting the good fight."

*   *   *

Far into the night, Cait sat on the edge of the bed, staring into the embers of the fire that had warmed her room, while she was at their strange dinner. Now, hours past midnight, the fire was dying and a distinct chill had crept into the room as she tossed and turned in the big feather bed.

She couldn't sleep despite the fatigue she felt. She'd always known there was more to life than met the eye. Known things others didn't know... seen things others didn't see... sensed events before they occurred... dreamed precognitive dreams. She'd assumed it was because of her Celtic roots, and maybe the caul she'd been born with, but she'd never consciously striven to enhance her abilities. In fact, she often fought down her innerknowings, so her rational scientific side could win out. Except... she hugged herself in the chilly darkness of the room... that wasn't quite true. How many times had she put her hands on a patient and known unequivocally what the diagnosis would be, before doing a single test or examination? How many times had she known the phone would ring and it would be Meg at the other end, seconds before the ring sounded? How many times had visions flashed before her eyes or hovered on the edge of dreams... visions that later became reality. Meg knew about all of it... Jack had known, too, and neither had ever questioned her gift or asked her to justify it.

And now she was an unwilling player in a game that would require whatever of these arcane skills she could muster and hone. Could Hugh have been right that this was her battle, not Jack's?

Just the thought of Jack brought tears to her eyes and reawakened the terrible emptiness she'd felt since his death, an emptiness that frightened her and made her feel inadequate for the business of simply living each day. For ten years every act of her life had felt part of a larger, stronger wholeness. Now she felt bereft, adrift in a strange cold ocean with no shore in sight.

Cait glanced at the cell phone on the bedside table. She desperately wanted to talk to Lark and to Meg. Her heart ached at the thought of Lark alone and fearful. Alone and feeling abandoned by both the people who were supposed to be her protectors against all harm. She did a quick calculation of time zone differences and sighing with disappointment, reached for the phone, but only to send texts to the two she loved best in the world.

Too restless to sleep, she decided to find her way to the chapel – maybe there, she'd find some semblance of peace. She drew on her robe, and on quiet slippered feet let herself out of the bedroom and made her way along the corridor toward the chapel. She was startled to find the doors open and the room filled with candlelight.

Curiously, she peered in and was startled to see both Prince Siegfried and Hugh, each dressed in a gold embroidered, snow white robe, standing before the altar. They were obviously engaged in some kind of ceremony she didn't recognize.

What startled her even more was the fact that each was surrounded by a soft nimbus of light that seemed to be emanating from the men themselves. She stared, immobilized for a few moments, then feeling she was an intruder on sacred ground, she turned and made her way back to her room, awash in questions without answers.

She sat on the edge of her bed trying to make sense of what she'd witnessed, then she simply took the wooly lap robe from the bedside chair, wrapped it tight around her shoulders, and knelt down by the side of the bed, to pray.

*   *   *

Hugh and the old Prince stood quietly in the sacristy of the chapel, having finished their prayers and put away their ceremonial vestments.

The older man scanned his nephew's so-serious countenance and decided to say what he had not intended to. But, the vision of the future he'd had while in the chapel had made him feel he must voice what was on his mind.

"You have recognized this woman from the past, haven't you, my dear boy?" he began and Hugh, startled, raised his eyes to his uncle's knowing and benevolent gaze. He nodded, but said nothing.

"You are still bound by your oath, then?" the old man asked.

"Another year," Hugh answered.

Seigfried nodded in turn. "A hard oath to live up to, and a harsh reason for having taken such a path, my boy. I admire your courage." He paused, collecting his thoughts.

"But if you'll forgive a bit of unsolicited advice from someone who cares deeply about you," he took a breath, then plunged on. "Life is short and hard for those of our calling. And old loves, such as that which I believe you have known with this woman in times past, are rare and precious."

"She loves her husband," Hugh said simply.

"In this life, that is true and commendable. But this is not the only life of which you are aware, my dear nephew."

"What are you telling me, Uncle?" Hugh asked, unsettled by the old man's words. "To violate my oath?"

"No, indeed," the old Prince replied, choosing his words with great care. "Never that. Only that should the moment come when you can reach out to her, do not let your vow, or her love for her husband, stay your hand. You must let her know your feelings, Hugh, and then let Cait make her own choices. If Divine Providence gives you the opportunity to speak your heart, do not remain silent. Take the risk, Hugh! You are both young. There may yet be a way for you to bring each other happiness."

Hugh nodded again, wondering at this strange advice from The Master of the Hunt. It was unlike his uncle to interfere with karma. He was a man known for his unwavering adherence to the rules of their Order.

Of course, he realized, as he turned the old Prince's words over in his mind, Seigfried von Hochberg was also a man known for his loving and compassionate heart.

58

Heredon. England.

Lark was hunched up on the bed bent over her laptop, so lost in the game she didn't see Mrs. Dunleavey watching her with concern from the doorway. In the time this odd little girl had been at Heredon the housekeeper had grown fond of her. Lark was a delightful child, Mrs. Dunleavey thought watching her, polite and good-hearted, but she was growing more and more obsessed with the computer game she played at, and left to her own devices she would have stayed at it night and day, without a break for food or sleep or exercise. It wasn't healthy, and it was getting harder by the day to get Lark to focus on anything else at all. Even the pursuits that had pleased her when she'd first arrived, were now forgotten. She suspected the game was Lark's escape hatch from all in her real life that had gone so terribly wrong, and it was her way to immerse herself in a universe over which she had some control. *Poor little thing.*

"Miss Lark, dear," the housekeeper called softly, not wanting to startle the child who seemed so engrossed in what she was doing. "It's a lovely, mild day outdoors, and Arthur was wondering if you might be good enough to help him exercise Excalibur this afternoon."

Lark looked up and blinked as if to remind herself of where she was, who might be speaking, and why.

"I have to figure this out first," she said looking back to the screen. "It's a really hard riddle and I can't go anywhere until I get to the next level. I'm stuck in the Dreadosphere and I need to get out before the Fractious Fractals find me. I've only got one more question to answer to get to the next level but if the Fractious Fractals get me I have to answer the horrific fractal problem about connectedness, and I don't think I can do it without my Daddy.

"I remember he said… when you leave the interval from -1 to 1 with a number x and plug it into the fraction $f(x) = x^2$ again and again, then you travel forever and ever off to infinity… to the right or the left… plus or minus infinity… but forever and ever… So, if x is on the boundary, like if x is either +1 or -1, then you bounce back and forth between 1 and -1 or you stay put at 1 and maybe that's better. I know why that's true, but if all the expanded domain of the imaginary world is my playground, what will happen then?"

"Oh dear," Mrs. Dunleavey said, shaking her silvery head, having not understood a word of Lark's explanation. "That sounds just dreadful, I'm sure. But I'm afraid His Lordship has grown a bit concerned about all the time you're spending indoors, dear, and today is perfect to get some fresh air into those lungs of yours. You know I've been charged with keeping you in fine fettle whilst your Mother is traveling, and I fear I may be failing miserably at my task." She smiled benevolently at Lark and walked toward the bed to see what a fractious fractal looked like. She realized today's children were all becoming slaves to electronics, but in Lark's case, it was worrisome, and Mrs. Dunleavey felt quite out of her depth.

"Do you think perhaps you could leave the Dreadosphere for an hour or two to have lunch with His Lordship, my dear? He's asked you to join him, and I wouldn't want him to think I'm derelict in my duties." She tilted her plump little face to the side questioningly, hoping Lark's compassionate nature would kick in and she wouldn't want to cause a problem in the household. "And then perhaps a short ride would be in order?" she added hopefully. "I know Arthur relies upon you now to help exercise Excalibur – he's told me what a fine rider you are."

Lark looked reluctant, but didn't want to hurt Mrs. Dunleavey's feelings. She was such a nice little woman and she was trying so hard.

"I guess I could come back later," Lark said, obviously disappointed at having to quit the game even for a few hours. "It's not easy to get out of this swamp," she added, to explain her reluctance. "But maybe I'll figure out the riddle when I'm riding. My daddy says sometimes you have to let your head just figure things out on its own, and stop trying so hard."

Mrs. Dunleavey heard the wistfulness in the child's voice and understood how very much she missed her father. "What a smart fellow your father sounds." Her voice was soft and kindly when she responded, careful to couch her words in the present tense. "I expect he would like you to give that fine head of yours a bit of a rest from time to time, don't you think? Perhaps, you could let a bit of wind blow through your hair whilst you're riding – to clear the cobwebs, so to speak?"

Lark closed the laptop and climbed down from the high bed.

"My riding helmet doesn't let too much wind in," she said in her usual literal way.

Mrs. Dunleavey shook her head at the analytical response and laughed, "I'm certain it will be just enough! Why, it wouldn't surprise me at all, if when you get back to it, you'll find your way out of that dreadosphere place in a heartbeat."

Lark looked unconvinced. She cast a rueful glance back at the closed laptop, and with a sigh, followed Mrs. Dunleavey down the hall.

59

Sunlight poured through the morning room, gilding the soft toile of walls and upholstery with a benevolent shimmer. Delafield had chosen this room for his chat with Lark, purposely for its coziness. It had been his wife's favorite spot.

"My dear, Lark," he greeted her enthusiastically as she entered the room, and looked tentatively around. "I'm so very glad you've decided to join me for lunch. With Hugh gone, it gets a bit lonely in this big old place, wouldn't you say? I thought we might keep each other company, whilst he and your mother are traveling, eh?"

Lark nodded, not knowing what to say.

"And I have a favor to ask of you."

She looked up startled. Lord Delafield had servants to do everything for him, what could he possibly want her to do?

He watched her interest sparked.

"Did you know I have a cousin who is a bona fide Prince?" His eyes twinkled as he saw hers widen, so he waved her to a seat at the small table.

"Hugh told me you have a rather extraordinary knowledge of chivalry for a young lady, and it occurred to me that Siegfried is an authority on that very subject, so I propose we introduce the two of you. What do you think about that?"

Lark wasn't sure what she thought, so she answered, "Does he have a castle?"

Delafield chuckled.

"One of the better ones, I'd say. Crenellated battlements, fortified towers, flying buttresses... all the very best castle accoutrements. He could bring photographs if you'd like, and after your mother returns, I'm sure you could visit him there. Would you like that?"

"Yes. I've never been in a real castle before."

"Excellent! And Cousin Siegfried has become a friend of your mother's as well, Lark. She's been visiting with him in Germany, and he's promised her he would come visit us whilst she's abroad."

"I miss her," Lark said simply. "I wish she would just come home." Her voice faltered, and Delafield reached his large hand across the table to cover her small one.

"Of course you do, and Siegfried has told me how very much she misses you. In fact, he's bringing you a letter from her and a small gift he thought might cheer you."

"Really?" The child's face lit up.

"Indeed he is. And now may I ask you for the favor I mentioned earlier?"

Lark's eyes met his, and she nodded.

"Will you let Siegfried and me help you with your puzzle?"

"You want to learn to play Lark's Labyrinth?" The idea startled her.

Delafield smiled. "Hugh tells me its quite challenging, and you know they say one can't teach an old dog new tricks, but perhaps if *two* old dogs put their heads together..." he left the possibilities to her imagination.

"Are either of you any good at math?" she asked, unconvinced.

Delafield pursed his lips, composing an answer.

"Not bad," he said finally. "But I'm rather good with ciphers. Used to do quite a bit of that sort of thing in the war, you see? Siegfried... I've called him Siggy, from the time we were youngsters, but most people find him far too princely for that now, I suppose… Siggy and I used to communicate with each other in Atbash when we were boys.

"No way!" Lark blurted.

"Way." Delafield said with a smile of satisfaction.

Lunch from that point forward was, Lord Delafield thought, a smashing success. When it was done and Lark had scampered off with Mrs. Dunleavey, he picked up the phone and called Germany.

*   *   *

"We're in! Siggy," Delafield said, when the Prince picked up. "She is a most delightful child, infinitely complex, and greatly in need of a father-figure or two. How soon can you be here?"

"By the weekend, I should think," Prince Siegfried replied, pleased by the news and the invitation. "Shall I bring anything along?"

"Some of your old cipher books, perhaps, and as many photographs of your castle as you can carry. And, Siggy, could you perhaps find an appropriate gift of some sort that would please a lonely child, hmm? And I wouldn't plan on leaving any time soon."

"I see…" the Prince answered thoughtfully. "If you think it wise for me to be there, I shall be at your disposal. And Tony, you should know I've already put several Amici in place for their journey. Best discussed in person, but a heartening response from one and all."

"Excellent. Until the weekend then." Delafield hung up the phone. His own grandson would have been around Lark's age, had he lived. And Siggy's grandchildren were long grown, but he was certain neither of them had forgotten how to be a grandfather. It would be lovely to feel needed in that tender way again… and awfully good to be back in the game.

Watch out for Dragonspawn

Part IX

Logic n.

*The art of thinking and reasoning in
strict accordance with the limitations
and incapacities of human mis-
understanding.*

Ambrose Bierce

60

On Friday morning, Lark appeared in Delafield's study with her laptop in hand, and invited him to enter the Labyrinth for his first lesson. He seemed delighted by the challenge and when introduced to Pythagoras, made quite a show of his delight in meeting so famous a thinker, and to Lark's delight, attempted to speak to him in Greek.

A pyramid of numbers bounced into view ahead of them.

"Do you recognize this and do you know its secret?" asked Pythagoras in his deep sonorous voice.

Lark, greatly heartened by Lord Delafield's enthusiasm for the game, turned to him and whispered. "This isn't geometry, just plain old math, so don't worry, OK?"

"Absolutely no worries, here," Delafield replied with a smile.

Lark looked closely at him to make sure he didn't feel embarrassed by his ineptitude. Anybody could see at a glance this was Pascal's Triangle.

Delafield was touched by her concern, and also by how starved Lark seemed for someone to play her game with her. Perhaps it was good he was such a neophyte. It gave her a chance to be the teacher and show off her skills.

She addressed the figure on the screen and typed in her answer, too.

"It's Pascal's Triangle," she said confidently, "and the secret is it goes on forever! The sides are all 1's and every number is the sum of the numbers diagonally above it."

"I want to take you to the library," she told him eagerly, after they'd passed Pythagoras. "It's a really cool place to go next, OK?"

"Lead on Milady," he said with enthusiasm. "I'm yours to command."

An Elven creature, naked except for a tassled hat and a tiny tabard, opened the great door to the Library, and as it swung back creakily on its ancient iron hinges, Lord Delafield glimpsed a magnificent round tower room beyond. It was filled, floor to ceiling, with shelves overflowing with leather-bound books of conspicuous age, many with gilded lettering on their spines. A fire crackled in the great stone hearth, and Delafield chuckled despite himself.

"What are you laughing at?" Lark asked, looking up from her screen.

"It looks rather like *my* library, don't you think?" he asked. "I should feel quite at home here."

Lark giggled. "Except that it's round and yours is a rectangle."

The old man smiled indulgently at the child, who was so very literal, yet capable of such whimsy. He wondered if her father, seeing the serious and literal bent of his daughter's mind, had purposely made the Labyrinth whimsical, to teach her light-heartedness.

"You'll have to answer a logic question and a math question to get in," she said as the Elf acknowledged their presence with a low bow.

"Logic or mathematics?" the small creature inquired politely. "Choose one." And both words swooped into view on the screen, their large letters hovering in front of the elder Knight's avatar.

"Click on whichever one you want," Lark prompted and when Delafield clicked *logic,* the Elf unfurled a scroll that read:

> *Some bacteria in a bowl divide themselves*
> *every minute into two equal parts that are the*
> *same size as the original bacteria, and which*
> *also divide the next minute and so on.*
> *The bowl in which this is occurring*
> *is full at twelve p.m.*
> *When was it half full?*

Let me ponder that a moment..." Lord Delafield mused. "I think I was rather decent at logic at Oxford, back before the dawn of time, you know... so I'll say the bowl was half full one minute earlier. Let's see if that's correct, shall we?"

He typed in the answer and the scroll fluttered back to its place in the corner of the room. Lark clapped her approval and her Princess avatar clapped too, and said, "Well done, Sir Knight."

"Mathematics!" intoned the Elf immediately, and a book zoomed from the shelf and opened itself in front of them. It read:

> *You have eight books.*
> *How many ways can you arrange them*
> *left to right on the shelf?*

"Oh dear," Delafield said, "that's a bit harder isn't?"

"Don't worry," Lark whispered, as if the Elf shouldn't hear. "I know how to do this one!" She jotted down some quick numbers on a pad, remembering that the answer is 8 factorial, and said with a note of triumph in her voice, "There are 40,320 ways to put the books on the shelves!"

Then she typed in the number, and both the Elf and the book applauded noisily.

"How on earth did you *do that?*" Delafield asked in genuine amazement.

Lark's eyes were shining with delight when she turned her face to him. "It wasn't so hard – this is only Level One. Watch this..." she used her pencil as a pointer. "See... you have eight books to choose from for the first book, seven for the second book, six for the third book, and so on, all the way down to the last book, so its really just a simple equation... see?" she showed him what she had written on the paper.

$$8 \times 7 \times 6 \times 5 \times 4 \times 3 \times 2 \times 1 = 40,320$$

Delafield shook his head. "I think I'd best go slay a dragon to redeem myself, or you'll soon lose all faith in me," he said ruefully.

"There's a nest of Dragonspawn just a little way from here," she replied matter-of-factly, "you can kill as many as you want to. They're not very nice and they serve the Dark Lord. But first you have to get our Library Card from the Elf and then I'll take you there."

"However did we get a library card?" Lord Delafield asked with genuine curiosity.

"We just won it because we got two right answers," Lark said happily, as the Elf promptly tucked a Library Card into the pocket of the Delafield knight's doublet.

"We collect tokens every time we get an answer right," Lark explained, "because if we get into trouble on the path, we might need them to get us out of the Dismal Failure Swamp or some other scary place."

"I shall remember that henceforward," the old man said with a smile. "I'd wager no one wants to spend any more time in the Dismal Failure Swamp than is absolutely necessary!"

He wondered what Siggy would make of this remarkable child.

"You know my Princely Cousin, Siggy, will be arriving this afternoon," he said, delighted to make the announcement. "He's led a very adventurous life and I have a strong feeling he's going to be a very good player of your game."

Lark checked his expression. "You're not tired of playing with me already are you?" she asked worriedly.

"The truth is my dear," he said heartily, "I haven't been this excited about playing anything in more years than I can count!"

61

Anthony Lord Delafield was eating his breakfast with Lark sitting across from him at the table. He had intended to read his morning newspaper, but he could see she had something she wanted to say, so he laid down the paper and smiled at her.

"You appear to me to be brimming over with news of some sort. Am I right, my dear?" he asked, the twinkle in his old eyes making them seem young again.

She nodded eagerly and put down the spoon with which she'd been eating her oatmeal. She thought oatmeal tasted better in England than at home, or maybe it was just that the name porridge made it sound much more interesting.

"I've been wondering..." she began. "How did anybody ever find the Spear in the olden days? I mean, before computers and all?"

Delafield leaned back in his chair, surprised by her question.

"My dear child," he said, "has no one told you of the Spear's magical journey and why it is so important to the world?"

She shook her head no.

"What a dreadful oversight!" he said emphatically. "I do apologize. Wait 'til I tell your Uncle Siggy that we have been so remiss. Here you are on a grand spiritual quest..."

She giggled. "I think you're mixing me up with my mommy," she amended.

"Indeed I am not!" he asserted. "She is on a great quest as well, of course, but you will nonetheless be called to do your part. Who else but *you* knows the secrets of Lark's Labyrinth, after all? And that's where we may find the key!"

He almost smiled at her startled expression but didn't want to puncture the gravity of the moment. "One doesn't have to travel by car or plane to go on a spiritual quest you know. One can be called on to travel in the mind and heart."

"Wow!" she breathed. "That's really cool! So how do I do it?"

"But you already *are* doing it, my dear child. Every time you enter the Labyrinth, you are doing it!"

"Awesome," she said, and now he did allow himself a smile.

"Awesome indeed. And I believe that just as Hugh is your mother's champion, so Siggy and I must be yours – and our very first duty will be to instruct you in the history of the Spear.

"We shall begin today. What say you meet Siggy and me in the library in – shall we say twenty minutes?"

He watched her scamper off happily, and rose from the table to go in search of a Prince, who would be most pleased to know he'd just been awarded the role of co-champion on a quest.

*   *   *

Nearly a week had gone by since Uncle Siggy and Uncle Tony had begun the stories of the Spear. Lark lay on the floor, clutching the giant cushion that was her favorite. She was listening, enraptured by the tale she now felt part of. The Uncles had said they'd take turns telling her the tales of the Spear, one each day until her mommy came home.

They'd already told her about what happened to Jesus on the Cross, and how Longinus had given the Spear to Joseph of Arimethea, and how it had had to be hidden to keep it from the bad guys. Today, she was going to find out where it turned up again, and how everybody found out it was really magic! This was sort of like watching a miniseries on TV, except it was even better because you had to use your imagination and you could ask questions if you didn't understand something. And besides, she liked the sound of their voices and the fact that they really *believed* the stories, and they used a lot of grown-up old-fashioned words that made her feel kind of important. And it was cool that they seemed to believe in things like miracles and angels.

She snuggled in by the fire as the story began. It was Uncle Siggy's turn to tell the tale:

Golgatha A.D. 324

Helena stood in the broiling desert sun and surveyed the ruin before her. She, too, was a ruin, she thought, as she watched the diggers toiling in the stifling heat. She had embarked on this pilgrimage despite her age, because her soul was drowning in sorrow and remorse, and she knew of nowhere else to turn for solace but to God. Standing here, exhausted, made miserable by the heat, sand and insects, painfully aware of every anguish she'd suffered in the past two years, she did not feel like the mother of an Emperor, but rather, the mother of an arrogant fool. She loved her son, now called by the world, Emperor Constantine, or Pontifix Maximus, but how hollow and meaningless his rarefied titles seemed to her. He was so like the man who'd sired him – a brave soldier, but a feckless husband and father.

Helena had been an innkeeper's daughter, more beautiful than most, when the handsome Roman General Constantus had taken a fancy to her, and wooed her away from home and family. She'd been gloriously happy for a time, reveling in the birth of this son, who was now called an Emperor, and in the love of her dashing husband. Those were the days when her husband had still loved her more than he loved his own ambition. Before Constantus had cast her aside to marry Flavia Maximiana Theodora, daughter of the Western Roman Emperor, and had thereby bought an empire, at the cost of Helena's happiness.

She hastily made the sign of the cross on her brow and breast to banish the hatred that welled so easily in the wake of her life's latest tragedy.

*Her grandson Crispus lay two years dead, by his father's own decree, his sweet wife and son banished from Helena's sight, forever. What curse was it that blighted the loves and marriages of the men of this tainted lineage? How could Constantine have believed the lies his wife Fausta told him, when she accused Crispus of the most terrible treason? How could he **not** have understood the vile deceit of this woman whose ambitions knew no bounds, and whose self-serving falsehoods were legendary in the palace? His loyal, loving son Crispus would never have betrayed him in such a way as she had claimed.*

It had taken Helena a year to prove Fausta's perfidy to Constantine. A year of searching, documenting, following the money-trail of bribes that lay in Fausta's wake, as she'd woven the tangled web that brought Crispus to his doom, and put her own brats next in line for the Imperial throne.

*Constantine had sentenced Fausta to death, then, but he'd let her die by the kindest sentence available – allowing her to expire in an overheated steam bath. The death Fausta had chosen for Crispus – chopped to death by the Imperial Guard – had not been so kind, and the sentence of **damnatio memoriae** that had accompanied the death decree meant Crispus's name was stricken forever from all mention, and his wife and son, Helena's only grandchild, banished from any contact with the Imperial family.*

And so, here she stood in Palestine, having undertaken this pilgrimage as a penance for the fierce vengeful rage that had tainted her soul since Crispus' death. She'd promised her Confessor she'd find the True Cross, but instead she'd found this ancient Spear...

Helena hugged herself despite the heat, as she watched the digger shovel away the last of the dirt and debris beneath which the Spear had lain for centuries. As she knelt and pulled it from the sands that held it, a vision began to unfold before her eyes...

Helena was no longer on the Hill of Skulls. Instead, she was standing in a golden landscape, not of this world. Before her stood a great warrior angel in full battle dress.

"Hail, Caretaker!" the angel greeted her, and she did not know what he meant by that, or how to address him properly, so she merely said in a trembling voice, "Hail to thee, Great Angel of the Light."

"The Spear you hold is that of Longinus, the Centurion. It carries power you cannot dream. Men will sense its greatness, but understand it not. They will fight to possess it, to use this power for rulership, yet it's true power is that of a Way-Shower."

"And what is a Way-Shower, great Angel?" Helena asked wonderingly.

"Humankind is greatly flawed, yet greatly gifted, Caretaker. When free will was bestowed by Creator upon your kind, the choice of two Paths was opened to you. Light or Darkness – you are free to choose, and free to suffer the consequence of that choice. A Way-Shower is meant to lead you toward the Path of Light."

"And if the power of this Spear were to fall into the hands of evil men?" she asked, for she had seen what temptations power brought to men, and the corruption that followed in its wake.

"It is the task of the Caretaker to see this does not happen," was his solemn reply.

Helena looked into the Angel's face and saw great beams of Light radiating from his magnificent eyes.

"Am I to give this Spear to my Son, the Emperor?" she asked, hesitantly, wondering why she, of all people, had been chosen for this task..

*"**You** are the Caretaker, now, Lady. Only you can be the judge of your son's worthiness."*

*"But **I** am unworthy of such a trust!" she protested, frightened by such responsibility. "I cannot bear such a task alone."*

"On the path of goodness, there will you find friends and allies. So shall it always be. Choose well, Caretaker. Your

immortal soul and the lives of many will depend upon it. I, Michael, Captain of the Angelic Army, bid you peace and farewell."

The Angel unfurled his wings and the light that blazed out from them was so dazzling that Helena could no longer see a form at all, but only the blinding light, where he had stood...

Lark sat listening wide-eyed. She loved the way Uncle Siggy's voice sounded when he told a story – it was almost like he had been there when it happened. Even though he couldn't be *that* old.

"Do you believe in Angels?" she asked him, very seriously. "When you tell stories it sounds like you really do."

"With all my heart," the old man replied, and she knew by the way he said it that it was the truth.

62

New York

Meg picked up the hall phone and barely recognized the voice at the other end.

"Sally? Is that you? You sound really weird."

"Meg, listen to me!" Sally's voice was frantic, terrified. "I found things... oh God, I should never have followed those threads..."

"What things? What threads?" Meg pressed. "Sally, what the hell are you talking about? You sound terrified. And I thought you said you weren't going to look into this any further..."

Meg motioned to Carter to pick up the extension phone, and her partner lifted the receiver in the living room.

"I *am* terrified!" Sally whispered urgently. "I'm pretty sure somebody's following me. I must have triggered a tripwire."

Carter broke in. "Sally honey, I'm on here too. Don't say another word on the phone, do you understand me?   Not one word!"

Meg broke in, "Meet me where we spoke last time, can you do that?"

"No! I can't," Sally snapped, panic in her words, "I know they're watching."

"*Who's* watching, Sally?" Meg urged.

"I don't know, for Christ's sake!" Sally blurted. "Somebody bad. When you follow the info I sent you, you'll *get* exactly how bad. This is big, Meg. Really big. Really dirty."

"You sent me something?" Meg pursued, trying to understand what was going on. "Did you send it here?"

"The *twins!*" Sally blurted, emphasizing the word, as if it were a code. "Carter's twins – you know, the ones she told us about! I sent it there."

Carter was waving frantically to say she understood. She mouthed *Damon and Pythias* to Meg, who nodded back, understanding.

"Smart girl," she said into the phone. "Now we need to get you some help. I'll call my cop friends – they'll help you, okay? Just tell me where you are so we can come get you."

"I need to know what to do next, Meg. I'm really scared and I have a really bad feeling about what's happening... After you read what I sent you'll get it... I should have stopped when I realized how bad it was, but I was so freaked by everything I was finding out so I just kept digging..."

Carter broke in, "I still have friends at the Bureau, Sally, they'll help you..."

"No! Not 'til you see what I sent you!" she was growing more agitated. "Read it, *then* let me know if you think they can help, or just make it worse."

"Sally, are you sure you don't want to come here for a few days. We're both armed and we've got friends..."

"No! I can't leave my Mom. She's in really bad shape again. Oh God, maybe I'm just being paranoid from lack of sleep and too much worry... but what I found really spooked me."

"I hear you, Sally," Meg said, worriedly. "I'm so sorry to have gotten you into this... whatever *this* is. I'll get Matt on it... he'll protect you."

"No! Just get to the twins. Get them on it first. Look I gotta go. I'll check in, tomorrow morning." Then the line went dead.

Carter had her safe-cell out calling Damon and Pythias – she was speaking in short clipped phrases. "You got something for Meg? Okay. It's important. We're on our way."

Meg had both their coats out of the closet, and was grabbing for her keys on the hall console.

"What the hell did she find?" she asked grimly.

Carter caught her partner's eyes and locked there. "And who else knows about it?"

63

Carter banged on the loft door and waited impatiently for the locks to click open. Damon looked relieved to see her.

"Got the envelope?" she asked, her voice taut.

"Right here – it came an hour ago."

Carter nodded acknowledgement. "This is escalating, guys. The intel in this envelope scared the bejesus out of the person who got it for us. It may make you change your mind about helping us. If that happens, you have to tell me straight up, OK?

"Not very likely," Pythias said. "This is just starting to get good."

Carter ripped open the envelope, scanned it, her expression turning from frown to genuine dismay. This was much more disturbing and much more detailed than what they'd already found – no wonder Sally had freaked. Her notes were meticulous and detailed. A dozen names of Top Secret Projects spawned by Paperclip, and all the tendrils she had unearthed. She'd outlined what each project appeared to have entailed – wherever she'd hit dead ends, she'd given the boys clues to where they might find more. Names like MK Ultra, Project 63, Safehaven and Eclipse were here, and every piece of intel seemed to point to something nefarious, illegal, clandestine or all three. Carter was reading the pages says aloud now, her voice taut.

"It ends with a list of questions," she said, her voice serious. "Listen up:

- Who in government is protecting Gruner, and who in the private sector? She read the names that followed, aloud. They were all well-known.
- Who *is the real enemy here?* Gruner, CIA, NSA, others you don't yet know about?
- How do the Neo Nazis tie in? Are they just the visible ground troops, or is there still an actual hierarchy of Nazis, much higher up and more dangerous than the skinheads and bikers?
- What links this Spear quest to the Middle East and terrorism?
- Is Al Qaeda involved?
- Is the U.S. military tangled up in this, and if so, *how?*
- Are all those nut-bag conspiracy theorists right, and we just never knew?
- What is *The 13* and who are its members? *There were even more prominent names listed here.*
- Why were so many of these files still Top Secret after more than half a century?

- Is it possible these programs never got shut down, but just went Black with the sanction of government?
- Is it possible there are government programs still in play that are progeny of Project Paperclip?
- Have some of these programs morphed into businesses that now appear legit?
- How many other tendrils of Black Ops, dating back to the 40's and 50's, are still operating? A list of corporate names followed. Many of them worldwide giants. There was also a list of hospitals, and research facilities.

The boys' demeanors had grown more intense as she talked, hunting dogs who'd caught the scent. A torrent of cryptic phrases were exchanged rapid fire. Pythias was already tapping keys at warp speed. Damon's big eyes had grown wider still, as he turned from his screen to face Pythias. She could see they were straining now to be let loose.

64

Lark sat on the floor, her ever-present laptop at her feet, the fire crackling cheerily in the hearth and sending dancing shadows to the wall beyond her. Lord Delafield and Prince Siegfried sat in the big leather armchairs that flanked the fire, drinking brandy from funny looking glasses they called snifters. The Prince had been at Heredon more than a week now, and both he and Lord Delafield had played in the Labyrinth with her every single day.

They were kind of like two almost-Grandpas, she thought watching them, even though they'd said she should call them Uncle instead of your Highness or *whatever*, even though they were very elegant and royal, which was pretty cool. She thought they were Knights of some ancient secret order, like Hugh, which, of course, wouldn't be too weird considering they were a real Prince and a real Earl.

Lark observed with interest the ease of their conversation, the hearty laughter and the frequent references to things they both understood and she didn't. She didn't feel left out, or that it was rude of them to converse this way, she thought it was just that they were really old and they'd done a lot of cool things together. They'd told her they'd been BFFs ever since they were her age and they were so old now that really was *forever!* The thought made her stifle a giggle. They always invited her to sit with them in Lord Delafield's library after dinner now, and that made her feel a little less lonely, because loneliness was worst at night. When they were all together she loved the stories they told. And sometimes they just played the game with her.

Her mommy had said she could talk to Lord Delafield about the clues if she wanted to, but she hadn't decided to show them *everything* she'd collected yet. Uncle Tony said both he and Uncle Siggy knew a whole lot about encryption from their war in the olden days, so she was beginning to think maybe they really could help her after all, but they weren't all that good at computer stuff because computers hadn't even been invented 'til they were pretty old. They were good at math and logic though and they were pretty smart like Hugh. She hoped maybe they could help her figure out her father's solution and then she could surprise her mommy when she got back. *If she ever got back...* the sobering thought brought her up short, but she sensed a lull in the old men's conversation and piped up, "Uncle Tony? Uncle Siggy?"

Both men looked at the child questioningly.

"I was wondering... do either of you happen to know anything about Bacon's Cipher?"

The two men exchanged glances. "We know it rather well, leibchen," Uncle Siggy said. "Why do you ask this?"

Lark looked relieved. "Because I think that's what this means, don't you?" She took a crumpled piece of paper out of her pocket, worked to unwrinkle it and handed it to Uncle Tony, who was closest to where she sat.

"This was the last Atbash clue I won," she said eagerly.

Gsv Gvnkozi Giryv
Rh mlg blfi Nfhv
Hszpvhkvzi'h hxiryv
Rmhgvzw, mld fhv.

"When you disencrypt it, it says:

The Templer Tribe
Is not your Muse
Shakespeare's scribe
Instead, now use.

"So I figure that means Bacon, right?"

"Very good, my dear!" Delafield applauded. "I believe it might, at that. How ever did you know Sir Francis Bacon had created a cipher?"

Lark grinned. "My real Grandpa told me about lots of ciphers, especially the ones from olden times before they invented computers." Then her face turned solemn again. "But I don't remember exactly how this one works, so I was hoping you might know. I could probably get it disencrypted online but I didn't want anyone else to know what it says. You know, in case anybody has hacked me?"

Prince Siegfried leaned forward in his chair and tapped the paper Delafield had handed on to him. "Very wise, my dear child. Very wise," he said. "And I am most pleased to tell you that Sir Francis Bacon's cipher was my favorite when I was a boy. My tutor told me he was one of the greatest intellects of his age, and so I wished to follow the pattern of his thoughts to see where they would lead me. Alas, they did not lead me to produce the works of Shakespeare, as so many believe Bacon did, but my studies did leave me with a working knowledge of his cipher. Do you have the next clue, so we may try our skills, perhaps?"

Lark pulled another crumpled scrap from her pocket and handed it to him.

"It's just a zillion A's and B's," she said as she handed it over.

The Prince laid the paper in the center of the table.

"Ah... yes," he said with obvious delight. "Baconian, without a doubt! Now, we must fetch paper and pencils and see what we can see?"

```
BAABBAABBBAABAA AAABBABBBAABBBABAAAB BAABBABBBA
BAABAABABBAABAAAABAAABBBB ABAAABAABA
BBAAAABBBABABAABAAABBAABA
AAAAAABABBABBBAABBABAABAA BBAAAABBBABABAABAAAB
BAABAAABAAAAABABAAABAABAABAABBBAABA
ABABAAABAAAABAAABBBB
BABBAABAAABAABBAABBBABAAAABBAB BAABBAABBBAABAA
BAABABAABBABBBAABBABAABAA AAAAA
AABBABABAAAAAAABAAABAAABBABAAAAAAAABBAB
BAABABAABBAAAAAABBABAAABBBAABA BAABBAABBBAABAA
BABBAABBBABAAABABABBAAABB
AAAAAAAAABABBBABABABAABAA AAAAA
AABABAAAAABAABBAABBBAABAABAAAB BAABA
AABBBAAAAAABBABAAABBBAABA
ABBBBBAAABABBBABAABBAABAAAAABABAABB
BABBAABAAABAABBAABBB ABABBABBBABABABAABAA
BAABBAABBBAABAA AABABBABAABAABBBABAABAAABAABAA
BAABA ABBBBBAAABABAAABBAABAABAA ABBBAABBAB
BBAAAABBBABABAA AAABBAABAAABBBBAABAAABBABAAABBBAABA
BBAAAABBBABABAABAAAB ABBBBABBBABABBAAABAABAAAB
ABABBABAAAAABAABAABA BABBAAABBBAABAABAAABAABAA
ABBBABAABBAABBBAABAABAAABBAABA
AABAAABBABAAABBBAABA
```

Twenty minutes later the disencryption lay before them on the table.

The door to sleep
Is yours alone
Your secrets keep
Within the Stone.

A guardian stands
The world above.
A father's hands
Protect with love.

The Future's prize
On you depends
Your power lies
When others' ends.

"Does this mean something to you, little one?" the Prince asked, studying the words.

Lark shook her head no, sadly. "It's the longest clue yet, though. Almost like three clues. But it still doesn't tell us where the stupid Spear is!"

"Perhaps not, leibchen," Prince Siegfried answered, "but it assures us you are on the right track and following the path through the Labyrinth as your dear father intended. So you must not lose heart." But he could see she'd been hoping for a revelation from this clue and now felt deflated. He looked at Delafield, who nodded that he, too, understood the child's dismay.

"Would you like to hear a tale about a time when the world was in grave danger and it was saved by people who did *not* give up just because the odds were against them..."

"And because they understood magic," Delafield added with enthusiasm.

Lark looked up, interest sparked. "You mean *real* magic? Is this a true story or a fairytale?"

"My dear child," the Prince said, leaning toward her, "Why do you not pull a chair up close to the fire and your Uncle Tony and I will tell you a tale of magic that we ourselves participated in, so we know it is quite *literally* true."

Lark's eyes widened, and Delafield got up from his chair and motioned for her to take his seat, as he tugged another upholstered armchair toward the hearth, making a cozy circle.

"My Daddy said there isn't any such thing as magic," Lark said judiciously, "except maybe Mommy has some."

Delafield and Von Hochburg exchanged amused glances. "Did he, now?" asked Delafield. "And what do you suppose he meant by that?"

"Well, he was a math person, you know, so he said he wasn't supposed to believe in anything math or science couldn't prove, but that Mommy knew things other people didn't. Like when stuff was going to happen before it did, and when the phone was going to ring. And she always knew when the people she loved were trying to reach her, even if she didn't have her cell phone..." Lark screwed up her face in the effort to remember more, then brightened. "And when our dog got hit by a car after he crawled under the fence, she knew exactly where to find him, even though he was two miles from home and we couldn't hear him barking."

"Yes, yes," Delafield said enthusiastically, "Uncle Siggy and I suspected as much about her from the start! You see magic is very real, my dear, but quite misunderstood. That's partially because few people have a true gift for it. Many *pretend*, of course, and that rather muddies the water. And, sadly, for hundreds of years, those who were the most gifted practitioners of the Magical Arts were hunted down and burned at the stake, so most were smart enough to keep their gifts secret, as you might imagine.

"But always, through the ages, there have been secret societies that protected the great knowledge and worked to use it for the good of humankind. We refer to it as the Great Work."

"Are there evil wizards, too, like in Harry Potter?" Lark asked, enraptured by the grown-up turn the conversation was taking.

"I'm afraid there are such men, leibchen," Prince Siegfried answered. "The Dark Arts were preserved by those greedy enough to seek power through selling their immortal souls. So another of the tasks of those who pledge their souls to the Forces of the Light, is to protect the earth and humanity from those who would use their powerful gifts for selfish ends."

"Wow!" Lark breathed fervently. "That's really cool."

Both men chuckled at the response.

"And so perhaps a story is in order here..." said Delafield. "One we saw with our own eyes."

Lark snuggled herself deeper into the big armchair in happy anticipation.

65

"The time was 1940," Uncle Siggy began, "and the Great War had already caused a good deal of suffering when Herr Hitler decided to send airplanes to drop his terrible bombs on London. So many bombs fell and so many people were killed and buildings smashed, that people thought the world was ending. Hitler called his air attack a Blitzkrieg, which means lightning war in the language of my country... but the Brits have come to remember it simply as the Blitz."

"Quite right," Delafield agreed. "And it was both devastating and terrorizing, Lark. Buildings falling, fires raging, smoke, chaos, injury and terrible loss of life..."

"Kind of like what happened on 9/11?" Lark offered.

"Very like that, I'm afraid," Delafield replied. "It was meant to cow us, you see," he saw a puzzled look came over the child's face and chuckled. "To make us *cowards*, my dear, not bovines. Sometimes our shared language is quite amusing don't you think?"

Lark giggled, but looked eager for him to continue.

"It became clear to us that Herr Hitler's plan was to subdue our fighting spirit with those lightning raids, and then to send occupying forces to invade our homeland itself, and make us prisoners. But there was something about us he wasn't expecting. An old secret you might say. You see, many of us, who were part of the war effort, were also from the old families, the ones who had various ties to elements of what you would call Magic."

Lark's eyes widened.

"But there was a bit of a snag in using it properly, you see, because there were so many rivalries among those secret societies who had genuine knowledge of the old ways."

"You mean like some were Black magicians and some were White?" she blurted.

"That, my dear, was only part of it! We had to make the assumption that the Black Adepts would be on Hitler's side, so we didn't want them at all. But even among the White Magic groups there were rivalries, some quite ancient. We had, after all, Druids, Witches, Pagans of all sorts... societies like the Golden Dawn and the Ordo Templi Orientis, the Priory, the Rosicrucians, the Knights of Malta and St. John and so on..."

"And the Knights Templar, too, right?" Lark added eagerly.

Delafield smiled benevolently at the precocious child. "Oh yes, my dear, the Knights Templar played a stellar role in all that transpired.

"At any rate, some of us decided to call a meeting of all the Good Wizards and Worshipful Masters and High Witches we could find, and ask that they put aside their petty squabbles and ancient rivalries, to protect this sceptered isle, as Shakespeare called it.

"I wasn't there in physical form, of course," Siegfried interrupted, "because I was under surveillance by the Reich at the time and couldn't leave Germany. But I attended the ritual on the Astral Plane, as did many others who serve the Light, the world over. However, I've heard many people in the years since, speak of your Uncle Tony's eloquence and diplomacy, in finding a way to get all these extraordinary, but obstinate beings, to agree to his plan."

"What was his plan?" Lark asked, eagerly.

Delafield continued, "I asked them to agree to come together on the one night of the year when the doorway between the worlds stands open..."

"Halloween!" she guessed excitedly.

"Precisely!" he answered. "But most of those assembled called it Samhain, and considered it a quite sacred time. We asked that all rivalries be put aside for this one night, and that every spiritual leader prepare the most powerful Adept of his Magical Art, to raise a cone of protection over the British Isles. A cone whose sole purpose would be to keep the Germans from invading our islands! The great ritual took place right here at Heredon, and a most wondrous night it was. Just imagine all those Witches and Wizards, Druids and Mages in full ceremonial regalia calling down the powers of The Light."

Lark, ever practical, wrinkled her nose.

"Maybe you should have just asked God to get rid of Hitler," she said, and both men burst out laughing.

"An astute thought, my dear, but you see, God does not *win* our battles for us by doing in our enemies – more's the pity. He does however give us help in helping ourselves. We felt this warding of our islands against invasion was allowable within Universal Law, because it would give us a fighting chance."

"And it worked?" she pursued.

"It did indeed! Each time Hitler planned to invade, he changed his mind at the very last minute. No one has ever been able to explain just why, although many have tried."

Lark nodded sagely. "Could you *see* this cone of protection? With your earth eyes, I mean?"

"Oh, most definitely!" Delafield answered. "It was like a vast network of golden filaments and stars, flung like a great fisherman's net into the night sky – a most glorious vision. Even those who didn't have The Sight, saw a strange golden glow in the heavens, but they thought it was from bonfires set to celebrate Samhain, you see."

Lark thought for a moment before speaking.

"That was a really nice story..." she said, judiciously, "but I think my Daddy would say you couldn't really *prove* it worked... like Hitler could have changed his mind for some *other* reason..." She saw their disappointment then added, "But I think my Mommy would believe you."

She smiled at the two old men, then hugged each of them goodnight, and headed for the door, but turned with her hand on the door knob.

"And I believe you, too," she said quietly. Then she slipped through the door and was gone.

66

The following morning, Lark re-read the clues she'd collected so far and her forehead wrinkled with annoyance. As far as she could see, they still meant nothing at all.

Where Care commenced
Is minus one
Justice dispensed
'til time is done.

The game is long
The road is steep
A promise strong
Is yours to keep

The trials once passed
The Feathers furled
The secret solved
Can save the world

His greaves are gold

His heart is fire
His power holds
Eternal ire.

She'd had to look up two words to even understand that one!
Now she copied in the latest clue and committed it to memory.

Be brave and bold
The secret keep
The truth is told
Before you sleep.

With a sigh, Lark relocked the book and put it back under her
pillow, then changing her mind, she snatched it up and left her
room.

She knocked tentatively at the door of Lord Delafield's study
and waited for his deep kindly voice. She pulled the heavy door
open, then closed it behind her. The light from the huge window
and the snow scene outside it, shone on his white hair making him
look like some kind of angel, or maybe a wizard.

"Good morning, my dear Lark," he said in his usual
affectionate tone. "To what do I owe this unexpected pleasure?"

Lark held out her diary, opened to the last page written on. "I
keep all the clues in here," she said without preamble. "I decided I
should show them all to you."

"Is that your journal, Lark?" he asked, and she nodded.

"In my experience, journals are rather private places where
one puts one's most important thoughts for later contemplation. Is
that true of yours, my dear?"

"I think so," she answered, "but I call it my diary."

"Ah..." he replied thoughtfully. "Then here is what I
propose: I will give you pen and paper to write down the clues and
you will keep your diary to yourself, so we don't impinge upon
your privacy. How does that sound to you?"

The child nodded vigorously.

"I assume you meant the clues for both Siggy and me... is that
right?"

She nodded again and he smiled.

"Excellent. Then why don't I ask Albert to let him know he's needed, and perhaps, while we're waiting, he could also ask cook to prepare a tray of cocoa for us all. Would that suit you?"

"Could we have tea instead?" Lark asked. "My Mommy and I used to drink tea a lot together."

"And so you shall again, my dear," he said, understanding the deeper need, unexpressed. "Tea is a splendid idea." He reached for the velvet cord that would summon the butler.

"In the meantime, why don't you take this pen and paper and copy out your clues. I'm most anxious to see if we can make something of them."

*   *   *

Lark had already been tucked into bed, when later that evening the two old men once again put their heads together over the accumulated clues. Each sat in his accustomed chair by the library hearth with a glass of brandy warming on the small table in front of him near the fire.

The table was filled with scraps of paper on which they had been scribbling possible letter configurations for the past hour.

"Has it struck you, Tony," Siegfried asked, after having reread the verses one more time, "that there isn't a single clue that has to do with an actual *place*?"

Delafield nodded. "It has," he said. "At first I assumed it was some manner of steganography – you know, new clues hidden within the old – or perhaps these few clues contained another letter sequence entirely, like that old gambit the Ruskies used to be so fond of using. But if it is that, I haven't found the key to it."

Siegfried cradled his glass, warming the bowl between two long-fingered hands, and said, "I have had another thought entirely. Let me try it out on you, Tony. Do you think it possible that Jack had no intention of providing specific directions within the game? He might have been concerned that others equally skilled could gather all the clues – or perhaps, some future computer software program would exist, capable of solving the riddle and therefore finding the Spear..." he took a sip of the golden liquid in his glass before continuing.

"Could it be possible that he was planting in the game, not *geographic* clues at all, but rather psychological and emotional ones that only his daughter could unravel? Clues meant to trigger for her, in some inspired moment, a sort of psychic epiphany about the Spear's whereabouts?"

Siegfried shook his head, "I'm not at all certain *precisely* what it is I'm suggesting here, Tony, but the utter absence of anything to do with geographic or material placement, makes me want to ask – could these clues be pointing our little Lark, by a circuitous route, to some knowledge *only* she and her father, in all the world, possessed?"

"So without Lark, no one and no artificial intelligence could ever solve the riddle?" Delafield finished.

"Would it not then be the ultimate perfect cipher?" Siegfried asked, warming to his own hypothesis. "What if the answer resides in Lark herself, and not in her game?"

The Game is Afoot

Part X

Knight: *You play chess, don't you?*
Death: *How did you know that?*
Knight: *I have seen it in paintings and heard it sung in battles.*
Death: *Yes, in fact I am quite a good chess player.*
Knight: *But you can't be better than I am.*

Ingmar Bergman
The Seventh Seal

—————————— **67** ——————————

Linc Tremaine, a man given to serious introspection, had been in a more than usually introspective frame of mind since Meg's visit. The Spear business had loosed memories that went far beyond his time in Germany.

He stared absently out the window of the limo taking him to Georgetown, but the landscape he was seeing in his mind's eye was rural Alabama. A sharecropper's cottage. Two dirt-poor women sacrificing everything to give him a shot at something better. It was his grandmama, who'd taught him to read... taught him pretty much everything of importance, he thought now, with a sigh. Child of a slave mother, who'd gotten "book larnin' " only because the plantation owner's daughter wanted company in her studies, his grandmama'd treasured the precious knowledge, and passed it on to him, knowing it was what made everything *better* possible. He thought about his father, murdered by the KKK... about his mother working as a charwomen until she died of some wasting sickness that was really just poverty and heartbreak... about his grandmama struggling to get him raised and educated, alone and poor and absolutely stalwart in her belief that she could do it, that he was worth it, and that God would help.

So many memories that could still flood his eyes with tears, still set his heart to pounding... so much firsthand knowledge about injustice, and so many years of learning how to fight it with the Constitution of the United States. Even looking back, it was impossible to fathom how anything but the grace of God and his

Grandmama's indomitable courage could have brought him to his seat on the United States Supreme Court.

What a long dusty road it had been, he thought, as he walked up the pristine steps of Senator Rudd Dandridge's Georgetown home: the road that had brought him to be General Patton's aide, and to the Spear of Longinus. Where would the road take him now, he wondered as he rang the ornate door bell.

A servant led Tremaine to an elegant drawing room.

"Good to see you Lincoln," Senator Dandridge said with his usual firm handshake and politician's meaningless smile.

"Always a pleasure, Senator," Tremaine responded in kind.

Rudd walked to one of the long tufted leather sofas that flanked the library fireplace and motioned Tremaine to the facing one. "To what do I owe the pleasure, Mr. Justice?" he asked with feigned affability. "Just what was so hush-hush it could not be spoken of on the phone?"

Tremaine glanced unhurriedly around the heavily wood-paneled room, noting the impressive array of photos of Dandridge with the greats and the near greats. Not surprising, of course, if your son is President of the United States, as Rudd's was, and you yourself have occupied a Senate seat for four decades. But Linc was in a strange mood this morning and he took his time before replying.

"I'm afraid that 'damned old relic' as you once called it, may have surfaced, Senator," he said finally, settling back to watch what effect his words would have.

Rudd sat up a little straighter and put down the glass he'd been about to sip from. "I told you a long time ago, Lincoln, I wanted nothing to do with the damned thing then, I want nothing to do with it now."

Tremaine nodded, his mouth in the thin line his law clerks had come to understand meant he was holding in words that wished to escape. "Be that as it may, Ruddy," he answered choosing for the first time to call the man by his old nickname. "You should probably know there have been three murders connected to it in the past week or so. John Monahan, his wife and son are all dead."

The senator's eyes nailed the old jurist's. "And you know this, *how*?"

"The tale grows stranger still," said Tremaine, utterly unfazed by the stare meant to intimidate lesser men. "I had a clerk a while back... smart as a whip. A young woman out of Harvard who went on to the Justice Department and then to a big New York City firm with a very fine recommendation from me, I might add. Hadn't heard from her in several years, but for the occasional Christmas or birthday card. It seems her sister was married to John's son, Jack. At the funeral Delafield spilled the beans about us to her..."

"Son of a bitch!" the senator exploded. "And why in Hell would he do such a damned fool thing?"

"Because Jack was the new Caretaker and he knows whoever tortured and killed him would put his wife Caitlin – my clerk's sister – next on the hit list."

"We might be on that list, too!" Dandridge interjected, obviously unconcerned about the Monahans' demise and very concerned about his own.

"So we might," said Tremaine, allowing himself a small twitch of the mouth at Dandridge's expense. Ruddy had never been known for his courage.

"Which is why I'm here. Just a heads up, so you'll know what's afoot. If I learn more, I'll let you know."

"I want nothing to do with this matter, Lincoln," Dandridge said softly and somewhat menacingly. "Do you understand me?"

Tremaine cocked his large, mostly grey head a little, and looked at Dandridge. "I've always understood you, Ruddy," he said, then got to his feet, to leave. "This call is just a courtesy."

Dandridge recollected himself – Tremaine was, after all, a Supreme Court Justice, not the aide de camp he'd once been. "Yes. Yes, of course. Forgive me, Lincoln, for sounding abrupt. This is just very disturbing news. I do appreciate your coming by, of course. I'm sure it'll all turn out to be just a tempest in a teapot...

nothing to concern us after all these years. After all, John was the Caretaker, not the rest of us."

Tremaine nodded. There was really nothing left to say.

*   *   *

Standing at one of the floor to ceiling windows that flanked his entry hall, Senator Rudd Dandridge watched the resolute old black giant walk down the steps to his waiting car. He'd always felt like a coward about this whole affair of the Spear. The others, he suspected, had each pulled his own weight in the Caretaking role over the years, in some fashion he couldn't even imagine, while he had always abstained when any issue arose.

Just like being in the Senate, he thought, with a wry smile – you can vote *aye, nay* or just *present* – a perfect way to avoid ever being hung with a decision's consequences.

He could call over to the Oval and ask his son for some Presidential-level protection, of course. But that would mean he'd have to explain things about the past that were maybe better left unmentioned. Some muckraking journalist might cause havoc with it now, he thought – his son's presidency and his own next senate race didn't need that.

Why the hell hadn't he asked Lincoln for more details about John's murder? He obviously knew more than he'd let on. Had John been tortured before he died? Had he spilled the names of the other three conspirators? Why the hell hadn't he just told them where the damned thing was, so nobody else would be in danger? Why had they ever agreed to the conspiracy in the first damned place!

Dandridge pulled the heavy lace curtain aside and scanned the nearly empty street with a sudden sense of danger. If John Monahan had spilled his guts under torture, which was damned likely, they were all marked men. *Was that van supposed to be parked there? Who was that man standing with his back against the lamppost? Who just loiters like that on a Georgetown street?*

The senator felt his heartbeat suddenly escalate, and dropped the curtain. *This was just foolish paranoia.* He'd have to get a grip. There was no evidence of anything to worry about – not a shred. This was just unexpected and disturbing news, nothing more serious than that. Certainly nothing to warrant telling an unsavory old story to the President of the United States.

He wondered who would be the next to die.

68

Linc thought about the Senator's reaction, as his car moved onto the Beltway. It was entirely possible that John Monahan had given up the names of the conspirators before he died. Linc had seen reams of data about torture in the years since Rumsfeld had championed changing the laws to allow it. Surely no man could withstand seeing his wife tortured in front of him – and, if that was what had happened to John, they could all be targets. Unless of course, John had also told them that only one of the conspirators knew the truth and that's why they'd gone after his son. From the beginning, Linc had made the assumption that they'd moved on to Monahan's son's house because they knew he was the heir to the secret. But, he realized as he now assessed the possibilities, that didn't mean they thought he was the *only* heir.

It struck Linc as interesting that he felt none of the physical fear he'd read in Ruddy. He'd lived a long life of rich experience, and whatever God had in mind for his remaining time on earth was just fine by him. But common sense did suggest that a little extra caution might be prudent under the circumstances. And perhaps it wouldn't hurt to see what he could find out about this famous Dr. Gruner. If Gruner really was a war criminal who not only had escaped justice, but had managed to insinuate himself into a position as political advisor to the President, he had to be unmasked. Or at least neutralized. Better still, he should be brought to justice. Not that it would be an easy task.

What was it Sun Tzu had said... something like '*if you know the enemy and know yourself, you need not fear the result of a hundred battles. If you know yourself but not the enemy, for every victory gained you will suffer a defeat.*' It appeared it was time for him to get to know the enemy. That Sun Tzu, was a smart old boy, but Gruner – *if* he really was Guttman and head of The 13 – was smart, too. Linc would have to be very discreet with his inquiries.

Lincoln knocked on the window that separated him from his driver. "I've changed my mind about our destination, I'm afraid," he said to the man behind the wheel. "If you don't mind, son, I'd like to head on over to the Library of Congress."

He realized after he'd said it, that it had been dogs' years now since he'd had to do his own research – all those fine young clerks of his had been only too happy to get him anything he'd needed in case law. But this was different, and needed the kind of discretion best understood by *old* men. He hoped Arnold Peabody was still alive and still at work as an archivist at the Library. He was just the kind of man to point him in the right direction, while keeping the inquiry tucked away in the vault that was his remarkable librarian mind.

*   *   *

Lincoln did not find Arnold Peabody at the Library of Congress. Instead he was told the man had retired nearly ten years before, and now resided with his granddaughter and her two young sons in Bethesda. When he followed up by asking for Peabody's address, the spikey-haired young girl behind the desk had quite rightly, although somewhat rudely, refused his request. Finally an older manager of some sort, who had recognized Linc, told the young woman she was speaking with Justice Lincoln Tremaine of the Supreme Court of the United States. The girl, now thoroughly embarrassed, blurted out, "Oh no, I thought Justice Tremaine was dead!" which made Linc laugh so loudly, he was soundly shushed by the head librarian.

69

Matt knocked on the door of the Captain's office, wondering which of the current homicides he was working had piqued the man's interest enough for a meeting. Captain Ferguson, a street cop in his youth, seldom interfered with his men unless they screwed up.

"You wanted to see me, Captain?" Matt said, entering the small crowded office, cluttered with papers and file folders on every surface. His boss looked up, an unreadable expression on his square, pugnacious face. He was good-natured as bosses go, but it was always hard to read his mood.

"I've gotten the word from the higher-ups that you've been nosing around in a few places that may not concern you, McCormack. Is there some case you're working I don't know about, that can explain why you'd risk stepping on big toes?"

Matt riffled through his mental Rolodex fast, trying to figure out which of the many phone calls he'd made on this Spear business could have provoked both an immediate response, and a rebuke.

"Sir, I'm not sure I know which inquiries you mean. I've got a number of actives, as you know, but I don't..."

"Cut the crap McCormack!" the Captain barked, interrupting. "You've been asking questions about a VIP named Gruner, and that's ruffling feathers at One Police Plaza, which means it's already ruffled feathers somewhere higher up the ladder. I don't know what this is about, but whatever it is, I suggest you cease and desist, unless this has something vital to do with one of your ongoing homicides?" He cocked an eyebrow at Matt, as if to ask if that were the case.

When Matt didn't volunteer any information, Ferguson made a harrumphing sound, then pinned Matt's eyes with his own. "I thought that might be the way it is. And by the way, just so you have a really clear picture of what a heavy foot just landed on my neck, even if it *does* have to do with a legitimate case, you are being ordered to *back off Gruner*." He emphasized the last words.

Matt's eyebrows came together in a puzzled frown. "Did they say why, sir?"

The Captain put his pen down on the desk with an exasperated thump. "They did not. And I didn't ask, based on the less than cordial tone of the message. Whatever bone you have in your teeth here, McCormack, I'm ordering you to drop it and bury it. *Now!* Gruner has friends in high places, that you and I don't. Do I make myself crystal clear?"

"Yes, sir."

"Then you're dismissed."

Matt walked out of the captain's office puzzled and worried. How the hell had the higher-ups heard about his inquiries so damned fast? Most of his calls had only been made in the past two or three days. And why had they come down so hard on the Captain? Had he accidentally requested some file that would have shed light on this mess? He would have given a month's pay to know which file it was that had set off the alarm.

Croce looked up from his desk as Matt passed by, a quizzical expression on his face, but Matt signaled with his eyes and body language that a conversation right now wasn't a good idea. Croce nodded and glanced at his watch. Lunchtime was only forty minutes away and should be interesting.

*   *   *

"So who did you tap about Gruner, who might have blown the whistle? You think it was the old lady?" Croce asked after he'd heard a replay of the conversation. They were walking on Fifth, headed toward the park. The smaller man pulled up his coat collar as he spoke. The damp wind was biting and they were walking directly into it.

"I hit up Richardson, another lawyer who's with NCIS, two guys at State, checked the dead records office, did a computer search, *and* talked to the old lady."

"She sounds like your bell ringer to me," Croce said with disgust. "The CIA's pet law firm knew where every skeleton was buried since the '40's. They even knew where the skeletons buried their skeletons."

Matt nodded. "You got that right. And the old broad was some tough case. How about you? Rattle any chains that could have caused repercussions?"

Croce snorted a puff of steam into the cold air. "Yeah, I rattled a few. The word could be out there that I'm nosing around."

"If you want out of this," Matt said evenly, "that's not a problem for me, Croce. It's starting to look like a career ender and you don't need that."

"You're kidding me, right? Nobody comes down on you this hard and fast if they ain't got nothin' big to hide. It pisses me off that this Gruner jerk has everybody bowing and scraping, when he's a murdering lowlife son of a bitch."

Matt let out a small wry laugh. "Yeah, there is that."

The two men walked in silence for a few steps before Matt spoke again.

"Maybe Carter or her cyber snoops got some place for us to poke around that won't lead directly back to the precinct. I'll stop by there after work and see if there's anything new. Wanna come with me?"

Croce looked distracted. "Nah. I got another place to try. I'll call you if it looks promising, OK?"

Absentmindedly, Matt pulled the scarf Meg had given him last Christmas up around his neck, before he spoke again. "Just do me a favor and watch your six, ok? This whole thing feels really weird to me... disproportionate, you know? Like the girls might have really stepped in it this time. I don't like it when I can't get a grip on what's going on."

"Yeah, I'm thinking the same thing, boss. But we need a helluva lot more intel and I've still got a bunch more people I can put the arm on..."

"Discreetly, right?"

Croce laughed out loud. "Ever know me not to be the soul of discretion?"

The men parted company and Matt headed back toward the precinct house alone.

*   *   *

Just before the shift ended, Croce stopped by Matt's desk, his voice was low and conspiratorial. "I got something small but interesting for you on that matter of mutual concern."

Matt's brain flipped from the case he'd been working, to Cait's. "OK," he said, "Shoot."

"You know your feisty old lady?"

"What about her?"

"She's been on the government payroll since 1950!"

"So? She could have a pension..." Matt began.

"No pension. I'm talking *payroll*. From the Feds. While she was working her other gig at the law firm, and ever since. The old broad just never came in from the cold."

"How'd you find out?"

"I got Carter's guys to hack her bank records. Right after your visit, the old lady got a nice bonus. So we gotta figure she reported back to whoever the fuck she works for."

"OK. So maybe we shouldn't be talking about this here."

"Yeah. So back to the salt mines. But this is getting real interesting."

70

The Skinhead Bar was grungy even by the standards Croce had come to expect of this ugly area of the East Village. "God bless the First Amendment," he murmured sarcastically to himself as his eyes focused through the gloom and cigarette smoke, on the giant Swastika that adorned the wall behind the bar, and the garish posters that emblazoned the other walls. In a place of prominence was a flag with a giant number 14 sewn on it. He knew 14 was code for the 14 word manifesto of terrorist David Lane, that had become the battle cry of the whole white supremacist movement. Another showed a huge 88, the code for Heil Hitler. Pointy-hooded KKK figures burned a cross in a poster that read ORION, the acronym for Our Race is Our Nation. *Fight Jew Lies* was a banner running across the wall. *Sheesh!*

He scanned the room for the face he sought, and spotting him at a booth at the far end of the bar, he locked eyes with the man for the briefest of moments – just before a huge skinhead, who had to be the bouncer, barred his way with a mountainous beer belly and biceps the size of steel-belted radials.

"Man, I don't want no trouble," Croce said, trying to sound like a guy who'd stumbled into the wrong door, and was scared to find out where he'd landed. "This place ain't what I was lookin' for."

The big man grinned, two missing teeth making his huge face a Halloween pumpkin. "What was it you was lookin' for, *exactly?*" he said with exaggerated articulation, tapping Croce's chest with a meaty finger.

Croce held up his hands, palms forward, as if to nervously ward off whatever the jerk planned to dish out next.

"Nothin' man!" he stuttered, backing toward the door. "I just wanted a beer is all. I'll just get outta your way..."

Amused by the smaller man's obvious terror, the behemoth shoved him toward the door so hard, Croce stumbled.

"We ain't got beer for no Jews here," he said raising his hand for a second shove, but before it landed, Croce grabbed the arm in an iron fist of his own, and twisted it violently backward into an Aikido elbow lock. It was a particularly effective move against an aggressive giant because it used the opponent's weight and momentum against itself, causing maximum pain and incapacity. The unexpected anguish forced the big, stunned man's knees to buckle.

"I ain't no Jew, Motherfucker," Croce hissed at the astounded bouncer, "I'm a WOP and I don't want your stinking beer."

Men were pouring off the bar, but Croce was out the door in a sprint, and around the darkened corner before most of the crowd had decided whether to chase him, or go back for another round. Only three men kept up the pursuit down the dark village streets until they lost sight of him two blocks later.

"He ain't worth it!" one of the chasers pronounced, puffing his way to a breathless halt.

"Who'd 'ya think he was?" the other asked, panting frost clouds into the air. "He had some real good moves, for a little guy."

"Ex-military is my guess," the first one pronounced. "Let's not worry about it. No way he's comin' back tonight." He wheeled back toward the bar and the other man turned with him.

"You comin'?" he called out to the third man, who'd peeled out the door just after them – a tall, rangy guy in military camies. "Nah," the man called back, shaking his bald, tattooed head. "I had enough for tonight. I'm gonna hit the rack."

"Suit yourself, Ace," the first guy called over his shoulder, as he and his sidekick ambled back toward the bar. "Its cold as a witch's tit out here – we're headin' back in."

The tall man grunted an unintelligible response, and then turned in the opposite direction. He walked two blocks, then turned back to where he'd spotted Croce in a darkened alley.

The man looked around as casually as he could, although his honed instincts had already told him no one had followed. But staying alive in deep undercover work meant you never took anything for granted.

"Swell show you put on back there, dude," he said to Croce. "Real impressive."

"Yeah, well he pissed me off" Croce replied.

"I got that. The question is why stick your nose in there to begin with? You were expecting to get welcomed into the fold, maybe? You shouldda Seig Heiled, if you wanted to join up."

"I needed your input," Croce said, "on a sorta-kinda case I'm working."

"Ah..." the big man said with a snort, "so lemme guess... you figured sorta/kinda cases are my specialty?"

"Something like that," Croce said.

"And you didn't think a cell phone would be maybe a less conspicuous way to communicate?"

"Cells get tapped," Croce said, "and you hang with a paranoid crowd of scumbags, JC."

The big man laughed softly, "True enough," he acknowledged, "so what exactly can I do for you, my man?"

"Would any of those aforementioned scumbags know anything about a missing spear?"

JC's posture went rigid and still. Of all the deep cover cops Croce had worked with over the years, JC was the one he respected most. Undercover assignments tended to change men, or maybe bring out something that had lain dormant in them, waiting for an excuse to take over. JC was still righteous. At least he had been about a year ago when Croce had last made contact.

"The Heilege Lanze," JC answered. He'd dropped the street patois, and sounded serious. "Yeah, I heard something."

"So spill," Croce nudged. "What do you know?"

JC checked the street again, now on high alert.

"There's a legend about the Heilege Lanze," he said. "It's like the Grail to these dudes."

"Yeah, yeah, I know all that crap," Croce cut him off. "But what's going on *now* about it?"

"Shut up and listen!" JC said the words with quiet menace. "I tell it my way or you can take a hike, Croce. The legend is part of the hit."

"Somebody's ordered a hit?" Croce interrupted again. JC skewered him with a death stare that said *interrupt me like that again and I'm out of here.* Croce held up his hands in a gesture of surrender.

"Hitler thought this Holy Spear had magical powers," JC began again, his voice barely above a whisper. "The real one disappeared after the war. A lot of my scumbag set would kill to lay hands on it. Word on the street is it's surfaced recently and some people have died, and some woman might know where it is, so there's this bounty somebody's placed on it. Mostly rumors. Nobody knows for sure if the bounty is really a million bucks – that's the number being bandied about – or a buck fifty. You know, inside the scumbag regime there are circles within circles and only the inner circle knows the whole story. But the rumors are flying hot and heavy that some higher ups have started a search. The scuttlebutt is you're not supposed to kill the woman until she gives up the Spear – if you kill her before that, you're dead meat, but you should feel free to mess her up as bad as you want to get the Spear info out of her." His eyes wise and cynical, fixed Croce with another stare. "That the Spear you're talking about?"

"The very Spear," Croce affirmed. "And how about the name Gruner? Does that ring any bells?"

"Are we talking *the* Gruner?" JC asked. "Everybody's favorite dinner guest?"

"Yeah," Croce answered. "That's the very Gruner."

JC pursed his lips, impressed. "I hadn't connected *those* dots before," he said thoughtfully. "But that's about as high up the chain as anybody gets. You think he's the one ordered the hit?" Croce shrugged.

JC made a move to leave the alley. "I'll keep my ears open," he said. "Just don't come near the bar again. You get me killed, I swear to God I'll take you with me."

"So how will I stay in touch?"

"You won't," JC snapped. "I will, if there's a reason."

He was gone so swiftly and stealthily, he might never have been there at all.

71

Germany

Fritz lay back against the pillows of the great Jacobean bed that dominated his dark, oppressive bedroom, and sighed with satisfaction. By God, she was a magnificent fuck, he thought as the sweat he was drenched in began to cool on his skin, and he reached across Marta's body absently, for the 1000 thread count sheet he intended to pull up to cover them. Indefatigable, and an utterly perfect physical specimen. Breasts, hips, waist, legs, all faultless. And she was possessed of more skills than any whore he'd ever had, at any price. What a find she was! What a fine fucking find, and right here in his own household. How on earth had he not noticed her before?

"Have you ever been to the states?" he asked her suddenly, as he felt her reach again for his semi exhausted penis. The lascivious look in her eyes almost made him hard again, but he brushed her hand away and opted for a few more moments of leisure before the next bout. She'd graced his bed for enough nights, and a few days, too, so he had no doubt that another bout would follow. And then another after that, if he so desired.

"The States?" she asked, seemingly dazzled by the idea. "I've never been!" She said it in the sexy, breathy voice he found so very provocative, like everything else about her. "But I have always dreamed of going there one day, Fritzy. I want to see the Statue of Liberty and Disneyland." She laughed musically and he laughed, too, at her simple tastes, and her pleasantly simple disposition that seemed to want nothing more than to have him fuck her brains out as often as possible.

"My father is going to the U.S. for a few weeks, and there is business for me to attend to there. Would you like it if I were to take you with me, Marta?" he asked it, knowing what a great treat he was offering. He was also feeling a little thrill of the forbidden. He knew the suggestion of taking Marta to Bedford would make the old man dyspeptic.

Marta propped herself up on one elbow, with childlike adoration in her eyes. "You could do that?" she exclaimed. "Your father would let you do such a thing?" She planted the bomb, hoping she'd not gone too far in invoking the old tyrant's obvious domination of his son. But men were never at their sharpest right after sex. She imagined the blood from the brain had found other places to be that were more fun, so she thought she might be able to provoke him without antagonizing him too much.

Fritz frowned. "I do not have to ask my father's permission!" he snapped. "If I choose to take you there, I will take you there! I am the one who chooses."

"Oh, Fritzy," she cooed. "I would so love to go with you! Oh please, *please* find a way to do this, *liebchen*. I know such a trip would stimulate my imagination so much I would think of *so* many new ways to please you." She began to lower her hair to his groin to underscore the promise, but she felt her head jerked suddenly backwards as his fingers tightened their grip. She yelped in pain.

"We do what *I* want, when I want it!" he growled, "do you understand me?"

Marta tried to answer, but he was forcing her face down onto the bed so she couldn't breathe. Still holding her helplessly by her hair, he slapped her viciously across her bare buttocks. Then, he hit her again and again and again, until she begged him, sobbing, to stop.

And he did. But when she tried to rise, he threw her back down onto the bed and took her from behind, driving into her with such frenzy she had to grab the bedpost to keep from having the force of his thrusts crash her head into the lavish oak headboard.

When he'd climaxed, Fritz collapsed on top of her and lay there, like a dead man. Marta waited, stunned by the ferocity of the attack, and not wanting to provoke another until she'd had time to think how to deal with it without blowing her cover. She had ample skills to protect herself in an ordinary situation, but this was far from ordinary. Her Grav Maga techniques could take him down but would also blow her cover and end her op.

When she finally heard the soft snores that indicated Fritz was asleep, she wriggled carefully out from under his large body, and made her way to the bathroom.

It wasn't that she hadn't known that he had a capacity for violence, but, up to now, she'd felt she could control it with sex. She'd have to proceed carefully from here on. It was the mention of his father that had opened such floodgates. What rage this man must keep bottled up inside, in order to keep the old man's trust and money. She wondered what horrors Fritz's childhood might have held, and filed the thoughts away in the psychological profile of the man she was constructing for her handler.

Marta sifted through the details of what had just transpired, as she stood later in the shower and the stinging hot water sluiced over her body. It hadn't been pleasant to endure, but it had shown her how rapidly things were deteriorating. Something was afoot, and if she could keep her wits about her, and not let Fritz kill her in one of his rages, she might just be able to do the job she'd come here to do. If bringing down Gruner meant putting up with some risky sex from his psycho son, it might even be worth the pain. Her grandmother had died at Gruner's hands and her mother had never recovered from losing her entire family in the camps. That was motivation enough for her to put up with a little rough sex. And in the end, if she were really lucky, maybe she'd get a chance to give the bastard a taste of his own medicine.

72

Ruddy Dandridge loosened the collar of his shirt, then took a sip of his hastily poured whiskey. He was almost certain someone was following him and just the thought had ratcheted up his blood pressure. If only he could be certain it wasn't just some frightened fantasy... but he had always had an overactive imagination when it came to danger. Even as a boy, he'd made it a point to avoid dangerous games, a skill that had later served him well in Washington.

It was all the fault of that damnable Spear – he'd always known it was a bird of ill omen. John or Jack Monahan must have cracked under torture and given up the names of the other conspirators, and now he himself, was on somebody's radar. *No! Stop that,* he admonished himself. If Tremaine and Delafield weren't being harassed, why would anybody be after him? He'd never known a damned thing about the *damned thing*!

If he could only be sure about the tail... He didn't want to look like a paranoid old fool and he didn't want to have to divulge the story of the Spear, so there really wasn't anything to do about all this except to take extra precautions. And maybe speak to his son.

But he'd have to think a bit more before doing that – some stories are just better left buried. How could he tell RJ he'd stolen one of the spoils of the Second World War, implicate a long dead General in a theft, and a conspiracy of silence so bizarre it bordered on the ludicrous? Who would believe him? *No one!* But it could precipitate an investigation and lots of media speculation about both his honesty – if they believed the story – or his sanity, if they didn't. It was a lose-lose situation. *Shit!* Ruddy polished off the clear amber liquid and poured himself another. He was just acting like an old fool. He reached for the remote control for the television and tried to calm down.

73

Aunt Nell woke from the disturbing dream with a start. It hadn't been an ordinary dream, but rather the revelatory kind she'd had from childhood, the ones that had marked her with what her Irish family called the Second Sight.

For the most part, she cherished the gift. It had, after all, provided her with a very fine living in the years since her husband's death, and she believed she had used it always for the good of others, never maliciously, never for inordinate personal gain. Not once had she asked for tomorrow's lottery numbers.

In childhood it had been a different matter, of course. Nell'd had to learn early not to greet anyone until she was absolutely certain that person was also visible to others. It had taken quite a while before she could differentiate on her own between the corporeal and the non. She'd also had to keep her communication with angels to herself, and not share their messages in the schoolyard. And she'd had to learn what to tell to whom, and under what circumstances, because people for the most part couldn't bear to hear the truths that came to her, about the future, about life, and most especially about death. The information she received about impending deaths had always seemed to her more curse than gift, but today she thought it could maybe help her protect Matthew.

Nell blessed herself and sighed. There was serious trouble ahead for Matt and for people he cared deeply about, that was clear. In fact, his whole life was about to be upended by his generous attempt to help a woman and a child, but she couldn't see clearly how the difficulties would unfold. Some things were simply blocked from her vision, because they had to be played out without her assistance. She'd learned *that* long ago. Sometimes, a soul was tested in some crucible that demanded all decisions be made alone – other times, intervention might be permitted, or even mandated, and so she applied her gifts to those cases in which the Almighty had chosen to use her as a messenger.

Nell got out of bed and stood at the window, trying to sort her memory of what she'd just been shown in the dream vision, before any of it was lost. She struggled, too, to figure out what had been veiled from view, because sometimes knowing what had been hidden from her, helped her understand the Big Picture.

The dream had taken her to the Library – the Akashic Records – where all life on earth had been stored, past, present and future. "All is already written on the Eye of God," her mentor in all things spiritual had told her many years before.

Although knowledge came to Nell in many different ways, when something of great consequence was to be revealed to her, she would sometimes find herself in the library, in the company of the august Librarian of all Time/Space, and he would show her a page in a book, or unfold before her eyes, a scene that explained what was expected of her, or show her a pre-cognitive glimpse of a moment to come. Of *those to whom much is given, much is expected* – she had been told this by the Librarian, whose name she knew, but was not permitted to reveal, for his name was the key to accessing the truths that lay within the Library itself. The visions had never, in all her long life, been wrong.

But last night's dream had been unusual. In it, the Librarian had taken her on a journey to a variety of places, in multiple time-frames. All were connected in some way to the Spear that was a Way-Shower – the Spear that awarded both power and holiness, but which had been, too often, in the grip of those who wanted only its power. She'd been shown that each Owner could have chosen to use the Spear's magic for the common good – so, it was a test of conscience. Seen, too, that each time the Spear came into play, mankind stood at some moral crossroads. Compassion or Power. Good or Evil. The Spear could tip the balance, but the choice was always in the hands of the possessor. And too often, they chose wrong.

Nell hugged herself against the chill in the apartment, or perhaps the chill of what she'd just seen. She hadn't been told what would be expected of Matt, or of her, for that matter, but she had seen glimpses of scenes to come, all of them unsettling. And she had seen the Angel of Death quite clearly. She'd seen him often enough in this life to know that when he appeared to her like this, he didn't leave empty-handed. She just didn't know whose soul he was coming to collect.

She thought about calling Matt... warning him... but of *what*? What could she say that would make any sense to him?" The only thing she was sure of, was that something much bigger than the Spear itself was involved here. Bigger than the small human lives that were pawns in this game. But one of those lives meant a great deal to *her*, and another seemed to mean a good deal to *him*. And, she knew all too well that souls are tested, sometimes cruelly, sometimes even sacrificed, on the road to salvation. She hoped some terrible sacrifice was not going to be exacted here. But she wouldn't have wanted to take odds on it.

Gather the Players

Part XI

"The object of war is not to die for your country, but to make the other bastard die for his."

General George Patton

74

Cardinal Andretti, when he chose to intimidate subordinates, had a habit of barreling through the Vatican corridors. He was a large heavy man who was known for grand entrances, as well as grand tantrums, so in deference to his august status, his famous irascible temper, and his bulk, underlings generally scattered before him like hens in the barnyard.

Andretti was in high dudgeon today and no one had the temerity to wonder why. He had long since earned his right to any mood or any conduct he wished to display. Power was always recognized and admired in the Vatican.

In fact, his annoyance had been caused by a singularly unsatisfactory meeting about Pacelli's cause for sainthood. Damn the Jesuit Postulator for his judicial timidity, and his unspeakably conciliatory manner toward these obstructionist Jews. Just because yet another delegation had been sent from Israel to protest the idea of canonizing Pius XII, there was no reason whatsoever to slow their plans. Damage control was what was called for... not a pusillanimous display of molly-coddling and spineless capitulation.

Andretti stormed into his own office and slammed the outer office door so hard his American secretary dropped the pen he'd been writing with, and disappeared under his desk in a futile effort to retrieve it.

"Leave the pen where it is, for the love of God!" the Cardinal thundered at the young priest, who thought he'd grown impervious to Andretti's unpredictable tantrums, but was still occasionally unnerved by the explosions. "I have no interest in staring at the posterior of your cassock while you root around like a truffle hound."

The young man clambered back onto his chair, returning his posterior to a properly dignified position.

"You will clear my calendar for this evening immediately, and summon the people on the list I'm about to give you," Andretti ordered. "And I suppose there is no need to tell you that both this list and the fact that these men have been summoned, is not to be grist for the Vatican gossip mill? Your discretion, I assume, is above reproach, Father?" he fixed the young man with a ferocious glare.

"Oh yes, sir... I mean Eminence," the young man stammered. "They won't get the names out of me with thumbscrews."

Andretti eyed him again, to see if this last remark was evidence of some unseemly American humor, but he saw only contrition and a touch of terror in the boy's blue eyes.

"You may come for the list in seven minutes," he said portentously, then turned and entered his elegantly appointed office. Generally, his meetings of Deus Vult were conducted outside the grounds, but he'd had his office swept for surveillance devices earlier today, and there was some urgency about this meeting. The information he'd received about the Spear business had started the day off on the wrong foot. It seemed every Intelligence Service on record was now involved in the damned Spear hunt.

*   *   *

Andretti yanked the folder from the top drawer of his desk and snapped it open, to peruse it one more time. The process of Beatification and Canonization was as familiar to him as the rosary tucked under his cassock, but it never hurt to refresh his memory on specifics before addressing the *Deus Vult* delegates. They were a damnably scholarly lot – none had less than one doctorate – and he couldn't afford any mistakes.

The process of making a saint usually began at the diocesan level, where a Bishop with jurisdiction – usually the one from the place where the candidate for sainthood had been born or died –

gave permission for an investigation to be opened into the virtues of the individual to be canonized, who was from that point forward called "the Servant of God." Five years were supposed to elapse after the Servant's death, before the process could begin, although occasionally this rule was not followed.

Once enough ecclesiastical investigation has been done, the Bishop then presented the case to the Roman Curia's Congregation for the Causes of the Saints, and a Postulator was assigned, who then took over the investigation. In the case of Pius XII's petition for Sainthood, the Jesuit Postular General had been chosen.

It was only natural that the Church's elite cadre of intellectuals and strategists had been given this task. The Jesuits were known for their competency, their relentless adherence to their own code, and their loyalty to their own Governor General. Strict obedience to the Vatican, had never been high on their priority list.

Nonetheless, Andretti had to admit the choice of the annoying Jesuit Postulator General, to further the cause of Pius XII had been an inspired one. After all, twelve Jesuit priests had already been formally recognized by *Yod Vashem*, the Holocaust Martyrs and Heroes Authority in Jerusalem, for having risked their lives during the war to save Jews from the Holocaust, and another 152 Jesuits had been honored for giving their lives during that time.

And, truth be told, the Jesuit P.G. had so far done a credible job fending off the dissenting Jewish voices, who had sought to derail Pius' Canonization. He'd gotten the old boy as far as Beatification – probably because, unlike Andretti, he actually believed Pius deserved the honor. Having already proved him "heroic in virtue," to get him past the Venerable stage of the process, the Jesuit who was now working diligently on the Beatification stage, had even somehow managed to document the necessary *bona fide* miracle without any help from the Cardinal, whose name was now popularly linked with Pius XII's bid for Sainthood.

Soon, another miracle would be required – one attributed to the direct heavenly intercession of the deceased candidate for sainthood. After that, the process was inevitable with all its attendant hoopla, cheering nuns, hawked artifacts and prayer cards – then, equally inevitably, a waterfall of new miracles would sluice in, and Eugenio Pacelli, aka Pius XII, would be given his own Saint's Day on the calendar, and the whole tedious process would prove to have been worth all the trouble because of what it would do for Andretti's career. It was his ticket to the Papacy.

No man got to be a Cardinal without being either unusually holy or a consummate politician – having failed at the first possibility, Andretti had succeeded at the second. He had worked and cajoled and schemed and plotted to be in the forefront of every media event that allowed him to proclaim the impeccable *holiness* of His Holiness the wartime Pope, believing utterly that he would finally be rewarded for his endless efforts, by achieving St. Peter's throne. He would not allow anything to upset his applecart now.

He picked up the disturbing article from the Israeli News Service, that sat at the rear of the dossier, and reread it for the sixth time. He intended to make use of it, too, at tonight's meeting.

Beatification of Pope Pius XII is Halted by Vatican was the bold headline on the lengthy article. That cursedly thorough reporter had touched on every single sore-point in this whole contentious mess! Inflammatory statements told the tale of a pontiff who had studiously skirted denouncing Germany's heinous acts against humanity, throughout the war. Never once had he spoken of the extermination of Jews or called for Catholics to defend those who were being brutalized and slaughtered. Even after the war had ended, Pius had never clearly denounced the atrocities.

The article quoted a spokesman for a central organization for Jewish groups as saying, Pius XII had been worried about burning bridges with Germany, and had therefore never denounced the monstrous extermination of millions of Jews, either during or after the war. He said the plan to beatify Pius XII, who was Pope between 1939 and 1958, would deal a severe blow to relations between the Catholic Church and the entire Jewish world.

Cardinal Andretti stared at the article thinking about his infuriating conversation with the Jesuit today. The man, a conciliator by nature, intended to slow the process until this newest assault could be handled. This was the opposite of what needed to be done and Andretti had told him so in no uncertain terms. But to no avail.

So he would bring *Deus Vult's* most useful, clever and devious members up to date, and make certain they would then light a fire under the Jesuit. Any pressure this annoying Postulator General might be feeling from the Jewish delegation, would seem like child's play by comparison. Andretti liked to think of it as his *Death by a Thousand Mosquito Bites* ploy – a manipulation by minutia that could drive any man mad.

A sudden thought occurred to him. He'd better make certain there was no damning evidence findable *anywhere* in the Vatican archives that could in any way corroborate the stories the Jews were telling about the Pope's ties to Hitler. All tales of complicity could be dismissed as cruel gossip, if there were no proof to back them up.

He knew just the man for the job.

75

The old Librarian, Father DeFeo, made his way to the Cardinal's office. He had not been summoned by a Prelate of this stature, he realized with a wry internal smile, since the *sede vacante* – the time when Peter's chair was vacant, after Pope John Paul's suspicious death. There had been no doubt in DeFeo's mind then, nor was there any now, that John Paul had been murdered by the same agents of Lucifer who had attempted to discredit Pope John XXIII, and his reforms. Of course, there was no way to prove either.

As chief Vatican archivist and keeper of the *Secretum* with all its 2000 years of secrets sacred, vile, and otherwise, DeFeo knew where most of the Vatican's skeletons were buried, and also who had buried them. He could sniff out an ecclesiastical lie with one brain lobe tied behind his back, he thought with a small chuckle, as he hurried down the corridor.

Lie after lie had been told after the Pope's assassination, and poor Sister Vincenza, who'd had the misfortune to find the dead Pontiff, had been forced to keep silent about whatever it was she had seen and whatever it was she knew. It was no less than a Cardinal who had imposed an immediate vow of silence on the nun, most likely to cover up the fabrication that had been so hastily woven over the truth. A body removed with unseemly haste, no autopsy permitted, conflicting death certificate diagnoses – why, the entire episode smelled of an act of assassination and its meticulous cover-up had been worthy of a Borgia. Glasses, slippers and Last Will had conveniently disappeared... embalmers had been called an hour *before* a doctor, and when a physician was finally brought in, it was *not* John Paul's personal internist, but some unknown outsider to pronounce a cause of death for a Pope? Preposterous. All letters, notes, books and personal mementoes of John Paul's 33 day Papacy had been removed and "lost," and no blood had been permitted to be drawn for forensic purposes. A clean sweep and a dirty death most likely. The only question was which poison had been used, as the glass of champagne the Pope had been given before bed had mysteriously disappeared. The glass later emerged, washed of all traces.

In the midst of all this, the then-Cardinal Camerlengo had called Father DeFeo to ask refreshment of mind, on certain obscure points of historic precedent. Exactly *what were* the protocols to be followed on the death of a pope? – of course he'd been asked this only after it was entirely too late, for any of them to be observed.

Father DeFeo reached Cardinal Andretti's outer office and found the man's secretary missing, and Andretti's door open.

"You may enter," the Cardinal intoned, as if bestowing a great honor on an unworthy peon. DeFeo once again swallowed the humiliation of being subservient to one of such meager spiritual and intellectual gifts. It was small price to pay for being left alone with his beloved books, and perhaps it was a penance he deserved for thinking such unchristian thoughts about so many Princes of the Church.

The Cardinal eyed the ancient threadbare cassock, and the seemingly even more ancient priest who wore it, with undisguised distaste. His own personal wardrobe was made by the finest tailors in Rome.

"I am concerned," Andretti said without preamble, "about certain impediments to the progress being made in the matter of canonization of our Blessed Pius XII."

DeFeo nodded, but didn't speak. Andretti barely noticed.

"I wish you to look into certain archival references for me, regarding alleged dinner parties held by His Holiness with certain members of the Nazi High Command, during the war years. And any correspondence with the Reich had best be segregated, too. These dinners and communications would be too easily misunderstood by our enemies, if they were to come to light. Needless to say, the Holy Father found it necessary to placate forces he could not overcome, in his effort to protect the Church from the Nazis, but I think it best that any such references you might find, be consigned, for the time being, to the Index. And while you're at it, it might be best to remove all references and correspondence between the Vatican and the Reich during the time of His Holiness serving in Berlin as Papal Nuncio. There's no point in leaving anything that could be misinterpreted by our enemies, where prying eyes might seek for ammunition."

DeFeo's own eyes came up with interest. "You know, of course, Eminence, that, officially, the *Librorum Prohibitorum* no longer exists. It was abolished in 1966," he said.

"Don't be a dolt, DeFeo!" Andretti snapped. "Of course, I know that! It hardly means the Librorum ceased to exist, does it?

The point is the old secrets must remain secret – you can tuck them under your bed for all I care. But the material I require may be, shall we say, incendiary, in the wrong hands, so I wish you to bring it to me for vetting, and then see that it is conveniently misplaced. Do I make myself clear?"

"It will not be easy or quick, Eminence," DeFeo said, playing for time. "The task of codifying has been woefully slow because we have so little help..." he paused for emphasis. "And there were so *many* dinners with Nazis..."

The Cardinal glared at the impudent old fool.

"And if I may be bold enough to ask, Eminence," the little priest said with feigned humility, "and in the interest of serving your need, of course..."

Andretti looked at him wondering *what, now.*

"There are other things you may wish to consider, perhaps... For example, how do you wish me to handle the fact that His Holiness never once decried the Holocaust, and that he imposed sanctions against the only German bishop who had the courage to do so? And then there is the question of all the money and art works that the Nazis saw fit to leave in our hands..."

"Find me what I *require*, DeFeo," the Cardinal answered in a low and menacing voice. "*All* of it. That *is* your job, is it not?"

The old priest nodded. "Indeed, Eminence, it is my job... and I will do my best," he said, mentally cataloguing all the ways he could procrastinate. "As it is so urgent, may I begin?" he said innocently, and turned to go.

"Not yet!" Andretti snapped, now certain of the man's impertinence. "I'd like to see what you can find for me on two other subjects, as well." This was said a little too casually, DeFeo noted. "I want whatever you can find on a statesman named Gruner and on the old myths about the Spear of Longinus."

DeFeo's attention was definitely engaged now. *This* was a most interesting combination – one to be discussed with Mother General. Most interesting. He left the Cardinal's office with a lightened footstep. What game was afoot here, he wondered? The

Cardinal's interest in hiding incriminating documents about Pacelli's papacy was only to be expected. But the other two requests were intriguing.

DeFeo returned to his library in half the time it had taken him to get to the Cardinal's office, humming all the way there.

76

Washington, D.C.

The trip to Bethesda was both pleasant and fruitful for Linc. Arnold Peabody not only remembered him from the old days, but it seemed, he'd followed Linc's career through all the decades since they'd first met, when Linc had been a young law student with an abiding interest in the Constitution. An interest that had taken him so often to the Library of Congress for research, refuge, and just plain pleasure, he'd become a fixture there.

Truth was, in those days, Linc had no money and little time for the kind of pleasures other young men pursued, so his passion for the Constitution and the uncommon geniuses who had framed it, had been his bulwark against the loneliness and poverty and prejudice that were his life's other realities. Within the walls of the Library of Congress, Lincoln Tremaine, the sharecropper's boy from Alabama, had spent his time in the company of giants.

In fact, Linc had spent so many days and nights in the main reading room that Arnold Peabody, then an erudite and conscientious young librarian, had started keeping an eye on him.

The ten foot high allegorical statues that decorated the room, each surmounted by an inscription about the ideal it represented, seemed to fascinate the young black giant, who had a habit of standing beneath each in turn, lost in contemplation.

"Why do you keep doing that?" Arnold had finally asked, when his curiosity got the better of his manners. "Standing there... just looking. You must have them all memorized by now."

And Lincoln had replied, "It's all up here, isn't it? The best of what we humans can aspire to be. Look there, above Bauer's statue of Religion – read what it says *'What does the Lord require of thee, but to do justly, and to love mercy, and to walk humbly with thy God!* And over there..." he pointed to Paul Wayland Bartlett's statue of the Law. "I do admire that one so."

The young librarian had raised his eyes to the stone engraving and read aloud 'Of Law there can be no less acknowledged, than that her voice is the harmony of the world.'

"I see what you're saying," he'd responded as the answer dawned on him. "Its really like a Ten Commandments of civilized thought isn't it?"

"And *deed*," Linc had replied emphatically. "It will be the *deeds* these thoughts engender that make us a great nation. We must have the courage for the deeds, and not merely admiration for the words."

Arnold Peabody, in all his years with the Library of Congress, had never heard the like, nor forgotten the words.

There'd never been a question in his mind that this strange black boy was going places. And now, after all these years, Lincoln Tremaine had come all the way to Bethesda, to ask his help. What a remarkable honor! He thought at first, that perhaps, like himself, Tremaine was an old man revisiting ideas and ideals of a youth long gone. But the intellectual vigor with which the questions were posed made clear that age had not dimmed the man's intellect or curiosity. And then, when the Justice had asked for secrecy and discretion...

It had been a rigorous and exhilarating day for Peabody, if the truth be told. Just like in the old days, when he'd felt needed. The questions hadn't been easy ones, without all the reference tools of the library at his beck and call. God bless the computerized references online, of course, but still...

The War, the CIA, the Nuremburg Trials, Secret Societies, famous men... the list of questions the Justice had asked was gargantuan. What a brain that man had! Peabody thought, as he watched the old jurist trudge down the brick walk, back to his car, after the day's search had ended. What a heart, as well, for he had even taken the trouble to recall the name of Peabody's long dead wife, and of his son, who had died in Viet Nam.

Tremaine hadn't explained his mission. He had simply asked the man's word that he would speak of their conversation to no one, until he received a phone call releasing him from that promise. The old Justice hadn't asked Peabody to sign a Confidentiality Agreement – just asked for his word. Imagine that... in this day and age. Peabody had been deeply touched by that gesture.

*   *   *

Tremaine was thoughtful on the drive back. Linc had scattered the unimportant in with the important, in hopes that an inquiry by an old man, a former librarian, would be able to escape scrutiny in so vast a sea of information as the Library of Congress. What he'd really been after was the information about where the more inaccessible material lay buried in the archive, about who had written closest to the bone on certain subjects, about threads he himself could follow up on, in as discreet a way as possible – this was the kind of invaluable information a man like Arnold Peabody knew how to find. He had to think now, about just how to proceed. Perhaps by dividing up what he needed to know among different researchers... perhaps by calling in a favor or two of long standing... perhaps by taking this fine old archivist into his confidence... he'd be able to lay his hands on the information he sought without raising any alarm bells.

There was much to learn, but very, very carefully.

77

Senator Dandridge walked down the Capitol steps with a jaunty step. The day was cold but sunny, and the winds that had been keeping everyone indoors for two weeks had died down.

The man who suddenly gripped his arm as he neared the center of the steps was well-dressed enough to look as if he belonged in the throng. The hoarse whisper was another story.

"Don't get in the way," the man rasped. Did he mean on the steps? Was he talking about the Spear investigation?

The man was gone so suddenly it might never have happened at all. He could just as easily have pushed the old man headlong down the Capitol steps, but instead, he'd simply whispered words that might be a warning? Or might they simply have been the hasty words of a rude pedestrian in a hurry? By the time Ruddy recovered enough to turn around to see the face that has been averted, all that was visible was a rapidly retreating back.

Dandridge stood and tried to make his heart stop pounding. He was fine. He was not hurt. He was just scared shitless.

78

Rutherford Dandridge waited for his son, the President, in the parlour of the residence at the White House. He'd almost called for an appointment three times in the past week, he'd been *that* agitated ever since Lincoln had laid the bombshell on him, and the odd things had started happening. But each time he'd thought better of it. He didn't relish telling his son about the Spear or the General – in fact, he'd never said much about his experiences in the war at all, except to occasionally brag a bit with the boys at the Club, about how hush-hush his very important work had been in the European war theatre. People had commended him for being so modest. Little did they know how much he had to be modest about.

Truth was, he hadn't done much of anything worthwhile back then, and what he had done that was useful, was classified. Which, on reflection, had worked out very well for him. If you never claimed to have taken some god-forsaken hill, or carried a buddy on your back out of enemy artillery fire, you could never be caught in a lie. If, on the other hand, you deftly alluded to having been privy to secrets that had helped win the war, but couldn't be talked about... well, *that* was just the ticket for launching a successful career in politics.

Truth be known, because of his family's money and prestige, and his own not-inconsiderable charm, the War Office had used Ruddy Dandrige as a sort of dashing young officer-at-large while he was stationed in London and Berlin. He was the perfect cocktail party guest at any Embassy. His impeccable French from all those summers in Paris, and his quite-passable Italian and German, picked up as pillow-talk or ski-slope chatter in Gstaad, had meant that he spent the war in drawing rooms, not danger zones. Still, he'd always suspected his father had pulled strings in Washington to keep him out of combat.

"Senator Dandridge, sir," a very boyish looking young man whom he knew to be his son's latest protégé-aide, interrupted his reverie. "The President will be with you in just a few moments, now," the boy said in a soft southern drawl, "I'm afraid he got caught on a call from Mr. Putin, and it's taking longer than he'd hoped. May I get you a refreshment of some kind, while you wait, sir?"

Ruddy eyed the youngster with approval. You had to go far to find this level of courtesy in the young these days. "Bourbon on the rocks will do just fine, son," he answered graciously, as if bestowing a gift of civility on the young man. "I take it, the President will have a few minutes to spare me, once he's given Mr. Putin his marching orders?"

The young man smiled appreciatively at the humor. "Indeed he will, sir," he answered, intending to pour the drink himself, rather than calling for someone else to do it. He knew the President and his father enjoyed their private time together. "He's cleared his calendar for the next hour for you, sir. So if nuclear war doesn't break out anywhere in the world before eight o'clock this evening, I think you two can have a nice long chat." He pulled a bottle from the well-stocked bar and set it on the marble serving counter, he now stood behind.

"We've just gotten in a supply of lovely Tennessee Whiskey, sir... would that suit you?" the young man asked.

"Hell, no, son! None of that girly whiskey for me... have you got any Baker's 7, or Bookers, maybe?"

The young man smiled, pulled up the proper bottle, poured and handed the asked-for drink to the senator. The older man raised his glass to the younger in pleasant salute.

He was glad the call from that wily old bastard in Russia had intervened, it gave him a little more time to figure out what he really wanted to say to his son, Ruddy thought, as he sipped the fine old bourbon... and a little good whiskey would help settle his nerves. He'd been more shaken by Tremaine's visit than he liked to admit. Fact was, that old boy had always unnerved him just a little, even when he was just a young buck, back in the war days. There was something downright unnatural about a man who could keep his cool, walk the tightrope of politics, and make you believe he'd never told a lie in his life – as if such a thing were even possible. Ruddy'd seen it all in Washington in his 40 years on Capitol Hill, and one thing he'd never seen was a completely honest man. Diogenes might as well blow out that damned lantern he'd been using to seek out the last honest man, at least if he ever came to DC – Ruddy'd told his wife that very thing, on more than one occasion. This is a town where you'd better learn early on how to chop off a man's arm and convince him he looks better without it, if you intend to make a name for yourself. But, that just wasn't the way of old Lincoln Tremaine – he was cut from some other self-righteous cloth, and damned if he didn't have the ability to make a man feel fucking *inadequate. God damn!* He said out loud, to the empty room, just as his son entered.

The younger Dandridge let out a laugh. "Was it something I said?" he asked, walking over to shake hands with his father. It didn't occur to either man to embrace. "And here I thought Putin was a hard case."

The elder Dandridge chuckled. "Just because he was head of the KGB is no reason to think he's not a Commie pinko wuss, son. Did you give him a piece of your mind?"

The President of the United States shook his head and chuckled. "Didn't think I could spare any pieces today," he replied. "I've got nothing on my plate at the moment that looks even vaguely capable of being improved on, never mind, solved. But enough about me, Dad – you said you had something you wanted to discuss with me? I've got about 45 minutes, if that'll do it for you."

The senator looked at his son and saw the deep dark circles under his eyes, and the filigree of new lines in his face. No matter how you cut it, the Presidency always took a toll on a man, he thought. He'd seen them all come and go since the war. Truman, Nixon, Kennedy, Johnson, the Bush boys and all the rest of them. The Presidency never left a man where it found him. Nobody got out of the Oval unscathed. Hell, some of them didn't even make it out alive.

He reconsidered his decision to let the cat out of the bag about what Lincoln had told him. If he did, he'd probably have to fess up to that old S.O.B. Farnsworth at CIA and God alone knows who else. Better to keep it buried and be just a little extra careful around town for a few more days... at least 'til he was certain there really was something to be afraid of. He took a breath, polished off the whiskey, and handed the glass back to his son.

"I could use another one of these," he temporized, framing what he would say. "I had a visit from Justice Tremaine the other day that unsettled me, that's all – nothing really. I may have overreacted, I suppose. He brought up some things that happened overseas at the end of the war..."

"Which war are we talking about here?" the President asked, suddenly alert.

"Not any war you need worry about, Mr. President," Ruddy said, smiling proudly at his son. "He was talking about *my* war... all those years ago. Anyway, there was this incident he and I witnessed back in '45, and we thought it was ancient history, but it seems to have surfaced in some way, shape or form, and there have been a couple of murders that may or may not be connected..."

"Murders?" his son asked, his voice suddenly concerned. "Does this mean you're in some kind of danger, Dad? Do you want me to put the FBI on it, or the Secret Service?"

The old man shook his head emphatically. "Not yet, son," he said, "and definitely not the FBI. This thing may have CIA tendrils, I'm just not sure, yet. And it may just be a tempest in a teacup – I'm not sure of anything at the moment, and I confess I was just looking for a sounding board..."

A knock interrupted the thought and the young aide entered the room. "Mr. President, I'm so sorry to interrupt, sir, but I've got General Armstrong on the phone... it seems they need you in the Situation Room." He looked ruefully at the Senator, but the older man was already on his feet.

"Duty calls, son," he said easily. "What I have on my mind can wait... matter of fact it's probably a good idea if I find out more about it before I burden you with any of it."

The President had risen, too, and was putting on the jacket he'd thrown over a chair when he'd entered the residence.

"Thanks, Dad," he said. "Let me know if you need me on this. *Whatever* this is. You know where to find me." He touched his father on the arm and turned toward the door. They never embraced, as he'd seen other fathers and sons do. Well almost never, the President thought, as he left the room. They'd embraced at his mother's funeral.

79

Germany

"Take a housemaid to New York with you?" Gruner stared incredulously at his son, "Have you lost your senses completely?"

Fritz stood his ground. His time was coming, he reminded himself. Perhaps it would come in the U.S. "You take your Stasi lapdog-butler with you when you travel. Is that senseless, too?"

Gruner eyed the younger man coldly. "Don't be impertinent, Fritz, Hans is my bodyguard. It would be insane *not* to have him travel with me."

Fritz smiled. "Ah, but you see this housemaid serves my body in other ways, no less necessary, Father."

His father's eyebrows raised at that. Was the boy flaunting his youth and sexual stamina, perhaps?

"I have no interest in training another to my needs at the moment," Fritz went on, "nor do I wish to go without those needs being met while I am in New York. You have your toys, Father, I have mine. I no longer am of an age to require your permission to indulge my particular proclivities. I shall, however, remain discreet as ever, and my pleasures will in no way impinge upon yours, I assure you."

Gruner deliberated a moment, but seeing his son's determination, decided the fight was not worth it. "So *this* is the hill you choose to die on, is it? The company of a whore?" he mused in an ironic, bantering tone. "If that is the case, Fritz, let me say I applaud your choice. She's a succulent morsel."

"I have no intention of dying, Father," Fritz replied icily, "on this hill or any other."

Gruner assessed his son's demeanor. Something had changed in the boy since the Summit of The 13, but he wasn't yet certain what form this new confidence was going to take, and just how he might use it to his own advantage.

"Very well. If she's that good in bed. But don't take her on the G5. She can fly commercial and coach." He had no intention of letting the crew and attendants see his son make a fool of himself with a housemaid.

Now, Fritz's eyebrows rose. "As you wish, father. She can fly on a broomstick for all I care, as long as she is available to me in Bedford."

Fritz left his father's study, elated that he'd gotten his way, furious that he'd had to ask permission.

80

Brooklyn, New York

The Brooklyn bar was dark, noisy and far enough off the beaten track so Matt thought he could hold the necessary conversation without too much fear of being overhead. Truth was, he was really pissed. About the dressing down he'd gotten from the Captain, about the old bat who was still on the CIA payroll, about his friend Chris, who'd said the old woman could be trusted. About being so far from Cait and where the action was. About an asshole who could really be above the law. About the whole fucking situation.

He saw Croce standing at the door, searching the crowd for him. He stood up to signal the man, and Croce, seeing him in the corner booth, headed in Matt's direction.

"Ya got something to tell, right?" Croce said without preamble. "Me, too. But you go first."

Matt took a mouthful of beer and looked around for the umpteenth time, to see if there were prying ears anywhere close by. Not that you had to be close these days, with all the sophisticated surveillance gear that was available, but what the hell, they had to talk somewhere.

Seeing Matt's uneasiness, Croce grinned. "You looking to find a snoop-free zone?"

Matt chuckled. "If they can bug us in all this noise, more power to 'em," he said raising the bottle toward Croce. He'd ordered one for him, too.

"I think maybe the reason everybody has gone bat-shit over exposing Gruner," Matt said in a carefully conspiratorial voice, "is not just because of the fact that he's a Nazi and he got saved by the CIA, but because of the specific work he sold to the spooks, and continued to help them with, once he got his new identity."

Croce took a long slug of the Harp the waitress had set down in front of him on the table. "Which was or is?"

"Gruner was an interrogation specialist and a torture expert, among his other talents. The story goes like this: part of the information he used to buy his new identity and the cover-up that went with it, had to do with the techniques he'd developed to coerce confessions and bend minds or wipe them out completely. Drugs, torture, brainwashing – the full delight."

Croce frowned. "OK, but everybody knows the military has been studying, aka *practicing,* all this stuff for decades. Like waterboarding isn't their first rodeo – so what's the big deal about Herr Doktor's stuff?"

"You're right," Matt agreed, "but what isn't common knowledge is that 25 or 30 well-known universities and institutions were involved with Gruner's covert research. They did experimentation and testing, here and in Canada, on unwitting U.S. citizens. People got drugged, brainwashed, maybe even killed – all with CIA approval. Remember, after we were in Korea, Asian torture and brainwash techniques were front page news, so the military was hot to understand how it all worked, and figure out how to outdo the Gooks.

"So the whole thing seems to have ballooned into a bunch of other acronymed projects that were taken over by the military, and the research kind of mushroomed into not just torture, but projects aimed at mind control of sleepers, who could be put in place to do certain tasks and infiltrate governments..."

"Like the Manchurian Candidate?"

"Yeah, exactly. He also evidently sold them on the idea that controlling whole cities or countries looked like a great 'weaponless' weapon of war. Gruner told them maybe you could use this stuff to mind-bend on a broad scale."

"I thought that's why they invented television," Croce quipped, and Matt laughed, but only a little.

"So you think Gruner was involved in all this, all the while he was busy becoming the bon vivant political sage and dinner party guest du jour?" Croce asked, the magnitude of the deception dawning.

"It looks like he helped design and *carry out* some pretty heinous clandestine experiments that the government now wants to forget ever happened, and his son may still be running some of those programs. With Rendition pulling out all the stops on torture, I think he's still in the thick of it. Which is probably why all this ancient history is still classified Top Secret, and why we're all taking flak for having tried to peek under the covers," Matt responded.

"*Marrone!*" Croce said reverting to childhood street-speak, "*That* kind of crap coming to light would definitely put the fox in the henhouse."

"And the henhouse," Matt finished the thought, "belongs to The Company."

"CIA," Croce said and took another gulp from the bottle. "That's not good. You sure about your intel?"

"Carter's über-geeks followed up on that stuff from Sally. They went digging in their own inimitable way, hacked into classified files God knows where..."

"Ok. This all makes sense of what I got, which is about the fruit of Gruner's loins – *sheesh*, talk about fruit of the poisonous tree – anyway, this Fritz Gruner it seems, is a trained psychologist with a specialty in psychotropic drugs and behavioral modification.

"So the apple didn't fall far..." Matt added.

"Yeah, but it seems our boy Fritz is a multi-tasker. He's got an MBA from Wharton and a Doctorate in Economics from The London School of the same – so he helps his daddy with the finances of their business interests, and the financial press claims he uses his behavioral smarts to manipulate markets, and second-guess exactly where the economies of developing countries are headed. So far, he seems to make uncommonly good guesses, so he has added substantially to the family fortune. But maybe his real talent is in this behavioral modification stuff, which he does for the military?"

"And do we know how Fritzy feels about dear old dad?" Matt asked, working on conjuring up a mental picture of both Gruner and son.

"Deferential. Cool. Enigmatic... are the press-flak words I found describing their relationship. My bet is he hates the old man's guts and is wondering why the fuck it's taking him so long to die. The old geezer's over 90 and going strong."

"Sounds probable," Matt said finishing his beer. "And it also sounds like any milk of human kindness in that gene pool curdled a while back."

"Ya think?"

Croce looked at Matt as if deciding whether or not to say what was on his mind, then spoke. "You know, it occurred to me these charmers might decide to use some of Fritz's interrogation techniques on Cait or Lark..." He let the thought hang, watching Matt's eyes. He had a hunch Matt liked this woman more than he was willing to let on.

"So, I guess that means we'd better make sure that never happens," Matt answered, in a tone that said he meant it.

Croce told Matt about what he'd learned at the Skinhead bar. He said he hadn't heard more from JC, but he was pretty sure he

would. The men talked a few more minutes, finished their beers
and left.

81

Gruner's connection to the Neo Nazi movement was deep,
long, and worldwide, but he had put so many layers of
intermediaries between himself and the White Supremacist ground
troops, that they might have lived on separate planets. His social
position and media high profile made any Nazi association, neo or
otherwise, anathema, but that didn't mean he didn't value their
competencies and usefulness.   This worldwide underground
network, snaked into a thousand low-end places and was a superb
information gathering, courier and strong-arm service. Gruner had
made use of it countless times since the war's end, and in many
countries, always through a complex baffle of intermediaries.

Actions could be mandated to these troops that could never
be traced back to his doorstep. Propaganda and disinformation
could be disseminated via the rumor mill that was always active.
Which was precisely why he'd decided to have his underlings
spread the rumor of an apocryphal million dollar pay off among
them, just to set wheels in motion. He didn't expect the foot
soldiers to actually *find* Cait or the Spear, but he wanted them
buzzing about the subject, wanted them on high alert for scuttlebutt.
Information dropped in bars or bedrooms, sometimes proved more
valuable than phone taps. Not that they couldn't do that, too, if
he'd asked for it.

And then the aura of mystery and mysticism that surrounded
Hitler's Spear was just the kind of esoterica that excited the masses,
and re-invigorated the spirit of the Reich and the mystic powers of
der Führer. Something good would come of this little financial
incentive program. There was nothing like the scent of money to

incite a feeding frenzy. Especially in the U.S., a mongrel place. Americans, like all inferior polyglot races, would stoop to any level of depravity for money. It was despicable, but it was useful.

He made a mental note to have Fritz up the ante by adding a bit more substance to the rumors.

82

Croce walked briskly down the street, his hand deep in his coat pocket because he'd left his gloves in the office and it was damned cold.

He glanced right and left, as casually as possible when he hit the stoop of his building. *Nobody.* That was good. He was cold and tired. The triple homicide he'd been working had kept him up most of the night and the follow up and paperwork had consumed the rest of a long annoying day.

The hand that reached for his as he opened the inner vestibule door shocked him.

"Relax dude," the hoarse voice said in the semi-darkness. "It's me."

"Holy shit, J.C.," Croce hissed back. "How'd you get in here? You scared the crap out of me."

"Its what I do, dude," was the amiable reply.

Croce shook his head with disgust, silently cursing his own stupidity in not checking the inner vestibule. Fatigue made you stupid. It could also make you dead.

He opened the door to his apartment quickly and ushered the man in.

"No lights," J.C. said pre-emptorily.

"Yeah, yeah. I figured you weren't here for dinner. What'dya got for me?"

"You debugged lately?" J.C. answered looking around expertly, as Croce's eyes adjusted to the dark.

"Daily now," he answered. "I got this new gizmo from a friend – it's supposed to jam anybody's signal."

J.C. looked unconvinced. "Let's use the john."

"OK. I hear you." Croce answered.

"Just so nobody else does." J.C. replied.

The running water in the sink and tub seemed to make the man less jumpy.

"They're upping the ante on the Spear chase."

"Who?"

"Dunno. Higher ups. The guys who circulate rumors. The Spear story's everywhere, man. Propaganda up the ying yang. Magical powers. Hitler's mandate. Stolen by evil forces. The whole nine yards."

"And the money?"

"Supposed to be a million in Krugerrands, no less. Like a big pot of Nazi gold delivered to the bank of your choice."

"Yeah. Like that's gonna happen."

"Right. But who cares. I think the whole thing is just meant to get the whole network looking for this woman who supposedly knows where it is."

Croce nodded. "And Gruner?"

"Nada. Not a fucking word about him. And no way I can unobtrusively insert the name in a conversation, ya know? But there is some guy whose name surfaces with some regularity. They call him the Painmeister. He's like an expert torturer, old school, new school, whatever-works school. The legend is he learned from his father who learned in the Fatherland, and now he plies his trade for governments, military, black ops, etcetera, etcetera. I never put it together until you laid Gruner on me and I did a little research. His son, Fritz, could fill the bill."

Croce nodded. "You watchin' your back, J.C.?" he said carefully. "This is pretty fucked up stuff we're talkin'."

"Whatthefuck, Croce," J.C. said with a mirthless laugh, "I'm a dark-shit specialist. I thought that's why you sought out my special talents."

"No way," Croce replied. "I just missed your winsome repartée. Want a beer?"

"Can't. Got work to do. Miles to go before I sleep." The door opened and he was gone.

Croce smiled in the dark. He'd once heard Matt say about J.C. that he could disappear while you were holding his hand. He'd probably been right about that.

Into the Dreadosphere
Part XII

"Opportunities multiply as they are seized."
Sun Tzu

83

Hapsburg zu Bergenfeld Estate
Outside Vienna

The old woman was regal in the way of fairytale queens not princesses, and seemed too perfect to be real. She also seemed arrogant, cool and distant.

Good breeding and fine plastic surgeons had kept the lines of jaw and throat perfect. Genetic luck and a disciplined nature had kept her slender as a reed. The arrogance of long privilege was apparent in her clipped orders to the servants, and in the way her world had been organized to supply her every need. But underneath, Cait sensed a rich reservoir of something harder to categorize in Maria von Hapsburg zu Bergenfeld.

"I was born a Hapsburg," Maria began, after Cait had been introduced to her by Hugh. "It is a heady gift and a heavy responsibility. I carry a thousand years of secrets in my bloodline."

"I appreciate your kindness in seeing us," Cait ventured, a bit awed by the woman and her surroundings.

Maria dismissed the pleasantry with a wave of her manicured hand. "There is regrettably little time for social niceties. I understand the urgency of your mission. I know the players and the game. So let us begin."

Surprised by her directness, Cait merely nodded.

"How much do you know about my family?" Maria asked.

"Not enough," Cait replied.

"I know a good deal, Aunt," Hugh said at the same time, "but perhaps not what we *need* to know, now. This is why we have come to you."

The snowy, perfectly coiffed head nodded regal acknowledgment. "Our family was originally from Switzerland," she began. "We first reigned in Austria where we ruled uninterruptedly for six centuries. A series of dynastic marriages brought Spain, Bohemia, Burgundy, Hungary and assorted other countries under us. We Hapsburgs supplied the world with all Holy Roman Emperors between 1452 and 1740, as well as the rulers of Spain and Austria. I tell you all this merely to let you know that few secrets, from the 11th century onwards, have escaped Hapsburg notice. We survived Napoleon and Hitler by the judicious use of such secrets.

"Some joke that our family motto is '*Let others wage war, we shall marry!*', as we seem to have a special talent for felicitous intermarriage with other Royal Houses. Marriage is a tried and true way to keep the royal bloodlines protected, as everyone is aware. But what is less well known perhaps, is that these tangled skeins not only provide political protection in difficult times, they also provide access to extraordinary secrets. I have spent a lifetime in the pursuit of such private revelations."

Cait's eyes widened – the woman was a living history book.

"My family had another talent," Maria went on. "We were steeped in magic and religion, two sides of the same coin, of course. Our library contains more priceless knowledge of alchemy, witchcraft, astrology, sorcery, the dark arts, as well as the lighter ones... than does the Vatican, whose greed for power was similar to our own, and predicated on similar ambitions and knowledge.

"We have at varied times in history possessed most of the Hallows of Christ..."

Cait interrupted, "And what are they, please?"

The dowager turned her head to regard Cait closely before speaking.

"Sacred objects, each possessed of mystical power," she replied, "the number of them varies in different legends. There are said to be 13 that constitute the entirety of surviving artifacts sanctified by Jesus himself, but the Spear you seek may be part of a far greater quest. Which is why I believe I know what Herr Gruner is really after."

"Is he not after the Spear of Longinus, then?" Cait asked startled by the thought.

The imperial head shook in annoyance, as at a needlessly stupid remark from a bright child who should have known better.

"Of *course*, he is after the Spear," the dowager replied. "But I believe it is only a means to an end for him. "He wants *immortality*. To win *that* prize, he needs the Spear, in order to possess the Grail!"

"Immortality! The Holy Grail!" Cait burst out incredulously. "Well, I suppose its good to set one's sights high, but isn't that just a bit preposterous?"

"Don't be a fool!" the old woman snapped, imperiously. "Immortality is the ultimate goal for us all. The Grail confers it. It has been rumored among mages and alchemists for centuries that one of these Hallows puts the Grail within reach, which is why Adolph tried so desperately to get his grubby paws on them, by fair means or foul. I believe he somehow learned that your Spear was the *one*."

Cait, annoyed by the peremptory chiding, opened her mouth to argue, but Hugh grasped her wrist and she felt his energy move through her again, but this time she didn't protest.

"We must hear her out, Cait," he admonished, "we have to know the truth."

Cait turned, pulling her arm away instinctively. "I'm a doctor, Hugh. I know far too much to believe immortality is possible."

"Try not to be an ass, child," the old woman admonished condescendingly, but with a not-unkindly twinkle in her eyes. "You know *nothing* of what is possible. Do you think we've kept our fortune and our heads for a thousand years by political means alone? We are masters of the arcane! We understand how energies are manipulated. In another generation or two, your scientists will catch up to us... perhaps. One century's magic becomes the next century's science, after all. Alchemy becomes chemistry... qi becomes quantum physics. Yet every century's scientists are arrogant and stupid enough to think they have all the answers, only to be proved wrong again and again."

"As arrogant as you, perhaps?" Cait said in the same cool tone, annoyed by the condescension of this imperious woman.

Maria von Hapsburg zu Bergenfeld burst into delighted laughter. "Touché, dear child!" she said, clapping her hands. "I was hoping to see some spark to let me believe you are up to this formidable task. Now, how much do you know of the Grail? I ask again."

"Only that no one knows if it's real or not. And no one even knows for certain what it is... a cup, a chalice, a stone, a bloodline... I've heard it called all of these things. As a child, I was in love with King Arthur and the Knights of the Roundtable, so of course, I know many of the stories of the Grail Quest, and over the years, whenever I've come across a new story about the Grail, I've read it. For a time I even entertained a fantasy that I'd once lived at King Arthur's court."

Maria looked at her speculatively. "And perhaps you did," she said looking speculatively at Cait. "Do you know then that Arthur's illegitimate daughter M'Lara carried the Spear of Longinus into battle, and, for a time pursued her own Grail Quest?"

Cait's eyes widened. "No," she said, genuinely startled. "I've never read any such story. I thought Mordred was Arthur's only child."

"She was his identical twin," Maria said. "Hidden by Merlin and the Lady of the Lake – raised in magic and given a mission, which she chose to ignore because she loved her father."

"But this isn't part of Camelot's history," Cait argued.

"Victors write the history books," Maria said with imperial certainty. "But M'Lara is a story for another day. Your task is an urgent one and your foes are many. So permit me to enlighten you about the Grail. The legends are legion, and so are the descriptions of what the Grail looks like."

"A Chalice is the most accepted description, of course. Either the Cup used at the last supper, or a cup used by Joseph of Arimathea to collect the actual blood of Jesus after his crucifixion, which I find a bit too ghoulish.

"Others believe it to be a great emerald dropped by Lucifer in his titanic battle for control of heaven with Archangel Michael, God's champion.

"And of course, there is the Jesus' blood line theory, very popular at the moment. Is the phrase *San Graal*, really a homonym of Sang Real, or Royal Blood? As my family is born of this line, I find it a charming theory – and quite true of course. The reasoning is, of course, that Jesus Christ had children by Mary of Magdala, and their lineage of the Royal Blood continues to the present day. This part is most certainly true, and has been known by the Royal Houses of Europe forever. In Jesus' day, Rabbis had to marry and sire children, and via the Merovingian kings, his blood runs through all the Royal families via intermarriage over the centuries, within a small gene pool. The *Sang Rael* is true... but it is not the Grail.

"The shape the Grail takes doesn't matter.... All that matters is this: In every single story, the Grail bestows immortality, and I assure you it has been sought for *that* fact alone, rather than for any spiritual gift it may bestow.

"Adolf Hitler and Heinrich Himmler believed utterly that immortality was possible. You would be surprised how many of the concentration camp medical experiments were devised as part of a quest for immortality. I have personal knowledge of the fact that Adolf dispatched the mystic Otto Rahn first, and then that scoundrel Skorzeny to collect any Hallow he could lay his hands on, and find the Grail. It seems he needed the one, to find the other.

"I believe Skorzeny may have actually found the place where the Grail resides, but couldn't access it for some reason – perhaps because he was so corrupt. After all, if one small indiscretion on Galahad's part kept him from achieving the Grail, a man with Skorzeny's moral decrepitude, should have been struck by divine lightning for even aspiring to touch the holy object!

"The most plausible scenario is that the war ended too soon for Skorzeny's expedition to return to Berlin to get the Spear from the bunker Hitler had placed it in, and so it was inconveniently found by Patton, who removed it from the Nazi's reach. The Spear that was returned to my family at the War's end was, of course, the forgery.

"I believe Hitler had somehow solved the mystery, and that Gruner knows where the Grail is hidden, and needs the Spear to access it, or to complete some arcane ritual of immortality he and Hitler knew about. There's rumored to be a Book of Secrets that explained the ritual – perhaps Hitler's henchmen found it. Gruner grows old and his need grows desperate. It is the only plausible explanation for this mad quest to find the Spear. We cannot let him get his hands on it."

Cait's eyes met Hugh's – she saw in them, utter acceptance of his aunt's story.

*   *   *

"Now," the elegant woman said, rising effortlessly from her chair. "I'm told you wish to see the Spear your General Patton returned to my family after the war, yes?"

Cait stood, too. "Yes," she said, "I hope that seeing it may inspire some notion of where my husband or his father could have hidden it. And, in truth, thus far, its more an idea than a reality for me."

Maria nodded.

"I've had it brought here to save time," she said loftily, as if liberating ancient treasures from museums was an everyday occurrence. She rang a bell, and a tall, liveried servant came in carrying a burgundy velvet cushion of considerable size. Atop the cushion lay what appeared to be an ancient spearhead about 16 inches long, attached by leather thongs to the 18 inches or so that remained of a lance, broken off in the haft. A band of silver and gold wrapped the artifact and Cait leaned closer to see if she could make out the words inscribed on the band.

"Place it here, Herbert," Maria directed, indicating the table between them. "And then you may go. I'll ring when it is time to return it to the Schatzkammer."

The man bowed wordlessly and retreated.

Cait, trying to be objective, gazed at this object, whose twin had cost her husband's life, and still might claim her own, her child's and her sister's.

"The band reads 'Nail of Our Lord,'" Maria said, watching Cait. "In 1084 Henry IV, one of the many kings who have possessed the Spear, had it made to commemorate the fact that Constantine the Great had added this so-called Crucifixion Nail to the Spear. His mother Helena found both Spear and Nail, you know."

"The genuine spear and nail are encrusted with what is said to be the actual blood of Jesus. *Whose* blood adorns this forgery that Hitler had crafted, I can't speculate. God knows, he had plenty to choose from. The phenomenon of blood and water spewing from the wounds of the man on the cross, onto the Centurion Longinus' Spear was considered to be a miracle in itself, and the fulfillment of a prophecy, as noted by St. John in his gospel."

Cait automatically responded as a doctor. "It wouldn't be odd for such fluid to escape under the circumstances," she said. "If the pericardial sinus was pierced on its way to the heart, fluid *and* blood would have drained in some quantity."

Maria smiled. "So you do not believe in miracles, then?"

Cait looked up at her, "I'm all for miracles. I just haven't witnessed any lately."

"That may change," Maria said portentously. "So tell us... has seeing this imposter Spear helped you imagine the *real* Spear's current whereabouts?"

Cait shook her head, sadly. "It's bigger than I'd imagined, even without the entire haft intact. Unfortunately, it still looks fairly easy to hide." She sighed in frustration. "But I am grateful. Seeing this makes it real."

"Excellent!" said the old Matriarch. "Then on to Wewelsburg, and after that, to Rome."

"Why Rome, Aunt?" Hugh asked. "I'd thought to take Cait to the Priory in Paris, after Wewelsburg."

"No," Maria said empathically. "Not yet. You must follow the path. Each person to whom you are sent, will be told where you are to go next. You must not deviate. Father DeFeo is expecting you at the Vatican. He is of no importance there, merely an old archivist whose political power died with John XXIII. But for you, he holds important knowledge, and he is an old friend of the Hunt. Go to him swiftly. If you must detour to Wewelsburg, take no more than a day to do it."

84

Outside Vienna

Dusk was darkening the road ahead and purpling the sky beyond the mountains as Cait and Hugh left the zu Bergenfeld estate behind. Cait was trying to sort out whether anything in all Maria had said was useful to their search. It didn't matter whether immortality was plausible, all that mattered was that a ruthless 90 year old man, with all the resources in the world at his disposal, *thought* it was possible, and was willing to kill anyone who got in the way of his achieving it. *That* scenario was easier to accept than the possibility of magic.

"If you thought immortality was possible, Hugh?" she asked suddenly, shaking loose from her reverie, "would you seek it?"

He turned his head to look at her, a slight smile tugging at his lips. "I think that's a decision that would most likely be based on whether those I loved most would be immortal, too. Eternity alone, watching those I love wither and die, wouldn't hold much appeal for me, I'm afraid. And you?"

As he asked the question, the car engine suddenly sputtered ominously, and Hugh's grip on the wheel tightened, as his eyes darted to the dash. "Bloody hell!" he snapped, as the engine died entirely and the vehicle rolled to a hesitant halt, "that's not possible!" Pointing at the fuel gauge he said to Cait, "We just filled her up with petrol."

Hugh was already opening the car door, as he spoke, and Cait, startled, watched as he jumped free of the car and lowered himself to the ground so he could look under the chassis.

"Get out of the car, Cait, *now!*" he barked urgently, as he made the effort to push himself upright. "The fuel line's been cut. Somebody wants us on foot." She saw he had his mobile out, but judging by his frustrated scowl, she knew there was no cell service here.

Cait scrambled for her door handle, then a flash-thought stopped her. She kicked off her pumps, and reaching into the back seat, yanked open her duffle and grabbed sneakers from the bag. Whatever was to come, better it not get here while she was in three inch heels, she thought grimly, as she pulled on running shoes, yanked the laces tight, and exited the car. She was barely out the door before the black sedan pulled alongside them and two men emerged, flanking them on either side of the disabled car.

One of the men was tall and broad as a linebacker, the other shorter, more wiry, with a narrow rodent-like face. Both were dressed in black and there was no mistaking their intent; the larger held a semi-automatic pistol in his hand pointed at Hugh. The man closing in on Cait displayed no weapon, just malice. *They want me alive and Hugh dead,* flashed into Cait's head.

"There is no need for you to die," the big man said to Hugh in a guttural German accent. "We want only the woman. If she comes quietly, we'll just knock you out, and you won't have to play the hero and get yourself killed trying to save the bitch."

Cait was in the process of registering that the gun the man held was a Beretta 92F, her sister's favorite handgun, just as the ferocious kick Hugh launched at it smashed the weapon out of the man's meaty fist and sent it flying into the gathering dusk.

This unexpected attack moved the smaller man into action. He grabbed Cait's arm and swung her toward him with a painful wrench that slammed her forcefully into his chest. His other arm went round her body, wrapping her in a python grip that pinned one arm to her side. *Don't let them overpower you.* The words of her long-ago martial arts teacher were in her head. *Once they've overpowered you, you're as good as dead.* She smashed her sneakered heel down onto the man's instep so hard she could feel bones crunch. The unexpected resistance and pain made him drop his grip, and Cait launched a palm strike to his nose that staggered the man backwards. *You're a woman,* her teacher had said, *an attacker won't expect you to fight back. That can give you a momentary edge.* The loosened grip gave her courage. She shrieked a *kiyae* that would have chilled a banshee, and swept the man's knees with a crippling round kick, sending him sprawling before he could unholster the gun he was now groping for.

Cait heard the sounds of heavy combat beyond the front bumper on the driver's side, but couldn't take her eyes off her own assailant long enough to see how much trouble Hugh was in. She'd noticed where their larger assailant's gun had landed, but it was too far from her to matter, so she kept her attention riveted on her own attacker, and saw he'd now managed to get a grip on the gun from his shoulder holster. Time slowed to the strange slow motion that precedes an accident or death. The whole fight had taken only seconds, but as the man's gun cleared leather, slow motion or not, she saw there was only one inevitable ending now. There was rage in his ugly shattered face, rage that hadn't been there before. He was going to kill her because she'd humiliated him.

The shot rang out just as she'd known it would, but to her astonishment she felt no pain, saw no blinding flash of light to signal death. Her assailant, not she, crumpled to the ground. A second shot came on the heels of the first, as she registered they were rifle rounds, not pistol shots. The huge man who'd been grappling with Hugh on the other side of the car grunted as another shot slammed him backwards off Hugh, and a final round finished the job.

This time she'd seen the muzzle flash at the ridgeline of the woods... had seen, too, a large male figure emerge from cover, as Hugh crawled out from under the dead weight of the giant's fallen, blood drenched body.

"Holy Mother of God!" she breathed. "That's some shooting from that distance. Is he one of ours?"

Hugh, covered in blood and limping badly, made his way toward her. He was favoring his leg enough to make her wonder if it might be fractured. She saw him strain his eyes in the gathering dusk toward the figure at the tree line, then watched him make an arcane gesture. The unmoving figure did not return it.

"Not one of ours," he said quietly.

"Just a good Samaritan," Cait quipped, brushing dirt and blood from her clothes, "who just happened by with a scoped sniper rifle?"

Hugh shook his head to say he didn't have a clue, but he kept his eyes on the figure at the ridgeline.

"Are you alright, Cait," he asked, glancing at her quickly, "are you hurt?"

"Just shaken up. But what the hell just happened here?"

"Damned if I know," he said, watching the figure that still stood immobile, 500 yards away. "Who are you?" he called out, impulsively to the man. But the figure simply melted back into the trees and was gone.

*   *   *

Vincenzo shouldered his rifle and thought about what had just transpired. He thanked God he had been keeping the doctor and her friend within in his sight, just as the Cardinal had said he must. He wondered who the two men were, who now lay dead at his hand. No matter. The scrawny little one had intended to shoot the *dottore*. He had read that clearly in the man's body language. He was a little man, and had been humiliated by her attack – a scared little man, caught off guard by the woman's bravery, so he had wanted revenge. Vincenzo could see she was not a trained professional, and would surely have been killed if the little man had been better at his job. But she had courage and *some* training... and that was to be admired.

If people were going to start threatening his little dottore, he would have to stay alert, for she had not yet led him to whatever it was the Cardinal wanted. Perhaps this would not be as disturbing an assignment as he had feared. The child was not in play, thanks be to God, and the woman was... interesting. His mama was also the kind of woman who would fight a man with a gun, if the need arose. A brave woman, not given to surrender. Yes. He was coming to think of this one as his strong little dottore. He would light a special candle to Santa Lucia that God would not require him to kill her.

Vincenzo began to sing a hymn to his favorite Saint.

There was nothing to fear in the woods now, and the music sounded lovely, carried over the cold night air in the untroubled forest. There was no need for stealth at this moment and singing always seemed to him a good way to praise God. With the hand that did not hold the butt of the rifle, now propped on his shoulder, he fingered his rosary beads. Vincenzo no longer went to mass as he had done when he was a child, but that did not mean he didn't pray.

*   *   *

"So, my dear Caitlin," Hugh said as they made their way back toward the zu Bergenfeld estate on foot, "it would appear you know how to defend yourself." She couldn't determine what it was she heard in his voice – surprise, admiration, amusement all jumbled together, but perhaps something else, too. Not that figuring it out was at all important. The attack had drained her and added to the strain of the day, but she had to admit the whole encounter had convinced her how thoroughly Hugh was on her side. She wished he didn't unsettle her so.

"Not as well as you," she answered him with a short laugh. "If you hadn't kicked the gun out of Gargantua's hands, I'm afraid neither one of us would have lived to fight another day. That was a pretty gutsy move and gorgeously executed." There was genuine admiration in her tone.

"I think their plan was to kill me and kidnap you, Cait," he said skimming over the compliment, but pleased by it, nonetheless. "That's why your assailant didn't have his gun drawn. And they never expected you to go on the attack, as you did. It probably didn't occur to either of them that they couldn't subdue you easily, if I were gotten out of the way."

"And, our friend in the woods?" she countered. "He must have been following us, too. But why?"

"I haven't the foggiest, but I'd say it suggests you and the Spear are on more than one person's wish list. And it appears everyone needs you to stay alive... at least until they find what they're after."

"I wonder why that doesn't comfort me," she responded, suddenly realizing how cold she felt now that the adrenaline rush was gone, and the sweat of the fight had turned clammy on her skin in the frigid night air. Cait hugged herself as she walked, not so much because of the exterior cold, but because of how suddenly real the danger was that she might never make it back to Lark alive.

Hugh watched her from the corner of his eye, wanting more than anything to put his arms around her to keep her warm. Knowing instinctively how much that would spook her, instead, he shrugged out of his jacket and put it around her shoulders without saying a word.

85

"Those imbeciles have failed again, Fritz," Gruner's words were an explosion of loathing and frustrated rage. "My patience is truly at an end."

Fritz painted the appropriate sentiment onto his own face – concerned, not overly curious – and answered.

"Is there some way I can help, Father?" he offered respectfully. "You have so many more urgent matters on your plate...." he let the thought hang.

Gruner eyed his son's angular face and body. Fritz was a fine specimen.   Tall, lean, Aryan to the bone.   Mentally, he congratulated himself on the woman he had chosen all those years ago, as his breeder. She had brought superb genetic material to the construction of his son's physical body. He, himself, had seen to the boy's mental strength and his sense of purpose, after disposing of the woman. He had considered keeping her for a time, but the possible   contamination   of   their   perfect   creation   by   the unpredictability of emotional attachment, was just too great a risk. No. He'd made the right choice.

Gruner weighed his options now and came to a decision.

"It appears the man is a more formidable opponent than we had imagined. He is trained – a former Para, it seems, in some elite regiment or other. A one man protection detail. And the woman, while not a professional, appears not easy to subdue. It seems the men sent to abduct her made the assumption they could quickly dispose of the man and easily overpower the woman. They were wrong in both assumptions.

"Perhaps it's merely a matter of the wrong people having been dispatched to deal with this?" Fritz suggested, help-fully.

"Hmmm," his father made a non-committal sound. "Perhaps. But I suspect there's more to it. Serendipitous interventions of some sort keep getting in the way. I shall have to make enquiries on the Inner Planes. And of course, there is the matter of discretion and the complication of disposing of him, while keeping her alive for questioning."

Fritz nodded. "And I assume you've considered kidnapping the child, as an incentive to the mother's cooperation? You so much enjoy children."

Gruner's eyes narrowed, studying his son's handsome face, now blank of expression. A curious remark, the last one. Perhaps a subtle slander about his own parenting. But he saw no hint of irony in the younger man's placid gaze.

"I do," he replied, "they alter the balance of the sport." Abruptly, he tired of the discussion.

"I may require your assistance with this matter, Fritz," he said, his voice cold and even. "Perhaps you should familiarize yourself with the issue."

Fritz rose, knowing his father's cues so well. He had suffered a good deal in boyhood, during the learning process, as mistakes had never been gently dealt with.

"You may be assured I shall give it thought, Father, but of course, I'll need access to the specifics of what's been done so far..."

"Hans Kolb will brief you," Gruner said. *Ah...* Fritz noted with interest. *It was his father's own security advisor who had failed thus far.* The man was usually quite competent. That upped the ante a bit. If this were a path to undermining his father's confidence in Kolb, it could serve his purpose. Getting rid of the Stasi would go a long way toward making his father's untimely demise easier.

He'd almost revealed to his father his idea about contacting the child directly through the Internet, but was now pleased he hadn't let it slip. He'd had one of his computer specialists get the IP address, and he'd worked out an interesting experiment, but now he'd wait to tell his father, until he had proved his hypothesis.

Fritz smiled to himself. It would be interesting to see just how vulnerable the child would be to the kind of mind manipulation he was adept at. And, it appeared his father had just welcomed him into the chase.

86

Heredon. England.

A gate marked with a glowing Roman numeral marked the entrance to the newest game level. Lark had Milady ring the gong that hung beside the gate, and an echoing reverberation boomed then faded, as the Gatekeeper's large form materialized.

"Have you been formally introduced to Charlemagne?" he asked without saying hello.

"Not yet, Gatekeeper," she answered.

"He wishes to tell you about the man who invented the game of chess. Do you wish to learn?"

"Oh yes!" she said, excited by the idea because maybe this Gate could be all about the Wheat and Chessboard Problem. Her daddy had told her all about that one. It was hard, but she knew she could do it. He'd said the man who invented chess had offered to sell the game to some king who was maybe, Charlemagne, but nobody knew for sure. When the king asked the price of the game, the inventor said it was very reasonable... all he wanted was one grain of wheat for the first square, two for the second, four for the third, each square doubling the amount on the one before it. The king wasn't so good at math, or maybe he had other stuff on his mind that day, like conquering the world, or something, so he said OK, but then the final amount of wheat was so huge, the king got mad and threw the inventor in jail instead! Her daddy said math students all over the world knew about the Wheat and the Chessboard problem.

It would be a whole big formula, and that could take a while, because of the 64 squares, but she'd started scribbling down ideas even before Charlemagne finished telling the story.

Twenty-eight minutes later, Lark typed in the number 18, 446, 744, 073, 709, 551, 615 and was rewarded for the right answer, with the newest word clue as it materialized ahead of her on the path. It said

An icon stands
The truth to cloak
The secret rests
Within the Oak.

Not much help, she thought, disappointed. But she dutifully wrote it down in her pink patent leather diary, with the other clues she'd already been awarded.

Lark clicked out of the game and into e-mail, feeling cranky and disgruntled. There was a message from Aunt Meg, but there was another message from an unknown sender. She was about to delete it because she knew she wasn't supposed to read e-mail from strangers, but the subject line read *Your Daddy Always Talked About You.*

Lark stared at it for a minute, trying to decide. The sender was somebody called Big Wiz Kid.

She hit the *read* icon and started to do just that.

87

Gruner donned the black silk hooded robe and tied the red cincture at his waist. He placed the Thule torc around his neck and donned the ring of office. He intended to gain contact with the Inner Realms in ritual, something he hadn't done in considerable time. In truth, he was not particularly gifted as a medium, or in any other specific psychic discipline. He had learned the Dark Arts by rote and ruthlessness, not talent, once he'd seen the authority that could be gained by those who tapped the Dark Powers.

He had applied himself to his black magic studies with the same assiduous, some would say manic, determination he had used with all other valuable studies throughout his lifetime. His superb memory had made spell-work easy and ancient tongues accessible, and his own nature that had not balked at even the vilest and most deplorable black practices, had made his a swift climb through the 10 Initiatory Degrees necessary for mastery.

Adepthood had served him during the War, in his accumulation of vast wealth and in a sophisticated understanding of those within The 13 who owed their fortunes and powers to their allegiance to the Dark Lords. But beyond the pleasure of being able to best and control even such as these, the actual practice of the Mystic Arts themselves gave him no genuine pleasure. Unlike Hitler, Himmler, Haushoffer, Eckhardt and the like, who were gifted occultists, he found the practice of Black Magic a useful tool, like a computer or electricity itself, not a passion. Other than the ritual sacrifices that involved sex and blood, he took no great pleasure in its duties.

But at the moment, he must overcome his disdain for arcane ceremony and see what he could learn on The Inner Planes, either about the whereabouts of the Spear itself, or the path of its Caretaker. As he robed, he cast about in his mind for something suitable he could offer the Dark Gods in return for what he sought. Remembering that Fritz had several test subjects incarcerated in the lab, he thought a blood oblation might be just the thing. He would have preferred a hunt, but there really wasn't time.

Gruner rang the bell that summoned Kolb, told him of his need, then set to work with the theurgical tools he'd need for the invoking ritual he intended. He'd scry first – the black scrying mirror would give him information before approaching the demon he sought. It was always dangerous to bind a demon to do your bidding, so he began the ritual to steady his breathing and focus. From this point on, any misstep could mean death or considerably worse.

*   *   *

His ceremonial robe in place, Gruner entered the dedicated circle and inverted pentagram. He now knew which demon could serve him best but this was a formidable creature and had to be approached with precision. He'd dealt with him before.

Black candles burned at all five points of the star and a blood red candle in an elaborate golden receptacle that had once graced the palace of a Borgia, flamed brightly at the center. He had decided precisely which spell from the many possibilities would best suit his purpose.

Scattering appropriate incense on the flame, then, tossing back the hood of his robe, he intoned the words of power that would summon the demonic force to do his bidding. Care had to be taken to contain the creature so it could fulfill its task without escaping. It was essential the beast be banished back to Hell once the deed was done, but demons who had tasted freedom were sometimes hard to handle, particularly this one. He'd dealt with it before.

The dark smoke billowed and writhed as a huge sulfurous form began to coalesce in the center of the separate summoning pentagram Gruner had constructed for it earlier.

"You called?" an insolent and sepulchral voice asked.

"I have a task for you," Gruner replied, satisfied that the right creature had answered his call.

"What would you have me do?" it asked, breathing out a stench of decay.

"There is a woman," Gruner replied. "She seeks the Spear of Longinus..."

The apparition hissed and recoiled, inflating itself to much larger stature in the process. "Are you not aware, fool, that I cannot traffic with a sacred object of the Light!" it thundered.

"Take care whom you call fool, fiend!" Gruner spat back. "I hold the chain that binds you to my will."

"For now, you hold the chain," it replied archly. "But for how long, arrogant mortal?"

"Beware, demon," Gruner said with quiet malice. "I could see you chained forever, and choose another for my bidding."

"But you won't," it said, its tone now thoroughly bored. "And can the fucking melodrama. Nobody's listening, least of all me. You know how well I perform for you. More than well enough for us to continue our, shall we say, relationship?" It smirked and malevolent calculating yellow eyes were suddenly visible in the roiling column.

"Here is my bidding, then," Gruner said, annoyed by the creature's obvious lack of respect. "Help the woman find her Spear, then see to it that she cannot keep it. I have other plans for its use."

The apparition seemed to ponder that a moment. It liked when a human, thinking he had the upper hand, floundered into a trap. This one's request had possibilities.

"And what do I receive in payment?" it asked, as if undecided.

"Human flesh to consume. If you can gorge on the souls as well, so be it."

"This is a difficult task," it countered. "I will require more payment than usual."

"Are you a demon or a rug merchant?" Gruner snapped.

"Do you wish the deed done or not?" it responded, bored again. "Summon me tomorrow and I will tell you my price."

"Name your price now or return to your pit and await word of your punishment!" Gruner ordered, standing his ground.

"A half-dozen virgins suitably sacrificed," it said, having already seen the fatal flaw in what had been asked of him. The virgins were just a delectable extra treat. Humans, especially the smartest and most vicious, frequently made the mistake of thinking they could best a demon. This ass had not specified where the Spear would land, if the woman could not keep it.

"Two lives," Gruner countered. "I don't guarantee virginity."

"Four, and we have a bargain," it answered, "I'm feeling a bit peckish."

Gruner agreed, smiled, performed the banishing ritual, then left the chamber.

The demon was smiling, too.

—————————————— **88** ——————————————

The drive to Wewelsburg in central Germany's Alma Valley was long, but the picture postcard snowscape somewhat made up for the tedium. It was obvious from the way Hugh spoke during the drive, that he knew a great deal about the old Nazi fortress at Wewelsburg, now a youth hostel and museum. Cait was surprised when they were met by an elderly guide just outside the castle wall, apparently awaiting their arrival.

"Herr Schnabel has extraordinary knowledge of this place," Hugh explained after introducing the frail old man. "No one knows more."

Cait saw Schnabel smile sadly in acknowledging the compliment, but he said nothing, until Cait spoke to him directly. "Thank you for taking the time to indulge us, Herr Schnabel. I have so many questions..."

"And, I have so many answers, Frau Doktor," he replied. "Let us hope they are the correct ones for your quest." His educated English was accented, making his s's and th's both sound like softly sibilant z's.

She nodded. "Please, Herr Schnabel, as Hugh tells me you understand our needs, tell us whatever you think it's important for us to know."

The old man nodded, thought a moment, then began. "Ya," he said, "from the beginning, then. In 1933, S.S. Reichsfuhrer Heinrich Himmler, head of the SS, and the second most powerful man in the Reich, declared this stronghold to be "The Center of the World," a vast storehouse of magical energies that would protect the 1000 year Reich."

He raised his head and pointed to a tower on their left.

"Some still believe the energies collected in the North Tower of Wewelsburg Castle were so powerful all the Allies' efforts to destroy it at the war's end, were unsuccessful."

He began to walk as he continued speaking, so they followed him.

"Himmler leased the Castle for 100 years for the grand sum of one Reichsmark per year. The site was considered by locals to be an ancient place of dark occult power. Witch trials had been held here and many women had been tortured in the castle... so the place had a history of suffering."

He pointed them toward the tower. "Of course suffering was something for which Himmler bore particular responsibility, despite the fact that he was known to be a fastidious little man of meager physical courage. On the one occasion when he observed some of his own handiwork at Auschwitz, he became physically ill, fainted, and never again personally inspected any of the death camps, which he both administered and funded."

The old man led the way as he spoke, Cait marveling at how nimbly he navigated the rocky landscape, the paths, and the tourists.

"You know every nook and cranny of this place, don't you, Herr Schnabel?" Cait prompted, intrigued by the old man, curious about his knowledge and his dignity.

"Ya," Herr Schnabel grudgingly agreed. "I helped build this fortress of the damned, you see. I was one of the boys who survived the Niederhagen Concentration Camp from which the laborers for the fortress were taken. It was our labor that transformed an old ruined castle into the Nazi Headquarters that became the corrupt heart of the Third Reich. It was here the SS took their blood oaths, and a most ancient evil was raised by their dark magic and allowed to enter this world."

Cait looked skeptically at Hugh, but he signaled her with his eyes and an almost imperceptible shake of his head, to wait and listen.

"To have contributed to this in any way, is not so easy a burden to bear, so I salve my conscience by remaining here to bear witness," Schnable said the words simply, then began to move again. "People forget, you see," he called over his shoulder.

Cait glanced at Hugh and saw compassion on his face, but he quickly turned away from her gaze. She was getting used to the fact that he frequently tried to hide the evidence of a soft heart, and she found the trait endearing.

"Himmler's plans were always evolving," Schnabel continued, waving his expressive, bone-thin hand toward the North Tower. "This tower was to be its cosmic center – in it was constructed the Obergruppsenfürhrersaal, a sacred chamber into which a massive oak round table was installed to mimic King Arthur's. Himmler and Hitler fancied this to be their Grail Castle, ya?" Cait's eyes met Hugh's at the mention of the Grail. Seeing their interest, Schnabel added, "Der Fuehrer was *obsessed* by the Grail myth, and with Wagner's opera *Parsifal*, which portrayed the mystic quest for the Grail.

"Hitler wanted this to be a place where one could connect to one's Aryan ancestors, study the runes, and so forth. A school of racial doctrines that declared the Aryans superior to all other races was established here, and all SS officers were taught of their *genetic superiority*." Contempt dripped from the last two words.

The old man unlocked a great wrought iron gate, and led the visitors into a vast stone chamber. "We keep out the tourists," he explained, "but I have been given the privilege of a key for special guests, as I am a 'renowned expert'." He made a rueful sound, as if to say this was not an expertise he had ever aspired to.

"The SS Marriage Consecrations took place here. The Master Race was to be conceived through these marriages of the blond, blue-eyed Aryans that Hitler so admired, despite the fact that he looked nothing like them. He and Himmler carefully chose the male and female specimens for their breeding program." Herr Schnabel beckoned them to a staircase.

"The place below is important to your store of knowledge, Frau Doktor."

They followed him down into a dark circular crypt. Schnabel waved his hand about the dark cold space. "Welcome to the Land of the Dead," he said.

Nausea had been creeping into Cait's consciousness ever since she'd entered the Tower. Now, suddenly it increased exponentially, and she found herself swaying a little, sick, dizzy, thoroughly disoriented. Hugh gripped her arm to steady her.

"I'm sorry," she breathed, confused. "I feel quite nauseated. If you'll just give me a minute to collect myself..." She saw Hugh and Schnabel exchange knowing glances, and was suddenly aware of what felt like an icy-electrical current surging up from the ground, invading her body.

"What took place here?" she managed to ask, unable to quell the roiling unwanted current of energies inside her, that were making her want to vomit.

"It was to be a burial place for the elite SS officers," said Hugh, watching her carefully, "and a place to keep their Death's Head rings, which were to be stored forever in the castle. There were 11,500 of those cursed rings that went missing at the end of the war. Presumably they are still worn by believers all over the world."

Images were flickering in and out of Cait's consciousness now... images she couldn't hold back and didn't understand.

"Please – I'm seeing disjointed images... I think you have to take me to where some Book was kept..." she blurted the words suddenly, not having thought them first.

"It wasn't here," Schnabel said quickly. "Come. We go to the West Tower." Hugh was half holding her up as they stumbled out into the chill air of the courtyard together. Cait didn't try to brush away his grip. She would have fallen without it. Nothing around her looked solid any more – everything seemed in a kind of gelatinous slow motion.

They stepped inside the West Tower and Cait felt propelled on auto-pilot toward an empty niche cut deep in the stone wall.

"It was kept here, wasn't it?" she whispered. "The Spear and a book that resonated with it. A Book of Secrets, but not a Grimoire. The Grimoires were kept elsewhere." She looked around, then pointed to another wall. "Over there," she said with sudden conviction.

Schnabel nodded. "This is all true, Frau Doktor. I had to take them to the crypt from time to time myself, those evil books."

Cait shook her head vehemently. "The Book I'm seeing isn't evil... it has light shining from its pages. I see words, sentences, but I can't read them – there are symbols, a cipher of some kind... and drawings... diagrams and maps... like an alchemist's journal..." her words trailed off, for the images were fading as she spoke. The world around her was again coalescing into firm reality, and she realized she no longer felt ill, only terribly drained. She shook her head and blinked her eyes in an attempt to clear her vision.

"What just happened to me?" she asked finally, certain both men knew.

"This place is a portal between dimensions, Cait." It was Hugh who spoke gently, "a place where the veil between the worlds is thin and permeable.

"It grips everyone differently, but those who have the Sight see images. I take it you saw things... felt things. I think the tower is a collection point, not a generator – some kind of huge natural accumulator and capacitor for earth energies. I think visual images are stored here, as if on a computer chip."

"We couldn't warn you, my dear," Schnabel said in a kindly tone, "because we didn't know precisely how, or if, you would be affected."

"What's most unnerving about the experience," she said, trying to force her thoughts to collect themselves, "is that everything I saw seemed to have enormous meaning, but it was all beyond my grasp. I don't know what was expected of me in this place, but whatever it was, I've failed us completely."

"Ah, but you are quite wrong about that, Frau Doktor," said Schnabel. "What you have seen tells us you are indeed the One. Therefore, I can now tell you what I know, without fear of that knowledge falling into profane hands.

"Come. We have a cup of tea, and perhaps a little Schnapps, ya... and I will tell you what I have waited, all these years, to tell *someone*."

89

Their drive to the nearby town of Buren was silent. Hugh and Schnabel exchanged a few sentences, some of it in German, but Cait tuned them out and just leaned her head back gratefully against the car seat and tried to recapture all of her strange vision, willing it to make sense. She could remember much of what she'd seen, but the message of the Book of Secrets kept eluding her. The words were there, beaming light – she just couldn't read them.

"Is there no place closer?" she asked once. "I'd like to write down all I can, before I forget any details."

"I'm afraid we must go to Buren, rather than into the village of Wewelsburg," Schnabel answered. "In Buren, we will find the privacy we require."

The small but charming house they finally stopped in front of was not actually in the town of Buren, but rather on its outskirts, near a wooded area. The well-tended garden in front was filled with the winter remains of summer roses, and a variety of wild flowers. Cait saw that a geometrically arranged herb garden was positioned to catch the afternoon sunlight, and the corner of an orderly vegetable garden was visible to the right of the house. A light frosting of snow lay over all, making it seem too picturesque to be real.

"Welcome to my home, Frau Doktor," the little man said with a formal bow. "Here we have no fear of prying eyes or ears. Hugh and I have conversed here on a number of occasions, and his father and uncle have been my guests as well."

He settled them into a small cozy library, filled floor to ceiling with overflowing shelves. Books and manuscripts littered every surface.

"Would you be so kind, Hugh," he asked, over his shoulder, as he moved toward the kitchen, "to light the fire in the hearth for us, while I fetch our tea."

"It will be my pleasure, Professor," Hugh called back, and Cait looked up, surprised by the title.

Hugh smiled as he struck a match to the already laid logs in the old stone hearth. "Professor Schnabel prefers not to use his academic title in the proximity of the Castle," he told her in a near whisper. "He says it's because he doesn't wish to be pestered by all the youth hostellers asking questions, but I suspect the truth is that when he's there, he sees himself not as the acclaimed academic he became after the war, but as the desperate slave boy who was forced to leave his childhood behind to build a temple to evil."

"Is there a Frau Schnabel?" Cait asked looking around the room at the decorating touches she thought showed a woman's hand.

"Hilda passed away five years ago. She, too, was a survivor of the camps, and one of us."

By the time Professor Schnabel returned minutes later with a well-laden tea tray and a bottle of his favorite Schnapps, the fire was blazing, and the room was bathed in its soothing, flickering glow. The scent of the fragrant logs filled the small house with a powerful pine essence.

"What is that marvelous scent, Professor?" Cait asked appreciatively. "I've never smelled a fire so fragrant."

He smiled, "It is wonderful, is it not? The pine from this forest is famous throughout Germany for its lush scent. You cannot help but feel you are one with the Earth herself, when you breathe in such beauty, ya?"

He turned to Cait. "Will you do us the honor of pouring our tea, my dear," he asked, a little self-consciously. "It is seldom since Hilda passed that I have the pleasure of seeing a beautiful woman perform this lovely task. It is so much more nourishing and graceful when tea is poured by a woman's hand, I think. Perhaps Hugh would agree?"

Cait smiled, accepting the charming invitation, and thinking how many of the simple graces of life we take for granted. She poured their tea and placed the tiny, succulent-looking pastries on plates for each of them, then sat back in her chair, wondering if this had been Frau Schnabel's accustomed place at the tea table.

"Now, let our story begin..." the old man said gravely. He took a deep breath, girding himself for a difficult task, then started in, "I was a lad of 12 years when my family and I were taken. My Father was a respected scholar, my beautiful Mutti was a hausfrau, but also a painter of some skill, and a quite gifted musician. These talents had been passed on in varying measure to me, to my brother Gunther, and to my little sister, Aloise." He paused, and she thought it was to gain control of his emotions.

"We were taken one terrible night of pain and terror, by the Gestapo, torn from each other's arms, and sent to separate camps." His tear-bright eyes rose to Cait's.

"Do you know the word *zerissenheit*?" he asked, and she shook her head no.

The professor nodded. "I speak seven languages and in none of them but ours have I found such a word, so there is no real translation. But I believe you could say it means *torn-to-pieces-hood.*" He paused. "Do you understand this?"

Cait felt tears rise at the thought. "I understand this very well," she said softly.

He reached over and patted her hand. "Ya," he said with a sigh. "I see that you do." Then he withdrew his old hand and continued.

"I later learned that my Mutti and Aloise were murdered very soon after this night of *zerissenheit.* My father died in Buchenwald, my brother and I were sent first to Sachsenhausen, and then later to Niederhagen, where I saw my brother Gunther hanged on my 13th birthday. He was accused of stealing a crust of bread. If it was true, it was probably for me he had stolen this food, as many around us had already perished from starvation." He paused again, looking deep into the fire.

"At first, we were merely laborers, forced to work on the reconstruction of the castle, but two strange serendipities – perhaps you would call them this – kept me alive, when so many others perished. The first, was that it was somehow learned I was both musician and artist, so I was detailed to serve inside the castle for the many dinner parties that were given there for the SS elite. Sometimes, I played the violin, and sometimes I was merely a kitchen boy. Sometimes, after they had grown accustomed to my presence, I was allowed to be a server at table. We who worked inside the castle, fed on table scraps and therefore lived when others did not." He stopped and took a small sip of tea, to regain his composure. "This is how I was present at times when certain plans were discussed."

"Often, I was allowed to play my instrument to entertain the SS men, but when I did this, of course, I could not hear so well their conversations."

He sighed. "My second reprieve I owe also to my dear Mutti's gifts to me. I could draw very well – far better than I played music – so I was next given duties to help the architect render copies of Himmler's ever-changing plans for the edifice at the *Center of the World.*" He emphasized the last, as if to say how utterly ridiculous this pretension was.

"I was always a boy of small stature, and looked even younger than my meager years, so I suppose I was hardly considered a threat to anyone, small mouse that I was. And, too, we workers were all to be killed once the work on the Castle had been accomplished, so perhaps things could be said in my presence that surely would never have been said before an adult." He breathed in a long deep inhalation. "So do the Gods decide our fates, ya? Gunther and Aloise die and I live... who can say why?" He sighed once more and went on.

"Could it be, I wonder, is *this* very moment, here in this house with you, Frau Doktor, the reason why I was spared the fate of my brother and sister? That I might tell you now, what I heard from the lips of terrible men?" He shook his head, and wiped the moisture from his eyes brusquely. Professor Schnabel cleared his throat, embarrassed by his own emotion.

"An important man named Haushoffer – one, who along with Dietrich Eckart, had founded the infamous Thule Society – was one night, a guest of Himmler's. On this night, I was chosen to serve as a footman – one who carried dishes of steaming vegetables to the table, and then stood along the wall, with my heavy dish quivering in my puny hands, trying to stay upright while the dinner wore on and on, in case any officer should require more gluttony.

"Himmler was regaling Haushoffer – who was der Führer's own personal occultist, astrologer and prophet – with his mystical plans for the Wewelsburg Castle. Haushoffer, an arrogant aristocrat, was in return regaling Himmler with tales of Thule, an island like Atlantis, that he said had once been the center of a great and magical civilization. The Germans and some few Scandinavians, he said, were the only survivors of this lost magical world of Aryan Supermen.

"In fact, he said, this was the very reason Hitler had been chosen to be der Führer... because of the need to communicate once more with this magical world! As you can imagine, my boyish ears pricked up at this strange statement.

"Haushoffer, who had taken too much drink, told Himmler that when he, himself, had been a very young man, it had been mystically revealed to him that in order to recreate the majesty and power of this lost world of magic, the right men must take charge of the world's destiny, and that he and Dietrich Eckart were among those chosen to decide the fate of the world!

"You can imagine Himmler's reaction to such a tale. He just kept pouring more and more wine into Haushoffer and plying him with questions, while this self-important "mystic" was only too happy to pontificate.

"Haushoffer said that he and Eckart realized they needed a brilliant *medium* to establish a firm connection with the energies of this ancient lost civilization, so it could be reestablished in Germany. And *that*, he said, was how the mystical destiny of Adolf Hitler was revealed to them! All of this, was, of course, music to Himmler's ears. He pressed Hauschoffer for endless details.

"Can you even imagine how such a conversation had me mesmerized and terrified at the same time? Just hearing such words could surely be my death warrant!

"Haushoffer said he and Eckart knew immediately that Hitler was *the One*. Destined to be able to summon the dark power of the Old Gods, he must be designated the Leader... *der Führer*.

"According to Haushoffer, for this reason, he and Eckart began to train Hitler in the Dark Arts, and while Adolf was – Haushoffer's own words, mind you – '*a wild, semi-literate non-entity*' when they began to train him – he was also a genius – a *savant* – a great medium who could be trained do to their will! He said it had taken only three years to initiate Hitler into Dark Magic Adepthood, then with the help of their ancient Gods, Hitler was transformed during this time, to the master leader he was meant to be. He said that their Secret Society met always at the house of their idol, the composer Richard Wagner! I have always since believed this explains, at least in part, Hitler's obsession with Wagner's opera, Parsifal.

"'*We are Hell and Darkness*,' this travesty of a human being said that night. '*And through Hitler, we will overrun the world*!' With my own ears I heard him say this!"

The old man stopped a moment, pursing his lips thoughtfully, then said, with great solemnity, "And of course, they very nearly did just that."

Cait began to speak, but Schnabel held up his hand to stay her. "Please, my dear Frau Doktor, allow me to complete my story, for it does not end here, and I must not forget a single word of what I am meant to impart to you.

"From this night forward, I continued to serve every dinner I could volunteer for, and to make my drawings as perfect as possible, so that I would be given access to more conversations... more knowledge. I was a boy on fire to know their evil plans and to survive that terrible place, so that I could tell someone, *anyone*, who would listen, about their madness and their mission. I would bear witness!

"Thus, on another occasion, I served your Herr Gruner, a butcher of men who was then known as Herr Doctor Guttman. Would that it could have been strychnine that I served to him that night, but alas, it was only sauerbraten.

"Thus, did I hear of how the camps were being used for their occult rituals. How the most grotesque and horrific deaths served their purpose best, for fear and pain were the energies needed to raise the dark powers with which they sought to curry favor with the Old Gods.

"All through dinner, and through the following day, Guttman/Gruner set forth his plans to Himmler and others. If they would permit him to design the experiments he outlined, he would guarantee a level of suffering that would generate massive occult power. It was the same way in which blood sacrifice was used in the Black Mass, and the same way it had been used in ancient

Teutonic times, when blood sacrifice was how the fierce warrior Gods of Thule were propitiated.

"I, of course, did not hear *all* that was said, as I was in and out of the room a hundred times that night and day, serving, serving, serving these monsters until I could barely stay on my feet. But I heard enough and I remembered every word, in the hope of one day telling *someone* what I had heard! This was all that drove me and kept me alive."

He paused, took a bit of tea, cleared the hoarseness that had been prompted by his memory, then pressed on.

"Some time after Gruner's departure from Wewelsburg, a package arrived under elite SS guard from der Führer, himself. It contained the Spear you seek, and what appeared to be a very old leather-bound book – I saw both with my own eyes. For one whole day, Himmler sat in his private study with this book, and whatever instructions he had received from der Führer himself. I brought him food and drink, several times, which he barely touched. At one moment, when I entered the room, he was holding the Spearhead in his hand and studying it, or perhaps fondling it would be more expressive of his actions.

"'Do you know what this is, boy?'" he asked me. I nearly dropped his tray, I was so startled he would address me directly.

"No, Herr Reichsmarshall," I replied, trembling that I'd been noticed at all. You see, one *only* survived by *not* being noticed. Except for my drawings, I had succeeded at achieving this invisibility.

"This is the Spear with which you filthy Jews killed Christ!" he said. He was generally an even tempered little man, an accountant by profession, you know, and phlegmatic? This outburst frightened me.

"Yes, sir," I stammered. "I'm sorry, sir."

"He turned to look me up and down and seeing my small insignificant stature he said contemptuously, 'It does not matter now. You vermin will all soon be dead.' Then he dismissed me with a wave of his manicured hand, and I fled to the relative safety of the kitchen. All night I lay awake in terror that having been noticed, I would now be killed, like my brother. But as you can see, that did not happen." He sighed again.

"The final puzzle piece I can offer you is this one. I saw Himmler remove the Spear and the Book from the safe, before he left the castle for the final time. He had them wrapped in brown paper and string like a common parcel, and he left the castle with them under his arm. I never saw him again. This was late in 1943. What happened to either the Spear or the Book I have no way to know, but Himmler's driver told cook they went straight to Berlin."

The emotions rekindled by his story left Schnabel drained. He tried to maintain his role as gracious host, but he seemed utterly spent after unburdening himself of the knowledge he had kept through so many years – uncertain of why it had been given to him, hoping one day to know what to do with it.

Cait and Hugh, after tidying up the tea tray, left him asleep in his armchair by the fire. Hugh said this was how the old man often ended his evenings since Hilda's passing, and that it would be best simply to leave him a note of thanks, and to be on their way.

Cait covered the old professor with a knitted afghan she found neatly folded in the corner of the sofa – the work of Hilda's loving hands, she was sure. There were tears in her eyes as she tucked it in around the frail old man, and followed Hugh to their waiting car. Snow had fallen while they were in the house and the world around them was lightly dusted and glittering in the moonlight.

"Oh Hugh..." Cait choked as she looked up at the falling flakes. "It's almost Christmas and Lark is all alone..."

*   *   *

Cait hung up the phone in the hotel they'd stopped at, once the snow had made the roads too dangerous to drive. She was dead tired and the tragic stories Schnabel had told them had left her feeling drained, saddened and unutterably alone. She would have given anything to hold Lark in her arms so they could both cry out their loneliness and sorrow at the loss of the one person each had loved so unconditionally.

She'd phoned both Meg and Lark, needing to hear their voices, needing to love and *feel* loved, but the frustration of not being able to speak freely, when she wanted so desperately to blurt out everything she'd learned, and all that was happening to her, just made her feel even more frustrated than she'd been before making the calls. Meg said Carter was arranging for encrypted phones for all of them, and they'd somehow manage to get one to her, if she could figure out where she'd be by week's end. But she never knew where they'd be the next day, never mind at the end of the week, so it didn't give her much feeling of hopefulness.

The conversation with Lark had been even more unsettling. Her daughter had sounded so little-girl-sad and so terribly alone, they'd each just ended up crying, and then trying unsuccessfully to cheer each other up. Finally, Cait had promised she'd be home before Christmas whether they found the Spear or not, but she could hear in Lark's voice that her old absolute confidence in her mother's word wasn't there anymore, and that fact triggered every maternal fear of inadequacy Cait possessed. She wondered if there was a way to feel any more a failure than she did at that moment. She hadn't been able to save her husband, and now her child no longer believed in her. And the jury was still out on whether she believed in herself enough to think she could save any of them at all.

Thoroughly chilled and miserable, she slid under the covers, grateful for the promise of the oblivion sleep would provide, if she could just get there. Her nerves were so on edge now that she'd taken to waking every few hours, as if her mind was always on high alert to make sure no new danger had surfaced, no new threat was in the room with her.

God, how I hate sleeping without Jack beside me! She thought as she hugged the pillow to her chest, and wished with all her heart that her husband was there, folding her in, making her feel loved and safe. She'd reveled in the comforting warmth of Jack's large body next to hers for so many years, so many comforting entanglements of limbs, and lives... had she just taken all that for granted, she wondered? Or had she just so believed in their love and the foreverness of their commitment to each other that there was no blame to be placed in having felt such utter contentment. The sensuality of naked flesh on flesh, the just plain all-encompassing safety-net of feeling loved and protected had meant everything to her, and now it was gone for good. Nothing bad could ever happen to her with Jack beside her, somehow she'd always known that, and she'd been right. What she hadn't known was that it wouldn't be forever, and that he was the one who wouldn't be protected.

"Dear God," she sighed the prayer into the night air before falling into fitful sleep, "Please just let me save Lark. I don't care what happens to me... just let me keep my little girl safe." She decided she'd make the trip to Rome, but after that, she'd go home to the child who needed her so badly.

90

BWK is awesome! Lark thought, as she shut her computer for the night. He knew everything about Daddy and about his classes. He'd told her about how her daddy talked about her all the time in class, because he was so proud of her. He even knew when her birthday was and about her school and her teachers and Bitsy.

Lark felt her happiness drain when she thought about how far she was from Bitsy and from home. Why didn't her mommy understand how awful it was to be so far from home, and with no BFF to talk to, and only old people to play with? Why didn't her mommy *just come back*?

BWK understood how lonely she was. He felt so bad for her that he'd sent her things to take her mind off her troubles. At first, she felt a little guilty about checking out the links he sent, because they were pretty grown-up, but then BWK told her how her daddy had talked about how mature she was. So much more mature than other kids her age.

And besides, the sites were really interesting.

The Past is Prologue

Part XIII

"We learn from history that we learn nothing from history."

George Bernard Shaw

91

CIA Headquarters
Langley, Virginia

Director Farnsworth let the age-yellowed dossier fall heavily onto his desk. He'd read it cover to cover, for what seemed like the hundredth time. He probably knew every word of the document by heart now – and heart was unquestionably the right word to invoke in this ancient drama that had haunted him for damned-near a lifetime.

His father had been a man of great and stalwart heart. Not a man of privilege, but a man of courage and intellect and conscience. Just the kind of man a son looks up to, admires, wants to emulate. The kind of man who deserved better at the hands of his country than he'd gotten. Harry Farnsworth had been smart and honorable, steadfast, in the way so many men of his generation seemed to be. Summa from Columbia Law, half of it done at night so he could support a family while getting his J.D. degree. A fine husband, a loving father, who thought going into government service was a proper example to set for his son. It had been an example for Farnsworth, all right – just not the kind his father had envisioned.

Harry Farnsworth had been thrown to the wolves by the covert decision-makers of the very country he'd fought to protect. And all because of the likes of Gustav Gruner...

Washington, DC
1946

Harry Farnsworth couldn't believe what he was seeing on the Top Secret memorandum he held in his hand. Dr. Helmut Guttman was to be given every assistance in his escape from Germany. He was **not** *to be indicted nor sent to Nuremburg to be tried for his crimes against humanity. Instead, he was to be given a new identity, a white-washed past and a large sum of money with which to begin a new life. Helmut Guttman, the butcher of Sobibor, Buchenwald, Auschwitz, and more... the man who had constructed some of the war's most heinous medical experiments and exterminations was being given a free pass and a payoff. It just wasn't possible! Farnsworth reread the memo three times to be certain he was not misinterpreting the inconceivable orders he'd just received regarding the man.*

Harry had been there at the camps, traveling as legal liaison with the 3rd Army detail charged with liberating the death camps. He'd seen the worst of them first hand. It was not just the staggering reality of genocide that had overwhelmed him, but the inconceivable atrocities that had been perpetrated on the living skeletons and on the corpses in the mass graves... atrocities perpetrated by Guttman and his ilk. In the final days not even the crematoria could keep up with the disposal of the evidence, so Harry and the troops he'd been billeted with, had seen more of the truth than any of them could have imagined... truths that would never leave their nightmares.

He'd held the skeletal hands of women with festering craters in their bellies where uterus and ovaries had been destroyed by radiation. He'd seen limbless men, who'd had gangrenous debris sewn into a leg or an arm to see how long it would take before amputation was called for. He'd talked with amputees, who'd had limbs removed without anesthesia. He'd heard of women forced to watch their children buried alive. And, now, this man – this butcher – would go free?

No. That simply could not be allowed to happen. It didn't matter that Guttman had bargained with military and political higher ups, using scientific data as his bargaining chips. The only reason the man had this data was because of his butchery of innocents. Wasn't ridding the world of such conscienceless monsters a goodly portion of what this whole damned war had been fought about? Harry put down the memo and made a decision. Whatever it took, he would use all the legal skills at his disposal to make sure Guttman got the punishment he deserved for his crimes against humanity. It was the least he could do for the suffering and the dead. Somebody had to insist on justice for them.

Harry Farnsworth picked up a pen and began to make his notes: meticulous, analytical documentation of all he knew of Herr Dr. Guttman. It appeared, from the papers that had just crossed his desk, that the man was to be given a new identity – that of Dr. Gustav Gruner...

*   *   *

Top Secret
Memo
To Director OSS:
From Nightbird:
Re: Paperclip file #28

Attorney (H.F.) previously discussed, is causing considerable agitation regarding Paperclip 28. Suggest immediate action to deal with this problem, if it cannot be contained. HF has refused, thus far, to listen to reason regarding National Security issue here at stake. He insists the doctor (Paperclip #28) we have cleared for repatriation, be tried for his alleged crimes.

Paperclip 28 has already delivered the material bargained for to appropriate parties, and a passport has been secured from our spiritual colleagues in Rome, who will see to his prompt departure.

Threat to go public with Top Secret data is a traitorous offense. H.F., an attorney, has been apprised of the possible consequences if he does not cease and desist.

Please advise.

*   *   *

Top Secret
Eyes Only
To: Nightbird
From: The Director
Re: Subject 28

Contain or remove threat.

Immediate action sanctioned. Discreditation suggested. Discretion
and mis-direction appropriate.

Advise on method of containment.

New York Times
September 26, 1946

Suspicious Death of State Department Attorney

    Harry Farnsworth, head of the European desk at the
United States Department of State, fell to his death from the
window of a hotel room, two weeks after having been questioned
by the FBI regarding his suspicious contacts with Soviet
Military Intelligence, contacts that had not been sanctioned
by his superiors. The issue of his possibly having leaked
secret information to these contacts has besmirched a
previously impeccable reputation, and therefore came as a
shock to many in Washington and New York. Farnsworth was a
former Captain in the United States Army, and had been
commended for his legal liaison work during the last months of
the war, particularly his work on the legal issues involved
with the liberation of prisoners at several Nazi concentration
camps.
    Although police have ruled this death a suicide,
multiple questions have been raised about the manner of
Farnsworth's death, as he was wearing eyeglasses, galoshes and
a raincoat when he fell, and appears to have been carrying an
umbrella, all of which are unusual in a suicide...

Director Farnsworth removed his glasses, wiped his eyes, and leaned further back into the leather chair he had occupied so long it now conformed to every bodily contour. His father had been framed, silenced, killed, and vilified, and every bit of the trumped up evidence about the case stank like a week old carp. And none of that mattered at all to any but the people who had loved the man.

He had loved his father, and had never for one moment believed the suicide story or the alleged crap about his spying for the Soviets. Neither could have been less in character for the man, as anyone who knew him could attest. His mother and many high-ranking people in government had tried for years to clear his father's name. But to no avail. The fix was in. His mother had never recovered from the death or the scandal.

He himself had dealt with it all in his own way. He'd gotten his J.D. law degree with every conceivable honor, and then gone immediately into government service, despite his mother's horrified protest. He hadn't been able to explain to her that he had an agenda of his own, that would require knowledge he could gain no other way.

Learning about his father's death had been the central motivation of his long and successful career... discovering every dirty secret of every power player in the game. He had groveled and curried favor, he had worked longer and harder and better than his peers, he had pulled every string with the men who felt guilty over his father's demise, had attached himself to the ones who knew the secrets, no matter what sacrifice it demanded of his life or his conscience. And before he left this seat of power, which he had attained and maintained because of all he'd sacrificed, he would see justice done. Or some semblance of it. He had no illusions about happy endings, but seeing Gruner dead would be sufficient. To see him discredited would be the coda he'd waited a lifetime to attach to this dossier.

The Director was too old and too wise in the ways of covert intelligence operations to imagine he could clear his father's name. Too many lies had been told about his father's supposed disloyalty to his country, about his apocryphal bouts of depression and alcoholism. So much disinformational horseshit had been conjured up by covert ops brains to taint the memory of a good man who'd run up against a covert political agenda, and been swept away by the rotting tide of it. All "in the interests of National Security" that had never been at risk from Harry Farnsworth, a gentle man of good conscience, who had only wanted to see justice done.

Hell, the Director thought as he leaned back in his chair, a glass of Glenfiddich in his hand – he, himself had done the same thing to other men, during his long career. Finally, he had learned all there was to know about the covert business of governments, and the vulnerabilities and frailties of the men they manipulated. And, he had bided his time, waiting always for the opportune moment. In his gut, he knew that moment was finally near at hand.

I've been waiting in the tall grass for you Herr Doctor Gruner, for a long, long time... he murmured into the whiskey glass, as he held it to his lips. *I only regret that you'll never know the part I played in your demise. But then neither will anyone else.*

Farnsworth sighed. He was no better a man than the others who played this conscienceless covert game, but he was a better man than Gruner. And that's all that counted now.

Now, it was just a matter of helping Livingston do the dirty work, without letting his subordinate know he was being manipulated. The man's Achilles heel was that he'd do anything necessary to curry favor at the top. He wasn't as wily as the Director, and he could be played. Which was why he wouldn't ever *be* the Director. That job required a very special set of talents. And a very, very long memory.

All Roads Lead to Rome

Part XIV

*"He regarded the Universe as a
cryptogram set out by the Almighty."*
John Maynard Keynes

92

The Vatican Library

Cait clasped the hand of the priest they'd been sent to find in Rome. Father Umberto DeFeo looked old and fragile, his spider-veined, spotted hands delicate as twigs, yet his grip was strong and warm, and his ancient face was alive with delight upon greeting his visitors.

"Si, si," he said, as if confirming his own happiness at their arrival. He exchanged a Latin phrase with Hugh that seemed some sort of fraternal greeting, then turned his attention to Cait.

"You are the so-beautiful *dottore*, Maria told me to expect," he said with an effusive Italian appreciation for a pretty woman. He made a sweeping bow that was both gracious and comical. "I welcome you to my cemetery of forgotten books. My companions and I delight in your presence!"

Cait smiling, looked around at the shelves and shelves of books, taking in the scent of old paper, leather and dust. "Is someone else here with you, Father?"

"Oh, si, si *Dottore!*" he said with a twinkle, so at odds with his frail, ascetic appearance. "A thousand times a thousand characters reside within these walls with me. My beloved companions. They tell me things," he put his finger to his lips in a conspiratorial gesture. "They confide in me their mysteries and secrets, back to the dawn of time!" As he said it, he waved his hand at the bookshelves and passageways, the ladders and book-laden platforms that overflowed with volumes of the written word.

"The *Archivio Secreto Vaticano* is my home of many, many years. Since il Papa died, I have been consigned here as my punishment for having believed in the reforms he sought to bring about in the Church, you see.

"When he lived, I was his secretary, his helper. When he went home to God, his successors were only too happy to see me brought low and banished to obscurity." He chuckled softly. "An obscurity that suits me to *perfection*, I might add. After il Papa, those who followed him on the Throne of St. Peter, were not to my liking." He wrinkled his nose in distaste.

Cait smiled at the strange old character. "I take it," she said, "that the Papa you speak of was Pope John XXIII. Am I right?"

Father DeFeo's eyes lit up and he crossed himself. "Of blessed memory, he was, my dear dottore. It is he who should be now awaiting sainthood... but of course, God has already seen to that, has he not? Whatever these *politicios* do with their pretensions of canonization for the eyes of the world, God alone makes saints. God alone sees into men's hearts and judges holiness."

Hugh was smiling broadly. "My aunt tells me that of all the Amici, *you* may be the one with the most comprehensive knowledge about what we seek, Father," he said, "so we want you to know how very grateful we are for your help."

Father DeFeo put his bony fingers to his lips again, in the universal sign for silence, then said brightly, "Your aunt... she is a fine scholar herself, and the dissertation she tells me you are collaborating on for the great University in America that I currently cannot recall the name of, sounds most interesting to me. It pertains to the Lateran Conclave, I believe? Si, si, there is so much for me to tell you on this obscure and essential subject. So..." he looked at them closely to be sure they understood his obfuscation of their real purpose.

"Tell me, precisely how much do you know of our great Biblioteca? It is most important that you allow me to take you on a tour, si? Si!" he answered himself, as he set off and gestured for them to follow.

Realizing the priest did not wish to discuss their true purpose in this place, they pursued his sprightly footsteps down a long flight of stairs and through a serpentine series of corridors that seemed to go on for miles. DeFeo continued with an endless barrage of information.

"There are many libraries here at the Vatican," he told them as he led them from corridor to corridor. "We will, perhaps, need to visit them all."

He rattled off an astonishing list of at least a dozen libraries, giving each a tour guide's view of their worth. The last of his soliloquy carried them to an outer door, which led to St. Peter's Square. Once out, he breathed in deeply, and said, "The walls have ears... and eyes, and babbling mouths. Surveillance cameras are everywhere in the Archivio, and beyond that there are many who would seek to curry favor with my enemies if they could catch me in a single misstep. Thus, I have become Claudius – the doddering old fool, whom no one need fear." He chuckled with a fair degree of mirth. "My position gives me freedom to browse and to find things that have been conveniently mis-placed by my predecessors, because of their various political agendas. Thus, I hold many secrets."

"So the Vatican really is a place of political intrigue?" Cait asked.

"Here, power is the substitute for sex, my dear Dottore," he said simply. "Not that there isn't more than a bit of that, as well, eh? But it is very cold in the Square and, as I have friends as well as enemies, we will go to a place of warmth and safety. There is a cloistered convent on the Via Allessandro. I go there weekly, as I am the Confessor to Mother General. She, too, is Amici. Come. Mother will be expecting us."

The old priest wrapped his tattered cloak tighter and headed out of the Square and onto the busy thoroughfare beyond. A ten minute walk brought them to a rabbit-warren of ancient small and winding streets. Not even the smallest car could have navigated the street onto which he turned, which was hardly more than an alley.

They stopped, finally, in front of a heavy wrought iron screening gate, for which the priest produced a key. A tiny, silent girl in the habit of a novice, answered Father DeFeo's ringing of the great bell, mounted beside the heavy oak door that lay behind the gate.

The ancient door creaked closed behind them, and the childlike young woman, who was obviously bound by a vow of silence, led them through a flagstoned foyer, into a courtyard invisible from the street, and across the yard to another oaken door, this one reinforced with iron hardware that appeared to have withstood the assault of centuries.

The priest wafted the sign of the cross above the girl's head, a thank you for her courtesy. She curtsied in return, then scurried away, her long rosary clinking as she went, reminding Cait of her Catholic school childhood. Father DeFeo knocked, and a formidable female voice intoned, "Enter."

An imposing woman in a traditional white habit rose from behind her desk to greet her visitors. Cait was 5' 10", quite tall for a woman, yet this nun was taller still, by inches.

"Mother General," the priest, who looked half her size, greeted her warmly. "May I present to you Dottore Caitlin Monahan and the Honorable Hugh Delafield, Earl of Urnbridge."

Hugh reached out a hand to the woman. "My father, Uncle and Aunt send greetings," Hugh told the nun, then the Latin words he'd said to DeFeo followed and Mother General nodded acknowledgement.

"You are most welcome here." She waved slightly in the direction of a small, but genteelly appointed sitting room that adjoined her office. "Tea has been summoned. We will chat in my parlor."

Cait caught Hugh's eyes questioningly; he seemed to know this authoritarian woman. He smiled and winked at her, and she was again reminded of childhood, when all little girls lived in terror of the nuns, but the boys endured their rules with rebellious amusement.

After they'd been seated, the nun spoke again, her voice autocratic, her English superb. "I'm delighted to be of assistance to you both, and to Father DeFeo. There is little an old woman can do for the cause, living in so cloistered a world," she said with the first hint of a smile Cait had seen, "but the one thing such a world assures is absolute privacy. So you may speak freely here and you may consider this a safe house, should the need for one arise while you are in Rome. Not the Pope himself would violate the sanctuary of this Mother House. And even the spies of Deus Vult would not dare to breach our walls... and if they did so, it would be at their own peril."

Cait wondered what on earth *that* meant, but Hugh interrupted before she could ask.

"Most gracious of you, Mother," he said. "We hope to fly beneath the radar enough so that sanctuary will not be necessary, but not everything goes as anticipated, so we're grateful for an offer not given lightly – we realize sheltering us could put you and the sisters in danger."

Mother General smiled benignly. "This Convent has sheltered Jews and gypsies, resistance fighters, and all whom Divine Providence has seen fit to deposit on our doorstep, for generations. It is the task of our Order to do battle with the devil on a daily basis. I assure you, there is no power in heaven or on earth we fear." She said the words with such quiet conviction, Cait had no doubt of their truth.

"You know what we seek, Mother?" Cait asked.

The woman nodded. "Father DeFeo and I can help you in two important ways, I believe. We are both most grateful God has given us this chance to use our knowledge in His service."

The old priest murmured, "Sí, sí, Madre."

"I have intimate knowledge of why the Spear is surfacing now," said the austere Abbess, "why it is causing such disturbance, and why so many seek to suppress its story. You see, it is a '*way-*

shower'... an illuminator of Truth. Few know this of the Spear of Longinus, but Father and I have studied carefully enough to be certain and can add this knowledge to your puzzle.

"We know that Deus Vult wants Cardinal Andretti on Peter's throne to further the interests of the cabal he heads within the Vatican's elite. Andretti sees the canonization of Pius XII as his launch platform for acquiring the Papacy, but he also knows that Gruner's obsession with possessing the Spear could place terrible old secrets in a spotlight. If Gruner is unmasked for the butcher he was in the war, the truth about the Ratlines that funneled Gruner and others like him to safety through Vatican diplomatic routes will become public knowledge. Andretti fears that could undermine both Pius' Canonization and his own chance for ascendancy to the power of the Papacy. He cannot allow that to happen."

She leaned back in her chair. "And this is, I'm afraid, just the tip of the iceberg. You see, there are *so many* stories that must stay hidden to preserve the myth of Pius XII's sainthood. And it isn't only the Vatican that has an interest in containing the toxic truths the Spear could bring to light.

"With the Vatican's help, your CIA saved scum like Gruner and Eichman and the Croatian dictator Pavelic, from prosecution. They, too, want this kept buried, and they have powerful friends everywhere, make no mistake. Gruner heads The 13, an organization with an agenda in every fascist country in the world, that needs anonymity for what it does with its vast power and money. *All* these formidable forces have reason to suppress the story of the Spear. And I doubt any one of them would have scruples about killing you to protect old secrets as vile as their own."

Cait looked into the woman's eyes with alarm. "Then, you believe our task is hopeless, Mother?" she asked.

"Certainly not!" the nun snapped. "You have the power of God on your side."

Cait responded with a spontaneous burst of laughter. "Well if that's the case, I wish He'd just tell us where to find the Spear and we could be done with it!"

"Ah... but you see, He does not tend to make things so easy for His Champions... no one sets the bar higher than God Himself."

After a moment, she added, "But He has not left us without resources, I assure you. I myself possess documents that prove beyond doubt that Guttman and Gruner are the same man! Documents that certify both his change of name and the date of his passage to South America." She sat back in her chair with some satisfaction. "To the best of my knowledge, *all* other copies of this information were destroyed by your government long ago."

"How on earth did you come by such documents, Mother?" Cait asked leaning forward.

"I was very young in the war," she replied, "but I was never stupid. And I was *never* a servant of the dark force. My father was a high ranking member of Mussolini's entourage. He was, in fact, the judge who declared all Vatican passports and those they obtained from the Red Cross, valid, and he was privy to many dark secrets. I was his obedient young daughter who had been forbidden to enter the convent as I wished to do, because my father feared this would anger the Nazi atheists, with whom his Fascist friends curried favor. I acted for a time as my father's secretary. And, I put that time to good use." She smiled with righteous satisfaction. "Herr Schindler was not the only one who made a list..."

Cait's eyes widened with admiration. "You copied your father's files? That took courage!"

"Indeed. At first, I intended to use them only to blackmail him into letting me follow my calling to the religious life. But later, after the war had ended, and he'd died, it came to me that perhaps I had been guided all along by the hand of God, and that this knowledge I possessed could someday be used in the continuing struggle between Good and Evil that rages now more furiously than ever."

"You are as formidable as I have heard, Mother," Hugh said with genuine admiration.

"We are all merely pawns in God's game," she answered. "He alone controls the board."

Father DeFeo cleared his throat. It was about to be his turn to reveal his part in the game.

"And the papers that are proof of Gruner's identity?" Cait ventured. "Where are they?"

Mother General smiled. "They are kept safe until you need them. When that day comes, they are at your disposal. We have resources that would, no doubt, surprise you."

Before Cait could pursue that further, Father Defeo interrupted.

"The secrets of evil men are not the only mystery to be unlocked by the Spear, my dear children," he said. "I cannot tell you where it currently rests, but I can tell you why you must find it before Herr Gruner does!"

He saw with some satisfaction that he had their full attention and said with a twinkle in his old eyes. "After all, no man lives within a library for fifty years, without becoming a storyteller..."

93

"What do you know of the Cathari?" Father DeFeo began, eager to tell his tale.

"Only that they were heretics, brutally destroyed by the Inquisition," Cait answered, looking to Hugh to see if he knew more.

"They were similar to the Gnostics in their beliefs, Cait," Hugh explained. "They were a religious sect that flourished in the Languedoque in France, in the 11th, 12th and 13th centuries. They were tolerant of all faiths, did a lucrative business with Jews and Muslims, and ran acropper of the Catholic church."

"Si, si, my son," Father DeFeo, agreed eagerly. "This is correct. For the Cathari, man's purpose was to renounce material desires and to transform the soul to its highest spiritual capacity. They were good and decent Christians, you might say, but they did not accept Christ as the son of God, merely as a great adept of spiritual correctness. An avatar, you might call him now, but not a God. They refused to accept the sovereignty of the Church of Rome, whose perfidy and ostentation were both at odds with the Cathari's idea of holiness... and, I might add, with those of Christ himself."

Hugh took up the tale, "The Dominicans were sent to give them the choice of conversion or death. When they didn't respond to that, a Papal Legate was sent with an army. You see the Cathari saw no need for priests as intermediaries to God – to the Church, this was heresy."

DeFeo broke in. "The Church could not afford to allow such heretical disagreement with its own teachings, of course. And, as was generally the reason underlying every crusade ever mounted against any group of so-called Heretics, the Church wished to possess the Cathari wealth, so in 1229, the Church established the Holy Inquisition to root out any remaining Cathars. The bloodiest, most profane era in Church history commenced. The Inquisition swept through Toulouse, Albi, Carcassonne, most of Southern France. The Pope offered eternal salvation to soldiers who served for forty days in the campaign, a heady incentive for the scum of Europe to volunteer to murder and pillage. Torture, hangings, burnings, and, finally, annihilation was the agenda –they pursued it with unholy fervor.

"In their final desperate days – from May 1243 to March 1244 – the last Cathari defended themselves by taking refuge in the great fortress atop Montsegur. When they were defeated, the last 200 Cathari, it is said, marched singing to be burned alive on stakes set before the fortress walls."

"But the night before the burning," interjected the Mother General, "a small party led by a young woman who may have been the daughter of the embattled Carcassonne Lord, escaped the fortress, lowered on ropes from the battlements, and following a secret route to safety. She took with her the fabled Cathari treasure."

"Didn't you say these people wanted no part of worldly wealth?" Cait asked, surprised.

"Quite true, Caitlin," replied Mother General, "but you see this treasure was *not* of this world. It was a sacred trust that had been left with them by the Templar Knights. The treasure they spirited away was the Spear of Longinus, the magical regalia of the Merovingian King Dagobert II, and the Gnostic Gospels, which gave a very different picture of the rise of the Roman Church, from what had been told to the faithful by politically motivated men. The true original story of Jesus had been told in *many* gospels, not just four... Jesus had honored women for their wisdom and compassion... Jesus was a married Rabbi. It could not be otherwise in those times.

"But it is said that a far greater treasure than *all* of this, was what they left behind," Father DeFeo broke in. "The Templars who trusted the Cathari's sense of honor had secreted it in a vault deep within the caves beneaeth Montsegur." He leaned forward, like a child desperate to tell his best secret to the grown ups.

"The Grail, my children!" he breathed with immense reverence. "The real treasure saved by the Cathari's was the Holy Grail and the secret of the Spear of Longinus, its companion in history. What I uncovered hidden away in a document in the *Archivio Segreto* was this: the vault that holds the Grail can be opened only by inserting the Spear of Longinus into the lock that guards it, and that Spear must be wielded only by the true Caretaker!"

The Spear unlocks *the Grail...* Cait felt herself suddenly grow dizzy and faint, as the words triggered a torrent of memories... The room around her was rapidly dissolving as a kaleidoscope of images flooded in, one image supplanting the next at lightning speed, as if being downloaded into her brain by some cosmic computer.

Montsegur, Occitan
AD 1244

The young girl looked back toward the smoldering ruins of her father's fortress atop Montsegur and forced back the tears and strangled sobs that threatened to undo her resolve.

The smoke from the fires of the 200 death stakes still thickened the air so every breath reminded her that on this hideous day, everyone she loved in the world had suffered and died, consumed in the flames, the hatred and the vengeance. Nausea rose again at the thought, and she forced herself to remember that her father had made her promise to escape and survive. "You must promise me you will bear witness, child. You must take the Holy Spear to the knight who will come from the Templar Priory. In his hands alone, you must place this holy relic. He has made a sacred vow to take it far, far from the hiding place of the Grail..." her father's desperate command was her sacred mission.

The tall figure of the knight approached, giving the sign of the Amici, with his gloved hand. The expression on his handsome, late middle-aged face was both grim and compassionate, he looked to be a man who understood suffering. The great red cross on his tabard marked him a Templar.

"I can see that you suffer because you and your escort are the lone survivors of your family and your race," he said gently, "You must find the courage to forgive yourself." He made a sign of warding over her head.

She nodded, but could find no words to speak in reply.

"You were chosen for this task, small one," the knight continued, "because it was deemed that you were strong enough to accomplish it. The protection of this artifact is the duty of the

Caretaker – it is not your fault that you were chosen. Who is to say where in eternity that pact was made? Those you love fulfilled their destiny, just as you have now fulfilled yours. When I leave, you must go to seek whatever peace you may find in this world, for you have passed the task to me. I will see to it that a thousand miles pass beneath my horse's feet before this Spear finds a resting place. You have my word on it."

The girl nodded and bit her lower lip. Her golden hair gleamed in the afternoon sun and the knight hoped her father had chosen her three traveling companions wisely, for one such as she could be sold into slavery for a huge and tempting price.

"Now, must you take this pouch from me," he said, handing a leather bag to her. *"It contains documents, letters of credit issued by our Templar Order, a new name for you and your companions. Perhaps a new life, if God wills it."*

The young girl looked into the face of this stranger who towered above her, and saw resolve there. And kindness.

"Thank you, Sir Knight," she managed to say. *"Wither do you travel now?"*

He smiled. *"That, young miss, no one can know."* He saluted, turned and retreated down the mountain, with the casket that contained the Spear tucked firmly beneath his arm.

"Farewell, Caretaker," she whispered, grateful to be rid of her terrible burden. Then she returned to her companions and the journey into the rest of her life began.

The images were so many and so rapid after that Cait couldn't consciously grasp or hold any, yet every one felt true, and every one contained the Spear. She saw herself in the garb of many centuries... in other bodies, yet herself, despite the fact that the bodies were sometimes male. The Spear's power consumed her and she felt herself dissolve willingly into it, as she toppled from her chair.

Hugh caught her as she fell. She tried to speak to him, but he, too, was in the garb of another time and the language in her head was not the one they had been speaking. Aramaic, Farsi, Italian, German, French... modern voices, too, interspersed with the ones in the vision. She tried to sort through the cacophony...

"Put her on the sofa," Mother General's voice was saying urgently. *Was it English,* she was speaking?

"She's a clairvoyant, Mother," Hugh was explaining, as Cait felt herself lifted, carried. Her head was pressed against his chest... the warmth of his arms was somehow familiar as he laid her gently on the velvet cushions. "But she's not yet trained in how to control the visions, and they're getting stronger, more persistent..." he was saying these words, *somewhere* in her head. The "other," ancient voices were fading, and she was swimming upward into her own body, toward the room around her that was coalescing once again into the only reality.

Three anxious faces hovered above hers.

"I saw the Spear," she said softly, carefully, the English foreign on her tongue. "I'm starting to remember..."

"Si, si, mio dottore!" said DeFeo as if that were only to be expected. "Soon it will *all* be shown to you. It is a journey of initiation, your quest. Do you not yet understand? You are permitted to see only what you have earned!"

Cait struggled to sit up, trying to comprehend...

"I believe you've passed through another Gate," Hugh gently held her hands in his own. She started to pull them away, but he held on.

"Not yet, Cait," he said. "My energy can restore you." As he said it, she knew it was true. *Warrior. Battlefield surgeon.* The words were suddenly in her head and she thought she understood why.

"There is more that you must know, dottore," Father DeFeo was saying. "One more piece of this great puzzle that I can give you..." He breathed the words with enormous gravity, "It was the Jews to whom they entrusted the secret of the unlocking."

"The *Jews*?" Cait said, thinking she must still be disoriented.

"Si, Si!" he replied, excitement re-animating his elfin face. "This I found in the *Archivio Secreto*. In the Index of the Forbidden, where they had placed these great truths." He put his finger to his lips and rolled his eyes heavenward in an exaggerated gesture of secrecy. "You see there were many truths of Christ's life that were suppressed or altered by the Council of Nicea in 325 AD, for the political agendas of powerful men, both within the Church and outside it. There was needed a place to hide these truths, in wait for a time when they could again be exposed to the light."

Comprehension began to dawn in Cait's eyes. "The Index..." she said, trying to remember. "Isn't the Index, the library of the books the Church owns, that *no one* is ever permitted to read, except for one librarian in each generation? I remember the nuns at school speaking of such a secret place, but I thought it was a myth."

"Si, mi *Dottore*, officially it was closed in 1966, but unofficially... that is another story. But I assure you it is not a myth," he said beaming. "And I *am* the *Librarian*!

Constantine and the Council of Nicea
AD 325

Flavius Valerius Aurelius Constantine was Emperor of the largest kingdom on Earth. His Roman Empire contained Britain, Gaul, Spain, and so vast a swath of territories from Europe to the Levant, that Byzantium called him its founder, and the great city of Constantinople had been named in his honor.

Within the Empire he was revered as a near-saint as well as ruler, and his embrace of Christianity had not only been a brilliant political coup, it had nearly won him back the forgiveness of his mother Helena. She had been angry with him over the foolish mistake he'd made in believing his wife Fausta, instead of his son Crispus. Could she not see it had been an honest mistake any man might make? Women were a great trial, Emperor Constantine thought with a sigh.

*Why did his mother not simply accept him as **her** ruler, too?*

Now, he had summoned all the Christian Bishops to Nicea in Bithnia because it had become clear to him that if Christianity was to be his power-base, he had to see to it that this Council defined precisely what the Christian church would teach, and what it would consider heresy, from this point forward. Constantine mulled all this over as he made his way across the marble floor toward the Council Chamber where the Bishops awaited.

Helena, clutching the offending draft written by the Bishops in her hand, hurried toward her son. She had to catch him before he entered the Council Chamber and made another dreadful mistake.

The Emperor came to an abrupt halt as his mother reached him. He was a man of immense stature, built with the breadth of a bull. His mother, not small for a woman, was dwarfed by him, but not intimidated.

"Constantinus!" she cried, waggling the parchment in front of his face. "Have you read this travesty, my son? This damnable document your Council of Bishops is proposing?"

*He cut her off with a sigh. "Calm yourself, Mother. **Calm yourself!** The Council is far from ended. Nothing has yet been decided. The wrangling over every detail is enough to drive a sober man to drink, and I have never claimed sobriety as one of my virtues."*

Helena gazed at her son in exasperation. She loved him, but it did no man good to be called Emperor by the populations of ten countries.

"I beg you, Constantinus," she pleaded, trying to hold his attention. "Do not let this fabrication become the official doctrine of Christianity!"

*"Mother!" the word carried all the exasperation he felt at her meddling. "We cannot have a thousand different versions of our faith, or soon there will be **no** faith. The learned Hosius of*

Cordoba has assured me we must competently codify the law of the Church."

*"But shouldn't that **law at least** tell the truth of Jesus' ministry? Mary was to be his successor as leader – this fact is clear in several of the firsthand gospels..."*

Constantine breathed another audible sigh. His mother was a formidable adversary in debate, and no one knew better than he, that she was occasionally right, but her continued nattering about the inadequacies of the Council was insupportable.

*"There are serious issues to consider here, Mother. Issues of Statecraft far beyond your ability to comprehend. It is quite clear to me that Jesus, knowing women's dispositions and frailties, would **never** have chosen a woman as his successor. No man who understands leadership would ever do such a damned fool thing!*

"We have gathered bishops from every region of my empire except Britain, to decide these great truths. Asia Minor, Syria, Thrace, Palestine, Egypt, Greece – all the great and revered scholars of theology are here today. Do you pit yourself against their superior knowledge?"

*Helena contained her hurt and anger, and drew herself up to her full stature before replying. "It was to **me** that Archangel Michael vouchsafed the Spear of Longinus as a Way-Shower – to me that the nail from the True Cross was given. Would he have done so, if he did not believe my voice equal to that of your Bishops?"*

Constantine shook his great head wearily.

"Enough!" he shouted, "I will see that your objections are raised before the group. But I must tell you, I intend to abide by their decisions!"

With that pronouncement, his Imperial Majesty, Emperor Constantine I, turned and left his mother standing alone and seething in the middle of the marble rotunda.

"Would that you remembered the destruction that ensued the last time you refused to hear my truth," Helena whispered into the empty hall. Then she, too, turned, and commending the outcome to

God, left the scene of their encounter, prayerful, but not in the least hopeful.

"I understand that the story of Jesus' life and ministry was radically altered by this politically motivated Council," Cait said, after hearing the story so well told, "but I'm sorry, Hugh, Mother, Father..." Cait turned a feisty expression on each one in turn. "I accept what you're saying, even if I find it a little perverse on God's part..." she hesitated, trying to frame the next thought, "but I don't see how this involves Jews or how Jews got involved with a Christian artifact or myth, or *whatever* the hell this Spear is? Why would they even *care* about something so connected to Christ and Christianity, when they've been persecuted by Christians for a thousand years?"

"Think, child! And I would prefer you do so without resorting to profanity," Mother General said, in the reproving nun-voice that Cait remembered so well from her childhood. "Jesus was a Jew, was he not?"

"Si. Si!" the old priest chimed in. "He was a Jew, and an Essene – the most esoteric sect in Judaism in his time –*not* the myth that Paul, the Council of Nicea, and later churchmen created about him for their own purpose. He was a reformer and a man of action. A great teacher who had been schooled in many ancient disciplines, not merely in Judaism. He was a seeker of *all* truths. A spiritual traveler taught by the greatest esoteric thinkers of the ancient world – schooled not just in Palestine, but in the monasteries of Egypt and India and Tibet, in the practices of magic and of healing. He was born of a line of kings like the great Patriarchs of old – a direct descendant of King David himself! And he was married to Mary of Magdala, also of royal blood, and a priestess of Isis.

"Have you not wondered why the history of all those years from 12 to 30 in Christ's life are *missing*? They were stolen from Him by the Church, so it could invent the myths it needed to market a religion suitable for empire-building purposes. A religion, I'm sad to say, that in many of the succeeding centuries, bore less and less resemblance to the goodness of Jesus' own teachings, or the true scope of his knowledge and training.

"All this was discovered by the Knights Templar while they were in the Holy Land! Not only did they find scrolls, similar to those of the Dead Sea, but they exchanged learned views with Gnostic thinkers, and with the great scholars of Persia and the Far East, who knew many of the truths beyond the myths. But these truths were at odds with the Church's narrow doctrines. In Jerusalem, the Knights learned facts the Church could not afford to make public – truths about a royal bloodline that had been denied and suppressed in order to continue the myth that the Church had the *only* power to save men from Hellfire.

"They learned that Jesus and Mary had married and that a pregnant Mary Magdalene had fled to Southern France after the crucifixion to save their children from the rabble and the Romans. The Cathari and the people of the Languedoc had always known about this, for the Languedoc had been Mary's place of refuge! But, of course, the people who knew these dangerous truths had been forced to remain silent for fear of Church reprisal.

"*Think*, child, of what having such knowledge would mean to the Church of Rome!" Mother interjected. "If the *only* way to save yourself from an eternity of torment was to believe *exactly* what that Church told you, and to follow their orders implicitly, would you not, out of terror, do precisely the Church's bidding? Terror is a mighty goad – perhaps the mightiest of all!"

"The Jews, too, knew much of the story, I've told you," Father DeFeo went on "which is at least part of the reason they have been so hated and hounded by the Church for a thousand years."

"But, I've *always* had the strongest devotion to Jesus," Cait said defiantly. "I've always felt connected to him in the most powerful way. What exactly are you telling me to think about him now... about *all* of what you're saying?"

"Jesus was a Bringer of the Light," Hugh said emphatically, understanding her concern. "Of *that* there is no question whatsoever. He was a teacher of the Laws of Righteousness and a preacher of a gospel of love and kindness. He was *never* one who would sanction pogrom or torture or Inquisition. He would never have kept women from positions of influence in his Church. Instead, he made Mary Magdalene his consort and his head disciple, until the Council of Nicea destroyed her gospels, along with those of Thomas, Martha of Bethany, Salome, Phillip and many others. Jesus meant Magdalene to lead his Church after he was gone. Women were *never* to be excluded from the priesthood. Remember, it was the two Mary's and John who stood at the foot of the cross – not the great burly fishermen disciples who had scattered like chaff before the wind to save themselves. Yet, later these same fishermen claimed that their power had come directly from Jesus. 'Upon this Rock I will build my Church,' is the wording they've used ever since, to maintain their power-base. That *rock* – that Peter – was nowhere to be seen at the Crucifixion! But both Mary's were there."

Cait looked defiantly at DeFeo who was watching her intently.

"You *know* all this," she said incredulously, "and yet you remain a priest of this tainted Church..." She turned on Mother General, "And *you* Mother? You know this, too, and yet you serve this Church, despite its lies and its history of cruelty?"

"I do *not* serve a *Church*!" Mother General responded, in a voice that left no room for question. "I serve *God!*"

"Si, si, mi *dottore*," the priest put in gently, "The myths made by later, lesser men, do not diminish the truth of Jesus and his life, nor the truths of what he preached. He told of a God of Love, not punishment. He added a new Commandment to the 10: *Thou shalt love thy neighbor as thyself*! He spoke the Beatitudes. He *never* preached hatred of any kind – he never preached, 'an eye for an eye' or that his was the *only* way to God. He preached the supremacy of goodness over evil! *Love God, love your fellow man is the whole of the law*, he said to the Pharisees, and many, *many* have lived these precepts by staying *in* the Church, not by abandoning it. They do this, not for the trappings of pomp and power that adorn a fallible Church, but in the name of this humble Jewish preacher, this activist reformer, this Jesus who took on a degenerate empire and tried to change it!" His voice was thick with emotion.

"Think of his life, Dottore! Jesus lived a public life for only three years, and died ignominiously on a cross between two thieves, and yet no man who has ever lived has changed the world as much as he! Not all the armies, nor all the philosophers, nor all the political might ever wielded has had as much impact on civilization. Does that not smack of the Hand of God?" He paused for breath, then continued.

"Yes! There have been terrible atrocities perpetrated in His gentle name by a Church *not* of his design. You must not forget, mi dottore, the Church is a vast *institution*, run by *human beings* – both good ones and bad ones.

"But just as there have been terrible atrocities, so too have there been a million acts of kindness and charity done in Jesus' name, by men and women of good faith who believed in *everything* he preached. Jesus was not merely a Utopian dreamer, and neither are we who serve him and do our best to navigate through the landmines of politics and greed and corruption that are *inevitable* in the corridors of power."

The little old man paused again and squinted at her, seeking some sign that she understood his impassioned speech. "All this is why John XXIII declared it was not His *death and resurrection* that made Jesus, our Savior, but the example of his *life* that did so.

"The Church has nurtured saints as well as sinners, you must remember that. Within the church there are always power brokers, and the merely self-serving – but there are also good men and women who sacrifice their own lives to the service of God and humanity on a daily basis. The Church is not merely an institution that grows fat on the simple faith of its followers. It is *more* than that! And so are we!"

Cait's voice was filled with emotion when she spoke, but the emotion was hard to read and the words non-committal, "Where do we go to seek these Jews who know the truth, Father?" she asked, instead of responding to his fervent explanation, because she truly didn't know what to say.

"They are in Spain," Mother General answered, having watched the exchange with deep understanding, "where they found refuge in the time of The Inquisition. You are expected there by a Rabbi friend, who knows many secrets. But you cannot take the usual route. You must drive, and with great care. And you must set out today, before all borders are closed to you. The noose tightens as the Quest escalates. Sister Rosaria has mapped your route, and awaits you now in the antechamber."

94

The passionate voice of Father DeFeo remained in Cait's head, along with the confusions his revelations had provoked in her, as the circuitous route they traveled into Andalusia become more and more austere and beautiful.

"Sister Rosaria must have been a travel agent before joining the Convent," she said absently.

Hugh smiled, wishing he knew how to cajole her out of the heavy mood that had kept her silent most of this leg of their journey. "Actually, Mother General told me Rosaria was in Military Intelligence before chucking it for the convent. Evidently what she'd learned of the real world left her longing for a better one."

"Can't fault her for that," Cait replied with a short laugh. "My world seems to be growing more incomprehensible by the day.

I spoke to Lark last night on the phone. She sounded terrible... distant. I'm worried sick about her, Hugh, and I miss her so much it hurts." She stared out the window at the unspoiled mountain terrain. After a while, she said wistfully, "I would have loved to have the chance to show this wild beauty to my little girl. I would have loved to make her life safe and pretty and filled with all the things I always dreamed for her..."

Hearing the sadness in her voice, Hugh turned his head toward her to reply. As he did, the car window imploded in a hail storm of shattering glass. A second shot zinged in fast behind the first. High powered rifle rounds, their sound unmistakable. The third and fourth rounds took out their tires, sending the car careening across the road, slaloming over the bumpy rockbound shoulder, and straight toward the trees beyond. Hugh managed to jockey them to a stop opposite the hillside from which the shots had been fired, but the car lost balance as it slammed to a halt – the pitch of the shoulder and a small ditch beyond causing it to tilt precariously.

"Get out and stay low," Hugh shouted to Cait, who was crouched below window level, her hands, face and arms bleeding from a dozen tiny glass cuts. "Out my door and hope we can make a run for those woods." Unable to get the door fully open, Hugh wriggled free, and then kicked at the partially wedged door so Cait could escape behind him.

"The car won't give us protection against those rounds for long," she breathed, searching the hill opposite for a glint off a barrel to indicate where the shots had come from. "He's a pro."

"Better than nothing, but you're right," Hugh answered, his voice low and tight, "we're sitting ducks if we stay put." She nodded grim agreement, as they crouched, waiting for the next barrage, scanning right, left and behind for better cover, but finding only the possibility of the woods and the near-impossibility of reaching them. Just ahead to their left were several boulders that could provide protection, but they'd need to cover a dozen feet in the open to get there.

Another volley smashed into the car before he could say anything more. Hugh had a gun in his hand, Cait realized, but where had it come from? DeFeo? Mother General?

"Do you have another one of those handy?" Cait demanded, but he shook his head. "I'm lucky to have this one. We'll have a chance, if we can get into the trees, Cait. It appears there's only one sniper, and those rocks look like our only possible cover between the car and the woods. When I give you the word, run like hell and I'll lay down covering fire – it's not as easy as you'd think to hit a moving target."

"It is for a trained sniper!" she snapped back at him.

Hugh grunted weary agreement. "Be that as it may, there aren't any other options. We run for it and hope to lose him in the woods, or we sit here and wait for him to come get us – or ignite the gas tank with one of those high powered rounds."

"I don't mean to be a pain in the ass," she apologized, her voice low and hoarse, "this is just scary as hell." Hugh nodded.

"I'll run on your signal," she said, forcing her body into position to make a break for it. She thought of Lark, as she willed her heartbeat and breathing to steady.

"On the count of three, then. One... two..."

"Wait!" she blurted, "what's that noise?" A faint rumble that hadn't been there a moment ago, was causing the ground beneath them to hum.

"A heavy vehicle," Hugh breathed, as the engines sounds got louder. "Our sniper must have called in reinforcements. This road is usually deserted..."

"No! It's a bus, Hugh. Look! Its a tour bus of some kind. We can make it to those rocks as it passes between us and the sniper – maybe even get to the woods..."

"What the bloody hell..." he started to say, then broke off in mid-sentence, as a large battered bus lumbered into full view.

The bus halted directly between their disabled car and their hillside assailant. The face in the driver's seat window was topped by a huge white wimple, and a flock of similarly coiffed nuns came scrambling down from the idling vehicle, waving their arms and shouting. The habits they wore were the old-fashioned kind, black ankle length dresses, topped by astonishing white wimples that made them look like a flock of exotic birds, spilling from the bus and starting to run toward the disabled car.

"Hello, the car!" a voice shouted in a thick Irish brogue. "Are you in trouble over there?"

"Stay back, sisters!" Cait yelled, "someone's shooting at us!"

"Jaysus, Mary and St. Patrick!" the nun snapped. "Well, he'd better not shoot at me, lass, or God will have something to say about that, you may be sure! He hasn't forgotten how to smite, you know." She turned and waved her fist in the direction of the sniper. "Get along with now, boyo!" she shouted "These are not the droids you want!"

Cait burst out laughing. An improbable Irish nun was rescuing them from near certain death, and quoting Obi Wan Kanobi as she did it? *No way...* She heard Hugh's laughter echoing her own.

"By God, sister!" he managed to get out as the woman reached them. "You are the most beautiful sight I've ever seen."

The nun laughed heartily. "Go on with you now, lad. I'll bet you tell that to all your rescuers!"

The dozen or so nuns completely surrounded them and the car now, a gaggle of black geese protecting their young.

"You're a bloody genius, sister, and brave, to boot," Hugh said with real admiration. "The sniper will have to take all of you out now to get at us."

"We've only a heartbeat, darlin's," she answered, sharp eyes scanning the opposite hillside, "we're praying he's not been paid enough to kill us all without new orders. So hurry along now, stay to the middle of us, we'll keep you out of his sight 'til we're all on the bus. Away with you now..."

She herded them all across the road and onto the bus, then shouted a terse order to the driver. "Warp speed, Sister Margaret, if you please."

The bus lurched forward, and the nun smiled reassuringly at Cait and Hugh. Then she yanked off her wimple to reveal a mop of close cropped pepper and salt hair. She lifted her arms to free herself from the confines of the habit's headdress, and Cait saw an old Colt 1911 in a belt holster, next to the long rosary that rattled at her waist. Free of the wimple, the woman reached from under her seat and yanked out an AK47. She checked the breech to see it locked and loaded, before turning back to Cait.

"How in the name of God do you suppose all those generations of holy women bore the heat in these old habits?" she asked in non-sequitur.

"You're not a nun?" Cait blurted in surprise.

"Oh, I'm a nun alright, dear heart," the lilting Irish eyes were full of mischief. "Sister Teresa Concepta at your service. But I spent my novitiate in Belfast, you see – me Da and me brothers were with the Provos, so I know a thing or two about snipers. By the grace of God, Mother General finds these skills useful from time to time and she keeps a supply of habits from a bunch of other religious orders, for when we need them. We've been following you for a while now, at Mother's suggestion. But since Vatican II we aren't stuck in these medieval torture garments, thanks be to God – the habits from hell the older sisters used to call them. I expect they offered up the misery of it for their past sins, or for the holy souls in Purgatory, God rest them. Ah well, I suppose they were better than flagellation, but only marginally, mind you. You know they're hot as Hades and itch like an army of bedbugs have taken refuge in your underpants. Now, we just wear dowdy old outfits, and ground-gripper shoes, but there's nothing like these old wimples to put the fear of God into anyone raised a Catholic – which in this part of the world, is mostly everyone – assassins included!" She laughed at her own story.

The near-death attack, the adrenaline rush, the Monty Python scenario they'd just played out, was all too much – Cait and Hugh began to laugh until they couldn't stop and had to hold each other 'til the spasm passed. There was relief in the laughter, but something more as well – an acknowledgement of how close they'd come to death and how much they had come to trust each other. The nuns joined in, except for the two who were scanning the road with sniper rifles held in competent hands and utter concentration on their faces.

The rosy cheeked Sister Teresa was suddenly serious. "So let's get back to business. Seville is lovely this time of year. It's our next stop."

95

Win Livingston reread the surveillance information, with annoyed fascination. Why the hell were all these players on the field? So far, intimidation, political pressure, a near-murder, and several kidnapping attempts had resulted in nothing more than a trail of failures, perpetrated by more factions than you could shake a stick at. This was turning into a Keystone Cop farce.

And now a busload of *nuns* to the rescue? *Really!* How utterly preposterous. The Almighty must have quite a perverse sense of humor. A quote he'd been taken with, as a boy, came to mind, "*I'm appalled at the behavior of nearly everyone in the Old Testament, including God,*" some wicked British wit had quipped.

Livingstone took up a yellow lined legal pad and one of the dozen #2 pencils his secretary always made certain were on his desk, sharpened to a perfect point by her own compulsive hand each morning. Meticulous listmaking was a habit he'd developed as a boy at Choate. List the possibilities, the probabilities, the impossibilities of any puzzle, and then whittle them down to handleable size, ticking off the useless or the already accomplished from the list, with precise checkmarks, and deal expeditiously with whatever was left.

Win began to make very deliberate notes. The Old Man wanted results, and he would provide them. There was no need to run his plans by anyone – he had all the authority he needed to get this job done and was certainly not going to leave it in the hands of bumbling fools like the ones he'd just been reading about. Although, all the bumbling had not only shown him what *wouldn't* work with this elusive woman, it had also shown him what would. It was time to take her into custody *and* to get rid of the meddlesome Brit.

He was finally beginning to see the bigger picture emerging. It had been a difficult task to bring any semblance of cohesion to this puzzle, but finally, a picture was emerging. That was how it worked, after all. One gathered intel from as many places as possible, and then one made sense of it.

Win now knew the Director had history with Gruner. Or rather his father had. In fact, his father's death had probably not been a suicide at all, but a necessary piece of wetwork, of the crude sort that used to be relatively common in the earlier, less sophisticated days of the Company. Men who couldn't be reined in, were either discredited or spirited off to a mental hospital where electric shock treatments assured that they couldn't remember their own names, much less state secrets. Or after their reputations had been destroyed, they suddenly became conspicuously depressed and committed suicide.

Damned sloppy work Win thought. Imagine leaving the man's galoshes on before pushing him out a window.

So there might be a good deal more to this story than met the eye. Did the Director see this as an opportunity for revenge? A chance to expose Gruner, without having to actually dirty his hands bringing it about?

He picked up his pad and pencil again and began scribbling possibilities:

- Dr. Monahan might cause Gruner to overplay his hand and reveal himself? *Not very likely.*

- One of the several factions in play might let the cat out of the bag? *Marginally more plausible.*
- Some of the factions now looking into Gruner's past might unearth the truth and leak it to the media? *Quite possible, particularly if the Director purposely didn't take the proper pains to keep the old secrets secret anymore.*
- Dr. Monahan or her gallant companion might have to kill Gruner, to keep him from harming the little girl? *Now **that's** got legs.*

Livingston chuckled as he assessed and numbered the individual possibilities neatly on his pad. The old man was one clever old bastard, and this circle in a spiral was just convoluted enough to be the kind of thing he would engineer. Use Gruner's obsession against him? Very clever.

He allowed himself to contemplate for a moment precisely what the Director had in mind for his own role in this drama. If Win played it just right, the Director was sure to recommend him for successor, if and when the old boy retired.

Now, to the next list, he thought with a smile. *List the best ways to help the Director get what he wants, without letting him know that I've figured out his true agenda. At least until such time as that information might prove useful to my own career path.*

Win reminded himself he had to do all this without leaving his own handprints all over it, because in this line of work you just never could be certain how it would all play out.

*   *   *

"Let's turn up the heat," Winfield Livingston said into the secure phone, while drumming his long slender fingers on the desktop. "This woman is resourceful and she appears to have more friends than expected."

He frowned at the response on the other end of the phone.

"*Nothing* that ties to us in any way," Win said curtly. "I want our hands completely clean on this. Any further contracts you may expect to have with the Company are riding on both your discretion and creativity with this matter. I'm assuming you and your group are at least as clever as our suburban doctor-mom and her aristocratic escort?"

He smiled at the reply, satisfied he'd struck a nerve.

"I'm issuing an international watchlist flag on both of them today, to amp up the pressure and help keep them contained. What I want from you is twofold. Scare the bejesus out of them and the sister, too, while you're at it – but don't kill them. Let's keep the doctor alive for now, but frightened. His Lordship's life doesn't interest me, although I'd rather not cause an intentional incident unless we have no choice. And find out why Herr Doktor Gruner wants the damned artifact, will you? Just in case this all goes south, I want as much intel as you can get me that would allow us to discredit either or both of the doctors involved."

He listened a moment. "Yes. Yes. You heard me correctly. I want enough dirt on *both* Monahan and Gruner, so whichever one we decide to take down, hasn't a leg left to stand on. Yes, *yes*, I know you've handled this kind of thing for us before. That's precisely why we're having this conversation – a conversation which, of course, we have never held. Do I make myself perfectly clear?"

He tipped the encrypted receiver away from his ear and waited for the self-serving diatribe to end. "No. *I'm* handling this for the Director. No need to trouble him, until we have all our ducks in line. And let's get on with it. Christmas is coming and I have my in-laws to deal with, and they're far more formidable adversaries than the ones I'm giving you a shot at."

Win smiled at the enthusiasm for the task he heard clearly on the other end of the line. There were mercenaries and then there were *mercenaries*. This group was top drawer. Now, that he'd given them their marching orders, he had no doubt they'd come through expeditiously and bring this ridiculous project to a happy conclusion.

Rearranging the Deck Chairs

Part XV

"The Prince of Darkness is a gentleman."
William Shakespeare
King Lear

—————————— **96** ——————————

Meg hurried down the cold empty street, remembering how much she hated the whole Wall Street scene at night. The Real Estate Section of the Times kept proclaiming that Battery Park and its surrounds were the next hot address in the City, but from what she could see, it just never seemed to happen. Few Yuppies wanted to be this far from the action or the good schools, and once the bustle of the big brokerage houses and law firms quieted down after eight or nine at night, it got dead as the graves in Trinity Churchyard, anyplace south of Murray Street or west of Water.

She pulled her muffler up around her cold ears and cursed herself for having forgotten to change her shoes before leaving the office. She wore the *de rigueur* high heels that went with the unspoken-but-clear dress code of Kramer Crowley Crookfield, everyday, in order to look as chic as the upper class clients she served there. But she generally changed into flats or running shoes before making her nightly trek to the subway.

I'm way off my game, she thought, ruefully, regretting the shoes and several other small details that had slipped between the cracks today. She was worried sick about Cait and Lark since she'd heard about the latest attack, and not feeling all that sure of her own safety or Carter's, for that matter. She had to pull it together and put all the pieces they were gathering into a workable action plan. Where the hell was that stupid Spear, and why the hell did such vile and powerful men want it? And why had Jack left Cait in this impossible situation? He may have been the world's sweetest guy, but for all his smarts, he was obviously a horse's ass about this Spear business.

Meg turned at Pearl Street and Park Row, her mind so cluttered with swirling, useless fragments of knowledge it was making her head pound. This might be one of those nights when she should have taken a cab instead of walking the four blocks to the subway. She felt uneasy, as if someone were watching her. She glanced left, right and behind, but the dark street was deserted. *Shit!* Paranoia wasn't going to help anything. Annoyed by her own foolishness, she picked up her pace, high heels clicking on the silent pavement.

With relief, she saw taxi lights come round a corner two blocks away. She made up her mind not to let it get past her, as there might not be another along anytime soon. Just as she hurried to the curb, and put up her hand to flag him down, a voice came out of nowhere behind her.

"Tell your sister we want the Spear or you're all dead. Last warning."

Meg started to turn but the shove that crashed between her shoulder blades was so violent, it sent her sprawling directly into the path of the oncoming taxi, lifting her off the curb and snapping her head back so hard she saw stars and blinding light. She heard herself scream and heard a weird crunching sound somewhere in her upper body, but there was no time for a coherent thought, before she felt her head hit something hard and cold and very, very painful. The bumper of the cab... the pavement? Time slowed and then it stopped altogether.

97

Carter sat on the edge of the gurney in the ER of New York Downtown Hospital and watched as Meg opened her eyes for the second time. The first time she'd just stared blankly for a few seconds, then lost consciousness again. This time, Carter could see she was trying to figure out where she was.

"It's OK, baby," Carter said quietly, leaning in to kiss her face, then brush the matted hair off her injured cheek. "You got hit by a cab, but the driver called 911 and they got you here pretty fast for New York City. Thank God traffic downtown this time of night is nonexistent. It's a wonder you even *found* a cab to get hit by." She smiled at her own wan attempt at humor and reached out to touch Meg's battered face again.

Meg's head throbbed like an Irish marching band on St. Paddy's Day, and her left arm was in some sort of a sling, while the right had an IV dripping into it. She hurt everywhere. The noise of the bustling city emergency room sounded cacophonous and deafening in her ears, and she was nauseous as hell. She moved to sit up, but the pain that speared her head, plopped her right back onto the pillow.

"Do you have any idea what happened?" Carter asked. "The cabbie said you came flying off the curb like you had wings, and he saw some guy in black run past you like he was on fire. He figured it was a mugging, but your purse was still on the ground. He's a nice little Pakistani who's on the verge of a coronary over all the trouble he's going to be in with his boss over hitting you, which he says was not his fault."

Carter took a breath, and reached for Meg's hand.

"How bad do you feel?" she asked, knowing the answer.

"Really glad to be alive enough to feel this bad." Meg said trying to smile, but her face was so swollen it was just a grimace.

"It couldn't just have been a mugging, right? I have to ask because the police will."

"No way! I thought somebody was following me, but I couldn't see anybody – that's when I decided to take a cab instead of the subway."

Carter nodded. "I figured. So now I guess we know the sideswipe by the van on the Merritt Parkway and the push down the stairs at the subway station weren't accidents either? But those incidents seemed meant to scare you, not kill you, Meg. Sorry to be practical here, but those downtown streets were plenty deserted enough for a hit. If they'd wanted you dead, that's what you'd be. Whoever *they* might be." Her voice didn't sound as sure as her words.

Meg tried to nod agreement, but winced as the pain hit again. "He said 'Tell your sister we want the Spear or you're all dead.'"

Carter grimaced. "Son of a bitch. I'd better tell Matt. He's on his way. He said he'd handle the cops' questions for tonight."

"Can I go home?"

"They need to x-ray your arm and shoulder to see if anything's broken, you're pretty banged up, but maybe no breaks. You've got a concussion, so they'll probably want to watch you overnight, but I'll see what I can do to spring you fast as possible. Matt and I will stay with you tonight, if they won't let you out of here, so not to worry – we're not leaving you alone for an instant, that's for damned sure."

Meg would have said more, if she could have done so without her head exploding. She watched Carter's worried expression, then saw her stride determinedly toward the nurse's station. She knew her partner's assessment was right-on. She could easily have been dead, not just injured. She wondered what that meant for twenty seconds or so before she drifted back into uneasy sleep.

98

Carter closed the door to their apartment, shrugged out of her coat and leaned against the closet door after closing it, as if she needed to catch her breath or collect her thoughts. Then she pulled the clip from her hair, and bending over, shook her head as if shaking out all constraints. She was very upset, that was obvious.

Curious, Meg looked up from the sofa where she'd been camping out for the 24 hours since she'd left the hospital. She saw the bleak expression on Carter's face, and stood up, gingerly nursing the pain that hit whenever she moved too fast. "What's happened?" she asked, knowing it was something really bad.

"I have something awful to tell you, Meg. It's about Sally."

"Sally Kittridge?" A chill started up Meg's spine at the stricken look in Carter's eyes.

"What about Sally, Cart?"

"She's dead, Meg. Your pal Annie, from the DOJ called you and when she couldn't get through, and your secretary told her about the taxi incident, she called me. She said Sally died in an accident... only it wasn't." Carter's voice was clipped with contained emotion. "It's got to be connected to all this Spear shit. What the hell is going on here, Meg, and how are they tracking every move we make so fast? And who are *they*? And how do we get to them?"

Meg headed toward Carter, and wordlessly wrapped her arms around her. Carter laid her head on Meg's shoulder and they stood for a long moment, neither saying a word.

Meg finally spoke in a hoarse whisper. "I could see how scared she was about accessing the information I'd asked for. I should *never* have pushed her. She must not have dropped it there... she said she had other leads to follow... I should have told her not to..."

Carter almost said *don't blame yourself,* but the words caught in her throat. Maybe Meg was to blame for making contact, but someone else, someone *somewhere,* was much, much more so.

"What happened to her?" Meg asked, thinking of the moments she remembered just before the taxi hit her, wondering if Sally had known what was coming.

"They said she tripped and fell down a flight of stairs in her building. Her neck was broken on impact. They *said* her heel broke and she lost her footing on the way to the laundry room. But it's all crap! Nobody does laundry in high heels at midnight, and why was she on the back stairs when there was nothing wrong with the elevator? And why was she doing laundry still dressed in her work clothes... and... and... and... there are about 20 things wrong with the picture."

"Shit! Carter! This is so bad. And I'm so, so sorry to have gotten us all into this mess."

"*You* didn't get us into it, Meg! Some Nazi butcher war criminal, who's rich as Croesus, and thinks he's above the law because he can pull everybody's strings – *he's* the one who got us *all* into this. I want to find that son of a bitch, and I want to let him know he's not going to win this one. I just wish I could get some one of the government agencies I do work for involved, but I'm not sure how, and after everything we've uncovered about cover-ups, I *don't* know whom to trust..." She let the thought wind down, in frustration.

"I'm really worried about your safety and I'm not sure what to do to protect you, Meg. I need to get out of my work clothes, and then we should figure out what our options are." Meg nodded, knowing exactly what would happen next. Carter would head into the shower, stay there long enough to wash away enough of her worry and anger at the situation that her usual laser focus would return. Then they'd figure it out. Carter had such an Old Testament sense of justice and she always felt it was up to her to make sure the world got fixed.

Hearing the water turn on in the shower, Meg, let out a long sigh and picked up her cell phone. Tapped or not, *screw* it, she had to call Matt with the news about Sally. What the hell had her friend found out that could get her murdered? And who had blown the whistle on her? Because *that* person knew what she and her side needed to know.

99

Forty-eight hours after the taxi incident, Meg entered the lavish wood paneled office of the firm's senior partner, and waited for him to put down the telephone. Arthur Crookfield was a named Partner in one of the finest law firms in Manhattan, and it showed.

He waved her to a seat, cradled the receiver he'd been talking into, telling his secretary to hold his calls, then studied Meg's badly bruised face for a long moment before speaking, his usual perfunctory and meaningless half-smile firmly in place.

"Good of you to come, Megan," he said genially, as if there'd been a choice on her part.

"Of course, Mr. Crookfield," she responded with a smile of her own – the serious smile she reserved for senior partner interchanges when she had no idea what the agenda might include. "I understand there's something you'd like to discuss with me?" her voice trailed up at the end of the sentence, so it became a question.

"Yes, yes, that's true," he responded thoughtfully. "Although its more a series of certain disturbing events that have come to my attention recently, that I wish to discuss with you. By the way, how are you feeling, Megan? I understand you had a bit of a scare a few nights ago."

"I did, but I'm fine, actually. Thank you for asking. Nothing broken, just one bruised shoulder, some ripped cartilage, and a bit of a headache to show for it. I was lucky."

Arthur Crookfield nodded sagely, as if taking that all in and considering it.

"This hasn't been a good month for you, as I understand it. That unfortunate incident at your sister's home... now this traffic accident. And I believe there was an unauthorized trip you made to D.C. for some mysterious purpose you chose not to share with your secretary?" he crinkled an elegant eyebrow at her to suggest he'd unearthed a major secret. "I suppose it's not so surprising that your workload has been short-circuited somewhat in the wake of all that."

Meg felt her stomach tighten. "Sir, its been less than three weeks since the death of my sister's husband and her in-laws. I took only two days off to help with the funeral arrangements, and one, after my own accident. I'm not aware of any work that's fallen through the cracks..."

"Quite so," he replied, steepling his fingers and looking judicious, "but, it might, mightn't it? If this matter persists, of course. You are aware that your sister may be a suspect in her husband's death?" he asked in too-casual a way.

Meg's shock propelled her out of her seat. "No, Mr. Crookfield. I most certainly am not aware of that! Nor, as far as I know, are the police. What on earth gave you that idea?"

"Sit down, Megan," he said gravely. "I want you to listen very carefully to what I'm about to say to you, as it won't be said twice. I like you. And I like the work you've done here. You came to us with stellar recommendations and we've had no reason to disagree with those appraisals. That said, word has reached me that you and your sister are involved in something far beyond your comprehension. And I might add, far beyond your ability to control.

"You have been making inquiries about someone who not only has enormous international resources at his disposal, and an impeccable reputation, but, also, I'm afraid, has the ear of the President. I'm told this statesman is of the utmost value to our national security, and I have been charged with telling you that any attempts to compromise his name or reputation will be dealt with by Homeland Security. Furthermore, I feel duty bound to remind you that *any* scandal – be it a breach of national security on your part, or an unsavory murder investigation of your sister, cannot and will not be tolerated by this firm. Thus far, you have been on the fast track for partner, but needless to say such a scandal would scuttle any such hopes.

"I trust you will consider yourself warned and behave with the kind of prudence one expects from an attorney at this firm."

Meg had to struggle to keep her fury under control, but she forced her voice to courtroom steadiness, before replying.

"My sister, her husband, and his family, have been the *victims*, not the perpetrators of a heinous crime. As far as I know, despite the recent assaults on our Constitution, it is not yet a crime to be the *victim* of a crime. As to the inquiries you spoke of, surely you, as one of the finest trial counsels in the country, understand that this kind of reprisal for a simple inquiry, suggests there's something big and terrible that's being kept hidden..."

"And that damned well better stay that way!" he completed her sentence, all geniality now replaced by ice. "Whatever you *think* you know, you are a fool to *think* you'll be permitted to expose it. I've never thought you a fool. I trust I wasn't wrong in my judgment."

Megan realized she was biting her lower lip and quickly composed her face.

"I understand," she said, simply, wishing with all her heart that she didn't.

Arthur Crookfield nodded, stood and extended his hand. "Some things are best left undisturbed, Megan. I have assured the Attorney General that I'm certain there's no truth to the rumor of your sister's involvement in this murder, or of her husband's involvement in any breach of National Security. My sense is that the A.G. will back off, if you do."

Meg, her head spinning more from the unexpectedness of this threat, than from the odious tone of the conversation, shook the proffered hand perfunctorily and walked from Crookfield's office, heading for her own. Then, on impulse, she ducked into the ladies room and stood for a moment at the sink, struggling to quiet her breathing. She turned on the cold water and ran her wrists under the icy stream, forcing herself to regain her equilibrium.

The full implication of the threat flooded her as she gripped the sink and struggled for control. Just how high in the government of the United States can this man Gruner reach to pull the strings that could destroy all their lives.

And what the hell could they do about it?

Evil is as Evil Does

Part XVI

"Never, never, never, never, never give up!"
Winston Churchill

100

Seville, Spain

The old Rabbi peered at his two somewhat bedraggled visitors with amused interest. "I was *not* told I was expecting a priest and a nun," he said, a smile animating in his eyes.

Hugh chuckled. "Nor did you get either one, Rabbi. We needed to change our appearance after a scuffle on the road and these were the most available garments."

The old man, nodded. His glance at Hugh's ring told Cait this man, too, was Amici or aware of them.

The house was very old, its edges softened by centuries of prideful wear, well-tended and pristine. The Rabbi led them through a tidy, book strewn sitting room to an interior garden, where a tiered fountain trickled water into a blue ceramic basin shaped like a giant seashell. An abundance of herbs in careful rows, and a variety of small shade trees, now winter-bare, appeared to be flourishing there. A tenacious vine snaked up the adobe walls and over the roof. The old man gestured them to a table and chairs that had been carved from some gnarled and curving wood Cait didn't recognize. The day was mild and the air sweet.

"I have had word from Mother General regarding your need," the old man began, "and I am aware of the urgency of your mission, so I will not waste what little time you have, with rambling. But to make you understand *why* you have been sent here, I must tell you a tale that happened long ago. What do you know of the history of mysticism among the Jews of Spain, may I ask?"

Hugh glanced at Cait, and seeing her shrug, answered for them both, "Only that the Sephardic Jews have been known for centuries, for their fearless exploration of the great Mysteries, and that they have preserved an unbroken lineage of mystical exercises which date back to ancient times."

The old man nodded, pursing his lips, thoughtfully.

"In the first and second centuries of this epoch, it was not only Talmudic *scholars* who practiced mystical exercises, but every man who considered himself a pious Jew. Communicating with the Divine was a very personal act that a man demanded of himself. He had to seek the visionary experience of his God, through his own considerable efforts, not merely through a teacher or intermediary.

"Consequently, our lineage of Kabbalah is a rich, unbroken chain of transmissions to individuals, dating back to Talmudic and Biblical times. The Zohar, for example, our most revered and influential text, was attributed by its author, Moses de Leon, to the revelations of a second century sage, Simeon bar Yochai – but the Zohar includes the revelations which de Leon, himself, experienced, as well. Our Hebrew Bible is, of course, filled with visions and prophecies derived from the work of more ancient times – Ezekiel, Elijah and Enoch are fine examples. And then we must consider the dreamer patriarchs, Abraham, Jacob and Joseph, as the revelations from the dream state are very important in our studies. And let us not forget the visionaries like Moses, Samuel and Jonah. The word Kabbalah means *receiving*, and one receives from one's inner gazing.

"I thought the Kabbalah was based on the Tree of Life?" Cait interjected. "Madonna seems to have made it the new hot spiritual practice in the U.S."

The old Rabbi smiled at her naiveté.

"Many forms of Kabbalah have emerged in recent years, which have focused on the Sephiroth, doctor – the energy spheres of the Tree of Life. Or on Gematria, which analyzes the numerical values of our Hebrew letters. But Madonna notwithstanding, I'm afraid people have been given a very distorted view of Kaballah's true meaning. It would be a bit like thinking you have explained the message of Christianity by giving someone a chocolate Easter bunny!"

He sighed and resumed his explanation. The particular focus of *our* Kabbalah, and the practice of *my* lineage, is mystical and experiential. And while the Kabbalah of many traditions is only transmitted to men, in Sephardic families such as ours, the women sometimes have played pivotal roles, both in carrying our lineage, and in the interpretation and understanding of the great mysteries."

He chuckled as he explained, "You see, during the times of persecution by the Christian Church, when we were forced to convert to Christianity against our will, our men would go to mass on Sunday in order to escape arrest, and the women would stay home to teach our truths. Do you understand?"

He laughed softly, shaking his head at the impossibility of explaining all he wished to say. "One does not learn Kabbalah in an afternoon, my friends, nor by tying a red string on one's wrist. It is a vast body of knowledge. But I shall tell you what I can -- enough to give context to what you need for your current quest.

"In the time when Europe was emerging from the Dark Ages, there was already a flourishing intellectual and commercial community centered here in Spain – and Spain was still under Islamic rule.

"The most accomplished thinkers of that time – be they Jews, Muslims or Christians – were attracted to Spain for study – it was all part of an elitist spiritual and intellectual movement that was burgeoning in all three societies. Seekers converged here! It was as if all the mystical knowledge of the ancients was being re-awakened after centuries of lying dormant – or, at least, hidden from view. During this Golden Time, the Kabbalists and the Templars formed ties of friendship that were later to be of great consequence to both groups.

"Alas, the notoriety of this Jewish Center of learning and influence soon became a thorn in the side of the Catholic clergy and the Catholic monarchy. We Jews were, at first, only persecuted – then we were expelled from Spain, entirely. It was only much later that a few of the old families managed to return.

"But you must understand that before our expulsion, there had been centuries of friendship, commerce and intellectual give-and-take among the mystical students of all three major faiths. The three schools of Hermetic philosophy had shared vast amounts of hidden knowledge. The Arabs had contributed mathematics, alchemy, astronomy, and the last vestiges of the magical secrets of Egypt and Persia, that had been thought lost with the burning of the great Alexandrian Library. The Jews had contributed knowledge of medicine, surgery, and even astrology, plus the mysticism of Kabbalah. The Templars had provided not only the scholarly and mystical knowledge of their own native countries – do not forget that the British Isles were rife with pagan mysticism and the Roman Church practiced powerful magic of its own – but the Templars, who had created both a banking system and trade routes with the East, were also the keepers of secrets they had brought back from as far away as China and India!"

"I do remember that the Templars provided sanctuary to the Jews in many places, during the purges and expulsions," Hugh added, his voice thoughtful as he turned to Cait. "You see Cait, the Jews and the Templar Knights were the only sanctioned money-lenders – bankers if you will – in the middle ages. So Jewish funding, and Templar Letters of Credit, created the great banking systems of Europe and the Middle East. That's what allowed commerce to stretch from Europe to Asia. It makes all the sense in the world that the Jews and Templars knew and trusted each other."

"This is quite true," the Rabbi agreed. "People forget that for several hundred years, Jews in Muslim countries, because of their wealth, skill, connections and ambitions, were sought out by those in power, and gained power of their own. From the time of the Abbasid Caliphates in the 9th century, all the way through the apex of the Ottoman Empire in the 16th century, this was true all over the Middle East, North Africa and in Moorish Spain. We Jews created an entire class – a hierarchy, if you will – of socially elite and well connected Courtiers. These Court Jews, as they came to be called, flourished as a highly effective social network in medieval royal circles."

Cait looked surprised. "I've never known where the great Jewish dynasties came from."

"You must remember to 'follow the money' as your American detective stories would say!" the old man said enthusiastically, and was amused by the startled looks this statement provoked on his guests' faces.

"Yes, *yes*, I do sometimes allow myself to be frivolous and read something other than the Zohar!" he explained with a chuckle, before returning to the seriousness of his story.

"Other Christian countries also, enjoyed the cultural, intellectual and social gifts of Jewry. But you must remember that all this Courtly acceptance was just a by-product of our central power-base. We were *rich* – we were the *bankers!* We controlled *everyone's* money for centuries!"

The Rabbi had warmed to his story.

"We Jewish bankers funded Rulers *and* their wars – a most lucrative trade, considering the frailty of human nature. And with our extraordinary wealth, came extraordinary tastes. Needless to say, jewelry and jeweled artifacts were desirable commodities at the Courts of Kings. The artists and craftsmen who could create such treasures became the darlings of the Kings and their courtiers, so many of my clever and artistic ancestors took up jewelry making and gem-dealing. Very often, watchmaking and locksmithery went hand-in-hand with these crafts, of course, so when we add those skills to the mysticism I have already described, I believe you will understand why the Templars found in Jewry, precisely *who* and *what* they needed to secure their treasure!"

He sat back and rested both hands on his knees to take in his visitors' growing excitement.

Cait's eyes widened as the full impact hit her. "Are you telling us the Templars entrusted the Jews with their treasure," she asked, the pieces falling into place, "and one of your people created the magical lock that guards it?"

The Rabbi's eyes sparkled behind his thick glasses, as he sat back in his chair and smiled. "One of our most gifted ones was both sage and jeweler. He received a vision – it was the design for a warded lock, the likes of which had never before been constructed. He was told it was a magical means of protecting *that which should never be found* until the world reached enlightenment."

Seville. Spain
AD 1238

The jeweler looked up from his workbench and tried to find the source of the strange music. Itzak was a man of many gifts and had played the lute since boyhood, but he had never heard the likes of this music. It was so faint he had to reach out with all his senses to distinguish its distant strains from the sounds around him in the city. But where could it be coming from?

Reluctantly, Itzak rose from his worktable and made his way to the door of his shop. He took immense pride in the tiny shop that was the source of his livelihood, his growing fame among the courtiers, and most wonderfully of all, it was the source of his beautiful life as a scholar, a husband and a father. **Thanks be to G-d**, *he breathed as he stuck his head out the door to see if the musicians might be at the end of this winding little street in the Jewish quarter. He saw no one, but realized that the strains were becoming more distinct and that, oddly, they now seemed to be coming from somewhere above him.*

Itzak shook his head in puzzlement and started back toward his worktable.

His father had been a great scholar and philosopher. A kind and generous man who had not been disappointed when his son

Itzak chose not to follow in his rabbinical footsteps, but to become an artisan, a jeweler, a locksmith, and a sometimes musician.

"Your talent comes from G-d, my son," his father had said. "Would you question his gift or his choice of your path? You can return no greater gift to him than to be the best at your craft. Once you have achieved mastery of your gifts, perhaps, you will one day understand why you have been so directed."

Itzak wiped the tear from his cheek, for the memory of his father, dead these past two years, had reminded him of how much he missed the man's generosity and wisdom.

The music was more audible now, and extraordinarily beautiful, Never, in all his life had Itzak heard music so exquisite, so delicate, so... celestial. That was the word he was searching for. The music of the spheres must sound like this... He hurried to his workroom, intending to put away his tools and go to seek the source.

The workroom, when he entered it, was ablaze with light, and the music was somehow entwined in the brilliance, and in the midst of it all, stood an angel.

Itzak's first thought was **I wish my father could be here to see this!** *He remembered Zachariah 1:18 said something about an angel visiting a craftsman, but he couldn't remember which angel it had been, or what had been said.*

"I am the Fire of G-d," the presence said, or rather the words were suddenly inside Itzak's head. "You have been given a task. I bring you the means to honor it."

He noted that the Being wore a golden belt and greaves, on which strange letters were blazoned. He seemed more a great warrior, than a messenger, and was covered in what appeared to be copper chain mail, although the brilliance of the light he emanated made it hard for Itzak to be certain what he was seeing.

"I will do my best," the awestruck young man managed to stammer.

"You will be called upon to create a lock that will guard a great treasure," the angel went on   "It must be warded in a

singular way by the power of G-d. You have been deemed worthy of being the instrument by which this comes to pass..."

Itzak felt as if he, himself, were dissolving, every particle of his being melting into the pure light of the angel, and he was afraid, and awestruck and grateful all at the same time. And then he was no longer in his shop, or in Spain, or even in this world...

The sun had long since set, the street beyond his shop was dark and empty, the celestial music had ceased many, many hours since. Itzak stood alone in his doorway staring up at the stars in the night sky, and knowing exactly how the lock must be constructed. In his hand, he held a book that glowed with lettering as golden as the sun. It contained the secret of the lock's magical warding.

Now he must wait until he was called upon to use this knowledge, for he had been shown the date and the time at which he would be summoned to a certain mountain and given the commission on which so much would depend.

"Oh, Papa," he breathed into the sweet night air. "How I wish you could have seen him."

The old Rabbi smiled at the rapt faces of his listeners.

"Just as the Arc of the Covenant was protected by God's highest magic, so too, Itzak had been told, the Grail must be protected," he continued. "The immortality which the Grail granted, was too great a temptation for venal man until – *and if* – an age of enlightenment made appropriate restraint possible, it had to be hidden. According to the vision vouchsafed to our mystical locksmith the Grail must remain lost until humanity had overcome its warlike and greedy nature. So perhaps we shouldn't stand on one foot, waiting, eh?" The last thought was accompanied by a wry chuckle.

"You see, we Jews, the Cathari and the Templars, not only shared dangerous knowledge, we shared tolerance for each other's belief systems.   That was why, I believe, those who guide humanity's progress placed into our collective hands, these sacred objects, along with the means to keep them hidden.

"Remember, my children, the Templars possessed both the Grail *and* the Spear. Our locksmith's vision had told him to create a mystical lock that could only be opened when the Spear was placed within its mechanism – and moreover, it had to be placed there, by one who had been chosen by God as its Caretaker! Angels do not create easy tasks, you may be sure.

"Certain rituals were necessary for this mystical warding to take effect, of course, and certain magical rituals would be needed to dissolve the warding at some future date. These had been set in Itzak's own hand, as he was being instructed by the Angel, in a magical Book of Secrets that could be read only by Adepts. The lock was constructed, the Grail was hidden in a cave beneath the Cathari stronghold, the warded lock was secured, and the Spear was spirited away, to be hidden elsewhere, along with a book, until such time as the world was ready for what the Spear could unlock."

"That must have been just prior to the time all Hell was unleashed on the Cathari," Hugh said, sorting the puzzle pieces in his own mind. "The Church and the monarchy annihilated the Cathars in 1244, and then all but destroyed the Templar Order itself, in 1307. The Inquisition they'd created to perpetrate those decimations, was then used to subjugate or kill any who dared disagree with Church teachings. The Templars who survived the torture and burnings were forced underground. In the guise of various secret societies, we have remained there ever since."

Cait was eagerly leaning forward, both elbows on the table now, her hands covering her mouth as if to hold back the thousand questions that were surfacing.

"And the Spear we seek..." she said finally, "what became of *that*, Rabbi?"

The old man watched her face. "It began a long journey into, and out of, the hands of powerful men... the kind of men who thought the power to be holy far less desirable than the power to rule the world..."

101

Seville. Spain

The restless night of fitful dreams finally ended. Cait sat bolt upright in the bed she'd been led to by the Rabbi's wife the night before, too tired and too bedazzled by all she'd heard, to care where or if, she slept.

But then the dreams had come... or were they dreams at all? She couldn't tell anymore, they were becoming so vivid. Ghettos, battlefields, palaces, churches, ships at sea... image upon images. And always running, always hiding. Always afraid of what lay around the next corner.

Cait had awakened with only one certainty – she was sick to death of feeling afraid. She had to find a way to shake off the fear that dogged her almost as much as the sorrow of loss did. For a few moments she just sat in bed, staring at the wall in front of her, without really seeing it, trying to remember the dreams that just a moment ago had seemed too vivid to fade. The knock at the door startled her.

"Cait?" it was Hugh's voice. "We need to make an early start and Rabbi ben Ibraham wants to talk with us before we go. It seems he's had a dream..."

"Dreams must be contagious around here," Cait called back, getting out of bed wearily and padding toward the door. She glanced down at the tee shirt and shorts she'd worn to bed, and deciding she was decent enough, opened the door.

Hugh's body filled the doorframe made for smaller people, in other times. She frowned as she realized how awful she must look, bed-headed with no makeup, then dismissed the thought as inappropriate, as quickly as it had surfaced.

"Sorry to wake you, but the Rabbi seems really agitated about whatever it was he dreamed last night. He's fairly brimming over with something he'll only tell to both of us together."

"Give me five minutes..." Cait answered with a short laugh. "Just please tell me the Rabbi drinks coffee or tea. I'm desperate for caffeine."

"No worries," Hugh replied with a laugh of his own. "The coffee they brew here would put hair on your chest, as you Yanks say."

"Well, that's about the only surprising thing that *hasn't* happened to me yet, I suppose," she murmured as she shut the door and turned toward her duffle and the small stack of clothes she hadn't even bothered to unpack. But the minute she heard her words, she knew how very far they were from the truth. There was *plenty* that could still happen...

* * *

There was excitement in Rabbi ben Ibraham's demeanor as he welcomed Cait and Hugh to his small study, and motioned them to sit down.

"I have had a true dream!" he announced, excitedly and with no preamble. "I have been informed that there is a new stop you must make on your journey – one you had not intended. It is connected *to* your quest, but is not precisely *of* this quest." He emphasized the words. "I do not know exactly what this means, only that it is important!"

Hugh frowned. "We're grateful for all your help, Rabbi, but our mission is urgent and Cait needs to get back to her daughter before Christmas. I'm not certain we can be distracted for anything non-essential..."

"Yes, yes, I *know* all this!" the old man interrupted impatiently. "But this knowledge must *be essential!* It would not have been given to me in such a way, if it were not of the utmost urgency that you heed it! You must go to Israel and..."

"Israel!" both his visitors blurted simultaneously.

"Something will be given to you there – *something* crucial that may close the circle!"

Cait's eyebrows drew together in a puzzled frown. "What circle are you talking about?" Cait asked with exasperation.

The Rabbi shook his head in frustration.

"I do not *know!* This is all that was told to me. *The gift you receive can close the circle.* I saw this circle burning before my eyes. A fiery sword inscribing a great circle on the earth, around this gift – *what* this *something* is, I was not permitted to see. There is more at stake here than your Spear, I was told. Your Spear is merely the Way-shower! It propels you on the Path, but something larger, more important, is at stake."

He looked beseechingly at his visitors, willing them to understand the gravity of this message.

"And you cannot go by the usual routes," the old man added urgently, as if just remembering this fact. "There is a friend – a private plane. This plane will take you. But you must hurry. Go now, before the way is closed to you. Where the light grows brightest, darkness redoubles its effort to bar the way."

The man and woman exchanged weary glances, deciding.

"Give us your blessing, Rabbi," Cait answered for both of them. "We'll do exactly as you say."

102

New York

Meg and Carter had arrived with Chinese take-out, Matt and Croce had brought wine and beer. Damon and Pythias had pulled up chairs for them on the far side of the computer nest, where they now sat surrounded by blinking screens, including one that looked like a huge flat screen TV. Matt wondered fleetingly if these guys ever emerged from their perches back there, with the electronic blitzkrieg from which they seemed to draw their power. Did they ever have sex? Had they ever seen the sun? In the next generation, geeks like this would probably have physically mutated, so they could just plug their fingers into their computer CPU's like those guys in Avatar plugged their tails into the giant pterodactyl thingies they flew around on.

Damon was pointing to the big screen. He reached up and started spreading things around directly on the screen, as if it were a giant iPad, zooming in on details and enlarging them.

"We started this data tree to keep track of all the disparate threads. Over here is the doc's travel route so far, with what we know about why she went where she went, and what she might have learned when she got there." He looked at Meg and Carter disapprovingly. "If you'd gotten the special phone to her like we asked, she'd have been able to keep us more clued in."

Meg started to protest, but Carter cut in placatingly. "Not like we didn't try, boys, but she's a moving target."

"Yeah, yeah, we got it covered," Pythias piped up, as more lines and connections appeared on the screen.

"Over here we got the Gruner files," Damon said pointing. "He wasn't just dirty *then,* he's been dirty ever since, so there's lots of data..."

"Where'd you get it?" Matt asked.

"You don't wanna know," Pythias replied, "but those tips from Sally made all the difference. Governments, immigration, military, Pentagon, NSA..."

"Ok, enough!" Damon cut in as he saw Matt and Croce's eyes widen. "Remember you're talking to cops... We got what we got, *where* we got it is irrelevant. You can arrest us later."

"Over here is the CIA strand," Damon said, pointing. "They're in this up to their dark glasses, but we think its not just business as usual – you know, like mercs and cover-ups and dis-information? The Director has a link to Gruner through his father, who supposedly committed treason and suicide right after trying to blow the whistle on Herr Gruner, back in the day."

"Ok, *that's* new," Matt said.

"And maybe *really* good to know," Croce added.

"The Sinclair woman's thread goes all the way back and intersects, too, but she's a flunky, and there's much bigger fish to fry here."

"Any idea who the big shaggy guy is, who seems to be acting as my sister's guardian angel?" Meg asked.

"No clue yet," Damon said, "Unless he's employed by one of these other players. But doing *what*, we're clueless. He just seems to pop up randomly like a wack-a-mole."

"How about my Skinheads?" Croce asked.

"Not just Skinheads. We got Neos, White Supremacists, Aryan Brotherhood, and a shit-load of other fascist types. They got threads at all levels of this. The Skinheads look like the bottom rung, but they do dirty work for the higher ups, and they act as couriers and worker bees all over the world. And it looks like they've got serious ties to Al-Q and sympathetic other factions all over the Middle East."

"How exactly does the Middle East tie in?" Carter prompted. Pythias hit a few keys on his computer and a bunch of interwoven threads lit up the screen with the number 13 in red at the top.

"The Order of The 13," Pythias said portentously. "Based on what we've scrounged, we think the old guys were right, Gruner is head of the Order of The 13 and those guys collectively pull more weight than the Bilderbergs, Trilateral Commission and CFR combined. And war is the biggest money-maker on the planet for the guys who pull the strings. We *think* we've identified a bunch of them... He hit another key and a list of names appeared containing a staggering roll-call of power-players, politicians, military leaders, philanthropists..."

"Come on guys! Are you on crack? This sounds like a load of bullshit to me," Matt interrupted with a smirk. "You're letting your conspiracy jones skew the way you're looking at this. You *can't* be serious about these names. You're talking about some of the most important people on the planet..."

The two geniuses looked at each other and sighed collectively, before Damon answered, obviously trying not to let his irritation get the better of him.

"Look, dude. I know you're law enforcement, so you gotta *think* the world works a certain way, or you can't do your job. We *get* that. But you're a babe in the woods if you think you and the rest of the world aren't being manipulated on a minute-to-minute basis by powers so complex, and so far beyond your understanding, you'd have to throw away your badge if you grokked what's *really* happening out there.

"We follow data and we extrapolate intel from that data. End of story. If you want fairytales like the press is neutral, the government is on the side of the little guy, the law is always right, and money doesn't pull the strings that make the world go round, you can just get your asses out of here and find somebody else who'll go along with your bullshit."

"Whoa, boys!" Carter interjected. "Let's put our rulers back in our pants, and focus on why we're here, ok?"

"This isn't dick measuring, Cart," Pythias shot back, with more fire than she'd ever seen the man display. "We're putting our asses on the line for you guys. We are snooping on the Prince of Fucking Darkness here and we're not gonna keep on doing it and get dissed in the process."

Matt put up his hands in the universal gesture of surrender. "OK. OK. I got it. I apologize," he said sounding like he meant it. "It's just I did a lot of things when I was in the military – and I believed I was doing them for all the right reasons. Now – since all this stuff we're finding out about – I'm not so sure about anything and I'm a little shook up about some of this shit, alright? But I didn't mean to take it out on you. I'm really sorry."

"Apology accepted," Damon said without waiting for Pythias' pronouncement. "So let's get on with it."

"For now, it doesn't matter who's ruling the world. It just matters that we find the fucking Spear and get the doc and her kid out of the target zone. OK? After that we can argue politics."

Meg took in the high tension testosterone zinging around the room and pulled out her best negotiator voice. "Guys, we *get* it! Everybody's on high E because everybody's trying so hard to help, and everybody's laying it on the line here. So we need a little peace in the valley right now because I for one, believe every word you've said. And I'll bet I speak for everybody in this room. If you're right, and truly terrible people are pulling the strings, we need all the intel we can get on who's doing what to whom. And most of all, we need to *support each other*. We're like David up against Goliath here. We need to have each other's backs so the Philistines don't win."

"More like Sarah Connor against Skynet," Pythias corrected. "These guys have already got the world by the balls... we're just the Insurrection."

"Food!" Croce thundered, startling everybody. "We need pasta – maybe a little salad. Some tiramisu. McCormack here gets all fucked up when he's out of carbs. Chinese ain't gonna cut it tonight. We need serious Guinea food to get our blood up."

"Right," Carter piped up. "Do you two have menus from the local Italians?"

Damon and Pythias looked at her as if she'd come unglued. "You mean like take-out?" Damon said incredulously. "We don't let strangers in here with takeout." He shook his head, as if it were inconceivable that *anyone* anywhere would ever do such a stupid thing.

"OK, then," she answered, "Tell me where I'm going and I'll be back with food in half an hour. I have a feeling you've got a lot more for us to see, so Croce's right, we need sustenance."

Croce stood up. "I ain't lettin' you out in this neighborhood after dark by yourself, kid. Besides, you need a wop with you so you don't screw up the order. Come on!"

Carter flashed a look at Meg that said 'rein in Matt while we're gone,' but she could see he already regretted his earlier outburst. He knew as well as the rest of them that Damon and Pythias knew what they were doing, but she could see what it did to his heart to have his version of reality questioned.

When they got to the pavement outside the building, Croce pulled up the collar of his jacket against the bitter cold wind and turned to Carter.

"You gotta know some things about the big guy," he said, weighing his words, careful not to betray any confidences.

"He was Special Forces, ya know? The kind of kills he racked up are harder on some guys than others. For a guy like Matt, with a big conscience, about the only way you can deal with that stuff is if you believe you're on the side of the angels, ya know? Finding out your government sometimes protects the bad guys and sacrifices the good guys has to get him in the gut."

He looked hard at her, to see if she understood. "And all the lies and cover-ups to protect scum like Gruner... that's really fucked up, ya know what I mean?"

Carter thought a minute about her reply then said. "Somebody once said 'A patriot must always be ready to defend his country against his government.' – but sometimes it gets really hard to figure out if that time has come for you, doesn't it, Croce? It's why I left the Bureau. I didn't want to find out the day had come to make that choice."

Croce shoved his hands deep into his pockets and looked at her again. He nodded his head inside his turned up collar as if to say *OK then.*

"Life's a bitch," he said finally, his words sending frost clouds into the air.

"And then you die," she answered matter of factly. They both smiled.

"Yeah," he said, "so in between you eat Italian, and you try to make it through the night. Right?"

Carter nodded, understanding perfectly. "Sounds like a plan to me," she said and took his arm as they walked into the dark of Dumbo.

103

"Hi, Bird," Meg said to Lark on the phone. "How are you doing, kiddo? I really miss you." Meg, with no children of her own and no plans to have any, had a really special relationship with Lark. She and Cait had always been so close, it worried her that Lark had no sister to be her confidante.

"I miss you too, Aunt Meggie," Lark said, sounding more distant and lethargic than usual. "Do you know where my mommy is? I don't really, and when she calls me, she doesn't sound so great and she never says when she's coming back. I'm pretty lonely here except for two nice old guys and some horses..."

Meg smiled at the childlike assessment.

"I can imagine, sweetheart," she said, "but your mom will be back soon and then everything can get back to normal."

"Not *everything*!" Lark blurted and Meg bit her lip. "What about my Daddy!"

"You're right, sweetie, I know it won't ever be the same without your Dad. I guess sometimes life just needs us to be brave for a while and this is one of those times." She took a breath. "I called because I met a couple of gamers who want to learn about the Labyrinth... after you get back home, I mean."

"Really!" Lark squealed. "Are they geeks?"

"The geekiest, kiddo," Meg answered. "Carter says they're totally cool and really know their stuff. They've read your Dad's math papers and they're the kind of kids he taught in grad school. You'll like them."

"Awesome!" Lark said.   "So did you show them the Labyrinth yet?"

"I didn't know how to do that, Bird, but I thought maybe you and Carter could make it happen for them, when you get back, OK. I really miss you, and I miss your mommy."

"Yeah, I miss her, too, but I'm really mad at her too!" Lark said with sudden heat that startled Meg.

"Why, sweetie? Why on earth are you mad at your mom?"

"Because she doesn't even *care* about me anymore and she doesn't care that I'm all alone here and I want to go home! Couldn't I just come stay with you and Cart for a while?"

Meg heard the distress ratcheting up in Lark's voice and wondered what had triggered the outburst.

"Listen to me, Bird. Your mommy absolutely adores you! The *only* reason she's gone is to find that secret thing we know about..."

"How come it's such a big *secret* if a whole lot of people know about it?" Lark interrupted defiantly, and Meg remembered how literal her niece was and how analytical.

"Let's just say there are *some secret things* we shouldn't talk about on the phone – and the reason you can't come stay with Carter and me right now is because we work all day and you'd have nobody to play with and nobody to keep you safe all day. Your mommy left you in the safest place she could think of, and she didn't *want* to do it – she *had* to. I thought they were really nice to you there, Lark. Has anything happened you need to tell me about? Did somebody hurt your feelings?"

Lark felt suddenly guilty about making it sound like the uncles weren't being nice to her.

"No," she said reluctantly. "The old guys are really nice and they're trying hard to play with me and all – it's just that they're really *old* and I'm kind of sad a lot, and I miss the way things used to be..." She almost told Meg about BWK, but didn't.

"How about if I get Carter on the phone so you two can talk geek talk to each other – that always cheers you up, right? And I promise I'll see if I can find out *exactly* when your mom will get back, because I know she's missing you just like you're missing her. How's that?"

Only partially placated, Lark asked, "Is mommy *ever* gonna tell me what's really happening and why I'm stuck here?"

Meg tried to think how to answer that. "I know she *wants* to tell you everything, Bird," she said, treading carefully. "But it's hard to do that when its only safe to talk about things in code like we're doing. But as soon as she gets back..."

"I hate codes!" Lark blurted, unexpectedly cutting her off. "I have enough codes to think about already. And, besides, pretty soon I won't even care if my Mommy *never* comes back!"

When Meg hung up the phone a few minutes later she had one more thing to worry about.

104

Bedford, New York

Marta dressed for her outing, the first since her arrival in the U.S. She'd been able to manage just a brief encounter with the contact sent by her handler, in the ladies room at JFK International when her flight landed. Kolb had been sent to collect her at the airport, and had watched her like the evil hawk he was the entire time they were in the terminal. She and her contact had little privacy in the ladies room, and barely time to exchange a few words, plus the makeup case which contained her handler's message.

The house in Bedford was guarded and fenced, the message had told her, she'd be searched, so weapons would have to be gotten to her by other means. A stash had been buried just outside the grounds, the place indicated on a tiny map, which she'd then flushed down the toilet with the rest of the message. Marta would have to contrive to get to this stash as quickly as possible and then smuggle what weapons she could into the house. The note said she could leave her own communications in the weapons box and it would be monitored as often as possible. She was given an address in Bedford where she was to make contact with them, whenever she could contrive a way to get out of the estate for an hour or two. They had specified a date she was to try for, as well.

Today, Marta's first day off, since arriving, was the appointed time for the meeting, and she was increasingly desperate to make contact. Fritz was escalating, she needed to let them know that. Needed to tell them what small intel her pillow talk had gleaned -- needed to put a contingency plan in place, in case the whole op went south.

Marta put on her coat and muffler, then headed for the door, looking forward to her escape from this place more than she dared admit even to herself. Even a few hours away would make a difference to her flagging spirits, and, perhaps on the way back, she could scope out the area she believed to be the one where the weapons were stashed. She also intended to scope out the guards, and had to figure out a plan to make that possible without triggering either distrust or jealousy on the part of the hair-trigger Fritz.

She opened the door from her room and almost as if her thoughts had conjured him, she collided with Fritz's large form blocking the doorway. *Gott in himmel*! It was a good thing she didn't talk to herself when she thought she was alone.

"Where are you going, Marta?" he asked, eyeing her outdoor attire.

Regaining her composure, she smiled up at him. "This is my day off, remember, Fritzy?" she hoped her voice sounded more playful than she felt.

"So it is," he said, unbuttoning her coat and slipping his hand inside to find her flesh. "I have plans to enjoy your freedom in special ways today," he whispered into her ear as he bent to kiss her neck.

Marta's heart sank. "But Fritzy, I have to go to town," she wheedled. "I need things from the drugstore. Woman things. And I want to see something of this place. You know I have never been before to America." She hoped she sounded charmingly pouty.

But she could feel his arousal against her belly, and she groaned inwardly. The man was damned near priapic. Every time he came near her, he wanted sex. More and more of it. Rougher and rougher, especially if his father's name had been mentioned, or he'd had an encounter with the old Nazi that day...

"But, Fritzy, you will grow tired of your Marta," she said seductively, "if you have sex with me so constantly. You barely give me time to seduce you with my womanly wiles..." she tried to avoid the groping but knew it was futile.

"And you mustn't do this here," she whispered urgently, pushing his hands away. "If we are seen, I will be fired!"

"You're right," he admitted. "It isn't prudent to be indiscreet. Come to my study in ten minutes. I'll see we are not disturbed for the rest of the day." With that he turned and sauntered back down the hall.

Marta closed the door of her room and leaned against it for a moment, seething with impotent fury and utter disgust. He was nothing but a rutting animal and she was his unwilling prey. And now she'd have to find some other way to get a message out of this elegant prison camp. She allowed herself a moment of cursing silently in four languages before she felt composed enough to do what she must.

Sacrifice

Part XVII

"A lie gets halfway around the world before the truth has a chance to get its pants on."

Sir Winston Churchill

105

Tel Aviv. Israel.

Seven hours after Cait and Hugh had been arrested at the airport in Tel Aviv, the Israeli detective with the small, wiry body and Levantine face, eyed them both appraisingly across the grey metal table in the interrogation room. He seemed to be deciding which one he would begin questioning. Cait saved him the trouble.

"Why are we here?" she snapped, tired, hungry and furious at their detention. The police had been waiting for them at the private airfield. "Why have we been given no food or water? For that matter, why are we *here* at all?"

"I alone will ask the questions, doctor." The man's curt words showed no semblance of civility. "You are in a great deal of trouble, are you aware of that?"

"See here," Hugh interjected, "Doctor Monahan is a U.S. citizen and I am a citizen of Great Britain. We demand to see representatives of our respective Embassies."

The man shook his head, as if it saddened him to be talking to imbeciles.

"You are not in a position to demand anything at all," he said with weary and deliberate coldness. "Your names are on our terrorist watch list, you are being sought by your own governments, you will answer my questions or you will be interrogated by far less agreeable people than myself."

Cait's frayed temper was apparent in her voice.

"We are *tourists* in your country. We have no political agenda whatsoever. Whatever you may *think* we've done, is wrong! Whatever it is you want from us, we cannot give you. You're treating us as criminals, which is absolutely insane! I demand that you call our Embassy. I demand legal counsel, and while you're at it, I demand a glass of water and the use of a ladies room!"

The expression on the man's face was almost one of amusement at the woman's ridiculous audacity. He would let others deal with her. He reached across to an intercom and pressed a button. The door opened and two muscular men with sidearms entered the room.

"Take this woman to an interrogation cell," he ordered, "let Simon deal with her."

Hugh rose in an instinctive gesture of protection – it was dangerous to be separated. The two men ignored him and grabbed Cait roughly by the arms, intending to force her out the door.

The detective turned on the struggling Cait.

"You are being a fool, doctor, if you think we will not extract the information we want from you. We have means at our disposal you could not dream in your worst nightmares."

Hugh was suddenly over the table and onto the burlier of the two guards. The man was so taken by surprise, he dropped Cait's arm to parry the attack. Cait screamed, "No!" A sickening thud followed her scream, as the butt of the detective's pistol crashed into the back of Hugh's skull.

Horrified, Cait watched blood erupt from the deep scalp wound, as Hugh slumped and fell. She redoubled her struggles, trying to get to him, but she was being yanked unceremoniously toward the door by the two guards, and didn't have a prayer of escaping them. What the hell had impelled Hugh to take on two heavily armed guards inside a police station, for God's sake?

"You will not be able to keep anything from us, doctor, I assure you," the detective repeated his threat angrily.

"Three weeks ago I would have believed that, you sadistic son of a bitch!" she spat back at him from the doorway. "Now, I'm just not so sure, so go ahead and give it your best shot!"

Then she ceased struggling, and straightened her tall body. "My friend needs medical attention, *now!*" she thundered at him. "You may have caused a concussion or a fracture. I'm a doctor. Let me at least look at him before you drag me out of here..."

The detective opened his mouth to say no, but a heavy-set man in a dark rumpled suit had appeared in the doorway, blocking it with his bull-like bulk. He was surveying the scene with eyes as hooded and drooping as a basset hound's. The sad eyes dominated a lined and jowled face of somewhat more than middle age. He pursed his thick, semitic lips and frowned, addressing the detective.

"I will be taking charge here now," he said, in a quiet but commanding voice. "Kindly release the woman and let her determine what damage has been done to her companion."

The two guards hesitated, looking to the detective for their instructions. Cait tried to pull away from them but they kept their grip.

The man in the doorway shook his head, wearily, as if dealing with recalcitrant school boys.

"You will hand them over to me eventually, Ari," he said to the detective, shaking his big head, so the flaccid jowls flapped. "Why not do it now, before any further mistakes are made and we have an international incident on our hands, eh?"

The detective's eyes narrowed as he considered his options. He knew this Mossad man well, and didn't relish tangling with him. He had seniority and clout. And what were these two foreigners to him after all, but trouble and paperwork?

"Let the woman go," he ordered, his voice sullen.

Cait wrenched free and bent over Hugh. The scalp was rich with blood vessels, so scalp wounds bled copiously and he'd need stitches. "Do you have a medical emergency kit here?" she demanded. "I'll need gloves, sutures, bandages, antiseptic."

The detective, with a disgusted, but acquiescent inclination of his head, sent one of the guards in search of what had been requested.

"They're on the watch list, Rafi!" he complained to the older man, a whiney note in his tone.

"Yes, Ari," the man said patiently. "Which is why I shall take them off your hands, as soon as the doctor has finished. You'll have no further problem with this matter, I assure you."

"But I must make my report..." the detective countered.

"Consider that you have already made this report to *me*," was the reply. "Unless of course you wish to embroil yourself in the matter of how this man was injured. He is considered a minor royal in England, as I understand it, and the Brits, as you may recall, can be difficult when it comes to the treatment of those they consider their aristocracy. I realize, of course, that you may prefer to do this by the book..." he let the thought trail off with a shrug of his heavy shoulders.

The detective knew a prudent offer when it was placed on the table. "Take them," he said magnanimously, "and good riddance. I have no further need of them."

The man with the hooded eyes moved his lips in what might have been the semblance of a smile – just enough to end the conversation pleasantly.

"Good decision, my boy," he said just as the guard returned with the supplies Cait had asked for.

"Now, doctor," he said addressing Cait directly. "You will kindly dress this wound swiftly. Your presence is wanted elsewhere with a certain urgency."

She looked up at the man, not knowing if he were their savior, or their ticket out of the frying pan into the fire. As there was nothing she could do about it either way, she decided that getting Hugh back on his feet quickly, was her best course of action. What on earth had he been thinking, coming to her rescue like that? Maybe it had just become conditioned reflex. His eyes were open now, and he was struggling to rise, but she pushed him back down, "We're moving on," she said to him, "but first I'm going to see to your head."

Hugh nodded and winced, focused his gaze on the man in the doorway, then settled back to her competent ministrations.

— 106 —

"You're going to have a whopper of a headache," Cait said as she finished dressing Hugh's wound. It had been bloody and would be painful, but it wasn't serious, unless a concussion followed.

"You may have a point," he said, wincing as he gingerly touched his hand to the goose egg that had risen under the bandage.

"Time to go!" The voice of the man who'd freed them pre-empted further conversation. "We've lost enough time." He marched them down the corridor to a desk where their possessions were retrieved, then on to a waiting car and driver. He snapped an order in Hebrew to the man at the wheel, who closed the heavy glass partition between them.

"I am Raphael Weiss," the man said as they lurched into traffic. "Many factions seek you now. There is more than one game being played. More than one agenda."

"You are Mossad?" Hugh asked.

"I am, but that is of no consequence for the moment, except that it has afforded me a way to free you with relative ease. We meet because I am part of a group whose mission is the apprehension of those who escaped us at Nuremburg and it is as part of *this* work, I have come for you. We have a mutual enemy in Herr Doktor Guttman/Gruner."

Hugh started to speak, but the man silenced him. "Waste no time on lies, Mr. Delafield, your other business here is of no consequence to me. But there is a place where your business and mine intersect and it may serve us both if we cooperate.

"As to the butcher-in-sheep's clothing who pursues you, we have had him in our sights for decades, but until now, there has been no misstep great enough for us to be able to use what we know, to bring him to justice. His fabricated reputation is too great, his money has bought too many powerful allies, his organization guards him too well, his own ruthlessness has left alive few witnesses to his crimes. Moreover, time seems to be on his side, God alone knows why. The last of those whom he brutalized will soon be dead. It is of great personal importance to me to see him brought to justice before that happens. Do you understand me?" His voice had gone from gruff to grim.

Both somewhat bewildered passengers murmured yes.

"We have reason now to believe his obsession with the Spear you seek – whatever misshugge importance it has to this maniac – will cause him to make a blunder large enough so that not even his friends or his undeserved reputation can save him. We believe you are perhaps being used as an instrument of his well-deserved destruction. You don't have to be a Jew to know how mysterious are the ways of God."

He reached into his breast pocket.

"I have for you a copy of a document we have waited decades to find the right use for. The original is kept safe in Jerusalem. If Gruner/ Guttman's wall of protection is ever breached, we believe this document will put the final nails in his coffin."

Cait and Hugh exchanged looks. "And you haven't used it before... *why?*" she asked.

"Of itself, this is not enough to bring him down. But added to other things, and in the right hands at the right moment, it may tip the scales..." he let the words trail off, then cleared his throat. "We believe, for reasons I can not disclose, those hands could be yours, doctor. If not, we have lost nothing but a little more time."

"Are we to read this now?" she asked, "or are you taking us to meet someone who will explain further."

He shook his head. "I imagine you do not read Hebrew. I'm taking you over the border to a waiting car, doctor. In the envelope, along with the document I speak of, you will find passports, papers, money. Airports, bus and train terminals, are closed to you now, but we believe certain borders can be crossed using these papers. A route has been mapped. There are friends who have been alerted, and you have your own allies. We cannot be certain you will succeed in returning to your own country, but you have the best chance of doing so, if you follow this route."

"And this document?" she asked riffling through the envelope, "You say it's in Hebrew?"

"You're more fluent in Yiddish, maybe? Of course it's in Hebrew," the man said with a small laugh, "There is also the name of a woman in New York who can translate it correctly for you."

"And what am I to *do* with it?"

"This, I do not know. Perhaps the way will be shown to you."

The man's rumpled face took on a determined expression. "The outcome is in the hands of God," he said with finality. "We do not know why He has waited so long to mete out justice for what was done to the innocent. We know only that we are expected to do what we can, to achieve this justice. We follow orders when we receive them." He didn't elaborate on the source of such orders. "The car will take you to a private airstrip, the plane will take you up the Atlantic to the West Coast of Ireland."

Cait, wonderingly, tucked the envelope into her bag.

"Why Ireland, not England?" Hugh asked.

"The Irish have no love for those who issued the warrants for your arrest. They have the means to get you quietly to England, by fishing boat and truck. From there, we assume certain friends of yours can get you home."

"How long will all this take?" Cait asked wearily, thinking of how lonely Lark had sounded in their last phone call.

"Four days," he said. "Maybe five. I assure you, there is no other way."

107

Heredon. England

Lark stared at the screen, an expression of puzzled concern on her face. She'd figured out the math problem, despite the rapidly escalating difficulty of this level of the game. But the increased complexity of the problems wasn't why she was furrowing her forehead and biting her lower lip.

It was the weird fact that a whole new layer of meaning had sneaked up on her just now. As if there were another game entirely hidden inside this one – sort of like steganography, where important data could be embedded in other data files, or in a picture, even, in such a way that it was really hard to find, or remove, or *anything!* That had simply not occurred to her before, and now that it had, she really needed her Daddy or Grandpa to tell her if she was right and what to do about it. Or maybe Carter would know. What if another whole game was hidden here somewhere or even just some big important clue? But was it safe to tell Carter on the phone or over the internet? What if this was the key to *everything* and somebody was watching and waiting for her to figure it out and now they'd be able to find the Spear before Mommy did?

The first eight levels of the Labyrinth were just a game, she told herself, trying hard to be calm and to work out the probability of what she thought she saw here. Lark's Labyrinth was an increasingly difficult challenge, but it was one anybody with a brain for math could play.... maybe not beat, but at least play. Like all computer games, it altered with the player and his or her ability. And it had a seemingly endless stream of possible variations – the different galaxies, dimensions, time-slots and levels of difficulty were what made it exciting for people of different ages and talents to play.

This problem had been the hardest by far. It had taken her two whole days to work it out. *Can you find positive numbers a and b whose cubes are the same as the cube of another positive number?* had been the question asked. It was a special case of Fermat's Last Theorem, namely for the exponent 3, but it had been really, really hard to figure out and she was proud of herself for having gotten through it. Once she'd solved the problem, Lark thought her troubles were over, but then a whole new Labyrinth had appeared!

It was different. *Really* different. If she was right and this was steganography, it would make sense of why all the other clues had been so vague... they were just a way to hide the *real* clues. But if that was true, she might need serious help to figure it out. But where could she get that kind of help now? She didn't think Uncle Tony or Uncle Siggy would even know what steganography meant.

The hidden clue she'd just found wasn't any more helpful than the rest – just better hidden. But why? And how could it say the clues were done when there was still another level to the game? She read it again. *Why* was this one important enough to hide even deeper than all the other clues? Was it just because the Path was nearing the center of the Labyrinth, so the end was getting close? Or was it something else entirely?

> *No man can find*
> *What you can see*
> *All are blind*
> *But you and me.*
>
> *The clues are done*
> *The talent shows*
> *But you're the only one*
> *Who knows*

108

The emails from BWK were more exciting every day. She looked forward to them now – rebelliously. She knew she should tell Mrs. Dunleavy or the Uncles, but it was sort of fun to have a secret. And feeling guilty was a little bit fun, too. Like an imaginary playmate or a sin, or something. She wondered if it would be OK to ask BWK about the steganography.

BWK was cool. He knew stuff kids knew, and liked stuff kids liked. He had sent her links to sites her parents would never have let her look at, and he understood how unfair it was that she'd been left behind. She'd told him all about it. About how her dad got murdered and how they'd escaped. And how then they'd come to this big castle-y place and she'd been dumped there. His word, *dumped.* But it was exactly true.

So sorry you got dumped like nobody cared what happened to you, kid... he'd said in his email. *Your dad would never have done that.* And he was right about that, too, because he knew her dad really well from being his student, so he was really smart, too, or he'd never have been in her dad's class in the first place.

Maybe your mom just wants to be alone with this Hugh guy, he said. *Maybe she's going to marry him and forget all about your daddy. And you know what they do with kids in England, right? They send them off to private boarding schools, where the headmasters beat them and nobody gets to go home except at Christmas. And the kids all have sex with each other and the teachers, so you'd better go to this site and find out how to do it...*

Christmas. Lark looked away from the screen and sighed. It was almost Christmas and her mom didn't even care enough about her to come home to her for *that.* She couldn't imagine what Christmas would be like without Daddy, anyway. Who would chop down the tree with her, like they always did at the Christmas tree farm? Probably at Heredon they just made the servants do it all.

Who would dress up like Santa Claus and make her laugh like daddy did?

No. BWK was her own secret friend... someone she could say what she really felt about *everything* to, and not get yelled at or told it wasn't polite to say stuff like that. She could tell BWK about how Mommy had left her behind to figure everything out by herself, and how really, really mad and sad she felt about that.

109

The phone conversation was static-y, distant. And there was a weird lag-time screwing up the rhythm of the conversation, because you were constantly talking over each other's last thought. The frustration of separation, the inability to tell Lark exactly when she would be home, and the damnable phone problem was driving Cait crazy. And Lark sounded terrible.

"Please come home, Mommy! Please..." the sound of her daughter's pleading wrenched at Cait's heart.

"I'm *trying*, Sweetheart. I'm trying so hard!" Cait replied, not able to explain why she wasn't already there. "I'm on my way home right now, but I can't just get on a plane for complicated reasons, so it's taking longer than it should, but I'm trying to get there fast..."

"You said a week!" Lark practically screamed the accusation at her mother. "You *promised* you would be home in a week, and then you broke your promise and you never came back. I don't believe you anymore!"

Cait, now thoroughly alarmed, blurted, "Did something happen, baby? What happened to upset you so much, sweetheart? I thought you liked Lord Delafield and you know I only left you there because I wanted to keep you safe..."

"You don't care if I'm safe. You don't care about me at all!" Lark shouted. "You just care about that stupid Spear and you'll never come home because you'll never, *ever* find it!"

Cait heard an emphatic click as the line went dead. *Oh my God*! she thought. *What could have happened*? She started to redial, then realized there was absolutely nothing she could *say* to her child that would make a difference. She just had to get back to her immediately. *Screw the Spear*! God could take care of that on His own. She put her pounding head down on her folded arms, and sobbed out all the misery, sorrow, frustration and loneliness she'd been battling. *Was Lark really so wrong in what she'd accused her of? What kind of a mother was she that she'd left her broken-hearted child all alone with strangers?*

110

Dingle Peninsula, Republic of Ireland

The journey out of Israel – every border, every exchange point, every search of documents – had sent Cait's already frayed nervous system into hyperdrive.

She was desperate to talk to Meg, and find out what was wrong with Lark. She'd been able to do so only for a brief moment, before leaving Tel Aviv. Weiss had assured her his phone was secure, but she knew it was monitored by his own people. The way Lark sounded had frightened her – cranky, distant, *angry*... not in the least the child she'd left behind a month ago. Thank God they were finally on their way back to Heredon.

Hugh, too, had made use of the phone to reach his father, presumably to alert those along their proposed route, who would need to know they were on the move, and would be returning through Ireland.

*   *   *

Cait stood alone, silhouetted against the bleak and rock-strewn expanse of Irish beach, waiting for Hugh to make the exchange of documents with the hard-looking men who had met them at the trawler, and then taken them to this deserted stretch of strand. The water that met her gaze was fierce and dark as it smashed unrelentingly against the great rocks that were the hallmark of the Dingle Coast. The water had the look of turbulent slate, and the icy cold that rose from its salty spray made her hug herself for warmth despite the fisherman's sweater, one of the men had tossed to her before beginning his conversation with Hugh. She had wandered away from the urgent male voices, no longer interested in every word, as she most certainly would been at the start of this awful journey to nowhere. Now, all she cared about was getting home to Lark as fast as possible.

She heard the men leave, heard Hugh walk toward her, felt him standing just behind her, but for some strange reason she couldn't make herself turn to go and only hugged herself harder against the cold that seemed to have seeped so deeply into her bones and psyche. She didn't want him to see the tears running down her cheeks, didn't want him to know she felt as desolate as the seascape around them.

But he knew. And to her surprise, he put his arms around her and pulled her in close to his body. No hesitancy this time. No permission asked. She felt the strong, hard warmth of him course through her and was shocked at her own response. Shocked at the comfort it provided and at how very much she wanted to stay in those arms. Except that she knew she couldn't let that happen...

"Hugh, no," she whispered urgently, and tried to pull away. But for once didn't let go.

"You know there's something between us, Cait," he said, his voice low and husky with emotion. "I can't feel what I do this strongly, if you feel nothing for me..." She turned to meet his eyes and the earnestness in them stopped the quick words she'd meant to say. Instead she answered him just as earnestly, from someplace very deep within. "I know that, Hugh..." she breathed, realizing for the first time that it was true. "But I just can't let that be." As she said the words, she felt the disappointment surge through the man, felt the effort of will it took for him to take her at her word and let her go.

"Please, Hugh..." she began, stricken by the pain she saw in his eyes, searching his troubled face and wanting desperately to explain, but not knowing how. "Please understand... I loved my husband. More than I can even begin to say. He felt like the other half of my heart. He was entangled in every memory, every dream, don't you see, Hugh? Until a few weeks ago it never even occurred to me that I would ever have to live a day without him. Never entered my mind there could ever be another man for me..." She stopped, breathing hard, trying to be bedrock honest. "And then he was gone... in the most terrible way! And I was alone and afraid and vulnerable in ways I had no strength for... ways I didn't know how to navigate." She hesitated before going on. "And then there was *you*. With your kindness and your strength, and..." she smiled ruefully, "and those eyes that seem to see straight through to my soul..." she drew another deep breath. "Don't you see, Hugh? I'm afraid of you. Afraid of what I might feel for you... it seems such a betrayal of Jack and my commitment to our love and our life together. And when that guilt crashes in on me, I just want to run away! To escape you and all the questions you force me to face. Questions I have no answers to. I hate the fact that I'm drawn to you... don't you see?"

The desperation in her voice wrenched at his resolve.

He looked beyond her for a moment unable or unwilling to speak. Finally he answered her, his voice gentle as she had ever heard it. "It will be alright, Cait," he said. "I don't know how, but if we survive this journey, we'll find our way. I promise you. Somehow, we'll find our way."

Tears shone in her eyes and she looked so distressed there was nothing more he could say to help her or himself. Nothing he *should* say. So he simply reached up and tenderly brushed back the hair that was blown across her face by the seawind. Then he encircled her again in his arms and as she did not pull away this time, he felt the soft warmth of her against him and buried his face in her long loose hair as they clung together, the roar of the waves on the rocks around them nearly drowning out the pounding of their hearts.

*   *   *

The Irish landscape outside their car window was rock-strewn and barren as a moonscape. They'd been picked up by a fishing trawler that made Cait feel even her hair smelled of halibut, and been landed on that deserted stretch of beach in Dingle, where they'd been met by an old, battered car and two hard, taciturn men who hadn't seemed trustworthy to her, although she couldn't say why. She'd thought their arrival in Ireland would make her feel safer, but every nerve was still on high E. Maybe it was just that they still had no Spear to show for all they'd been through and she was bone-weary.

Cait remembered how very romantic it had all seemed to her years before, in what now seemed another lifetime, when she and Jack had honeymooned in Ireland, drinking in its poetry and passion with every blissed-out breath. Now, the Western Irish coast seemed cold, bleak, and scary as hell.

The day was dour and grey, the wind bitingly damp as only western Irish winds can be, but they were nearly home, she told herself for consolation. Nearly back with Lark. Her heart ached with longing for her daughter.

This was the last leg of their bizarre journey to nowhere. As the dreary landscape whipped by, Cait tried to comfort herself with the thought of seeing her child, but the knowledge that they hadn't found what they'd sought, kept distracting her, as if her brain refused to allow her to feel anything except anxiety. And depression, of course, don't forget *that* she amended, with an internal grimace. She felt thoroughly depressed, which was unlike her.

Hugh, too, had been quiet and pensive most of the time since they'd held each other on the beach. She knew he'd been dosing himself with aspirin for the headache she suspected was far worse than he was letting on. She'd seen him rub at his eyes several times, obviously trying to clear his vision. He had a concussion, she was sure of it now, but he insisted there was nothing to be done about it until they were in the clear. He was probably right. She wondered if he were as weary of the quest as she, and just as homesick.

The dilapidated petrol station due east of the small village where they'd picked up sandwiches and water, was so antiquated it seemed more geared to the horse-drawn jaunting cars that used to travel these isolated roads, than to the service of automobiles. But they'd asked about where to acquire petrol at a roadside food store, and been sent to this relic of a by-gone day, so she assumed it must be functional, even though it appeared deserted.

"I'll see if I can fill the tank," Hugh said, getting out to stretch his long legs. She saw him wince with pain as he stood up, then grab the pump to steady himself, but he smiled at the concern on her face. "Just a bit road weary," he said to reassure her.

"And Cait... would you mind asking inside, if they might have a more recent map than this masterpiece we were given?" He waved the crumpled, endlessly folded map toward her. "Several roads seem to have been digested completely by the years."

Cait nodded, then looked dubiously at the beaten-down structure that appeared to serve as an office. "It'll be a miracle if they even have *petrol* here, never mind a map," she said, straightening her own long limbs, still stiff from the boat, the truck and the terrible beds they'd experienced in the four awful days and nights that had passed since their sleepless night in Israel.

The door was locked, the window shade, half-drawn. As she turned to let Hugh know, the man with the hunting knife came flying at her from the side of the building, catching her totally off guard. But Hugh must have seen him, or sensed the danger, because before she could take in anything other than the size of the blade coming straight at her, he was flinging her out of the way, just as the knife slashed down.

Cait heard a terrible sound of slicing flesh and cloth, then the agonized groan that escaped Hugh's throat. Blood fountained as the knife slashed up again and down. "Sweet Jesus!" she breathed as she launched herself at the back of Hugh's assailant. Pounding at the man's head and shoulders, she saw Hugh had managed to draw the gun the IRA man had given him. She leaped backwards out of the way, and he struggled to get off a shot, just as a second man – this one with a gun – rounded the corner from behind the station. A tire iron was lying on the ground, and Cait grabbed it, and brought it down onto the first man's skull. Hugh, on one knee now, and obviously in terrible pain, fired at the second man, driving him back toward cover. She heard the man grunt and curse.

"You got him!" she gasped, dragging the badly wounded Hugh to his feet. Adrenaline pumping, heart pounding, she pulled him toward the passenger seat of their car and pushed him inside. He was holding his jacket tight around his body, trying to staunch the blood. She grabbed the gun from his dripping fingers and slammed the car into gear. Hitting the gas pedal, screeching out of the gas station and onto the road, she heard the splat of gunshots the wounded man was firing in their wake. She swerved in an attempt to dodge both the bullets and the pelting rocks spat up by the gunfire. In the rearview mirror, she saw the man run into the road behind them, but fall back onto the gravel and lie still. *Thank God!*

The road ahead was completely empty, woods on one side, barren rocky fields on the other, but there could be other men trailing them now, and Hugh needed immediate attention. *What to do?* Cait's mind was racing, her heart in her throat. If she could make the next town, she could get help – *or would there just be more assassins waiting there?* She could go to the police. *No! There was a warrant out for their arrest...* A glance at the blood puddling at Hugh's feet, and the ashen color of his face meant there was no time for indecision. If she didn't stop he would bleed out.

They needed cover. Cait scanned the road for any cutoff that might give her access to the woods before they ran out of gas. The first road was too obvious, but maybe the sheep path a hundred yards further on could get her into cover. She spun the car off the road, over the impossibly rocky and rutted dirt path, hearing Hugh's grunts of pain as she crashed unceremoniously into the cover of the trees and thick undergrowth. The engine stuttered at the strain... *could any axle take this pounding?...* and the gas gauge read nearly empty. Cait pushed the car as far as it could go, worrying they were still too visible from the road. *Damn it to Hell!* She had only a few more rounds in the gun. She glanced at Hugh. *Very, very bad.* Her heart sank and tears welled in her eyes. She blinked them away to scan the landscape desperately. She'd have to get him to a place where she could stop the bleeding *now.* She jerked the car to a halt.

The blankets! The man had said there were two blankets in the car, in case they had to sleep on the road. Cait shook out the bigger blanket on the ground next to the car and struggled to ease Hugh's nearly unconscious form off the seat and onto it. He was trying desperately not to cry out in pain. She used the smaller blanket to rig a rough pressure bandage, cursing at the inadequacy of what she had to work with, then remembering Jake Many Feathers' admonition about being grateful for whatever Creator supplied you in time of need, and said a fast prayer of thanks they had anything at all.

Mustering all the strength she could, she dragged the makeshift travois as far into the cover of the woods as she could go.

Holy Mother of God! she breathed into the darkening forest around her, feeling as Irish as she'd ever felt in her life. *"Don't let him die. Please! He was only trying to help us..."* She had no breath for more, barely enough for dragging the blanket and Hugh's body without exhausting all the strength she had left...

111

Lark waited in the darkness of her room until everything had stilled in the huge house. Only the wind whistling through the chimney pots, just like in the story of *The Selfish Giant,* made a continuous whoosh-whoosh-rattle-rattle sound to disturb the silence of the old manor.

Gingerly, she eased out from under the covers. The frosty air made her reach for the wooly robe Mrs. Dunleavey had left her on the bedside chair. Lark slipped her feet into her fleecy slippers and softly pattered to the desk. She grabbed her laptop, then scampered back to the warmth of the big down comforter. They called them feather-beds or eiderdowns over here in England, Lark thought as she snuggled under, but they were just big fluffy comforters, really. A pang of loss suddenly hit her, as the thought of her own toasty pink room with its just-right bedspread and its perfect pillows came to her. She missed *everything* about her old life and just wanted to go home! Why didn't her mommy come and take her back home? Why did she have to leave her all alone here and afraid? It wasn't fair! And now she might not even be home for Christmas. The thought fueled the child's growing misery and anger. Defiantly, she booted up the computer and logged in.

She knew the emails were forbidden even though no grown-up had told her that, because they were all secret, and that was the very best part about them. BWK had told her not to tell anybody, and he'd been right. On TV, kids hid things from their parents all the time. Especially teenagers, and she was practically a teen, or at least a tween now. BWK knew she was pretty grownup – that's why he had sent her to those sketchy websites about sex and very interesting grownup stuff. Even though some of the stuff she saw on them was pretty disgusting, it was still interesting. She couldn't wait to tell Bitsy about them when she got home.

If she ever got home! The uncles were great and she had fun with them but they were practically a hundred years old, and she wanted a friend her own age to play with, and she wanted her old life back, and she never wanted to have to leave home again, *ever!* And BWK understood all that. It was almost like he could see inside her head.

BWK knew a lot of stuff... games and math puzzles like she used to do with her Dad. He knew all about her because Professor Monahan had talked about her so much. And he wanted to meet her because he had a book that had belonged to her dad that he knew would mean a lot to her. He'd sent her a photo of himself and he was really cool looking, too. Kind of like a movie star.

BWK said he was coming to England for a family vacation, so if she could just get out of the manor without telling the grown-ups, even it was only for a minute, he could give her the book.

Lark had wondered, in the beginning, how BWK knew where she was, until she remembered that computer geeks knew how to trace your IP anywhere on the planet, and all her Daddy's students were really smart geeks.

And now he was actually here and she was going to meet him!

Hi, LWK... this morning's email had started,
Jst landd. Wl Bn yr naybrhood 2 moz on d wA2 scotld.
Cn u sneak ot? Ive a QL pic of yr dad nu, n a surpriz,
2! C U 2 moro?
BWK

She stared at the screen. It was fun having somebody to talk to in geek-speak – somebody like Daddy. Fun having a secret of her own, instead of always having to worry about everybody else's big fat stupid secret. And maybe, if he turned out to be nice, BWK could help her figure out what the steganography meant in the game. Except, she wasn't allowed to tell anybody about the clues... but maybe if nobody knew she'd told him...

A little voice inside her head said, "Tell Mrs. Dunleavey about him. Tell Uncle Tony. Tell Uncle Siggy," but she knew if she did that they'd get mad at her because she'd kept it a secret for weeks already, and she was afraid they might take her laptop and then she wouldn't have anything left of her Daddy at all.

Hi BWK, she tapped the keys. She'd been thinking about where she could meet him. There were people everywhere on the estate and the dogs would go crazy if a stranger came anywhere near the house. There was only one possibility: the place they all called the Dollhouse. She could take Excalibur for a ride *really* early while all the grooms were still asleep, then meet BWK at the Dollhouse because he wouldn't have to go through any security gate to get there, and it was pretty far from the Manor House.

Lark was very careful when she typed out the directions. The little thrill of guilt and rebellion made her feel very, very pleased with herself.

112

Dingle Peninsula. Republic of Ireland

Hugh's knife wound could turn septic in a matter of hours, in these conditions, if the blood loss he'd suffered didn't kill him first, Cait thought as she examined him. And the knife had sliced his leg as well as his upper body. There was no question he'd sacrificed himself to save her, absorbing the vicious slash that would surely have killed her. The game had obviously changed. Now they wanted her dead, not captured. Whoever *they* were. Or maybe this was the work of a whole new set of pursuers bent on murder, not kidnapping. *No matter.*

The knife had caught him in the shoulder first, slashing through muscle to bone, rendering his arm useless. The second gash had ripped into his back just above kidney level. The gash on his thigh had missed the femoral artery, so was not life threatening like the other two, but it was bleeding badly, nonetheless.

Cait forced herself to think beyond her own pain, which was so minor by comparison. She'd wrenched her back badly and scraped her knees, when Hugh had thrown her out of the knife-path. But what she cared about was Hugh, and the gathering darkness. She knew there was no hope of getting help before sunup. She didn't fear the woods, she respected them, and knew that in strange and hostile terrain she'd never find her way in the dark. And besides that, she couldn't leave this man who'd become so dear to her. She was his only chance for survival.

Cait worked rapidly to stem the bleeding and make a plan. *Thank God he's unconscious,* she breathed into the woods around them. *Pain can kill as well as sepsis.*

Feeling her mind as sharp as she'd ever felt it, terrified she would lose him, she kept pressure on the worst of the wounds... taking in facts. *Nearly dark. No instruments, water, bandages, antiseptic, meds. No shelter.* Temperature already cold, would drop sharply as night fell. *Options?* Whatever she could find to alter the odds, she had to find *now*, before all light was gone and whatever prowled these woods caught the scent of blood. *"Ok,"* she said aloud, forcing herself to show courage she didn't feel. *"We're not without resources. Thanks, Dad... thanks Jake... Keep an eye on us, will you?"*

She pulled Hugh's belt from his pants for a leg tourniquet, checking her watch as she did so... it would have to be loosened in 20 minutes, but that would give her time to work on the other wounds. Hugh was groaning now, coming out of unconsciousness. She needed to accomplish the most painful parts of her ministrations quickly, while he was still groggy.

She ripped away his impeding clothes, and in doing so was momentarily startled to find one of Lark's blue hair ribbon in his pocket... she held it wonderingly for a moment, then was distracted by the thrill of finding a hefty Swiss Army knife in another. She grabbed it, checked out its tools, gratified to find the knife blade was substantial enough to help her. She'd need a fire to sterilize it, but that would have to come later. Using the fabric from her own shirt and his trousers for packing, she bandaged his wounds with strips that had once been clothing.

Have to get him warmer, she thought, her eyes scanning every direction for possibilities. *Leaves.* Leaves and pine needles would have to do until she could rig a shelter. Hastily, racing the dying sun, she piled leaves around and over him, careful to keep the wound areas as clean as possible.

She felt his forehead, then on impulse touched her fingers to his cheek. Clammy and damp. Shocky. Not a good sign, but maybe better than fever. *If* she could keep him warm... "I'll be back, Hugh," she whispered close to his ear, sure he couldn't hear her, but willing him not to feel abandoned. "I have to get wood for a fire." She also had to get back to the car. She thought she might have that little sewing kit she usually traveled with in her bag. If so, she could suture some of his wounds. Then she was up and moving.

"*The woods are silent dark and deep and I have promises to keep and miles to go before I sleep...*" the words of the poem played in a sing-song loop in her head as she foraged for anything that could help them stay alive 'til morning. Branches for a lean-to of some kind. Without anything to drape over them it would be horribly primitive, but better than no shelter at all. Wood for a fire, twigs for kindling, brush for warmth, *anything*, everything she could find that might help. Back and forth to the car and the woods. Check the watch. Make sure the bleeding has stopped. Check the vitals. *Do what you can. Sometimes it's enough,* her Emergency Medicine prof had said eons ago. Jake had said the same. *The woods are filled with tools, if you can recognize them.* Moss only grows on the north side of trees, animal tracks usually lead to water, all healthy bugs and birds can supply protein. *How do you know if a bug is healthy?* she remembered asking Jake, and he had laughed and ruffled her hair.

113

Now that she was out of the house by herself, Lark didn't feel so good about it. It had been spooky in the stable, but it had felt like an adventure at least, and it felt like she was smarter than the grownups, who were all still asleep.

It hadn't been too hard to tack up Excalibur. He was gentle and she'd been practicing with Billy, the youngest groom, who wasn't much bigger than she was. He wanted to be a steeplechase jockey, so he was OK with being small – that was better for the horse anyway. So he'd shown her some tricks he used to get the saddle up over the horse's back and how to tickle the horse's nose to make him sneeze, so you could tighten the girth enough so the saddle wouldn't slip.

But now, standing here holding the horse's reins in the mostly dark, it didn't feel right... or even like an adventure. And she didn't feel brave. Maybe she should have said to meet her in the hedges of the big garden maze – that way, if anything was weird about BWK, she could just hide there and he'd never find her.

Lark whispered her worries to Excalibur, and he watched her with his lush dark eyes, looking sympathetic. Then he whinnied to tell her somebody was there and she turned to look for BWK but a man and a woman were running towards her and she knew right away she'd made a terrible mistake.

Lark grabbed Excalibur's mane to pull herself up onto his back, but an arm came around her from behind and even though she screamed and screamed nobody heard her.

114

Excalibur clip-clopped into the stableyard, riderless. He stood, reins hanging, then lifted his head in a demanding whinny, and pawed the ground. Arthur had just gotten to the stables. He was a very early riser and liked to get there before the lads assembled. He saw the horse from the window in front of his desk and called to Colin, the head groom.

"Is little Miss going out for a ride with you this early?" he asked sharply. Leaving a horse tacked up, with his reins dragging, was absolutely not done. What had gotten into Colin to allow such a thing?

"No, Sor," Colin replied worriedly in his thick burr. "I have no' seen the wee bairn today. You dinna suppose she got the tack on him hersilf, do ya? I'm right worried, if she did tha'."

Arthur was out of his chair in a heartbeat, and reaching for the phone.

"Mrs. Dunleavey," he spoke urgently into the receiver, keeping his gaze on Colin. "Is Miss Lark with you, by chance?" He frowned at the unwanted answer.

"No," he said quietly, "I haven't seen her at all this morning. I was rather hoping you had. Mrs. Dunleavey, I don't wish to alarm you, but we have her horse here, saddled up and loose. I think you'd best alert staff and tell His Lordship." He waited for a verbal barrage from the housekeeper, then frowned. "You're right, of course, Mrs. Dunleavey," he said, "I didn't realize he'd been called away on an emergency. Don't try to reach him yet, let's wait to see if we can find her first. We'll explain when he returns."

"Tell the lads to saddle up – all available hands, please, Colin. And wake up the later shift. We'll search the grounds. Every man knows which quadrant is his to search. And, Colin... bring Excalibur – he may be able to lead us to her – and the dogs, they're very fond of her. If she did somehow manage to take the horse out by herself, there may have been an accident..." he left the thought unfinished.

"She's a bonny wee rider, sor," the man said. "Ya dinna think she's been taken?"

"Just *find* her!" Arthur ordered. "If we find her, there'll be no need to speculate, do you understand me, man?"

"I do, sor," the groom replied gravely. "I'll see to the lads..."

Arthur watched after him for a moment, collecting his own thoughts. The child was an excellent rider for her age. A natural. The horse was well schooled and gentle-natured. If Lark had somehow fallen accidentally, Excalibur would, more than likely, have stayed with her until help came. It wasn't a good sign that he'd returned without her, and how the *hell* had she gotten a saddle and bridle on him and taken him out without anyone seeing her? To do that, she would have had to go hours before dawn.

Arthur pulled on his jacket, picked up the shotgun from beside his desk and put a handful of shells into his pocket. Something was very, very wrong.

115

By the time Cait had done all she could do, the dark was heavy and complete. She'd dragged Hugh's large body on the blanket a little further, toward the small shelter afforded by a nearby rock outcropping, then covered their tracks as best she could. Thanking heaven for her own physical size and strength, she'd propped branches for camouflage and protection around the space formed by the rock's overhang, and made a crude shelter large enough to hold them both. She'd riffled through the car and both their pockets in desperation, and by the grace of some benevolent god, had found a package of matches in his jacket. Hugh didn't smoke, so the unlikely bonanza seemed an act of divine providence. Maybe he'd picked up the matchbook, as she sometimes did, to remember the name of a restaurant. No matter. There was a fire now. The warmth and the psychological comfort it provided against the unknown that lurked in the dark just beyond the fire's small circle of safety, was enough to keep her courage up.

She'd tried her cell a dozen times to no avail. Hugh's phone was satellite connected, so it *might* have worked, but she couldn't find it. Maybe it had been lost at the gas station.

He was conscious now. The pain from the wounds and the shattered ribs beneath, had to be nearly unbearable, but when he'd regained consciousness he'd begged her to prop him up a little, against the rocks. "Whatever comes..." he'd managed to say with enough conviction so she didn't have the heart to argue. "We face it together..."

He'd drifted in and out of consciousness then, which made her grateful for the small respite it gave him from pain, but also left her feeling terribly alone.

"So much to tell you, Cait..." he'd whispered once, when she'd returned from adding wood to the small fire. She'd draped her coat and his jacket over both of them and crowded her own body in as close over his as she could, both the better to hear his faint words, and to keep him from hypothermia 'til morning, and the help she had to believe would be sent.

His breathing was labored, but at times, he was able to speak. "My ring..." he'd said, in one of the lucid moments. "Take it... Amici will help you..."

He'd tugged at the ring with so little strength, she'd closed her hands over his and gently pulled it from his finger and placed it on her own. "...power in the ring... trust it..." then he'd begun to cough and had to stop speaking.

She'd soothed, "we'll talk in the morning, when help comes."

"No!" he'd blurted with surprising force.

"I care for you..." he'd whispered. She'd started to protest but he'd moved his hand beneath hers, to stop her. "Please..." he'd begged. "...can't stay conscious long..." She'd nodded, tears filling her eyes and throat as she watched him gather strength to speak and realized, shocked by the thought, how much she cared for him, too.

And then in tiny disjointed fragments, he'd told her about the wife he'd loved and the son they'd both adored and how they'd both died because of the Hunt. A retaliation of some kind that had put him in a coma and when he'd returned to consciousness he'd learned they both were gone. He told her of the guilt he'd suffered, as well as the loss. How others told him it was a sacrifice he'd been called on to make for God, but all he'd felt was remorse and rage.

I railed at God, he'd said, *an unconscionable thing because I knew better.* His voice was so ragged, labored, and determined she was afraid to interfere or interrupt although she knew the effort of speaking and the anguish of these terrible memories were draining what small strength was left in him.

He told her that within their Order, there was a ritual of purification. The Knights in other times had done this to prepare for the Grail quest. Finally, as an act of desperate expiation, he'd accepted this ancient trial in hope of forgiveness, although he wasn't certain who it was he sought forgiveness from – God, his wife, his son... perhaps, himself. *Celibacy... fasting... my sixth year of seven,* he told her, his voice faltering and then most of the rest of what he said was lost to her, as his speech deteriorated into delirium. Sometimes, she thought she understood the words, but didn't believe they were meant for her – perhaps they were meant for his lost love, or for God.

Cait folded her body in around Hugh's, feeling every breath, every movement as if they were her own. In her mind, and sometimes out loud, she held a long conversation, first with Jack, then with her father, then with her own soul. After that, she cried herself to sleep.

The boy who woke her just before dawn was wearing an Amici ring on a chain around his neck.

116

Lark drifted in and out of consciousness. She was floating, drifting... felt a car bumping along and then another prick of the needle. The sting of hot pain, then nothing for a long while. Over and over. She thought there was a woman's face, then a man's, somewhere above her, looking down and mumbling. Then she was in a dark *someplace...* a tiny room?... a big closet?... a box? No, that couldn't be, could it? And she was nauseated, cold, thirsty. And then she was gone again, down the rabbit hole... under the water... no place she'd ever been or dreamt. Grotesque shapes and sounds were all around her in the dark. She was terribly afraid. She was bumping and flying and hearing sounds like an airplane. The drone of a big engine... the stomach-churning lurch of landing. And then there was shouting in some foreign language she didn't understand.

Hands were touching her, moving her like she was a rag doll or a piece of luggage. Then she was suddenly being tied up... hands, feet... Oh no! *No!* Please no! She struggled against her captors' hands and someone slapped her hard. And then the sting came again, but this time she fought against the blackness it brought. *Mommy, Mommy! where are you? I want to go home!*

What have I done? were the last words in her head. *What have I done?*

117

Marta groaned as she attempted to rise from the bed, despite the pain she felt in every muscle. She cursed inwardly, and forced herself toward the hot shower she knew would restore her at least partially. Between the athleticism of Fritz's sexual demands, and the fact that she'd managed to convince him she needed to spend an hour a day running and doing the workout that kept her body in shape, she hadn't hurt in this many places since boot camp.

She turned the shower on to the hottest she could stand, and let the water sluice over her, willing herself to be cleansed by it. She felt contaminated *everywhere* – by Fritz, by this place, by the other servants who behaved like automatons, and by the one really sicko-in-residence, Gruner's Stasi bodyguard/butler, who looked at her as if he were measuring her for a coffin.

Gruner's eyes followed her, too, now that he knew of his son's conquest. Envy? Unwillingness to let his son possess anything of his own choosing? She wasn't certain. All she knew was that everyone in this household knew whose bed she spent her nights in. And that everyone hated her for it, each for his or her own reasons. Now it wasn't just Fritz's moods she had to contend with, it was the malice she felt from the rest of the household, too.

The streaming water was doing its job, making her feel human again. She'd instigated the exercise routine in a desperate bid for freedom of some kind, as a way to learn the ins and outs of the estate, so she could have access to the weapons cache her handler had planted. Freedom to get to know the outdoor guards and their routine. She'd have to be very careful with that group, as she didn't know yet where their loyalties lay, but she was counting on the fact that most men's motivations could be manipulated by their sexual appetites. That, and the good fortune that unlike the house in Germany, here the guards were Americans. Men with no agenda, as far as she could see, beyond their paychecks.

It irked her that she still hadn't figured out how to get anything concrete on Gruner. She feared the most damning evidence was back in Germany, and hoped her making the move on Fritz hadn't been a big mistake. Maybe, if she'd stayed behind, once Kolb had left for America, she'd have been able to find Gruner's safe, or papers, or *some* kind of evidence that would have put a nail in his coffin. But, there was no use crying over spilled milk, she'd made her decision to wheedle what she could out of Fritz and now she'd just have to make it pay off.

Marta turned off the water and assessed herself in the steaming bathroom mirror. Satisfied with what she saw – all this exercise was useful at least, as she might need all her strength to defend herself one of these nights. She took a deep breath and began her day.

118

The monitors at Hugh's bedside droned and clicked, digital readings flickering on screens of varied colors and sizes, measuring blood pressure, oxygen saturation, heart, lung and brain function in an endless staccato tedium.

After their evac from the woods, when they'd landed in England, they'd been driven by ambulance directly to the hospital. Lord Delafield had been there to take charge.

The hospital had only let Cait into the Intensive Care Cubicle because she was a physician and because Lord Delafield was a philanthropic contributor. There really wasn't anything she could do for Hugh now, other than pray. He'd lost so much blood, the wounds were so grievous, and one of them had gone septic, but at least now he had proper care.

Cait had been sitting here holding his hand, and speaking words of comfort, too worried to sleep, ever since he'd gotten out of surgery. She, herself, would have to sleep soon, she knew, but she was still too wired, and besides, she sensed that seemingly comatose patients were far more cognizant of their surroundings than the text books claimed. She'd listened to many patients during her years of practice, describe conversations heard around them while in a comatose state, even during surgery. So she sat and talked to Hugh.

Cait hadn't been back to the manor yet, had not yet seen Lark, as she so desperately wanted to. She'd insisted on waiting until Hugh was stabilized before leaving him, so Lord Delafield had returned to Heredon to retrieve things Hugh would need when he woke up. When he got back he'd relieve her vigil at Hugh's bedside, and his car and driver would take her back to Heredon and Lark.

Waiting anxiously for Delafield's return, Cait spoke in an endless stream-of-consciousness, to Hugh, unburdening herself of sorrows and fears, in ways she hadn't been able to, before. Until she'd heard it said aloud, she hadn't realized how desperately she'd needed to put all she'd been feeling into words, but the floodgates had been pried open in the woods and there seemed no way to staunch the torrent now.

Cait heard Lord Delafield's voice asking urgent directions of the nurse, before she saw him in the doorway. His stricken face was haggard, and showed such alarm her heart went out to him.

"It's alright, Tony," she said, rising to go to the old man. "Hugh's past the crisis point. It's all going to be fine. You don't have to worry..."

The old man gripped both her arms as she reached him. "No, Cait, *NO*! It *isn't* fine, and it isn't Hugh! It's Lark!" His eyes were desperate, stricken, brimming with tears. "She's gone, Cait. They've taken her. I don't know how it could have happened. Mrs. Dunleavey..."

But Cait had already torn her arms out of his grip and was running down the hall toward the lift. The old man put his hand over his mouth and bowed his head to his chest, tears flowing freely onto the silk cravat at his throat. He reached for his son's leg and squeezed it hard in a gesture of profound love, "Oh Hugh," he breathed to his son and to God. "What more can be asked of us..." Then he was following in Cait's wake, his heavy steps echoing in the silent marble corridor.

119

When Cait tore through the great doors of the manor and nearly collided with Mrs. Dunleavey, the note was waiting for her.

"Cait!" Lord Delafield called after her. "Wait, please... let me gather the staff so we can learn whatever details we can."

She tore open the elegant envelope and one of Lark's hair ribbons fell into her hand.

Your daughter misses you dreadfully,

the note read,

return to New York immediately for directions.
Delicate birds are so easily silenced.

It wasn't a note you could take to the authorities. It didn't say a word about kidnapping, didn't make a ransom demand. She stuffed it into her pocket with trembling hands, then ran into the powder room and violently vomited up the coffee she'd drunk in the hospital.

Cait packed her bag for the flight home with hands that trembled so badly she could barely make them function, as His Lordship's arranged a private flight and pulled strings somehow to get her through Passport Control despite the warrant hanging over her.

Her mind and heart an exhausted, terrified jumble of raw emotions and soul-curdling guilt, she was on her way to the airport within an hour, and texted Meg from the car on the way to the plane.

Lark taken
Awaiting instructions
Landing at Teterboro at 11:10

Meg and Carter were at the Gate when she arrived. Without a word, the sisters wrapped their arms around each other and wept. Carter, her own eyes flooded, texted Matt, who was waiting in short term parking with the car, to say they were on their way out of the terminal.

Into the Woods

Part XVIII

*"We are all in a small boat in a stormy sea
and we owe each other a terrible loyalty."*
G.K. Chesterton

——— **120** ———

Gruner Estate
Bedford

Gruner watched the man and woman who had kidnapped the child, as they prodded her into the room. The 9 year old seemed disoriented from the drugs they'd subdued her with, and her clothes were torn and dirty. She kept blinking her eyes, trying to focus.

"Untie her," he growled at the woman. "Or did you fear she would overpower you, drugs and all?"

The woman looked belligerent. "You gave me no specific instructions, Herr Doktor. We did as we thought best. She fought like a wild thing. And she cried incessantly." The last sounded like an indictment. Children of the Reich did not cry.

Gruner's eyebrows rose, taking in the child's slender stature and her drug-induced pallor. There was no need to say anything further about this foolishness.

"She is here now. I do not feel threatened, so you may remove her restraints, and then leave us, until you are called."

To the child he said, "Good evening, Lark, I have been looking forward to meeting you."

Lark, tried to make sense of all that was happening to her. She looked around the room and tried to force the fuzziness in her brain to recede.

"Where am I?" she asked finally. Her voice was small and frightened. "Why did those people bring me here?"

"Let us try this again," Gruner said evenly, the smile on his lips not reaching his eyes. "I said good evening to you, Lark. What is a child's proper reply to this?"

Lark blinked to clear the blurry vision that even her glasses didn't help. She knew she was in terrible danger. The hair on her arms was standing straight up. She didn't know exactly what kind of danger it was, but she knew it was very, very bad. The kind that happened to kids sometimes, when they didn't obey their parents and they went somewhere with a stranger. She had been *so stupid* to run away. So *stupid* to keep logging onto that forbidden site. But she'd been so *mad!* Mad at everybody. Mad at her Daddy for being dead, and at her Mommy for leaving her all alone with strangers, even if they were nice strangers. Most of all she'd been mad at herself for not being able to figure out the riddle of the Labyrinth, so her Mommy could come home again. Everybody pretended it wasn't her fault, but she could tell they were lying to make her feel better. She knew now that the biggest anger of all was the anger of stupid failure – but she hadn't known it *then*. *Then* she just knew she was mad at everybody and everything that had gone wrong with her life.

Now, she just wanted to go home to her Mommy. *Oh Mommy! Where Are You! I need you so much!*

She looked up into Gruner's ice blue eyes and wanted to scream for help. He was a very bad man. She could see that right away in those eyes that were missing something she couldn't name. They were glittering like a snake's.

"Good evening," she managed to say, finally, her throat dry and her words thick. "It would be polite to say good evening *Mr. Somebody*, but I don't know what your name is."

Gruner smiled approval. "You may call me Doctor," he said as if bestowing an honor.

"What kind of doctor are you?" Lark asked, thinking of her mother.

"The kind who holds your life and your mother's in my hands, Lark," he answered with equanimity.

She didn't know what to say to that, so said nothing at all. She just wanted to go home.

Gruner's demeanor shifted suddenly as he glanced to his right where a chess board with a half-played game was displayed. Lark's eyes followed his.

"Would you like to play a game with me?" he asked, obviously attempting a more agreeable tone.

Lark looked at the board for a few moments before replying. "Don't you have to finish that game?" she asked. "White has four more moves before it wins."

Gruner's eyebrow rose again. "Oh, yes, of course," he said, trying to hide his excitement at the prize he'd trapped in his snare. "Why don't we do that while we wait for tea."

—————— **121** ——————

Gruner Estate
Bedford, New York

The young American security guard standing outside the guardhouse, stomped his feet against the cold. Even his insulated boots were inadequate protection in the damp penetrating freeze that had settled over Westchester for the past week. Sporadic snow and sleet had left frozen puddles under foot and the trees were all hung with ice crystals. It would all be beautiful, he thought, if it wasn't so goddamned cold his testicles were halfway up to his throat by now. You could barely breathe in this air without turning your lungs as brittle as the ice-encrusted trees.

He saw the white-hot German maid in all her spandex glory running on her morning route, punctual as clockwork. Why the fuck anybody would run in this weather was beyond him, but he welcomed the sight of her everyday, nonetheless, perfect muscles working unbelievable legs, boobs bouncing despite the layers that covered them. Guess they didn't have sports bras in Germany. He waved as he always did in appreciation.

To his surprise, this morning she waved back and turned in his direction.

——————— 122 ———————

New York City

Meg and Cait sat in Meg's living room, a breakfast tray untouched between them on the coffee table. Cait seemed to have aged ten years in a month, her sister thought looking at her, and more, since they'd picked her up at the airport, near midnight. It was easy to see how little she'd slept.

Cait had just finished blurting out the painful details of all that had happened to her in Europe. They'd disclosed basic facts to each other on the way from the airport, but both had been too exhausted and agitated to take in all the details. There was so much to tell and Cait was talking so fast now, it wasn't easy to understand all she was saying, but Meg knew better than to stop her for questions, yet. Cait so badly needed to unburden herself; to dredge up all the pain and fear and horror that was damned near killing her. Meg knew her sister could barely breathe for the burden of what she was carrying. Grief. Terror. *Guilt.* Terrible guilt about having left Lark in danger. *Fear.* Abject, bone-chilling fear for Lark's life.

The detailed story of what had gone on in Europe was mind-blowing. The cryptic phone calls they'd been able to make to each other over the last weeks had been unsettling, unsatisfying, almost worse than none at all, but she could see now they hadn't told a fraction of what had really gone down in Europe. It took every ounce of restraint Meg could muster not to interrupt, so many questions roiled in her own brain. But Cait seemed to be winding down, finally nearing the end of her awful story.

"I guess even if you have all the money in the world, the one thing you can't buy with it is immortality," Meg said with revulsion, and Cait just nodded wearily.

Meg had been trying to think of some way to talk her sister down off the ledge. Not easy, when she felt she was pretty close to the edge herself. Usually, at least one of them could stay centered when the other was in trouble, but not *this* kind of trouble, and not today.

"Do *you* think we should go to the police, Meg?" Cait asked urgently, "I'm so afraid he'll kill her if we do."

Meg shook her head. "Matt's already doing that, Cait. He went to his boss this morning on the QT – the Captain said he'd try to sound out the higher-ups, but he was pretty sure the diplomatic immunity thing would make it tough to investigate Gruner, even if we had evidence of his involvement, which we don't. The Captain's already been warned off anything to do with Gruner, so he's going out on a limb even asking. Remember, we still have nothing that ties Gruner into all this... no proof he wrote the kidnap note... no proof Lark's even with him..." she stopped, to collect herself, then not wanting Cait to have to argue the point, she hurried on. "We don't have any proof she's even in this country." She took a breath.

"Carter reached out to an FBI contact she thinks she can trust, because kidnapping's their jurisdiction after 24 hours, and I posed a hypothetical at the DOJ, but nobody, and I mean *nobody* believes Gruner could be a kidnapper, and because of his diplomatic status everybody's treading *very* carefully. Mostly they offered to go talk to him, but you know he'll deny everything and it'll just tip him off we've gone to the authorities, so I think we have to be really careful about what we say to anybody at this point."

She paused a few seconds, then added, "If anybody *did* believe our story, that would mean they'd know how dangerous he and his cronies are, and that they'd be risking their asses to help us, which is just as useful as not believing... People who know the stakes, just don't want to get involved. You almost can't blame them, Cait. It's not *their* families at risk."

Cait wished she could clear her head enough to think straight, but she was so damned tired, and so terrified for Lark.

"I keep running this loop in my head, Meg. I go over and over everything that's happened, everything we learned, and none of it solves *anything*! And then I remember, it isn't Lark he wants," she said, her eyes on her sister's. "He wants *me.* And then all the guilt crashes in on me and I know I should *never,* ever have left her alone..."

"You *didn't* leave her alone, Cait! You had no choice but to go, and you left her in a fortress with a staff of 20 to take care of her, for God's sake!"

Cait ignored the offered reprieve. "Don't you see, Meg? If I hadn't fought so hard to stay *out* of his clutches, he would have me now, *not* Lark."

"No, he doesn't want *you,* Cait! He wants the damned Spear!"

"But he thinks I can get it for him. He thinks Jack must have given me some clue..."

Meg shook her head at the futility of arguing with such raw guilt. It was the anguish talking, not Cait. She tried another tack.

"Matt says kidnappers always make demands, so if we just wait for Gruner to make his, *then* we can nail him. "He thinks we'll hear within 24 hours. Carter's got our phones recording everything – as if that's even necessary with everybody else on the planet bugging us, too – but dammit, *then* we'll have *proof.* And with proof, we can get law enforcement into the act to help us."

Cait locked eyes with her sister's. "Not with his diplomatic immunity, we won't! And *not* if he's protected by the CIA, we won't. Some nameless agency will cut a deal with some other nameless agency and he'll go free, like he always does. Lark will be gone, and we'll be lucky if we don't end up in Guantanimo, and he'll still be above the law. You know I'm right!"

Meg took in a deep breath and held it, knowing better than Cait, how right that assessment probably was – she just wasn't willing to believe there was no way out. There was *always* a way out. You just had to be smart enough to find it. And tough enough to see it through.

"Everyone who loves you and Lark is on this 24/7, Cait. Carter's got the boys hacking everybody in Christendom. *Somebody* knows *something* that will change the odds to our favor. We'll come up with *something we can use for leverage,* we just need to do this one step at a time."

"But it's got to be *fast*, Meggie," Cait interrupted. "He's had my baby for 24 hours already, and you know what Matt always says. If you don't find a kidnap victim in 48 hours, you'll never find her alive."

"This is *different!*" Meg snapped. "Lark's a *hostage*, not a kidnap victim – he only has her to torture you into capitulating."

"I would give him the Spear, Meg. You know that, right? If I had it, I'd trade it for her and take my chances with Heaven."

Meg only nodded. Now she knew just how close to the edge of the ledge Cait was standing.

123

Gruner Estate
Bedford, New York

"She's extraordinary, Fritz!" Gruner said with more excitement in his voice than his son was used to hearing. "She reminds me of myself at that age. Raw genius waiting to be shaped correctly."

Fritz paused the breakfast forkful of eggs on its way to his mouth. "And does she remind you of *me,* as well, Father?"

Gruner looked with mixed indulgence and annoyance at his son, formulating a careful answer. "You were gifted, Fritz – superb raw material – how could it have been otherwise, considering the breeding– but you did not show the genius I see in this specimen. Her abilities are entirely left brain, entirely mathematical. Yours were, shall we say, *more varied,* which is why I insisted on a subtler and more comprehensive curriculum of study for you. And, of course, that has paid off brilliantly in the scope of your multi-dimensional abilities." He smiled at his son, having found precisely the right words. Fritz had a temper and could take umbrage at small slights. He had no time for such nonsense now.

Damned with faint praise yet again, Fritz thought looking at his father, trying to be sure his loathing didn't show on his face. *Taking credit for my triumphs, yet still managing to let me know I never quite measure up.*

"Is she bait to draw in the Mother, then, or a wonderful new toy?" Fritz asked, a certain acerbity in his tone. "Or do you think she knows the whereabouts of your Spear, perhaps?"

"I'm well aware of your contempt for my desire to possess this artifact, Fritz," Gruner said without rancor. "You must indulge an old man's fancy in this, or perhaps simply accept the fact that I do few things on whim alone. The Spear is priceless, and represents power. That is more than enough motivation for seeking it. I intend to interrogate the child to find out if she has possession of any useful information about its resting place. If she has none, she still has value as bait. I've already composed an appropriate communication with the Mother – an offer to exchange the girl for the information I want."

Fritz's gaze focused on his breakfast a little longer than was necessary. He kept his voice casual. "Perhaps, *I* should be the one to interrogate her, Father. After all, interrogation is my specialty. The mind-control and coercion techniques I've developed for the military could be easily adapted..."

Gruner touched his napkin to his lips delicately and dismissed the suggestion with a shake of his head. "I see no need for your methods at the moment, Fritz. Let us try my brand of subtlety first. Later... we can decide about more painful possibilities. But for now, I'm enjoying mapping her mental abilities with my own methods... it isn't often one has the pleasure of interacting with such a unique intellect."

"But, Father, surely you realize electronic and chemical stimulus could far more easily map her brain function," Fritz countered evenly, "as well as eliciting the information you desire."

"And perhaps damage her irreparably in the process? Making the retrieval of information, should she have any, impossible? I think not. I shall proceed until I tire of her, or until the mother comes – then she's yours for the taking. I don't care what you do with her."

Fritz nodded and rose from the table, rather than letting his irritation show. Arguing with his father was futile, he'd learned that in the first two decades of life.

"As you wish, Father. I'm just pleased that I was able to be of help to you in securing the child." Gruner looked up at his son.

"I'm well aware of the ingenuity you showed in luring her, Fritz," he said patiently. "And grateful, of course."

Fritz eyed his father coldly. At least he'd made his point. "I have several important monetary matters to deal with today, so I don't need any more trifling distractions. I'm sure you'll call, if I'm needed. When do you expect the mother will appear?"

"The message will be sent today – it won't be long after that."

"And if she doesn't come?"

Gruner smiled. "You forget I have a good deal of experience observing mothers and their endangered young. She'll come."

Fritz rose from the table and left the room, wanting to escape his father before the seething anger he was feeling spilled over into visibility. He headed for the front door, then abruptly turned in the opposite direction. He pressed the button for the elevator that would take him to his laboratory. He needed a place to express his rage before daring to meet with the bankers, who were on his agenda for this morning. He'd find something in the lab. He'd known how to achieve catharsis in these situations since he was a boy. But now the tools he could call on were somewhat more sophisticated than those he'd used on the neighbor's unfortunate cats and dogs.

124

The test subject sat strapped to the large metal chair in the laboratory, wires sprouting from an ominous looking leather band that held his head rigidly in place. Similar wires ran from arms, legs, torso and genitals to an array of electric display panels behind him. His terrified gaze watched Fritz shrug out of his suit jacket and don a white medical coat from the rack behind the stainless steel door to the lab.

"Please," the man gasped, thirst and the effects of screaming making his voice barely understandable. "No more. In the name of God..."

Fritz eyed him coldly, utterly unmoved by his plea.

"Speak only when I ask a question," he said and the man shuddered at remembrance of other questions and their aftermath. "You are aware of the rules."

"But I've told you..." he blurted in desperation.

Fritz frowned and hit a button that sent 50,000 volts of electricity through the man's kidneys as his agonized shriek filled the room. *Why do they never learn?* he thought with exasperation. It was always the same.

A young Chinese man in a white lab coat entered from a door to the left of the giant display screens. He carried a clipboard and waited patiently for Fritz to acknowledge his presence. After some seconds of watching with clinical interest as the bound man writhed in agony, Fritz turned a questioning eye towards his assistant.

"We have gotten from him whatever small bits of relevant information he possessed," the newcomer said in Mandarin. "The new equipment elicited his most private and personal fears. They turned out to be rather banal. It appears he is phobic about spiders and crawling insects."

Fritz's eyebrow raised with a modicum of interest. "Excellent," he answered in the same language. "We have no further use for this subject, so he can be disposed of today. But let us do so by bringing his nightmares to life. Fill the chamber with arachnids and monitor his dying carefully. I find those who die in abject terror emit substantially different brain wave patterns and pheromones from those who've been tortured to the point where they welcome death. See if this subject has anything more to teach us."

The younger man nodded, made a note on his clipboard and departed briskly.

Fritz looked disdainfully, at the suffering man, now sobbing in utter terror and despair and moved a step closer, then slapped him hard across the face. "Stop sniveling!" he commanded, "It won't do you any good."

He then turned as four men entered on the other side of the chamber, two large glass tanks filled with hairy arachnids of all shapes and sizes, carried carefully between them. Before turning the door knob, Fritz hesitated, watching as one of the men removed the lid from the first tank and an orderly parade of Black Widows began their climb from the tank. He was smiling with satisfaction, as he closed the door on the victim's ear-splitting shrieks.

125

Marta had left Fritz's bed, with every instinct on high alert. The girl who'd been brought onto the estate was part of why Fritz was in such a state of contained fury and weird elation. She'd tried to wheedle information out of that old bat, Mathilde, the housemanager, about what was happening here, but so far most of it was barely useful. The child was here against her will, she was a special project for Herr Doktor Gruner, no one was permitted to interfere... *Duh!* Marta had seen the poor kid being tied to a chair by some creepy Brunhilde, so it was hardly news that she was a prisoner.

She'd asked Fritz, and while he'd gotten hostile at first, she'd finally been able to get him to open up a little. The girl was part of his father's favorite obsession, he'd said, but of course, that could mean anything. The old Nazi had more than one obsession. She shuddered to think of a child being exposed to any of these self-righteous psychopaths. She'd pressed to get more information, so he'd told her his father wanted something from the girl's mother, and the child was bait for a trap. Something in the way Fritz spoke of the girl made Marta feel sure he was jealous of her, but that made no sense, unless he was actually envious of the attention she was getting from the old man.

After their pillow talk about the child, the sex had gotten rougher, more brutal, as it always did when any discussion involving his father preceded it, and Martha had to keep her wits about her to avoid getting seriously hurt. He was a cruel, cold fuck, but in some ways she almost felt sorry for him. What kind of hell would it be to grow up in the shadow of a demanding madman like Gruner – what kind of hell, to have to wait your turn to kill your father. Every instinct told her *that* was Fritz's plan.

And something had definitely changed since Germany. There was a new sense of empowerment in Fritz that hadn't been there before. A new anger and determination, so something must have shifted the odds in his favor. Maybe he finally had some dirt on the old boy – leverage that would give him the upper hand. Maybe he'd just reached the moment when one more humiliation would be the trigger.

Marta would have to make it her business to find out more about both child and mother today as their existence seemed part of why Fritz was so keyed up. He was planning something, and the child was part of it; she just didn't yet know how the pieces fit. But, he'd started to open up a little, and her experience told her that once there was a crack in a man's armour, she could find her way in. One small confidence would lead to another. Marta thought she'd better start putting all her ducks in line fast. She'd have to be ready to make her move when opportunity came her way.

The Germans in the house were either too well trained or too frightened to tell her anything useful, and she couldn't be certain they wouldn't repeat her questions to Fritz or his father. But the Americans among the security guards – *they* were a whole other ballgame. Now that she'd gotten to know them all on her daily runs, she'd need to assess which were the weakest and the most likely to be lust-driven. Fritz wasn't the only one who'd noticed her assets and in a pinch, these security guards might be her best defense, and her escape hatch if her handlers couldn't get her out in time when the shit hit the fan.

126

Marta scanned the road for any sign of cars before diverting her route toward the solitary guard who patrolled the farthest section of the estate. He was uniformed and armed, but at least didn't have one of those damned guard dogs on a leash today. The Dobermans and Rottweilers on the estate had been trained for blood, she could tell. Poor creatures had probably been tortured into brutality, but they reminded her too much of her Bubbe's stories of the dogs in the camps, for her to feel too sorry for them.

She sensed this guard was feeling the small freedom of being on his own today for a change. The cold weather had guaranteed that the men with least seniority would be out walking the fences and he looked like the youngest among them.

Her own temporary sense of freedom was occasioned by the fact that both psychos were out of the compound for the day. Some kind of meeting at the U.N. in New York, along with Kolb as their bodyguard. She felt a thrill of excitement at finally having time to put her plan in motion.

Marta let out an audible exclamation as she pretended to slip on a patch of icy ground. She made a noisy show of attempting to scramble up, only to be overwhelmed by the pain from an injured leg. The guard responded instantly to her distress, as she knew he would.

"Are you OK!" he called as he hurried toward her. "That looked like a bad fall you just took. Running on this frozen ground is dangerous."

"I twisted something, I think," she said, sounding pained and embarrassed. "It's slippery out here... I think I pulled a muscle. How stupid of me!"

The man halted in front of her then bent to see the damage. "Why don't we get you over to that big rock," he said pointing at a nearby low ledge, "so you can sit long enough for me to get a better look. I played a lot of sports, so I'm pretty good with this kind of thing."

"I'm not sure I can walk that far," Marta said plaintively, turning her eyes to his in a silent plea for help.

"Don't you worry, miss," he said gallantly, "I can carry you. No trouble."

"Could you really?" she breathed admiringly. "You do look very strong. I'd be so grateful..."

The young guard was tall and broad as a linebacker – he lifted her easily. Marta put her arms around his neck and making sure her breasts crushed into him, cuddled against his chest.

"You *are* very strong," she whispered as he moved in the direction of the rock. She saw his jaw muscles relax into a smile of pleasure at the compliment. *I think I have a new friend* she said to herself as he reluctantly set her down on the rock.

"What's your name, my dear rescuer," Marta asked, her smile now playful.

"Mike," he answered. "Mike Ericsson."

"I can't tell you how grateful I am for your help, Mike Ericcson," she replied in her breathy voice. "But I must ask you yet another favor, I'm afraid..." she let the thought hang. "I hope you'll not think badly of me when I ask it of you..."

"Anything I can do for you," he offered eagerly, "just tell me what you need."

She thought he might be 25 or so, and chock full of the idealistic gallantry young American men were famous for. A stroke of luck.

"I must ask you to not tell *anyone* we've spoken like this, Mike Ericsson. You see, I'm not allowed to talk with *anyone* outside the house. I'm afraid the rules are very strict here and they are *always* enforced. I can't afford to get sacked."

He nodded. "I get it, Miss," he said, "I've noticed how uptight these guys are about everything. I won't tell a soul."

Marta smiled her most ingratiating smile, then reaching down to touch her "injured" leg. With a sharp intake of breath, she made it clear the movement was very painful.

"Do you want me to get you to a doctor," he asked, concerned. "Or maybe back up to the house?"

"No!" she blurted, sounding frightened. "No. *Please!* I'd get in terrible trouble if they knew we'd talked. Do you think perhaps you could just massage my leg a bit, Mike Ericsson? The pain starts in my calf and goes all the way up to my thigh... I think I've pulled something that will make it hard for me to walk..."

Marta opened her legs to give him a better view of her spandex clad lower body. She watched his eyes travel up her leg to her crotch, then quickly back down, as he colored slightly with chivalrous embarrassment.

"Please," she whispered urgently. "I think I'll be alright if you'll just rub my leg to warm the muscle..."

And so he did.

127

Meg rose from the sofa after her conversation with her sister, trying to contain the intense agitation she was feeling. She needed to call Matt and the others about all she'd just learned from Cait. Somewhere out of her sister's earshot, they could make a plan, depending on how much help they'd been able to scare up. She didn't want to lay out the odds or look at a worst case scenario around Cait.

"I hate to leave you alone, Cait," she said, "but I really have to put in an appearance at the office for a little while, much as I don't want to, in order to keep Crookfield at bay. I don't think I'll have a job after this, and I'm not sure I care, but right now, I don't need him hassling me." She looked at her sister's haggard face, and frowned. "You look beyond exhausted, Cait. If I go, do you think you could sleep for an hour?"

Cait nodded absently, knowing sleep was impossible, not wanting to argue the point. Then she remembered something that had fled her mind because of all the more urgent matters.

"Meg, if you're going back to your office, could you do me a favor?" Meg nodded. "I forgot all about the document I got in Israel, and I don't want to just keep carrying it around with me."

Cait wiped her eyes with the back of one hand, as she dug into her handbag with the other. She couldn't seem to keep herself from crying, no matter what she did. She pulled out the thick envelope and handed it to Meg. "The Mossad guy, Weiss, made me promise to get it translated. I don't really know why he gave it to me but both he and the old Rabbi in Spain acted like it was important. There's a name on the envelope – she's some woman at the Anti-Defamation League in New York – Weiss said she'd translate it for us." She shrugged apologetically, "I gave him my word."

"No problem," Meg answered, taking the envelope from Cait's hand and stuffing it into her briefcase. "But you look half dead, Cait. Could you please just lie down 'til I get back here? I promise I'll bring the others with me and then we'll make a plausible plan, OK? You won't be any good to Lark if you're down for the count..."

Cait just nodded yes again, numbly, and Meg, impulsively reached over and hugged her sister hard. Cait felt so much skinnier than she remembered. She'd lost weight in these last few weeks – her muscles were like wire beneath her clothes, and her heart was beating like a trapped bird's.

Meg left the apartment, uncertain it was safe to leave her sister alone, but needing to go. She couldn't bear to see her in this condition and not know how to help – maybe if she and the others could talk, away from Cait's distraught presence, they could come up with something... *anything*. She pushed the elevator button and blinked back tears. She thought they probably only had a couple of hours to figure out what should come next, before Cait took it into her own hands and did something rash.

128

Meg hurried down the green carpet at Kramer Crowley Crookfield. The wool runner seemed to stretch into infinity, past all the plush offices on her floor, toward the lavish corner offices the partners occupied. She no longer cared if she got fired over this – as a matter of fact, it was probably to be expected, maybe welcomed, after that cozy chat with Arthur Crookfield.

She stopped briefly at her secretary Emily's desk, grabbed a 9 x 12 mailing envelope, scribbled the name and address Cait had given her onto the front, stuck the old envelope from Israel inside and sealed the package, marking *Personal & Confidential* on the front.

"Messenger this over to the ADL, for me, will you?" she directed Emily, "and see if you can get me Jerome Halloran at Intellicorps, please. After that I have several important calls I need to make, so if you could run interference with anybody who wants me, I'd really appreciate it."

"Hot new case, Ms. Fitzgibbons?" Emily asked con-spiratorially.

"Something like that, Emily," Meg answered, knowing Emily was too polite to press further, and no longer trusting her one whit, since she'd passed the word about the DC trip up the line of command. Meg entered her own office and closed the door behind her, gratefully. She thought of closing the blinds on the glass panels that separated her from the rest of the office staff, but knew that could raise questions she didn't need right now.

She hung her coat and scarf on the coat rack in the corner, then sat down behind her desk, and thumbed her Blackberry for the numbers she needed.

The intercom buzzed and Emily said. "Mr. Halloran on the line for you."

Meg picked up the phone and composed herself before speaking. She had a favor to ask.

Jerry Halloran was Chairman of Intellicorps, an import/export company that was big and profitable. Four years ago, she'd saved his company from an embarrassing lawsuit that would have harmed Jerry's personal reputation, quite undeservedly. He was a pretty good guy, and he'd been wrongly accused of something that would have trashed his reputation if she hadn't been able to exonerate him. He'd once told her if she were ever in need of help, he was to be her first phone call. Today was that day and this was the call.

Even if no kidnap demand had been made yet, Meg had a hunch it would turn out Gruner had taken Lark to his house in either Bedford or Georgetown, and Bedford was far bigger and far more private, so it was a better bet. Where else could he be assured of the kind of stronghold he'd want and need? Georgetown was too far to worry about, but she thought she knew a way to check out Bedford, just in case.

Jerry had a small corporate air force, she knew. He'd been a pilot in Viet Nam and had not only kept up his skills, but had found ways to get the jump on competition in the early days of his business, by using his own planes for deliveries. She knew he also owned a chopper. If she could talk him into doing a little aerial recon over Gruner's estate without his asking too many questions, it would give her a place to start. Google maps were great, but nothing beat getting somebody who understood combat to eyeball the terrain.

She picked up the receiver and told Jerry what she needed.

"Are you in some kind of trouble, Meg?" he'd asked, with concern.

"I can't explain, Jerry," she answered, "but this is really important to me. I wouldn't ask otherwise."

"That's all I need to know, kid," he said, then asked her to spell out exactly what kind of intel she'd need.

129

Bedford, New York

More than twenty hours had gone by since Lark had been deposited in Bedford. She'd played so many games of chess with this scary old doctor, she'd stopped counting. He was really crazy and very, very mean. Alternately cranky and then nice, then mean again. And he kept asking her questions, mostly about math, or about the Labyrinth or about where the Spear was, but he didn't seem to listen to her answers. And when he didn't feel like playing chess any more, he had them tie her up, so she hurt all over and she was really, really scared now.

"Now, that we have gotten to know each other, Lark," Gruner said to the frightened child, as casually as he could manage, considering his level of frustration with her. "I think its time for you to tell me where to find this Spear your Mother is searching for. And, then perhaps I will let you go home." In order to test the parameters of this brilliant, annoying child's mind, he had played multiple games with her last night and today, and he was growing bored by his lack of success. He was on the verge of letting Fritz employ his research methods on her. Even if the damage he inflicted was irreparable, at least he'd know for certain if she had what he wanted. And, she would never go home, which was the one fact that gave him a modicum of satisfaction. As long as she was alive, she could be used to coerce the mother.

She was a human calculating device of some kind, that was obvious. He had tested her skill at numbers with varying problems, at many skill levels, and it was apparent that her gifts in this regard far exceeded his own. Indeed, they exceeded any he had ever seen. She was a savant. Nimble and lightning fast. Absolutely accurate. But it was not this skill that irritated him. It was her strategic sense, and the clever deviousness of the strategies she applied to gaming, that were of interest to him. He'd felt certain when she'd arrived

that her innocence and lack of guile would be her Achilles Heel –
he was no longer so certain. Now, he saw that the guilelessness
was more than compensated for by her strategic ability to stay one
step ahead of an opponent in a game. He doubted it was a
conscious calculation at all, simply another manifestation of her
gifts, but it meant she might keep finding strategies to protect her
secret. It was Heisenberg's Principle at work. His own actions
were triggering changes in her ability to obfuscate. Wretched child!
But she was born to gaming, that was a given. Perhaps her father,
knowing that, had created Lark's Labyrinth as the ultimate
challenge for her skills. Or perhaps he had made it the route to the
Spear's mysterious hiding place. *Or perhaps none of these!* It was
an infuriating conundrum.

Lark wrinkled her freckled forehead and peered at him
worriedly, from behind her eyeglasses.

"I don't know where my Daddy put it," she answered without
elaboration.

"Really?" Gruner asked, an expression of disbelief on his
face. "But you are very smart, and your daddy put this information
in your game, did he not?"

Lark shook her head. "I don't think so," she answered
honestly. "Everybody says he must have, but I know everything
about this game and I can't find it." She stopped, then added, "And
besides, if I *did* know, I wouldn't tell you, I'd tell my Mommy."

Gruner cocked his head to one side. He wanted to beat the
little brat senseless. But that pleasure could come later, so he
composed himself and said casually, "And if I were to tell you I
will send men to kill your mommy if you do *not* tell me the truth –
what would you do then?"

Lark's eyes widened. "Then I would have to tell you, if I
knew, but I still wouldn't know!" Now, she was agitated, too.
"Maybe my Daddy didn't get it finished yet! He put new stuff into
the Labyrinth every year, but maybe he didn't get a chance to put it
all in, yet! I looked on every level. I went to the Dragon Brood
and the Necropolis, and the Gargoyle Roosts, and the Sun Bonnet

Bushes. I went to Castle Perilous and the 14 Heavens of the Buddha, and the Flame Pit of Terranabis..." she paused to think of the other places she'd searched. "I even went interdimensional and intergalactic and I *still* didn't find it!"

"Enough!" Gruner thundered, cutting her off. "If you cannot find it, you are useless to me! Why should I bother to keep you alive at all? I know a thousand terrible ways to kill you. Why should I *not* do that?"

Lark's face seemed to fold inward on itself, genuine terror making her heart race in her chest. He probably meant it. Tears welled out of her eyes and magnified by her glasses, spilled down her cheeks.

"Because my Mommy's coming to get me," she said softly.

Gruner blinked in surprise.

"Just so," he said, after a moment. "Perhaps I will wait to kill you, until I have you both."

The mother was the one he needed. It was absurd to think a nine year old, however gifted, would have been made the lone keeper of such a secret. The child was merely the bait to get the mother to come to him, he mustn't forget that.

"Tie her up again!" he snarled at the uniformed woman who hovered at the edge of the room. Lark cringed. She already hurt all over from sitting tied to a chair. Her arms hurt and her back ached and her shoulders felt on fire when she had to sit in one place for hours and hours. And her wrists and ankles were cut and rubbed raw. And they wouldn't even take her to the bathroom, so once she even had to pee in her pants. Just thinking about it made her cringe.

Gruner turned to the frightened, miserable child.

"You see, Lark," he said coldly. "You are no longer of any great interest to me." Then he left the room.

Cue the Ferryman

Part XIX

"It has been said that man is a rational mind. All my life I have been searching for evidence which could support this."
Bertrand Russell
Popular Essays

——————— **130** ———————

The morning had dawned cold and damp, with the scent of impending snow in the air. Fritz pulled up the collar of his jacket against the bone-chilling wind and smiled with satisfaction as he left the house, his mind seething with plans for how to use the kidnapping of the child to his advantage. He welcomed the time outdoors alone to sort out his options.

When he was a boy, his father had insisted he participate in a wide variety of strenuous body building regimens to perfect his Aryan physique. Daily Gymnasium, as he called it, followed by lengthy forced marches were required, regardless of the weather. So, Fritz had dutifully walked or run five miles per day, rain, snow or heat notwithstanding. Not that heat was often a problem in Germany, France or England, the countries in which he'd spent most of his youth. Now, it amused him that his own insistence on continuing this daily practice had made it possible for him to commit to memory every inch of the large property in Bedford. It had also given him the chance to spend time getting to know the security guards who patrolled the property.

In the beginning, there had been two sets of security guards on the estate – the mercenaries who were part of the military underground of The 13, and those from a local American security company, chosen because it was the one relied on by most of their wealthy neighbors in Bedford, New York, and therefore not at all conspicuous. But for the past year his father had felt there was relatively little danger here in Westchester and no need to call attention to themselves so the American security company had been left with all the responsibility of protecting the property.

When heads of state or the inordinately wealthy and prominent visited, they generally came equipped with their own little armies, so all that was necessary for adequate protection was that they have security staff of the most proficient kind Westchester, had to offer.

Fritz had read a most enlightening book on the subject of the personal security needs of America's elite class, by a quite knowledgeable fellow who'd been endorsed by the NRA, as an expert in the field. Bill something or other, was his name. The part of the book Fritz had liked best, was the chapter on the likelihood of one's own bodyguards being bought off by an enemy. Evidently bodyguards themselves were the most serious chinks in the security networks of the rich and famous in the U.S. It was easy to suborn men who made inadequate salaries and were, most often, treated like little more than lackeys and stood in endless boredom on the periphery of vast wealth and self-indulgence.

Fritz had tucked this piece of useful information away and had begun to go out of his way, on his daily constitutionals, to observe each guard and to assess which ones were most likely to be seduced by money. He'd even made a boast of it to Marta in their bed, telling her exactly how he'd deduced which men to put on his payroll.

The time had never been quite right as yet, to make use of this potential vulnerability of his father's. He'd had to be stealthy because of Hans Kolb. Gruner had often told Fritz admiring tales of the Stasi Secret Police, most of them were ex-KGB who'd been both hated and feared throughout Europe.

Fortunately, Kolb was as disliked and mistrusted by the rest of the staff, as he was by Fritz, so while he did his job superbly, he had no friends in the house.

It had taken Fritz a little more than half a year to choose the men whose psyches he had vetted for appropriate weaknesses. He'd had several of them on his payroll for months, now.

It had been money well spent, he thought, as he walked briskly back from the sentry station farthest from the house. The few thousands it had cost him were pocket change to him, yet more than their yearly salary, to his chosen ones. Fritz had made it a point to let them know that his father would not live forever, and that once he was gone, Fritz would be the new Master here, so any pangs about disloyalty to their current employer had been easily put to rest.

He'd even befriended the dogs – Dobermans and Rottweilers all trained in Germany by the best canine behaviorists. Fritz had never been permitted a dog, when he was a boy, his snake had been his only pet. And then, of course, there had been the animals he caught and tortured, but they were experiments, not pets. He'd grown quite adept with trained dogs in the past few years. Mind control was mind control, after all – be the minds human or canine, all minds were exploitable, if you knew the right pain thresholds and the right commands.

131

"Fritzy," Marta began in the soft, seductive voice she knew turned him on, as she let her fingers trail down his naked belly toward his groin. "How long will the little girl be here before her mother comes for her?"

He gripped her hand hard to stop it where it lay.

"Why do you want to know this?" he asked, more wariness than the harshness he'd intended, in his question.

"She cute, that's all. And she's tied up, which is so weird, Fritzy. And the servants are afraid to speak to her." She wriggled her body in closer, so her nipples brushed the side of his chest. "And besides, I like children, don't you? I want to have some, someday. I would like to have your child, leibchen, he would be so smart and so strong..."

He let go of her hand and she felt his body relax again, as she played a little with the dark hair that curled at the base of his belly. Why not let her fantasize about something that would never happen. Her touch was delicate, teasing. Then, when he didn't respond to her in the usual way, Marta pulled her hand away and rolled away from him onto her back.

He eyed her, deciding what to say. He didn't like it when she pouted but he knew that was something women did when they didn't get what they wanted. If the stupid cow imagined he would have children with the likes of her it wasn't worth a response. And besides, truth was, he couldn't care less what she had to say about anything, least of all the little girl. But he felt like talking, felt like venting his spleen about this whole situation, at the endless series of small humiliations he suffered at his father's hands on a daily basis. *Fritz do this. Fritz handle that for me.* Never a *Fine job, son* – only being told how he could have done it better.

Fritz considered his options and let his hand stray idly to Marta's bare back, now turned to him. He didn't trust her, but he wanted, *needed* to sound authoritative to *someone* over whom he had some control. What real danger could there be in talking with this whore about it, after all? Whom could she tell about his secrets anyway? he reminded himself, rationalizing. Marta had no one here in the states to whom she could divulge his confidences, and if she ever proved troublesome, he could simply have her disposed of. In such an eventuality, she would never return from America and if anyone inquired, which they most likely wouldn't, he would simply say she had been dismissed with cause and had promptly disappeared.

"My father has an absurd obsession," he said finally. "He's using this child as bait to lure her mother here, because he believes she has an object he desires."

"What kind of object, Fritzy?" she asked, turning back to him and trying not to sound too eager.

"A stupid Spear," he answered impatiently. "A stupid fucking ancient Spear."

"Why would he want such a thing?" she asked. "He has so many weapons on his wall already."

"He's going senile," Fritz said viciously. "He thinks it has some kind of power..."

Marta felt a small thrill run through her. This was progress. Real progress. To reward him, she let her fingers wander down his belly again.

"What will he do with these people if they give him this Spear, leipchen," she asked as she touched his balls in the gentle, practiced way he liked and he groaned a little with pleasure. Instead of answering, he grabbed her hair and prodded her head toward his crotch. But Marta pulled away, and with a lascivious smile said, "No. *No!* Leibchen... not so quickly today. I have something new to show you..." Fritz wasn't the only one in the bed who knew methods for controlling men's minds.

And then they didn't talk about the little girl or her mother or the Spear, for a very long time, but Marta knew now that soon they would talk again, about them. Because Fritz had reached the turning point and she would find a way to use this to her advantage.

132

"Something's going down," Pythias said, staring at the screen in front of him. "I got a lot of activity in the Bedford house."

"You're inside his security system?" Damon responded. "Cool."

"Yeah, I'm in. The security system was easy, it's the rest of his encrypted files that've been giving me agita. This guy should be giving the NSA tips. But I'm all over it now. We were so right about The 13, ya know? He's hooked into the ones on our list and more. They're like a shadow government, so invisible and protected by their public personas and their mega-billions there's no way to bring them down. That's why he's got such sophisticated encryption for somebody who's supposed to just be an ambassador."

"Ambassador to Hell maybe," Damon answered with a grunt. "I got a shit-load on this torture/mind control stuff he helped design, and on his military connections. It's pretty gruesome and there's no question it's being used by governments, including ours – but there's no hard evidence we could nail him with. Unless you've got some smoking gun stuff that's irrefutable, all we can prove is this guy has a helluva lot of powerful friends, a really strong stomach, and absolutely no conscience."

"That's the problem," Pythias said, quietly. "I'm pretty sure he's got the kid at the Bedford Estate. There's some communications satellite imagery that looks like somebody being carried in there on a stretcher, and there's no action whatsoever at his other houses. The Bedford place is fortified, guards on shifts, guardhouse, electrified fences, dogs, you name it. I could take down the security system, no sweat, but then you still got the humans and the canines and somebody's got to go in and find her. And the place is huge. I'm gonna see what I can get with thermal, then call Carter."

133

Aunt Nell jolted out of her meditative state and tried to reorient herself to the earth plane. She reached for a piece of Godiva chocolate from the plate she always kept near at hand in her meditation room. Nothing grounded you like chocolate, after an astral journey.

This wasn't good at all. She grabbed for her cell phone and pressed the speed dial for Matt. It went to voicemail. "Damn!" she said aloud, as the stupid mechanical voice told her to leave a message.

"Call me, Matt!" she barked into the phone. "It's important and not for an answering machine. Call me *now!*"

Then she grabbed a pen and paper and scribbled down all she could remember of the images she'd been shown. It was a genuine pain in the ass that psychic messages were generally fragmentary and symbological, thus open to interpretation. It was easy enough to miss a nuance that could be critical, and she couldn't afford that now.

On TV and in the movies, mystics looked omnipotent, except for that sweet blond medium with the nice family, Alison something or other. *Her* messages were never clear, and they were often as confusing as Nell's. It was the closest to the reality of what being psychic was really like, that she'd ever seen on TV or anywhere, for that matter.

OK! She made herself concentrate. *A betrayal. A child in terrible danger. Chaos. Misinterpretation. Terror. Blood. Death!* And something really important about Black Magic. She'd have to go to a really High Source to get more information. And if it was Black Magic being used against Cait, she'd have to get advice on the Inner Planes about how to help her.

"Dear God, Matt!" she breathed into the empty room. *Call me now!*

134

"Senator," Ruddy Dandridge's driver said in a carefully neutral voice. "Do you think there's any possibility somebody could be surveilling you, sir?"

Ruddy looked up from his copy of the Financial Times and blinked. He'd always had the ability to read a newspaper in a moving car without getting nauseated. You had to be a news junkie, if you were going to succeed in politics. You needed to know every tidbit that could be spun to your advantage, and to spot every word that could be used against you. He read four papers a day, and he'd never had a single staffer work for him, who could match him for picking up on really important minutiae.

"Why are you asking, Hank?" the Senator responded, carefully.

"Well sir, there's been a tag team of vehicles on our tail for the last two trips we've taken. I wasn't positive this morning – thought I might just be imagining it sir, but this afternoon the same two vehicles cropped up again and that's a little too much coincidence for me. When I was on the job, I got pretty good at spotting a tail..."

Hank was a retired DC cop and a Marine before that, and Ruddy liked both those things about the man. He was tough and street smart, a winning combination. Not that he'd ever needed those particular skills in the Senator's service before.

"You want me to put the PD or the Secret Service on it, Senator?"

Dandridge thought a moment, calculating who would get tipped to what, by such a call. "Secret Service sounds like a better bet to me, Hank, unless you think otherwise. But I'd like to give some thought to who it might be before we take any steps at all... maybe talk to the President. Can you lose them?"

Hank smiled. "You bet I can, sir," he said as he stepped on the gas.

So he hadn't been just *paranoid*! Ruddy thought with a mix of relief and anxiety. But what could they want with *him*? And who were *they*? Who on earth would even know he'd been one of the Spear conspirators, unless Monahan had broken under torture. He'd better call Tremaine and see if he was being followed, too. If so, he'd tell the President immediately and call in the cavalry.

"You carrying, Hank?" Ruddy asked, trying to sound casual, despite the hammering of his heart.

"Yes, sir," Hank answered. "My wife says I always got a Glock in my sock, Senator. Drives her crazy. Like I'm never really off duty, ya know? But after all those years on the job, I guess I just don't trust DC all that much, unless I'm armed."

"Well, I hope your sock isn't really where you stash your piece, son," the Senator bantered, trying to keep his voice under control. "I'd hate to think you couldn't get to it if you needed to."

Hank smiled into the rearview mirror and fixed his cop eyes on his passenger. Odds were the Senator knew what this was all about.

"No worries there, sir. Cocked and locked and ready for action. Always."

"Semper Fi, my boy," the senator said trying to sound jovial. "Nothing I like better than a man who's prepared for the worst."

He didn't feel jovial, and he didn't like being followed, not one little bit. How much had John Monahan and his wife told those bastards before they died? Probably everything. He just hoped part of that *everything* was that Ruddy Dandridge didn't know a goddamned thing. Otherwise, he could be in deep shit.

135

Carter burst through the door, breathing hard enough to have run up all fourteen flights of stairs.

"They got it! You were right about Bedford" she gasped triumphantly. "Damon and Pythias... they hacked into Gruner's server and a pile of other things and they're sure she's there."

"Anything definite enough for a warrant?" Meg pressed. Carter, shook her head.

"But you're sure Lark's there?" Cait asked, shooting up from the sofa.

"Ninety-five percent sure, Cait," Carter answered. "I'm just not sure how it helps us yet. Like, what do we do about it, if we don't have any proof? The note he sent is totally ambiguous and there are no fingerprints. The British police are treating this like an ordinary missing persons case. You're still sure about not getting the cops and the FBI involved, officially, right?"

"I think I've got to go get her myself," Cait said evenly.

"Okaaay..." Carter dragged out the word, looking to Meg for support. "And what?... you think if you walk in there he'll just hand her over to you and let you both waltz out?"

"I'll offer him a trade," Cait said as if what she was saying made some kind of sense. "He must know by now *Lark* doesn't know where the Spear is – he doesn't know that yet about me!" Cait pulled her coat from the closet.

Meg was suddenly on her feet, placing herself between Cait and the door. "You can't do this, Cait!" she pleaded, intent on stopping her sister. "You've got to get a grip on yourself! *Now,* we've finally got something concrete to go on! And if Damon and Pythias have gotten this, they'll get *more.* And maybe just *this* is enough for a warrant, if you'll give me an hour to pull some rabbits out of hats. Carter can go to the FBI with what we know now, and Matt's got friends who may be able to help us. *Shit!* We *all* do. We just need another hour to get it all together..."

As if he'd heard his name called, Matt was banging on the door. As he opened it, Cait tried to push past him, her coat half on her body, the handbag she grabbed from the hall table, slung over her shoulder.

"You can't go!" Meg shouted to her sister. "No, Cait – wait! This is insane!"

"Matt, don't let her out of here!" Carter yelled to a bewildered Matt, who instinctively grabbed for Cait.

"What the hell is going on here?" he demanded, body blocking her, as he said it, not knowing what else to do. "Where are you going, Cait? And what the hell is this all about?" he asked incredulously, as she actually threw a punch at him to get free of his grip.

"For Christ's sake!" he yelped, grabbing both her arms and using his superior strength and training to yank her towards him. "Will you just *not* go *anywhere* until somebody tells me what the fuck is happening?"

Cait drew in a deep pained breath, and finding herself pinned, stopped struggling. "Carter's guys found Lark," she snapped, looking up at him. "She's at Gruner's estate in Bedford. Matt, don't you see? My little girl is an hour away from here and nobody can go get her but me."

"Have you lost your fucking marbles?" he shot back, unnerved by what he'd just walked into. "The only thing you can accomplish by going to *wherever* the hell it is you think you're going, is to give that bastard *two* hostages instead of one!"

"Don't you *get it?*" Cait shouted up at him, her voice so overwrought he barely recognized it. "I've got to go to her! I can't just leave her all alone there. I should never have let her out of my sight in the first place! I don't care if I *can't* get her out of there, I have to try. Don't you see, even if I can't save her, at least she has to know I didn't leave her there to die alone! She already hates me for leaving her in England!"

"No, I fucking well *don't* see! This is *not* the way, Cait. Gruner hasn't made a single fucking demand yet. At least wait for *that*... buy us some time for Christsakes, so we can do this right. We'll only get one shot at this – don't you fucking-well blow it!"

"We don't have any time!" she screamed back. "If I go now maybe I can surprise him..."

"*Surprise him?*" he said derisively, "*him* and his bodyguards and his dogs? Maybe you can *surprise* all of them, ya think?"

"I *think* I'm going to do what I damn well think is the right thing to do!" she shouted back, but everyone in the room was looking at her as if she were a lunatic, so she stopped yelling. And then everybody else in the room started yelling at once.

"I can't lose both you and Lark!" Meg blurted, tears of frustration running down her cheeks. "We'll figure out a way to get her out of there. Carter, Matt, all of us..."

"*I'll* find a way to get Lark out safely, Cait, if you'll just let me handle this *my way!*" Matt thundered, trying to be the voice of reason, but just sounding authoritative and macho. "I have *experience* with kidnappers. I know how they work, and I have friends who are skilled hostage rescue guys. I don't know for sure if I can organize the kind of op we need on such short notice, but at least I've got a shot at it. *You* don't have the chance of a snowball in Hell."

"Please, Cait," Meg begged. "Just give us a little time to come up with a plan that *could work.* I know people with money, influence. I've a friend getting aerial photos of Gruner's estate right this minute... Let me call Tremaine... I need to..."

Cait shook her head adamantly, tears flying in all directions. "Why doesn't anybody understand what I'm saying?" Her voice sounded near hysteria. "Lark's all *alone* with that pervert. *There isn't any time...* You've got to listen to me. *All of you!* All my life I've known that if I ever got thrown into Lubyanka with no hope of escape, there were two people on this earth who'd walk barefoot across Finland, if they had to, to get me out. You and Jack, Meg. Do you honestly think I'd do any less for my baby? I've got to try to help Lark! And I've got to do it *now.*"

Meg stared at her sister, knowing truth when she heard it. She drew in a breath, let it out slowly, trying to think of a way to slow everything down. The insanity... her own pounding heart... the headlong rush to disaster. Cait was the impulsive one. She was *not. She* had to de-escalate this right this minute to give them all time to think.

"I understand that you're scared to death, Cait," she said trying to control her voice so it didn't sound as terrified as she felt, "and I *know* your heart is broken." There were tears in her voice now. "I *get* it! I really do. I also know you don't *know* what to do, so what you're planning makes some kind of sense to you, because you don't see any alternative. But to just walk in there... to put yourself in a madman's hands. You can't just throw your life away like that! I won't let you! We've got no leverage in this situation, *yet*. We've got to *get some*, before you try to *get* her back. Don't you see that? You *must* see that! Please, Cait. *Please see that!*"

Cait saw the anguish in her sister's face, so she fought to sound calmer. "I've thought of a possible edge, I *might* have, Meg," she said breathlessly. "I've been thinking about what we found out about his obsession with hunting people... maybe if I could just bait him into playing his game with me, I could shift the odds. I'm not as good as you are in the woods, but I'm not bad either..."

"Holy Christ on a crutch!" Matt shouted, cutting her off, the incredulity and anger in his voice making it thunderous. "Are you two out of your fucking *minds?* Do you two lunatics think this is some kind of *game*? Gruner's a brilliant fucking psychopath with trained men, guard dogs, and a lifetime of experience hunting human quarry. You'd have the lifespan of a gnat on that compound, even *if* he gave you the chance to be hunted, and he has absolutely no fucking reason to do that! All the cards are in his hand, for Christsakes! You've never dealt with a conscienceless, murdering prick like him. I have. *Let me handle this!*"

Meg, just as overwrought as Cait, turned on him and lashed out. "Don't speak to her as if she's an idiot!" He was her friend, but that didn't give him permission for this. "Cait's *not crazy!* You've never seen us hunt, goddammit! We're *good* at it, and Gruner doesn't know that, so maybe what Cait's saying isn't as insane as it sounds. And I *get* why Cait can't leave Lark alone there! So will you just wait a minute and let me think this through. Maybe there's a way..."

"Don't be an ass, Meg!" Matt shot back. "You two mean well, but you're way out of your league here. He could have an army on that estate for all we know. What are you going to fight him with, that Girl Scout bow and arrow you keep in the hall closet?" Matt was trying his damnedest to keep his cool, but this lunacy was way out of bounds and he had to get it calmed down enough to get out of here and find Croce. Together, they'd figure out what to do. Either the Captain would help them, or they'd do it themselves.

"If the fox fights for his dinner and the rabbit fights for his life – bet on the damned rabbit!" Meg spat back at him, all the frustration and fury of this impossible situation in her voice. Carter watching horrified, saw how seriously pissed off Matt was at what he saw as their naiveté, and how over the brink with worry, Meg was.

"Matt!" she shouted, interposing her body between the two of them. "Why don't you go find Croce and bring him back here, *right now*? Cait and Meg obviously need to take a minute to sort their options, OK?" Her eyes pleaded with him to de-escalate this fight.

But he just shook his head in disgust. "They're both fucking unhinged by this!" he spat, and then regretted it the second the words were out of his mouth, but couldn't un-ring the bell. "Oh, *shit!*" he blurted in disgust, knowing any more talk was worse than useless. He turned on his heel and slammed the door shut behind him. He had to get the hell out of here, before he said something he could never take back. *Out of here* he could do something useful, and organize some miracle of his own. *Just as soon as he thought of one.* He fought his own testosterone-fueled temper for control, then turned back, opened the door and stuck his head in again.

"Just do me one favor," he said hoarsely, "Try to calm down and don't do anything *stupid* until I get us some real help here. *Please!*" then he was gone.

"I guess nobody ever told him the one thing you *never* ever say to a woman is *calm down,*" Meg said ruefully, trying to defuse the fury in the room.

"No matter *who* goes in there to rescue her," she said gently, reaching for Cait and wrapping her arms around her, "we need to *know more* about Gruner's estate. You agree with that much, right?"

She didn't wait for a reply, but turned toward Carter. "Can your cyber snoops get us terrain maps, house plans, alarm system info, *anything* that can help us if we go in there? My friend Jerry is getting us aerial reconnaissance photos as we speak. He said he'd have them to us in an hour."

"They'll hack the frigging White House if we need them to," Carter answered, meaning every word. "Give me an hour..."

"I'm so *sorry*, Meg," Cait blurted through tears, the hopelessness of it all in her voice. "He's got my baby and I just can't wait for Matt or anybody... what if he's done something horrible to her already?... what if she's so scared she can't breath? What if she's *dead*?" Cait buried her head in her hands, as Meg tried to control her own tears. Carter had to turn her face away from the terrible scene, but she already had her cell phone in her hand and the boys on the line.

"*Please,* Cait," Meg whispered, urgently trying to get Cait to look her in the eye. She'd never seen her sister this out of control, not even after Jack's murder. "You've got to give me your word you'll wait just a *little* longer to let me see if I can alter the odds some. That's *all* I'm asking here! Matt can be a horse's ass when he's mad, but he loves us. He'll pull out all the stops – you know he will. He'll come up with a rescue plan, and we'll at least have a shot at making it work because he knows how! All that male chauvinist *let me do this* crap pisses me off, too, but we all know his heart's in the right place, and he does this for a living. You know *he knows* I'd never survive losing you and Lark! *He won't let that happen.*"

Know Who Your Friends Are

Part XX

"317 is a prime, not because we think so, or because our minds shaped it one way rather than another, but because it is so, because mathematically reality is built that way."

Godfrey Hardey

136

The helo was one of Jerry Halloran's favorite toys, and a damned useful one at that. The Bell Long Ranger was a terrific combo of room, range and power. For a civilian helicopter, it was a honey. Having his own little airforce to play with was the best perk that came with being CEO of a successful import/export company.

In Nam, Jerry had flown Hueys, probably the most famous helicopters of all time, made immortal by their rescue work and about a thousand Hollywood versions of chopper-pilot heroics, none of them exaggerated, as far as he was concerned. The Huey or UH1 was made by Bell, as was the helo he was in at the moment, and they hadn't forgotten how to make a near-perfect machine in the 40 years since he'd first encountered Bell's choppers. The Long Ranger IV had been worth every penny he'd paid for it.

It was perfect for what they were up to right now, he thought as he focused his long range camera on the terrain below. *Whatever* the hell it was they were up to! The likelihood of anybody bothering to be perturbed by a helo flying over Westchester was practically nil. Westchester Airport was a hop and a skip away, and plenty of the local estates had chopper pads of their own, to get execs into the city without the bother of traffic on I-84 or the Saw Mill.

He didn't know exactly why Meg Fitzgibbons needed these aerial shots of this particular estate, but why wasn't important. He was just glad finally to be able to repay what she'd done for him and his company.

She'd seemed pretty desperate and trying hard not to let on just *how* desperate, when she'd called. She hadn't pressured him or offered details but hearing her unaccustomed level of agitation, he hadn't asked for any. He'd known her to be a young woman of both smarts and integrity, and he owed her this favor. If there turned out to be any flack about today's mission, he'd have his lawyers handle it. And besides, this was fun.

It had been four years since Meg had saved his bacon and she'd never asked for a thing in return. Hadn't even over-charged him like most lawyers would have. That was good enough for Jerry. He'd decided to take the photos himself today, just in case. He could trust his pilot Frank, for discretion, but it didn't pay to let too many prying eyes into anything that smacked of a need for secrecy.

Halloran turned his full attention to the task at hand.

Damn, that's one big piece of property, he thought, as he stared down at the Gruner estate and started snapping. Had to be a couple hundred acres. Huge house, pool, tennis courts – that was normal. But more than one guard station, dog pens, and trained men patrolling... that was not. And there were miles of heavy woodland, backed up on some kind of protected wetlands. Plenty of room for privacy. Or mischief.

He hoped Meg wasn't in some kind of trouble. But, if she was, he'd have her back. She was a good kid, and he liked a good scrap.

"Swing her around low enough so I can get what I need in two flyovers, Frank," he told the pilot through the speakers in his flight helmet. "Any more than that could alert somebody and I'd rather not."

"Roger that, boss," Frank said, happy to oblige. It was a perfect day for picture taking.

137

Lark felt just plain awful! She was sick to her stomach now most of the time, and so tired of playing stupid chess games with this scary old man, but she was afraid to let the games stop because she didn't want to stay tied up all the time. But the playing was getting harder. She had to concentrate now, on not beating him too easily, and on not letting him win too easily, either. Both made him mad. *Everything* made him mad. He was smart and he knew how to play chess pretty well – probably because he was about a million years old, she thought, looking at his mean old face and his mostly white hair. But he wasn't as good at game theory as she was – that was for sure and he, too, seemed to be tiring of the chess playing. But gaming was her specialty and she had to keep him interested so he wouldn't kill her like he said he might.

"Do you know any other games?" she'd ventured to ask. "There are some really good ones you can play on a chessboard – like maybe the Eight Queens Problem? You just have to figure out how many ways 8 queens could be placed on the board so that no two attack each other. It's kind of like Euler's Knight's Tour Problem, and it's really fun to try..." She could immediately see by his scowl of disapproval that he wasn't buying her idea. Lark cast about in her mind for something he might like and an idea popped into her head that maybe he'd be willing to try.

"Do you know the Angel Problem?" she asked hopefully. "It's really cool, 'cause you play it on an infinite chess board, so it's kind of like amazing to try to figure out..." she saw he was almost smiling as he shook his head, but it wasn't a good smile, it was creepy.

Lark thought maybe it was because his smile was so horrible that she thought about how much she wished her daddy could be there to protect her.

Her mind was playing tricks on her now – she thought it was because she was so afraid. It was like sometimes she felt herself slipping away into another reality – like she could do in the Labyrinth. Someplace safe. And someplace where Daddy was. She'd been remembering things about how Daddy made her feel safe... like when he always said the same thing as he tucked her in at night. She hadn't let herself think about how very much she missed *that* for a long time because it hurt her heart too much to. Daddy was gone, and his strong, kind hands would never again tuck the covers in around her and make her feel safe and warm. *"Good night, Angel. Never forget that the Angel always wins."* And she'd thought he meant in the Angel Problem because his math students usually liked to play that game a lot, but when she asked him, he said *no, its not that, its about real life, like the Labyrinth. If you ever need to find your way out of the Labyrinth, just remember the Angel always wins.* "How come, Daddy?" she'd asked and he'd said, "Light gobbles up darkness, sweetheart, doesn't it? If you go into a dark room and turn on a light, then the dark is gone, just like that, right? And Angels are made of light aren't they?"

Angel... light... labyrinth... *angel... light... labyrinth...* kept swimming around and round in her head after that. But it wasn't until later that night that she finally knew what it meant. It meant Daddy was the smartest man in the world, because he made sure that nobody – no matter how geeky he might be – could *ever* figure this out, because she was the only person in the whole wide world who had the final clue. And the clue wasn't in the game at all. It was only in her head.

She felt so proud of her Daddy that he was *that* smart.

She just wished she herself hadn't been smart enough to finally figure it out. Because now that she knew, it might just make things worse.

138

"Let me have a go at her, Father," Fritz offered. My new research is impeccable. And I've been gathering intel on this child ever since you asked me to be prepared. I know her inside and out and believe I now have the means of finding her Achilles heel. I won't harm her, I give you my word. I'll just use my methods to search out her greatest fear. You know how useful that kind of knowledge can be in an interrogation – you're the one who taught me. I'll simply make her more vulnerable for you. I can see you're tiring of her anyway, and want to get on with it. The mother is far bigger game for you."

Gruner looked up at his son, from the papers he'd been pretending to read when Fritz began speaking.

"I want her mind intact," Gruner admonished. "No impairment. She must be fully functional when the mother gets here."

"And when is that?" Fritz asked, trying to conceal his excitement.

"Sometime tonight." Gruner replied.

"Then let me have the girl for an hour, no more. I'll get what you need and return her to you, in perfect readiness for whatever you're planning."

Gruner looked thoughtful. "Alright, then. One hour. No damage."

Fritz nodded, satisfied. He'd been hoping to get his hands on the little brat who was the object of so much of his father's infatuated attention. His father might think Lark was smarter than his own son, but Fritz knew better.

139

Matt stormed out of Meg's place knowing the second the door closed behind him how badly he'd handled the whole situation. But they'd caught him off guard and he'd blown his cool. For Christ's sake, he wasn't a saint and any man would have said what he'd said. Both women were stretched beyond the breaking point by all of this, and they had no idea what kind of bastard they were up against. Hell, *he* didn't even know for sure. But he did know what he had to do next to get Lark out of Bedford clandestinely, and how fast it had to happen. There was just no way to explain it to two overwrought women who hadn't seen what he'd seen, and couldn't in their wildest nightmares imagine what they were up against with a guy like Gruner, who'd kill them as soon as look at them, and then jump on his private jet with his diplomatic passport and never look back.

He'd rather try to do it by the book, but after the Captain warning him off Gruner, there'd probably be no help there...

Matt had been in Special Forces in the Gulf, and was still in the Reserves. If it hadn't been for 9/11, he thought grimly, as he took the stairs two at a time rather than wait for the elevator, there'd have been no way to put together a team of specialists fast enough to do an undercover op like this. But the Special Task Force Guiliani had drafted after the Towers went down, meant there were trained men and equipment right here in the city right now. Military backgrounds, Police and Federal. Between himself and Croce they knew most of them, at least well enough to put the proposition to them.

Matt ticked off the snafu probabilities in his mind, rapidly. Gruner's got diplomatic immunity so the cops can't touch him. The CIA has its own agenda, so the odds on the Company or the Bureau being friendly are next to nil. There's no viable proof that Gruner snatched the kid, or even that she's in this country. They could show the authorities whatever the Cyber Snoops had found, but that could land Damon and Pythias in jail for hacking. These ops could go FUBAR pretty damned quick and fucked-up-beyond-repair was not what they needed tonight. Even if they could try for a warrant, there was no probable cause. *Shit.* Some odds. God *better* be on their side. Which reminded him he'd better call Aunt Nell back as soon as he could. She might know something useful.

Matt hit the steps of the precinct at a dead run. There were good guys on the Task Force – guys who knew how to pull the kid out of there without taking anybody down permanently – if the captain said OK, or if they'd do it for him or Croce. Most of the guys he knew would go to the mat for a kidnapped kid. This wasn't the kind of risky op anybody volunteered for unless they owed you, respected you, and knew you'd never ask, unless there wasn't any other choice. A couple of these guys owed him alright, but this would rain down heavy shit if it went south.

Matt spotted Croce coming out of the men's john. "I need to get some guys together on the QT, real fast, for a real dangerous op," he said simply. The men's eyes locked long enough for Croce to assess Matt's seriousness on a scale of 1 to 10.

"I take it we know where she is, but can't get her out by the usual means?" Croce responded quietly.

Matt nodded yes. "I'd try the Captain, but he's already been warned off..."

"Shift's almost over – I'll have them at your place in an hour after that." Croce said, his expression grim.

"I owe you," Matt answered evenly. "I'll owe them, too, if they'll do it."

"Yeah, yeah," Croce answered with a crooked grin. "So what else is new?" He was already in motion.

—————————————— **140** ——————————————

Fritz sat across from the child, deciding how to accomplish the task his father had failed at, delighted he'd finally been asked to assist. He'd observed his father's efforts to pry out the information they sought, and had thought them rather clumsy. But then his father had no understanding of children, whatsoever. He wondered idly if his father had ever actually been one. The probability was that once the man's prodigious gifts had become apparent in his youth, he'd been little more than a lab rat. A spoiled lab rat – made to feel omnipotent by his mother's pride and his father's overweening ambition – but a lab rat nonetheless.

For a lifetime, Helmut Guttman/Gustav Gruner had gotten everything he'd ever wanted – and all because of a fluke of fate that had supplied him with a superior brain, ambitious parents, a total lack of conscience and the resources of a Reich that valued such qualities. Fritz thought he, himself, had probably studied psychology so intensely, because he'd hoped to understand both the differences between his father and himself, and, the one vital missing ingredient in his own upbringing. No doting parents had given him omnipotence – nor even a semblance of approbation. Quite the contrary, his father had made him feel inadequate every day of his life.

That would soon end. Whether by the simple time-bomb of old-age overtaking the old man, or at Fritz's own hand, his father's days were now numbered. He hoped he'd have the pleasure of dispatching him with his own hand... of seeing in his father's eyes the final realization of betrayal, both by his perfect Aryan body and by his perfect Aryan son, but the results would be most satisfactory, either way. *At stroke of midnight, God will win* – the line of poetry popped into his agile mind, unbidden. Fritz didn't believe in God. But he did believe that midnight was approaching for his father.

But now to the task at hand.

"You are rather bright, hmmmm...?" he said to Lark, matter of factly.

She eyed him with suspicion. "Who are you?" she asked. "Do you play chess, too?"

"I do," he answered in the same uninterested tone. "Why do you ask?"

"That old man unties me when we play chess," she said.

"Is that right?" Fritz feigned consummate unconcern. "I don't do that," he said. "I like it when you are tied up. Does it hurt?"

Lark looked up sharply. This man was different. He wasn't pretending to be her friend.

"I don't like it," she said finally.

"Does it *hurt*?" he thundered the words and, shocked by the sudden fury she heard in his voice, Lark instinctively tried to move backwards, to get away from him, but she was constrained by the chair she was bound to. Her heart rate shot up.

"Yes," she answered softly.

"I can hurt you a great deal more," he said, "and your Mother isn't here to help you."

Lark's eyes turned defiant. "My mother is coming to get me!" she said.

"Really?" Fritz's expression was contemptuous. "She doesn't seem all that interested in you. First, she leaves you with strangers, then she lets you get kidnapped. Now, she hasn't even tried to find you."

Lark's eyes hardened. "I don't believe you," she said defiantly. "I'm not stupid, you know!"

"You were stupid enough to believe I was BWK," he said, triumphantly.

Lark's horrified eyes met his. If he was BWK, he knew *everything*... all her secrets.

"My father sent her a note," Fritz went on. "Would you like to see a copy? We told her exactly where you are, and that all she had to do to save you was to come here, herself, and she hasn't even had the courtesy to respond." His voice had the purposeful sing-song cadence of a schoolyard bully. Sounds were important in breaking down a prisoner. Sounds, like smells, reached below consciousness, below efforts to resist.

He stood up suddenly and turned toward the door. "Think about it," he said. Then he was gone.

Lark let her head sink forward on her chest as tears began to fall. She'd been trying not to cry anymore, because with her hands tied so tightly behind her back, she couldn't wipe her eyes or nose and her glasses fogged up, too.

Despite her best efforts not to, she cried and cried and cried. Small hopeless sobs. Fritz, watching through the two-way mirror he had often used to observe prisoners, smiled with satisfaction as the child's glasses slipped off her bent hand and clattered to the floor. Good. She'd be more disoriented without them, more vulnerable. Lark was exhausted, terrified weakened and alone. It wouldn't take much more to push her over the brink. Then he would see to it that her real torment began.

——————————— **141** ———————————

The Vatican.
Rome

Andretti slammed down the phone and tried hard to calm himself. This day had held nothing good so far. He should have known better than to try Gruner when the stars seemed completely out of alignment, but he'd wanted an update on the man's efforts to collect the Spear. Vincenzo would call tonight to get new orders, and Andretti needed intel, before instructing him. Vincenzo had lost track of his quarry in Spain, then had tracked her to Israel, only to lose her again. It wasn't like the man to fail.

And then this insult from that despicable Nazi tyrant just because he'd had the temerity to broach the Spear subject. How dare any man, no matter how rich, speak that way to a Prince of the Church! He'd been so caught off guard by the ferocity of Gruner's verbal assault that he'd tried to cover his own shock by offering the Church's help in the quest. But Gruner had told him coldly, that *his* people were more than capable of retrieving the object, and that the Church had no business whatsoever involving itself with Gruner's affairs, when it was apparent they couldn't even deal with a few noisy Jews who seemed able to scuttle Andretti's plan to gain power through a canonization that now might never take place!

The only good that had come of the entire conversation was that he'd learned that the Spear was *not yet* in Gruner's hands, but that the woman seemed to be closing in on it. At least he could tell Vincenzo *that,* and hope the man had managed to find her. It might be time to reel her in.

He glanced at the ornate clock on his desk and made a decision. When Vincenzo checked in, he would tell him to take the woman into custody and dredge from her the Spear's hiding place, by whatever means were necessary. Now he knew for certain that Gruner couldn't be trusted *not* to do something stupid that could blow the lid off everything. Andretti was not going to chance *that* under any circumstances. Besides, it would serve the arrogant bastard right to be beaten at his own game.

142

Marta wiped her hands on her jeans and tucked the gun into her waistband, thankful her jacket was heavy enough so it wouldn't show. The knife, she slipped deep into the top of her boot. She'd spotted the place, finally, a week ago, on her morning run, but hadn't been able to get to it until today. The landmarks she'd been told to find by the woman in the airport ladies room, had been hard to spot under the covering of ice and snow, but her reconnaissance runs had finally paid off. She'd found the box stashed beneath a thin layer of dirt, old leaves and ice. She knew that because she'd failed to meet them on her day off, her handlers would be aware now that she was in trouble and needed weaponry, but she'd been relieved just the same, to find exactly what she needed in the stash. Now, at least, she was armed, and she had a place to leave messages.

It was never easy to slip out of the house unnoticed. Only the fact that Gruner and Fritz had taken to going to Manhattan occasionally on the same day, and that Gruner sometimes chose to take his human watchdog along, had made it possible. She'd left the note in the box where the weapons had been, and could only hope her handlers were monitoring the box daily, and that they'd try to find a way for her to make further contact fast. She needed to know if the child's presence altered her orders in any way.

She'd bribed the friendly young American with a blow job, and he'd let her outside the gates today. She smiled at him now, as she made her way back onto the grounds. She thought she'd made enough of an impression so he'd be a future resource for escape.

Hastily, Marta made her way back to the house. Now, she'd have to find a way to conceal the weapons from the prying housekeeper. A pity she couldn't use sex on that old rottweiler bitch, too. She looked like she could use some to sweeten her disposition.

143

Senator Dandridge hurried down the dark Georgetown Street, only a block from home. Why, *dammit*, hadn't he waited for Hank to drive him back from his weekly card game? It was only a three block walk, and he needed to get more exercise according to his doctor, and it was the safest neighborhood in the whole DC area... But he should have waited for Hank.

The game had gone later than usual, and Hank had been called home by his wife, who was ill.   The Senator had magnanimously told him to go, expecting him back by game's end, but Hank was now stuck in traffic, and three blocks hadn't seemed too far to walk alone.

Dandridge looked up and down the deserted street and tried to calm himself.   He was just being stupid.   There had been absolutely no contact, no threats, to either himself or Tremaine. He'd just *imagined* footsteps behind him on the deserted street, imagined that the man in the baseball cap was the same one he'd seen outside the National Cathedral on Sunday morning, and again, on the steps of the Senate building. *Ridiculous!* And all because of what Lincoln had said when he'd called about the car Hank said was following them.   There'd been more deaths, Lincoln had told him.   More deaths connected to the Spear.   But he hadn't seen the connection the way Lincoln seemed to, and even Tremaine had to admit there was no proof whatsoever about *any* of it, that was worth a tinker's dam in a court of law.   But still....

He was nearly home, thank God.   Already on his own street. Another three minutes and he'd be in his pajamas, a glass of bourbon in his hand.   He hurried his pace but that made his heart start to race so hard it made his ears ring with a *ga-slurp, ga-slurp* internal sound he'd never heard his body make before.   It was like the sound you heard when you were about to pass out.   His house was only 50 yards away, but he had a sudden sharp pain in his chest, and it was growing sharper... making it harder to breathe. There was his house, all lit up on the other side of the street. *Safety.* Tomorrow morning he would let the President know what was going on here, even if it made him look like a paranoid old fool.   It was time to get a full-time Secret Service bodyguard, not just rely on Hank.

The man in the baseball cap stepped out from between a parked car and a van. He had something black and ominous in his hand that seemed pointed at Dandridge's belly. *Oh, God,* Dandridge breathed the words audibly. It looked like a gun and he was all alone. He'd never make it up the steps to his door...

The Senator stared at the man for a moment, then he blurted, "I don't know anything about the Spear. *I never did!*" That was just before the terrible, searing pain crashed through his chest and forced him to his knees on the pavement. He tried to scream for help... but no sound emerged. Tried to reach for his cell phone, but his hand didn't obey his command. He thought he heard the man speak something into a cell phone, then the darkness took all thought away and he slipped silently onto the cold pavement and then into some other place entirely.

144

"Matt darling! *Thank God!*" Aunt Nell said breathlessly when she finally reached him on the phone. "I have important information for you. I got a psychic hit that's really unnerved me..."

"I'm so sorry I didn't get back to you right away, Aunt Nell," he said contritely. "I'm up to my ass in a really big problem and..."

"Yes, *yes.* I *know* all that dear," she said hurriedly. "In fact, I know it better than you do. I've been monitoring you."

Matt took an uneasy moment to digest that – he loved his aunt but there were plenty of places in his life he wouldn't want her snooping. "That sounds like we better post some 'No Trespassing' signs around my sex life, Aunt Nell," he answered.

"Oh, shut up you big idiot!" she snapped. "This is no time for levity *or* modesty. I don't give a rat's ass about your sex life – I only care about your *real* life. And what I saw was serious, Matthew, so are you ready to listen to what I have to say or not?"

Matt let the air in his lungs puff out into his cheeks, and then out altogether. "Go ahead... lay it on me," he said, serious now. "I can hear in your voice that you've got something big on your mind."

"Damned right, I have," she said. "Here's the bare bones: There's going to be a can of whoop-ass opened around you within the next 24 hours. There's a death – I don't know who's – there's a big, crazy scene with the police coming and going. And then it gets even crazier because everything gets misconstrued and..." she groped for words.

"Fucked up, bigtime?" he supplied.

"Precisely, Matthew. Fucked up bigger than you can possibly imagine. And there's Black Magic involved... Is it possible this has something to do with Washington, DC, and some celebrity, so the press gets involved, too? And that your friends are right in the thick of it, but it's all upside down and nobody gets it right? And there's some kind of betrayal here, or more than one betrayal, actually..." she let her voice just die off.

"I don't know Aunt Nell," he said, "you're throwing a lot at me."

"There's more, darling, I'm afraid, but it doesn't make any sense to me. There's somebody running in the woods – it looks like the damned forest primeval you know? There's snow and tall trees and rocks, and I hear dogs barking and I hear a child screaming..." she sounded really upset.

"Oh, Matthew this is bad!" she said. "I'm really afraid your friends are in the worst kind of danger."

"I hear you, Aunt Nell," he said solemnly, "and I believe you."

He did believe every word. He just didn't have a fucking clue what he could do but wait for it to happen.

"And Matt, darling," she said, choosing words carefully. "I'm afraid your friend Cait is out there on her own. Some kind of cosmic test..."

"She's not alone," he said emphatically. "Not if I can help it!"

Nell held the receiver in her hand after the line was dead. She wasn't sure if this situation needed magic or prayer.

She kicked off her shoes, entered God's Bedroom and knelt down to try both.

145

Fritz stared out the window at the lavishly manicured, lightly snow-sprinkled lawn, the old growth trees and exotic specimen plants that gave life to the landscape of the huge estate. He wasn't really seeing them, just using them as a resting place for his gaze.

He could break this hostage child in hours, but in truth he couldn't care less about what she knew. He was just sick to death of the old man's arrogance and condescension. The Spear was nothing but some kind of sick chimera, anyway, and it certainly wasn't *his* priority. Just his opportunity.

His last conversation with his father had been the final straw. He was sick to death of waiting for the old man to die. *This child, this woman. They* were the key to ridding himself of the old bastard once and for all. His father's obsession with the Spear was the weakness that would make it all possible, but the child and the woman were the key to pulling it off without having to get his hands dirty. He'd already planted the seed about the hunt, now he just had to help it along. And he had to plan exactly how his father's unfortunate accident in the woods would happen. A cracked skull, a fall into a ravine... there were plenty of options for an accidental death.

He'd carefully built his own alliances with The 13, and now that those relationships were all in place, he could make his move. It had taken decades of manipulation and planning, but it was *fait accompli* at last. At this year's Summit he'd read their admiration in their body language, the complexity of their questions, the side glances at each other as he spoke, and in the strategy meetings several of them had arranged with him, after the larger meetings had adjourned. The only allegiance any of them felt toward his father was based on fear or financial entanglement. And they all knew his father wouldn't last forever...

The long, long years of learning and absorbing were nearing an end. The skillful use of bribes and the clever redistribution of power he'd fostered within corporations, the insidious infiltration of governments, the amassing of quite a sizable fortune of his own... all these had been essential building blocks for the carefully laid foundations of an empire of his own, now successfully in place. And all while playing the obedient, obsequious, dutiful son. The seeds of destruction he had sown and nurtured right under his father's self-satisfied gaze were about to bloom.

The Spear would be his father's downfall, and the woman was the way to spring the trap. Every instinct said she was the catalyst. Best of all, the payoff would be so enormous, not even Fritz could be certain how far it would reach.

"Yes, indeed, *Father*," he murmured. "You're quite right. My gifts are *not* the same as yours. More *multi-dimensional*... was *that* today's deprecating assessment? I know how disappointed you feel about my inadequacies. But don't despair, yet, Father. You may soon have reason to alter your appraisal."

Marta, lying in the bed behind him, was pretending to be asleep. She strained to hear what meshuggah thing he was mumbling now – something about his father – he sounded like a whiney adolescent. Neither one of these Gruner fruitcakes was a mensch. This one liked inflicting pain, and he liked throwing off the constraint of having to appear civilized. There was nothing civilized about either one of these Gruner maniacs. It galled her that she hadn't been able to nail down any definitive evidence against them, but now, maybe she could use this kidnapping against him. She'd have to cajole him into telling her more details.

Fritz was losing control, that was clear. Which made him all the more dangerous. She'd have to figure out a way to arm herself from this point on with something more than her Grav Maga skills. She was good with her hands and legs, but he was a big guy, and he was mentally imbalanced.

Marta heard him turn from the window and stand over the bed, watching her, to make certain she was still asleep. She prayed silently that he wouldn't try to fuck her again. It was getting harder and harder to endure and she hurt everywhere after the last bout of sexual excess.

With great relief, Marta heard him turn away from the bed and toward the bathroom. When she heard the bathroom door close behind him, she slipped out of bed and headed for the door.

* * *

Fritz heard Marta's good-bye, muffled by the running water. His mind was occupied with more important matters than a whore. The Monahan woman was coming, assuming she took the bait, and then the final game would begin.

He turned off the shower, walked naked into the now empty bedroom and tried to control his excitement. Tonight was the night he'd been waiting for all his life.

146

```
Washington Post
December 12, 2010
Senator Rutheford Dandridge Suffers Massive Coronary

    Rutherford P. Dandridge, father of President R.J.
Dandridge, and fifty year veteran Republican Senator
```

from New Hampshire, suffered a massive coronary late last night, while walking near his Georgetown home.

The senator, former war hero and near legendary party pundit, is a graduate of Choate, Harvard and Harvard Law. An often quoted spokesman during the Reagan years, his advocacy of the 'peace through strength' initiative and support for the massive tax cuts that Reagan believed would energize the economy, helped give Republicans control of the Senate for the first time in decades. His proponents claim the programs he championed provided unprecedented economic growth - his detractors say his major contribution to politics was the ability to spend fifty years in the Senate without ever sponsoring a major piece of legislation.

Senator Dandridge's condition is guarded, and sources at the White House say the President has been put on notice that his father may not recover. Speculation has already begun about the most likely candidate to pursue Dandridge's senate seat in the event of his death.

147

Eight men sat around the coffee table in Matt's living room. A Dunkin Donuts Box 'O Joe, paper cups and varied fast-foods sat, mostly untouched, in front of them. Meg's Intellicorps surveillance photos were scattered all over the table, and most of the info Carter's cyber snoops had emailed was printed and sitting next to them. An 18 x 24 scratch pad was propped up on a chair, criss-crossed with Matt's diagrams that matched photos, and a laptop was opened to show electronic files of the floor plans and alarm system info. The estate had been chopped into sectors on the big pad, each sector now had men's names scrawled across it.

Matt looked around at the group Croce had assembled. An electronics expert to interface with Damon and Pythias, the surveillance cameras, electric fences, and in-house communications system... two Hostage Response Specialists to locate Lark and take out the body guards... four ex-Special Forces guys to secure the perimeter, without use of deadly force... one man to silence the dogs with tranquilizer darts... Croce to back up Matt finding Gruner and his son.

Old military ties, especially Special Forces, were tough to break. Matt had saved the lives of two of these men in Desert Storm – one had later returned the favor. One of the ex-FBI guys had served with Croce in Desert Shield, and he'd brought one of the Hostage Rescue guys onto the team, and vouched for him. There were no FNG's in this crowd. A Fucking New Guy could get everybody killed.

Matt did a mental checklist about what they'd need to pull this off. All the guys had weapons and NVG's. Counterterrorist operations tended to get real personal, and each man put a lot of faith in gear he trusted, modified for his own sub-specialty to give him the edge he'd rely on for survival. You go dressed right for a takedown or you don't go, was the rule of thumb.

He knew the men all had their own mission-specific gear. Eagle Tac III Kevlar assault vests, Nomex coveralls and gloves, 9mm Beretta or Sig Sauer sidearms, flash/bang grenades, rappelling harnesses were standard. At least one suppressed H&K 9mm MP5A3 submachine gun with a three-lug barrel allowing easy on and off for the 'can,' and equipped with a Navy Seal pack was needed. The Navy Seal Pack would allow for one-shot or three-shot bursts in addition to full-auto, to keep the firepower contained unless all hell broke loose. One tranquilizer gun and darts for the dogs was another essential tool. A Benelli M4 12 gauge with an Eotach holo sight in case they had to blast any doors from their hinges. They were pros. They'd know what was needed.

"The plan is simple," Matt said looking at the grim faces around the table. "Four men go over the wall first, tranq the dogs and take down the two guys patrolling the perimeter. Two more follow closely to scan for lasers and trip wires and to disable any electronic surveillance equipment and phones that haven't already been taken out by Carter's guys. Gruner must feel pretty secure here in America. He's got all those acres around his property that separate him from prying eyes, *and* he's got his government connections. I'm hoping his over-confidence can work to our advantage here. He has security and a personal bodyguard – the good news is there's not a lot of them – the bad news is we don't know if they're all just rent-a-cops or if any are military trained. He uses both. Carter's guys are hacking the security company to see who's on duty tomorrow night. She says he doesn't appear to want to look suspicious to his American colleagues, so he doesn't keep the military guys on all the time. The only one to really watch out for is the butler. He's ex-Stasi.

"Bobby and Vinny, you'll peel off toward the main house, disabling cameras and lights as you go. Jose and Smitty are hostage rescue – they'll head directly for the interior. Once the walkers and dogs are down, the first two men will hit the gatehouse sentry station.

"We'll need Jake to work out a way to fool the surveillance cameras for eight minutes before we disable them completely. We don't want to alert the guards inside the house too soon, or give them time to harm Lark.

"Rich and Herb have plenty of search and rescue experience. We need to get them inside ASAP, to find and secure Lark's safety. Worst case, Gruner already has her buried somewhere on the estate. He's known for live burials, so if there's a bunker anywhere, we have to hope surveillance can spot it. We could really use the AlCan thermal imaging, so Damon and Pythias are on that. If we can't get hold of it fast enough, we'll need all the search time we can get, and maybe some canines of our own.

"No need to say this out loud, but I'll say it anyway. The object here is to get Lark out without incident. That's all. No lethal force unless there's absolutely no other option. We've got no housekeeping here. We don't want to end up with any dead bodies we need to explain."

He watched the heads nod imperceptibly around the table, before proceeding.

"You men all have your own equipment, if you need anything beyond what's been outlined, I need to know it, now." He did a quick mental inventory knowing the job required decent night vision, a Cyclops goggle system maybe. Sidearms with silencers. A suppressed SR25 equipped with a Munz unit with a PRT tube. Howie's M24, tranq darts, stun grenades... They'd know and they'd come prepared.

"We need to figure out exactly where the trip wires are," he continued, "and disable the lasers as fast as possible once we're in, so speed and accuracy are paramount. If the kid's hidden somewhere, we'll need search time, and we'll have eight hostages on the ground who have to be kept alive and incapacitated while we do that." He scanned the faces again. "Now's the time for questions or for anybody who wants out to make that known."

"So how much time do we have for rehearsal?" Croce replied quietly.

"Only one tactical run-through possible because of timing, and no on-site rehearsal, obviously. We have to do this tomorrow night, so that means we make our plans now and work the kinks out with just the recon. We have aerial maps and house plans, and we can do a drive-by and maybe surveil from the perimeter, but that's about all we can do 'til the real thing tomorrow night."

Heads nodded, assessing what they'd heard.

For the next four hours, the men worked on the plan. Each made suggestions, and everyone listened with respect to what the others had to say. They were putting their jobs, as well as their lives, on the line here, because Matt or Croce had asked them to. And because there was a kid at stake.

148

The envelope was slipped under the door. Cait picked it up and grabbed the gun from the entrance hall table drawer where Meg had stashed it, then opened the apartment door and peered out. No one. She picked up the building intercom and dialed the doorman. "Jimmy, did someone just enter the building to leave me a note? This is Dr. Monahan."

"Jeez, no, doc. Nobody came in, nobody asked for you, neither. Why?"

"A note just got pushed under the door here, Jimmy. *Somebody* must have delivered it?"

"Sorry doc," he said, sounding genuinely concerned. "I don't know what to tell you. Should I call the police?"

"No, that's OK, Jimmy," she said, hastily. "I'll just tell my sister when she gets back and she can decide what she wants to do about it."

Her fingers were shaking as she tore open the envelope. The note was made of letters clipped from newspapers and magazines. Still nothing to tie it to Gruner.

I have no interest in birds, only artifacts.
Drive North on the Saw Mill River Parkway to Exit 38 at 7:30 tonight.
Pull off the exit ramp and turn right.
A car will be waiting to lead you to your destination.
Come alone or the bird loses a wing.

Cait let the words sink in for a moment, nausea rising, and glanced at her watch. Not much time with rush hour traffic. She picked up the phone to call Meg, then realized the chain of events that would be set in motion and put the phone down again. This was her job to do, nobody else's. Enough people she loved had been hurt already because of her mistakes. She couldn't let Meg sacrifice herself.

Meg would try to keep her from going, and she had to go. Even if there were only one chance in a million, she had to go.

Cait glanced longingly at the handgun. She'd never get a gun into Gruner's house, but maybe she could hide it in the car, to use in case she and Lark got a chance to escape. Could any other weapon be hidden where she could get to it? A knife maybe. It might be better than nothing. And there was that innocuous little Swiss Army contraption she always kept in her wallet – it looked like a credit card but housed a tiny knife and scissors. They'd missed that at the airport security check point, on her last flight. It was absurdly tiny, but it was *something*. If she were home, she could have taken the necklace she and Meg had bought at the last gun show they attended – it looked like a decorative pendant, but had a little push-dagger hidden inside. Maybe she could find Meg's...

No! No time for that now. Meg would be here any minute. She'd write a note, take her car from the garage. The keys were on the hall table.

Cait dressed as fast as she could, wrote a note to her sister, tears spilling down her cheeks. She wanted to say so much more... but Meg would understand all that could never be put into words.

149

Fritz was a firm believer in cash. Not promises or checks or wire transfers, unless the amount was too unwieldy or the recipient not of the laboring class. Just cash. He'd never known anyone to turn him down once they saw a hefty roll of bills in his hand.

He'd made certain the guards on duty tonight were the right ones for the job he had in mind. It was a relatively simple task he would be demanding of them, after all, but it would be easier with the rent-a-cops than military-trained men.

They wouldn't have to do much in return for the very generous cash payment he was about to make. It was more a matter of the things they *wouldn't do* tonight. Rounds they wouldn't make... checkpoints they wouldn't monitor. Timing of the dog's release....

──────────────── **150** ────────────────

Cait tried to concentrate on the road.

My plan is just as stupid as Matt said it is! she told herself over and over in rhythm with the windshield wipers that were clearing away the lazy snowflakes that couldn't seem to decide if they wanted to become a real snow storm. She wished she'd checked the weather map before setting out. *Funny how stark raving terror can make you forget the little things.* Not that the weather mattered.

I have no plan! What am I going to do? The fear and uncertainty seemed to be draining her resolve, and whatever small confidence she'd mustered when she'd left the city. No plan. *No plan.* The words kept time in her brain with the windshield wipers' relentless rhythm.

Then her father's voice was suddenly in her head. *"Any plan is better than no plan at all, sweet Cait. If you're ever in trouble and you don't know what to do, just do what you can. Don't let fear paralyze you. You can always correct what you do, as long as you're not paralyzed."*

And then Jake's voice was there, too. *"Movement is life, Cait. No movement is death."* She knew it was just her memory playing tricks, but that didn't matter. The message mattered.

And then the idea was in her head about how to bait Gruner. It was probably crazy... probably useless. But it was an idea, and it was better than no idea at all.

— 151 —

Meg's cell phone rang as the doors to the elevator of her building whooshed shut behind her. She was on her way back upstairs to Cait, but alone for the moment in this small paneled privacy of the elevator, so she answered when she saw Matt's number.

"It's done, Meg," Matt said. "We can make it happen tomorrow night." Meg exhaled an audible sigh of relief.

"Thank God, Matt!" she breathed into her iPhone. "And you, and Croce. I'll tell Cait. I think I talked her into getting some sleep while I went out. She's dead on her feet and beside herself with worry."

"I've been trying Cait's cell for half an hour, but it goes to voicemail – I'd feel better to know she's just asleep," Matt answered, sounding worried and weary.

Meg stepped off the elevator and headed down the hall to her apartment. "Let me call you from inside, OK? I have information you'll need but I don't want to talk in the hall." She stopped in front of her door. "And Matt... just one more thing... You know I'm coming with you, right?" she waited for his reply and braced herself, while putting her key in the lock.

"I *know* you're *not!*" he exploded. "Don't be an ass, Meg. There is no way in hell you are coming with us. My guys can't be expected to pull this off and babysit you simultaneously."

"I can outshoot you at the range," she replied, wiggling the key in the lock. She'd known he'd say no, and that it didn't matter what he said. She'd already decided she was going with them.

"Yeah, that's right, and that's at the *range,* not in a combat situation. You can only fuck this up and the guys will go apeshit if there's a civilian in the woods with them."

"We'll talk about it later," she said, cutting him off. "I'm home. I'll call you after I talk to Cait."

She knew when she opened the door and saw Carter's stricken face that something worse had happened. But what could possibly be worse?

152

Fritz studied the child in the chair. The device was too large for her small frame and he made a mental note to have a smaller one fabricated for future use. For now, this would have to do.

Lark, tethered by straps and wires, was watching the scary man who was the son of the mean old man. The metal was cold against her skin and the straps that held her were painfully tight. Her head ached from trying to figure out how to save herself from this scene. She felt like she was in some horror movie – the kind her Mommy and Daddy would never let her watch. She wished she had seen at least one, because maybe people in those movies knew how to escape.

"I don't know where it is," she offered, without being asked. "I swear."

But the scary man just put his finger to his lips for silence.

"Here in my laboratory," he said, "we speak only when spoken to, and we only speak the truth. If we disobey, we suffer pain." To underscore the words, he hit a button and electricity coursed through the child, arching her back and causing her to shriek in pain.

"Do you understand me, Lark?" he asked in a calm cold voice.

The child nodded her head and tears fell in silent streams down her cheeks. She realized she had wet herself. It made her feel ashamed.

"I am not interested just now about where you are hiding the Spear. I am interested in finding out more about *you*. Even more than you told BWK. What I want are your deepest darkest secrets. Do you see the screen in front of you? Pictures will flash onto that screen. Pictures of many, many frightening things. Things like snakes and spiders and earthquakes and falling off buildings and war and torture. Do you understand?"

The look in her terrified eyes replied eloquently.

"Now Lark, here is what is going to happen next. As you see each of these terrible pictures, we will be monitoring your responses. Your blood pressure, your brain waves, your breathing, and so forth. At the end of the show, you will have told us by your reactions, which of these scenes is your worst nightmare, do you understand? Because your terror will be visible on our monitors." He smiled as he saw the realization dawn in her eyes.

"You will try not to give us true readings, of course, but the more you fight, the more we will know of your true fears. That way, when I finally do decide to ask you the whereabouts of the Spear, you and I will both know precisely what your punishment will be if you lie to me, hmm?"

He turned to the Chinese lab technician and waved him toward the controls.

"Let the show begin," he said, as the image of a boa constrictor opening its jaws to swallow a bleating goat whole, filled the screen and Lark tried desperately to turn her head away, but failing that squeezed her eyes shut.

"No, no, no!" Fritz said in a tone of firm admonishment. "We must have none of that. If you do not keep your eyes open voluntarily, I'm afraid we must keep them open by another means, and I assure you, you will not like that at all."

Reluctantly, Lark opened her eyes a slit to peek at the screen. She saw an army of fire ants surging into the eyes and nose and ears of a writhing naked man staked out on a jungle floor.

Twenty interminable minutes later, Fritz left the lab and reported to his father.

"You'll be delighted to know, Father," he said as he entered the man's study. "That the child's worst fear is the one you most enjoy."

He didn't wait for a response. He needed to set the bait to get them into the woods. Not that it was ever too hard to interest his father in a hunt. Then he turned on his heel and went in search of Marta.

Worst Nightmare

Part XXI

"The mistakes are all waiting to be made."

Chessmaster
Savielly Grigorievitch
Tartakower

153

The man at the gate waved Cait and the car she was following onto the estate. She drove slowly up the half mile long driveway toward the house, trying to memorize every detail along the way. She heard dogs barking, saw two men, shadowy figures flanking the road, registered that lights were flashing on and off, obviously on motion sensors, triggered as she approached and passed. She counted six of them. She was trembling so much she had to clutch the wheel tightly to keep the car steady on the path. She was scared to death. She couldn't even imagine how scared Lark must be.

The house was old, elegant, immense. It loomed in front of her, as she rounded the final curve. It was one of those magnificent Victorian mansions built by some robber baron in the middle of the 19th century. This part of Westchester was littered with them. Railroad fortunes, shipping fortunes, even whaling and slaving fortunes, had dotted this landscape with the architectural rewards of ill-gotten gains.

A tall man, neither young nor old, but built like a refrigerator, greeted her formally at the door. He had a faint Middle-European accent and eyes as colorless and cold as concrete. If her heart could have sunk any further, it would have, as he closed the house door behind her and she heard the lock engage.

She *knew* that coming here was insane, knew neither she nor Lark would probably leave here alive. But she also knew she had to try. Had to hold Lark in her arms one more time and let her know she hadn't been abandoned. And, she was tired of running from this monster and from everyone else who wanted the one thing she couldn't give them. It would all end tonight.

The butler checked her expertly for weapons, and finding none, led her through the grand entrance foyer.

Gruner stood in the doorway of a large, elegantly appointed drawing room. She knew him from the thousand photos she'd seen in newspapers and magazines, and his many appearances on TV. Always the pundit. Always the sage. *Always the monster,* she thought as she studied him now. It seemed implausible that the man before her was over 90. His face and body looked more like those of a 70 year old who'd taken good care of himself.

"How very brave of you to have come," the man said, extending a well manicured hand to her. The idea of touching him was repugnant.

"I would have called it foolhardy," she replied, ignoring the hand. "You said you have my daughter and would harm her if I didn't come. You left me no choice."

Gruner smiled and it almost reached his icy eyes.

"You have a point, doctor," Gruner replied, assessing her. "I expect you'd like to see your child?" He saw she was watching him as closely as he was watching her.

"I've had tea prepared for us," he said, changing tack. "Perhaps, we can discuss our negotiations in a civilized manner?" Gruner gracefully gestured her into the impeccably decorated room. A magnificent sterling tea service sat on a Queen Anne table between two graceful Scalamandre-upholstered armchairs that flanked the fire.

"This is a negotiation, then?" Cait asked, slightly heartened by the word. She seated herself on the edge of the chair he'd indicated.

"Would you care to pour, doctor?" Gruner asked looking at her with undisguised amusement. Cait shook her head no.

"I prefer to think of it as a game, really," he said leaning forward with an athlete's unstudied grace, and pouring the tea himself. "You have something I want, I have something you want.

There's no reason to believe we cannot come to mutually agreeable terms."

Cait said nothing. She found she could barely breathe. One *misstep...* but what were the *right* steps? What possible leverage did she have in this bizarre game of cat and mouse?

"If you release my child," she said finally, "I'll tell you everything I know."

"Really?" he said with a dismissive smirk. "And, here, I had been led to believe you were the Spear's champion. Its *Caretaker*. Surely your God expects more of you than such easy capitulation?"

"I have no idea what my God expects of me," she answered evenly. "And as to my being a champion of anything, I assure you I have no such pretensions. I was thrown into this crucible against my will, and I've done the best I could with it, no more, no less. I do not believe any God worthy of the name would trade a child's life for an artifact, however precious."

Gruner tilted his head to the side and pursed his lips. He hadn't anticipated such an answer. Anger. Pleading. Tears, yes. But this was more interesting.

"Have you forgotten what God demanded of Abraham, then?" he asked, rebuke in the tone.

"Are you equating yourself with God, now?" she tried to control the edge in her voice.

He looked up. "In this situation, perhaps this is not so far-fetched? I hold the power of life and death, after all."

"But in the end, God relented," she said, "and an angel intervened. In the end, God did not demand that Abraham go through with the sacrifice of Isaac, did He?"

"Hmmm," Gruner mused. "He did not. Do you think then, that God will relent in this case, too? Shall I tell my butler to expect a heavenly visitor?"

Rage flared in Cait, but she willed it to recede. She had to control her urge to leap across the table and pummel this arrogant madman to death with his own weighty tea pot. Lark was somewhere in this hell house. *That* was what mattered. That was the *only* thing that mattered.

That and engaging his interest. Since getting back to New York, she'd read every word of every dossier all her allies had collected. Gruner was an egomaniac. A brilliant sociopath, who liked to play games with his victims. He had only one weakness to exploit. She prayed to God she was up to doing that. It was her only hope for saving Lark.

154

"She's gone, Meg," Carter said, as Meg shut the door behind her. "I got here five minutes ago and tried to call you, but got bounced into voice mail, and I knew you were on your way home anyway..." She took something out of her pocket. "She left you a note," Carter held the paper out in front of her.

> *Dearest Meggie,*
>
> *He made contact. I'm on my way to somewhere upstate. I'll be met by a car that will show where I'm going. Please don't come after us. I can't let anybody else get killed because of us, and I can't leave her there alone. Please try to understand. I love you all there is. There's never been a better sister in this world.*
>
> *Cait*

Meg sagged back against the door behind her and tried to breathe. When she looked up, Carter thought she'd never seen such unmitigated anguish in anyone's eyes.

155

Carter put down the phone and listened to the frenzied movements in the bedroom. Meg was pulling things out of closets and tossing them onto the floor. This was definitely not a good sign.

She'd just called Matt and told him, and he'd gone ballistic. She couldn't blame him. There was no way the team he'd assembled could go tonight – no equipment, no rehearsal, no time to gather what they'd need or make arrangements... Not even Matt could ask that of the men who'd volunteered to help them.

So Carter had told him to keep going with his guys, to get tomorrow night's op down cold. They'd just have to rescue two hostages instead of one. And he'd told her to keep Meg from following Cait, no matter what it took, and she'd agreed. But of course that wasn't an option, so why argue about it. All she could do was not let Meg go alone.

156

The bedroom door opened and Meg walked into the hall. She was dressed in black turtleneck, camouflage pants, boots, hair pulled up and under a black wool ski hat she'd bought in Aspen two winters ago when they'd spent a great ski holiday there. She had her Beretta 92F in her waist holster, and her 85F, barely visible at the top of her right boot. A hunting knife was in the other one.

Meg frowned when she saw that Carter was similarly dressed.

"You're not getting out of here without me," Carter said simply, to head off the protest.

"No!" Meg answered emphatically. "I need you here. This is *my* fight, not yours."

"The hell it is!" Carter flung back. "We go together or so help me God you'll never get out that door."

"You forget I'm armed," Meg said with a short laugh.

"So am I, *and* I have PMS, so don't even think about trying to get past me. You were trained at Harvard... I was trained at Quantico." She handed Meg the winter camo jacket she knew she'd want to wear. She'd pulled it from the hall closet where Meg kept her hunting gear, moments before.

"I have a right to risk my own life, Carter. They're my family. I have no right to risk yours, especially on something that's probably hopeless."

"Cut the crap and put on the damned jacket, Meg. We don't have time for this. The only question is, do we tell Matt? He's got his own op planned for tomorrow night. Do we tell him we're going *now*?"

"No way!" Meg shook her head emphatically. "He'll only try to talk us out of it and waste our time. We'll leave him a note."

Carter nodded and picked up a pad and pen from the table to scribble something. She stuck it in an envelope, licked it quickly and wrote Matt's name on the front.

"I'll leave it with the doorman," Carter said. "Matt said he's coming by here after his guys finish their rehearsal for tomorrow night." She hesitated, then said, "Just so we're clear, here, kiddo... you *know* he's a good guy, Meg, and he's really trying to help us. You *know* it would make sense to let him handle this, right?"

"Cait and Lark could both be dead by tomorrow night," Meg answered, looking her partner in the eyes. Carter pursed her lips, then nodded. Then she checked her Colt Delta Elite, her favorite handgun, stuffed it locked and loaded into the back of her jeans, and Meg almost laughed despite herself.

"Why you don't use a shoulder rig or a belt holster like normal people is beyond me," she said trying to ease the tension that hung between them in the room.

"Yeah, well I'd rather blow my own ass off than have to wear a shoulder holster," Carter replied, knowing gallows humor was sometimes the only thing you could rely on to keep you rational. "Besides, I've got a.380 in my boot and a belt holster in the car."

Meg had pulled her hunting bow out of the closet then a quiver of steel tipped wooden arrows. Carter opened her mouth to protest, thought better of it, pulled on her own jacket and followed her partner out the door. Who was she to quibble? In a fight, the weapon you knew best was your best ally.

They were in the car and on the road before she spoke again. "You know this is fucking stupid, right?"

Meg didn't look at her when she answered, "Of course I know that. What's your point?"

Carter smiled just a little, and settled back into the leather seat. "Just wanted to make sure we're on the same page," she said, then turned to stare out the window as the Bronx slid by.

157

Gruner sat back in his armchair, deciding how to proceed. He so enjoyed playing with his victims, and the woman was pretty, desperate and angry, a combination he found particularly pleasing. But there was work to do, and the Spear was nearly in his grasp. His plan had worked remarkably well, at the end. He should have handled it all himself from the beginning, instead of leaving it to underlings. They were, after all, underlings for good reason.

At the same time, Cait was taking the measure of the man and his world as well, hoping for some inspiration that was better than her own feeble plan. The walls of the palatial room were lined with photographs of Gruner with many of the most influential people on the planet. Heads of governments, religious leaders, media moguls, Hollywood stars. The President of the United States. She said a silent prayer for help, and waited for him to lob the ball over the net one more time. She'd been pretty good at sussing people out when she'd done her psych rotation in med school, and at the moment, her psychic, or whatever you wanted to call it *intuition*, was at its peak. Somehow she *knew* she could throw him slightly off his game, if she waited for him to speak.

"What...?" he said finally. "No begging for your child's life, doctor. Or your own, for that matter?"

"Would begging help?" she asked, trying to keep her voice steady. "I thought you said this was a negotiation. I came here to negotiate."

"And how do you propose to do that?"

"You let Lark go, and I stay. I'm the one who has what you want. You took her to get me here, and here I am. You've won. Almost."

He cocked an eyebrow, finding her quite entertaining.

"And is that *all* you have to bargain with?" he asked with amused disdain. "After all, I seem to have you *both* now, don't I? Why should I bargain at all?"

"People know I'm here," she replied. "If Lark is returned, they won't call the police. Otherwise..."

He smiled. "You must know by now that the police are powerless because of my diplomatic immunity. And because of a few judiciously placed phone calls, made earlier, I might add."

"I'm banking on the fact that you don't need the firestorm my friends can instigate. There's no way you can spin the idea that a child came here alone of her own volition. There's no record at immigration of her having left England and she's been reported missing to Scotland Yard. People's sympathies are easier to manipulate if a nine year old is the victim. A kidnapping charge could get ugly – why risk it when there's an easier way? With me... I'm an easier story to spin..." She shrugged her shoulders, "You can say I'm just some crazy woman who stalks famous men." She waved at the pictures on the wall.

"Tell me where my Spear is," he ordered.

Cait weighed her options and settled for truth. "I don't know," she answered. "But I have clues I've collected all over Europe. I'll give them all to you. Added to what you already know, maybe it's enough for you to find it."

He thought that over for a moment, then rose.

"Perhaps, the problem is that you simply don't understand how dangerous I am," he said, "and how close to death your daughter is." This was not going quite as he'd planned. "Perhaps it's time you learned."

Fritz watched the interchange from the doorway. *Very good.* This woman was more than he'd hoped for. She'd fold when she saw what he'd done to Lark. Now, he just had to wait for the perfect moment while his father's mind was occupied with his victims... He made a slight alteration in his plan, based on what he'd just seen, and moved to where he knew his father would take her next.

158

The shaggy-haired man watched from his carefully chosen vantage point on the periphery of the Gruner estate, where it backed up on the wetlands. He'd lost his dottore for a time but had found her again. He would not let such a thing happen ever again. He had found an appropriate perch for the waiting and watching that would now be necessary. How many years had it been since he'd learned the patience of his trade, he wondered idly, munching on a handful of the nuts and dried fruit he always carried to keep his energy and alertness at the correct level.

His camouflage was as perfect as his stillness. The guards had passed within 50 yards of his perch twice. The dogs would be harder to elude when the time came... but only at first, and they were not an insurmountable obstacle. They would be subdued, not killed, despite the fact that they, like all such guard dogs, had been brutalized by their training into killing machines, cowed by pain, and tortured into compliance, so they were strictly speaking, no longer dogs, like his little Sophie. And he would kill them if need be, but ever since the invention of tranquilizer darts, which he liked very much it usually was unnecessary.

He had seen his dottore enter this house of hard men. He knew she had come for her child, a foolish, but nonetheless, brave thing. He had also observed the men digging a large hole far to the rear of the house, and the size and shape of it had raised the hairs on the back of his powerful hands and arms. Large enough for a coffin, or a body. He himself had dug many such holes. Vincenzo knew such holes were best filled in full darkness so there was still time to sit in stillness.

The Cardinal had told him to capture the woman, but there had been no time for that since she had returned to the States. Or perhaps he'd dragged his feet, just a little because he did not want to do this thing. Now, the decision had been removed from his hands for the moment, so he must remain alert until a time for decision came again.

Vincenzo waited and watched, engraving in his memory the topography of the grounds, the movements of the guards, their schedule, and their habits. One large and lumbering, one smaller and quicker, one who slacked off to smoke, and one who had no talent other than a big mouth and ego to match, who filled the air with much needless laughter. A buffoon – no more, no less. And so on, and on, he mentally catalogued each man and detail. Uniformed amateurs, from their lack of alertness, the casualness of their discipline. They most likely worked in eight hour shifts, guarding a house that was a fortress, had a man in a gate booth who watched TV and talked on his cell phone, or dozed intermittently.

Vincenzo had memorized the pattern of the lights that were on timers, the ones on motion sensors, the ones controlled by the dozing man in the little glass box. He had never understood why men in his line of work sometimes complained of the boredom of surveillance. There were an infinite number of things to know, so a man's brain must remain always alert, a computer for the random possibilities. When the computing was done, Vincenzo liked to say his rosary, asking the Blessed Mother to guide his hand in the service of her Son. How could there be boredom he wondered, as he saw the lazy guard slip away from his rounds, a cigarette pack in his hands, when there was so much you must learn about your prey, in order to do your job well.

159

The basement Gruner led Cait to was vast and very different from the floor above. The walls were native stone. It appeared the foundation for the huge mansion had been blasted out of the solid granite that was the bedrock in this part of Westchester. The lights blinked on and then off, as they passed through a long corridor, as their motion activated and then deactivated them. The fixtures shed an eerie blue-grey light that made the place seem even more sinister, if that were possible. The temperature felt nearly as cold as if they were outdoors, but Cait shivered more from fear for Lark. This was the kind of place that would evoke a child's worst nightmares... to say nothing of her own.

Gruner opened a steel door and flipped on an array of blinding fluorescent lighting. Cait's eyes took a moment to adjust, then she saw what he had brought her here to see.

In the center of the room, which looked like a cross between an operating theater and laboratory, Lark lay strapped into a box, immobilized, nearly naked and shivering, reduced to utter nine year old embarrassment and terror. There was duct tape over her mouth, but her eyes filled with tears of relief, the moment she saw her mother and she began to struggle hard against the restraints.

Reality sluiced through Cait – she had imagined the worst and now it was happening and she was helpless, and for a moment paralyzed by the enormity of it she couldn't move, breathe or think. The room swam out of focus and then in again, and then she was in motion, running toward Lark, screaming, trying to reach her terrified child, as hard male hands grabbed at her and pulled her back. She fought and kicked and shrieked – useless promises – to her child. *I'm coming, Baby. I'm here. I love you!* What difference did it make?

The men slammed her body to the floor. They were handcuffing her, lifting her, tying her to a chair, but she felt and saw nothing but Lark's eyes and the utter hopelessness in them now.

Gruner walked to the struggling child and laid one hand on her bare flesh, as with the other he pulled the tape from her mouth.

Lark began to scream, words and sobs tumbling over each other. "Mommy. Mommy! He's going to bury me in the ground and I won't be able to breathe. Mommy *please!* Don't let him do that. *I'm afraid of the dark...*" the last words were drowned out by Cait's own screams as she struggled uselessly against her bonds, cursing and screaming at the madman to let Lark go... that she'd tell him everything... anything... *do anything...*

She saw him smile as he filled a hypodermic syringe and plunged it into Lark's arm, saw Lark's eyelids flutter and close, as Gruner slammed down the lid on the coffin-like box and fastened it.

"Where is my Spear?" he asked calmly. "I assume you would like to tell me now?"

Cait tore her eyes from the horrific box and focused on Gruner. "You sick filthy son of a bitch!" she croaked, her throat raw from screaming and thick with tears. "Don't do this! I'm begging you! No human being could do such a thing to a child!"

Gruner pondered that for a moment. He had always been particularly excited by the anguish of mothers and children in mutual distress. He'd never really been certain why that particular cruelty pleased him more than all the others, his own mother had adored him, after all. He'd despised her for it, of course, perhaps that was it. Not that the reasons mattered. It just would have been interesting to know his own motivation.

"Let me tell you exactly what will transpire now, Doctor Monahan," he said, seemingly energized by what was happening, his cold eyes glittering unnaturally as a cobra's.

"There is exactly one hour of air in that box. I have given instructions that it be buried in the woods beyond my home. There are over two hundred acres of woodland on this estate, so do not imagine you will find her without my help, even *if* you were somehow able to overcome me and my guards, which is highly improbable.

"I will continue to question you during this hour. If I receive the answers I wish to have, the child will be freed before she dies of suffocation or fright. But you should be made aware that the drug she has received will wear off in half that time, and as she will be terrified and will fight and cry and scream as children do, she will use up what little oxygen is left more rapidly. You are a physician, you understand the process. I should tell you we were able to ascertain that her worst fear is that of being trapped alone in the dark where you cannot find her. And that since your husband's funeral, she has been haunted by the idea of his being buried beneath the ground."

Cait's mind was reeling, the bile in her throat was threatening to make her vomit. Fury at his sadism, and abject terror for Lark made it almost impossible for her to think at all. Maybe the others would come in time... maybe her plan would work... maybe God would intervene... a kaleidoscope of maybes raced through her in a chaotic jumble, but she knew they were only the desperate fantasies of a mother who had failed to save her child. Her heart was racing so fast and hard she could barely breathe and she had to struggle not to pass out.

Gruner motioned to the men to remove the box. As they did so, he set a timer on the table in front of her.

"We have somewhat less than an hour, doctor," he said briskly. "Shall we begin again?"

160

Gruner watched implacably, as Cait shrieked and cursed and flailed against her bonds then, when she seemed to have exhausted herself, he tapped the timer and the realization of its inexorable movement snapped her back into some semblance of rational thought. With it came a hatred so intense she could barely contain it.

She had to goad him, had to instigate his fury bit by bit, until he could not control it, while she herself appeared to sink deeper and deeper into the helpless victimhood he got off on.

Gruner enjoyed tormenting his victims psychologically even more than he enjoyed inflicting pain, *that* was in every dossier she'd read. *He has to believe he's defeating me – so close to the truth.*

At the twelve minute mark, Cait began to sob and beg for Lark's life again, the hopelessness she exuded so raw, Gruner could not doubt the sincerity of her suffering. Her plan seemed so pathetic to her now. But it was all she had.

At the fourteen minute mark, he hit her so hard across the face her head felt it had exploded. She thought he might have dislocated her jaw. Then he hit her again and again and again, until she lost consciousness for six very precious minutes.

161

Fritz watched the scene with an almost sexual excitement rising along with the anticipation. He would make no further move until he saw which way this would unfold, but all the pieces were now in place. He did a careful mental checklist. He had armed himself and had warned the guards that this was the night when they would earn the money he'd paid them. There might need to be an electrical problem that short circuited the alarm system. Bonuses could be expected if they did exactly as instructed, no questions asked once he gave the word. Only one dog, König, his father's favorite, was to be loosed exactly 20 minutes after his father left the house. He smiled, remembering that he'd suggested the one dog idea to his father earlier. *After all*, he'd said, *this woman is such easy prey, you don't want the entire hunt to be over in minutes, do you?* And his father had so easily agreed.

No one, absolutely no one, was to enter the woods until he'd given the 'all clear' signal, as his father had plans to practice his night hunting skills and did not wish distraction of any kind. Fritz would not be part of the hunt, but would follow his father at a discreet distance, waiting for the precise moment for the *accident* to happen. A car and driver were to be waiting for him, to take him to the G5.

Satisfied that he'd covered all bases, Fritz, on high alert, determined the whereabouts of each member of the household staff. Only two concerned him at all. Hans Kolb and Marta. Each would most likely die tonight.

162

Marta had watched the woman arrive – she was pretty but haggard-looking. Her hair, which could have been nice, was tied up in a careless knot at the back of her head, tendrils falling willy-nilly.

This was the mother of the captive child, Fritz had said, which explained her condition and demeanor. He was being uncharacteristically forthcoming with her tonight, which put Marta's self-protective instincts on high-alert. He'd ordered her to remain dressed in street clothes after her shift was done, as he might require her services, possibly to convey a message to the guardhouse for him, at some point in the evening. He'd even given her the names of the two guards who were on his payroll and could be relied on.

Fritz was inordinately keyed up, like a man on cocaine, and when she'd pressed him for specific details, instead of rebuking her, he'd said he intended to leave tonight and take her with him. He'd told her to pack her things for a journey. She assumed this meant that whatever it was she would witness, would mean he'd have to kill her. Or try to.

Marta pulled on her jeans and sweater, and waited for the moment when she could make her move. The staff had been ordered to remain in their rooms after dinner and under no circumstances was anyone to leave the house. Herr Doctor Gruner was planning a night hunting party, testing new equipment, and it would be dangerous for anyone not so equipped to be in the vicinity of the woods.

Marta intended to seize the moment to get into Gruner's study, or Fritz's, but first she'd have to find out if the Stasi was in the house or in the woods.

163

The anesthetic had worn off in minutes and Lark had awakened, trapped in terrible darkness. She'd shrieked and cried and fought against the restraints that held her until she had no more strength to do anything but die.

And then the strangest thing had happened. Everything had slipped away quietly into the darkness, so that even the fear now seemed somehow far away.

Lark twirled around and around in her mind as though a sine curve was enticing her to follow it. *Round and round... up and down, up and down... twirling and twirling... never stopping...*

She drifted in a near catatonic state, a place of safety her mind had found when the final horror had set in and everything inside her head had exploded. She thought it might be the place where the "other" Lark – her Secret Self – lived when she wasn't needed. Some part of her knew she was dying and Mommy couldn't save her now. But another part of her had pushed all that back and back and back... until it was far enough away so it couldn't touch her anymore. Couldn't make her heart break any more. Absently, she wondered why nobody ever told you that your heart could break over and over again and never stop breaking.

She was drifting in the darkness and things were drifting with her. Numbers were everywhere. Formulas. Equations. Words. Thoughts. Rhymes.

Where Care commenced
Is minus one...

Floated with her...

The game is long
The road is steep...

Without meaning to she began to recite the clues in her head, a mantra that would help keep everything else far, far away, while she drifted. After that she thought vaguely, she would say an Our Father, a Hail Mary and an Act of Contrition. She thought maybe that's what people did when they were going to die, but even that seemed unimportant to her now.

Soon she knew what all the clues meant and that she'd been right about where the Spear was. Daddy had told her in the clues, but she just hadn't understood everything before. After he came to get her, she'd be able to talk with him about it. The Spear didn't matter anymore, but being with her Daddy mattered more than everything else in the world. She could almost feel him coming toward her in the darkness she floated in. He would find her... she knew he would... and she would tell him all she'd figured out and he would be so proud of her...

Where Care commenced
Is minus one
Justice dispensed
'til time is done.

That one was easy. Care commenced when they hid the Spear. Uncle Tony said there had been four men, but only three were in the game.

The game is long
The road is steep
A promise strong
Is yours to keep

That was just a fluff clue – of course it was hers to keep. Who else?

The trials once passed
The Feathers furled

The secret solved
Can save the world

The feathers belonged to the angel! The secret was supposed to keep everybody safe. Even if it didn't do such a good job of that, really...

His greaves are gold
His heart is fire
His power holds
Eternal ire.

She should have understood because of the greaves. Archangels were warriors, and Michael was the fiery one. And he was always mad at Lucifer. It said so in the Bible.

The Place is near
The Guardian far
His home beyond
A distant star

Michael lived in heaven, but the hiding place was really in Greenwich all the time.

An icon stands
The truth to cloak
The secret rests
Within the Oak.

The cemetery was called Oakbridge. That's where the Michael statue was.

The answer lies
Within a stone
It can be prized

By you alone.

They'd built it into the statue so nobody could get it out. Kind of like Excalibur...

Good night, my child
I tuck you in
With every wile
You need to win.

It was all about Daddy tucking her in at night, because that's when he always told her about the angel.

The Clues are done
The talent shows
But you're the only
One who knows.

And it was true. Nobody else knew what daddy always said to her when he tucked her in. Not even Mommy knew about that.
It was the bedtime ritual that held the secret... she knew that now.

Go back to One
And think it through
Good-night my love
The Game is You.

Of course! The game was *her* game! Wasn't it called Lark... Lark... *Lark*...

164

The two men carrying the box with Lark in it trudged across the frozen acreage. They'd stopped to get warmer clothes and flashlights. The hole they'd dug earlier was far behind the house, deep into the wooded acreage. They lowered the box into the ground and retrieved the shovels they'd left there hours before.

The shorter one spoke first, his words carried on the crisp cold air. "This sucks, Arnie, ya know what I mean!" he said, blowing on his fingers to warm them. "I didn't sign up to bury no kid. And she ain't even dead yet! That's fucked up, man!"

The taller, broader one looked around to make sure they weren't overheard and their two-ways weren't on *send*. "Yeah, Joey, well she'll be dead soon enough, and besides, there's no choice. If we don't do what we're told, we'll be the ones in the box."

The short one shook his head, and blew on his hands again, stomping his feet against the cold and his own agitation. "Yeah, well I don't really give a fuck, Arnie. This ain't like killin' ragheads in Kabul. This is New-fucking-York and I didn't sign up to bury no kid alive. The old guy is one sick son of a bitch, ya know... this ain't right. Maybe we could tell Fritz..."

"Yeah, right!" Arnie said with a snort. "He already knows, and he's fine with it. I don't think he even likes the kid. So maybe you should just let me do it, if you're too much of a pussy."

Vincenzo listened to the sounds of the dirt falling on the small coffin in which the child lay. He would use the dog tranquilizer on the small one, to reward him for his compassion. As to the tall one... he would cut his throat. It would be quieter than the gun. *Bastardo!* So, willing to kill a child in this terrible way? But first, he would make certain this one had time to think of his sins on his way to Hell.

—————————— **165** ——————————

Anthony Lord Delafield dozed in his chair as Prince Siegfried shook his shoulder. He'd have to tell him about the call he'd received on the Inner Planes. It had been clear but curious. He hadn't recognized the small woman with the big auric field, who had stood in full ceremonial regalia at the gate of the Temple of Light, urgently calling his name, but he knew the danger was imminent.

"We must go to the chamber, Tony," he urged, as his cousin stared up at him, blinking. "We've been called."

Delafield shook the sleep from his consciousness, and rose from the chair. "No need to explain," he said, "I saw her in my dream, too. But I couldn't hear what was said."

The two elderly men made their way to the ceremonial chamber, pausing only long enough to open the wardings that guarded the entrance, and then reseal them, once they were inside the antechamber where they robed for ceremony.

"The woman is as yet in the physical world," Siegfried said. "A stranger to me, an American, but most assuredly an Adept. She knew her way about on the Inner Planes. Not one of ours, but certainly of the Light. She presented the Sigil of the Great Mother, and the Guardian immediately lowered his sword, so she could cross the Temple Gate."

"I saw as much," said Delafield, "curious indeed. What did she have to say?"

Siegfried knotted the Cord of Office about the waist of his robe, and looked up. "She said she'd been called to the game by one who cares deeply for Cait and Lark, so she'd therefore asked her own Guides and Guardians in the Light to monitor Cait's journey – yes, she knew all about the Spear – and to be alerted when a serious threat loomed. She said she'd been told in a dream that the danger had radically escalated because of the interference of Magic wielded by a powerful Black Adept, and that we needed to help level the playing field."

"By neutralizing the Adept?" Delafield asked with concern.

"No," Siegfried said, "by neutralizing the field itself, so Magic is removed from the board – theirs and ours. She said the adversaries have used blood sacrifice to control the forcefield. What we need do is back them off long enough for Cait to use her own resources of mind and body."

"The Test of the Abyss for Cait, then?" Delafield asked.

"It would seem so. I wish there'd been time for her Initiation into the Greater Mysteries – she would have more resources at her disposal..." Siegfried began worriedly.

"No," Delafield countered. "She has us. It will be enough. Did you believe this woman...?"

Siegfried stopped the question. "I confirmed it with the Master, before waking you."

Delafield nodded. "Then let us gather our forces and proceed to shut down their power grid."

The two men made the sign required of the Adepti, as they reached the larger chamber beyond, pausing reverently to make obeisance before entering the sacred space. Each was garbed in robes of white, with sigils in silver and gold embroidered on their ceremonial chasubles. An exquisite ancient gem-studded torq hung from Delafield's neck, and a golden breastplate, filled with precious and semi-precious stones covered the front of Siegfried's robe.

They wore identical emerald rings – arcane talismanic sigils, visibly engraved as intaglios.   Each now touched these rings reverently to his lips, heart and third eye, before entering the great sigil-laden circle that dominated the center of the room. Delafield lit the elaborately anointed white candles he had carried with him into the circle, positioning one at each of the four compass points that marked the realms of the Keepers of the Watchtowers of Creation. North, South, East, West. As he lit each candle he uttered a prayer, asking the archangels to hold the Light against all attack. Von Hochburg approached the sacred and eternal flame that burned in the circle's center, sprinkling incense over its intense blue violet flame. As the scent of Cinnamon, Myrrh and Sandalwood filled the ceremonial chamber each man took his accustomed place, and turned the eye of his soul inward to its Source, open to whatever form the answers to his questions would take.

The marble walls and ceiling seemed to dissolve around them, revealing a vast canopy of stars. They felt themselves transported through this to the Void and then farther on to a golden plane, beyond which a vast white marble temple was visible.

Prince Siegfried lifted his head and intoned with resonant authority:

"Immortal, Eternal, Ineffable and Uncreated Father/ Mother of All. Ruler over the Etherial Vastness, where the Throne of thy Powers is raised, from the summit of which thine eyes behold all; and thy pure and holy ears hear all, help us, thy children, whom thou hast loved since the birth of the ages of time.

"I, Siegfried, Master of the Hunt, ask that we may petition thy mercy for one of our number who is sorely besieged by the Darkness."

A vast Presence shimmered into visibility, within the immense incorporeal Temple, itself. The Presence appeared as a mighty column of iridescent pulsing light, waves and particles and dancing molecules so powerful its radiance seemed capable of shattering Creation.

"We give you leave to assemble your Huntsmen," said an authoritative voice from the Light.

Siegfried bowed low toward the Shimmering Light, then rising, spoke again:

"I, Siegfried, Master of the Hunt, summon all servants of the Light who have pledged their spirits to the performance of The Great Work, to attend this most sacred ceremony. Let all who have been called to serve the Light as Friends of the Hunt come now to the Temple."

On the Temple steps, a soft glow was slowly coalescing into multiple human forms, all clothed in robes of white or gold or emerald, each with a crown, or necklace or ring that seemed made of starlight adorning their persons. Hundreds of them began filing into the Temple, moving in an orderly manner toward the Great Presence, as Delafield's Light Body, no longer old, but in its eternal prime, took its place at the Prince's side and Siegfried began to address The Presence once again.

"Great One, I come before you as Master of the Hunt for our ancient Order, to present to you a petition on behalf of a candidate for Initiation, who has not yet completed her initiatory journey, yet stands at a crossroad where she must pit her life against a servant of the Dark Force far more skilled than she in the ways of Magic. She is a candidate for Huntsman, and has carried this honor in other lifetimes, but has not yet completed her training in this current incarnation. We ask most humbly that you guide us in whatever ways will be deemed appropriate within the Law, to assist her."

The voice of the Great Being was thunderous in response:

"What do you ask of us, Huntmaster? You well know the candidate must pass all tests before full access to the Light Codes can be given."

"We ask only that you even the playing field, Mighty One. Let our Adepts of the Light stand against their Adepts of the Darkness, so that this candidate and her foe meet as mere humans, the forces of High Magic held at bay, until they have played out their destinies."

The voice emanated from the great column of Light once again.

"So be it. This request is deemed just. Array your forces for the battle to come, Master of the Hunt. The Keepers of the Watchtowers will monitor the playing field. All magic will be intercepted. The test begins…"

166

Cait woke from the bizarre hallucination and tried to blink herself back into consciousness. People had been chanting in a place of brilliant light. She'd seen white robed figures, heard voices... she was going mad. She glanced at the timer, and saw only six minutes had elapsed – how could there have been time for such an elaborate dream? Trauma could cause hallucinations... that was it. Her ears were still ringing from the heavy blows. She'd lost another six minutes. It was now or never.

"If you don't know where my Spear is there's really no reason to keep you alive, is there?" Gruner was asking archly, as he swam into focus.

"Please...," she gasped, barely able to speak. "Please, I'm *begging* you, Dr. Gruner. Let me try to find my daughter. Let us die together, if nothing else. I'll do anything... tell you anything, if you'll just let me try to find her..." The sobbing that accompanied this was genuine.

Gruner looked mildly interested again.

"You have nothing to bargain with," he said, "as it seems neither of you has what I want."

"But if you just let me find her, talk to her," Cait pleaded, "maybe if we put our clues together... hers and mine... it might mean *something*..." This time she sounded just as pathetic and desperate as she felt.

Gruner pursed his lips a moment. "Have you by any chance ever read a story called, "The Dangerous Game?" he asked. "It's a favorite of mine."

Cait looked confused. "Is that the story where the man hunts his dinner guests?" she asked.

"It is," he answered, pleased by her response. "Have you ever hunted anything, Doctor Monahan?"

"No," she whispered. "I heal things, I don't kill them."

He pursed his lips. "A pity," he said, "I so enjoy a good hunt."

"What are you saying?" she blurted, pretending she was grasping at the straw. "Are you telling me you'd let me hunt for my daughter?" She hoped she sounded as horrified and incredulous as she felt, hoped she didn't betray her small elation.

"You hunt her, I hunt you," he finished with a satisfied smile. "There's only another half hour of air left in your daughter's box, doctor. And, it might be a pleasant diversion for me."

"And if I find her, will you let her live?" Cait pleaded. "Please, I'm begging you, Dr. Gruner. I'll do *anything* you say..."

"I will," he interrupted her pathetic rant. "High stakes make a better game."

167

Fritz watched through the two-way glass and smiled. His father was going to hunt the woman down before he tortured and killed her. Burying the child had been an exquisite torment. Of course she would agree to the hunt. What choice did she have? Not that it would do her any good. He'd witnessed similar debacles. First, his father would exhaust her while she still held out hope, then he would torture the truth out of her, before he killed her child before her eyes and then disposed of both.

His father hadn't staged one of his human hunts in years, but the temptation with this particular woman and child had been just too much for him to resist. And she had been so perfect in her supplication, so brave at first and then so despicably pathetic. He'd almost wondered who was playing whom, as he'd watched the tableau, but the woman could have had no knowledge of his father's predilections, so perhaps it must have been just as it seemed. No matter. It would only make his own task easier.

Luring his father into the woods without Kolb in attendance might have been a difficult proposition without the hunt.

Fritz knew the drill was always the same: his father would give his prey a fifteen minute start, then go after her. He'd rely on his dog König to flush her out, but wouldn't have him released until she was another 10 to 15 minutes into the hunt, depending on how much of a challenge he wished to create. No matter how resourceful she was, there'd be no possibility of escape, and his father's attention would be squarely on his quarry when the accident happened. Splendid. *Absolutely splendid.*

Fritz took the cell phone from his pocket to call his man at the gatehouse with further instructions, then remembered there was no cell service in this granite tomb of a basement, so instead went in search of Marta. He would tell her what his father intended, to play on her sympathies, then he'd have her warn the men they must not interfere with whatever went on tonight, in order to protect themselves should they be questioned later. He'd have to kill her after that – she was already a liability, and that was a shame. She had undeniable talents. But the moment he had waited a lifetime for was at hand, and no sacrifice – particularly that of a slut – would be too much to ask.

168

Cait blinked back the tears that clouded her vision, and nearly fell as she was pushed out of the basement, into the icy night. Her limbs were stiff from being bound, her jaw and head were on fire, her hands and legs prickly with the pins and needles of forced inertia. Or maybe it was just the bitter cold, that hit her like an ice blanket as she stood in the dark and tried to get her bearings. *I will not pass out,* she ordered her body. *I will concentrate on breathing.*

I will make my heart stop pounding. I will think clearly... I will find Lark... I will kill the bastard.

She didn't even feel fear anymore. Just fury. Intense, white-hot, suppurating, absolutely uncontainable rage.

She had to focus it... had to use it to fuel her plan.

Cait bent over from the waist, forcing her breathing to quiet, forcing her heart beat to stop trying to burst through her chest wall. Forcing every ounce of strength and courage she had left into every cell of her body. Then she stood up, willed herself to her full height, and in the whispered hiss of a voice she'd never heard before... a voice that emanated from somewhere in the depths of her soul... she spoke her intent into the frigid night.

"I am coming for you, Gruner. I am going to *end* you! As God is my witness, *I AM COMING FOR YOU!*

Then she started to run.

169

Marta knew, after Fritz gave her the message to give the guard, that she was as good as dead. He would leave behind no witnesses to this night's work.

She checked the Glock 29, racked the slide and slipped an extra magazine into the under-side of her bra. A lot of shooters dismissed it, but she'd been trained on Desert Eagles and Colt Delta Elites, and she loved the comfort of this smaller model in her hand. It had enough stopping power to bring down a bull elephant, and these new Glocks were lighter to carry than the Delta, and so reliable you could shoot them under water if you had to.

The little .380 she'd also found in the weapons stash, went into the boot beneath her pants leg and her knife was secured in a belt sheath. This was the first time she'd armed herself since arriving in America. It made her feel better, but she still had to get safely out of the house. The servants were hiding in their rooms and only Kolb remained unaccounted for. She wondered where he had positioned himself for the night's activities.

Marta heard the baying of the Dobermans and knew the game had begun. She hesitated, deciding where to go first. Try for the documents that Gruner might have in his office? Or Fritz's laptop, which she was pretty sure she could grab and stash? Find Kolb and gut him? She was looking forward to that. But then there was the unarmed woman in the woods and the child... She sorted the possibilities fast. If Kolb was not with the doctor, he could be watching Gruner's office. Fritz's laptop was on his desk, and Kolb stayed clear of Fritz, so that was a better bet. The woman played no part in her mission, and would be nearly impossible to get to with both armed Gruners in the woods, to say nothing of the dogs. But maybe she could check the basement in case the child was there. If so, she'd let her loose, but she'd have to find Kolb first. Then she'd steal whatever documents she could carry, and make a run for it.

She was sure the guard Mike would let her out of the compound – if not, she'd escape some other way, once the mayhem in the woods had everyone's attention.

170

I have to put ground between us, Cait thought as she worked her way through the undergrowth, forcing pain and cold and everything else that wasn't essential, into the dimmest recesses of her mind, trying to keep to places where the light sprinkling of snow hadn't reached, and footprints would be harder to follow. *Have to find water to throw the dogs off the scent. There must be a stream on this much acreage. I need a weapon... speed... stealth... high ground...* she ticked off every lesson her father or Jake had ever taught her. If Gruner caught her, the game was over. And he knew these woods. She didn't.

All she wanted on this earth was to find her child. But she couldn't let the thought of her buried, into her mind now... that thought would kill her before she could find her target. *If I don't kill Gruner, he can still kill Lark.* God alone knew where he'd hidden her. *No!* That wasn't true. His men knew, and with Gruner dead, she could get help for the search. Dogs. Men and women who were professionals. Cops, FBI. There'd be no way to hide the truth then. *Hang on, baby!* she willed the thought out into the freezing air. *I will find you. I will take you home!*

A few flakes were still falling, the air was sharp, cleansed by the biting wind. She reached out with every sense, intuiting the way toward higher ground. *Always get to the high ground*, she repeated the mantra in her mind. *See what you can see.* Assess the terrain. Map it in your head. Spot landmarks. Check the position of the stars. Find a weapon. Be ready for anything. She had to find Gruner, and double back on him, before he realized her gameplan.

She had only one advantage.

The filthy son of a bitch thought *he* was the hunter.

171

Marta stuffed the laptop and whatever else looked useful into her backpack. If Fritz saw the backpack, she'd say it was part of her packing for the trip. She'd searched the basement lab for the child, and finding no one, she had placed the bag on the floor next to the cellar door and opened it carefully to get the lay of the land. If all was clear, she'd retrieve the bag and head for the wall.

"What are you doing out here?" A deep voice demanded and she froze. "You were told to stay inside." It was Kolb.

"No," she answered insolently. "Fritz gave me orders to take this note to the guards with the dogs." She held out a slip of paper.

"Why would he not call them with these orders?" he asked, suspiciously. "It is cold as a Gulag out here, and you are up to something. You will empty your pockets!"

Marta saw the man reach into his own pocket, saw the handle of the garrot before it cleared his jacket. Stasis were famous for using a handled garrot that locked into place and was impossible to break through. Screw the pretense... Her cover was blown after tonight anyway. Everything was coming apart and there could be no turning back now.

Kolb didn't expect the knife. Didn't expect she was as good with it as he was with the garrot. The stunned look on his ugly face was gratifying but she knew he wouldn't be an easy take down unless her first thrust hit something vital. The knife caught him deep in the gut, but he kept on coming, and if she hadn't gotten her thumb into his eye socket, he might have overpowered her before she could yank the knife out for a second strike. His bellow from the eye gouge was cut short by the second knife strike that put him down like a felled ox.

No one seemed to have heard the struggle. Marta dragged Kolb's heavy body into the shadows, wiped the blade on his jacket, grabbed the backpack and sprinted for the fence. She'd get to her handler and see if they could help the woman and child.

172

Cait, cold, scared, weaponless but powered by fury, stopped to get her bearings and her breath. The woods were thick with large bare trees and thick, frozen underbrush. Rocks and boulders littered the landscape. Gruner had said he'd give her a fifteen minute start – she heard dogs barking in the distance, but none seemed to be coming toward her. Of course, they were probably trained to silence until they flushed their prey.

She centered her senses and strained to listen for sounds of Gruner's movement, forced herself to remember her father's survival words. *Breathe, dammit!* she told herself. *Breathe and* **think***! You can't lose it now. You're the only chance Lark's got.*

The snapping sound said Gruner was on the move and not far behind her. How could he have covered so much ground, if he'd really given her a 15 minute head start? Cait said a silent prayer and started toward the small frozen creek she'd spotted off to her left. She glanced up at the stars, and thankful for what small sliver of moonlight there was, reminded herself to note landmarks in her mind. She looked for weapons as she ran... a stick, a sharp edged rock... there had to be *something* in these woods she could use to kill the madman who pursued her.

Countdown

Part XXII

"Sift the Twos and sift the Threes,
The Sieve of Eratosthenes,
When the multiples sublime,
The numbers that remain are Prime."

Traditional mnemonic

173

Meg leaned over and hugged Carter. Best she could figure it; they were nearly two hours behind Cait. They'd parked the car two blocks beyond the Gruner gates with Carter's old FBI ID on the dashboard. She wished they both had Kevlar vests, but asking to borrow them from Matt would have tipped their hand. She had Cait's handgun in the pocket of her camo jacket, ready to be handed off. She checked her own weapons, then slung Matilda II over her shoulder. It was the second generation cross bow she'd been using for years now, ever since Mathilda I had given up the ghost after a lifetime of faithful service. Jake had been the bowyer for both weapons.

A compound bow might have had more power and speed, but as far as Meg was concerned, nothing on earth beat a traditional bow, made by a master bowyer like Jake. Hers was Snakeskin-covered for perfect grip, handcrafted to meet her every physical and mental requirement, strung to the perfect poundage for her pull, and then hunted with so long and so lovingly the bow became another appendage. Matilda had always been the weapon she relied on in the clinches, and it was a lot quieter than a gun.

"Archery," Jake had told her a million years ago, when he'd handed her the first Matilda, "is all in the spirit... your spirit and the spirit of the bow, child. You must learn the basic skills and then you must practice, practice until they are your second nature. But then you must forget all rules, and become the bow, become the arrow, become the flight. Too much thinking will not bring down the prey. Instinct, spirit, heart... these are the allies that will bring you victory."

"We need to find Cait and get her a weapon," Meg said urgently to Carter. And we need to find Lark. She's somewhere in that house. I think we have to split up. You go to the house after Lark, I'll head for the woods to find Cait. OK with you?"

Carter's large eyes were full of troubled questions, but she'd run out of arguments. If this is what Meg had to do, she'd be there for her and the gameplan had to be Meg's, because she'd have to live with the consequences of tonight no matter which way it went. She nodded assent, then said, "Just don't give that son of a bitch the benefit of any doubts, kiddo." She wished to say so much more.

"I don't *have* any doubts about Gruner," Meg replied, meeting Carter's eyes. "But we're just here to get Cait and Lark out. Nothing else, OK?"

"You look like an Aries in that gettup," Carter said with a short forced laugh to cut the tension, as she looked her partner up and down worriedly. She'd studied hostage situations at Quantico. They never went the way you thought they would.

"All litigators are probably Aries," Meg replied. She didn't believe in astrology, but she believed in her own fighting instincts, even in this awful situation. She was at her best in a fight, always had been. But she felt heartsick, now, and she didn't know whether to hope Cait was in the house or the woods. In the house, she'd be safer, but there'd be guards. In the woods there'd be guards, dogs and Gruner. It suddenly occurred to her that the dogs were barking and agitated while they probably wouldn't be, if they were already tracking...

She took her bearings, praying she'd intuited accurately where her sister's instincts would take her. There was a hell of a lot of ground to cover if she'd guessed wrong.

174

Gruner sniffed the air like a bloodhound. Adrenaline coursed through his system, pushing his heart rate, muscles, brain to optimal performance. He was far from young, but he was fit as a man half his age, and he knew all the routes the fools always chose. The exhausted or wounded ones would stick to the low ground, picking their way desperately through the undergrowth, hoping for a cave or ravine or rock ledge to hide them. The fit and smart ones headed for higher ground, hoping for a vantage point. The idiots climbed a tree and waited, breathless with terror, until he and the dogs found them.

He'd taken two of his favorite weapons with him this evening – the Mauser 696 with its useful shoulder stock. It amused him to think both Winston Churchill and Lawrence of Arabia had chosen this masterpiece of German engineering to use in battle. And his Luger, of course. He was seldom without his favorite sidearm. He didn't intend to kill her with either one. Merely to capture and intimidate.

He'd told Fritz to wait 20 minutes before releasing König tonight. There was no point ending the fun too soon, and the dog was a superb hunter. Fritz had suggested he join the hunt, but Gruner had declined his offer. He wanted to feel the thrill of the moment himself, and had no intention of sharing it. It had been some time since he'd allowed himself the adrenaline rush of hunting a human. And this one would be more fun than most.

This one is nimble and canny he told himself as he followed Cait's trail. She was instinctively choosing the smarter routes. She'd headed for the creek to throw off the dog. Smart. So she'd spent time in the woods somewhere. *Excellent.* The tougher the quarry, the more exhilarating the hunt. He would wear her endurance thin, then sweep her into his net and drag her back for the real fun with the little girl. There was actually air enough for several hours in the box – he'd lied about that – so the child would still be alive, however barely, when he returned with her exhausted and defeated mother. Mothers and children were always the easiest to manipulate once they realized there would be no hope and no mercy.

Gruner smiled and snugged his binoculars to his face again. He'd considered taking the AN/PVS-74A infrared night vision goggles that would give him a remarkably sharp green picture of all that lay ahead, but had decided against it. His own eyes were plenty sharp enough to spot one lone woman running for her life. This was turning into a most entertaining evening and he hadn't a doubt in the world about how it would end.

175

Fritz checked his weapon expertly and slipped an extra magazine into his pocket, not that he'd need it. The gun belonged to his father, one of many in a vast collection. It was a favorite of the old man's and Fritz had chosen it precisely for the irony. If he was forced to use a gun, he would make it appear his father had died by his own hand, an unfortunate hunting accident occasioned by falling in the woods. But there were other kinds of accidents possible, too. A push down a ravine... an old man stumbling in the dark... a rock to the side of the head. Who would question the accidental death of one foolish enough to plan a night hunt at his father's age? By the time the old man was found, all trace of woman and child would have been obliterated, Marta would be dead and he would be on his G5, or better still, already at home in Germany.

Fritz smiled at the how well it was coming together.

Now the trick was to make sure his father didn't know he, too, was in the woods. Fritz thought of a line attributed to

Napoleon, and smiled. *"Never interrupt your enemy when he is making a mistake."*

He'd already given the order about when to release König and provided the dog's handler with a piece of Cait's clothing for scent. He'd delayed the dog's release an extra few minutes beyond his father's orders, to give himself a few minutes more for surveilling the scene.

176

Meg lowered herself over the wall and waited for the onslaught of the dogs, bow at the ready, swift, silent, another arm. She heard them baying, but oddly, they didn't seem to be moving. Maybe it was Gruner's habit to give his quarry a serious head start on the dogs. Or maybe they were silent while they tracked, baying only when they found their prey. She'd never hunted with Dobermans and didn't know their hunting traits – only that they'd been bred from Rottweilers and Greyhounds, so they were fast, good trackers and lethal in a take-down. Some breeds tracked and treed their quarry. Some were trained to threaten or attack. Some to kill.

The woods were thick with frozen, brittle trees and fallen branches. The terrain was rocky and intermittently icy underfoot, but blessedly, the snow had been so sparse it wasn't leaving easy footprints. Stealth had never been a problem for her, but over-confidence could get you killed and one slippery stone could change the night's outcome. As she tracked, Meg mentally reviewed the way it would go, the mechanical processing of data that could then be discarded so that instinct could take over.

Trusting her skills, Meg moved toward the rock outcrop she'd spotted on the aerial map. *That's* where Cait would go. The place their father and Jake would have picked to get the lay of the land.

Cait would follow the water to avoid the dogs, and head for that rise to assess, then she'd backtrack, so she could attempt to take the man who was hunting her, by surprise. But where the fuck was Gruner?

Meg picked her way soundlessly across the frozen ground, listening, smelling, sensing every nuance of the woods around her. Creaking tree limbs, thick with frost, creatures skittering to a burrow, night sounds, owl hoots, twig snaps... everything that belonged to the natural order. Anything that didn't.

Minutes in, she picked up both trails, Cait's and Gruner. He was not far behind her sister, but her gut told Meg that Cait was already doubling back. It was her only hope... she would know she couldn't outrun him and the dogs. Gruner knew these woods and Cait was unarmed and alone.

Got to get the gun to her. Got to give her a fighting chance. She can't take him down without a weapon. Meg thought about Carter going alone after Lark and shuddered inwardly. If anything happened to Cart... *No!* She couldn't let fear in now. Fear would slow her down and screw up her focus... *Set your course, then go with it. Never second guess your gut.*

Meg set out in the direction she'd chosen, following tracks where she could and looking for shortcuts to where she needed to get to. She moved through the woods as if born three, but Cait left tracks. At that moment, that was both the good news and the bad news.

Five minutes later Meg was near her intended destination, and still had seen no sign of dogs. She needed more intel, needed to scope out who and what were where, and see if she could spot any canines in the frozen brush. The great hunting breeds ran silent as the grave until the moment they had you cornered.

Meg found the tree she needed and boosted herself into a low hanging branch as gingerly as possible. Brittle branch snaps would alert Gruner, dogs, or both. But she needed a vantage point now... needed to know if she'd guessed right and how much time she had to prepare. She'd spent a lot of time in trees waiting to spot prey, still as a limb, watchful as a hawk. Now, she needed to get a bead on her sister or Gruner or both and was settling into her careful perch when a tiny sound snapped her head around, and she saw the large dark-coated dog tunneling through the frozen undergrowth with the stealth and speed of a panther. A Doberman, silent, fast, fierce. A silent tracker and he had Cait's scent. She looked around frantically to see exactly where the dog's trajectory was taking him. Suddenly, Cait was dead ahead at 50 yards. Meg saw her sister turn at the cracked twig sound of the dog behind her just as the animal torpedoed toward her. She saw the hurtling Doberman leap for her sister's throat, 100 pounds of perfect predator. He would hit Cait with the impact of a freight train, sending her sprawling, then rip out her throat while she was down and helpless.

The bow was in Meg's hands without conscious thought. Weight, pull, feel so hers it needed no conscious thought at all, but the dog was fast and far, she had to kill him without killing Cait. *Full draw, full draw, solid anchor, pick a spot, pick a spot* and then the rules were gone, and there was no time to move or miss or think. No time for nerves or fear or intervening branches. Meg ceased to breathe and the arrow flew.

It skewered the dog in mid-flight, his single yelping cry was only for a heartbeat, and was followed by the sound of his dead weight falling to the ground at Cait's feet. He didn't move or moan.

Meg slid from the tree. "It's me, Cait!" she hissed in a desperate whisper racing toward her sister. "He's right behind you."

They flung their arms around each other for a nanosecond, then broke free feverishly looking behind them.

"I knew it was you! That unbelievable perfect shot..." Cait breathed. "I knew you'd come. Have you got a gun for me?"

Meg nodded, pressing it into her hand, "It's yours."

Cait grabbed the weapon, saw it was locked and loaded, shoved it into the back of her waistband. Her own .45 in her hand felt like salvation.

"You've got to go after Lark, Meg!" she whispered urgently. "He put her in a coffin and two men took her out to bury her somewhere on the estate. There's only a little air left. You've got to find her!"

"Sweet Jesus!" Meg gasped. "Any idea which way they went? Carter's gone to the house... we didn't know if you were in or out."

"Please!" Cait begged. "You've got to find Lark. I'll go after Gruner. Is Matt here, too?"

Meg shook her head. "He's got a team for tomorrow night, but I was afraid it would be too late. It's just me and Carter."

"Please, Meggie," Cait pleaded, "if you both look for Lark you may get to her in time! I'll get Gruner. If one of us gets out of here alive we can get help for Lark!"

"I've got a map," Meg said, shoving the crumpled aerial map at her sister. "We're *here*. The house is here..."

Cait stared at the map, closed her eyes, said a desperate prayer for guidance, then opened them and pointed to a spot in the northeast sector of the property. "Start here," she said urgently. "She's somewhere really close to here... don't ask me how I know!"

"OK," Meg said, "We'll find her, I promise you. Just promise me you'll stay out of Gruner's way.

"I'm *not* staying out of his way," Cait hissed. "I'm going to kill the filthy son of a bitch. You don't know what he did to her!"

Met thought her sister looked like she'd gone over the edge.

"We have to move, Cait. *Now.*" she said. "But you've got ot stay alive! So stay the fuck out of Gruner's way!"

"He's coming... I feel him! I love you, Meg."

Meg reached for her sister's hand, but Cait was already in motion.

177

Gruner's head whipped toward the sound of the dog's yelp. *Could that be König? No! That is not the direction the woman is running in.* He waited, taking stock for a moment, then detoured slightly to the left and regretting now that he'd left the NVG's behind, lifted his binocs to his eyes. He thought he'd spotted someone moving, but in the opposite direction to where Cait was going. Maybe an animal.

Could it be that his hunting instinct was off? That had *never* happened before. And where was his dog? König should have her run to ground by now. Damn Fritz! He'd probably been angry that he'd been left out of the hunt. He probably had not released the dog, as he'd been told to. How like him to be petty in his retaliation. Or perhaps, he'd gotten distracted by that slut he was bedding.

"Don't move!" a fierce female voice behind him ordered, and Gruner froze. It was *not* possible she was *behind* him. And *that* voice could not come from the terrified woman he had bested in the basement.

"Where is my daughter?" the words were deliberate, glacial.

"She's dead by now," he said evenly, without turning to face her. He knew she was unarmed, but that was no reason not to carefully remove his own pistol from its holster before turning to look her in the eye.

"Then there's no reason to keep you alive, is there?" the voice, still behind him, said and something in its tone made Gruner whip around, weapon raised. He swung the gun toward Cait just a fraction too late.

178

Vincenzo carried the sobbing child close to his heart. Her head was cradled on his left shoulder, his left arm holding her, so his right was free to shoot anyone in their path. His blood was up now. He had decided what to do after freeing the nearly comatose child from the makeshift grave. He would return her to her mother, and kill anyone who got in the way of that. He could feel her pitiful sobs through his coat now, and her breath gasping as if she couldn't get enough air. He tried to speak words of comfort to her but his English was somewhat limited, so he just kept saying over and over, "Mama dottore. We go to Mama dottore. Everything gonna be OK now."

"Put her down!" the order came obliquely from Vincenzo's left and slightly behind him. He would have killed the woman where she stood except that the child screamed, "Aunt Meggie, *no!* He saved me! He saved me!"

That was when they heard the gunshot.

179

Marta headed for the periphery of the estate as quickly and stealthily as she could. She knew now that Fritz had ordered the security men to stand down, and to keep the dogs except for Gruner's pet hunter in the kennels, no matter what happened. That could mean only one thing. Fritz would kill his father tonight, somewhere in the dense woods so the old man wouldn't be found immediately. Her own cover was blown but she had the laptop and all the papers she'd been able to swoop up from Gruner's desk and office. There'd been no time for the safe.

She'd have to count on everyone's attention being elsewhere to get the hell out of hell. She was armed and dressed warmly. Once she made it off the grounds, her handlers would find her and decide what to do next. She hoped they'd let her go back to help the woman and child.

Marta heard the crack of the gunshot just as she reached the road. She wished to God she knew which one of them had been killed.

180

Fritz stared as his father's body crumpled to the frozen ground. He'd been just minutes behind the old hunter and had seen the dog rush to the scent. And then this... Where had that woman gotten a gun? How was *this* even possible? He watched the blood trickle down the old man's face, and for the briefest of moments admired her shooting.

Then the full impact of what had just transpired hit him, and the elation of what it meant. His father was dead. Absolutely, unequivocally dead, and he was *free, free at last!* And she had saved him from even dirtying his hands. Fritz turned quickly and retreated toward the house, nearly giddy with the full excitement of the moment.

Maybe he wouldn't wait to kill Marta after all. Maybe he would simply board the waiting jet and leave. Why wait for Marta's death or Kolb's interference or anything else that could delay him in case some neighbor had heard the gunfire?

At the waiting car Fritz handed an envelope to the driver and they were out of the grounds and on their way to Westchester's private airfield before the first police cars were anywhere near the Gruner estate.

Fritz had just become one of the richest men on earth. His heart was pounding so thunderously he could barely breathe, but nonetheless he started laughing. First it was just a short nearly inaudible chuckle but then as all the bonds that had contained and distorted him were torn asunder a kind of laughter he had never before experienced burst from him in peal after peal of pure joy.

The driver was unnerved by the sound but kept his eyes on the road. The money in the envelope more than paid for driving a lunatic to an airport.

181

"I killed him," Cait's voice was a weird breathy monotone. "I shot him and he's dead."

"Shut up, Cait!" Meg screamed at her sister from six feet away. *"Not another word,* do you hear me?" The gunshot had caused the security guards to call in local backup, orders or no orders. Official vehicles jammed the driveway and colored lights seemed to be flashing neon reds and blues in every direction as if a carnival had come to town.

"No!" Cait shouted back. "No more lies, Meg. I want to tell the world what he was. He was a vicious animal and I'm glad I put him down!"

Meg wanted to strangle her sister and hug her simultaneously. Instead, she turned on the big cop nearest Cait.

"Officer," she shouted, "you *never* heard that! My client is in shock and she's been instructed by her attorney not to say another word, do you understand me?"

The cop seemed pained by the desperation he heard in both women's voices, but determined. The redhead was obviously deranged. "Look Counselor, I don't know exactly what went down here tonight," he said, "but I know what I heard. I gotta take her into custody. And by the way, what's with the camouflage get-up and that *thing* you got on your shoulder, it looks to me like maybe they should be taking you in, too," He glanced at the bow and quiver, but Meg stared him down.

By the time Matt and Croce reached the estate, the pandemonium was intense. A Crown Vic had pulled up and two detectives were exiting, an M.E. Van nestled in behind it, illuminated by the flashers on a half dozen black and whites. The Security Company alarm truck was somewhere in the melee and two overcoated Alarm Company execs were trying unsuccessfully to get their two cents in.

"Hey, O'Keefe!" a strong male voice cut through the clutter of sounds and Meg's head went up. It was Matt.

The lead detective looked up, saw Matt and smirked. "What the hell are you doing here, McCormack? Isn't this a little north of your jurisdiction?"

"I got a couple of friends here, Jimmy," Matt said. "It's a real long story..."

O'Keefe looked skeptical. "Yeah, I'll bet! And you just happened to be in the neighborhood at the exact right time to help your friends with the murder, maybe?"

"Murder?" Matt asked incredulously. "What murder?" He looked around, caught Meg's eye and saw the warning glance. "What the hell's going on here, Jimmy?"

"Look, McCormack," the detective said, "I like you, but I gotta do my job and you know I can't tell you nothin' til I know somethin', right? So why don't you just run along home and I'll call you if I need some big city backup. Howsat sound to you?"

"Come on O'Keefe, what're you scared of?" Matt was trying to keep his voice amiable, "Cop to cop... who's the stiff? Anybody I know?"

O'Keefe chuckled. "Not a chance of that, *compadre*. This one's a Big Fish... the kind that swims in International waters. We're waitin' on the Feds, so it's gonna be a long night.

"And we got somebody from Child Services coming, too," he said as an afterthought. "There's some little kid here who's pretty shook up, but we're not sure yet what she has to do with all this shit." He inclined his head toward the back of an EMT truck where Lark was being examined by the medical personnel.

"Look, Mike," Matt said urgently, "screw Child Services! I know the kid *and* the mother – her aunt's standing right over there. You don't need child services for Christsakes. I can take her home with me 'til we figure out what's going on here..."

O'Keefe cocked an eyebrow at him.

"*That* kind of friend, huh. And no, you ain't takin' nobody nowhere, *capisce?* You are just going to get yourself out of my crime scene, McCormack. And you can take Croce with you," he tipped his head toward where Croce stood near the EMTs. "And don't think I ain't noticed the two of you are dressed up like a pair of Ninjas. I don't suppose there's any possibility you were anywhere near this estate when *whatever* went down tonight?" He ended the thought on a questioning note then continued, "'cause if you were, you'd be accessories before the fact, wouldn't you? and you might even be able to shed a little light on what's what here? Am I wrong about that?"

Meg had joined the men. "They've Mirandized Cait and they're talking about taking Lark to protective services," she said to Matt without preamble. "I need to give them my bona fides, so they'll let her come home with me, then see about the arraignment and bail."

"I wouldn't count on bail here, if I was you, guys," O'Keefe interjected. "There's all kinds of international warrants out on this woman, and now the murder of a Big Shot international philanthropist... no judge I know is lettin' this nut job out on the street."

182

The morning after the shooting, once everything that could be done overnight had been handled, Meg Fitzgibbons sat down at the desk in her office for the very last time, and tried to calm herself and think clearly despite the fog of the awful sleepless night. Not only had she met a solid wall of resistance from the partners at the firm when she'd asked for help with securing a top flight criminal attorney to defend Cait, she'd been fired. Told to clear out her office immediately. Not a single word of sympathy, regret or understanding.

Meg knew she should have seen it coming. She should have known when she walked down the long green carpet, and every eye in every cubicle, office or outside secretarial desk had so studiously avoided hers. But her mind had not been on anything so mundane as her job.

Meg found her hands were trembling, as she packed the box of personal belongings and tried to control both her fury about how this had been handled, and her fear for Cait. They'd sent a security guard with her to make sure she took no files.

An envelope from the ADL was sitting on top of a mess of interoffice memos that had been in her in-box, memos that would now, never need to be answered. She lifted the envelope, with the words *Personal & Confidential* stamped in big black letters on the front. She called to the security guard to take a look.

"Do you want to read what's in this... its personal?" she offered, but the guard, somewhat embarrassed by his assignment shook his head no. He'd known Meg to be a nice lady all the time she'd worked here. Always a cheery good morning to the guys on duty, unlike a lot of the stuck-up WASP lawyer types. "They said if it's personal you can take it with you, Ms. Fitzgibbons," he answered. "That says it's personal, so it's OK by me."

"Thanks, Jimmy," she said and put the envelope in her handbag, then stood up, looked around one last time, and headed for the elevator.

As she exited the building, she tore the envelope open. Maybe the woman at the Anti Defamation League could recommend a heavy hitter defense attorney – one who would understand the special circumstances of Cait's case. It was worth a shot.

Meg pulled out the sheaf of papers that accompanied the original Hebrew document, and read the handwritten note on top. In very large scrawling script, it said simply:

Call me. There is more you must know.

A signature that looked like Miriam Leventhal, was scribbled across the page followed by several phone numbers, home, office, cell.

Intrigued by the peremptory message, and needing to do something to calm her overwrought emotions, Meg walked across the street to the little park, sat down on a bench and started to read the translation. It didn't take more than a minute or two before the words on the pages became blurred by her tears.

She finished reading rapidly, and thought for a moment about next moves. Then she stuffed the papers and envelope into her handbag, picked up the box of her belongings and hailed a cab to take her to Miriam Levanthal's office.

Lincoln's Law

Part XXIII

"De minimis non curat lex."
The Law is not concerned with trifles.
Legal Maxim

—————— **183** ——————

The woman at the ADL was deep into middle age and took no pains to hide it. She had pepper and salt hair, a strong face with a pugnacious jaw, and the kindest, most compassionate eyes Meg had seen since her father's.

"Miriam Leventhal," she said extending her firm hand, as Meg entered her paper strewn office. The file cabinets looked old enough to have come with the ark and the no frills office made Meg's former space at Kramer Crowley Crookfield look like something out of Architectural Digest. Meg sat down on the small upholstered chair from which Miriam had cleared a stack of law books.

"I don't know whether to offer my condolences on the plight of your sister, or say *mazeltov* that she had the privilege of executing that old Nazi," she said it in a voice that could have been offering Meg another piece of strudel. There was the faintest accent, but well overlain with American cadence.

"I appreciate your seeing me, Miriam. I came as soon as I could. I'm trying to get my sister out of jail, deal with my niece's trauma, trying to figure out whose jurisdiction this will be tried in, Westchester or Federal. My law firm just fired me, and I've got to find a really good criminal lawyer for Cait..." she ran out of steam and was surprised to see the woman smiling at her in a maternal sort of way.

"All this I know," she said, "and we will help you."

Meg's eyes met hers. "Who is *we*?" she asked.

The woman smiled again. "The ADL, the Wiesenthal Center, men like our friend, Weiss, others who care deeply. We will help you." She paused a moment to let that sink in, then continued.

"This will not be easy, you understand. There are many arrayed against you and your sister. I know something about what's happened, although I'm anxious to hear your account of it. But there is no time to lose – we must work quickly. The Westchester DA could get re-elected on such a high profile murder case, if he wins it. The CIA is involved and now the FBI is making noises so as not to get left out. The case may be remanded to Federal Court, in which case you and your sister are in for an even rougher ride. And then there is the matter of the diplomatic immunity, the UN, and the President..."

"Tell me something I don't know," Meg said, feeling the full weight of the legal system and her exhaustion pressing in on her, and knowing full well the power that could be brought to bear in such a high profile case.

Miriam chuckled. "But of course telling you what you *don't* know is my plan," she said. "That is why I asked you to come. There is much that we know of Herr Dr. Gruner that we could not use until now."

She pulled a rolling file toward her and waved her hand over it to say it contained only Gruner files. "There are many more," she said, "but let us begin with these..."

184

Carter pulled out an old textbook she hadn't looked at since law school. She needed to refresh her memory about the order of all the steps that would happen next. A homicide investigation and trial made for a grim, long haul and this one was so fucking complicated by the media, the high profile victim, Cait's confession... She sighed and opened to the page she sought, then groaned at the length of the chapter. So very many steps where something could go very, very wrong.

The simple legal definition of homicide was 'the killing of one person by another.' Whether it was intentional, accidental, justifiable – those issues were not taken into account until later. Excusable homicide, justifiable homicide – these were the definitions that kept law students up nights researching precedents. And were there witnesses to what had gone down? Maybe the son who had already hightailed it back to Germany, and claimed not to have seen anything, an Israeli operative who was in the country illegally and had disappeared like smoke, an Italian assassin, who seemed to have melted after saving Lark, a child who'd been drugged and nearly buried alive, who'd be assumed too traumatized to be viable as a witness. And a distraught gun-wielding woman who had been only too eager to confess.

And then the legal process itself was odious and interminable, humiliating and spiritually devastating. To say nothing of dangerous. The Grand Jury, the Indictment, the Trial... dear God, the thought of Cait and Meg going through all that for having rid the earth of scum like Gruner, was enough to make her want to put her fist through a wall.

She hoped to God the woman at the ADL had some hot shot criminal attorney up her sleeve for Meg, because from what she'd read in this morning's *New York Times,* the forces of evil were all lining up at the plate to get a crack at this ball.

She and Meg and Matt and their tiny band of allies had a lot of work to do, very, very fast.

185

The New York to Washington shuttle touched down at Dulles and Meg hurried from the plane, her briefcase clutched in her hand. She was afraid the Homeland Security guy, Thornby, might have sent his storm troopers to pick her up, so Carter was traveling to DC by car at the same time Meg was flying there. Each had an encrypted thumb drive the boys had made in her pocket. It carried a duplicate of the Israeli documents, the story of the existence of the Gruner birth and immigration records being held in Rome, and a monumental amount of meticulously collected data from both the Anti-Defamation League files and those at the Wiesenthal Center. If Meg was intercepted, maybe Carter would get through to Tremaine. If that didn't work, Matt, Croce, Damon and Pythias each had an identical thumb drive. One of them would get to Tremaine, one to the *New York Times,* and one to the *Washington Post.*

Meg also carried in her head the self-destruct code for the computer data file. If the Feds attempted to play it without the code, it would erase itself. They had the skill to reconstruct it, of course, Pythias had told her, but between the erasure and the encryption it would take them long enough so that one of the other drives could be gotten to the media.

But none of that would happen until Meg delivered all the knowledge she carried in her head, plus all that was in her briefcase, to Lincoln Tremaine. She said a prayer and hailed a cab.

186

The old jurist held the extraordinary printout Meg had given him and intently weighed his options. He'd spent a lifetime wondering why Fate had singled him out to be one of the Spear's Caretakers. Now, he knew what was expected of him, but this was to be no easy task.

There was so much legal and illegal maneuvering already going on about this case, that he'd have to pray for guidance on this one and hope he made the right moves, and only the right moves.

The CIA was intent on covering up its complicity with Gruner and the other Nazi war criminals, and particularly determined that MK Ultra's terrible projects never come to light. Because of Gruner's prominence and diplomatic status, they had managed to get a Federal murder warrant issued for Cait, and now even Homeland Security was in on the action. The fix was very nearly at the point where it would be unstoppable. Linc silently blessed little Arnold Peabody who had unearthed Gruner's ties to Director Farnsworth, and so much more.

Lark's kidnapping had been completely covered up and a series of stories had been leaked to the media making Cait look like a nutcase vigilante, who'd mistakenly thought Gruner was involved with her husband's recent death. He'd seen these cover-ups before. By God, hadn't he witnessed what happened with the Kennedy brothers and Dr. King? If you can cover up the murder of a president and get people to believe a ridiculous lone gunman story, you could pull off anything.

He'd been around Washington long enough to know exactly how these things were done, how lives got considered suddenly expendable, how injustice could always be covered by claiming "the interest of National Security," especially since the Patriot Act and the decimation of Habeas Corpus. The bigger the lie, the more likely it was to be believed.

He was not in the least certain they could win this case, despite what he'd said to that nice young lawyer who was so desperate to save her sister. Already, it was apparent how many people saw the case as a ticket to elected office, and how much the CIA was determined to keep its secrets at any cost.

But I will give this everything I've got, he said to himself and to the Almighty, as he rose heavily from his chair. *"And I will say to the Lord, He is my refuge and my fortress... in Him I trust, and He shall deliver me..."* The words of the 91st Psalm, his grandmama's favorite, were in his head and on his lips.

"Alright then, God," Linc said out loud, standing very straight and respectful, beside his own desk and looking out the window at the sky over Washington, D.C. *"You seem to have given me this job to do, so I'm going to make the assumption You will help me see it through."* Then he walked out the door of his office.

"Letitia," he said as he reached his secretary's desk. "I have one or two things I'd like you to do for me, right away. I'd like you to call on over to Director Farnsworth at the CIA and get me an urgent meeting with the man, and I mean within the hour. Then, I'd like you to place a call to the White House, and tell them I need to speak with the President on a *most pressing matter*, later today. Can you do that for me?" He smiled at the young woman who'd been with him for just over a year now.

She looked closely at him now.

"Most pressing, Mr. Justice?" she quoted him.

He nodded. "They'd be the words I'd use, Letitia," he said, knowing he'd be in the Oval Office before the end of business.

*   *   *

There was a certain amount to be said for growing old, Tremaine thought two hours later, as he left the office of the CIA's Director. Two old men could accomplish a lot together with relatively little wasted time.

He'd known the Director for decades, never as a friend, but long enough and well enough for each of them to know that this conversation, which neither would ever admit had taken place, had the power to alter the future of a good many lives and had better be taken seriously.

Lincoln told Farnsworth enough of what he knew, to get the man's full attention. Then he'd told him exactly what he wanted. There'd been no need for threats. When you were this old, and had spent your life in the service of your country as each of them had, you knew what had to be done here, and exactly what it would cost you. You knew what was right and what was wrong, because you'd lived through enough of both.

Now it would be up to the Director to decide if at his age he could afford one more terrible sin on his already overburdened conscience. As Tremaine left he told Farnsworth his next call would be on the President.

— 187 —

President R.J. Dandridge looked up as Justice Tremaine entered the Oval, then he rose from behind his desk and came forward to shake hands with the old man. They'd been on opposite sides of a great many issues. Their politics were markedly different, their political parties were different, and their approach to matters pertaining to the Constitution were different, but that didn't mean he didn't admire the old jurist's knowledge, and his unwavering sense of fair play, legendary in a city that seldom played fair.

President Dandridge gestured toward the two sofas that faced each other, and waited for Tremaine to take a seat. He saw the man hesitate before doing so, and wondered why he would have preferred to stand. This was obviously not a social call.

"I believe you have a pressing matter on your mind, Lincoln," the President prompted. "You don't often make this kind of request... so, what exactly is this visit about?"

Tremaine's voice was clear and steady.

"Thank you, sir, for seeing me on such short notice," he began. "I'm certain you are well aware of the media circus in New York about the death of Gustav Gruner, sir? I'm here because I have relevant facts about it at my disposal that I believe you will want to know."

Dandridge laughed shortly. "Well, you'd be wrong about that, Mr. Justice," he answered. "I believe that whole mess is being handled very expeditiously by nearly everybody in law enforcement in New York and D.C. It seems that by now, the PD, NSA, CIA all have their fingers in that particular pie, to say nothing of the media circus, as you point out... So no, I do not wish to touch that mess with a ten foot pole."

"Would I be right in assuming, sir, that the Director has briefed you about the fact that all this began because of the theft of a religious artifact by four men who were in General Patton's command?"

"Yes, yes," the President responded with exasperation. "I know all about the fact that the woman claims this Spear of Longinus was at the bottom of all this. Absolute nonsense, of course."

"I just wanted to make sure you have all relevant facts at your disposal, Mr. President." Lincoln Tremaine assessed the man in front of him. He was a better man than his father. A consummate politician of course, you don't get to the Oval Office without being that, but he was also a globalist, a tough negotiator, a smart judge of the nuances of government, and the best down and dirty strategist in dealing with the Congress he'd seen since Lyndon Johnson.

"...Beyond all that, Gustav Gruner was a friend of mine..." Dandridge was saying now.

"I'd like you to hold on right there, sir," Tremaine interjected. "Please forgive me for interrupting you, Mr. President, I mean no disrespect, I'm sure you know that. But you see, I have information at my disposal that I *must* make you aware of, lest you make any such claims of friendship to the press, and be embarrassed later. I feel certain once you know what *I* know, sir, the very *last* thing you'll feel for this man is friendship. And the further you can distance yourself in the public mind, the better it will be for you, sir."

The President's eye came up now to meet Lincoln's. "OK, you've got my attention," he said, a sharp note of warning in his voice. "This had better be good."

And it was. In fact, Lincoln thought, as he recounted the precise details of Gruner's double identity, his crimes against humanity, and his lifelong entanglement with the CIA, he'd never been more eloquent.

"I'm asking you Mr. President," he concluded, "to see that all charges are dismissed against Doctor Monahan. No good can come of the inevitable revelations, should this go to trial, sir."

The President stared at him coldly. A desire to shoot the messenger was clear in his expression.

"Perhaps you're right, Lincoln," he said carefully. "It might be best if we avoid a trial, and simply have this woman *disappear* shall we say, from public view." He, too, like his father before him had been playing high stakes poker in D.C. for a very long time. Venerable old jurist or not, this man had to be shown he was dealing with the ultimate power that held all the good cards.

"You see, Lincoln," he said carefully choosing his words and his use of the man's first name, "what you're describing is a political hot potato and a CIA hot button, and I have no intention of burning my fingers on either one, if I may continue the metaphor. Gruner is a, shall we say, *confrere,* of many of the biggest players around the globe, to say nothing of those right here in DC. You can't possibly expect me to cause an international incident by ignoring his murder. And even if everything you're telling me about his crimes is true, they happened a very long time ago, and people have notoriously short memories. And there's no real evidence a kidnapping ever took place, is there? Just the word of a hysterical woman and a high strung child who, the CIA tells me, were invited guests at that estate. And let us not forget that this woman took the law into her own hands, and murdered a very prominent man, and maybe his bodyguard, too!

"So, no matter what this woman *alleges* about Gruner's past," the President said, "which she'd have a damned hard time proving in a court of law – you *know* I can't condone this kind of vigilantism, Mr. Justice. Why, the law's been broken here, and, by God, the law must be served." The President seemed pleased with the fact that he'd said it all so well.

"No, Mr. President," Tremaine replied quietly, but firmly, "it's *Justice* that must be served here. If this woman goes to jail for killing Gustav Gruner, Justice will surely weep behind her blindfold. I cannot tell you how *strongly* I feel about this, sir, except to say this one thing...," he took a deep breath for emphasis before continuing, "if need be, sir, I'll step down from the Supreme Court of the United States to try one last case as a defense attorney, before I die."

Dandridge's eyebrows rose in an expression of utter disbelief.

"You can't possibly be serious Lincoln!" he blurted.

"I think perhaps I've never been more serious about anything in my entire life, sir," Tremaine replied steadily.

"May I take that as a *threat*, Justice Tremaine?" the President asked, coldly.

Tremaine pursed his lips and thought carefully before answering.

"Let's just say, you may take it as an opportunity to save the taxpayers a great deal of money on a needless trial, sir," he answered quietly, "and this octogenarian a monumental effort he's far too old to have to make."

Dandridge sat for a moment, digesting what he'd heard before speaking.

He finally responded. "You're playing a very dangerous game with me."

Tremaine nodded, accepting the rebuke, then said with conviction, "There comes a time in every man's life when he's called upon to choose between what is expedient and what is right, sir. That moment has come for me, Mr. President... just as I believe it has come for you." He paused, then said gravely, "You see sir, I know how to win this one." The voice was grave, the conviction unmistakable.

The President responded in his own most potent Presidential voice – the one that cowed most of Washington.

"And why exactly is that, Mr. Justice?"

"If I try this case, sir," Tremaine replied with great dignity, "I shall tell that jury of every injustice ever perpetrated by the Nazis on the weak, the suffering and the helpless. And then I'll remind them of those falling bodies at the World Trade Center. I'll move on to the people who pulled the strings of the terrorists who were responsible, and how all these strings seem to intersect at the deceased. I'll take them to Calvary, sir, to remember a man who was nailed to a cross because he sought to save humanity from its own evil. And if that isn't enough, Mr. President, I'll ask them to look into this old black face and *know* just how *easy* it is for those with power to victimize those who have none."

He drew himself up to the edge of the sofa and leaned forward toward the President, a force field seeming to emanate from him as he spoke. "And after all that, sir, *then* I'll tell them everything I know about how the CIA saved those Nazi butchers from justice at Nuremburg by means of deceit, self-serving corruption, and the wholesale hoodwinking of the American public. I'll give them chapter and verse."

Tremaine looked the President in the eye. "Long before Caitlin Monahan ever laid eyes on Herr Doktor Guttman/ Gruner, that travesty of a human being had been tried in absentia, and judged guilty of unspeakable crimes against humanity. He had been sentenced to death by a jury of his peers. Gruner escaped Nuremberg *only* because the CIA subverted justice. But God will not be mocked forever, Mr. President. Now, after half a century, the scales of justice will be balanced, sir. Fate has intervened, and this decent young woman, through circumstances utterly beyond her control, was chosen to be that man's executioner."

"What the hell are you talking about?" the President asked.

Tremaine handed him the affidavit Meg had given him.

"What we have here, Mr. President," he said quietly, "is not a question of whether or not Caitlin Monahan killed this man, but whether or not the son of a bitch deserved to die." He waited for that to sink in, then spoke again.

"I believe this document is your way out of this mess, sir. I'd appreciate it if you'd take a moment to read it."

The Auschwitz Dossier
Auschwitz 1945

The rain beat a relentless tattoo on the corrugated tin roof. The icy dampness cramped the bones of the skeletal men huddled in the freezing barracks.

Abraham Mendelssohn struggled to stand up straight and firm against the excruciating pain of his rheumatism and arthritis. I will stand erect this one last time, he instructed his pathetically wasted body. Weakness is out of the question. He cleared the phlegm from his throat; his voice had to be stalwart as his purpose.

Eleven other men rose around him, as if a claxon had sounded. Abraham saw that Chaim supported Raphael. It was doubtful the younger man would see first light. He knew that Raphael was keeping himself alive by a Herculean exercise of will in order to participate in what was about to transpire. The old rabbi allowed himself only a moment of regret for the waste of one so gifted – and he raised his blue veined hand for silence. The gesture was unnecessary.

"We are twelve this night, not the ten required by our laws. While we Jews accept the legality of the Sanhedrin that occupies this courtroom," he cast a contemptuous glance around the squalid barracks, "our friend Isaac reminds me that the rest of the world, too, must ultimately accept our judgment, if we are not to be considered vigilantes or murderers. Twelve is deemed an

appropriate number for a jury in most civilized courts of law, so tonight we must be twelve.

"We have selected the members of this tribunal with great care.

"I am a Rabbi, Isaac is a judge, Raphael and Chaim are lawyers, David, Bernard, Mordechai and Sigmund are doctors, Itzhak, Samuel, Shlomo, and Pieter are businessmen whose credentials, in other times than these of madness, would be considered above reproach.

"Some of us will be dead by this time tomorrow. Others will not live to leave this place of infamy. Our individual survival does not matter... our purpose does." He straightened painfully and motioned for the younger man to continue.

Raphael Rabinowitz tried to free himself from the arm that propped him, but realized he would fall without it. Then he began to speak in a soft voice, almost feminine in its mellifluous articulation. So sweet was this voice, that had sung in temple since childhood, seduced juries with its sensitivity and intellect, that the horrific words he intoned now seemed an unconscionable anomaly. Raphael recited the list of crimes of which Dr. Helmut Guttman stood accused, as calmly as was possible for a human being of decency, intelligence and compassion. He had memorized the heinous acts night after night, lying sleepless despite exhaustion, on the lice-plagued wooden planks that served as his bed. The inconceivable atrocities were like a litany from Hell. When the echo of his voice had died away, many heads were bowed, other eyes stared straight ahead, tears, the only profligacy left to them, streaming unabashedly. There was discussion... brief, decisive. Then silence.

Rabbi Abraham rose again. He felt as if righteousness had strengthened him.

"For his crimes against the Jewish people and their God, and for his crimes against humanity itself, we of this Sanhedrin, in accordance with the Law of Moses, do find Helmut Josef Guttman

guilty of murder in the first degree. For this we sentence him to death.

"We appoint ourselves, our heirs, or designees in perpetuity, his executioners."

A muffled murmur of assent rippled through the assemblage. The Rabbi cleared his throat to bring silence, then spoke again.

"I hereby swear before God that I will use any means at my disposal to destroy this murderer. Should I die before executing him, I will pass this obligation to my sons and daughters, or to any man or woman I deem worthy of carrying out the judgment of this court. I swear this on the soul of my Hannah, whom he murdered, and in memory of all the innocent and violated."

The labored words of Rabbi Abraham Mendelssohn, the gentlest of men, pierced the consciousness of every man in the barracks. Each man rose in turn and swore his oath in his own words. Each added the names of those he loved who had been murdered; some described the manner of their deaths. Some recited the names of others in the camp whose lives had been stolen by Guttman.

David Rubinstein was a poet as well as a doctor. "Medicine I practice for the brain and body, poetry for the soul," he had told his beautiful Leah when he met her. The word "doctor" had still seemed awe-inspiring to him then. Helper of humanity. Guttman, too, was a doctor. He had taken Leah from the woman's barracks when her labor began and delivered the child himself. Then he had made Leah watch as he gouged out the infant's eyes and pinned them to the wall like captured butterflies and let her hold the child until it bled to death. Mother and child were gone now.

All that had not been taken from David Rubinstein was his will to destroy the monster. This would not be murder, it would be justice. He was the designated scribe for this tribunal... somehow he would live to bear witness to this night and to leave the message of what took place here in God's hands to deliver.

Twelve signatures on a tiny fragment of paper that contained a death sentence, completed the document. Appended to it were affidavits, later sworn to by David Rubenstein and the few other participants in this Sanhedrin, who had serviced the camp.

188

The President finished reading and reached, somewhat self-consciously, into his pocket for his handkerchief. Hurriedly, he wiped his eyes, then returned the white monogrammed square to his pocket, buying time to recover his equilibrium before responding. He cleared his throat.

Still a political pragmatist, he began, "There are powerful forces at work here, Mr. Justice, and you must know this document, while very moving, has no legal value..." Tremaine cut him off.

"I'm afraid I must most respectfully disagree with you about that, sir. I believe this document has a great deal of value both legal and emotional. I can only imagine what the media would do with it... what investigative reporters would unearth... how many hits on YouTube might be provoked, and how many tweets – isn't that what they call those Twitter things, sir? – might go flying around the world. God alone knows what might crawl out of the woodwork after that... And as to the power of those who would like to see this woman silenced, they are surely no more powerful than *you*, sir."

The old man spoke again. "Cut a deal with The Company, Mr. President. I think the Director might be more willing than you'd expect. Call off the cops, the lawyers, and the media. Don't make me play my ace."

"Your ace?" the President repeated, with an expression on his face that asked *what more could there possibly be?*

"There were four men in the bunker with General Patton, on that day in 1945, when he found the Spear of Longinus, Mr. President. One of those men was your father."

The words hung in the air between them for a moment, the President searched Tremaine's eyes, stunned both by the revelation, and by the old man's audacity.

"And how exactly would *you* know about that, Justice Tremaine, assuming it to *be* true?"

"Because I was *there*, too, sir and because I've waited sixty years for God to tell me *why*."

It was some time before the President cleared his throat and spoke again. "I'll need time to think about all this... the ramifications..."

"There isn't any time, sir. A woman and her child are in terrible trouble, and the longer you wait, the deeper the hole they're in gets dug. You are going to do the right thing, Mr. President. I believe *that*, sir, so why not just do the right thing *now*?"

The President put up his hands in a gesture of *enough.*

"I'll see what I can do, Lincoln," he said, finally, his voice hoarse with the conflicting emotions he felt and all the unanswered questions he now needed answers to. "I will see if my father is in any condition to discuss this with me... they tell me he's near death. I'll need to see if a way can be found around this godawful mess. I'm concerned about the law..."

Tremaine nodded, rose and turned to go... but at the door of the Oval he stopped and as he turned said, "You know what they say about the law, Mr. President." Tremaine said with a slight smile. "The good people don't need it and the bad people don't follow it, so sometimes we just have to go with our own conscience. I believe your father will have a clearer one if we can see justice done here. And Mr. President, if I may presume to tell you something you have to be as old as your father and I to know. Death doesn't hold much terror for us anymore – not like when we were young. But the thought of what's yet to come does give a man pause. A clear conscience is a fine thing at our age."

The door to The Oval Office made a hollow sound as it closed behind him.

The President, stared out across the Potomac. Could this have been what his father was trying to tell him before the heart attack? How much more was there that he didn't yet know? Finally, he moved to his desk and hit the intercom button that connected him to his secretary.

"Get me Director Farnsworth on the phone, Alison, will you... and then clear my calendar for this evening. Yes, yes, I know all that, and frankly I don't give a damn right now. Just clear the calendar and then have my driver come round – I'm heading out to Bethesda to see my father. There's a story I think he might need to tell me."

Under His Wings You Shall Take Refuge

Part XXIV

"How far that little candle shows its beams
So shines a good deed in a naughty world."
Alexander Pope

—————————— **189** ——————————

During the entire transatlantic flight, Fritz Gruner had relished the thought of the one deliberate act he intended to accomplish the minute he returned to the German mansion that was now entirely his. His father's will had to be executed, his vast financial holdings be assessed, a decision made about which of the pieces of real estate to retain – but, all of these could wait for this one act.

Fritz sat now in the hidden chamber, surrounded by what seemed to be an acre of looted art masterpieces and treasures of every conceivable kind. None of them interested him, even mildly. The airtight archival box he held in his hand was another matter.

Settling himself into the armchair, he could imagine his father having sat there, doing just as he did now. He adjusted the lamp beside him to an optimal angle, opened the lid of the box as gingerly as if it held the secret of life and death, and began to read the translation that accompanied the Book.

It wasn't until many hours, and several glasses of cognac from his father's private collection, later, that he knew the whole truth – what he held in his hands was indeed the secret of life and death.

Fritz read and reread his father's translation of the Book of Secrets. He understood now, the old man's obsession with the Spear – he had needed it to insure his own immortality! And it was still somewhere out there. *Gott in himmel*, it had been a close call. What would his own life prospects have been if his father had actually unlocked the Grail, and become immortal.

But that was then. And this was now. And he, Fritz Gruner, would soon control one of the greatest fortunes in Europe, perhaps the world, and his accession to power with The 13 would be seamless, for they knew him to be a worthy successor to his father. And, he would leave his father's legacy in the dust as he created his own.

Fritz replaced the book and the cryptographic key along with his father's transcription of the material, back in the box, and took it with him to his own safe.

Strangely, he found himself wishing he could share this news with someone. Frau Ruder perhaps. But that was foolishness and she was long dead.

He wondered for a moment, if he'd had this secret back then, might he have saved her from his father's wrath? After all, would it be so wonderful a gift to become immortal all alone.

On the other hand, he was the only man now alive who knew the secret, and once he had the Spear, he could make *all* the choices about who lived and who died. There was quite simply no greater power than that on earth... for it was the power of God.

190

Winfield Livingston had just finished laying out for the Director's approval the final disinformation plan that would not only destroy Caitlin Monahan's reputation, get her medical license revoked, and put her behind bars for several decades if not for life – it would also insure the continued secrecy of all that must remain secret.

He was proud of the way he'd managed to fabricate a vast network of lies to implicate her not only in Gruner's murder, but in a whole series of treasonous collusions with her dead husband, that might have compromised National Security. The media disinformation campaign would follow all these allegations being made public, and there would be, as far as he could tell, no way anyone would be able to disentangle the web. Certainly not in Dr. Monahan's lifetime.

Livingston ended his presentation to the Director, which had been replete with computerized data trees and computer generated scenarios that assessed precisely the way in which the damage would be spread virally. He felt justifiably proud of what he'd accomplished. He'd taken a blameless private citizen with no political agenda whatsoever, and in the space of a single week had created a shadow persona in which she appeared to be damned near as much of a danger to the security of the United States as Osama Bin Laden had been. And she was so much easier to find.

The Director took it all in, asking pertinent questions as they occurred, making a note or two on his desk pad. Now, he sat well back in his high backed desk chair and nodded his head once or twice before speaking. Livingston thought the old man looked a little sadder than usual, and wondered if he were equating this, in some way, with what had most likely been done to his father.

"You've done a stellar job on this, Winfield," the Director said, finally, and Win relaxed. "Maybe the most comprehensive work I've seen you do, actually."

Livingston sat up taller in his chair. You never knew what the Director was thinking. Not for certain.

"That said," the old man continued, "I want you to shred every last bit of it. I want you to dismantle every tendril and neutralize every line of inquiry. In short, I want you to disassemble this fine piece of work, and I want it done today, do you understand me?"

Livingston didn't understand. "But Director," he managed to stammer. "I'm afraid I'm at a loss..."

"Not yet, you're not, Livingston," the Director said without a hint of good will in his voice. "But that remains to be seen, doesn't it? May I assume that you have not fielded anything or anyone that cannot be rescinded or recalled?"

Winfield Livingston did a lightning fast calculation and then said no, but he wasn't really absolutely certain that was the case. He'd given relatively open-ended orders to the head of that mercenary contract organization. He'd have some damned critical calls to make the minute he got out of this office.

"May I know *why*, sir?" Win asked, his voice as tentative as he felt. This made no sense at all.

"You may not," the Director said, with the first semblance of a smile Win had seen since he'd entered the old man's office. "But you may take it as a direct order from POTUS."

Jesus Christ! The President of the United States had given this order. Why in the hell...?

Livingston gathered his papers and his laptop and was surprised to see that his hands appeared steady. On the inside he was shaking, praying it was not already too late to un-spring the trap he'd set in motion. But on the outside, he didn't look at all like a man who now had to fear for his career, and perhaps even his life.

Director Farnsworth lifted the meticulously compiled dossier that was his father's, and, with a sigh, fed it page by page into the shredder. Then he put on his hat and coat. He thought he might just go on over to Arlington to see his father right about now. He wouldn't be able to tell him that what had happened to him so long ago would never happen to another American citizen. But he could tell him it wouldn't happen today and it wouldn't happen to this young woman. He thought his father might like to hear that.

191

Vincenzo paced back and forth, back and forth, a caged beast waiting for slaughter.

He had failed the Cardinal and must find the courage to confess his unforgivable sins of omission to the one man on earth he had intended never to fail.

Tears welled in his eyes, blurring the perfect vision he'd been blessed with, even in middle age.

Horrific pangs of conscience had now driven him to breach yet another of the Cardinal's rules: "You will never, not even in the direst circumstance, come to see me at the Vatican," he had told Vincenzo, many years ago, when their relationship had begun. "My safety and yours depend on it!" the Cardinal had said it in the gravest tones of admonishment. "It will be the greatest of *sins* if you were ever to compromise our work, Vincenzo. God demands this sacrifice of you – as do I."

Only the Cardinal would be able to tell him what to do now – the Cardinal whose orders he had betrayed, was the only one close enough to God, learned enough, holy enough, to tell him what he must do to save his immortal soul. If that was even possible now... Vincenzo hung his great shaggy head in despair.

If he committed suicide, his worldly suffering would end, but his eternal suffering would only be beginning, and he feared the fires of Hell as he had never feared anything on this earth. And if he lived, but could no longer do God's work for the Cardinal, what purpose would there be to his existence?

"What are you doing here?" Cardinal Andretti's fury echoed in the marble room. "You fool! Have I not told you, this can never be! You must leave at once. Who knows you are here? Whom have you told? Why did my secretary let you enter?"

"*No one* knows, Eminence!" Vincenzo gasped, horrified. "I need no one to help me enter where I must go."

"Then get yourself gone the same way!" Andretti thundered. "What in the name of God were you thinking, Vincenzo?"

But instead of leaving, Vincenzo lurched toward the horrified Cardinal and threw himself on his knees at Andretti's feet.

"I beg you, Eminence!" he pleaded, "You must hear my confession. I must tell you what I have done to betray your trust!"

Dumbstruck by his unseemly display, Andretti realized he had no choice but to hear the man out. The Cardinal instinctively scanned the room for cameras, even though he had his private sanctuary swept weekly for surveillance devices. He glanced at the door and saw it was closed, then reached for his phone and buzzed intercom.

"What can I do for you, Eminence?" the cheery American voice answered.

"You can show a little respect!" Andretti spat unnecessarily, his agitation making him surlier than usual. "And then you can see to it that *no one* – and I mean no one – not the Holy Father himself, enters this room for the next half hour. Do you understand me?"

Andretti slammed down the phone and struggled to get a grip on his temper. He must deal with this pathetic sobbing lunatic who was kneeling at his feet. The man was a loose cannon, but he was the one who had seen to all the other loose cannons of the past. *Basta!* this was a disaster. The Cardinal drew a heavy breath and reached for the chair behind him to steady himself. Then, resignedly, he sat down and forced his voice to a semblance of normalcy.

"What is it you must tell me, Vincenzo?" he asked with authority, but not anger. "How have you betrayed me?"

The shaggy head was bowed, so the man's words were muffled. "I disobeyed your orders, Eminence," he murmured. "I did not capture the Mother..." he swallowed hard before blurting out the rest. "And I saved the little one... I couldn't see her suffer so... and I gave her back to her mama and now it is too late..."

"What in God's name are you telling me, Vincenzo?" the Cardinal asked, confused and fearing the answer. "*What* is it too late to do?"

The big head came up and blood-shot eyes met the Cardinal's. "It is too late to get what you have sought, Eminence! Too late for me to capture the woman and question her. The *polizia* have taken her! They pulled the child from her arms, and they arrested her before my very eyes. *Madre mia*, it was all I could do not to kill them all! The sight was *tragico*!

"First the little dottore killed the bad man and she was very upset because she has not my experience of such things, Eminence. I would have cut off his hands, and fed them to him one finger at a time, for what he did to that little child, burying her in the cold earth – and to the mother, hunting *mi dottore* like an animal. For his many sins he had to die, of that there was no doubt, but the little dottore was not used to such things. And then I gave her back her child and she was happy once again, until the *Carabinieri* came and such chaos was all around us... *Madre Mia...* and they took this child away from her, and everyone was crying and screaming..." Vincenzo finally ran out of words and stopped for a breath. The Cardinal sat in stunned silence, as the man began again.

"I did not want them to find me, Eminence, for I knew that would displease you, so I melted away in the confusion, but I knew I had failed you and there was no way to fix this unless I killed all the *Carabinieri* and I thought you would not want that. And then I thought to end my own life, but I could not for I would go straight to Hell."

The Cardinal was no less astounded by this last sentence, than by the rest of the breathless soliloquy. "Vincenzo," he said, needing to understand, "after all the killings you have done in your life that God has forgiven you for, why on earth would you think you could not be forgiven for having broken your word to me?"

The great head bowed low again. "To be forgiven, Eminence, I must regret what I have done," he said, and the simple words lingered in the air between them for a long moment, as the old Cardinal struggled to comprehend.

"You do not regret breaking your oath to me, then?" he asked mystified.

"It is the saving of the child I do not regret, Eminence," Vincenzo whispered, "and, I do not regret not capturing mi dottore. My regret is only that I have failed you, Eminence. You were once a priest – you must know that this is not enough for absolution!"

Andretti sucked in his breath. *You were once a priest,* the man had said. What in God's name was he now?

He stared at the kneeling Vincenzo. *You are with the One on the Cross, or you are pounding in the nails,* his old Confessor had once admonished him. *You cannot be both.* What were all his own machinations, all his clever political strategies, all his huge ambitions worth, in the face of such simple, unquestioning faith? This man had what he, a Prince of the Church, had lost. Simple faith. Absolute belief in God. Even his utter devotion to the Cardinal had only been because he thought it served the one true Church, and that this Church served God.

With trembling hands, Giacomo Cardinal Andretti reached for the purple stole that lay folded pristinely on his desk. He picked it up and unfolded it, waiting until he could control his own trembling hands, then touched the stole reverently to his lips, and in a long practiced gesture, he placed it around his shoulders. *You were once a priest,* the words rang in his head, a terrible indictment. *You were once a priest.*

How long he wondered, had it been since he had, in truth, been a priest. How long since he had had the simple faith that fueled all the power and the pomp, and without which the rest had no meaning? How long since love of God had been his motivation, not self-aggrandizement and ego, fueled by the cunning of a Borgia?

You were once a priest. The words reverberated within him. He had no illusions about himself. These words, this man, had touched him, moved him. But would they make him a better man? In a momentary flash of self-honesty, he doubted that – for the die had been cast long ago. But perhaps, just for today, it would make him a better priest.

"*In nominee Patrie, et Fili, et Spiritu Sancti...*" he began the ritual words of confession, and as he did so, he was surprised to find the words were coming through tears.

Final Beckoning

Part XXV

"Not everything that can be counted counts, and not everything that counts can be counted."

Albert Einstein

192

Christmas Eve. Meg's Apartment.

Cait, Meg and Carter were knee deep in the Christmas tree ornaments Damon and Pythias had dragged up from the basement storage locker in Meg and Carter's building.   When the two reclusive boys had accepted their Christmas Eve invitation everyone had been stunned, but it was clear now, the two were just as willing to celebrate as the rest, and were getting a big kick out of sharing in the relief and merriment everyone was feeling. Damon had even bought a new tee shirt for the occasion that read "Santa thinks outside the quadrilateral parallelogram."

Matt was lying prone on the floor, struggling with the tree stand, as Croce held the tree and gave directions, chief of which seemed to be, "It's still tilting to the left... or to the right... or *"For C-sake, McCormack, what the hell's the matter with your sense of direction!"* which helpful hints Matt would have greeted with expletives, except for the fact that Lark was sitting on the floor nearby assessing the straightness of the tree operation with her own critical eye.

Matt peeked out at Cait from between the bottom branches, and let out a sigh that had absolutely nothing to do with tree placement. He'd been deliberating making a move on Cait – no that wasn't exactly it. Not making a *real* move, it was too soon for that, but at least trying to let her know that he'd like to make a move if the time ever got to be right. But he could see in her face that tonight wouldn't be a good time. She was trying to keep up a brave front for Lark and Meg and everybody, but he could tell she was hurting. It was Christmas and her husband had been dead six weeks and she'd been to hell and back. So whatever it was he planned to do would have to wait. He covered his disappointment by yelling at Croce, "Hey *paison!* don't you people have Christmas trees in Brooklyn? Could you get it together sometime soon? I think I hear reindeer on the roof already..."

Cait smiled a little, trying hard to be cheerful for Lark's sake. This would be their first Christmas without Jack, and it had seemed to her that after all they'd been through, it would be good for Lark to feel safe and warm and loved, *this*, of all Christmases. She was mending from her ordeal, but it would be a long time before the child was over it. In some ways, Cait knew, Lark would never truly be over what had happened, but children were amazingly resilient, and Lark was far from ordinary.

She and Meg had planned this little event, as a thank you – if that were even possible – for all that everyone in this room had done to save them. They'd even invited Justice Tremaine, but he'd declined with regret and said he hoped they'd come see him in Washington, when the cherry blossoms bloomed. He'd promised Lark a personal tour of the Supreme Court building.

They were going to spend the holidays with Meg and Carter, and then decide what to do about the house in Greenwich, Lark's school, and Cait's medical practice – all of which seemed somehow unimportant now. But it wasn't easy to stay cheerful, even if she wanted to so badly. How could she ever really repay what everyone in this room had done and given of themselves.

"Hey, guys," Damon called to the two men who were still wrestling with the tree. "If you two hulking elves *never* get that thing up into the stand, we'll never get it trimmed in time for Santa – at least not for *this* Christmas." He winked at Lark as he said it and she giggled back.

"I think it's fine now," she pronounced solemnly and a cheer went up in the room.

"Thank you God!" Carter said. "I'll get the wine," and made a beeline for the kitchen. Meg, saw Cait staring at the tree and knew she was thinking of Jack and all the other Christmases. She walked to where her sister stood and hugged her.

"I'm OK," Cait said, grateful for the hug. "I was just thinking that after all we've been through we still don't know where the damned Spear is..."

Lark looked up at her Mother. "I know where it is, Mommy," she said and all sound ceased in the room. "I figured it out when I was thinking about chess, but then a lot of other things happened to me, and I forgot about it again for a while, and then I thought maybe I could tell you for a Christmas present..."

As everyone stared dumbfoundedly at everyone else in the room, Lark ran into the bedroom, pulled a box out from under the bed and then scampered back to the dumbstruck group, and handed the box to her mother. "I made a picture for you, Mommy. To show you where Daddy put it."

Cait, wonderingly, unwrapped the package and stared at a childish drawing inside of the statue of Archangel Michael that guarded the graves in their family plot at Oak Bridge Cemetery. The statue was certainly big enough to hold the Spear, she thought, trying to wrap her mind around this possibility, but it would have to have been cemented into the base somehow, or maybe even into the great spear the Archangel held in his hand. Then she remembered that Jack had told her his father had commissioned the Angel statue for the family plot right after World War II, as a special kind of memorial, and that he went there often with flowers... and with Jack.

"I'm pretty sure it's there, Mommy," Lark said, her eyes shining with her knowledge. "Daddy told me the angel always wins and that he can always lead you out of the labyrinth, and he's the only angel we've got, and I can tell you what all the clues mean if you want me to."

Then everybody in the room started talking at once and they all sounded so silly that Lark told them how she'd figured it out, and Damon and Pythias high-fived her, and said there was this great new kind of sonar they knew about that could probably find out for sure, and they'd get on that right away... but Cait, listening, knew beyond a shadow of a doubt, that Lark was absolutely right.

Then they all hugged and kissed, and everybody seemed to be laughing and crying at the same time, and it was turning out to be a very nice Christmas party after all, Lark thought, thoroughly enjoying being the center of so much happy attention.

193

England

It was a few days after Christmas and Heredon Manor was still resplendent with holiday decorations. Magnificent wreaths graced the doors and windows, candles gleamed everywhere, and a tree that looked like the one at Rockefeller Center, heavy with decorations that went back centuries, stood in the Great Hall. Lark was in ecstasy at the magic of it all, and Cait was actually glad she'd come.

She'd been hesitant at first, the idea of leaving home again so soon had been unsettling, and there was so much to attend to now that the worst had passed. But there was still the pressing question of the Spear to deal with. If it stayed where it was, would she not remain its Caretaker, and therefore never sleep another night in her life? Or was it fair to give it to the Delafields, as they'd suggested, and place them in the same danger she'd endured? She couldn't trust this conversation to a phone call, not even after the boys had assured her the phone they'd encrypted for her would defy anybody's snooping.

Cait smiled as she watched Lark run toward Arthur, who had come to collect her for a morning ride. There were so many people watching over the child solicitously since they'd arrived, Cait couldn't imagine how Lark would ever be able to get back to just normal little-girl-hood. As if such a thing could even be possible after all that had happened to her. *I'll do a Scarlett O'Hara on it,* Cait told herself emphatically, *I'll just think about all that tomorrow.*

She was so grateful and so relieved that the worst was over. She felt safe here for the moment, before having to figure out the whole rest of her life, which now seemed to loom endlessly before her, full of question marks and loneliness. *Stop that!* She admonished herself as she made her way to the library where Lord Delafield, Prince Siegfried and Hugh awaited her. *Count your blessings, not your sorrows, Cait. You could have lost everything and you didn't, so gratitude is the only appropriate emotion to feel right now.*

Cait took a deep breath, smiled at the butler who had just opened the library door for her, and entered the room, once again struck by its beauty and grace. A fire glowed in the immense hearth, and Lord Delafield and Prince Siegfried both rose to greet her. Hugh tried to do the same, but she saw a look of pain flash across his face and instinctively reached out to touch him.

"You shouldn't even be out of bed," she admonished, in her best doctor voice, to cover her own embarrassment at the spontaneous gesture, and he smiled at her, as he settled back into the huge armchair. He looked pale and weakened, but he was on the mend, and his condition, too, merited gratitude rather than remorse.

"I didn't know you were here, Siegfried," she said warmly, as the old man first put out his hand to her, and then taking hers in his own, he drew her to him and embraced her soundly.

"Brava, child!" he said, and there seemed to be tears in his voice. "You did it! A remarkable feat. We are all so very proud of you."

Delafield, too, clasped her hands in both of his, and led her to a seat by the fire. "We have so very much to say to you, my dear

Caitlin," he began, "which is why Siegfried has come and Hugh has defied his doctor's orders to be with us for this moment." He looked toward his son with quiet pride apparent in his gaze.

All three men were beaming at her, and Cait feeling immense warmth toward them all, wondered why they seemed so expectant. She had anticipated a serious discussion about the Spear's future, but this was something else... she wondered what.

"My dear Caitlin," Siegfried began, "sometimes, the forces that govern the affairs of men, choose someone to be tested in an extraordinary process that supplants the usual journey to Initiation. You might say, it takes the Initiate through the labyrinth, in an unexpected way, and when that happens, the very unpredictability of the journey is what makes it so formidable and unique. We believe you have just completed such a journey. You were placed there by all the events of the recent past, and you have passed these tests successfully. Which is why we now wish to formally invite you to become a full fledged member of our Sacred Order."

She knew this was an extraordinary honor they wished to bestow on her, but it wasn't one to be taken lightly.

"If you accept this invitation, however," he continued, seeing her hesitation, "and we hope you will – we are duty bound to warn you that it is a commitment not merely to our purpose, but to learning certain arcane secrets you will need to know, in order to accomplish whatever future work is asked of you. There is serious training you would have to undertake, my dear Caitlin. There are tasks that could lie ahead of you that might be dangerous, and require esoteric knowledge you do not yet possess. Your gifts have been made apparent in all that has transpired, but you do not yet know all you must, in order to use them to their full advantage. Do you understand what I am saying?"

Cait, no longer astonished by anything, but weary of battle and longing for a "normal" life didn't immediately reply. Finally, in a voice thick with emotion, she simply said, "I love you all."

She said it gently, realizing as she spoke the words, how much she meant them. She felt a sense of family with these three men that she couldn't entirely explain, and it meant she didn't want to hurt them by refusing the great honor they offered.

"I'm touched to the heart and a bit overwhelmed by your offer," she said earnestly. "And part of me wants to say yes and to leap at all you can teach me. Now that I know so much more about the world's realities, and I understand the pervasiveness of evil all around us, I see the urgency and I want to help." She drew in a breath.

"But, another part of me is just a mother, and a woman who's lost her husband, and all the hopes and dreams for the future that were intertwined in Jack, and in my old life. Right now, I know Lark needs time to heal, and so do I. After everything we've seen and endured, I know that neither of our lives can ever go back to the way it was before, but I'm so uncertain of the future, that I feel I can't commit to anything right now. And if I do as you are asking of me, I'd be committing Lark's future to this, too. Do you understand my hesitancy?" She looked to all three and Lord Delafield responded.

"Not only do we understand, my dear, but we would have expected no less measured a response from you. This is not an invitation that can be taken lightly. So let me suggest a plan that may turn out to be for the highest good of all.

"I suggest you go back to America to sort the practical issues that need sorting, and then return to us in the summer and spend Lark's school holiday here at Heredon. By then, I feel sure you will have regained your equilibrium and have made quite a few decisions that are impossible now."

She nodded, thinking out loud. "I have to decide if I can stay in the house that contains memories of Jack in every room," she said, "and I need to decide what to do about Lark's special gifts – without her father and grandfather to tutor her, we'll need someone... Damon and Pythias have volunteered. And I have my medical practice..."

"Please, Cait," Hugh said, speaking for the first time. "*Please* just don't say no. It would mean *everything* to me if you'd promise merely to *think* about it."

She could hear in his voice how much her reply meant to him. And what exactly did this man mean to her, she wondered? He was her true friend, and perhaps had been much more than that in other times. There was some special soul bond between them, she was absolutely certain of that now -- but what did it mean for their future? What would it mean if she chose to stay in America? Thankfully, that was not a question she had to answer right now.

"There is the matter of the Spear, dear Cait," Lord Delafield was saying as she dragged her attention back to his voice. "Now that we know its whereabouts, we all realize that better disposition of it must be made, and quickly. We fear you and Lark may still be endangered by its Caretaking, and we think we may have come up with a suitable solution." He looked at the two Delafields for corroboration of the wisdom of the plan. "You see, my dear, we believe the best way to hide the Spear, is not to hide it at all..."

The only problem with what they proposed, she thought as they told her what they had in mind, was that the only man who could possibly pull it off would have to be willing to act as Caretaker one more time, if only for a little while.

194

When the two older men had left the room, Hugh and Cait sat together by the fire, the silence between them unaccustomed, new. Cait spoke first. "What are your doctors saying?" she asked, surprised by the huskiness of her own voice that betrayed the state of her emotions. "How long will it be before you're on your feet again?"

Hugh smiled at her, willing her to be more at ease. They'd been through too much together for awkwardness. "They're saying that I must have had some bloody good doctoring in those woods or I'd never have made it at all," he answered, then he reached for her hand, and she didn't pull away, but clasped his tightly in response.

"But that's not what I want to talk about, Cait, so I hope you'll hear me out, before you say a word." He smiled disarmingly and she looked at him quizzically.

"I believe you need to tell me *everything* that happened to you and to Lark after we parted, Cait," he said holding her eyes with his. "We know only the bare bones of it, from the newspapers, and from your sister's phone calls. I know you've been through hell after hell, and I also know from my own experience that one can't hold that kind of trauma and loss inside forever without being damaged by the enormity of it. You need to unburden yourself of the kind of details you can't really share with someone who hasn't been to hell, too, you see. I'm asking you to let me share the burden with you as we've shared so many others in these last months, and as it is meant to be shared by us. Surely Fate would not have brought us through so much together, if that weren't so..."

And so she told him all of it. The pain, the uncertainty, the fear, the desperate gamble. She told him of her worries for Lark's sanity and spirit after all the child had endured, and of her own confusions about the future that now spread before her so open-endedly. And she cried with him for all the losses and the terrors... and he understood it all, as he held her in his arms and let her sob out every terrible detail that had been eating away at her heart. He stroked her hair and patted her as if she were a wounded child, all the while marveling at the courage it had taken to do what she had done.

When the torrent had finally subsided and she pulled back from him, Hugh reached up to touch her tear-wet cheek with the backs of his fingers and Cait raised her face to his. Looking into his eyes she saw both love and understanding there, and for whatever reason that seemed more than enough for now.

Epilogue

"At stroke of midnight God will win."
William Butler Yeats

──── EPILOGUE ────

Abraham Lincoln Tremaine sat back in the large comfortable seat on Air Force One, and said his prayers. He'd been doing that a lot lately, he thought with a smile. Storming heaven, his Grandmama would have called it. He sighed at the thought of the stalwart old woman, so long gone now, who'd shaped his life in such significant ways, and in the final analysis had supplied all the answers they'd needed for the Spear.

"Swords into plowshares, Lincoln," she'd said to him a thousand times. "The Good Lord will show us how to turn swords into plowshares, one of these days. And then all the wars will cease to be, and man will love his brother, no matter what color his skin is, and the world will be a mighty fine place." *Swords into plowshares…* only this time it would be a Spear.

Comin' for to Carry Me Home, he hummed softly, remembering how every night after their meager meal they would read together from the Good Book and his Grandmama would explain to him about the goodness of God and the laws by which He ran the Universe. Then she'd tuck him into bed and sing that hymn in absolute faith that God knew what He was doing after all, despite the considerable evidence to the contrary in rural Alabama.

Linc Tremaine glanced down at the brown paper-wrapped parcel in his lap and thought how proud his Grandmama would have been, about his current mission. The Spear hadn't left his hand since they'd removed it from St. Michael's statue in the cemetery.

The President had approved his suggestion without hesitation. "A magnificent gesture of worldwide ecumenism," he'd called it –

in his usual media-speak. A perfect sound bite for the Six O'clock News. Then he'd added to Lincoln, as an aside, "You're sure you don't want me to give it to the Pope?"

"Asia's more of a tinder-box, Mr. President," Linc had answered judiciously, "and people of color everywhere will understand that you're reaching out to them." He was amused at his own ability to put just the right spin on an act – the legacy of a lifetime in Washington politics.

But this one time it was the right act, for the right reason. Cait and Lark would be off the hook, and the Spear no longer hidden and fought over by evil men. And, at last, the Spear of Longinus could help to rule the world as it always should have done – as a symbol of peace and unity. Jesus would have liked that.

He would take the Spear of Longinus to the Dalai Lama and his friend, Tenzin Rinpoche, the High Lama of The Bon Po Lamasary, which was said to be the true Shamballa.

Their Holinesses would take the Spear under their combined protection, and then invite Christian, Jewish and Moslem leaders to join them in declaring it the ultimate symbol of World Brotherhood – and by God, the world needed a new jump-start for its beleaguered spirit after September 11th and the ever-expanding wars in the Middle East that never seemed to find resolution, no matter who was in the Oval office.

Tremaine pushed the button that reclined his seat and closed his eyes. He was excited as a boy at the prospect of meeting the two Lamas. What an amazing world it was in which a sharecropper's son could render a service like this to humanity. The only ones who knew of his plan were the Conspirators and the President. No announcement would be made until after the Spear was safely in the Dalai Lama's hands. Reverently, he touched the paper wrapping he'd done up himself around his precious parcel and smiled contentedly.

"Would you like me to take that package for you, sir," the young Marine who guarded him, asked politely.

"No, indeed, son. I'm having quite a fine time holding on to this," he said amiably. "You might say it's a present for my Grandmama – something I promised to deliver a long, long time ago."

The two Marines locked eyes above the old man's head. If either questioned the use of Air Force One to deliver an old woman's package, it wasn't their place to say so. And how old could his grandma be? Justice Tremaine had to be at least 90, himself.

"Yes, sir, Mr. Justice," the one who'd spoken, replied.

"Justice..." the old man repeated softly. "Yes, indeed... every once in a while, I do believe there's justice." Abraham Lincoln Tremaine smiled a little as he settled in for the long ride. The two young Marines wondered what he could have meant by that.

"Thank you, Lord," he prayed fervently in his mind, as he drifted into peaceful sleep under the watchful eye of two young Marines who would never know they'd guarded the future of humanity. "Thank you for letting me be the one who carries it home."

Acknowledgements

In the course of nearly fifteen years of research and writing, a number of wonderful people have contributed to the store of knowledge contained in this book. Each has lent expertise and good will to my story, so I'd like to say a most heartfelt thank you to them for their help and their great generosity of spirit.

Rachel Allgood, gracious and good-humored computer wiz, who explained both the finer points of Internet Security and the personal quirks of the true digerati.

Dakota Cash, beloved daughter, who designed the Lark's Labyrinth book jacket, as well as encouraging me to keep on keeping on, every time I thought I'd never get Lark and Cait to safety.

Vera Haldy-Regier, superb memoirist (An Irregular Girlhood in Hitler's Shadow) and former Baroness, who helped name my German characters appropriately, and guided me regarding their language and manner.

Sandra Hayes, Professor of rarefied mathematics and renowned expert in Chaos Theory, whose mathematical expertise and perceptiveness about the mind of a greatly-gifted child helped fuel both Lark's game and her spirit.

Dolores Bolla Holt, whose understanding of the nuances of the Italian language as spoken by Princes of the Church, and the peasants who serve them, helped give voice to my characters.

Sally Moss, whose superb knowledge of weaponry helped equip my characters with correct ordnance. Be it firearm, bow, or appropriate gear, she helped get them ready to fight the good fight.

Nancy Nicholas, whose deft and intuitive editing was greatly enjoyed and appreciated.

Jamie Rubin, former attorney for The Anti-Defamation League, who gave me insight into that organization's fine work and dedication.

Steven Sadin, gamer extraordinaire, who helped me understand the passion of gamers for their art, and the kind of wizardry-mindset that would help keep Lark in the game.

Dr. Catherine Shainberg, renowned authority on Sephardic Kabbalah, who explained the history of why women were permitted into Kabbalah's secret teachings in 14th Century Spain.

Diana Zitnay, whose astonishing typing and organizational skills not only kept the manuscript in fine fettle through more than a decade of shifting chapters, research and ideas, but whose generous encouragement and belief in me and my story, helped both Lark and me find our way through the labyrinth.

Cathy Cash Spellman is the author of five New York Times and International Bestsellers. Her books have been sold in 22 countries, and her novel *Bless the Child* was a Paramount movie. She invites you to visit her website at **www.cathycashspellman.com**.

DEC X 2011

Made in the USA
Charleston, SC
29 November 2011

2/18